MW00934506

MINOTAUR'S MAZE OF MONSTER GIRLS: THE COMPLETE SERIES

MAIDENS OF MIXONIA

MARCUS SLOSS

ROYAL GUARD

Copyright © 2022 Royal Guard Publishing LLC.
All rights reserved.

No part of this publication may be reproduced, distributed, or transmitted in any form or by any means, including photocopying, recording, or other electronic or mechanical methods, without the prior written permission of the publisher, except in the case of brief quotations embodied in critical reviews and certain other noncommercial uses permitted by copyright law.

Any references to historical events, real people, or real places are used fictitiously. Names, characters, and places are products of the author's imagination.

MINOTAUR'S MAZE OF MONSTER GIRLS

MAIDENS OF MIXONIA BOOK 1

CHAPTER
ONE
KAMBRY

Mixonia - Minotaur Maze - Floor 2 - Combat Solo

K ambry crept over the forest floor, each footfall carefully placed. The *snap* of a nearby twig caused her to freeze. Her attentive pause revealed a foraging squirrel, allowing her to relax enough that her apprehensive breathing calmed.

It was just a forest critter. Calm yourself. You'll be relaxing at the bar in a comfy seat with a tasty drink, soon enough. Her concern faded and her joyful hope for an easy win returned. With the tension easing, Kambry continued walking. Suddenly, her peripheral vision caught a glint from the right.

A storm of frozen shards zoomed through the forest, seeking her demise. Her thighs pumped and she broke into a run, aided by her wings. She tucked them in and dove behind the cover of a fallen log. A surreal feeling washed over her as a single shard bounced off her armor with a *clang*.

Not again! She knew her victory of finding shelter was short lived. It was merely a prelude to the inevitable. No, she couldn't panic. There was still a chance.

She held onto hope. She didn't have a choice.

"Oh, Kambry. Come out, love," Thero said in a seductive attempt to woo her into the open.

He flung another barrage of ice against her cover. The shards cracked loudly as they shattered around her. When it was safe, she jumped up and sprinted deeper into the woods.

Fleas and pestilence!

Kambry knew she was in trouble. She knew Thero. He was a master mage, renowned for his abilities.

"Why are you running, darling?" Thero's footsteps crunched over the leafy forest floor, "I'll make you an offer. Sure beats dying and finding yourself on Min's shelves. I bet even your little figurine is worth leering at." His light laughter exuded confidence. He wasn't trying to be stealthy. He didn't need to be.

Kambry cursed her luck. She knew Thero was toying with her, he'd caught her in a bind. The mage snickered, "We both know your momma can't free you again. At least not anytime soon. Come work for me, be my toy. Or would you rather I pleasure your mom as she begs for tokens?"

Kambry knew better. She'd been in this disastrous situation before.

Desperate to pay her debts, determined to help her mom, and consumed by the thrill of combat, she'd ignored the warnings. Her presumption of easy victory was her downfall.

Min's Vault of Treasures were hers for the taking, at least she had hoped they would be. In her quest to strike it rich, she brazenly risked going into the labyrinth, becoming just another competitor in the Game of the Gods.

Most adventurers stuck to the simple levels, where you fought only the monsters that the labyrinth spawned. Kambry, however, had dared to compete against other champions. She'd squelched her inner voice of caution. A quick and easy pittance was not what she'd come for. She would repay her mother for making ever so many sacrifices, and she would do it sooner rather than later.

Kambry weighed her options. "How about I head to the entrance? You let me go, and you'll get ten easy tokens. Mom would let you do things that would make me shudder for ten tokens."

She heard a hiss, her eyes darting to the noise to see a large snake.

Oh, come on! Kambry bolted, and the angry snake struck at empty air where she had just been. She dodged an earth spike, then tumbled to safety behind a broad redwood.

At least he cornered me in a forest. Small victories, right?

"I'm afraid I can't do that. I'd be left dry, and you'd be free. Besides," Thero's chuckle oozed with evil, "your mom would never give me what I *really* want, right?"

Kambry didn't fall for his mind games. She needed to plot a way to the locket. If she could snatch up the golden locket and press it to the keyhole, she'd come out a hero. Honestly though, at this point, retreat sounded like a better option.

The floor she was on obviously allowed champion combat, hence the asshole flinging shards of ice at her. But this level's rewards for the bold were five times greater, too. Floor two offered a reward of ten tokens. For a champion, that was nothing, but for newbies like her, it was a fortune. She'd expected this floor to be free of other competitors, elite players usually avoided these lower challenges.

Usually.

I can't fail Mom, not again. I have to do this. Screw Thero, and his vile, perverted ways. If only her plan had worked.

"You've grown quiet," Thero teased from far closer than she anticipated.

Kambry tensed, waiting for the right moment. Her staff shot out from around the tree and set a flame wall between them. It was only meant to be a distraction. Her feet crunched across the forest's leafy floor as she weaved between the trees.

Limbs tore at her face as she flew recklessly back through the woods. Thero's ice magic dented her armor again. She knew he'd successfully cut off her only route to the final prize. He must have been waiting for her this whole time; she was just now figuring it out.

"Didn't you die on this pathetic level already?" he sneered, knowing the answer.

Of course, Thero had to bring that up. If he was trying to rub it in, that great rewards always entailed grave risks, he'd succeeded. *Prick.*

She reached her arm around the tree and flung a quick fireball without even looking; it came nowhere close to hitting the mage. Kambry never saw it land, however, thanks to another.volley of Thero's damned ice shards.

She risked a glance towards where she expected the end of this simple maze should be and felt a glimmer of hope. The locket lay on a pedestal, only a few hundred paces away.

Kambry knew there was only one way to get there, though, through Thero. She'd hoped an opportunity would present itself to make a run for the locket before she was forced to fight him. Today was not her lucky day. At least she'd have a fighting chance this time. Her first death hadn't even afforded her that.

"Escar got lucky," Kambry shouted defiantly, "it'll never happen again!"

Months ago, Escar hid on this very floor. He'd shot an arrow into her heart, at the exact moment her hand had wrapped around the locket. That sad day had not only dashed her ambitions, it altered her life.

The gods were heartless and uncaring with their punishments, but they were equally gracious with their rewards.

A death inside the Minotaur Maze left your soul bound to Min's Vault, your image rendered in clay. The six-inch figurine containing your soul would remain on the shelf until someone unlocked it with their tokens, if you were lucky. Those whose luck had run out simply remained there, for eternity. Kambry refused to leave her soul to fuel the magic that kept the peace. Not again.

"Back to your mother, Kambry. Tsk, tsk. She's going to be broken by this. I need a combat trainer of her caliber for my guild. Sure, her magic is weak, but between her pert ass and those dexterous hands..." His audible sigh of longing gave her shivers. "Yummy. The things that woman can do with a sword certainly make up for her lack of magic. I could watch her work a training yard for ages." Thero gave an enthusiastic wolf-whistle.

"Keep dreaming," Kambry muttered, sprinting to the next tree to keep him from getting an angle on her.

"If I get you into a contract with me, well, Anoka will do anything for you. Too bad there's no knight in shining armor to rescue you from Min's shelf." She heard Thero kicking leaves as he brazenly taunted her. "Your mother would have no choice but to turn to me."

His words cut deep, but mostly because Thero was right. There *wasn't* anyone to rescue her this time. It had taken everything her mother had to free Kambry after her first failure. She was in debt too deep to do so again—unless she sold her body. And there was only one buyer who had that many tokens. Thero.

I can't give up. I can't let him get inside my head with his mind games. She pressed back against a tree. *I need an opening.*

Her gut had warned her this adventure was a mistake. Even though she was a spirited fighter and a warrior by training, she was scared.

There is always hope, she reminded herself, *you trained for this. His high levels don't matter on this floor—a level playing field means his level is the same as yours. Only his skills give him an advantage. You can win!* She psyched herself up. *Make Mom proud.*

It was just her rotten luck that someone had found her on this run. Why was Thero even here? When he wasn't instructing, he was in the Maze's advanced levels, gaining ever higher floors. He had never known as a player hunter, before. *Unless...*

"You're obviously here for my mother," Kambry said, voicing her thoughts. Her shoulders deflated and her head banged against the tree with a thud. She sighed. "Demon piss, you knew."

"Who told you?!" She paused to regain her composure. "Was it Exom? I bet it was that filthy merchant."

Kambry glanced at the coiled rope attached to her hip. She remembered the merchant's leering gaze. She'd allowed the creep to look down her shirt while she bent over to get the rope. She'd done so slowly, hoping for a discount.

She knew her large breasts could be quite an asset, if used properly.

In reality, though, he'd openly ogled her body only to throw her off. Kambry wanted to beat her forehead into the tree—how could she have been so stupid as to tell the merchant she was attempting another run? She was simply too trusting.

If she managed to get out of this, somehow, she would never make that mistake again.

"Doesn't matter who told what to whom. Sure, my levels are capped on this pathetic excuse for a floor, but my skills are far beyond what you can handle. Make it easy on both of us. Submit to a quick death and I promise to help your mother. It is more than a fair offer, that I help her dig herself out of debt." Thero scoffed, "Anoka needs my help, or they'll soon force her onto floors she can't handle. "

"You don't want her to end up on a shelf beside you, do you?" The mage snickered. "Submit to my contract. The great god Min herself will oversee it and ensure I honor my word. You'll be treated fairly," he gloated, "and we'll both come out of this situation better than we came into it."

The crunch of his boots in the underbrush, just the other side of the tree she hid behind, let Kambry know it was now or never. She so desperately wanted to retort, but actions spoke louder than words.

I wound him, get the locket, and escape. I can do this. I have to do this. For mom.

She loosened her grip on the staff in her left hand and clenched the sword in her right so tight the leather creaked. Speed was her greatest advantage; the time to act was now.

Kambry flung the staff to her left and spun around the tree to the right.

Thero didn't take her bait, however, and unleashed a gout of flame at her torso.

She lunged forward, arcing over the searing cone of fire. It missed her by inches as she twisted over it. Kambry grinned as she snapped her wings together, closing the gap between them. Thero smirked, knowing she couldn't dodge his next orange inferno.

Kambry gasped and her eyes bulged in pain as his flames blasted through her right wing.

She tucked into a roll mere feet before the mage. When she sprang back to her feet, she swung her sword at his torso, scoring a slice across Thero's hip and opening a small wound.

She knew better than to give her opponent any time to recover, so she reversed her blow with a swift backswing in a desperate attempt to down her foe.

He parried her assault with ease. She recovered quickly, though, launching into an overhand chop with her superior strength.

But Thero was no fool, he sidestepped her attack and spiked her foot to the earth with an ice shard.

The combat had been so rapid she had no time to react when his wind spell knocked her from her feet. Her trapped ankle snapped like a twig as she fell forward onto her face. The loud *crack* was nothing compared to her cry of anguish.

She lay crumpled on the ground.

"I like your style! This was so much fun," Thero teased. "But you need far more training, little girl."

Kambry had been defeated so swiftly, it was embarrassing. A spike of ice streaked down through the moist air, slamming into her lower back, pinning her to the ground. She groaned as a growing numbness spread over her body.

I'm sorry Mom. This is for you. Min, or the Suca Gods, if you're listening, send me a savior. Not trying to be picky, here, but I like muscles on my men. She pushed her forehead into the ground in humble supplication. *Oh,* she added before finishing her prayer, *make sure this pile of pestilence feels this.*

She'd landed on her staff. Kambry knew she was doomed—her ankle and back were white-hot beacons of pain. She had only one play left. Only one way to get even.

The fire spell she cast was beyond unstable. When someone used magic incorrectly like this, it tended to leave a smoking crater where they'd stood, or lain, in her case.

Thero didn't noticed her staff, overloaded with power, as he arrived to gloat until it was too late.

Kambry tossed his evil laugh from earlier back in his face, but with far more enthusiasm. She'd found her last request to the gods that damn funny. Of all the final prayers to give, hers had been the best.

Thero stood over her. His frown, slumped shoulder, and weary eyes told her he was disappointed.

"I'll be picked off the shelves in an hour," the words poured from his mouth, "Cancel that spell or I'll torment your mother instead of doting on her. If you—"

Kambry only had time for one final thought. *At least I went out with a bang!*

A really big bang that would cost the prick twenty-five tokens to reclaim his soul.

CHAPTER

TWO

DEAN

Planet Oakley - 2542 AD - Larvian Sea

Dean slammed his feet into the ship's deck, arched his back and bent the pole in an attempt to control the running fish that fought him like a beast. The fishing line screamed as the gears fought to aid Dean in his efforts.

"Fook me, she's a hefty one!" Uncle Gordano hollered over his shoulder. The man was a professional fisherman and immediately tossed the water jets in reverse. The aft of the ship's hull flung sheets of water in the air as Dean regained line. "Atta boy, steady as she goes."

"I'm twenty-six, hardly a boy, and fook me indeed," Dean grunted with exertion. He pumped the rod and hand reeled the line in hastily. "She's turning!"

Gordano slammed the boat into neutral while Dean danced around the port wall. The ship pivoted forward and to the left once the captain gleaned the fish's new direction.

The reel screamed as the mighty beast peeled off line. Dean tightened the cinch down to maximum to slow the spool.

"There's no easy catch on this one, Uncle. She'll be a fighter and green for a while," Dean shouted.

He was fairly certain his uncle had already figured that out, from the sheer power this sea creature exhibited.

No doubt about it, this was going to be a knock-down drag-out fight and that wasn't always a good thing for a fishing boat.

"I miss the days when we weren't so regulated by them desk sitting bastards in Belmont. When'll governments learn, eh? Never! Stoopid fooks the lot of them," Gordano cursed, ensuring he diverted the boat to manage the fish's turn.

"Uncle, we both know there ain't no fun in auto-catching fish. The new rules help little guys, with the fishermen unionizing the whole damn thing; I'll agree with it, too. Sure hope this is a worthy haul," Dean said, struggling to keep the beast from stealing additional length on him.

A drone popped up out of the Forrester's Fancy Feline's roof. The device bleeped red as it recorded Dean in action. "Hey, Uncle! We've got a viewer! An extra few G-coins for sure."

Rarely did they get live viewers chucking down Galactic coins (G-coins) to watch them in action.

Dean ignored the viewer to focus on his task. His arms bulged from the contest. Dean had been doing this for years, though, building up incredible endurance and strength, particularly in his forearms and shoulders.

He worked the fish while his uncle handled the boat. They'd been a team that outperformed all others for the last three seasons on Oakley. Something that mattered far less now than it used to.

The Oakley government had shifted from a pure profit basis to a mix of socialism and capitalism. All catches were piled into a loot for all. The only bonus you got was after you exceeded your seasonal quota. If you missed your quota, you didn't have to worry, others helped you get paid.

Miss it five times in a row, however, and you stopped getting paid. While Dean thought it was complete bullshit someone could not toss a single line in the water for 5 weeks and still get paid, there had been that one time the duo had appreciated the help.

There had been a whole month when the fish had been scarce, Dean tore his rotator cuff, and Uncle Gordano had to visit his girlfriend's dying auntie.

Dean knew the expansion on Oakley wasn't perfect, but he was okay with that. What really kept him from bellyaching about minor problems was that, for the most part, his life was good. He earned a decent living doing something he loved; it afforded him plenty of time to play grabass with the ladies and to go on adventures with the lads.

The ever-present recording drone buzzed close to Dean who angrily tried to blow the obnoxious thing away. His efforts against the machine were futile.

"Damn Belmont nobles, always spying on us fishermen. Bugger off, ya damn thing," Uncle Gordano said in frustration.

"Focus. Full reverse!" Dean shouted. "Belay, starboard turn!" he corrected himself.

The catch was swimming away, and Dean couldn't let the line gain too much slack. The reel spooled line back in as the duo worked in tandem to keep the fish close to the boat.

There was always the very real chance a hook could pop free or the line could snap. The rules were the rules. Team Forrester knew better than to try to sneak anything by the observer drones.

"Whatchya thinking it is?" Gordano asked his nephew.

"In these waters, who the fook knows. I'd wager something ugly and poisonous. That's about my luck lately," Dean said with a scoff. His big arms torqued the pole back, denying the fish an easy line steal. "Tis a fighter, ay, no doubt about it."

Dean let the fish run as he scanned the horizon.

The sea around Oakley was green, that lime green you'd see in pictures from Earth. The waves were minimal in a gentle roll without chop. The clear sky let the yellowish suns beat down on a warmer than usual day.

The Forrester boys, as the other fishing crews called them, were on their forty-foot fishing hauler. A large ship like this was expensive and had been a fitting upgrade after years of hard work.

The bow of the ship had port and starboard claw cranes and an icebox hatch. Connected to the base of the claws were the Nevermiss™ fishing spears. The automations would gaff and retrieve the sea monsters of Oakley while the claws would snatch and dump the catch.

The stern was perfect for combating a monster catch on rod and reel with an expansive fishing deck penned in with thigh high walls.

Dean spun from port to starboard as the fish darted off in a new direction. He felt the jet propellers already swiveling to adjust, so he avoided wasting any breath shouting directions to his uncle.

He was feeling confident about this catch when a boiling of the sea a few hundred feet ahead caught his attention.

On its own, that was normal. A common effect of predators hunting prey in oceans across the galaxy. Except Oakley was drastically larger than Earth and its oceans only covered sixty-plus percent of the globe. While that equated to an excess of living area for humans, in comparison to the Earth, it really emphasized how different the seas were.

Sea life on Oakley was diverse and massive, Dean included the fish he currently struggled with in the latter category.

There were probably a few sea leviathans capable of swallowing this boat in one gulp. Would they? Probably never. Was there a risk? Certainly. Every season there were fishermen who never returned to the docks.

There were also those idiots who fished out of season and into the lightning storms of doom as the duo called them. Dean and his Uncle Gordano knew better, however, than to mess with those chaotic events. Dean also knew the boiling sea of baitfish was a bad sign for him and whatever was on his line.

"Ya seeing that?" Dean asked nodding over to the stirring surface.

"Aye, ain't good. Needin' to risk the line. Puttin' da Fancy Feline into neutral and getting the crane gaff ready," Gordano hollered, already moving towards the bow.

Dean immediately adjusted his line, causing the catch to shake its head angrily. A moment later the line went slack as the fish darted back in his direction.

Not good.

Dean had only a fraction of a second to react. His left hand left the pole locked into its rig while his right pumped the reel. He reached for a large trident gaff stored on the inside of the starboard wall. His hand found the shaft without ever taking his gaze from the line.

He ripped it from its container and stuck the weapon in a rod holder while avoiding the wire that unspooled with its release.

The rules for commercial fishing, compounded with multiple caveats and restrictions, permitted manually spearing a sea creature from any distance. It was literally one of the few no-holds-barred ways to snag a fish, assuming you hadn't baited the fish to the surface.

The crane gaff was different. There were distance requirements, and even line-off-reel requirements to prevent fishermen from simply driving up next to and gaffing a fish. Hell, there were even rules about how often you could shoot the darn things. All this led to the simple, yet incredibly dangerous fact that Dean was prepared to spear this monster himself, the old-fashioned way, if the gigantic fish at the end of his line didn't cooperated with the bureaucrats' long list of rules.

Years of fishing these seas had taught him hundreds of lessons—the kind learned only from experience. When a school of two-foot long fish jumped out of the water not thirty feet away, Dean was certain he had made the right choice.

He cranked the reel with vigor, desperate to get the line spooled back in. The fish was going to surface any moment and he had better be ready.

Dean dodged his head to the left as a large baitfish leaped into the boat.

The water lifted and the boat rocked, causing Dean to frown. His fish should only have displaced a fraction of that. Further out, fortunately, the surface stirred again from another goliath pushing water, reassuring him he hadn't accidentally hooked a ship killer.

"Here she be!" Dean shouted with a grin.

He'd spooled the line tight. A green icon flashed across the boat indicating the spear could be released. A twenty-foot Asroun breached the surface in a stunning display. Dean kept the line tight, so the indicator remained green.

Crack!

A spear rocketed out of the crane gun. The trajectory was sound, the aim precise.

Whoosh!

Dean fist-pumped at the epic Asroun, waiting for the spear to dig into the toothless fast swimmer.

Thump!

And then the joy fled his body and distress overwhelmed his senses as a second massive maw erupted from the water. A leviathan of the deep had arrived for an easy snack.

Oh no! Not a Voratin. We're doomed.

His heart pounded against his chest as the Voratin chomped the Asroun's tail clean off. The leviathan continued to reveal is hard shelled underbelly as it breached in an epic spectacle. This Voratin instilled terror in Dean; the difference between the two airborne sea monsters was staggering.

The situation left him in dismay. An Asroun in these waters made sense, it was a small school feeder with slimy green skin slotted with black stripes. The twenty-foot creature was a rare catch, but nothing unheard of.

The Voratin, however, was a sea monster of legend. It was rumored to be a boat killer and one of the top five things every crew was always taught to avoid. The ominous music they played when showing safety briefings about this creature was apropos for this very moment.

The beak on the creature's head was at least the size of the Asroun it hounded. If Gordano's shot hadn't yanked the prey out of its grasp there would simply have been a large fish, swallowed whole.

His well-placed spear gaffing of the Asroun was actually worse.

The ensuing splash of both creatures returning to the water rocked the boat and soaked Dean as water crashed back into the ocean.

He was in shock as the spear auto-reeled in what remained of the catch and the claw swiveled the Asroun into the icy hold in the short amount of time it took for a few heartbeats to thud against Dean's chest.

"No!" Gordano screamed at the automated claw.

The duo's eyes locked on to each other in horror.

We're so screwed. Before Uncle Gordano could even begin to rush the boat out of harm's way, the Voratin slammed into the side of the vessel.

Gordano stumbled into the captain's section while Dean grabbed onto the trident to keep his feet during the boat's violent shaking. Gordano recovered and switched the jets forward by inputting a steady acceleration.

Dean blew a deep sigh of relief when Gordano incrementally increased their speed and then finally gunned the boat's powerful engines. There was that welcoming familiar jostle of the boat cresting waves.

"Holy moon pies and yellow snakes!" Dean exclaimed. "I can't believe we got aw-"

Suddenly the Voratin's huge maw opened over the aft swim platform and snipped it off cleanly with a single bite.

"Faster!" Dean shouted with concern.

Gordano spun to look back over his shoulder and pointed at the controls. "She's on max!"

Dean snatched the trident out of the rod holder. He was not going down without a fight. The ship swarmed with drones, determined to catch their demise on record.

A maw opened up on the port side as the tail splashed water high into the air. The Voratin gained speed, eager to finish its metallic prey.

Dean didn't hesitate. He was dead without taking a drastic risk. He hopped onto the back deck and ran straight at the Voratin. His leap carried him over the tip of the massive beak preparing to crunch into the ship's hull.

Dean spun in midair with a half twist, so that when the trident line snapped tight, it caused both him and the spear to snap down into an eyeball as big as a buoy.

With his bulging muscles applying every bit of force he could muster, Dean plunged the triple speared weapon into the monster's eye.

The force of the Voratin speeding forward and the trident racing the other direction sank the weapon deep into the beast's ocular cavity.

Dean never got a chance to celebrate his amazing stab. The jarring collision with the beast sent him flying into the ocean.

The Larvian Sea was something no sane human went into willingly, ever. The depths were filled with monsters eager and ready to consume soft flesh. Even the beaches used multiple layers of reinforced steel netting to keep the copious predators out in the bay.

Dean plunged into the depths eerily far from his ship. The torrential current of the Voratin's wake sucked him after it.

Desperate to regain the air knocked out of him, he struggled towards the refracted sunlight above. When he finally breached the surface, Dean gulped in air with an urgency. With powerful strokes, he surged towards the boat in a determined swim. Gordano spotted him, shouting in vain as the boat was dragged further away from his nephew by a still-swimming Voratin. A preserver circle auto ejected from the retreating ship, soaring in his direction like a massive frisbee.

Dean adjusted his course and latched onto the device when it landed. He triggered the transformation button to convert it into a life raft. While the donut morphed into a lifeboat, he waited precariously.

He kicked off the waterlogged shoes that were impeding his ability to tread water but regretted the decision immediately.

Something long and slimy etched a jolt of electricity into his toes.

"Ya gotta be fooking kidding me!" Dean shouted to the drones above and below as they recorded him.

"Get in the raft immediately," a panicked voice from one of drones shouted, probably an emergency dispatcher.

Dean was actually calm and besides the cut he'd received on his right hand, somehow, he was surprisingly okay. The raft wasn't ready for him, yet, and he would destroy the transformation process if he flopped onto it now, ruining any chance of utilizing the life-saving tool.

"I'll kill it, quit being a pussy," Dean snapped to the drone operator.

He yanked the knife he used for fileting bait out of its sheath on his thigh. Dean ducked his head under the water, his weapon at the ready.

The visibility was about what he'd expected.

Shitty.

He saw several drones blasting indicator lighting off to his right. He noticed a pattern of them trying to aid his sight. Sure enough, from off to his right, an Eelraken shot for his torso.

He rapidly backstroked to shift his position. Rows of sharp teeth narrowly missed his nose. His left hand drove the knife into the side of the Eelraken as it twisted around to bite him. Dean's right hand was desperate to keep the head of the creature at bay even as his blade carved its body. He was stunned when his hand slid into the slimy body and his fingers clamped around something circular.

His entire body locked up from the intense electrical shock. At that moment, Dean died—megajoules of energy coursing through his body.

Yet a fraction of second later his functions returned. Sure, he pissed himself and sharted a bit, but somehow, he lived.

Dean knew he had to react quickly or drown. His feet kicked intensely, and he had a hard decision to make. Abandon the catch or dive deeper to retrieve the slowly sinking Eelraken's body. Dean knew there was only one choice for a diehard fisherman. One did not release a fish once caught.

He kicked down with powerful strokes until his arms bound the slimy creature tightly. Scissor pumps with his legs brought him back up to surface. With a whooping war cry of victory, he tossed the dead Eelraken into the now usable life raft. He sheathed his knife before hauling himself into the little round raft.

"Medical responders are on their way," a drone said.

Dean groaned at the person watching him. "Fook off, I can't afford it. I'm doing dandy," he complained to the drone.

"There is a volunteer on board and-"

"Great, great, but I'm fine," Dean said, weakly trying to bat the annoying drones away.

He found the craft's control panel and set the destination to his ship - the *Forrester's Fancy Feline*. While the little life raft got busy hauling its two passengers, he inspected his body.

"Oh, by the balls of Jupiter!" Dean cursed when he saw his chest.

His shirt was ruined. The body of the Eelraken had sent its full charge into him when they collided.

His outer skin was scarred by angry red puss-filled blisters. Oddly, he didn't feel the damage. The rational part of your brain that warns people not to mess with things had clearly malfunctioned for Dean.

He popped a nasty liquid-filled skin-bubble and heard the video operator gagging.

"Gross," Dean said at the sight of his chest, now oozing yellowish liquid.

When he glanced at his hand, he saw the wound from the Voratin was gone. A healed seam was in its place. As if magic had washed over his wound and left a raised scar.

Well, there were repair bots in this day and age that could do that, but not one that an Eelraken could hold and administer.

Must've been the raft had some healing bit built into it. How did I survive the electrocution then?

That was the last he thought about it as he was in for a surprise. The Fancy Feline pulled up to rescue Dean, distracting him from his self-evaluation.

On the front of the boat rested a hundred-plus foot sea monster. Its head and tail were both dragging in the water and the crane must be exceeding its maximum capacity, lifting the beast as high as it was. His trident stab through the eye and into its brain had been enough to end the mighty leviathan.

Gordano was brimming with a smile when the ship paused to pick up the stranded nephew.

"You're a crazy shit, Dean. That bastard dragged me even after it died. The bilge pumps were on overdrive as it flooded the aft from pulling me backwards. Right! A close call, close, for both of us. Worst part is, the news caught all of that. You're a legend my boy," Gordano congratulated him, when Dean flung the Eelraken onto the deck. "Da fook?"

"Unk. I guess if we're being recorded and actively watched I can clean up the slang. Uncle, this asshole ruined my chest," Dean said pointing at the dead Eelraken. Then he pointed at the big dead Voratin. "After that asshole flung me hundreds of feet. Damn, so much happened in a couple of seconds, it felt like a lifetime."

Dean laid down beside a still-flopping baitfish. He was too exhausted to give the deck dancer a merciful death.

Gordano kneeled beside his nephew and let out a long whistle of sympathy.

"You hurtin, lad?"

Dean swiveled his head and opened his eyes with a groan before batting away his Uncle's hands. "Tis nothing but a flesh wound."

"Ya've been watching those damn reruns at Patti's house, again. I thought you'd moved out? Seeing as how the two of you are not dating anymore," Gordano said, revealing juicy details to an eagerly recording set of drones. "Right?"

"Ugh, speaking of the Kendrick's house. Well, I almost died. So... umm, I want to come clean about something I've been hesitant to say in the open. I hate to do this on camera, but I've got a confession, Uncle. Patti and I stopped dating years ago— that you know. Even though I've been staying in her guesthouse, I was planning to crash at your place when you went on vacation at the end of this fishing season. I've saved up some funds and planned to get a nice crash pad, so I'd finally stop mooching. Honestly, I'm sitting pretty and could've moved out sooner. But I like Mr. Kendrick's, and Patti and I, we're still friends, and... it's complicated." Dean groaned.

"Aye, don't I know it. Fret not. I get you like him like a father, same as you do me," his Uncle chuckled. "Too bad it didn't work out with his daughter. Wait, is that pain or -"

"I slept with Candace. Few weeks back, she opened my room door and consented me. I'd have sent her away, if I wasn't so darn lonely myself," Dean admitted, his hands running through his short hair.

His Uncle snorted.

"Okay," he rolled his eyes, "maybe I was horny, not lonely. Feel awful about the whole ordeal. Everyone is going to be pissed."

"Tis the way to come clean. No sense in half-assing it, kiddo. How do you think Marty is gonna take it?" Gordano asked.

"Mr. Kendricks? I'm not too concerned about him. Orlith, though," he sighed, "she is a protective momma and I'm treated very well there. Patti, however, is going to go ballistic. All I want is not to alienate myself from the longest home I've ever known," I muttered, "beside yours, of course."

Gordano sighed with a sad glance down at his nephew's chest. "We don't get many redeeming chances. At least you came clean, and that's the right thing to do. Now, relax. Here comes your personal doctor."

Dean's eyes shot up to see a reflective ship's exterior lowering a medical professional down to the *Fancy Feline*. If he'd been hoping for a sexy nurse, well, Dean would've been disappointed.

A chunky lady with the features of a rat rushed to his side. Her hair was scraggly, her double chin thick, and she had food stuck to her cheek. To make matters worse, the first thing she did was to jam a ten-inch needle into his chest. The plunger dove down, and Dean stared at the audacious woman.

"The fook was that for?" Dean asked angrily, glaring at the needle in his chest.

When the nurse or doctor glanced down at Dean, she screamed in shock. Her eyes glazed in fright until Dean suddenly felt woozy.

"Oh, it's working... just slower," she said, seeing Dean's eyes fluttering, "he should already be down."

A jolt of energy coursed briefly through his veins that was swiftly put down. Blackness ensued.

CHAPTER

THREE

DEAN

Ola City

Dean drifted awake to the droning of the local news.

His blurred vision finally came in to focus, only to see Marty Kendricks seated in a hotel recliner watching a segment about a new influx of Earth immigrants eager to start a new life on Oakley.

The room was far from what he expected. He'd figured to come to either in a broom-closet sized hospital room or his Uncle's couch. It was a shock, because the room he found himself in had breathtaking views of the ocean. There were floor to ceiling windows his out left and a similar expanse of the city to his right. Either Mr. Kendricks thought Dean needed a super fancy hotel room, or something was afoot.

Dean shifted in the king-sized bed to sit up. He gave a throat clearing grunt to reveal to his guest that he was back with the living.

"So, Dean," Marty began with a meek smile, "not exactly how a father wants to hear about his daughters." He set the remote down after a quick power button press.

Dean shifted overt to the edge of the bed and paused, looking around. "Where am I?"

"Luxury penthouse of the Boisterous Tower. Biggest hotel in Ola," Marty noted with a pip in his voice, as if he was warming up to a sales pitch.

The actual name of their city was RootyCola, named after the famous beverage company, which had sponsored its colonization. Yes, no surprise that such sponsors remained particular about what they named everything. Not a surprise to anyone. The residents called the city 'Ola', however, in an effort to salvage some dignity.

"The catch?" Dean asked, running a hand over the thick layers of bandages and dressing that coated his chest.

Marty snickered. "First words out of your mouth are 'Where am I?' and 'The catch?'... nothing about my daughters or the shambles that your home life is in? Not a peep about your wounds? Your catch..." He paused to shake his head and let out another chuckle. "I wished you'd stayed at the office, Dean, you had a great thing going."

Years ago, Dean had attended the local college. Freshman year he was invited to an excursion in the woods for spring break. Oakley had a lot of the same old Earth traditions. He didn't get word at the last minute that there was a sudden change of venue—from the woods to the beach.

The original host was stuck at her cabin retreat alone, with Dean. That host was Patti Kendricks. After finding out what had happened, Dean skipped the beach for the woods—even ditching a potential girlfriend who was bummed he didn't come play in the surf with her.

Instead, Dean spent a week with Patti and her parents, who came to liven things up and make the situation a little less awkward. Dean and Marty hit it off right away. Dean and Patti's relationship slowly developed. While they did grow closer, they never really hit it off as a couple. Dean blamed the sex; she blamed his drinking.

When all was said and done, however, Dean was still the guy the Kendricks could rely on—a close friend of the family. Marty valued Dean's commitment to his earlier plans with Patti. He could've easily skipped the woods for the beach and Marty respected that. When Dean graduated, Marty had offered him a job at one of his accounting firms.

For three months, Dean did his best, trying to make things work at the firm. He was too restless to sit behind a desk and stare at a display all day, every day. To Marty's dismay, Dean resigned after those first three months. He spent the next three years fishing, seasonally. His off-seasons—the commercial fishing season was usually two months on and then two off—were often spent in the Kendricks' guest house.

Marty loved to remind Dean how safe the office was.

"I'd have jumped out a window if I'd spent another month behind a desk," Dean shuddered in remembrance.

All external planets ran off an Earth calendar, even when things didn't quite line up. Given its huge size, Oakley had thirty-hour days, and thirty-hour nights. Some colonized planets opted to stick with their own local times when it could work and keep track of two different systems. On Oakley they just ignored the planet's sunrise and sunset. Belmont, Ola and all of Oakley used Zulu Earth time. Confusing for a kid to understand, but you got used to it.

Dean changed the subject when Marty frowned without responding to his flippant remark about the office. "How did Orlith take it?"

"My wife is the least angry of the three, yet, still furious. Hence why I am here, at your side, instead of in my home," Marty said with a smile. He walked to the ocean window and peered down at the seafoam green water. "You should have been killed by the Voratin," Marty turned back and studied Dean. "And if some miracle kept you alive through all that, the Eelraken should have used up what little luck you had left."

"My wounds felt numb after I was zapped," Dean said, bewildered, "Look at my hand." He raised his hand, showing Marty the raised seam of a scar. Whatever that Eelraken had done to him, it still baffled Dean.

"I had you delivered directly here, instead of to a hospital. With those new injections and modern medicine, you were only unconscious for an hour and a half." He glanced at a clock on the bedside table. "Eh... closer to two."

"Anyhow," Marty continued, "the doctor lady cleared you after wrapping and bandaging your chest. Said that hand scar must be old. She could have removed it but didn't have the right tools with her. For a few thousand coins, you can have fresh clean flesh again... unless you want to keep the battle scar, that is."

Dean chuckled, admiring the evidence of his tussle with a Voratin.

"You're lucky you don't have insurance," Marty sighed, "Else they'd still be running a barrage of tests on you. Instead, a film crew wants to buy the rights to your footage to make a movie."

"What?" Dean grunted, his face twisted into scowl. "Gotta take a leak, hold that thought."

He walked toward a mirror in the bathroom. Dean had always been a big kid. He stood over six feet six inches and with his active lifestyle and fishing career, had bulked up to just under 250 pounds. With sandy brown hair and hazel eyes, his ruggedly handsome features suited him well.

He would never be an actor, or a model, but Dean couldn't care less about vanity. He was into fishing, hunting, camping, bar diving, digital fighting, dirt biking, and other exciting pastimes—things that tended to result in scars. He had a story to tell for every one of them.

A quick drain of the old bladder and he returned to the bedroom Marty.

"So... a movie, huh?" Dean said, hunting for clothes that covered more than the hospital gown he'd woke up in.

"I brought a change of clothes for you, in the top drawer." Marty pointed to a large chest-of-drawers against the wall. "I guess my first question really should've been how are you feeling?"

Dean slid into a fresh set of what he thought of as bar clothes, which included an Ola Pride t-shirt, some sweats, and a pair of sneakers that had seen better days. Perfect for when he just wanted to lounge at a bar, or chill on a couch.

"You may not believe me," Dean chuckled at Marty's wry smirk, "but I feel fine. Different, for some reason, but I am not sure how, yet," Dean said, rotating his upper body in a stretch to pop his back. "It's hard to describe. What exactly did the doctor say?"

"That you're a lucky, and I quote 'Handsome SOB,' " Marty said with a smirk. "Oh, and don't remove your ban—"

Dean, of course, was already unwrapping the chest covering. When it reached his bare skin, it was smooth with tufts of random chest hair.

"Dammit," Dean grumbled, "my chest is all patchy, now. I'm usually not a chest shaving kind of guy."

Marty came over and ran a finger over a patch of synth skin. "She did a good job fixing your wounds. For almost free, it's actually amazing. Sometimes I -"

"Almost free, you say?" Dean note, with some concern. He hated owing favors, even to good friends.

There was a huffing pause. "I paid it; you owe me a few hundred. I get it, we again go back to the desk job you should've kept. Money was tight. At least you can finally stop fretting. You survived a harrowing ordeal," Marty said, and his pocket jingled a tune.

He retrieved his iPhonie47 from his pocket, stuck a single finger in the air to pause their conversation, and answered. "Hello...? Yes, I'm beside him, right now... Yup, fit as a whistle."

Dean left him so he wasn't overbearing his space. Finding a clear spot, he flopped down, face first, onto the carpet. His weight caused a thud when he caught himself on his palms, his arms wider than shoulder width apart. He knocked out a dozen quick pushups; Dean felt great. The skin on his chest was smooth and new, his muscles handled the exertion with ease.

He still had a lot of unanswered questions about what had happened, so he found his phone on the end table and hooked into the interweb. He fretted about how he would pay Marty back for the hospital visit and shifted linked over to his bank account. His jaw bounced off the floor when he saw a fat three hundred thousand

Galactic coins more than he expected to in his usually anorexically lean account. He gasped and hesitated before he dove into his messages.

Did I win the lottery?

Trying to figure out how his account suddenly had hundreds of thousands of G-coins left him perplexed. Sure, he had a few hundred saved up for a rainy day, but this was far more than even the catch should have hauled in. He checked his income revenue and noted the numerous royalty deposits. Oh...

Normally, the odd drone footage brought in a few fractions of a coin. The infrequent guy or girl, normally a dude though, who tuned into their fishing show earned him a two percent royalty from whatever ad revenue the show attracted or a percentage of application subscriptions for those who spent a little extra for their views to be ad-free.

This amount was staggering and meant the video of his battle with the Voratin must have been watched by... A LOT of people. It had millions of views and that number kept climbing.

Uncle Gordano earns three percent royalties, light lordy...

His phone rang.

"Hello," he answered.

The voice on the other side was hesitant. "Dean?"

Ah, Candace. She sounded really timid, which didn't bode well for the conversation.

"Yeah, I'm here."

"They moved your stuff out, Dean. I'm so sorry. I'll try to find you tonight. Eek. Mom found me, gotta go," Candace hung up the phone.

Dean sighed and saw Marty was off the phone, also.

"That was Candace," he admitted. "Where's my stuff going?"

Marty slapped his young friend on the shoulder. "I love you like a son, Dean," he grinned, "that said, however, there's zero fookin chance you're shacking up at my place with angry hens in the roost. Gordano is heading out of town, tonight probably, at least that's what he said, when we swapped places at the hospital. You can either rent his apartment or find a new port, Skipper."

Dean plopped his ass down on the bed and grunted in defeat. "So, talk about rough sailing." There was a teasing hint of sarcasm in his voice. "Suddenly I have more money than I've ever seen in one account. I save my uncle's life and he flees for calmer waters. I come clean on Galactic television, thinking I'm about to die, and lose my crash pad while pissing off everyone else I give two shits about."

"Right! Actions have consequences," Marty said with a chortle. "Office jobs are much safer." His finger wag and an 'I told you so grin' got Dean to smile. "Can't say I feel bad for ya, though."

"I did this to myself," Dean said with a frown that transitioned into a grin, "And yeah, I made a bunch of coins, but so did Gordano. He finally gets to retire to the outer systems and cruise around, screwing old single ladies. A 'barracuda in a fish-bowl' as he liked to say."

Who was Dean kidding? The future was always brighter when you had coins.

"I guess I need to find a crew," Dean said with a grimace of determination. "We got four, maybe five more good fishing days. The Forrester's Fancy Feline is already at union quota. Oh shit, I'll have to buy the boat from him if he's skipping town." Dean started tossing his stuff into a pile on the end of the bed. "I need to talk to my uncle. Thanks for being here when I woke up."

Dean had already started for the door before Marty held him back.

"Two things before you jet off." Marty handed me a folded up digi-pad. "Since I'm your next of kin after Gordano, I got this offer. This is an offer for rights to a movie about your Voratin battle. They are offering a 300K advance, with five percent royalties. As an accountant, I was able to do some digging into the company's financials..." he paused, and a wolfish grin slid into place. "Counter with twelve percent royalties and no advance. Trust me."

"I do," Dean said without hesitation. "And the second thing?"

"Find a desk job, my boy!" He laughed at his own joke.

Dean smirked, knowing this was typical Marty.

"Seriously, though," Marty continued, "enjoy this vacation you've earned. This storm season is supposed to be bad."

Dean shrugged—he'd always found it impossible to sit still when he could be out fishing.

"Last thing," Marty frowned, "Candace is an adult, but you and I both know... she is not the right girl for you. Not hating on you, or going to stand in your way if you try to make it work, but..."

"I get it," Dean nodded, "Really, I do. Less drama the better. Twelve percent and I'm going to go hiking or big game hunting somewhere in one of the savannahs. Maybe convince Quincy's bar diving ass to join me." He smiled to himself. "Yeah, that is exactly what I'll do," Dean said feeling more confident.

He looked at Marty. "I'll always be there if you need me, though. Thanks for letting me crash at your place, and... um... sorry about Candace."

"She's a big girl and you didn't break her heart. Honestly, give it a few weeks and I bet they'll be all sappy about not having you around," Marty said, patting his friend on the back goodbye.

Dean left the hotel room but paused just outside the entrance to the penthouse. He digitally signed the offer with his counteroffer of zero advance and twelve percent royalties. They fired back three seconds later with ten percent royalties and a one-hundred K G-coins advance.

Hmm...

The immediate response screamed of desperation... ten percent? He stood firm at twelve. They met him at eleven and a twenty-five K advance. Looked like he was going to be earning a crap-ton of royalties for a movie about Oakley's sea monsters. The when was an as-yet-to-be-determined point in the future. A tidy little bonus for another day, he figured.

There was a skip to his step when he entered the elevator that finally came and pressed the 'Lobby' button. The damn thing shot electricity into him. Odd. At least it kept going, even if one of the lights burned out.

On the ride down, the elevator filled with people and he was that annoying dick who pulled out his phone and made a call in public. He ignored the irritated glares and dialed Gordano.

Uncle Gordano was still at the docks sorting out their catch. Apparently, there was a bidding war over the Voratin. This was the first one caught since the laws and regulations had changed on commercial fishing.

Dean laughed. No shit it was the first. They would never be caught with a mono line on a rod and reel.

Dean knew there would be some crazy adventure junkies who'd try to recreate his feat.

Why would people think otherwise? Some crazy fisherman killed a hundred-foot-long turtle fish creature with a trident. Yup, forty people were going to earn themselves a Darwin award. He'd simply done the impossible, trying to survive.

The sun hung directly overhead which reminded Dean about how awkward time-keeping could be on planet Oakley.

Dean's walk down Ola's streets to the docks was through a lively crowd. The Boisterous Tower was a waterfront hotel not far from the shore. Seeing as how he had no keycard, it was probably an hourly rental Marty had whipped up to hide from the trio of angry ladies in his home. Dean ingested the sights of the port city.

Tall buildings dotted this part of town with numerous air car balconies, big glass windows, and restaurants on the ground floor. Each of the nearby soaring skyscrapers proclaimed they had the greatest views available. Ola was packed and busy. Flying taxis, busy streets, and crowded sidewalks made it increasingly difficult to get around downtown. Drones zipped overhead, intent on delivering the latest purchases to impatient consumers. Dean had been in Ola for what felt like ages—and rarely was it ever NOT crowded.

Ola was on the orbital dropship route, and as such, tended to be busier than outlying towns and cities. An atmospheric shuttle the size of thirty story building whined overhead, its thrusters roaring above the normal sounds of the city as it eased the massive machine's descent into the space port. The newest batch of tourists from around the galaxy had arrived to visit the shiny port city of RootyCola.

Dean smirked and dodged a jogger. It was so easy to get distracted in this metropolis. Storefront ads begged for his attention; their neon signs tried to entice him out of his hard-earned G-coins. But Dean had seen and experienced it all, at least by Ola's relatively limited standards. Maybe that was his problem.

A vacation would help, but maybe a new port would help even more.

He sighed as he gave it some deep thought. He knew these fishing grounds too well. If he had scored his big payday, as it appeared he had, should he even keep fishing?

He felt conflicted and understandably so. So much had happened, and all so quickly. He didn't even know where he was sleeping tonight. Not like Dean couldn't afford a nice hotel for a night or two.

Assuming he got the opportunity to catch a break. For years he had wanted nothing more than to be the skipper of his own ship. Yet, now that the opportunity beckoned, he was somehow hesitant.

As he shifted his route across the street and made his final turn for the docks, the overwhelming perfume of the fish processing plant assaulted him. Even with the smell reducing ventilators positioned around the neighborhood, the stench was overwhelming.

Then again, he and his fellow fishermen had hauled in some big monsters today. Nothing went to waste here on Oakley. That was certainly one thing Dean could get behind.

Farmers would be happy when the fertilizer prices dropped. The number of useless byproducts from today's catch was going to be massive, and people didn't care if fish parts fueled the growth of their own food.

The crowd thinned out in this part of the town. That's about all the stink was good for. There were camera drones hovering around the massive body of the Voratin. Well, what remained of the body. Machines cleaved into sections of the vast beast with a tool akin to a chainsaw—just far less messy and operated by drones.

Workers efficiently processed the mighty beast. The docks had originally been built to handle these sized catches, back before all the rules and regulations stifled the size of an average day's catch—back when there were no rules. All that was left from those days were memories and images of massive sea creatures that still gave children nightmares after they'd been to the museum.

Dean stuck his hands on his hips and watched the rather gruesome task. This explained why there'd been no payday from the catch, at least not yet.

"Hey, Kiddo!" Uncle Gordano shouted from within a crowd of reporters. He waved Dean over. "Over here," he shouted, as if Dean was dense and couldn't tell that's what he wanted.

Dean didn't mind. His uncle was clearly riding a joyful high. The kind of high life rarely presented you with. For Dean, it still hadn't fully sunk in, how lucky he'd been. When the young man arrived the reporters and journalists abandoned Uncle Gordano to barrage him with questions.

"Please, wait a moment... I'll answer questions in a moment... Please..." Dean was rapidly losing his temper. He raised his voice and assertively belted out, "Back the fook up and let me talk to my Uncle, and then afterwards, I'll devote some time to answering your questions."

Dean pushed his way through the crowd of reporters, and Gordano surprised him with a massive hug. Yup, the man certainly was happy. Dean led him onto the *Fancy Feline* to steal a bit of privacy.

They clomped over to the real wood docks beyond a security point that held the press back. All the new cities were using that synthetic crap for their walkways, but Dean loved the sound of boards under his shoes.

The ship rocked as they hopped aboard and quickly moved to the captain's station, where drones were prohibited. When the door sealed behind Dean, his uncle let out an eardrum shattering whoop of joy. Dean plugged his ears while laughing.

"Hey!" Dean had to shout to pull his Uncle out of his happy dance.

Gordano let out a long sigh. One so long, he had to pause a moment to catch his breath.

"I'm retiring. At least for now. With age extenders, surgery enhancers, and proper exercise, I'm set to live the comfy life for the next one hundred years. I also got a cash advance from some movie place for thirty thousand and one percent royalty." Gordano caught his nephew's wince. "What?"

"Eh, I got eleven percent," Dean said with a shrug.

His uncle's eyes bulged. "Impressive! Speaking of which. I know you want to buy this old girl." He paused and focused on him with sad eyes. "The film crew asked to purchase this baby for triple the—"

Dean groaned at the suddenness of that statement. He went to the small table and slid into the bench seat. He ran his hands through his short hair in frustration and then let the disappointment go.

"Uncle, you raised me. This is your big payday times ten. Take the money—don't be a fool. Selling the *Fancy Feline* to me at cost ain't worth it. I'll need to go boat shopping for something smaller, anyway," Dean said with a genuine smile.

That meant the rest of the season was ruined.

"Any chance you can you make the sell contingent on me using her for the rest of the season? There's only seven days left of it, after all." Dean asked and his uncle tapped furiously on his iPhonie.

Dean went to talk, but his Uncle threw a hand up as he started a conversation on his phone.

Dean glanced around. The room down here had four bunks. There was another cabin with double that on the stern and bow. There was a shitter, a shower, and a sink for water. A small kitchen sat across from the table and a mini-fridge sacrificed a water bottle for Dean to quench his thirst.

"Sorry about that, I got you three days. They want to detail the boat before they start shooting next week. If you sink'er, which after five years of fishing on this pig is almost impossible, then you owe me nothin'. We insured her for the full value. Consider that cost covered as a thank you," Gordano said, and Dean grunted in thanks.

Then he remembered his Uncle got an extra percent of the video revenue and all he'd done was drive the damn boat. Dean smiled the thought away; he was truly happy for his uncle.

"So kid, what's next for you?" Gordano asked sliding into the booth across from him.

"Fook if I know. I fish. Then I get drunk and chase tail or go hunting for fun," Dean said, chugging his water. "Marty said I should see some new places, though, before I grace his sacred home, again." Dean chuckled, ruefully, "I almost died today, twice, thrice, and I'm feeling on top of the world. I AM upset that I pissed my friends off, though."

"Aye, man has a point. Sisters can be deadly when you pit them against each other. And Dean...there is more to life than fishing. You can be a pub owner or a pilot or—"

"A pilot?! Really?" Dean couldn't help the chuckle that slipped out; his uncle joined in.

"Sounded good at the time, you're a bright lad. This haul will be a big bounty. Go fishing, go adventuring... do whatever floats yer boat. I'm gone come mornin, I'll try an write... Who am I kidding?" He paused to laugh off his notion of writing. "You'll get the odd video message from me on a cruise, at most," Gordano admitted, setting the record straight.

Dean figured they were done, so he gave his uncle a hug. Gordano said, "Oh, they paid me for an interview with ya. Want me to send the pretty one down? She'll even pay to speak to ya. Ah, what a day it is," he sighed, "when a gorgeous lady pays a man to say hello."

Dean giggled at his Uncle's wistful look and the silliness of that statement. "Yeah, Uncle, send the cute one down. But no more. I'm doing one interview and one interview only, then heading over to see Quincy at the Oakley Doakley Saloon."

"I may just postpone my trip to join ya," Gordano said with a minor sniffle. "I can't tell ya how proud I'm of ya, boyo. Farewell my son. You're moving onto bigger things than being a deckhand." The older man stood up. "Off I go," he said gruffly, "before I start blubbering everywhere."

Dean exchanged another hug and watched his Uncle flee while trying to control his own manly emotions. He'd be back early tonight to check in on him. Dean knew it.

He followed him up top to give his interview on the deck of the boat. Three days of being its skipper would be enough.

"You Dean?" A young man asked from the gangplank and Dean frowned.

At first, he thought his uncle was having him on for a jest. Then he saw the trident in the young man's hands. Ah.

"Aye, Skipper Dean now, I guess," Dean said, walking for the weapon.

The fish cleaner handed the trident forward and said, "I don't know how you did it, but this was embedded in the back of the skull. If we hadn't seen the videos... we'd have never dug for it. And Dean, tip the guys for finding this. I got seniority, but the others swam in Voratin brains to fetch that out fer ya."

"Oh wow, umm... I'm new to dealing with the dock master, but you're right. A tip is certainly in order, and I honor my word. This will be rewarded. A worthy trophy." Dean spun the trident in his hand. "What's yer name?"

"Palmer."

"Well, Palmer, I'd like to get my hands on that Eelraken's skull, too. I killed it with my bare hands, you see," Dean said with pride. "I'd like to have it cleaned and delivered, please."

"A worthy trophy indeed," Palmer nodded, "I saw the size of the Eelraken." He stuck his hands in his pockets. "What'd you recommend for a person seeking a berth aboard a fishing boat?"

"Bulk up," Dean said immediately, with a chuckle that fell on confused ears. "No offense. I'd take you on if you had the upper body strength."

The young man sighed.

"Shit... tell you what, Palmer. You can come out with me, tomorrow, just watch and stay in the shelter. I'll let you drive while I fish with Quincy. You're the backup if he dodges his load of the job. That lazy fook always tries to get out of doing any hard work."

The clomp of high heels shifted their attention back to the dock.

Dean, pointing to the ship's deck, said, "Tomorrow morning at eight a.m. Earth standard time. You don't show, no biggie. Now, if you'll excuse me, I got an interview to do."

The young man from the processing center smiled and nodded excitedly.

"Thanks, Palmer." Dean spun the trident in his hand again. "Oh and stick the Eelraken skull on the Skipper's chair when it's cleaned."

CHAPTER

FOUR

DEAN

Ola Docks

Beauty is in the eye of the beholder, or so Dean had heard, often enough. This reporter was a makeup model, as he liked to call them. That didn't necessarily mean she wore lots of powder, but to Dean, a makeup model was a lady who enhanced everything they had with technology. Were they still pretty? Sure, but it never looked quite right to him and downgraded their beauty in his eyes.

This lady had extra-long eyelashes, hips for days with the trendy thick thighs of a soccer player, and a jaw line so sharp it probably cut her pillow. Was she attractive? Yes, just not to Dean.

"Mr. Forrester, I'm Wilma Artoua from Oakley Orbital News," she greeted him, "Permission to come aboard?"

Dean went to the side door she was struggling to open; it had an old school hatch and no automation. He flipped the metal catch up and slid it over for her. Her fake smile and ability to hold in her frustration were pleasing enough.

"Come on aboard," Dean welcomed with a sweeping gesture. He tucked the trident into its home and realized the wire from the boat to the trident had been removed at some point. A clamp applied with a crimper should fix that. Actually. "Mrs. Artova would -"

"Art. Wah. Pronounced like that, but I—"

"Wilma," Dean cut her off, "I'm going to work while we talk, if that's alright."

You make up stupid ways to say your last name and I'll swap to your first. Call me crazy for not being a pompous ass, Dean thought.

"I'm not a fan of being on the *Fancy Feline* without keeping my hands busy," Dean said and went to the back wall. Amid a section of cabinets, there were a bunch of latches that his fingers deftly popped. With a firm, rapid jerk, he extended the table and set it in the middle of the fishing deck.

"Are we safe here?" Wilma asked and Dean had to chuckle.

"Not a big risk taker, are ya?" he smiled.

Her team of drones, thankfully, focused on her for once. Dean had been doing a fairly good job of deliberately not noticing them. He wasn't a dummy. The Oakley Orbital, even though it was in orbit around the planet, was still the biggest city in the system.

Why people chose to live in space never settled well with Dean. Yet, it was commonly accepted fact, at least to the planet dwellers, that there were a lot of self-important people up there in orbit.

Wilma's hands flattened her tight power suit while she measured her response. Dean went down into the crew quarters while she hesitated. "I'm not going down there," she shouted as he ducked below.

"Ha! Ya ain't being offered the trip. Getting you a chair, that's all. I might be a brutal, hard man, but I'm not a savage. Plus," Dean hollered back as he tossed two chairs up top, "this one's for me. I'll let it slide because you're scared of the water—you and all your viewers should be terrified of the oceans here on Oakley."

Wilma surprised Dean when she set up the chairs after kicking off her heels. "Pause recording," Wilma said, and Dean froze.

He was going to get his reel cleaning kit, but he hesitated.

"Don't treat me like a little girl, I'm a miner's daughter who struck it rich. Rare, I know. Anyway, I paused the recording to go over our contract and to note that whatever your first impression was, I'm not a frilly little girl." Dean caught her muttering as she walked for the chair, "I hate these damn shoes, they rub all the time."

Dean nodded and went back down to retrieve his cleaning kit below. He tossed the bag with his cleaning kit up onto the deck, then the tool bag.

"So," Dean began as he came back up to the top deck, "let's talk money."

Wilma fidgeted a bit and said, "Let me be clear, this is not me hard balling you. The network wants to—"

Dean held up a hand, halting her. "Negotiate for me, then. The better ya do, the more thorough my replies."

"Three percent royalty on the segment, with a cash offer of three thousand Gs," Wilma blurted out.

Dean gave a hearty chuckle. Gs was pretty rough slang; rarely did a refined woman say less than Galactic coins with a haughty nose in the air.

"What?" she narrowed her eyes at him.

"I'd work a month for that. Fook yes, Madame Wilma," Dean grinned, and she rolled her eyes.

"No swearing on camera, alright? Look, this is a big interview for me. Even Earth will be watching this one. Earth orbital sent the hunky fake arms to—"

"Ugh, you mean where they add muscle appearance and it's nothing more than a shell? Gross. Why not just pump iron or swing an axe or something?" Dean said with a grunt. He stared down at the significantly shorter woman. "Why all the fake on you too?"

"The job," she shrugged, "combined with my significant other's pleading. Here's the real me." Wilma showed him a photo on her phone of her in a miner's outfit.

Her face was sooty, her spacesuit smeared with dust, and her smile sincere. And the best part was that her hair was a disheveled mess—that simply couldn't be faked.

She purred, "I thought a real man like you'd enjoy this. Glad to see I was right."

Dean shook his head. "Fine, you win. That picture makes me resent your fakeness a whole lot less. I went through some tribulations for work, too, so I get the urge to splurge and desire to make someone else happy. Let me know if you need me to pause while I work," Dean said. Just then, his phone rang. It was his uncle. "This is Dean, hurry up."

"We forgot to talk about my apartment, and my stuff. The lease ends a week after fishing season. Roughly two weeks... through the fourteenth of July. Okay, that's it. Have fun with your interview," Gordano said, eager to get off the phone. "Oh, I've already got a storage unit booked and movers handling all that. I love you, kiddo, enjoy the offseason and send me a photo of your new plane."

"Boat, it'll be a boat," he sighed. "Thanks, Uncle, be safe."

The call ended and he shoved the phone deep into his pocket. Dean grabbed his favorite combo rig and slapped it on the table.

"Before I turn the recording back on, are you ready?" she asked, and he nodded. "Good. We're going to get a ton of backstory to cherry pick from when we build our segment on you. So that's where we'll start."

33

He nodded.

"Rolling in three... two... one. Recording on. We're talking with Dean Forrester, aboard the ship *Forrester's Fancy Feline*. So, let's start at the beginning, shall we? Tell me about your younger years," Wilma began in a no-nonsense brisk tone that was very... reporter-y.

Dean pulled out the auto driver to unlatch the reel from the rod. Dean loathed talking about his younger years; there was a certain level of inner resentment that festered inside him when he did. Hate was too strong a word, but it came darn close to that. With a huff, he smiled at the drone and said, "Hi everyone. I'm Dean. Um... I grew up, well, was born, in the ocean city of Serenity on Earth. My dads—yes, I had two dads—were both workaholics. Somehow they thought a kid might save their relationship." He shrugged, "maybe they assumed I'd be easy to handle. Both assumptions, as it turned out, were wrong."

The reel disconnected from the rod and Dean began stripping the casing off.

He waited for the inevitable follow up.

"So, what happened?" Wilma asked and Dean smirked.

"The usual thing that does. My parents divorced and I was shipped out her to live with my Uncle G—or Uncle Gordano if I'm angry with him. My Uncle is stable. He has no drama in his life, and he likes it that way. I guess if people were to ask me what makes a good parent, my answer could be summed up in one word. Boring," Dean mentioned with a light laugh as he recalled how exciting life was about to get for Gordano. "I know ya going to ask it, people always do. How were you conceived? How were you a motherless baby?"

She indicated for him to continue.

"Yes, I'm different." He paused and chewed on the inside of his cheek, deep in thought. "I think that was part of the problem on Earth. Out here, in the undeveloped outer worlds, kids aren't just stinky brats who have to always know 'why'. Out here, no one cared if my gay dads purchased a cryo egg and cut out the genes that prohibit bad traits from developing." He sighed. "I hate talking about this stuff, but Oakley Orbital News is good people."

Dean said all this without lifting his gaze from his work. The casing was mostly off by now and he lubricated the gears with a spray bottle of oil. He knew the damn salt would eat them up if he didn't maintain his gear.

"What was life like with your Uncle?" Wilma asked.

"Well, I was seven when I arrived. I spent a week recovering from the cryo sleep and another few days processing through administration in Belmont. I remember thinking that this world, Oakley, felt the same as Earth. I'd had this crazy expectation that I'd be able to jump and fly hundreds of feet. Or there would be three suns, and aliens everywhere." He snorted. "Instead, there were flying cars, crowded streets, and advertisements telling me I should get bigger tits."

When Dean said this Wilma gave a genuine laugh. "Easy on the verbiage sailor," she warned. "What about school?"

Dean pieced the reel back together at this point and grunted, "Decent enough, I guess. I'm big, not huge, but always been big. That can lead to problems, sometimes. Knocking the big kid down is a status symbol. I'd avoid fights, minded my own business, but still, problems found me."

He looked around then dug in his tool kit for an autodriver to reattach the reel to the rod. "Maybe it's a facet of growing up. Grades were fine. Shi—" He stopped himself mid-cuss.

"Shoot, school has been so dumbed down these days, all so politicians can say kids are doing great, that I felt I was only going to class to spare my Uncle from my antics for the day, instead of gaining any real value."

"Ah, yes there has been growing pushback on the lowered standards in education. I recently did a piece on that very thing. The link can be found here," Wilma said, stabbing a place in the air with her finger. She turned back to Dean. "What of your final years in school?"

"Fairly basic, I guess. I tried to blend in and get good grades." He smiled, thinking back. "Uncle started fishing at that point. Funny, the man rails against the fishing union, but didn't go full time commercial until it was established. Catch twenty-two, you could say."

He reattached the reel to the rod with the auto driver. That bag went to the deck and he left his seat to retrieve a tackle box.

"Fishing is all I'd do when I had any free time. We'd venture out yonder and slay some small fish. Kept me outta trouble—well, mostly—and kept enough coin in my pocket to take the ladies out on a date come the weekend" Dean said.

"College next," the reported noted, "but first, what's all this?" Wilma's no-nonsense reporter masked slipped to reveal a spark of genuine curiosity. Her green eyes locked onto the clear tackle box.

"Oh," Dean grinned, "Most folks never see all the prep work."

His eyebrows bounced while letting the box hit the table with a *thud*. "I normally do this on the run out, folks can see it if you tune in early enough. But, if I'm running solo, with no crew, I may just end up having to both drive and fish on my own. So, doing the prep now makes sense." He shrugged and then winked at the drone camera, "and thank you Orbital news. I love tuning in to your broadcasts for all the latest topics."

Wilma rolled her eyes at the fact Dean was shilling her station. He chuckled, mainly because they were paying far more coins than he deserved for simply talking about his boring ass childhood.

"College was a breeze, also. I started out thinking I'd become a jet engine repair person. However, I stumbled upon a wise man who showed me the ways of accounting," Dean said, and Wilma held a finger up.

"A Mr. Marty Kendricks, correct?"

"Yeah. I swapped into doing a bunch more math, go me! And two years later, graduated at twenty-one. Had some flings, some heartbreak, and kept fishing for a side hustle. Accounting is good money that'll never vanish. People will always make coins, dollars, money, or whatever you want to call your current flavor of currency, and there will always be taxes, budgeting, payrolls, and such. A jet engine, however, can and likely will be replaced by some better piece of technology, over time, it's almost a guarantee."

"So why are you out here on a boat, and not spinning a wrench at the space port, or crunching numbers as an accountant?" Wilma pursued.

"The problem with accounting is that being a desk jockey sucks pineapples—with little plums smacking you in your chin. Those damn things told me, repeatedly, how brutal the situation was—I wasn't cut out to be working for 'da man' in a cubicle."

He finished the first rod and continued on to the second without a pause.

"I tried, I really tried," he sighed and smiled with a shrug at the camera, "sorry, Mr. Kendricks, but after several months of driving myself crazy staring day in and day out at a display, I came back to the Larvian Sea. From twenty-one to twenty-six, I made fewer coins than I'd made from the safety of my desk and slew fish with gusto."

He finished putting on a fresh leader and tied a new knot on the hook.

Dean snickered, "I'm a fish killer and I'm sure some hate me for the way I provide meat to feed people. I've learned to ignore the occasional dock protests. I do get a good chuckle, though, when I tell them they should protest in the water, out beyond the safety nets."

It seemed she had a call from someone, which halted their conversation.

The crimpers came out of the bag and onto the table. He slotted his combo in a top rod holder and shifted around to reach for the trident and some wire.

"The big finale," Wilma prompted, done with her call, "tell us what was going through your mind when you fought the first goliath Voratin."

Dean hesitated and pulled out his movie contract to check a few things. "Not to dissuade your fans or upset the network," he apologized, "but I can't go too in depth. Basics are okay."

"Not a newb Dean, we know this. Cut this part, Oscar." Dean shrugged figuring Oscar was some drone guy in a comfy chair in the orbital. She paused with a deep breath and reset herself. "The big finale, tell us what was going through your mind when you fought the first fish."

Dean flexed a smidge while setting the trident on the table. "A twenty-foot long Asroun swallowed bait and hooks meant for a fish about a tenth its size. These oceans are wild and insanely diverse," he grinned. "You never know what you're gonna catch." He frowned. "I hate not knowing what's on the line... and yet," his frown surged into a grin, "I love not knowing what's on the line."

Drawing out a long line of wire from the spool, Dean twisted the end into an eyehook, and slipped a cap onto the end of the trident.

"When it gutted my hook, I was uncertain as to what I'd snagged. A while back, they'd send a drone below the waves to monitor the fight with the auto-reeler, adjusting torsion and tack for the species, or if predators were nearby. New rules, though, can't do that anymore—got to keep things sporting," he snorted, "and fight the fish, the old-fashioned way."

"Anyway," he continued, "the contest was fun, and I generally believed I'd lose the Asroun at every turn or pivot. The big tell that something was amiss, though, was the boiling fish. You see," he explained, "a panicked fish on the line doesn't normally spook a school of bait fish unless by happenstance. The baitfish had me and Uncle G worried, and rightfully so."

Dean paused to connect the wiring to the trident. When it was time to crimp the clamp shut, his arms bulged from the exertion. His shirt almost ripped at the sleeves.

"Aye, these are real. When a man works for a living, he can toss a wee lass over his shoulder with ease, with their consent, of course," Dean said with a wink.

Somehow, Wilma kept from rolling her eyes.

"The fo- frustrating Voratin almost snagged our catch. For a moment," Dean paused with a stern look and furled brows, "I thought we'd wasted the whole trip."

He thought back to what had happened, as Uncle G sped them away from where the Asroun had been snapped out of the air. "Actually," he gestured to the front crane rigs, "I about pissed myself when the crane snagged half of the Asroun right out of the Voratin's mouth. The damn automation quickly and humanely freezes our catches, to avoid any needless suffering. That's great; until the day comes you find you need to return your catch to the sea and flee."

He shook his head. "Voratin are aggressive, even to video drones, and while they're not too rare in the deep, that's the first one I've ever seen up top. So here we were, making a loud ruckus up above it, and to add insult to injury, we stole its food."

"I honestly believed we would sink, and that the life rafts wouldn't save us from the beast's wrath even if we somehow managed to survive. So," he continued, "I did what any sane man would do. I sacrificed myself to the mercy of chance. I figured I was already dead, and life is about living. Ya ain't going to persist by being a coward —not when death stares ya in the eyes. So, I leapt into action and did what I thought might work." He chuckled, then. "I'll hafta watch the replay at some point."

Wilma's jaw dropped. "Oh wow, you mean you haven't seen yourself in action. That'll be a great reaction to catch for the viewers at home. Roll scene," Wilma said, and her phone flared to life as it emitted a holographic rendering of Dean's epic battle above the table.

Dean saw his near-death desperation leap. His epic burst of the monster's eyeball with a trident stab was impressive. The drones under the water gave him a real perspective on how massive the Voratin was. This wasn't even a big one for the species, the video labeled it a juvenile.

Hmm...

Dean was perplexed when the drones' video went to static the moment he sliced open the Eelraken's side.

"What happened there," Wilma asked.

"I killed that thing with my filet knife," Dean said, pointing at the image of himself tossing the Eelraken into the raft. "A simple dodge and the slithery eel racked its body down the blade."

"How did you not die?" Wilma wondered. "There are about thirty medical researchers on their way here to try to figure that one out, from all across the Galaxy."

Dean cringed.

He'd be forced to take a physical next fishing season, unless he skipped out and just did temp work. All skippers and registered deckhands were forced to take one.

Dean grunted and admitted, "Hell if I know."

He wasn't about to mention his sliced open hand latching onto the still-beating heart of an Eelraken and magically knitting itself back together. He definitely felt safer playing the dumb fisherman than saying anything more. Dean reached down and grasped the trident with a longing look.

"Uncle G is selling the ship. I'm going to take her out at least one more time, though. If you want to see some boring, normal fishing, tune in. For me, tis time to get a few drinks in me before sailing out in the morning," Dean said, closing off the interview. "Anything else you wanted to know?"

"End recording. Much, but you've exceeded the allotted time in our contract already. And a fisherman's story only needs so much airtime. My wife and I throw soirees up in our orbital penthouse. If you ever want to be the flavor of the night, among the local ladies," she winked, "you should visit. Here's my information. I'll be following your next moves with curiosity. You remind me of my father... and few men do that. Best of luck, Dean Forrester."

"Same to you, Wilma. And ma'am, I might just have a soiree—" Dean paused with a grunt. Leave it to the orbital queens to dress up a name for a simple get-together. "A fancy party down here, too, where you can be outcasts as space dwellers. It'd be only fair."

"Kelly would like that, a lot. She complains about wanting to get back to our simpler roots. Hell, I'm envious—you followed your passion," Wilma admitted.

Dean burst into laughter.

"Fishing ain't my passion. Hard work sure, but the ocean scares me, and rightfully so. I haven't found my calling yet. That three thousand will help, though. Until next time," Dean said, heading back down to the crew quarters.

"Cheers," Wilma replied. She slid her heels back on and returned down the dock from whence she'd come. The retreating clomp of her heels was music to Dean's ears.

Now he just needed a shower before he went on down to the Oakley Doakley for a night of debauchery. He'd love to party the whole night, but his celebration would have to be short lived, if he was to cast off early the next morning.

At least, that is what he intended: just a few hours of fun without getting stupid drunk. Reality had other plans.

CHAPTER

FIVE

DEAN

Ola Docks

Dean groaned from a pounding headache. When he sat up to race for the toilet, he bonked his head.

Where am I? The crew cabins? How'd I get here? What happened last night?

These were thoughts that frequented Dean, due to his stupidity when he started drinking. He'd blacked out again. He usually tried to avoid getting blackout drunk. He really did, and had even attended AA meetings a few times, but never stuck with the program.

His stumble revealed the long legs of a familiar female in the bunk on the stern side. Before he could check who it was, he had to duck into the shower room.

His vomit was some nasty bile reeking of Oakley firewater. That'd explain the blackout, then. That stuff was nasty. Where tequila might be a one-two punch combo, Oakley firewater was a kick in the nuts.

His second retching heave woke his guest. Light footsteps stepped over him and flicked on the shower, to keep the smell down. Dean noticed the parrot tattoo on the top of the foot that matched the perfectly manicured toes.

"Got a red pill?" Dean groaned miserably.

He shoved himself under the warm water and peeled off his wet boxers. Cassandra had already left to get him a sobering dose.

Red pills were a lifesaver for a drunk who still had to work. She stepped back into the small shower stall with a bottle of water and his lifesaver. She opened the bottle of water, dropped the pill in, and when Dean reached for the bottle, helped hold it up as he gulped it to completion.

"Da fook ya get that?" Dean said, noticing Cassandra's shirt.

She wore a t-shirt with a muscle-bound Dean flying in the air, trident poised to kill. At the bottom, it read 'Don't be a pussy!'.

Cassandra's blue eyes locked with his. She was rarely emotional. Without bothering to answer, she peeled the shirt off and hopped into the shower with him.

"So, ya ready to hear how your night went?" Cassandra asked.

"Cassie, if I wake up with you around, it's always a home run," Dean chuckled, already feeling better.

She snickered, "Except for last night. You failed a few times stud."

"Who me?" Dean quipped.

She rolled her baby blues.

"Never!"

Dean and Cassandra were friends. She was a powerful county attorney who'd gone through school with Dean. Cassandra grew up in a stable home, with a boring childhood, and after college, proceeded to have a very stable adulthood. Her only vice was vacationing, and for Dean, that worked perfectly.

Neither of them was into long-term relationships, nor felt the need for labels; when they wanted to, they had sex. There were plenty of times, too, where they'd also just spend time with one another, either just the two of them, or with other friends. They were comfortable being nothing more than friends. Five years' worth of fun times, though, tended to build up a strong rapport.

Rarely had either of them seriously dated during that time; to be fair they tended to scare off potential suitors. Nothing worse to a prospective girlfriend than to learn that one of Dean's best friends was not only a girl, but also his on-and-off-again, fook-buddy.

"Let's see," Cassie began, "it started with Candace. She was with Quincy, waiting for you at the Doakley. Summarizing a bit here... she bitch-slapped you when you told her you weren't going to pursue a relationship with her, though I've told her as much, many times," Cassandra sighed, using the auto dispenser to pump some soap into Dean's beard.

Dean clamped onto her hips and let his hands roam to her firm ass cheeks. Her toned body was a toy Dean never tired of playing with.

41

"Oh, and then there was you getting in a firewater shooting contest with some idiot who claimed your balls weren't big enough to have killed a Voratin." She adjusted the spray to rinse his beard and shook her head, "That ruined your night. Like big time. While I was watched the newest hero of Ola make an ass out of himself, some spacer sluts were plotting ways to claim their fifteen minutes of fame by screwing you."

"Cassie, did ya cock block me?" Dean asked teasingly, "Again?"

Her hands went to the patches on his chest and she sighed. "Guilty, as charged. I most certainly did. Sorry... I tried to drag you out before the shit hit the fan. At least you trust me when you're drunk. You picked me over the spacers."

She growled angrily at the thought. "There was almost an old school bitch fight. Well, you still pitched Patti and Quincy over your shoulder on the way out when they protested. You rented them a room at some fancy hotel and told them to meet you here on the boat at eight a.m. I'm still shocked you got that part right."

"I carried you here, didn't I?" Dean asked, guessing.

It was at this point Dean realized either his cock was really dirty or there was some ulterior motive with her cleaning. Cassandra washed his legs, with the briefest of kissing teases to his growing erection.

"You indeed hauled me here. You know," she paused for effect, "we've had sex in my attic, your Uncle G's shed... shit, even in the Kendricks' master closet. This was the first time, though, you brought me here. But you failed. I was even riding that cock of yours and calling you Skipper, just like you asked."

Her blue eyes sparkled with delight as she glanced up at him past his stiff boner. When she laughed at Dean, he frowned.

"When you passed the fook out. I had to dismount because my consent went away. I tried to snuggle with you, but these bunks are only meant for one," Cassandra said, and Dean chuckled. "So is this shower," she winked, "but if you pick me up, Skipper, I bet we can make it work."

Dean received a consent ping. After the marital laws of 2073, there was always a consent required from both parties before coitus. Regardless—whatever freaky scenario you could come up with, it didn't matter, sex required permission... every time.

Dean set his inhibitor to on while she kept hers off. Cassie liked the excitement. Dean never regretted turning his sperm killer on.

Dean hoisted Cassie by the waist against the back wall. She latched her legs around his thick torso. Cassandra was a natural bodied woman.

Did she run and have the long sleek legs to show for it? That she did. She also had a runner's small breasts with perfect nipples. Dean never complained that she wasn't modified to perfection; he knew she cherished him for it.

Her hands held his face. She kissed him deeply and then she started crying.

Now Dean had seen Cassandra cry before, he was her rock, her go to guy for problems. If Cassandra needed a man to support her, Dean was always there, if he could be. This was different, though.

"Out with it," Dean said, feeling the mood die.

"Don't you dare," Cassandra demanded, "make love to me this instant! You fooking owe me."

Dean reached down, grabbed his still stiff cock, and adjusted her positioning against the wall. He glided in easily with a smooth thrust. Cassandra's tight walls clenched as she arched back with a moan of pleasure.

She clutched so tightly onto his girth that Dean was impressed. When she used the wall to leverage her hips against him, he realized what she needed.

He snatched her hips, pulled her onto his cock to the hilt and bound their bodies into one. His hot kisses landed on her neck while he gave slow, rhythmic pumps of his hips. She shifted her ride to bury him slightly deeper with each thrust. The two of them entwined with the hot water lathering their bodies. Even though the sex was primal, it oozed passion.

Cassandra kissed Dean longingly while moaning for more, always more. She bit his lip as her first crescendo burst through her, her orgasmic climax long and loud. Dean didn't slow to give her a reprieve. He knew Cassandra always wanted more, and she did.

Right for the second orgasm, he went. He bit her earlobe, telling her how amazing her little pussy felt. He loved her tiny little cunny squeezing his big cock.

His fingers raked her ass cheeks giving her the exact amount of flaring pain she craved. As he worked her up for the next few minutes, he waited for the best moment to give her the trigger she loved.

He asked how badly she wanted his cum; she always got off to that, begging for him to explode inside of her.

Dean erupted, himself, when she screamed out for a second time. It'd been a while for him so when his panting calmed and he pulled out, his jizz trailed down her leg.

She shuddered, loving the feeling. When the mood was right, and she wanted round two, she would suck him hard again.

They were both cooling off from the sex when the intercom pinged.

"Hello, I'm half an hour early," a voice said, notifying Dean that he'd have to skip round two.

"Who's that?" Cassandra wondered, confusion pulling her eyebrows down in consternation.

"Activate intercom. Palmer, give me five minutes, permission to come onboard granted," Dean said. When the click of the intercom deactivated, he snuggled back into his shower partner, once more. "Cassie, it's been too long. Thanks for having my back last night. You mean the world to me."

"Dean, that video scared the shit out of me." She shuddered in his arms. "I get it, we're not a couple. Never been one and I can see why we both want something separate, but I've always got your back. And in cases like this, your front." She snickered and shimmied back to standing on her own feet. "This conversation is not even close to over, though, but for now," she chuckled, "go entertain your deck-hand, while I freshen up."

"Hey, I'll give the orders here. Why don't I go entertain the new kid, while you freshen up?" Dean replied with a smirk and was rewarded with a wet palm to his ass when he turned to go.

Cassandra rolled her eyes with a big smile and said, "Aye, aye Skipper. I'd like to join you, for fishing, if that's okay. I even signed the Dock Master's forms last night. You still need to approve them."

Dean hopped out of the small shower to towel off. "What about work at the office?"

"You going to be mad at me if I took some leave?" she grinned.

"Why would I care about that?" Dean asked, stealing the super awesome shirt she'd worn into the bathroom. "Did you bring a spare set of clothes?"

"I ordered some for a seven forty-five delivery. I wasn't expecting more than Quincy and Patti to be on the boat, though, and they've both seen me in a grungy shirt and panties before. Anyway, Dean," Cassandra said with a raised voice as he went back into the main crew quarters, "I freaked out a bit last night. You mean a lot to me, even if ours is not a traditional relationship."

"Cassie," Dean didn't hesitate to reply. "You've never let me down. Not once. I know you want more sometimes, but this has been what's best for the us... in the well, us. I couldn't imagine an orbit without you."

"Yeah, Dean. That's how I feel, too." She turned off the shower. "Except you almost died yesterday. What if the shoe was on the other foot?" Cassandra asked, as Dean finished equipping his fishing gear.

He actually was in the middle of putting on his waterproof shoes as she said this, causing him to find some levity in the idiom.

Cassandra said, "If I'd narrowly escaped a building collapse and should be dead, what would you be doing right now?"

"Freaking out, trying to cling to you... Alright," he sighed, "welcome to the *Fancy Feline*. I'm the skipper, you're on bait duty, deckhand Cassie, paperwork approved. Oh neat, approved deckhands Quincy, and Patti," Dean said hustling out of the crew quarters before she could reply.

When he reached the captain's station, he found Palmer sitting on an ice chest. "What's in the box?" Dean asked.

"My wife packed my lunch and some snacks. And then my mom brought a casserole dish for you, to say thanks," Palmer said, scratching at the back of his neck. Dean raised an eyebrow. Palmer couldn't be over twenty-one. "If it's too much, I can get rid of it, and well—"

Dean interrupted the young man's nervous rambling. "Hey Palmer, I won't mind if your mom uses her time to say thank you. A loving wife and mum are great." A trio of drones hovered around them at different angles. "Huh, did the drones follow you here?" Dean asked pointing at the machines that signaled they were broadcasting.

"Umm... Skipper, they're here for you. You tend to do video worthy things," Palmer said with a bit of a snicker.

Dean shooed the annoying robots away and then ushered Palmer off the ice cooler. He dragged it toward the crew quarters. His foot hit the hatch and Cassandra tilted her head up at the opening.

"Stow this stuff in the fridge, Cassie. When your clothes arrive, I'll toss them down," Dean said. Just then, a robot lost power, trying to fly into the crew quarters. "Ha! They deserve that for trying to see you in a towel. First catch of the day, my friends, was a free drone."

"Is that another deckhand, Skipper?" Palmer asked and Dean smirked.

He walked to the table and patted the top. "This needs to be stored there against the back wall. And yes, Cassandra is a deckhand for today. Bait girl. Woman really. She's a -"

"A lawyer for Ola County with stellar reports, excellent work ethic, enjoys reading, running, and tends to be a private person. Projected to be a lonely cat lady. Who writes this stuff?" Palmer asked. His phone was broadcasting the drone feed. "Oh, hey, they're offering a hundred credits for the return of the drone."

"Too fooking bad, you take those into private zones and suddenly they're no longer yours. Rules are rules, you dumbass operators. And no offense, an awkward shot of my friend in a towel is not worth a –" The number jumped by another zero. Oh, Dean thought, looks like those pricks at the studio started a slush fund to get the image of Dean's roomie in her towel. Dean powered down the video, before he became too tempted.

"Sorry, I had it on while you were busy downstairs. What first?" Palmer asked and Dean went to the Skipper's station and rang Quincy.

A text flashed back.

'In air taxi, be there soon. Need anything?' - Quincy

'Nope, Cassie has some deliveries coming, then we'll sail out. Should be dark here in an hour or so. Great time to get bait.' - Dean

He left the station for the stairs up to the crane. Around the main hatch were storage boxes for certain types of fishing rods. "Get up here, Greenie. Orientation is first and was trying to do it all at once."

Dean stood over the bow waiting. His phone showed seven forty-four. Sure enough, a buzzing sound darted for the fishing deck.

The delivery drone was so quick he hardly saw it. The package was gently set down and *boom*, off the drone went with a burst of speed.

Dean heard the crew hatch slide open. The drone from earlier was freed.

"No!" Dean cried out in mock anger.

Cassandra's hair was partially done, and she was wearing pants and a dirty shirt. She retrieved the box and hustled for the quarters again.

"Hold up, Cassie, real quick." Dean waved her over. When she joined them, he said, pointing, "That is the port crane claw and spear gun. I'll be firing it, if it's needed. The boat literally pings green when conditions are met for a shot. Red, you're too far out, reel the fish in more. Green is good, yeah?"

Cassie and Palmer nodded.

"I want you to see the rod chests, next." He pointed to the container on their left. "This left long box is for bait rods. This right one is for trolling," he guided them aft, "and here you have the three drops, right on the backs of the ceiling holders. Now, go on get changed. How much was the pot up to free the dastardly drone?"

"Four k."

He grinned.

"I expect all of it," Cassandra said and wagged a finger at Dean before retreating to get into some proper gear. Her hips swayed a bit more than necessary when she caught him watching.

"Hey, Dean," Cassie called, "what's the plan for this skull you were so proud of last night?"

Dean huffed, remembering the Eelraken trophy. Best if he gave it to Marty for safe-keeping. He had to hire an actual courier to pick the item up, though, which meant a trip to the docks was needed.

"Palmer when Deckhand Cassie is done down below, retrieve my trophy, and hand the Eelraken skull off to a courier on the docks. For now, though, grab the bait rods and stick them in the holders," Dean said to his new recruit and cursed himself for forgetting to haze him as a Greenie.

"Do we not need bait?" Palmer asked with a raised brow.

Cassandra left the crew deck in light waterproof shoes, a set of fishing coveralls, and her long brown hair pulled up in dual buns. Her blue eyes sparkled, and her mouth held a corner smile of pride when she said, "The bait is only ever netted or jigged for. Unlike other crews, the *Forrester's Fancy Feline* goes out without a crutch. Always."

"The lass has the right of it!" Quincy yelled. Dean saw him and Patti waving from the walkway. Their arrival was perfect. "Skipper," Quincy bowed, with a flourish, "requesting permission to come aboard."

Quincy was Dean's best friend. Ever since tenth grade, they'd been inseparable. Where Dean was bulky, tall, and all raw power. Quincy was of average height, lithe, and quick. The man had sharp, handsome features, blue eyes, and blonde hair.

They shared every passion they both sought: drinking, chasing girls, adventuring, and the list went on and on. The biggest difference between the two, was their work ethic. Dean was a workaholic, whereas Quincy had inherited money from some Earther great-grandfather who owned a ton of land—properties that grossed income for the whole family to live off.

Dean was never resentful. Even now that he was slightly rich, he was still going to work.

That said, Quincy, of course, showed up in his regular bar clothes.

Patti was in fishing gear that matched Cassandra's, which made sense. The girls were good friends. Even the small stint of Dean dating Patti for a few weeks had merely put their friendship on a brief pause.

This morning was vibrant with a full sun and minimal scatter clouds allowing Patti to shine with a radiance he rarely saw from her. Her black hair was in a neat shoulder-length ponytail and her brown eyes twinkled with the sunshine. She was happy, very much so, as she clung in a jostling walk with Quincy.

They both were brimming with grins that faded when Palmer exited from the crew quarters, a skull in his hands.

"The fook is that?" Quincy exclaimed. Not much startled the man. A skull, though, that did the trick. Dean tucked some prank ideas away, for later.

Patti scoffed with a squinting eye and asked, "Is that the eel's head?"

"Ding, ding," Palmer grinned, before jogging down the dock towards the awaiting courier.

"Who's the kid?" Quincy asked, watching him run.

Dean man slapped his best friend into a bro hug. He received a real hug from Patti who whispered "thank you" in his ear. *Guess she likes me setting the two of them up. Wasn't sure how she'd be, today, certainly didn't appear to be holding on to any resentment about her sister, Candace.*

Knowing they'd blush he said, "You two have been beating around the bush for a while. Glad ya both are giving it a try. Oh, newsflash, Cassie professed her undying —Ouch!"

"Did not!" Cassandra said defiantly, slugging Dean in the arm. "But I do love him." She stuck her tongue out to show him she wasn't truly upset.

Patti shook her head and tsked, sadly. "Deany," she said, and his head whipped around to give her a glare. "See? You don't like it, either. Call her Cassandra like everyone else."

"What? Not going to happen," he sniffed, "Cassie is her name to me. And I love her, too, just not in a get married and spend twenty years fighting over brats kind of way."

"Now," Dean grinned wickedly, "if she wants to start adding threesomes to the list or some lesbian orgies ..," Dean received a shove as he leered at her, "I happen to hear keeping a harem is not only cheap, it's effective for a home!"

"Keep dreaming," Cassandra smirked, and the group chuckled. "And we're talking later, boyo. About us, not a harem, stud."

Quincy waved both arms to get their attention. When they looked at him, he pointed to a returning Palmer. "Who's that?"

"Hey, Palmer!" Dean shouted to the man while ignoring his friend. "Why're ya fishin instead of going to school?"

"Money," Palmer said with a shrug. "My college girlfriend and I caught that New Texas flu. And... well," he blushed scarlet, "there was a lot of lonely time, which led to..."

"Your inhibitor's busted? Shucks man, I'm Quincy, nice to meet you, Palmer," Quincy said and the two shook hands.

"Boy or girl, and pictures!" Patti demanded with large, eager eyes.

Dean pointed to the magnetic dock locks and Cassandra went to unlock them with a minor pout. Everyone wanted to see the cute baby video. Dean fired up the jets and programmed a slow, steady pace to bringing them out of the harbor.

The harbormaster confirmed the *Fancy Feline's* safety net clearing time and Dean joined the group as the boat drove itself, which was well within the rules, as long as no lines were in the water or there was a declared emergency.

A cute little baby girl giggled from her back on the video. Her mom was tickling her, and the scene was adorable. Even Dean was drawn in by the baby's coos.

"Lora," Palmer chuckled, "my little demon. Don't let this sweet face fool you. She sleeps during the day and is up all night. We both had to drop out of college and now we're working, when we can. Mom is helping, after her shifts.

"Lilia's mom comes over every other night and we're living in my Mom's basement. All because some asshole scientists created some bioweapon that accidentally broke out of the lab," Palmer sighed and there were grunts all around. "Still, that little demon is my everything. My family has never been closer. Literally." He smiled, shyly and turned back to Dean. "Thanks, again, for the opportunity, Mr. Forrester."

"Just Dean's fine, but Skipper's preferred," Dean said, patting his back. "Now, go rig three jig lines for port and starboard. Weather is showing calm seas, but who knows how long they'll last."

Dean watched Palmer and Cassandra hustle to get the rods set up. Quincy pulled out a fancy iPhonie48.

"Oh, you upgraded?" Dean asked his friend.

Quincy gave a frustrated grunt and drew a finger across his neck with a deflated gesture. "Damned phone was busted after you dropped us off, last night. I swear you must have shocked me when you hauled us over your shoulder and back to the hotel. It was like you were filled with electricity, or something. I just about pissed myself and my phone died." Quincy shuddered.

His friend continued to grumble. "Part of why we stayed in this morning, was I need to be in one spot for this to get delivered." Quincy finally registered Dean's lack of expression. "You don't remember shocking me last night, while carrying me?"

"Hmm... Not a lick. If I did, well, then something is wrong. I'll have to get it checked out when I find the time. I kinda got stupid drunk last night and now we're going fishing, speaking of which, I need an intervention, Quincy. Please, I've got a bank full of G-coins suddenly and Cassie saved me last night. She wants to be here, but I'm not sure she'll always be at my side, not like you. No more heavy drinking," Dean said in a somber tone and there was pain etched on Quincy's face. "I mean it."

"You can keep Cassandra at your side, and you can quit being a retarded drunk," Quincy said with a tease, "But it'll change who ya are."

Dean chuckled at the tense moment. "Not if I take it in moderation. Honestly, after almost dying yesterday, I don't mind if Cassie clings for a bit. We probably need each other right now; we've been close before."

Quincy tapped suddenly at his phone.

"Hey," Dean wondered aloud. "Whatcha up to?"

Quincy showed Dean his screen. The girls had set up a funding pool for converting Lora the Demon into Lora the Angel. Quincy dumped in ten thousand. Dean gulped at the amount. That was enough to get a full-time nanny and go to school online. He reset the boat's course for the docks and informed the harbormaster they were returning one soul to port.

Dean checked his accounts. Four hundred and seventy-three thousand Galactic coins. He added thirteen-thousand to the 'make Lora an angel' fund. Quincy furled his brows immediately.

"Hey, what was that?" Quincy asked, confused. Dean was always poor.

Cassandra hopped off the starboard walk around with a *thud*. "Why we turning around, Skipper? And why the hell did you send me four thousand coins?"

Quincy showed Cassandra the growing funds that were being linked to my broadcast. "You said they forked over four k for your towel wearing selfie."

"Yeah, I looked great too. Was glowing with happiness," Cassandra said with a shrug. "I wasn't being serious Dean, keep the money. I've got more than I need at the moment. I know how hard it's been for you to get by with this job."

"Not anymore," Quincy quipped, showing her his donation.

"Everything okay?" Palmer asked.

"Yeah Palmer, I need the three trolling rigs up top and then come grab your ice chest. It's going to have to stay on the docks. I'll explain in a minute," Dean said with a terse smile.

When Palmer was gone, Dean showed them his account balance. It wasn't the first time he'd done so, but before it had always been for them to verify he was broke and him apologizing for being a mooch. Patti whistle, Quincy high fived him, and Cassandra groaned.

"I should've checked," Cassandra said, leaving to duck back below, "back in a bit."

Patti followed her, and Dean went to go, too, but Quincy stuck a hand to his chest to stop him.

"Patti's got this. It's minor, I promise," Quincy said, probably with an inside scoop.

The cooler was pushed up out of the hatch by Patti. "Wait, Patti," Dean said, popping the lid open and pulling out the casserole before closing it up again. He handed the dish to Patti to stick back in the fridge.

"What's the problem with the cooler, Skipper?" Palmer said, finishing his task.

"We're bailing you out, Palmer. Call it blind, dumb luck you asked two sorry saps for a job," he shook his head sadly.

Quincy nodded dolefully beside him, "and I happen to believe in luck. How about you Dean?"

Dean grinned and patted his friend's shoulder. "Bad luck? oh yeah, as a fisherman, I have to be a believer... And in this case, good luck, too." He gestured to Palmer, "Let me see your phone, friend."

Palmer looked confused but dug his phone out when Dean gestured again. The slush fund they'd made was growing and was linked to his accounts. With the press of a button, Palmer's life was forever altered.

Palmer gasped, shock freezing him in place.

Just then, they arrived back at the dock. Dean picked the young man up under his armpits, held him at arm's length and with a waddling walk to the side of the boat, set him on the dock with perfect timing. The magnetic locks secured the ship.

Quincy set the ice chest beside him. Palmer's phone was ringing, multiple calls competing for the young man's attention.

Palmer finally found his bearing and his voice. "I can still work the shift, Skipper."

"Sorry, friend, it's a double date, now, and you're a fifth wheel." He shrugged. "If you need a reference, well... I'm afraid you're fooked, I'm not a skipper come tomorrow. Lora was adorable. And we happen to agree, sometimes life can smack you in the face. This is us helping out."

Quincy shook his hand and then headed forward. "Have fun solving your drama, glad we could help," Dean smiled, and nodded to Quincy, who shifted the *Fancy Feline* back towards the safety net gate. "And Palmer," Dean shouted, as the dock fell behind them, "Grab life by the balls. Keep being a great dad. We wish you the best!"

The distance between them was growing to the point where Dean could barely hear when Palmer shouted back. "You... I won't forget this Dean Forrester. The Galaxy needs more men like you."

Dean shrugged and did not disagree. It also needed more men like Palmer. Dads who were determined to do the right thing, even if it made life overbearingly hard.

Patti slid the crew door open as Dean waved goodbye.

"This casserole is awful," Patti said, extending a plate to Dean and Quincy.

Two bites were quickly spit back onto the plate.

Dean chuckled and said, "Fook it, we toss it in to cheat on fish bait. I think I scored enough brownie points with grandma to say her cooking is mediocre for humans, but fantastic for the fish."

"What?" Patti said clearly confused as she ducked back down.

Quincy leaned down and showed her what they did. Patti gave the same *aww,* she'd given when watching Lora. Fitting really.

"Hey Cassie," Dean shouted, "breaking the duo out of their cute moment, "get your fine ass up here, you're going on a vacation with me."

The result was about what he'd expected. Patti had to jump out of the way as Cassandra rushed up to Dean.

"You've dodged a couple's vacations for years," she blurted out, cautiously optimistic, "Why now?"

"I need you more than ever, Cassie," Dean admitted, and she bit her lip, holding back her tears. He pulled her into his chest and rubbed her back. "Stay calm, Cassie, love. I want you to go to the outback with me."

Another snap reaction that Dean had also expected. Her tears suddenly vanished.

Her face squished up in a less than attractive way. He saw her working things out as she looked deep into his eyes. "

A hunting trip?"

He nodded.

"And I'm invited?"

Another nod.

"You've never invited a girl on a guy's trip with you before," she gasped, "not... ever."

"Hey, it's a bona fide invite—call it a chance for you and I to have this long talk that you seem to be wanting, without these guys hovering around," Dean said, gesturing out at the drones. "I can't promise they're excluded, though." He scratched at his chin. "Huh, that came out a bit odd. Who knows, they might come." He shook his head. "Probably better if they do..."

She nodded and grew determined. "I'm in."

"Great, one last trip of fishing. A full day of back breaking, arm cranking fun, and then we go off on an adventure. Just need to try not to die, today" Dean noted, scanning the horizon.

There was an ominous pause as they reached the sea gate. The interior walls opened, and Quincy sailed the *Fancy Feline* through. The interior walls sealed shut.

The exterior walls then opened, with the net lowering just enough to let the boat through without shearing off the propeller. When they entered the Larvian Sea, the nets sprang back up and the big doors snapped closed, quickly, with a resounding *bang*.

The four friends glided out into the Larvian Sea, to test fate one last time for the season. If Dean had known the monsters who lurked above were even more dangerous than the ones below, he would have kept the *Fancy Feline* back at the dock, with Palmer.

CHAPTER

SIX

Larvian Sea

T he *Fancy Feline* smacked into the slight chop on the clear blue day. The blue backdrop clashed against the green sea with a gorgeous setting sun.

Dean was preoccupied with a phone call as they cruised for his honey hole of a bait spot. He'd avoided fishing here, generally, because the goliaths lurked elsewhere. For a rookie Skipper with a green crew, though, it was perfect.

"Candace, I appreciate your honesty and accept your apology," Dean said to the digital rendering his phone projected. He didn't care at all that she'd slapped him last night in her anger. They were both well beyond that.

"Friends?" Candace asked, with a stern face.

"Friends," Dean replied. "No hard feelings. Now, please, I'd like to speak to your father."

"If it's about Patti braving the seas, don't bother. He's been watching your feed all morning with Mr. Rogan. They've been flipping between you and some other boring fishing show on Port Hope.

"They do shallow fishing there for lame small fish you'd use for bait," Candace said, and Dean chuckled. He checked out his video feed number and saw ten thousand people were watching him simply boat around and talk with Patti. In background noise, Dean heard Marty hollering something. "Never mind," Candace frowned, "He wants to say hello."

The sensory camera painted a picture of their home and Dean felt a sense of longing. That living room had been his favorite. Marty was in a big bean bag chair with a low table beside him, holding a glass half full of his favorite scotch.

"When you going to go all crazy, fishermen?" Marty's guest asked and the sensor included him in the view. "You haven't used yourself as bait this episode—not once!"

Rogan was one of Marty's many business partners. One of the perks of being an accountant was that you got to see who really made money and could ask if they needed investors. A key skill Marty had mastered, it seems.

"Mr. Rogan," Dean greeted the man, "We're just about to go get the little fish we recycle into cat food," he looked around them, "should be any moment, now. It's good to see you, Sir, sip one for me." Dean knew Marty hated Dean's slang around business partners, so he tried to keep his English Earthy clean.

"Nice gesture for the kid, Palmer Wilkinson. Great student, adorable little girl, and his family's barely getting by on Belmont's assisted basic income. Parents never went to school, and Palmer and his wife had to drop out—can't blame them, though. Got the regular flu, not the New Texas flu, at least according to public medical records. He had to drop out when she required bed rest," Marty said, giving Dean a long stare.

Dean shuffled his feet a bit, knowing what was coming. Patti went to save her friend, but Quincy held her back.

"An opportune offer for work, a sad story, and you dump a year's worth of income on the kid. You did really good, Dean." He shifted to see Quincy holding his daughter and raised his voice. "You both did something amazing with your spare coins and the donations of your followers. But! And it a big 'but' here... Don't be a trusting sucker. That research took me five minutes and less than a hundred coins. Do the right thing, if you're going to help someone, but make sure they need help and aren't swindling you, first."

Dean grunted and nodded. Marty always gave very good advice. The skipper's station pinged a positive school of bait fish on the radar with an echoing *pong*.

"I'll be more careful," he chuckled. "That sound is my cue, gentlemen, thanks for verifying I didn't goof," Dean said, and hung up the phone.

He trotted over to the storage bin and set his valuables into a locker. Not that he expected to go into the water again, but he had experienced splashes of ocean falling into a pocket, before, and phones weren't insured against saltwater on Oakley. Better safe than sorry.

Dean shifted his focus to the radar screen and enhanced the image. He frowned and gave a *hmm...*

"What's buggin ya?" Patti asked, trying to understand the situation. She was pointing at the school with her head tilted.

Cassandra went over to the image and swiped a second copy over to the first mate's station. Dean was watching the pattern of the fish. That spoke volumes to him. Cassandra was searching through the reading for bigger predators and bottom structures.

Dean wasn't in his honey hole, not yet, but he'd stopped here before. The bait was low and when he shot a glance at Cassandra's image the monsters were calm. The small fish were not here in large numbers, or aggressive, but the ping was a good sign that shallower water would be active. Dean dialed up an increase to their speed and let Quincy retake the Skipper's chair.

"Excellent question, Deckhand Patti. Catching fish is part science, part luck, and part skill. Catching baitfish is still catching fish. Follow me," Dean ordered, walking into the fresh whipping winds on the fishing boat's deck. "You ever watch my show? I know Cassie does. She'll even call me and ask questions about stuff on my trip home. Funny thing, is it's almost always when my shirt is off and I'm working out."

"Candace also has it on when you work out... Oh! Oh. Oh." Patti said with three different 'oh' sounds, as she pieced things together. "Besides that? No. Dad sometimes has your highlight reels on. I think he was one of your three subscribers before yesterday. At least you're skilled enough to catch fish, right! Else this boat would stay in port. Anyway, I'm here for Cassandra and to support you on your maiden Skipper voyage."

"Thanks... I think. I was wondering if you'd ever seen how the baitfish tank operated?" Dean asked with a raised eyebrow. Patti shook her head. "Give it a try Cassie."

Cassandra walked over to the back wall interface. While the *Fancy Feline* had plenty of old school, tried and true, features, the ship also had a great interface with advanced robotics for certain things—the bait tank being one of them.

Cassandra tried to open the panel from the touch screen and Dean had a *duh dummy* moment. He slid to her side and keyed in the password with his thumbprint. The ship required the Skipper's permission for certain things, unless he specifically authorized them.

"Thanks," Cassandra said, giving his cheek a quick kiss. "Skipper, are you blushing?"

"Aye, ten thousand fookers are watching. Not big on the PDA," Dean grumbled.

Patti laughed and said, "Candace will be jealous."

"You said that was weeks ago?" Cassandra asked.

"Twas, and nothing since," Dean said defensively. "Now get my bait tank up and filled, ya scurvy, rotten deckhand, with yer wily kisses."

Cassandra's cheeks puffed up and she smiled. A few inputs later and Patti squeaked as the decking she was standing on started to slide out from under her. She jumped back. The floor in the center of the fishing platform opened.

When the covers peeled back completely, a clear see through tank crept out of the hull. As it inched high and higher, water sloshed on the inside with its light green tint.

A moment later the four-foot-tall tank was filled with water and ready for bait. Dean went to a hatch on the aft wall and popped the lid open. He waved the ladies over.

"Grab the tools needed," Dean said, and Patti rolled her eyes. "Cassie will teach ya. I'll be needing to see how the honey hole is looking."

Dean left them to sort through the long nosed de-hookers and small tridents for gaffing the deck floppers. Quincy was slowing the ship as the radar went nuts. Dean's eyes drifted off into the distance to see the archipelago ahead that he called the Spring Breakers.

They were in shallow water—only twenty feet deep—as they neared the chain of small islands. This was a known getaway spot for Ola. Regulations allowed for only one-night stays, and no permanent structures. Dean had come out here in high school and remembered seeing all the small fish in the area. Which led to fishermen Dean knowing where to score easy baitfish.

Since the big monsters never came in this shallow, the baitfish schooled along these miles of barrier islands that dotted the horizon. The islands themselves were white sand with very little growth on them.

Small shrubs, short trees, and a few freshwater pools that nourished tropical trees. This chain provided a natural barrier to the mainland when lightning season arrived. During that time, the whole ocean, and even flights in this direction, shut down entirely.

After a trio of campers got stranded once for two weeks out here, Belmont had shifted the fishing season's end date a whole five days sooner, just in case. Dean noted a few partiers waving from the shoreline as they cruised by.

Even the shallows were feared in this area. The Larvian Sea was no friend to humans. If the hot day required a dip in cool water, best bet was to find an island with fresh water to hop into. The baitfish may not be hounded by monsters of the deep, here, but Eelraken and other hungry predators had no calms about coming into the shallow waters for a tasty snack or three.

"Where to boss?" Quincy asked.

Dean shifted closer to his friend and swapped from the directional map to an overview. "See this spot here?" he pointed to a location just before a series of islands. "There are tiny krill-like creatures, which live in this small deep spot. Occasionally big stuff will meander in here on high tide and gorge themselves on the fish that live on the little guys."

Quincy raised an eyebrow at that.

"You'll see the dead carcasses, occasionally, where they get stuck trying to leave during low tide. That's my honey hole. There are usually some nice, medium fish in the depths." Dean sighed, eyeing the ever-present drone cameras, "and while it's not a super-secret, it's not a secret at all, anymore."

Quincy set in a course. "Need me to manual drive?" he asked.

"Yeah, if we're not in a hurry, I like to troll through here. The white blooded sashimi fish tend to hunt here. Nothing amazing, but I'm not sure I want to go big game hunting. This is literally supposed to be a pleasure cruise, and honestly—"

"Bro, it's okay," Quincy said, trying to ease his friend's self-doubt, "A calm day of fishing and some island hopping is fine by me. We don't need to pull in some trophy fish on your first trip out as skipper."

"Alright, I'll go set the trolling lines. It's a few hundred to get a big drone to unbeach us, so keep a sharp watch on the seafloor," Dean said, heading to the bow.

He flipped open the trolling box and remembered he'd had Palmer set them in the high rack. He let the container *clap* shut and went back to the fishing deck.

The girls waved to some people while chatting. They both were so happy it brought a grin to his face. Boating tended to do that to people. Dean, himself, was elated—it was time to fish!

"Listen up, crew. We're in fishing grounds. There are spoon rigs and jig rigs. Cassie, you go to port and Patti to starboard. Grab a spoon rig; toss 'em out and reel 'em in. When I've set the trolling lines, I'll give ya a hand, if you're needin it," Dean instructed, pointing to the correct rods as he talked.

Patti asked Cassandra which side was starboard and then went to the right side of the boat.

Dean used his height to easily reach up and unseat the first trolling rod. This had his favorite mimic herring. The Oakley fish loved to chomp on some Earth fish. It swam like a champ and was almost always a great way to hook a white meaty predator.

Dean was just about to drop the herring lure in the water when Patti shouted, "I got one! Wahoo. Aw, it broke the fishing line."

He glanced over in time to note that her line was frayed before it snapped, it wasn't her fault. Small spoons were normally lost to the toothy predators if you didn't get the bait in quick.

"Watch Cassie, and don't get smacked in the face by a fish Patti. I don't want to explain to your dad how ya got a shiner," Dean said, letting his trolling line spool out behind the boat.

Patti was still pumped she lost the fish. "That was amazing, no wonder you do this. The big fish that ate the little fish was *pink*," she said enthusiastically. "*Eek!*"

Cassie flung a fish against the side of the tank. "The Krusan almost gobbled the little guy up, so I yoinked it out of the water."

"This is great. The Krusan and the Ornami are great value fish. We can make some decent coin if they're active here," Dean said, grabbing his second favorite troller. Sure enough, his favorite herring rod *whizzed* as the line screamed out.

Dean shouted over his shoulder, "Alright, halt the boat. Set the anchor foot. We're in calm waters with biting fish. Patti, bring that catch in. No, the rod that is angrily stripping line. Yes! That one. Pick it up, girl, turn off the clicking and reel for all ya got. I'll start chumming the waters."

"I thought you don't... oh, the casserole," Cassie chuckled, casting her topline back out.

The ship came to a halt and the electrical *whine* of four anchor feet sinking into the sand stopped quickly after starting. There were hours of setting daylight left.

With a nice beach not that far away and lots of fish to catch, Dean smiled as he retrieved the dish and tossed it overboard. When a nearby school of fish frenzied, he knew it was time for some fun.

He rushed back to the front of the ship. At the very bow of the boat, he kept his top-of-the-line spinner rigs. He pulled two out and hurried with them aft.

"Keep bringing in bait, Cassie. Quincy, use the net and stick this baitfish on that rod and toss it out that way," Dean said pointing toward the island.

"Uh, ya sure?"

Dean sighed and went to check on Patti. "Trust me, Quincy. Patti, how's that fight going?"

"It's so hard. How do I turn this clicker thing off?" Patti asked while fighting the fish on the trolling rod.

This was why he never chartered. Babysitting fishermen, or fisherwomen, in this case, was one of his least favorite activities.

Dean brought a second trolling rig up beside her. He let her see exactly what to do, showing her everything he did as he repeated the instructions. "Turn the notification drag off on the side. You'll want to keep the line tight on that fish, though. When it sees the boat and darts away with all it's got, either you loosen the drag, or it'll snap the line. Use your right thumb to do that." He verified she was absorbing what he was teaching "Up is tight, down is loose. Trust me. That is probably an Ursinfish. She'll tire herself out a fair ways away from the boat—they're stubborn fooks. Keep the line tight until the reel goes yellow, then loose, alright?" He smiled at her excitement. "You got this."

If the fish were this active it was no biggie if a few got away. They'd do so, even with Dean on the controls. Part of fishing was not catching anything. With a top water plug from the bow of the boat, he cast a spinning reel opposite Quincy.

Hand crank, jerk, hand crank, and jerk some more. The plug was *plunking* as it dove down and re-surfaced. His first cast came up empty. Quincy was waiting with his live bait chilling and Cassandra had a new baby Ursin on her spoon. The side of the boat cheated and unhooked her catch for her. Part of the new regulations were that only purposeful fish were allowed out of the water.

On his second retrieval, the boat flared green, telling Dean he was cleared for a humane harvest. "Keep it tight Patti! Clear the hatch!" Dean shouted, knowing the hatch was clear.

A lunging step connected him to the spear gun. The green pings stayed steady. He indented his thumbprint and a sudden *crack* sounded in the air.

The spear *whooshed* forward with its thin cable unspooling until it *splashed* into the shallow water.

Dean stayed the heck out of the way as the line zipped back into the container. A second later, the six-foot-long, fat bodied Ursinfish was snatched out of the water by the claw.

The ice hatch doors tucked in, allowing the opening to expand and the crane deposited the catch into the chilly morgue. When there was a *thunk* of the fish hitting the bottom of the ice, Dean grinned, and Patti cheered. Rightfully so. That was a hundred coin catch if you were over quota, which the *Fancy Feline* was.

"Fish on!"

Quincy shouted next, and Dean saw a breaching Krusan on the end of his line, shaking its head, trying to free itself. "What do I do?" his friend worried.

Dean was going to answer but he saw Cassandra calming Quincy. Patti went back to bait fishing and Dean went back to top water casting. After his fifth failed cast, he took a break to fix the first line that had snapped on Patti. Quincy had the hook pop from his catch, but he was not deterred. With a quick new live bait on, he eagerly rotated to fishing off the bow.

"This is great, thanks Skipper," Cassandra said, after putting her fifth baitfish in the tank.

Dean attached a new small spoon with a heavier leader before sticking the combo in a proper holder. He lifted Cassandra's chin to give her a peck her lips.

"What's that for?" she asked, knowing he was not normally the random kissing type. Even in private.

He sighed and said, "For when it turns from fun to work. I hope you brought some pain killers, with you." Dean scanned the horizon and noted infinite blues amid splotches of minimal white clouds. "I'm not the one and done kind of fisherman."

"Says the guy who—"

"Deckhand, it's imperative you do not finish that sentence," Dean commanded with a teasing wink. She smiled.

Cassandra went back to her corner in the fishing area. With the back swimming deck mostly destroyed, Dean used the roof to sight cast for bait. When he spotted a nice school, he chucked his spoon in and didn't have long to wait.

A moment later he had the eight-inch fish firmly in his grasp. He avoided the spikey fins, removed the hook, and chucked the lively swimmer over his shoulder into the tank. This happened another dozen times over the next thirty minutes or so.

He tossed one more Ursinfish into the hatch, but the bigger fish shied away after that. Even Quincy swapped to catching the little fish. The easier catch made for fun and less stress. When even the bait slowed down, they paused for a snack.

The girls stripped down to their bathing suits and used the freshwater rinse to wash away the day's sweat. Dean and Quincy put on their swim shorts.

Dean detached a dingy off the side of the boat and they went for the nearest island that an overview showed had a little lake.

Would Dean do this with Uncle Gordano? Not a chance. Yet, the sun was nice, the fishing pregame was done with a crowded bait tank, and Dean wanted to have some fun.

They ate a nice lunch on the beach, frolicked in the freshwater, and were back to the ship in less than an hour.

When the anchor feet lifted Quincy asked, "Where to next?"

"Well, ladies," he grinned, "we've got three choices, and yes you're a lady in this case, Quincy."

His friend rolled his eyes.

"We can catch more cat food," Dean said pointing at the small fish swimming beside him in the clear tank. "Or," he ticked the choices off on his fingers, "we go home and rent a penthouse, we go into the honey hole for medium fish or we go to some big clasts that house monsters of the deep and weigh his puppy down."

Patti and Cassandra giggled to each other and Quincy rolled his eyes.

"What?" Dean asked.

"That's four you goofball," Cassandra said. "The six thousand viewers are saying the depths." She paused when Patti checked a text. "Oh, Patti's mom says no to the depths and that she better convince you, or she'll never cook you steak again."

Dean figured it was better to please Mrs. Orlith Kendricks, after his recent transgressions.

"Ha! I owe her anyway. Medium fish for a few hours it is, then, and when the sun sets in an hour or two, we'll get that dark bite. Maybe be back at the Ola dock in six hours or so," Dean said with a shrug. "And I'm gonna turn off the video feed, sorry folks. Viewers are a side hustle—no offense to all those people watching." Dean addressed the nearest drone directly, "I'm grateful, really. Next season, when there's a new ship and less risk, I'll happily take ya back out to the depths."

Quincy cleared his throat and pointed at the map to the deep pocket Dean had marked earlier.

"Aye, Quincy. Nice and slow. We're going to troll to that spot. It's a twenty-minute ride from here, so there's no rush. Plus were speed limited in this area, anyway. There are sand disturbance prohibitors that make these channels off limits for power boating through. Partly why other crews hate diving into this island chain," Dean explained.

"Dean, we've got a question from an Earth charter captain. Why is the planet called Oakley, he wants to know, isn't it a corporate thing?" Patti asked.

Dean talked while he and Cassandra set out dual trolling lines.

"Oakley was a twenty-third century expansion project. The founders of this place holed themselves into the system hundreds of years ago," Dean said expecting his listeners to understand that by 'holed', he meant generated a wormhole through space for travel.

Space science was beyond him, but the principle was simple enough. You tied two points together and punched a hole between them for a direct route. At least, he thought that was how wormhole travel worked.

"So," he continued, "the planet back then was known as Patoria, that was on my sixth-grade history test. Yeah, Mr. Oland, see? I actually learned something, and it stuck in my thick skull," Dean said tapping the side of his head.

Dean congratulated himself with a fist pump now that the line was set. The *Fancy Feline* slipped between two barrier islands at a cool wind creating six knots. A smooth ride, perfect for sunbathing. No one had re-donned their gear for heavy fishing and Dean wasn't going to stress the issue if they were keeping things simple today.

"So, the orbital was, and always will be, the first thing built for a new colony. Patoria was a rapid expansion project. A planet this large, with nearly limitless landmasses, and an instant food source in vast oceans, meant it was a golden find. Corporations raced to assemble space elevators and connection shuttles from space to the surface. Oakley Orbital was known originally as," Dean paused for a moment, trying to remember.

"Berkshire Orbital," Quincy chimed in, bailing his friend out. They exchanged cheesy thumbs up while Quincy reclined in the skipper's chair.

Dean pulled on the trolling lines with slight tugs. They were in some fairly shallow waters, though, and he wasn't expecting a bite.

"Right, Berkshire Orbital. Way before our time. A rush job. Some inspector named Oakley had a gut feeling he followed up on—wasn't even on duty at the time. Felt the whole west wing had been slapped together haphazardly and approved way quicker than it should be."

"Maybe he was trying to rat on a fellow employee, or maybe he truly was concerned. Anyhow, Oakley found fourteen inspection points had been approved without proper, well, any inspections, really. One of them was already venting air and the exterior camera for the section had been disabled."

"It threw the whole project out of schedule for months. A few mega immigration ships were even forced to list in space, waiting for a docking slip. The new citizens demanded he lose his job—yup, he got fired for this, though that was eventually overturned, and he was restored back on the job. The government unanimously voted to swap the name of the planet and the orbital to his, in a final tribute when he died suddenly of asphyxiation, alone, in his room, under mysterious circumstances."

"Oakley has a dark history," Cassandra muttered. "Is this the spot? Looks like a lake."

"Yup, but it's not. Bring in the trollers and then, as much as Quincy, I, and our viewers like your thong bottoms, get back into yer fishin gear. We're going to have a busy afternoon. Only about a dozen or so minutes 'til the sun sets," Dean noted, pointing to the ball of gas sinking below the horizon.

The lines were reeled in while Dean slid into his fishing coveralls. Dusk on Oakley rarely lined up with Earth time's normal evening hours.

Dean had the small net out and the deep rigs in the side holders. Cassandra automatically went and stored the bait catchers. Before he went to drop a bait down, though, he wanted to check the radar ping. Fishing rules said he could inspect the area briefly and then the image would fade. The allotted sixty seconds was more than he would need. This honey hole was great for mid-water bait.

The scan revealed the long-term residents were in their common spots. Deep down, which only went a few hundred feet, he could find no goliaths lurking. A school of larger fish were present, though, and Dean predicted they were Ornami. Perfect. This place could be a gold mine sometimes; today was a great example of that.

"Drop deep," he instructed, "all the way to the bottom and then bring it back up thirty feet or so. Here is how this works. Give it lots of slack. Let the bait panic. The looser your bait is, the higher probability the Ornami will gullet the fish."

He mimicked a giant gulp.

"When your line zips angrily, stay calm. Slowly tighten your drag, about halfway or so. After five minutes, increase the drag in slow increments. We're in medium tide going to low tide, so unless an Eelboa slithers in, you're going to get all the time in the world to fight the catch. If you tire, rest the rod against the edge of the boat. Don't swap out with a fish on the line. Only a skipper can adjust a fish but may not fight it for more than a few minutes."

Cassandra furled her brows, "Why is that allowed?"

"There's no rockwork or artificial reefs around here. But in some cases, there are. If the fish wraps around a structure, an experienced fisherman or woman can fix the problem. Those kinds of things happen now and again, and the regulations provide caveats like this to allow for them. That being said, however, an Ornami—which is what I expect we're gonna hook here—is a decent fight that can last up to an hour," Dean mentioned.

He snatched a deep-water heavy rig from a portside slot and freed the hook from the holder. His hand dove into the bait tank and clasped a wiggling fish. The hook went through its nose.

"Always go top to bottom on the bait. That way you don't brain it going through the top. Quincy, here ya go," Dean handed him the rig, showcasing the flopping bait.

Quincy grabbed the rod and reel and sent the bait to the depths. Dean continued the baiting process and handed the girls each a baited rig. With lines in the water, Dean was forced to watch the minimal drift. Not like he needed to worry, though, with a medium tide and the gentle breeze.

Quincy's grunt was no shock to Dean. A glance over his shoulder told Dean the Ornami were hungry. This was feeding time for them. His friend's pole was doubled over with the line spooling out.

"Girls come up," Dean said. The two ladies on the starboard side huffed in annoyance. They weren't even down. Last thing Dean needed was three active lines with heavy fish and inexperienced people tangling them. "Faster before -"

"What the heck?" Both girls said in confusion as they fought against something slightly stronger than before.

"Don't sweat it, just bring those up quickly. You caught better cat food with your smaller bait fish, earlier. Cycle of the fish life. It'll be fine. Those, we can kill and toss in the ice box to prevent gulping up our bait," Dean said.

He watched poor Quincy struggling. The man was going to tire himself out long before the fish would. The veins in his neck bulged and his arms strained. He was pumping all wrong and overexerting himself. Dean stepped up beside him.

"Hand it to me, and before you say I'm built like a weightlifter, watch. There is a finesse to it," Dean said. Quincy removed the rod from his waist holder and Dean dug it into his hip. "This is stage green, not to be confused with boat green. The fish is full of energy. I don't pump too much here. I slightly jerk." The tip of the rod danced in agitation. "See the tip jiggling. That's the fish exerting a ton of energy. He's got nowhere to go. Watch."

Dean let the line run and then the fish slowed.

"I'd never do it like this around wrecks or rocky bottoms, but here, definitely. Okay, he calmed down. A couple of quick pumps to shorten the line, and away he goes again. Do this for the next ten minutes," Dean said handing the rod back to Quincy. "Let him be the dumb shit fighting a fishing reel's gears."

He shifted from the port side. The gentle breeze was barely pushing them, but they had drifted a few feet. He'd keep an eye on it while working. He went to the bait tank to slide his left hand into a staged chainmail glove. With his right, he snagged a long nosed de-hooker.

"Ship, open ice chest. Authorization Skipper Dean!" he couldn't keep the wide grin off his face. "Always wanted to say that," he chuckled.

The front hatch's servos *whined* as it opened. The medium bait fish were Vamprafish, but all the crews called them fangers. Nasty angler fish with two massive puncture teeth meant to bleed out prey as they held it. Dean was a veteran of these waters and he hated having to patch his skin with the quarter sized holes these fangers caused.

Patti had hers up first and the girls gave a tandem *eww* at the sight. Dean didn't blame them, not with the fishing orbs these things had and their excessive teeth. Most of Oakley's aquatic life was hideous.

The sun dipped below the horizon right as Dean grabbed the fish by the gills. The hook was released, and he walked the two-foot-long catch to the box. A quick toss into the icy depths and he went back for Cassandra's catch. Each fish was only worth a fraction of a coin. No sweat for Dean—even a simple catch like a Vamprafish was enough to buy a drink.

Dean grunted, realizing he was already craving the elixir of epicness. His mind stayed focused while he brought Cassandra's catch on board and tossed it into the frozen pit.

"Close the ice chest. Authorization Skipper Dean."

With that out of the way, the three of them relaxed to watch Quincy fight the Ornami. The side slots holding rods were removed to top rod holders. He ensured the walkways were clear and navigated the boat to the center of the honey hole again. Typical stuff a skipper did to help his deckhands succeed.

"What's next?" Patti asked.

Dean pointed to a nearby seat and chuckling, said, "We wait. This is the process for the rest of the night. There are probably a hundred Ornami down there, all bunched up. They will be rattled for ten minutes or so until that catch is stowed. Then the next greedy bellyaching fish will gobble one of those." Dean gestured at the fish circling in the tank.

Ten minutes later and the stars shined bright with an ever so slight wind stirring the surface. Dean was excited for more action, but that was common with big fishing, especially when you're the Skipper. He watched his friend fighting the fish and checked his phone.

Additional revenue was pouring in from today's viewers and people purchasing yesterday's video. His account had already recovered the money he'd donated to Palmer. There was a stack of messages from people wanting to be his agent.

Others offering him new deals through their own streaming services. He flicked them all into the delete bin. If someone reached out to him, in a few months, right before the next new fishing season, maybe he'd consider them.

Deep down, though, Dean wanted a quiet vacation. Doing side-hustles were not worth his happiness. A message from Marty came in, asking about his vacation plans. There was a coupon for a desolate tavern in the depths of the outback. A Bob's something or other.

Dean was in the middle of reading the message when his body surged with heat. The kind of internal feeling you get when you were about to vomit. Instead of spewing his fish lunch over the deck, though, a remarkable thing happened.

"Da fook!" Dean cursed as his hand shot white energy into his phone. The girls were facing Quincy, and only caught the flash out of the corner of their eye after it happened.

Dean was in shock and Cassandra hurried to his side, concern on her face. "You okay? Whoa, what did ya do to your phone?"

Dean's phone smoked in his hand, melted plastic dimpling the screen. "Involuntarily upgraded it, I guess. Do they build them to be lightning proof? Apparently, I'm discharging shock still from the Eelraken," Dean said and then cursed himself.

Nosy fookin drones needed to piss off.

He didn't regret deleting those offers at that moment. That subtle move actually improved his mood. Dean tossed his phone to the deck. The ship flashed yellow, telling him to get his ass in gear. He darted up the stairs for the port spear gun. The ship flashed green and then yellow.

"Tighten the line ya scrub!" Dean shouted, but he could hear the line peeling out. The Ornami had seen the boat. This'd be the last run. Dean knew it, from experience. "Now! Crank for all you got, hurry!"

The fish neared the boat and the ship pinged green. He put his thumb to the activation box.

Blinding white light flashed before his eyes stealing his night vision.

There was no crack of a spear firing. When the dots faded, and his vision cleared, the touchpad was smoking.

The controls were as dead as a doorknob.

"What's taking your slow ass so long?" Quincy clamored with a tired wheeze.

Dean raced down the walkway and balanced on the port wall. He snatched the rod out of Quincy's hands and his friend was shocked. He objected with a disgruntled, "Hey!"

Dean's upper body strength let him wrestle the fish expertly around the jagged broken section of the rear platform. When the fish ran, angered at having to go under the boat, he free spooled the line with a light thumb indent, letting the bitch run.

When it was deep enough, he latched down and two pump-chumped the fish to the surface. The ship blared red.

"Grab the fooking rod you newb," Dean shouted to an exhausted Quincy. "Hurry up."

Quincy trotted over and accepted the rod. The fish had all but rolled over, exhausted by the long battle.

It was ready for harvest and Dean saw the ship's lights ping green.

Dean ran for the starboard side spear gun and used his other thumb from his left hand. He figured if the damn Eelraken left him charged not using that hand would help.

Wrong.

Blinding light assaulted his vision again. The smell of burning electronics assaulted his nose and Dean screamed in rage at the sky above.

When his vision cleared, he ran for a trident. He already knew he'd ruined the other automated spear gun. It was time to revert to doing things the old fashion way. While the dots faded from his night vision, he snatched the trident from its horizontal rack on the port side and released the wiring clip. He caught Quincy flat footed and unmoving.

"Get that fish to the surface, ya lazy goof," Dean commanded, eagerly watching the water.

He was confused when Quincy stayed mute.

The water threw him off, too. It was calm, as if there was no breeze. Dean mind shut down and he hyperventilated when he caught sight of a reflection in the water's sheen.

His eyes slowly rose to lock onto a hooved foot standing on the water; its foot was the same size as his ship. His eyes continued up the hundred-foot-tall Minotaur who angrily glared down at Dean.

With the trident firmly in hand he braced to defend his motionless friends. A nudge to his friends' shoulders showed them frozen in place.

A tear in space and time ripped at the edge of the honey-hole's gleaming surface. Dean was thoroughly confused by the orange and black circular opening that appeared to drip tendrils of fire into the water—tendrils that continued to burn as they sank.

Either this is a prank, I got drunk, or fook me, the world is ending, he thought.

His confusion slipped into terror when a four horned Demon, wearing a metallic trench coat of all things, stepped onto the surface of the water and walked across it, as if it were dry land. Four Hell-Hound minions with beady red eyes leaped out of a crackling black portal that fairly screamed it had originated from the depths of hell. Each of them snarled for blood.

At that moment, Dean knew, something had gone terribly wrong.

CHAPTER

SEVEN

DEAN

Larvian Sea

Dean was mystified by the ten-foot-tall demonic monster in front of him. The abomination radiated fire, its blackened skin and clothing unaffected by the raging inferno that burned brightly against the night sky.

The minions that surrounded it were akin to Hell Hounds like you'd see in a movie. Four-feet tall, blazing red eyes, and slobbering spittle flying as they barked for blood. Nothing made sense, but his gut told him this was very real and very bad.

A human head with elven ears rose from the depths. The water parted as his height rocketed to match the Minotaur's.

Not a single drop cascaded off the god-sized arrival. Dean saw a man with folded arms wearing sweatpants and a boggy shirt speaking with the other enormous being. Oddly enough this was the most rational thing he was seeing. A deity in comfy clothes.

Their side conversation was finalized when they both pointed to Dean, who joined them in the finger pointing, promptly sticking a finger to his own chest in both question and denial. There was a *pop* from behind him.

Dean spun to see an angelic woman with wings sprouting out of her lower back. Her long blonde hair trailed down her back loosely. Her leggings clung tight to her body and her torso was covered in a shiny breastplate of a metal type unknown to Dean. She wore a whip on her left hip and a sword on her right. None of this alleviated Dean's fears or confusion. Pink eyes unrelenting in their hard stare, her chiseled face twisted in displeasure.

"Why're they frozen?" Dean asked rapidly, pointing to his friends and even the drones, which were rigidly stuck in time.

The angelic woman shook her head. "You've got three minutes. The water is a solid surface now. You can walk on it. Defeat that demon or your soul gets trapped in Min's Vault," she said. Dean's raised brows of confusion cued her into the fact he was not following the situation. "That... Demon... Kill..." Her finger pointed to the Demon thing. "Kill the whole team. Understand?"

Okay, Dean could understand that. Despite his desire to never be that pestering three-year old, ever again, he couldn't stop himself. "Why?" he asked.

The angel rolled her eyes and heaved a labored sigh. "Demons are bad. Nod if you understand."

Dean nodded. She continued. "Demons live in this planet's core, as they do on many other planets. You've been chosen as a temporary champion for this world. Far too much to cover in our remaining time. Let's just say, if you don't kill the demon, your soul becomes trapped for eternity."

"That's bullshit!" Dean exclaimed, clearly frustrated and pissed off.

"Gods play by different rules," she shrugged. "If you live, I'll see you on Mixonia. I'm Sable, demi to that hunky man who selected you. Twas you or some logging guy." She sighed uncaring. "In hindsight, you shoulda died to that Voratin, yesterday. Not all attention is the kind you want." She wagged a finger at him. "Good luck in your fight," Sable said, "You're gonna need it. Five against one," she snorted, "you're probably dead."

Dean titled his head in confusion and *poof*, she vanished. A million questions running through his mind all coalesced around one unanswerable thought.

When did I go out drinking again?

Dean hopped into the semi-tame waters to clear his clouded mind. Maybe the fanger had got him and there was poison on its teeth. Except...

His feet connected with the water and he scoffed in anger. He walked forward on the water until he bumped into an invisible wall. When Dean realized there was a block in place to stop him. His gaze shifted to focus on the demon across the solid water. Four Hell Hounds paced along their own invisible barrier, baying eagerly for his blood.

Oh shit, this wasn't some blackout dream; it was real.

Dean hopped back into the boat and grabbed a few baby tridents he loved to keep on hand for the odd flopping deck fish or Terrorsharks. Those bastards could be vicious on the deck of a boat. His big trident was too big and clunky to throw often or far. He'd need that too, though.

When he returned to the solid face of the water, the Hell Hounds charged. Dean was pissed. Five against one was bullshit.

Four of those opponents raced eagerly for his throat, while the big demon seemed content to lazily watch from afar.

Dean had limited options and no time to make up his mind. *Should I play defense? Let them run at me? No, that would let them close to the others. The rock star demon in the background needs to die first. How can I get over those infernal dogs? Maybe I...*

Dean sprinted for the Hell Hounds.

The Demon behind them laughed at the pathetic human; or maybe it was doing that evil laugh thing bad guys seemed to be contractually obligated to do —needlessly.

Suddenly, a fireball was cast from the end of the staff the infernal damnation held.

Dean spun to avoid the fire and he saw his foe cursing at the giant Minotaur as if it should have let him die. The Demon was beyond angry and raged against the unwavering, massive Minotaur.

Tearing his eyes from the distant scene, Dean noticed the Hell Hounds had slowed to flank him.

Not good.

He faked a throw of one of his spears at the waiting alpha hound. The creature actually flinched back, and Dean leaped forward in that split second of hesitation. Blind faith in the situation, as explained by the pink-eyed blonde angel, told him the water should act the same as dirt and he was right as he dug in and sprinted for his foe.

What he failed to notice, however, was another fireball zipping for his face. His run directly at the Demon prevented a fancy dodge. Confronted with the flash of fire directly before him, out of reflex, he twisted to the side. His attempt to avoid the orb of flame was only partially successful.

A searing pain cascaded over his senses. Dean's neck and ear burned with a *sizzle* and a *pop*.

Dean grimaced through the pain to close the distance.

When he was twenty feet from the demon, he shouted, "Eat spears you sack of shit!"

His arm cocked back readying a throw.

The Demon flung his shield up to guard his torso and face. When Dean tossed the clump of small tridents under hand at his opponent's feet there was shock.

Dean leveled the big trident for the demon's face, anticipating the reaction that unfolded. The Demon removed its shield for a split second in confusion.

The momentary opening allowed Dean to bury his big triple spiked weapon right into the centerline of his opponent's face. There was a sickening *crack* as its face caved under the power of his blow.

It fooking survived? I stuck a pitchfork in its skull... and it lived?!

The Demon was desperately attempting to free the trident Dean had simply abandoned in its face. The hell spawn tugged with short rapid jerks to no avail, all the while screaming so loud that Dean's ears felt like they were bleeding. That momentary distraction sent him into motion when he heard a loud snarl from behind him.

Dean dove to retrieve the javelins from the surface of the frozen water, tumbling with a tuck and a roll.

His hand snatched a small trident up and spun around with it defensively, guessing where the beast was coming at him from. The Hell Hound was less than a foot from his face when he drove the smaller trident into its neck with force enough to produce an echoing *crack*. He stood tall with a spin of the trident and a twist of his wrist to free the tip from the dead weight of the Hell Hound's body. The first dead Hell Hound slid across the water's surface like it was ice.

Dean kicked a Hell Hound back, only to have another lock onto his thigh. He stabbed down with his trident into the eye of the beast locked tightly onto his leg. There was no whimper, only the cessation of growling and a hundred pounds of dead weight he had to wrestle off his leg.

Two down. Two to go.

Dean was limping now. The two left were without their alpha or master.

Dean shifted until he saw the dead Demon sprawled on the surface, its arms splayed out to its sides.

He backpedaled for the weapon the Demon had somehow freed from its face before dying.

When he bent down to secure the weapon, though, one of the remaining Hell Hounds pounced. Dean tucked and rolled under the beast, stabbing it in the hindquarters before turning and thrusting the edge of his weapon into the final Hell Hound's open maw. The shaft of his weapon broke, though, as did Dean's collarbone when the Hell Hound chomped down around one of the tines to bury its teeth in his shoulder.

Dean twisted, valiantly trying to keep the hound from clamping down on his neck.

He whipped his filet knife out of its sheath and plunged it into the monster's bloody eye.

Dean cried out in agony when his fingers pried the dead animal's jaws off his shoulder. He heard a whimper off to his right. Not far from where his broken trident rested, a wounded Hell Hound crawled towards its motionless master.

Dean retrieved a javelin with his good arm. When he hobbled to the last of the beasts, its eyes pleaded for mercy. Dean was all out of pity. The javelin went into the beast's guts. He twisted and yanked his weapon back out. It was going to take a few minutes, if not hours, for it to bleed out.

When Dean walked to the dead demon, he tried to take its weapon first, but the staff was locked in its rigid, frozen hands. The purse on the demon's belt came off and Dean bounced it once in his palm; except that the item disappeared mid-toss, reappearing back on his dead foe's belt instantly, as if by magic. He tried to pilfer a fancy looking dagger, only to have the same thing happen, the dagger instantly returning to its owner's belt.

"That's some fooking bullshit," Dean muttered.

He retrieved his trident and trident javelins and went for the first aid kit on the Fancy Feline.

"It's rude to leave your foe to die slowly," a voice boomed from above.

Dean's eyes shot up to the Minotaur. He wasn't sure if it was a male or female. So hideous was its cow face and shaggy fur.

"Why can't I get his weapons?" Dean asked, not caring whether or not he was rude to his enemies.

The Minotaur snorted in anger and stomped its hooves. Yet, it did nothing else. Dean had a feeling the big brute was powerless in this situation. He tossed his weapons to the deck. He left a bloody trail across the boat as it flowed freely from his wounds.

He walked beyond his still frozen friends for the first aid box inside the seat of the Skipper's chair. Dean fumbled with the codes to unlock the damn thing as shock and pain started to set in. He mentally prepared himself for what was about to happen with rapid deep breathes when the case opened.

The first application was the worst. The disinfectant seared and he hollered for all to hear about how great his torment was. Next came the numbing application. Finally, the material filler and blood clotting foam. He would need to get to a real hospital or a fancy doctor when they got back.

"Human, shoot the hound with your electricity so I can end this farce," the Minotaur said with disdain.

"Huh?"

"Aim your palm at the sniveling mutt and blast it, I'm bound here until the fight is concluded and then I reward the winner," the Minotaur grumbled.

Dean leveled his right palm, aimed it at the Hell Hound, and wished a lightning arc to zap the minion.

A ball of white energy pushed him back as it soared forward. Dean stared at this palm in dismay. He actually hadn't expected that to work. The electric orb melted his foe, leaving tendrils of smoke rising from the now still body. The Minotaur shrinking down to a tenth of its previous size paused Dean's wonderment at his newfound power.

The smaller beast stood only ten-feet tall and walked to his ship to present the victor a locket on a necklace. A number was engraved on the locket—a clean one hundred etched on its cover. Dean went to accept the token, but the Minotaur batted aside his arms and placed the trinket around his neck.

With a flash of blinding light, the Minotaur was gone.

The hunky giant man with elf ears *clapped* in congratulations.

"I knew I picked right. A full demon team slaughtered. Wowzers!" the almost normal sized god proclaimed from beside him with such excitement that Dean's ears rang. "I bet you want some answers."

Dean nodded while slipping tiredly into the first mate's chair. "My back is bleeding," he grumbled. "I'll need one of them, or you, to help me patch it up."

"Beneath a god and against the rules. But..."

The god slid into Quincy's body. The fishing rod was set into the rod holder and his friend walked in a janky style for the captain's chair and the medical kit.

Repairing the bite marks on his back was just as painful as the ones on his front had been. When he'd finished treating Dean, the god exited Quincy and left him where he was.

"He'll feel worse than you will for about four days, maybe five. Sorry. I need to talk to you, though, and you needed healing, or you'd likely forget what all I'm about to tell you. You can explain it all to him," the god gestured to Quincy, "but I doubt he'll rationalize what he experienced."

Dean raised an eyebrow at the excitable deity.

"Ah, where are my manners? I'm Zued. A god of energy," Zued said with a wide smile.

"Demons are in the core?" Dean asked.

"Most certainly. This planet was theirs long before you humans arrived. Be grateful they never set up a Wixomia team until after you started banging around on the surface, else they'd be much farther ahead," Zued smirked, his hands spread wide, palms up with a 'so be it' shrug.

Dean, of course, had no idea what he was talking about.

"You will get caught up on all this soon enough, Dean," Zued continued. "For now, though, I need a favor. A really big favor or else expect some other poor sap to get challenged soon," he sighed, "and they probably won't be as lucky as you were."

Dean held up a hand gingerly. "I've got about a bazillion questions."

The god again shrugged, uncaring. "This Marty fellow recommended you check out an outback tavern," he smiled. "Go there. One of the other guests will introduce herself as a guard of Mixonia, sent to guide you on an adventure. Believe her," the god smirked, "she is. She'll answer some of your tedious questions, but be warned, she has been known to give half answers."

Dean wondered if he should be taking notes.

"I'll tell you why I'm here, though. I want this to be a world for the gods. Not the demons. If you ignore my advice, you'll never be able to cash in that necklace. Min's Vault of Treasures is filled with wonders. Wonders that keep many a gate master from ever going home. Again, you'll learn in due time what it is I'm referencing. The important takeaway for you," and here the god jabbed a massive digit at Dean, "is that because I chose you and not the tree cutter – the fate of Oakley rests in your hands."

The god gave a half-assed wave before blinking out of existence. Dean felt nauseous and he vomited, his bile mixed with blood.

His friends were so focused on the rod bent over in the holder they'd failed to notice him heaving in the first mate's chair. Dean recovered after a few final retches. He wiped his mouth with the back of a hand and stumbled past a groaning Quincy to reach for the rod. He reeled it in just enough to see the Ornami belly up in the water.

"Dean, what happened to your shirt? Is that blood?" Cassandra asked. "My god, your ear is almost gone!"

Dean ignored her to fetch a trident off the deck. The triple hooks sunk into the Ornami with the shaft pointing into the air. He prayed the crane wasn't busted. He dragged the fish to the front of the boat and like a miracle, the claw scooped the fish in its jaws. The icebox opened and the catch was deposited inside.

Even wounded, Dean knew his inner fisherman couldn't let the fish escape.

Cassandra was right in his face when he spun to check on his friends.

"Quincy is vomiting from his overexertion," Patti sounded worried from where she helped his friend at the Skipper's station.

"Give him lots of water. He's going to need tender care for the next five days, I've been told by a very solid source," Dean hollered loud enough for everyone to hear.

"What the fook happened Dean?" Cassandra gasped, her eyes showing that she was about to panic.

Dean groaned and shook his head, "I'll tell you everything once we're below deck. I need to auto plot us a route home, as in right this instant." He went to the autopilot router and input 'Ola docks'. With an ETA of forty-nine minutes, he selected go and the ship spun around and headed in a wide arc around the barrier islands.

Dean turned to give her a mock glare. "You never swear, Cassie, don't let me convert you to my vile ways."

His joke missed the mark, though, and she pulled him into a tender hug that still elicited a groan.

"I'm freaking out here, Dean, are you scared to tell me what happened because of them?" Cassandra asked, indicating the infuriating drones.

Dean ignored both her and the drones. "You'll have to be at the wheel for the sea gates," he instructed. He heard a concerned Patti fretting over Quincy from the crew station below. Dean stumbled down the hatch, using the railing to hold himself upright. When he reached the bottom, Cassandra hesitated.

"Let me clean the ship up and then I'll join you," she said and hurried off.

Dean grunted and went for the shower. He limped by a confused Patti who only just now noticed his wounds.

"What the hell?! What're those?" Patti exclaimed. "Is that blood?"

Dean ignored her and stripped, then flicked the shower on. She gave him some privacy when he closed the door. He sat in the shower folded in half as the water rinsed his blood off. Dean desperately wanted to check his medical tracker, but his phone was fried.

Cassandra barged in. She was a huffing ball of concern; Patti and Quincy were right behind her. Quincy was super pale and looked like shit. Dean stopped the water and leveraged himself off the floor. Cassandra handed him a towel he rapidly used to remove the water.

"Book a doctor and a hotel room we can fly directly into. The kind the rich kids use with the balcony docking ports. One night. Do that while I tell you what happened," Dean said tossing the damp towel in the sink. He hobbled by his friends to slide into a stiff bunk bed, pulling a pillow under his head. "So, get this," he began, "Demons and Gods are real."

He was expecting dropped jaws, shocked exclamations of denial, and just about everything—everything, that is, besides the blank gazes and flat faces they returned him.

"A Demon did... that? How?" Cassandra asked, he saw her eyes darting around trying to come up with one of her logical deductions.

"Let me tell the story, because I'm still full of questions too. After I fried both spear stations—man the insurance company is going to be pissed. Well, they'd probably disable them for filming, anyway."

Cassandra cleared her throat to get his attention and get back to his tale.

"Sorry," he apologized, "after I went around Quincy to trident spear the Ornami for the front claw—well," Dean shrugged uncomfortably, "yer not going to believe me, but that was when time just fooking froze. You three were stiff as boards.

"There was a hundred-foot tall minotaur. A hundred-foot tall hybrid elf dude and his daughter who was our size, but with angel wings coming out above her hips. On the water, which froze solid as the ground, were a demon and four of his Hell Hound minions. They were not very friendly. Angel chick said I had to kill the demon and his hounds, or my soul would rot in some place for eternity. Not sure the where, how or the why of anything—besides the fact that the big ones claimed to be gods," Dean said, sucking in a big breath after the words just poured out.

"Penthouse booked, decently reviewed doctor for animal wounds on the way, and I purchased some O-Neg plasma," Cassandra reported, reading from her phone. "You owe me."

"You're a lifesaver, Cassie. So," he continued, "I fought the demon spawn. Apparently, this planet has Demons living in its core."

Patti's eyebrows climbed into her bangs.

"Eh," Dean chuckled, "that wasn't the oddest thing. So... I won a fairly quick fight. Got lots of wounds, but I won. I gutted the final asshole of a Hell Hound, letting it fester in its mortal wound. This angered the Minotaur God, who ordered me to, and I quote, 'zap the thing'. So, I pointed my palm at it and shot a ball of lightning from my hand to kill it. After I'd won, the Minotaur God gave me this locket and necklace as a trophy, with the number one-hundred on it."

Cassandra picked the locket up off Dean's chest and examined it.

"Whatever that means," he snorted. "The humanoid elf-hybrid God shrank down to our size, possessed Quincy's body to repair my back. I think it did that to fook with Quincy and torment my wounds."

Quincy's pale face lost what little color it had regained since being possessed.

"Sorry, mate, the god said you'd feel like shit for the next five-day, then basically said the fate of Oakley rested on my shoulders." He pressed his palms to his face, as if that could block out the past hour.

"The god said I'm supposed to go to some shitty tavern in the outback that your Dad recommended, Patti, where I'll be escorted to some place called Mixonia. And then time resumed."

Three blank stares at him. Quincy went first. "By Jupiter's tits! Unfooking real. My mind is blown. But deep down, don't ask me how, but I believe ya? I ain't never felt this horrid in my life. One moment I'm fighting a fish and the next I'm a dozen feet away in feverish torment. I think I'm going into a cryo pod for five days." Quincy shook his head determinedly, "Yeah, I'll meet you at this tavern after."

"There are demons and gods," Patti repeated in disbelief. "Some really weird shit happened to you—that somehow included losing your ear in a battle that required nearly the entire first aid kit to patch the holes in you afterwards—with no valid explanation. I witnessed, with my own eyes, you both suddenly shift to different places. This, this is..." she shook her head in denial. "Gods vs Demons is a bit much, you've got to admit."

"Dean doesn't lie," Cassandra said with a deflated sigh. "I'm freaking out on a million levels internally but that won't help. Were still out in the middle of the ocean and not home safe, where I can scream into a pillow. For now, we have to stay calm."

Dean grunted and replied, "Hey look. I need you, Cassie, even if I'm delusional. Especially if I'm delusional. I'm done with the ocean for this season. Later this week we fly to check out this tavern. After I get seen by a medic and get a new phone." He closed his eyes, "And a good rest."

"It was a thousand for the private penthouse," Cassie winced, and Dean's eyes bulged at the price. "We're staying for at least a day, regardless. My vacation, my rules. You owe me a full twenty-four hours snuggled up to you, to ensure you are better," Cassandra huffed, bopping his nose with her index finger.

"Sounds wonderful. I wonder what this Minotaur guard at the tavern wants? The God said I wouldn't be able to collect my reward unless I went with her," Dean mumbled, and Quincy laughed.

"So much for a quiet offseason of debauchery. You got a vacation girlfriend and world ending problems on your hands. Oh my!" Quincy said with a hacking cough.

Patti caught him as he stumbled. She walked him to the bunk across from Dean's.

"I'm sure it'll be nothing. There'll be no guard, no treasure, and you were bitten by a poisonous fish. No," Cassandra muttered, "some fish released a gas we all inhaled. Everything will be completely normal by this time tomorrow and this will be behind us. After all, if there really were gods, we wouldn't have all these problems."

Dean chuckled and said, "You're right. We'll prove you right, and me wrong. While also getting away from this blasted sea for a few weeks. Cassie, as long as you are by my side, I'll be just fine."

Cassandra pecked his forehead with a tender kiss. She pulled the covers up to his chin and sang him a sweet song. Quincy was out first, though it wasn't much longer before Dean felt his eyes growing heavy and the wall of black swallowed him whole.

EIGHT

DEAN

Ola City

"**M**r. Forrester," the Doctor frowned, "You're damn lucky to be alive. I had to inject you with three plasma bags just to get your blood pressure stable. Your coursing electricity fried three of my devices."

Dean hoped that wouldn't happen. Shit, this was going to be one hell of a medical bill.

"You need to be seen by about every professional in the Galaxy more qualified than me," Doctor Hersa sighed. His stethoscope was still draped around his neck and he was packing his things.

"Vacation tomorrow?" Dean asked and the grouchy old man actually busted out a smile.

"Fook if I care what you do. Your body is fine for it. Nothing strenuous," He said eyeing Cassandra with a warning glare. "Keep him off the bottle. His liver is not doing so well. Not anything serious, but his counts are low. Seeing some sights and staying out of trouble is all this doctor can recommend."

"Thank you so very much Doctor Hersa, we appreciate your time," Cassandra said with a charming smile that matched her sincere blue eyes.

"Well, I'm not cheap, but I'm honest. And you're in better condition now than when I arrived, which is all I need to feel my charge worthy of my efforts. Take care Mr. Forrester and try not to ever call me again. I mean it. If I wasn't a privacy doctor, you'd be in a barrage of testing facilities getting more blood drawn than should be possible."

Dean watched the doctor walk out of the room for the landing pad on the balcony. Distant recording drones were only allowed on the outskirts of the property, though this didn't stop them from trying to glean information about why Dean and his friends had rushed home. He was sure the doctor wouldn't help the rumor mill.

Cassandra closed the sliding glass door to the exterior and sealed the curtains closed. Her mischievous smiled caused Dean more than a little concern.

"You heard the doctor," Dean warned," nothing strenuous!"

She mock-pouted, but only briefly. "I'm thinking of something better than sex: ice cream, a romantic movie, and snuggles with my beau," Cassandra said, and Dean grunted in acceptance. "He did a great job, fixing up your burns and wounds, but you'll still have a lopsided haircut for a while and a tender ear. How does it feel?"

"Numb. My body feels numb. Thank god for science though," Dean said, shifting his position, leaning back and lifting his arm for her to snuggle under.

He gave her a long, hard stare. Her blue eyes sparkled, a second bite of heaven from her expensive pint halfway to her full lips. "What?" She managed with a mouth full of frozen deliciousness.

"You're not freaked out?" Dean asked.

She shrugged and burrowed into his side. "I don't want to talk about it until we know more. I also want to hold off talking about us until we know more. I'll tell you one thing, though," she grimaced, "I'm not Patti. After that scheming doctor left us a fourteen thousand G-coin bill, I knew the truth. You've got electricity in your veins. That's enough for me to rationally accept the rest."

"I need to control it, I can't keep blasting phones and electronics," Dean said with a huff. He lightly smacked his forehead. "I should've asked the gods about my electric power. What it means, at least."

Cassandra kissed his forehead with icy lips. "Silly Dean, I'm sure a lot was racing through your mind at the time. I'm here for you. I even booked our trip already. We vacay, starting tomorrow." She looked down at her ice cream and then considered Dean carefully. "You think getting an icy blowjob would be considered 'strenuous'?"

"Nope!" Dean replied instantly with the biggest grin he could muster. "But Cassie, it's mellow if you want to just watch this chick flick."

"Fine," Cassandra agreed, "afterwards then," and put a movie on that Dean cringed his way through.

The evening did include a sensual blowjob, a nice delivered meal, and a long snuggle session where Dean drifted in and out of consciousness. The next morning, he swam in the balcony pool and still felt slightly ill, but by the time their flight for the Outback arrived, he was ready to leave the lavish penthouse.

When they boarded their private air taxi Dean asked, "So what's the name of this place we're heading to? I was reading about it when my phone fried."

"There's no city name. The tavern is Bob's Beer, Burgers, and Beds. Our suite sleeps a dozen and the place as a whole is barely up to code. I think the liquor licenses are cheaper outside established counties. Who knows? You excited to collect your reward?"

"Yes and no," he sighed.

She grinned. He could tell she was really excited about their vacation—whatever it may lead to.

"Hey Cassie, thanks again for being here. No offense... Hmm..." He stopped, frowned, shook his head and tried again. "Starting out with that is probably not the best way to thank someone." He pulled her in for a hug. "I'm just grateful you're here. End of statement."

"You'd do the same," Cassandra said, with a single raised brow. "Remember Mittens?"

Dean chuckled. "Your cat died while I'm in bed with another woman. You called me like 3 times, but that was enough to get me to stop and answer. Did I drop Lena? Or was it Beatrice? Yeah, it was awkward for everyone, but us. Either way, I left them—mid-sex ditched and ran right to ya."

Cassandra beamed.

"Gotta be honest," he smirked, "Never thought I'd do that, but the decision was easy enough. Just like when I got my first assault charge and had my attorney friend get me out four days after lock up."

"You shouldn't have hit him more than once," Cassandra scoffed. She entered the data into the air taxi and their flight took off.

Dean studied Ola during the long night cycle. The sun wouldn't be rising for a few more hours, but people were already out and about. Big delivery trucks cycled between locations, people shuffled about, and night lights everywhere blasted the dark away.

The city was so bright they'd drawn the curtains for most of their stay and essentially killed half the reason for an expensive hotel room. Dean smirked when he realized they were going to a dump and would miss the luxury soon enough. He shifted to see his Cassie eyeing him with a stern gaze.

"What!? He super deserved the second and third hit," Dean said while watching Ola drift under him.

"Dean, he was getting handsy, not rapey. And I knew him. We'd slept together a month earlier on a drunken bender," Cassandra sighed with a toss of her head. "I did tell him no, though, so it flared the area with an alert when he persisted."

"I'm still shocked he pressed charges. Fooking pussy. You were going to drop your charges if he dropped his," Dean said, letting it go. "I still get all angsty about it, five years later. Was a hell of a way to meet a new friend."

"Yeah, well, thanks Dean, and for being there for me every time I've needed you after that," Cassandra said.

Dean shifted his focus back to the interior of the air car when the last of the buildings vanished beneath them. "I wish I'd rescued you from that New Years' party on Oakley Orbital." Dean bit his nail in frustration.

"You were too drunk to fly, but so was I. I survived. Speaking of surviving. Have you seen what there is to do at this shithole of a tavern?" Cassandra asked and Dean shrugged. "Ah, shit, yeah. Scared to zap things. Let me put on the tour video."

The air car was compact, just big enough for two and some luggage. The windscreen converted into a video screen with a few taps. Dean reclined his seat and Cassandra did the same, nestling into him.

Flight time was showing four hours. Yup, that should mean daylight morning on Oakley.

A video beeped and showed what must have been Bob.

"Welcome to Bob's Burgers, Beers, and Beds." The short, portly man smiled, and Dean heard a 'close enough' comment in the background. "We've got all the best accommodations for the weary city slicker looking for some rustic charm."

Alarms started going off in Dean's head at the word 'rustic'. Those were verified when the video showed an original structure—as in, two hundred years old and handcrafted, in wood. Oh wow, he thought, was it ever a dump on the outside. No wonder it was offering bargain discounts.

"I know, it's hard to keep the outside pretty but on the inside, she shines," Bob smiled, and Cassandra fast forwarded to the part where he went into activities.

Dean frowned and then relaxed. He'd see the inside of the place later.

"We've got hunting, spelunking, river monster fishing, and even some rapid riding. Fair warning, though, the water is not safe! Actually," Bob chuckled, "none of it is. The outback is not for the faint of heart. So, we encourage you to walk some nice trails in the humanity preservation and enjoy a disconnect from your busy lives.

Disclaimer, the preservation may be overrun with Aringos and closed without warning."

The video ended and Dean looked out the window to see the first blush of dawn and a slowly rising sun.

"I get why he built this place. A short human preserve walk sounds nice," Dean said, bouncing his eyebrows with a teasing chuckle, "maybe you can wheel me around."

"This section of the outback is no laughing matter. There are one hundred and fourteen animals, insects, and other wildlife that can kill you. Seriously, I laughed at the thought of there being a human preserve, like really hard," Cassandra said with folded arms. She wasn't angry, merely serious.

"Then I realized that during the early colonization of this planet, the death rate was a staggering twenty two percent in this area," She said widening her arms as if measuring a big fish. "People would go out to the shed and be killed by a snake type scorpion. Piss on a tree and get killed by dart flinging lizards. Chase after your dog who is acting a little crazy, only to find out it got infected with a rabid poison and it bites you, killing you dead."

"My love?" Dean winced, it felt odd, calling her something besides Cassie. She hated hearing Cassie from anyone else, besides Dean.

He cleared his throat and tried again. "My lovely Cassandra? I'd be remiss to not acquiesce your request for some easy time. I've two months of offseason and a bundle of money saved. How much is this place?"

"I booked us a week in the largest room for six hundred coins. I'm sure there'll be upcharges and whatnot. But," she smiled shyly, "Dean I've got a lot of coins. The only partying I do is to see you or the girlfriends. Most of my lawyering money is piled in a big bank account. Not trying to brag, but I'm not worried if I have to relocate or skip a month or two of work." She paused, expecting Dean to react poorly.

"That's great, not the money thing. I always knew you were a whizz with money. Honestly," he sighed, "I should put you in charge of my money..."

She smirked.

Dean noticed her smirking. "Why that look?" Dean asked.

Cassandra fidgeted a bit and said, "Remember when you couldn't get that loan and you called me to see if they were breaking some law by denying you?"

"Yeah," he remembered, "for the small boat I wanted to get in the interior. I had this whole plan to do paragliding on the lake during the offseason. They shot me down real quick, though," Dean said with a sigh. It was hard to get a loan as a fisherman. "What about it?"

"I had you sign a form granting me power of attorney to seek alternate means of financing."

Dean nodded, remembering.

"Yeah, well," Cassandra continued, "I'm still on your accounts with a power of attorney. Never done anything wrong and only peeked in a few times. One of them was to balance your accounts earlier on the boat."

"Ah, you've been checking up on my spending habits. I'm not upset," Dean said, slapping her knee lightly enough not to trigger a violence alert. "Oh, I see... that look was because you're already in charge of my money."

"Yup, it's not as much as mine, but far more than you've ever had before. Not trying to emasculate you," she held her hand up, palms out. "I just want you to know it's in good hands."

He snickered.

"That statement came out weird," she grinned at his antics." Do you want me to remove myself?"

Dean shook his head. "Cassie, I've been meaning to slow down on the partying. If I get a regular dose of waking up to your smile and a bed wrestling partner with your skills, I can lay off the womanizing somewhat," Dean admitted, and she kissed his cheek. "My point is, I know I need help. I'm trying to build a better me."

"I'd love to help. I'm just worried that if we get too close, we'll fall apart like you and Patti did," Cassandra worried, resting her head on his shoulder.

"So, what did she tell you?"

"You had sex a few times, went out a few times, and then for some reason, you transitioned from being great friends to distant friends," Cassandra said.

Dean winced and muttered, "The sex was bad, and I hated it. Don't you dare tell a soul!"

"Aw, that I can understand. The thing that takes a friendship beyond friends is sex. How about we shift gears while we watch this lovely view?"

Dean's eyes scanned dense trees slowly transitioning into the savannah up ahead. Here there were still pockets of forest, lakes, and general non-desert biome scenery. Up ahead, though, the landscape shifted to where less rain fell, and the terrain supported much less life. A few abandoned homesteads and the odd ghost town or two stuck out among the thinning trees.

Settling on Oakley was tough. There was so much land, it was hard to manage it all, let alone to make it profitable. The Orbital served as the ultimate realtor, parceling out every section of land. Luckily, only counties collected taxes—so if you owned where there was no county, there was no property tax.

Value added, income, transaction, fair, and union taxes were all still there, though. But as far as property tax went, it was the wild west for the majority of Oakley. This made immigration lucrative and people tended to stick claims out in the bush only to be drawn into the cities over time.

Shoot, Uncle Gordano had a distant hidey hole until Dean showed up. No taxes, no school. So, his Uncle had moved to where there were taxes, because even Uncle G had been happy to hand Dean back to his teachers.

Now that he'd earned enough to semi-retire or buy his own boat, he needed to consider what he was going to do. He knew Cassandra was correct in waiting for answers. Still, he wanted to see about buying a place somewhere—save a bundle on rent, in the long term. He could always get a smaller vessel or be a deckhand on someone else's boat.

"Did you buy your condo?" Dean asked, changing the topic.

Cassandra's smirk turned into a grin. "It's too early to talk about moving in together."

Dean stuck his tongue out at her. "I need to make some life changing decisions, here. My storage locker can't hold more than a dozen sets of clothes and a few boxes of junk. Most of my money is tied up in fishing gear. Which, I think conveyed, ugh. I should send -"

"It didn't and it's going into your storage locker. All five thousand coins worth of the gear is insured. Our catch netted a few hundred coins and is already processed. Oh, and the insurance company is fixing the fritzing spear control panels.

"What else, there was something else that came in while you were sleeping," She paused tapping her chin. "Oh right, about a million offers for sex, a short-term contract to follow you around on vacation, and a licensing company wanted to use your image for their new advertisement about being brave."

"And?"

"And I handled your affairs and declined the offers, just like you'd have done," Cassandra said with a cocky shrug. Dean pulled her in for a long, deep kiss that they had to pause for a stupid consent approval.

"As far as my condo goes, I bought with cash. That way, you pay no one extra for rental or for interest. So yeah, I own my place." She turned to look at him closely, "What were you thinking?"

"That I should get a middle of nowhere home. Taxi in to work, sleep on my ship during the season, and taxi home again for the off season." He rubbed his face. "What do you think I could afford?"

"Would this be a long-term home?" Cassandra asked, renewed interest lighting up her face.

Dean bit a nail and said, "I'm not having kids anytime soon. I want a nanny on lockdown. Separate rooms. It's a huge deal to be a parent and for now, I'd rather get a dog or a cat. Since you're the crazy cat lady."

"Dean, I," Cassandra paused and leaned into Dean. "More to follow... later. After seeing the list of activities at Bob's, are there any items we need to get?"

"Besides what we've got stuffed in the suitcase? I doubt it. Drone delivery probably takes less than half the time it takes to shuttle my heavy ass out here," Dean said seeing the start of the outback's thin short scrub trees.

"Well, you're right. We can always adjust, and this cheap taxi is dreadfully slow. A few sets of clothes, some water backpacks with standard camping gear should be enough. Hmm..." She paused and typed in some information. "I splurged and bought us some protective suits."

"Like the spaceship kind?" Dean asked with an eyebrow. "I'd be ridiculed for ages in one of those."

"The outback is no joke Dean. They have air conditioning, thick armor, and will assist you in your movements."

"I guess, though it's not exactly my style," Dean said with a shrug. "The tavern probably has a shop with some for rent."

"These were pricey and new; meaning I don't think a rundown tavern has fancy survival suits. If I'm plastering my fine ass in an empowered suit, it's going to be new. I bet Bob has all the flashlights we could need at 39.99," Cassandra said. She noticed Dean biting his nails and raised an eyebrow. "Can I cut those for you?"

"Ha! I get it," he chuckled, "we're shifting towards becoming a couple, but no. I'm not giving up my nail biting—least not just yet. Also, is it Bob or someone else who even owns Bob's Tavern?"

"Let me look up the deed. Huh, imagine that. It's up for sale for two hundred K. Sold as is by a Jaeger Manfield. So... Fook me," Cassandra said.

"What?"

"Just a bit too convenient, is all," she sighed. "You're meeting a mysterious being sent by a god to redeem some reward and it's inside a joint that fits your requirements for a quiet non-city life. I'd never be a lawyer out here, though" Cassandra said with a longing sigh. Her scheming face came alive with excitement. "Or could I?"

"Yeah, so. I know we've had this conversation before. Why'd you become a lawyer? And does it make you happy? Also, couldn't you hop out on weekends if you wanted to?" Dean fired off a barrage of questions.

"How about we save these questions for later?" Cassandra said, ending the conversation, "I'm excited to meet this Jaeger character. I bet our room is epic."

Dean let her win, for now. He leaned against the window to check out the landscape drifting by below. Time would tell if he was making the right decision, coming out here. In the end, it's not like there were many other people he could turn to, to find answers. Dean had an avid distaste for government testing facilities and rightfully so. They didn't have the best track record of returning people in the same shape they'd borrowed them in. Or so all the conspiracy videos said.

Answers, he wanted so many answers—the reward was just a cherry on the top. Or so he thought.

CHAPTER

NINE

DEAN

Planet Oakley - Outback Bob's Tavern

They landed in a protected square, sectioned off by a tall stone wall with an entrance made out of an old school Land Rover's rear lift gate.

Dean's boots *crunched* in the loose soil when he exited the air taxi.

Cassandra completed the transaction with the interior interface while Dean fetched their luggage from the trunk. Once the self-carting bags were out and trundling along behind them, he inspected the building.

The exterior was even rougher than it had looked in the video. He guessed the building to be about forty-feet tall and at least three times that wide. The slatted wooden boards of the exterior were rotting in places. The paint chipped and peeling.

Through a few rotted holes, Dean could see the chipcrete foundation beneath the boards. He knew that material was impervious to the weather. The asteroid munchers built chipcrete cheap and most prefab or hasty construct buildings were made of it—even Uncle Gordano's apartment was made of it.

There were no flower beds, nice trees or decorative items to welcome them.

A solid chipcrete staircase led to a set of big double doors. A sign hung over the doors that looked to have been hand etched, *Welcome to Bob's*. This place was probably sound to sleep in, but it sure needed a woman's touch. Or a man's, if they were into that thing, though it was evident Bob was not.

Their arrival had probably triggered an alert because a haunted man with sunken eyes and visible signs of overusing life extenders exited the main double doors.

"Welcome, welcome!" The old man hollered, and Dean was shocked when he navigated the four stairs with fluid movements. "Would've been out sooner if it weren't for those darn sensors. The Orbital crew that installed them messed up the whole system. They're the worst, I'm telling you."

"Jaeger Manfield?" Cassandra asked and his brows furled for a moment.

"Indeed, but I go by Bob out here. Mainly because the last four owners all went by Bob. If I don't use Bob, the customers' bitch and moan. Not fine folks like you, understand, but the locals who want everything for free. I take it you're Cassandra and Dean," Jaeger said, offering to the guide the self-moving luggage bags.

Dean gave an odd corner eye at Cassandra, curious at what she'd thought. Her fake smile was plastered on her face. She seemed thrilled as she spun, taking in the empty desert wasteland. The words that came to mind, Dean thought, were bleak, desolate, and lonely.

"Yes, we're thrilled to be here. We're expecting a visitor, has anyone else showed?" Cassandra asked, looking to see if there were any ground or air cars were parked around the side.

"Afraid not. I got Beth and Rick drinkin at the bar. They ain't got many coins, be wary of their offers. Consider yerself warned," Jaeger said with an awkward frown. "Times are a tad rough out here since that explorer died last week. Hence why it's fer sale! Low price too. But don't let my need to pawn this place off deter you."

The old man spit to the side before leading them up the stairs. "I told him not to go tromping into the savannah as if he owned the place. You'd be surprised how few people listen. I tend to always be right and them always wrong." He squinted back at them. "You ever meet those types?"

"Too often," Dean chuckled.

"Learn from his lesson," the old-timer continued, "no wild drunk trips to the river for a late-night fishing session. His vacation drone caught a video of a scorp fish catching the poor man, instead of the other way around." Jaeger folded his hand to a point and jabbed the air rapidly. "Barbed him twice before dragging him down to the deeps."

"Yes," Cassandra said patting Dean's back, "we bought protective suits for exploring in. Dean here is a bit of an adventurer himself."

Jaeger nodded, impressed. "Those suits aren't cheap; the nice ones get mighty expensive. Been meaning to add some rentals to the business, but never seen 'em on a discount I could afford. I may have some work for ya. Get ya some free drinks for a wee task. We've an Aringo problem. Cat sized acid spitting gerbils. They busted into the preservation last week and—"

"Will the suits hold them off?" Dean asked.

Cassandra nodded, yes.

"Sounds like fun," Dean mused, "any particular laws on killing em?"

"Don't put holes in my barrier walls, that's all," Jaeger snorted, and Dean grinned. "We can discuss the details later. Sun is just up and it's already hot out. How about I show you around and we stick your luggage away?"

Jaeger spun around to lead them into his establishment. The door triggered open with their arrival revealing a vast bottom floor with a vaulted ceiling, twenty feet up. In the middle of the back wall sat the half circle of a wooden bar, with two patrons slumped on their stools.

The older duo gave the newcomers a quick glance before returning to their drinks and conversation.

The rest of the floor had tables with chairs perched on top of them so you could sweep under them. A stage filled most of the left wall and a big view screen played the local news to the right.

The alcohol arrayed on the shelving behind the bartender had steel locking lines securing the bottles, with locks on the end. A rag sat on the countertop and some light banjo music played from overhead speakers. The lighting was set to a rustic dim.

Based on the outside Dean expected the inside to be ratty and deteriorated. He was pleasantly surprised to find it was fairly decent on the inside, though, and well maintained. Even the tapestries looked to have been washed relatively recently.

"Welcome to Bob's Beer, Burgers, and Beds. Before you asked the repeated question all my guests ask - why is the inside so much nicer than the outside?

"Know that regulatory laws protect that old natural wood. Proper removal would cost a fortune. As would adding a new exterior. As you can see, we're not exactly raking in the coins," Jaeger said ignoring the man at the bar shaking his glass for a refill. "Give me a minute, Rick."

"So," Jaeger said with a deflated huff, "when I bought the place twenty years ago, I did so with high hopes and remodeled the interior. Figured that would be enough to get city folk to visit," he sighed. "Pipe dreams. Up for sale now to the next sucker simply because the upkeep costs keep piling on."

"My clients never complain, though, and my service is five stars, literally. Please review this room when you're done," he smiled, "you'll get a next visit voucher, if you do. A personal fault of my own. I go somewhere nice and have a great time and then say nothing. Find one cockroach and game over."

"I'm a good reviewer, Dean, not so much. I love the feel of this place. It's so cozy," Cassandra said with wide, excited eyes.

Dean picked up on what Jaeger was doing. His tactic was fairly common in small places. A random clerk at a big hotel would never give them a spiel about their reviewing habits being inferior. This was one of the main reasons why Dean never chartered. He was too brash and often overly critical, which would lead to him never getting repeat clients. He was honest enough to admit to himself that he'd been working on the last bit, though he still had a ways to go.

Dean couldn't help but give Cassandra the look for her exuberance.

She caught on and hip checked him playfully. "What? I live in a tiny one bedroom. Didn't you see, there was a real fireplace under that video screen. There is so much potential, here."

"Yeah, can't burn real wood, though, because of the anti-pollution laws and due to the historical classification of the building, you can't remove any of the real stone framework. You'd have to build into it with an electric or gas replica. It can be done—almost did it myself—but not really worth the effort. Adds to the rustic charm, though," Jaeger said, walking with them over to the elevator nestled in the back, by the restrooms.

"Only three floors and a basement. You'll need a key to use the below ground pool. Your phone will have one. You'll notice some off-limit doors down there. They're owner's rooms—where I live and store stuff for this wonderful establishment," Jaeger mentioned.

Dean caught on to him playing off Cassandra's elation.

He'd gone from sour to proud of his building, awful quick. "I have to say they're private because you'd be surprised what people do when they've had too much to drink." He shuddered. "Please don't get drunk and try to get in 'em after ya been in the pool, I ain't gonna be letting ya in. You got the biggest room in the building, anyhow, with the nicest views of the deadly desert of despair."

"Maybe taming the wildlife is what is needed," Dean muttered.

"Seriously, don't head out without your suits on. Don't say I never warned ya," Jaeger giggled, then his old ass farted, which made him near double over in laughter.

Dean and Cassandra groaned and happily exited the elevator when it opened for the third floor.

"Sorry," the old timer apologized, "getting old sucks saggy balls. Your enthusiasm is delightful, ma'am." He nodded to Cassandra. "You'd have to get permits to expand the preserve and while doable, it can get expensive. You'd basically have to build a new habitat addition in space to add to the zoo up top.

"Then if tourism doesn't cover the bills, they drop animals back down for you to sustain or rehome," Jaeger said, and Dean opened his mouth to say something but the old man continued. "If you're in self-defense, eliminating a pest, or helping the local ecological balance you're good to go. Belmont and Oakley Orbital have some dense rules, but they're not all retarded."

"Such a strong word," Cassandra said with a sour face.

"Sorry, strong willed with bad ideas is better. I apologize for the crass slip. Here's your room," Jaeger said opening a door at the end of the hall. "I'll be downstairs if ya need me. Again, sorry for the crass language."

"All is forgiven. Thank you for the tour. Ring me if our suits or guests arrive," Cassandra said in a dismissive tone.

The door slid closed with a *thunk* as it sealed. Cassandra *squeaked* for joy, running in place while pumping her fists.

"What's the commotion for?" Dean asked, scratching the side of his head in confusion.

Cassandra failed to answer. Her joy twirled her deeper into the suite. The narrow entryway expanded into a large lounging area with a big screen on the left, a large table on the right, and an expansive view of the savannah ahead.

There was a large balcony and Cassandra skipped into a kitchen area behind the table. He saw a full kitchen tucked into the back wall running down the side. A door Dean inspected had a smaller suite that was probably to stuff annoying children into. Dean rotated to the other end by the view screen to find another bedroom behind a door with a deadbolt.

He walked in and saw a huge four post bed with far more dresser storage. His exploring led him into a massive closet so big he was lost in it. Soft footsteps on the lush rug said his lover was behind him. When he turned, he saw a very naked Cassandra.

"Um... Yes!" Dean said, stripping off his shirt. He was never one to let an eager lady down.

"I love it! I love it! My apartment is smaller than this fooking closet," Cassandra said fidgeting with his pants. "After I ride that mighty cock of yours, I'm going to do my due diligence on this place. But first," she grinned lustily, "Time to reward my handsome man for taking me on vacation with him."

They exchanged consents quickly before she yanked his trousers down and his cock flopped out. His foxy babe was certainly in the mood, she dropped straight to her knees and sucked his growing erection into her mouth. "I wub it."

Dean grabbed a clothing hanger for balance as he pushed her head down on his cock.

"Weasy, now," her muffled reply was ignored. The sound of her gagging on his girth finally caused him to let her up, and he popped out of her mouth as stiff as the metal rod holder he hung on to. She gave him a stink eye as she gasped out, "Nothing crazy for you. Now go lay down and let me do the extraneous exercising part."

Her bouncing eyebrows were followed up by Dean staring at her snapping hips as she sauntered to the bed. The tease was more than enough for Dean to follow after. He rolled onto the bed that she kneeled on.

"I need to recover more often, I think," Dean said with a smirk. "The past two days have been some epic tenderness I can most certainly get behind... or under," he grinned. "Time for you to ride this one-eyed rollercoaster!"

"You're so damn cheesy," she snickered, putting a finger to his lips to silence him.

A slobbery wet kiss to the head of his cock left it glistening. She threw one leg over his hips and used his wet tip to tease her entry with a sway of her hips until he pulled her down by the hips, plunging deeply into her hot core.

His hands reached out and locked onto her breasts. She swayed down and out to hilt his cock. When she finally pressed her clit against his pubis, she held him tight inside her, rocking her hips in slow, perfect circles. Dean loved the way she could take his whole length with her small frame and yet grip him so firmly.

She worked herself into an early climax, biting her lip to keep from screaming. He twisted her nipples to help her cum. When she'd finished coming down from her first fix of yumminess, she stared down at Dean with a fire in her eyes.

Cassandra leaned down to softly kiss his bandaged neck. She swapped sides to nibble his flesh. He grabbed her tight ass. He loved it when she twerked his cock rapidly. Her pussy *slapped* down hard into his hips. Each subsequent *slap* was louder, and her tunnel grew tighter. Dean never lasted more than a few minutes like this and his lovely lady knew that.

She whispered huskily into his ear, telling him how eager she was for his cum. To feel his seed leaking out of her little tiny pussy. He was on the precipice of exploding into her when he saw a warning that his inhibitor was off.

No!

Too late Dean pumped gouts of his seed into Cassandra who kissed him lovingly. Dean's eyes flared open in panic. For the briefest of moments, there was a flash of a face beside Dean. Zued winked at him with a shit eating grin before vanishing.

Dean shuddered and groaned. "I'm not ready," he moaned.

"Ha!" Cassandra chuckled. "We can wait for round two, I'm going to take a shower, then maybe a soaking bath in the tub while we wait for the suits. I saw the tub was big enough for two."

Dean couldn't hide it, she'd know. She needed to know anyway.

"If I said my inhibitor was off what -"

"You'd never," she stated dryly until she checked the consent logs. "What the fook Dean? I tease you, you... fook me."

"If I hadn't just -"

"This isn't a joke. What did you do?" Cassandra was getting angry.

"Wasn't me," Dean scowled and said, "I've never intentionally swapped my inhibitor off and I never would. Also, you know the second their two inhibitors are off, both partners receive a notification. I can't slip live sperm into you without your approval."

She bit her lip in frustration and then her eyes shot open when she connected the dots.

"Your God did this? It must have been him. I had a high school boyfriend once who was so deeply in love with me, he swapped his inhibitor off once, and yeah, it tells me. Same with girls doing it to guys. I've heard there is even a warning before the volcano blows when couples are trying to conceive. This time," she frowned, "there was nothing."

"I'd not call him my God. Zued was his name. And yeah, I'd blame him. He was winking at me from right there as I creamed into ya," Dean said, nodding to the side of the bed.

Cassandra scrunched her face up at his term.

Dean wasn't the sharpest man. At times too trusting and at others, oblivious. But he understood something immediately with this situation.

"If you report a failure on your inhibitor it will raise flags and I'll have to go in for a checkup. Shit, I'll have to get a medical for next fishing season so seeing a public doctor is inevitable, but I think that's the point.

"I'm supposed to go do whatever it is to save Oakley. Not fish. As to giving you a baby, it locks me down. Grounds me from staying a retarded drunk like I'd planned to until I was in my mid-forties," Dean said with a loud and long deflated sigh. "Come here, Cassie."

She frowned but snuggled into him. "I'm irate Dean. I like you. I like the idea of a long term us, and I want to help you. On the other hand, being toyed with by the gods is flipping bullshit." She growled and pretend bit Dean to alleviate her frustration.

This triggered a laugh from him, helping to ease the tension.

"You think the one time was enough?" she asked. "That is generally not how making babies works. You usually have to go at it with abandon during peak ovulation..."

"A deity literally spawned beside my head to wink at me as I ejaculated into you. So yes, Cassie," Dean sighed, "Yes, I think we're going to have a baby. Bullcocks!" he exclaimed, blowing a raspberry as he blew out a breath.

"It's bollocks," Cassandra said, "unless you were thinking of a bull's cock, which would be a little odd, given the context."

Dean pulled her close.

"So," she began, "I never got to tell you why I was so happy." Dean one arm hugged her tighter before jostling the answer out of her. "I want to buy this place. My apartment costs about the same."

"Yeah that was kinda evident, given how in love you were with the tour, but he probably loses a lot, just in maintaining this place every month."

Cassandra pouted.

"Well," Dean said, thinking it over, "don't rush into it. But this is a much better place for a kiddo than your tiny apartment in Ola. I would've terrorized this tavern into a ruined mess if I grew up here."

"I'd need to see about doing some work from home type tasks with my boss. Maybe go back in, occasionally, for the odd day in court. But if we maintained both—"

"We?" he asked, startled, pulling back slightly.

"Dean," she sighed, "you've always been a player. I get it. Your consent list is pages and pages long, every off season." She tilted her head back to look up at him. "But you are still a good man. Mostly..."

He smirked.

"You'd not abandon your pregnant lover," Cassandra said, and Dean grunted in agreement.

He stared at the ceiling fan in frustration. Unable to take it any longer he said. "Jetted tub, just you and me."

"Deal," she said.

They soaked until their skins pruned. Cassandra's phone pinged an hour later. Their explorer suits had arrived. Dean smiled. He felt like killing something and a few Aringos should do the trick.

CHAPTER

TEN

DEAN

Bob's Outback Tavern

Dean couldn't help the fact that he was brooding. The man had an outline of his life, all pre-planned out, years in advance. His forties were for popping out offspring with a stable woman he could trust. The issue wasn't Cassandra, he knew, it was him.

His stomach twisted into knots; he was filled with angst and self-doubt. Dean was confident and courageous enough to leap into the maw of a mighty sea creature, but scared shitless about being a father. He couldn't rationalize his fear as anything more than wanting something better for his child than he'd had himself, growing up. Two loving parents.

He knew that wasn't a bad attitude to have, and hopefully that meant he'd be a loving father. It dawned on him slowly, that if he never went back to fishing, and this Zued god never sent their messenger, he could quit working and be a stay-at-home Dad.

That calmed him the most. Cassandra had her life together enough they could do this without a lot of pressure on him.

Dean let his simmering resentment of the situation fade. Cassandra was spot on about one thing, he'd kill for her now, not chuck her to the side. He'd never pawn off his children on someone else, not like his own fathers had done. There was nothing more to think about.

The spacesuits that Cassandra bought, weren't cheap. They arrived in massive coffins cases that the delivery guy hauled up to their suite. The boxes were large and the casings themselves were something Dean couldn't afford to stow his fishing gear in.

How did Dean know they weren't cheap? Well, they were made by Mercedes Tesla, for starters. That company was the pinnacle of twenty-sixth century engineering and Dean knew they were synonymous with expensive. Which spoke volumes about Cassandra's wealth, and finally prompted Dean to prod the issue.

She was opening the first lid when Dean nonchalantly asked, "Cassie, how wealthy are you?"

"I'd say that it's a rude question to ask of a friend." She mock glared at him. "There are stigmas about wealth my father drilled into me. You may notice how I normally dance around the subject; that's the reason why. I get it, though, we're at *that* point," she said, placing her balled fists under her chin while batting her eyelashes. She gave a cute *aww*, to go along with her adorable pose.

"Well," she got serious again, "I went to school on a full scholarship and was a paid intern. I graduated two years earlier than you did. My medical is covered, I get a housing bonus for living in Ola, and per diem for food. My groceries bills are low, I get bonuses for work performance, and for being healthy. My income, not including the per diem or housing allowance, is three hundred thousand a year and—"

"The fook?" Dean said with curled eyebrows. "You work a desk job for the county?"

Cassandra finished unwrapping her exoskeleton suit. She tapped a few codes in she found in the instruction manual, and then thumbed the chest plate. There was a *hiss* as the suit unlocked. She paused now that she had finished, turning to Dean.

"Dean," she snapped, "don't play ignorant. You worked a desk job yourself and knew fishing was a big pay cut. I love my job and, yeah, I probably do get paid too much—but that stays just between us." Her pointed finger at his chest elicited a nod in reply. "With the investments I've made and the value of my apartment, I've probably got almost two million Galactic coins in my accounts."

Dean's jaw bounced off the floor.

"That is me mostly just me being a frugal bitch, though. Now, Dean, I'm all for sharing a bed, managing your finances, and having a baby. I dreamed about this scenario. Like a lot," she smiled, "mind you, I knew I'd have to wait until you were ready. My momma clock, which I never expected to have, though, is ticking." She stuck her hands on her hips. "And it looks like we'll get to see in the next few days, if it's going to be satisfied. I am not, however, your sugar momma."

"This begs to differ." Dean pointed at the spacesuit.

"Touché. Sure, they have good, eh, decent resale value. And if I buy this place, I can keep them here, for rentals."

Dean let out a long, low whistle. "You like this place that much. I admit, I like the middle of nowhere vibe, the immense space, and the interior charm. It just has that money pit vibe."

She put her hand to her chin with a loud *Hmm*.

"While you were soaking in the tub, with your eyes closed, I hired some inspectors and general contractors to give me some quotes. They should be here by tonight."

He couldn't help the chuckle that slipped out.

"I'm thorough Dean," she glared back at him. "I'd likely only need to encase the exterior of the building, to convert it into a lovely looking modern home with a fake fireplace and a landing balcony for our suite."

Damn, he thought, she's serious.

"If I buy a high-end air car, I can get to Ola in an hour," she smiled. "That's not bad. I'd gladly sell my little condo, which has increased in value forty thousand since I bought it. But you are right, we need to figure some things out, and then can go from there. Just know I don't want to open my accounts to you fully, not yet. Not that I'm saying I'll keep 'em closed forever."

"Aye, I get it," Dean shrugged, "Maybe we can do an 'us' fund and match deposits or something."

Cassandra beamed at him and did a little happy dance.

"That was very sweet of you. Come on, I need to show you something," Cassandra said, sticking out a hand, which he accepted. He was led into the bedroom and she paused.

She dropped the instruction manual she was holding. When she bent over to pick up the paper, she wiggled her juicy booty at him teasingly.

"Round two?" Dean asked and she winked over her shoulder.

Ten minutes later they were back in the shower after some sweaty sex. Dean had to inject a backup plasma dose to stabilize his repairs from the exertion.

Doctor Hersa noted the usage, billed another backup, and sent it on its way. After the shower, they finally were ready to get into the exosuits.

Dean was handed an instruction manual to attune the suit to himself. Cassandra got into hers while he fiddled with the controls, hoping that he'd not fry the machine. The suits were supposed to be immune to electrical strikes. Then again, so were the spear gun turrets.

The casing recognized his thumb and opened with a *hiss*. A waft of new robot smelling air washed over him.

He laid inside the suit and the servos *whined* as the front half flipped back over and enclosed him. A minute later, he found he was locked inside the armor. A diagnostic ran his vitals from a HUD on his interior clear faceplate. It warned him his reproduction inhibitor was off.

No shit.

He turned it back on for the fifth time in the last ten minutes and it swapped right back to off. He ignored the issue for now and let the system go through its bootup process. When the armor was ready, he stepped out of the coffin like case it came in and joined Cassandra.

"So please buy mine for me with my funds," Dean said, and Cassandra fidgeted. "What?"

"They're two hundred thousand a pop."

Dean stumbled while walking towards the door in shock. "This suit costs more than this fooking building?"

"Yeah, you can't die in it easily. You can go mining in space with it," Cassandra said stabilizing his tilt. "You'd probably even last a while in the oceans, in this. It has laser sidearm for self-defense, air recycling, air conditioning, and even bio cleaning. It does it all. There was a reason we hopped in them in the nude, and a reason your butt feels off."

His brows crawled for the ceiling at the last bit.

"But why buy these?" Dean wondered. "Why not some knockoff or a simpler version?"

"Dean," she sighed, "I love exploring. Most of this planet is timid and open to humans. The outback, however, is the opposite. The less abundant life is, the more deadly the animals are. At least that's the theory."

Yeah, he thought, *I can agree with that.*

"And Dean, since we aren't hiding any secrets here, I have a majority share in Lexso Mining and More. That means these suits are getting tested by a board member and her sexy partner. If our vacation here ends with us going home after a few weeks of fun, the corporation buys these back at cost and we got to play in them for a bit."

Dean nodded his understanding. "Miss Lexso, huh? I love 'Cassie' so much more. Honestly, not to deflate your ego, but I've never heard of the company. Is it big?"

"Well, I'm the same person," she grinned mischievously, "and that's twice in a short period you called me love! And size is relevant," she waved away the question. "Profits are good, and my investment is making me decent G's."

Her teasing ended with her opening the door. Dean followed her out. Her shapely hips remained hidden below the modern spacesuit frame.

The exoskeleton suit was a metallic gray extension of one's body. There was no learning curve or stumbling. Well, other than when his girlfriend mentioned they were wearing suits worth more than the price of a house. Dean knew they only weighed about ten pounds heavier, so the elevator was fine for them to take to the ground floor.

The exit out of the front of the building revealed a few paintings of medieval warriors from Earth that Dean had missed seeing earlier. He found it wonderfully odd, seeing a man on a horse, wielding a lance in a twenty-sixth century foyer in the outback. He felt drawn to it. The whole concept just seemed fun, natural, and uniquely beautiful, all wrapped in the one amazing image.

"Do you like horses, Cassie?" Dean asked, entranced by the portrait.

She eyed the painting. "I know the New Texas initiative has bred some mighty horses. I ride them in gentler vacation spots. It's different; soothing. Simpler times. My thighs chafe and I'd be lost trying to care for one, but it could give you something to do if you have to give up fishing. Not sure if there is good money in horses, though."

"Would you rent rooms, still? That'd require staff and all sorts of expenses, wouldn't it?" Dean asked with a grimace.

"You seem to keep adding tasks to your list," Cassandra chuckled.

Dean joined her moment of levity and retorted, "As long as I don't turn into a crabby old man, that'd be A-Okay. Maybe get a stripper pole for that stage."

Cassandra bumped him for attention and bounced her eyebrows. "We got the liquor license which is almost worth the bar itself. I wouldn't mind some delicious long legs on the stage. I wonder why they haven't converted this into a pleasure tavern."

"Probably because there are a million of them on the planet. Hooking has been legal on Oakley since the start. This building was billed as hunting and adventuring for the brave. Not a place for the lazy to get their sex on.

"And talk about upkeep, probably have to pay working men and women to dance here at the start until a regular clientele came in." His face twisted into a grimace as he thought through what that might entail. "I could get behind a hooking tavern, though. Seein as how adventuring here has dried up."

"I see that smirk on your face, Dean. I'm a very open kind of gal. I did let you bone other girls while I played the long game," Cassandra noted breezily.

"But there were other men than me," Dean said feeling guilty. "Right?"

"Sure, Dean. I'm a catch, and we both know it. I was courted often, and I shot them all down. Maybe I wasn't ready, either. And there were a few times when I asked you over and you were on a date. What did I say?"

"Bring em on over, and I did. Twice. Both times the new girls saw how we looked at each other and vanished." He stopped and gave her a look. "You were always so nice to them, too."

"Dean, I told them we were fuck buddies and friends. I told them I was game to hop in the bed for a threesome and they split. Not the right girls for it, I guess," Cassandra noted, "which is fair."

"Why not get me to ask?" Dean wondered. "I'm convincing."

"Sure, but I did it mostly to cockblock the clingers off of you. I've wanted you for a while. Would I share? Sure. But it'd have to be with the right woman or... man." She giggled at her tease. "You did say that Zued was hunky."

"Yeah and his daughter was fine. I'm not blind, Cassie. Men can be attractive without me being attracted to them. Egor is different from Prince Charming. While I'd love to have a threesome or spicy bedroom encounters, I'm content at the moment. You're actually all I need right now, Cassie," Dean said and that triggered her to walk away, muttering furiously to herself.

Dean followed after her, not sure if he'd wowed her or upset her. They walked by the empty bar; Jaeger was nowhere in sight. Dean noticed a robot vacuum cleaning the rough tiled floor when it beeped at him. There was a lot to this building he still wanted to check out.

He actually enjoyed cooking fish, and a nice kitchen would be awesome. There'd be other times to explore the interior, though.

Once outside the scattered clouds allowed for a warm day that registered already in the nineties. Dean watched Cassandra observing the view.

"So, the preserve?" Dean asked and Cassandra sent over a ping.

Dean opened the notification and saw a biography of the Aringo. They were small-ish, fast, and rarely deadly to humans unless they walked into a nest of them. Their spitting would leave nasty infectious wounds if not treated promptly. Chances of breaching the spacesuit were .01%. Everything started with a .01%, so Dean could rest easy.

"You sure you want to go hunting these little assholes instead of just going for a walk?" Dean asked, not wanting to upset Cassandra with his pew-pew-pew tendencies.

She waved him forward and pointed at a rock. "We can low energy test fire at that rock. If you—"

Dean rapidly selected test fire for his sidearm and it *hissed* out of his thigh holster. He snatched the weapon in a fluid maneuver and brought the barrel to aim at the rock. A few slight squeezes and harmless bursts of energy bashed against the rock.

"Dean! You're supposed to get behind me until I feel your other gun digging into my butt, tell me how I need to squeeze the gun just right until it spews love onto the rock!" Cassandra said teasingly. "That's how it always goes in the romance movies. Yet, you whipped yours out and shot your load in less than three seconds." She giggled, "Only a little less than your average, actually."

He chuckled, holstering his weapon. He walked to grant her wish when she used some swift dexterous movements to unload on the rock. Dean nodded his head impressed.

"You shoot before?" Dean asked.

"No, it's a freaking laser gun!" Cassandra scoffed and said, "Aim, pull the trigger, and then guide the beam. So easy, a fisherman can do it!"

"Hey, what's with the 'pick on Dean' all of a sudden?"

She snorted. "I'm just messing with you. Sometimes you make it too easy."

He frowned. She usually didn't get like this.

"Sorry," she apologized, "trying to blow off some stress. Be the hero Dean, take my punishment, and then you can punish me later, in return."

Dean's thoughts ground to a halt. "What... you wanna get some kinky toys?"

"Do I ever! What were you thinking?"

"How about a sex swing and cat tail?" Dean asked, scuffing the dirt with his foot. He wasn't embarrassed, just worried about her reaction. "If it's okay with you."

Cassandra smirked, her eyes giving a mischievous gleam under her clear visor. "I'd like that. You want one of those ones that are an extension that I can control?" Dean nodded and he realized she was very excited about the idea. When her eyes glazed over, he figured she was shopping. "Fluffy or smooth?"

"Fluffy," Dean said.

"And do you want fluffy or smooth?"

"Fluffy," Dean said, not picking up on what she was inferring.

Cassandra chuckled at Dean as if she'd won some game. "Hey," she nodded towards the preserve, "those Aringo are spreading soldier. Time to clear the breach. You want to take point?"

"How many movies do you watch?" Dean asked, eyebrow raised suspiciously.

She shrugged. "Too many," she admitted, "Should make for some interesting role play, at least."

Cassandra pointed to the entrance of the preservation, which was a massive plexiglass type structure meant to keep the wilds out. Dean went for the door at a trot. There were a couple of signs warning him not to enter. A keypad blocked his entry until a face materialized from a projector.

"Oh, you're actually going in, already. Good luck, I hope you do better than those overpriced rip offs," Jaeger said *buzzing* the lock control, so that the bolt unlatched.

"Real quick," Cassandra asked, "how'd they get in here?"

Jaeger shrugged, dragging a napkin over his mouth. Apparently, they'd caught him eating an early lunch. He shook his head, causing his combed over hair to dance with the movement.

"Through the front door. The previous owner was tired of guests complaining about the code when they forgot their phone. Anyway, the Aringo eat leafy greens, and with no predators, they tend to bounce back after a harvest, because they burrow deep to bear their young.

"I hired a crew once," he grumbled, "a year later, the little ones converted into big ones. Turns out, you need to pay for exterminators a couple of times a year. After two failed cleanses, though, I gave up. Not worth the money. You have to be really careful who you hire, too. Everyone's out to rob you, these days. Being a business owner means you see the worst humanity has to offer. And if I were—"

"Appreciate the information. Thanks, Jaeger," Cassandra said, stepping into the enclosure and bypassing the image. The man grumbled some more but closed the connection.

Dean followed her in and ensured the door sealed behind them, waiting until he heard the lock *click*.

"This says the Aringo are territorial and aggressive," Dean reported, looking over the display sheet. "At least the adults are." He looked around them at an overgrown forest. "What a mess this place is. It's like a jungle. How does this preserve thing even work?"

"It uses fancy clear screening, meant to look like glass. Think of it like millions of tiny fishing wires, except clear, that lets air flow through it. The technology is pretty amazing, actually, it can expand when undisturbed and contract if need be.

"With a few expensive suits and some small arms, we kill the infestation and beat back this jungle overn—"

Dean let out a surprised *eek* when the bush he was inspecting suddenly lunged at him. A long, furry animal snarled at him with its small fangs and a mouth full of molars. Two clawed paws, primarily meant for digging, scratched ineffectively at his faceplate. The creature was about the size of a cat, if a fair bit rounder, and... sassier, if that was possible. Undeterred by the clear armor blocking its strikes, the Aringo persisted until Dean yanked it off his suit and held it up to get a better look at it.

When the furball twisted to bite his hand, he snapped its neck.

"Fook me," he muttered, "they blend in like master ninjas."

Cassandra was laughing, "I got that on video. Oh, it's priceless, your reaction was perfect."

"Aw, yeah he spooked me. I'll get my revenge," Dean said with a finger wag. "They're good hiders. Are the bodies worth anything?"

Dean tossed the corpse near the door to start a pile.

"I can do a search if you want to play bait," Cassandra said, waving Dean forward.

Dean rolled his eyes and replied, "Yes, I'd rather pew pew than geekily find a buyer for acid spitting long jumping gerbil bodies. But! We need to clear something up. Nothing major, just in situations like these I'm the boss. Mainly because I do dangerous shit like this for a living."

Dean expected an eyeroll, but she simply nodded that she was fine with him being in command.

He continued, "As you've seen, even when I'm hurt, I can be a useful play toy. I just don't want you walking all over me; I promise I will try to treat you like an equal. Just getting that out on the table now, so we don't end up fighting about it, later."

"Oh! Is this a pre-fight, fight, then?" Cassandra mused with a devilish smirk. "I hear you, dear partner, and likewise promise not to shoo you off to go and fight valiantly like a peasant."

Like a peasant?! Dean wagged his finger at her.

She cleared her throat and straightened her back, throwing the back of her hand to her forehead.

"Oh! Dean," she dramatically exclaimed, "there are hundreds of the dastardly critters, halt them, please, before they audaciously whisk me away to their evil lair."

"Why would they dare do something so heinous to such a fair maiden?" he played along. "Those vile little beasts. I'll save you, have no fear, my lady!" Dean shouted, running off into the bush, heedlessly.

Shit!

Thirty little acid-spitters assaulted him suddenly. If he'd been in regular clothes, he'd now be dead, Dean realized. Soon, he was going to be overwhelmed.

The Aringo latched onto the rigid boxy contours of his suit. He had to assume that this was a winning strategy for the little buggers, somehow, at warding off predators; they sure were determined.

His hand snatched his pistol free of its holster only to have it knocked to the ground. There was zero-fooking chance Dean was calling for help, though, because of a gerbil attack.

He bent his knees and hopped sideways into the air as high as he could. That did the trick. About half of the beasts flew off and a quarter of those who still clung to him were crushed under his suit as he landed on his side.

Rapidly scrambling back to his feet left him free of the writhing mass of fur, paws, and teeth.

Dean sighted his laser pistol, the glint of its metal barrel reflecting back up through the crowded bodies. Sweeping his foot out in a wide kick, he knocked a pile of the little monsters out of the way for a few seconds. His hand shot into the area where he expected to find the pistol until his fingers wrapped around the back straps. Those precious seconds were enough to grip the weapon.

A vibrant yellow light spit out from the end of the pistol. Dean was again quickly overwhelmed, his body weighed down with dozens of the critters. He only managed to roast a few of the little beings before needing to throw himself onto his back, crushing six more Aringo, to get some space again.

"You okay over there?" Cassandra called, hearing Dean's grunts and struggles.

"Peachy!" Dean hollered as he jumped up again, to clear the little furballs off his body.

The crushing pressure of Oakley's gravity caused numerous *cracks* as little bones *snapped* left and right. Finally, with some wiggle room, he roasted a dozen of the creatures while back peddling slowly towards the entrance. They let him flee.

"Okay," Dean finally caught his breath, hiding behind Cassandra. "Charging into this place is worse than Founding Day at your Mom's place."

She turned and swatted his butt.

"You had a great time with my family," she said. "Ugh, they still ask when you're coming back."

A dastardly Aringo charged out and Cassandra blasted it in two.

"I liked your parents," Dean admitted, and then groaned. "Oh, fook me. They're going to be pissed, aren't they?"

Cassandra tried to shrug it off but failed. She started sniffling behind her helmet.

Dean wrapped her up and said, "Hey, it's gonna be okay. We'll get through this, together. Your parents will forgive me… eventually. Just blame it all on me."

"You sayin it's not your fault?" She reached up with a gloved hand to wipe a tear off her face, but her helmet stopped her. She stomped a foot down and Dean dodged her heel. "Sorry. Being pregnant in this day and age when you're in your mid-twenties is unheard of. My career. I worked so hard to get to this point. The county has stuff in place to help me but… And… and then there's my parents…"

"It's all good. Remember what your Mom said and we both laughed about for the whole flight home from the orbital?"

"Give me grandbabies! She even hollered it out in front of everyone at the spaceport. I'm kinda surprised I don't have more siblings." She sighed and looked up in frustration. "Look at me jumping to conclusions. You did great with my family. Everyone loves it when I bring you around because you have this ability to light up a room. My mom has even been hounding me to lock you down."

Dean tilted his head at this. "Oh really?"

"Yeah, she liked you a lot, and I was hoping you'd see my family as something you wanted to spend more time around," Cassandra confessed, laying some more truth to their friendship.

"Wait, you said everyone needed to bring a plus one," Dean said with a teasing finger wag. "Did you con me into a family outing?"

"It helped, didn't it?" She asked meekly, cringing slightly.

"Aye, I loved that time. What did I say as we parted?" He smiled, "Do you remember?"

"If I ever needed a plus one, that you'd always be there. Dean I didn't invite you to the Holiday Winter Festival because I didn't want to drive you away," Cassandra said, getting a wee bit sappy.

"I get it, I wish I had a family to drag you around to. Oh wait, I kinda do and you've seen 'em all." He grinned at her. "So, are we good to get back to blasting some little furballs?"

"We only stopped because I needed to get a video of you losing to the little stinkers as they swarmed you."

"You saw that?" Dean asked teasingly.

"And recorded it for posterity. It didn't take me long to find out the bodies were worth a few fractions of a coin. Animal feed and fertilizer buyers will pick them up. Get a few hundred, though, and it adds up. Not going to buy us the Inn, killing these things, but they're great target—" she fired a shot into the bushes, "—practice."

Dean bobbed his head in agreement. They walked a pace or two forward and waited. Without fail, every time they did, a little furball would come flying out aggressively. This lasted for over an hour as they trekked deeper along the overgrown path. Eventually, Dean broke the companionable silence.

"I wonder if they're scared of anything," Dean asked, stepping half a step further in. His pistol *buzzed* as it discharged angrily at a trio of Aringos. The dismantled bodies were left for future collection. It might take weeks to clean this place out.

"They tend to remain stationary unless there is some big invader clomping through their turf. You know the last reported cleaning here was eighteen years ago. Unchecked, there should be a lot more of these things," Cassandra mused. "Maybe they do that thing bunnies do?"

"What's that?" Dean asked, slicing an Aringo in two before it could leap at him.

"Bunnies self-population regulate. Just something I remember from biology class. Squirrels too," Cassandra said, and Dean shrugged.

Science class had Becky Martin in it, and Becky had the biggest natural tits in the school, and always wore tube tops. He hadn't missed a single class and still only got a B-.

"Maybe a predator got in at some point," Cassandra frowned.

They froze, suddenly realizing how far away they were from the door. "Umm... that's possible," he allowed, "What predators eat these furballs?"

A branch shifted from Dean's right causing him to spin. Nothing should be that high up. A movement caught his eye and he blasted an Aringo as it leaped down onto him. After its death he waited patiently.

He heard Cassandra scraping her feet behind him, trying to lure more of the little buggers out. There was more scraping, rustling, and a minor commotion followed. He grew concerned she wasn't answering his question and turned to see a crocodile head on a snake's body, not five feet away.

Cassandra's top half was in the monster's jaws and her feet kicked a trail in the dirt as she sought to free herself. Dean didn't hesitate. He max indented his trigger and sliced his laser beam up the predator's neck. His body reveled in the sudden feeling of searing heat cascading through his being. The beam blasting from his pistol thickened as his own energy magically fueled the weapon.

The monster's hide melted under the powerful beam as it seared a glowing seam through its neck. The stunned monster's head split off the rest of the creature. Both parts of the beast crashed to the trail with a resounding *thud*.

"I'm coming," Dean shouted, "stay calm."

When he tried to pry the jaws apart, though, he found they were locked solid. He aimed his blaster for the hinge and carved out a connecting piece of the jaw. A body shaking *crack* sounded as the pressure Cassandra *snapped*.

She wiggled out and Dean pulled her back, helping her to stand up. She was a panting mess, but finally stood tall with a red-faced angry glare.

When she was finally up, she shouted, "And that is why you fooking buy the expensive suit when adventuring with Dean fooking Forrester! I got all that on camera. I even stayed somewhat calm."

Dean held his hands up palms out.

"To answer your question, Sir," she eventually continued, "A Titangator is the most common and effective predator against Aringo, as it is completely stealthy. It tends to hide in trees and strike from above. There could be dozens more of them in the trees, that missed inspection, during our ground-based invasion."

"How about we head back to the room, my fair maiden," Dean said, trying to cheer her up. "I'd rather not have both of us get eaten at the same time."

"Caught alive, they are worth about a hundred coins per. Their eggs are worth two hundred. They are fan favorites at zoos across the Galaxy. Dead," she frowned, "not worth so much."

Cassandra teased Dean's greed. "There is a trap we can buy to lure them in; it's a quacking duck lure that releases gas to knock them out. That's all that's needed because they'll scramble to gobble them up, every time."

"When did you have time to learn all this?"

"When I was in that damn thing's mouth! I even sent ya a text... didn't ya get it?"

Dean shook his head, dumbfounded.

"Dean, love," Cassandra said tightly, "your suit is patched directly into your phone."

Dean gave a long *ohhh...*

"Out we go," she decided, "we can come back later and continue the fun."

"Can the Titangators hurt us?" Dean asked.

"If you get an arm up at a bad angle during the constriction, sure. This one was so fat and big, though, it tried to swallow me whole. Explains where the missing Aringos went, doesn't it?"

Uh, Dean," Cassandra said pointing to the space where all their kills should be. The bloodstains were all that was left on the trail. "Yeah, maybe we trot our way out. The Titangators aren't very fast."

As they picked up the pace Dean saw evidence of smaller versions of the creatures resting in the tall trees. Their inchworm progression into the preserve made for only a five-minute run back to the entrance. Dean knew one thing for certain on his way out of the cage—this was just about the furthest thing from a human preservation that could possibly exist. It was a trail of doom that could be used to feed death row inmates into.

With the door locked firmly behind them once more, they laughed at the sheer craziness of the place. The last Bob had been a dick to leave that door open.

Dean felt his stomach rumbling angrily. It was past time to get some food in them. He had to wonder if that Zued guy had been just a figure of his imagination. They'd been here for a few hours and no guide had showed up.

The duo decided to make the most of the situation. They had a nice late lunch that was delivered to their room. A half hour away lay Noxi, a small town with a few thousand people in it. She ordered a few 'surprises' that could be sent from Noxi.

Dean waited for their guide while Cassandra paced impatiently, waiting for her sex toys to be delivered. The way she kept eyeing him hungrily made him savor this moment.

CHAPTER

ELEVEN

DEAN

Bob's Outback Tavern

The next six days zipped by for Dean and Cassandra.

Dean would wander into the doom pit to kill more than just time, while Cassandra dealt with the building inspectors and contractors. The duck trap arrived, and a local animal handler set up pens for him to dump his live catches into.

The handler grumbled at the sheer amount of work Dean was making him do. There were at least a dozen traps filled daily. This Harvey guy the company had sent out would vent endlessly about his shitty pay, then he'd complain about how much he hated Titangators, whining how they could kill him, if they got out. For some reason, however, he refused to wear a protective suit. By the end of a seemingly endless parade of building inspectors and contractors, Dean had come to despise the sour little man. He was being paying fairly; there was no need for his incessant complaining.

When the traps finally stopped triggering, Dean started clearing limbs and leaves off of everything. He had plenty of time, there was no rush, so he methodically destroyed all the plant life inside the structure. If he gave the little Aringo bastards nothing to eat, then they wouldn't come back. At least that was his firm opinion; Cassandra agreed.

Scorched earth, at least in this case, was a viable tactic. The preserve enclosure itself cost more than the tavern, if they had to add a new one from scratch. With the predators mostly gone, and places for them to hide greatly diminished, Dean became a furball killing machine.

If he wasn't shooting, killing or trapping inside the preserve, he'd pop out to listen in on some professional's over-inflated opinion about what Cassandra should get quotes for. Dean was no dummy, even if the results came back negative, and she was not pregnant, he knew she had fallen in love with this place. Occasionally his advice was solicited, like when Cassandra wanted to know how the gym should be expanded, but for the most part she handled everything just fine.

The building appraised for a hundred and ninety thousand Galactic coins and the estimates for the upgrades they'd agreed upon came in anywhere between an additional thirty to forty thousand coins. The exterior remodel was too costly, though, and so was not included in that quote. Too costly, as in not worth it—the old wood, for example, needed to be sealed in an expensive clear preserving foam, so that it could be recovered, later. And that was before any real exterior remodeling could begin.

Cassandra almost lost her patience with that one. Dean chuckled when she stormed off to the preserve to take her wrath out on the Aringo, all the while screaming about the inefficiencies of ineffective, useless bureaucracy. He bit his tongue every time he was tempted to remind her that she was, in point of fact, a lawyer for that same bureaucratic machine.

Dean had avoided vacations with women, before. Hell, he dodged every effort or attempt at cohabitation with the numerous girls he dated. A few had tried to bring over toothbrushes or shampoo, claiming it was just a temporary thing, but Dean hadn't been fooled. Those were pretty words, meant to lull a guy into complacency while subtly claiming more and more counter space in the bathroom.

He'd put his foot down, quickly, with every single one of them who'd tried such tactics, either sending the girls home with their stuff, or tossing their things unceremoniously out the door. His flings had never lasted long after that, but he didn't mind.

Those conquests had become too clingy or sappy. Which meant he was pleasantly surprised with how Cassandra was different; she let him have his space. When they went grocery shopping, they paid for some things from their new joint account, and other things they'd purchase with their own funds. Dean scored some nice steaks that he grilled in their en-suite kitchen and cooked something new every evening. He limited himself to a single alcoholic beverage each night as he weaned himself from his previous heavy drinking. Not once did he feel anything other than a natural connection with her.

The two of them found a happy rhythm to their lifestyles that just... worked. Dean was happy and Cassandra was beyond ecstatic about the situation. Dean thought she was so stinking cute when she'd ramble on every night about all the neat things she had planned for the next day.

Every day she'd take secondary blood tests to see if she was pregnant. Dean had no idea how it worked with modern medicine, but Cassandra said with such tests, you could determine a pregnancy fairly early in the first trimester. It was on the fateful day that Quincy called to tell them he was on his way out to join them, that they learned she had been wasting her time with the extra tests.

Her biochip, of all things, alerted her of the need to start taking prenatal vitamins and to schedule a visit to the hospital for her doctor to install an anti-miscarriage enhancer. Suddenly, Dean and the last six days of bliss got smacked back into reality.

Dean was going to be a dad. He put on a brave face and danced with Cassandra, but inside, he was terrified.

"Dean, you here?" Cassandra said with a wide smile as she snapped her fingers right in front of his face. "I'm off to the hospital. Can you keep an eye on the suits while I'm gone? I'll let you know everything I know, the moment I know it."

She was talking so fast, the words just tumbling from her mouth, that Dean was in a bit of a haze. Her blue eyes darted all over the place and it took Dean a moment to focus thoughts enough to form a coherent response.

"Huh, yeah, sure. Excellent." Dean stared at the wall with the painting of the knight. The longing for a horse suddenly consumed him. The why, lost even to him.

"Babe," Cassandra smiled, using a nickname he'd grumbled about, "It's okay. We've got this. I need to talk to my boss and figure a few things out with work. I'll need to keep my job, especially if we buy this place. The building is amazing, but the upkeep is more than we can afford, unless both of us keep working."

She locked her lips with his in a long tender embrace and he wrapped her up so tight, she squeaked and had to pinch him to ease up a little.

"Come back safe, okay," Dean mumbled as she skipped out to the air car. He waved as her ride shot off for the Ola Sacred Heart Hospital. He muttered to himself, "Where is that damn guide when you need him?"

Just then, a ring came from his phone notified him Quincy was calling. Dean answered, grateful that he'd finally gained enough control over his weird new powers to stop frying expensive technology. Every time he was in the doom pit, he'd practiced channeling his electricity into the laser pistol to increase the beams torrent. How he was able to do so remained an unknown. That he couldn't come up with a decent explanation for the excess electrostatic energy his body harnessed each day frustrated him to no end. The saving grace of his anger, however, was that he realized using the weapon was the perfect outlet for his internal charge, which meant fewer phones he had to replace. In fact, he'd only had to replace his phone once, since learning that trick.

"Quincy! About fooking time," Dean said excitedly, "Where are ya!" He was eager for his friend to arrive. Quincy had spent four days in cryo therapy and another three dealing with family stuff. Dean was fairly sure his friend had been busy taking things to the next level with Patti and hadn't been in a rush to dip out right away.

"So," he chuckled, "you're not going to believe this, or maybe you will. I had to rescue a woman from the desert. Caught a glimmer of her dark skin against the reflected rays from the light toned sand and rock. She says she is a guide for one Dean Forrester. We're inbound in about ten minutes. Get some water ready, please."

Dean winced.

"Well, shitballs," Quincy muttered, "I've got an incoming emergency call from Patti. See you soon!" Quincy closed the connection.

Dean sighed with a smirk. On his way into Bob's Tavern he bumped into Jaeger who was smiling for the first time.

"Can I get two pitchers of cold water, Jaeger?"

"Fook off, I quit!" Jaeger said in a joyful tone, even if his words were a tad offensive. "Some daft idiot bought the place for one hundred eighty thousand credits!"

"That would be us, Jaeger," Dean admitted, knowing Cassandra was no longer on the fence about having a bigger home.

"Oh," Jaeger said, handing him an old school skeleton key, "was going to leave this under the mat, but I guess it's yours, now." He beamed. "I'll let you into the booze storage. The rest is code accessed, and you should have no problems with it, now that you're the new owner."

"I was wondering why you putting so much effort in, working full time in cleaning up the death trap, as I call it. The movers should be hauling my stuff top side to the orbital over the next week. Good luck Dean."

"Aye, death trap is probably a better name than 'doom pit'." Dean smiled. "I hope you find... happiness, Jaeger, whatever it is you find yourself doing," Dean said, slipping past him to find some waters.

"I doubt I will," the old timer sighed, "but at least I'm finally free! Damn place has been up for sale for three years, now, you know."

At least he was honest. Bitchy, full of groans, and a constant complainer, but never a liar. Dean went to the bar to find Rick sitting on a stool wiggling his cup back and forth for a refill. Rick was probably expecting Jaeger to come back and serve him. Bad luck, Rick, Dean thought.

"Hey Rick," he began, "I bought the tavern. No longer is this Bob's place—and it may never be open to the public again. That was your last drink. You'll have to go, now," Dean said, hopping over the bar. He found two beer pitchers and brought them to the sink.

When they had filled, Dean plopped the pitchers onto the counter before vaulting back over the wood. Once back on the other side, he walked a confused Rick to the door, who kept mumbling some ridiculous nonsense about his drinking rights. Dean quickly realized Rick would need an air taxi and dialed one up for him. When the automated reply responded that it would arrive in less than sixty seconds, Dean was confused for a moment.

Then, Quincy's air taxi zoomed in from the horizon. Dean waited with Rick for the air vehicle to land. Quincy hopped out with a tall woman, who looked both exhausted and horribly sunburned.

She stood almost six feet tall, with freckles, brown hair, and brown eyes. She wore a plain white shirt and a brown kilted skirt. Dean wordlessly handed her a water pitcher. She gulped and gulped until she'd drained two-thirds of the pitcher, then drenched her hair with the rest of the water.

"There is more inside," he explained. "Quincy, take her in while I send off this final patron of what was formerly Bob's Beer, Burgers, and... shit, something else, I think." Dean shrugged nonchalantly. "In ya go Rick," Dean muttered, "pushing the drunk's head down and inside of the vehicle. The moment he shut the door, the air car lifted off.

Quincy had decided to stay outside and wait for his friend.

"It's good to see you brother," Quincy said.

They bro-hugged with some hearty thumps on the back. "My emergency conversation was all about you, my friend," Quincy smirked. "Patti had some very, very interesting things to report." Without warning, Quincy slugged him in the shoulder, "You've been holding out on me."

"Well, uh, yeah," Dean ducked his head sheepishly, assuming that Cassandra had told Patti, who'd immediately spilled the beans to Quincy. "We even broke out some condoms last week, going old school, but it's a done deal. Enough about my internal terror, come, let's meet our guest," Dean said walking them towards the woman, who'd already found the other pitcher of water at the bar into the cool air-conditioned building. "She say much?"

"Nothing, actually," Quincy snorted, "besides the bare minimum of 'I must find Dean Forrester at Bob's Burgers, Beers, and Beds.' Oh, and something about Sable being a bitch and this place being way the hell further away than she was told it would be. She was still at least a full day's walk out from here," Quincy noted with mild concern.

The door creaked as he opened it, and Dean mentally added a new task to his every increasing list of chores.

"Whoa, got to admit it's much nicer on the inside. I thought Patti was bullshitting me, when she said you two had gone and bought a house together," Quincy quipped, and Dean winced.

"What?"

"I didn't buy this place," he frowned. "Although my accounts are still growing from continuing video royalty revenue, this was all Cassie." Dean's phone chirped at him and he glanced down at the text.

"Looks like she left the hospital. Probably on such a high right now," Dean thought fondly of his... well, girlfriend wasn't going to cut it anymore, and baby-momma sounded almost disrespectful. He paused when the door shut behind them. A quick glance at the bar and he noticed the woman had her face under the sink faucet.

"What about you?" Quincy asked, rocking on his heels with arms folded before him.

"I'll be fine," Dean snorted, "I'm a big boy. It'll take some getting used to, but I swear I'll do right by her and the baby. Apparently, I should have seen this coming. The more we talked about our relationship, the more it seems she's been grooming me for marriage, playing the long game until I was ready. She is a very patient and understanding woman." He shook his head ruefully, "I can kick and stomp my boots about it all I want or be honest with myself and admit I was kinda doing the same thing with her." The taller man rubbed the back of his neck, "though my play was on a bit of a longer timeline."

"I'm glad you're happy, mate!" Quincy clapped a hand to his shoulder. "Half surprised you aren't skipping planet in a panic, though." He grinned mischievously, "We all know you'd come back, eventually, but you seem really calm about it—whatever this internal terror bullshit you're spewing. Hells, the Dean I knew hardly every fooks the same girl twice in a row."

Dean had to laugh and said, "Hey, you know those cat tail sex toys that you can pull on; the kind that won't come out and your partner can control?" Dean asked and Quincy nodded with a 'sure do' shit-eating grin. "We got a spare one upstairs that you're welcome to, never been used, and still new in the box. Someone thought it'd be funny to buy one for me."

"That's fooking hilarious, you're such a prude. If it's new in the box, we'll take it for sure." He smirked, "Was it fun?"

"Delightfully so. She even meowed and purred for me. Enough about me, though, tell me all about your recovery."

Quincy clapped his hands with bouncing eyebrows and rising excitement and said, "I got in good with Patti's parents. I know there was a bit of a void there, with you leaving and all, but it went really, really well. We're all happy in our ignorance."

"Good on ya, Quincy," Dean congratulated his friend.

"Oh hey, speaking of which," Quincy blurted out, "Patti wanted to come, but said she needed to work this weekend and that it would be a few days before she could get some vacation approved. Is it cool if she joins us out here?" he asked, then chuckled. "And big caveat here, she may just quit her crappy job with this news. Wouldn't surprise me one bit for her to suddenly appear at your doorstep, ready to support her pregnant girlfriend. Girls! Am I right?"

Dean shrugged and replied, "Yeah, no worries, we have more than enough room. Hell, we haven't even seen the owner's suite on the first floor. I kept meaning to sneak a peek during the inspections, but I zoned out in the death trap—which I need to show you, by and by—along with my neat, cool trick the Eelraken gave me."

"What?" Quincy screwed up his face at the odd statement.

"It'll make sense, all in due time," Dean said with an underhand gesture for them to walk to the bar and the woman Zued had termed 'the Minotaur gate guard'. "Let's go meet your desert refugee, shall we?"

They had barely started across the room when the woman stripped off her shirt and soaked it in the sink. She wore no bra and her small, firm breasts were exposed. On some planets a crime was in process; on Oakley it was merely a show.

"Miss!" Dean called out, loud enough to cause her to grunt. "Follow me, please."

She twisted her shirt into the sink before following Dean. He stepped down the stairwell until he reached the basement changing room that was connected to the pool and the gym. They passed a few open lockers and Dean flicked on a shower for the woman.

She had no shame. In seconds, she was nude. Dean bit back a chortle, the bush that girl had was an afro for the ages. Dean and Quincy ducked back, turning around to give her some privacy as she ducked her head back under the cascading water.

"Thank you," she groaned, "I take it you're Dean Forrester?"

"That'd be me," Dean responded, tossing a hand up in the air, but not turning around.

"I'm Felna. Sable sent me. By the grace of Min," she groaned, "please tell me this planet has more of those instant travel cars." Felna scrubbed her hands through her hair. Dean looked on the shelf and found a bottle of soap, scooped it up and backed up a few steps to hand it over his shoulder to her.

"What's this?" she asked.

"You squeeze a bit out of the tube and use it on your hair." He paused, "how do you not know what shampoo is?" Dean wondered.

"First time of being a human in this age of technology," Felna confessed.

Quincy gasped, "You're not human?"

"Well," Dean elbowed his friend, "let me start by answering 'yes' to the air taxi. We'll get you a direct flight back—no more long treks through the desert, filled with death and despair." Dean grabbed a fluffy white towel from the rack. "Tell us what you are, first, and we can go from there."

He flung the towel over his shoulder over close to where she stood under the cool water. By this point, she'd found enough modesty to face the other way, as she washed layers of grime away.

"I'm a Minotaur guard. I guard the entrance to Mixonia, as the surface fighters call it, or Wixomia, if you come from the core. I find myself on rotation between the two every few years and once in a rare while, I get to go home," she explained, "to relax and recoup."

"So," Quincy blurted out awkwardly, his tone laced with doubt, "you're a Minotaur —or a Minotress, I guess—but look like a human woman who runs a lot?"

"Yes," she laughed, her voice warm and rich, "when I leave the cavern of transition as many term it, my body is converted into what is most acceptable to the local population. If I entered from a Wixomia gate, I'd appear as a demon, lava hound, or some other core creature. Same with you. If I took you home to visit my world, when you left the transition gate, you'd be converted into Minotaurs.

"Generally speaking, if you're impressively big as a human, you'd be impressively big as a minotaur. Hopping around to other species' planets sounds like fun, until you violate some local custom and end up in jail, or worse, die." She grinned, "best to stick to your own race and play by the rules you know best. Inside the transition cavern, however, you're you—same in Mixonia. Don't worry, you'll never set foot in Wixomia," Felna said, building up a thick lather in her hair. Dean saw a clump of dirt disintegrate in the water and suds.

"How did you not die on the walk?" Dean asked, with a grunt, impressed. The Vigian Desert was extremely inhospitable, and that was putting it nicely. "That is most definitely not some nice terrain you must have crossed, out there."

"By the trapped souls! You are not kidding," Felna sneered. Dean picked up on 'the trapped souls' as being a Minotaur swear, of sorts. "I died five times. That's why it took me so long to reach you."

"What?!" Quincy gasped, astonished, "There is life after death?"

"Ugh... how to explain this one?" she snorted, explosively. "It always flusters the ignorant. You've got a lot to learn." She rinsed the shampoo out of her hair. "Minotaurs manage the war between the Gods above and the Gods below. The two sides battle it out in a game of sorts, though it is a game with very real consequences. We Minotaurs are neutral judges... I guess you'd call us referees, of sorts, if I remember right and am using the term correctly."

"Since Minotaurs tend to lay their labyrinths between the surface and the core of a planet they were the chosen mediators. In exchange for our services, my kind is allocated protected space by both parties.

"I was ordered by a demigod to fetch one Dean Forrester. Since I see that you wear a necklace, with tokens for Min's Vault, I'm duty bound to lead you to where you can claim your reward." Dean had forgotten all about the trinket around his neck. It'd vanished at some point, but suddenly it was there again, when she pointed directly at it. Felna continued with a chuckle at his look of shock, "It hides itself, unless summoned. So, to fulfill my honor-bound duty, I went trekking into the desert with nothing but a weapon and a water sack."

"Where'd those disappear to?" Quincy asked and Dean frowned.

"I was about to tell you." She quipped, shooting him a glare. "Are all humans this impatient?"

"Excuse my hasty friend," he glared at Quincy, "please continue. Patience is not his strong suit."

Quincy shrugged; not like he could deny the truth.

"I'm bound to the Oakley surface gate that leads to Mixonia," Felna stated, "I operate by a different set of rules than you surface dwellers or even core dwellers. Since there are as many core species as there are aliens on planetary surfaces, you're categorized into a group termed 'Suca'."

"Suca Human is what we Minotaur would call you. You, Suca Human Dean, defeated a Core Demon named Lozarak. You following me?"

Dean nodded, with a bob of his head.

"I'm a minotaur masquerading as a Suca Human. While I am on my mission, my body is entombed in a magical power granted to neutrals, supported by the trapped souls of those who have lost in the war games. I can't perish for but more than a few minutes. If I do die, I drop what I'm carrying, and rematerialize at the Mixonia Gate I guard. So... I learned the hard way that this Suca Human planet is quite deadly." She ticked off what she had learned on her fingers. "Don't swim, don't pee in bushes, and run rapidly from the lizards. I was even killed once by a massive bird that drowned me. Each time I died, magic returned me to my gate, and I had to start my journey over again."

Dean chuckled at this. She must have traveled the desert at night, when water bats were known to snatch humans up when they found them and drown them. Still, she had returned to the land of the living—multiple times, it seemed.

"Magic?" he asked, confused.

"Magic?" Felna repeated, and then scoffed. "Painful magic, but yes, magic. In order to have their games for planetary dominance, magic that is powered by the souls of the vanquished fuels everything we do. You'll learn of the great original sacrifice that started the whole thing, if you choose to, once inside Mixonia. I've walked for seven long days and nights to get here but would prefer to rest a bit, before we return to the cavern." She growled. "Sable is watching my post. That bitch laughed at me every time I died and had to return to the cavern."

"Dean?" Quincy asked, feeling bad.

"Go ahead and get out of the shower," he instructed. "I've got a nice bed for you, upstairs, and have no issue with making Sable wait a few hours or a few days in exchange for some more information about this Mixonia place you come from." He sighed, wondering what Cassie might say about all this. "I'll need to get some things in order anyway. How long do you expect I will be gone for?" Dean asked, shutting off the water for her.

"That is up to you. Some never leave, while others are too timid to ever claim their bounty. Only one master can use a gate at a time, and there is no other master to the gate I monitor," Felna said.

Dean pointed at Quincy with a raised eyebrow, asking if he could go. "Allowed," she chuckled, "if he is contracted to you, which could be as simple as a contract to carry your goods for a seven day."

Quincy beamed.

"There is a maximum of four guests, however, because team events are limited to a total of five participants. But a contract is required, nonetheless, and if it expires while you're still inside Mixonia, the contractee is removed."

"Okay, I can take friends, but there are rules we have to abide by," Dean said, understanding the concept. "While I have a lot of questions, I respect your strenuous effort to get here, and will provide you a nice place to rest, first." She wrapped herself up in the towel. "Follow me, Felna."

"What do you eat?" Quincy asked, as they slowly walked for the stairwell.

"I'd love a fresh salad. With tomatoes," she clapped her hands, "it has been eons since I had a human salad." They both shot her an odd glare. "I've worked at a gate on Earth before. The masters there were actually kind to the guards, which is a rare enough thing itself. A salad would be amazing."

"I'll have one ready for you when you awake, then," Dean said, bounding up the stairs.

He reached the second floor before the others and keyed a door open ahead of his guest. He could hear Quincy making small talk with Felna as their voices drifted up the confined stairwell.

The door accepted his authorization, and Dean walked into a medium sized room with a single bed, a small bathroom, and a sealed window with the curtains open. He drew the curtains, untucked the bed, and cursed.

He was going to need to hire a maid, or become one himself, if he had guests. Maybe he could hire Patti, she was currently working as a roller-skating food server, having quit the latest nine-to-five desk job Marty had set her up with.

Felna scooted by Dean and tossed the towel onto the end table, before snuggling under the covers, naked.

"An actual bed, nice. This accommodation is almost too much for me to accept as a gift. Thank you," Felna said sincerely, causing Dean to wonder what kind of shit-hole she lived in, that made a so-so hotel room look nice. Then again, he remembered she had said she also served Demon type races.

"I'll meet you downstairs," she continued, "when I awake. Thank you for this. Because you've been so kind, I will suffer your questions later with a smile."

"I like her," Quincy said as Dean closed the door behind them. They stood outside the room, uncertain of what to do next.

"Where to next?" Quincy bounced on his toes in excitement.

"The bar," Dean said, leaving his guest to rest, "and before you warn me, I know, we are not out to get sloshed." He grinned, "But a celebratory drink is definitely in order."

His phone buzzed and he picked it up "This is Dean."

"Miss me yet?" Cassandra purred, and he rolled his eyes with a smile.

"You know it," he chuckled, "so I've got some news. Quincy brought in our expected guest, and well, she had some interesting information to share that will have to wait for your return." Dean paused. "I want you to come with me. She said it's allowed."

"I was calling in to check in with you. My Mom and Dad wanted to come visit our new home, immediately. I told them to hold off until I had a chance to talk it over with you. Patti kept me in the loop about the guide arriving. I should be back at our home in a few hours, tops, a—"

Dean interrupted Cassandra. "I didn't know the home was ours," he blurted out.

"Down the middle, Dean. There's a clause in the title, that if one of us wants out, we first have to start an injunction, to come to terms on the house. If you or I still want out, after forty-five days, we're free to buy the other out. If we can't come to a deal, we sell."

Dean was shocked speechless.

"I figured you'd want to be an owner, love. You made one hundred thousand coins this past week we spent here, anyways," Cassandra told him. He'd noticed his bank account had been getting downright fat. Checking his growing bank balance had become a new hobby of his. Trapping Titangators was fun, he had to admit, every time he watched his balance numbers tick up.

"You still there," he heard, "you went silent on me."

"This is exactly what I wanted to hear," he laughed, relieved. "In a few days, Jaeger's stuff will be gone, and we can start turning this place into our own little fortress of awesomeness." He heard Cassandra cheer on the other end of the line. He could almost picture her doing a little happy dance. "I need to head into Noxi to pick up a salad for our guest," he said, "text me if you need anything from town."

Quincy was bent over, wheezing, he was laughing so hard.

"Oh," Dean continued, wishing he could have told her in person instead of over the phone, "don't come home in a taxi, please. Buy us a transport shuttle and a speedster for yourself, in case you require quick medical care or need to jet in for work. Wherever my guide is taking me is pretty far from here, and dangerous. We don't want the location showing up on the public record."

Even after the privacy communications act Belmont had enacted, there were still plenty of prying assholes, who didn't give two shits about the fines for violating privacy laws.

"Got it, I'm guessing you are going to want to stock up the gym, seeing as how you've complained endlessly about it lacking any good equipment?" Cassandra quipped. Quincy snickered some more behind him.

"I'll dump fifty thousand coins from each of our accounts to use for upgrades. Anything else, before I get off the phone?" she asked, "Oh! My sister's calling me."

"Be safe and see you soon babe."

"Bye, babe."

Quincy mimed sticking his finger down his throat and pretended to vomit as Dean hung up.

"And so, they came to the end of an era, the mighty vagina slayer, Dean Forrester, calling a woman a pet name," his friend intoned.

"To be fair," Dean glared at his friend's silly antics, "I've called her Cassie instead of Cassandra, since... I don't know, forever." Dean took a play swipe at his friend.

Quincy dodged, easily.

"After this drink," Dean said, turning for the stairs, "we're going to go into Noxi for a grocery run. Shit might as well order a taxi now." He pulled his phone back out. "Going to be nice," he admitted, "not having to taxi everywhere."

"Ha! You never needed a vehicle until your dumbass moved out into the boonies. Eh..." he paused briefly, "desert, but my point is still valid. Now unlock one of those damn bottles so we can go bottoms up," Quincy huffed, tugging on the chain in frustration.

Dean unlocked the bar and Quincy deftly poured them two stout shots of whiskey. "To the future," Quincy toasted, "and whatever glories it may hold."

"Now that, my friend, is something I can agree with," Dean said, clinking his shot-glass with Quincy's and holding it high, "To the future and whatever glories it may hold." Down the hatch the drinks went, and the friends switched to water while catching up as they waited on a taxi.

Dean started a mental list of questions he had for Felna, when next she was able to chat. He was very curious about what Mixonia was and thrilled by the idea of claiming a reward fit for the Gods.

CHAPTER
TWELVE
DEAN

Forrester-Lexso Estate

W hile shopping, Dean fielded calls from Uncle Gordano, Marty, college buddies, ex-lovers, sex partners, and even the movie producer. The whole time they were shopping in Noxi, he was on the damn phone. Finally, he simply powered it off.

Most of the calls were to congratulate him on settling down. A few, usually from an ex-lover or previous flings, somehow managed to squeeze anger, denial, and remorse into their rather backhanded compliments and well wishes. The movie producer was thrilled and said this was the perfect happy ending for his film. Dean chuckled as he mentioned it was more of a beginning than an ending, and the producer instantly shouted "No sequels!" and closed the connection.

With enough groceries to feed the four of them for a month, they returned home. It felt odd, that Dean realistically considered Bob's Tavern 'home', but he did. He and Cassandra had only spent a week living in the upstairs suite, but he could already fathom it being his home of homes.

Quincy had been talking to his mom the whole time about how crazy Dean was. There were friendly barbs tossed back and forth, but they were both happy for him. Dean had always gotten along well with Quincy's family.

When they finally hovered into the parking area in front of Bob's Tavern, Dean immediately noticed the new fancy Mercedes Tesla speedster. Dean expected to have to give a tissue sample for a DNA scan or a retinal scan for it or something incredibly secure and high-tech—at least a thumb scan—but no, it was just there. After they landed and crunched over to the vehicle, Dean swiped his code across the door, and it unlocked. Score!

"You wanna help me get these groceries inside or are you going to stay out here and ogle your sugar momma's new ride," Quincy snickered.

Dean left the air car to help Quincy with the overloaded grocery auto hauler. Dean and Quincy stacked everything onto the self-moving cart that then automatically sought out the ramp to the doors. A luxuriously stretching Felna opened the front door for them, as they followed the heavily encumbered hover cart inside.

"That wasn't a long sleep," Dean grinned.

"It was amazing though. I feel so refreshed. We Minotaurs require far less sleep than you humans. This body may have the same limitations, but our minds are different," Felna said with a shrug, "and most sleep is really just to recharge your mind." She said this as if Dean should have known it already.

Quincy tilted his head in thought to the side and said, "So, you're saying that if I become a Minotaur, I'd have to make up new excuses for my tens hours a night of beauty sleep?"

"Pretty much," Felna laughed. "I will help you make this excellent salad. My tummy is rumbling, already." She turned to Dean. "When were you wanting to leave?"

"Patti gets here when? Tomorrow?" Dean asked Quincy who pulled out his phone to check his messages.

"I think she is shuttle shopping for us at Ola's lemon lot. At least that is the rumor I heard, and that she was pressured into quitting her job with a sign on bonus of a full year's pay," Quincy chuckled, "to help run some new brothel out in the middle of nowhere." They passed through the door and walked straight for the kitchen. "Like twenty thousand G-coins or something similarly preposterous," he chortled.

Dean winced. "Starts to add up awful quick, doesn't it? I'm going to need to find a regular revenue source. Question number one, for you, Felna. Can I convert these hundred points of whatever is on this locket into money here?" he asked.

Felna gave a loud *hmm* and wave her hand back and forth a bit.

"If you don't know," he grunted, "it's okay."

When they reached the kitchen, Dean and Quincy started putting items away while Felna sifted through the many sacks to find veggies for her salad.

"It's not that I don't know. We've not set up a bank here on Oakley, yet. There is a lot that has yet to be worked out." She pinched the bridge of her nose. "There is just so much that you need to understand, and much of it is pretty complicated. At the same time, however, everything in Mixonia lives and breathes on simplicity."

Already Dean was getting confused. Sounded like a paradox—complicatedly simple.

"Two different sides battle to control a planet, you see," Felna started. "It's important, first off, that you understand I'm a neutral party so—"

"So," Zued interrupted suddenly, showing up by the kitchen door, "what she is about to say is heavily biased to one side—the middle." He crossed his arms with a flourish, playing up his showmanship, and suddenly, Felna's salad was diced up to perfection. "Can't stay long, but you especially, Miss Felna, should be careful. That response tiptoed awfully close to the borderline of deceit."

Felna lowered her head and said nothing, as if she was ashamed. Dean glanced at her before turning to face Zued.

"She is going to give half-truths and some full truths. Not only is she neutral, but she is also not your friend." Zued held a hand up, to stop her rebuttal. "Polite and cordial yes. Merely trust me when I say take her words are something to build from, not to imprint in a hand guide.

"And yes Dean, a hundred tokens could be redeemed for gems. The currency of Mixonia is gems that you can import or export. There is an old school secret trading company that will wash them for you on Earth. Have your Cassie find Capital Chase on Earth and mention she found gems in an asteroid she mined named Mixonia. They'll get the picture.

"Very rough estimate but the gems you could exchange that locket for would probably be worth around ten million Galactic coins—give or take a few hundred thousand. You'd exchange it for a few, big rare gems, vendor those to a gem seller, and then siphon the funds here into your accounts. After that, just buy smaller rubies and sapphires to use in Mixonia." The pointy-eared god muttered something under his breath about grubby money loving humans.

"Only do this at the start," he warned, "And Dean!" The god paused to ensure he had my full attention. "Hear me loud and clear on this. Do not use your Mixonia career to ruin your future gains by using your tokens to ill effect. Save them for statues and pets."

Gems, statues, pets? What the hell was Zued going on about?

"Telling you this will not help that much actually, it's more of an experience kind of thing. There is a rotational exchange, however, so you'll need to be patient regarding gem exchanges. Probably best to use Cassandra to help you as much as she can with her corporate ties. Why do you think I knocked up that little mining beauty for you?"

Dean's face flushed angrily.

"Right," the god muttered, "probably could have phrased that a little bit better. Anyhow, she's a keeper, for certain." He cleared his throat. "My advice to you, my friend, is to ask a few questions of Felna and then go see Sable, as quick as you can. Sable will get you situated."

Without warning, suddenly, he was just gone.

Dean stomped his foot in frustration. No explanation given about the god's interference in their personal lives, other than 'she's a keeper' with a mining company he could use as a front. He wanted to ensure it was his kid, and not some demi-god growing in Cassie's tummy.

"So, it did happen!" Quincy blurted out, his jaw hanging opening. "I wanted so hard to believe you, Dean, but... Hey! My inhibitor just turned off."

Dean chuckled at this and knew his friend was repeatedly smashing his inhibitor's 'on' button, only to only have it turn off again.

Felna scarfed down her food with abandon, relatively unfazed by Zued's appearance. "This is so good," Felna moaned, "Now, pay attention, prettier one."

Quincy smirked, finally dropping his inhibitor issue and giving her a thumbs up.

"Where was I?" she wondered.

"Two sides," Dean quipped.

"Yeah," she swallowed a mouthful of greens and cherry tomatoes. "Having only two sides fighting over something almost always results in a stalemate. Always has been, and almost assuredly always will be." She nodded emphatically and scooped up a huge fork full of lettuce and cucumber.

"Why? You might ask," she chewed noisily for a moment. "Think about it from a god's perspective for a moment. You can't openly fight your foe, due to the planet ending consequences a direct confrontation of powers at that scale would produce, but you still have an opponent you hate." She paused to suck down half a pitcher of water.

"A god's power, you see, is unique in its ability to interact with the universe. While they can be planet shattering powerful, they're far more limited than they like to admit." She laid a finger alongside her nose and winked.

"Sure, they'll alter this or affect that. But those minor interactions take ages to build up the power to do. To this day, they haven't found a workaround for their consumption problems. Souls, victories, and even drugs don't help. While gods are insanely powerful, it's for a limited time, only."

Dean raised a finger and asked, "Limited by whom, though?"

"Limited by a mighty demon, if you ask the Core gods; or limited by a mighty creator, if you ask the Suca gods." She shrugged. "So instead of direct confrontations, there are competitions and events between the gods to pass the time. Cities are built for the gods to meddle in and create their half breeds."

"Is there any way my unborn son is Zued's demi?" Dean worried.

"No," she snorted, "you'd still be in a fever like this one complained about the whole way here." Felna pointed another fork full of veggies at Quincy and waggled it around. "That was for the nice meal and the bed, by the way. Not too many people know that little tidbit."

Dean nodded his thanks, a load of angst lifted from his shoulders.

"Okay," Felna continued, "you got two sides. Above," she gestured around them, "and below." She pointed at the floor.

She paused to gobble up some more rabbit food, before continuing.

"Long, long ago; when this Galaxy was in its infancy the gods were born. The how, why, and exactly where are lost to time. Inner planet versus outer planet." She frowned and then took another bite. "We Minotaurs found ourselves stuck in the middle and are relatively powerless. Incapable of defeating either set of gods, we were forced to resort to trickery with our labyrinths."

"As you can imagine, a few of the first gods hid for long enough to conserve their power to a bursting point." She shuddered. "A fully charged god has horrible powers, capable of destroying planets filled with the very life that both sides seek to control. When both sides lose, nobody wins."

"So, the surviving head gods who reigned over many planets ordained a meeting between the two sides, adjudicated by the neutrals." Felna swung her hands together with a resounding *clap!* "And thus, were the great games born, and gods prohibited their own from destroying planets."

Dean's phone rang, and Felna went back to munching on her delightful salad.

He answered immediately. "Hey pretty lady!" Dean said, feeling better knowing he wasn't going to be stuck raising some pompous ass's son as his own.

"So," Cassandra sighed heavily, "I got roped into other things, Dean, after Patti talked about it with me." She hesitated. "I'm not comfortable going to a new vacation place that might be dangerous, in my condition. Would it be okay if I join you on your next trip?" Cassandra asked tensely.

The fact she hadn't video phoned him, told Dean she was really nervous. He bet she was worriedly working at her lip or chewing the inside of her cheek.

"Uh... Yeah, that's okay," he tried to ease her fears. "I've got Quincy to haul around. I completely understand." He grinned as he heard her mutter, not quite under her breath, 'thank the gods'. "Let me scope things out, this time," he continued, "and see how dangerous the situation is. Two... no, three things... though. First: When is the shuttle getting here?"

"Any minute. Nope, it's there. I bought two used shuttles outright and financed the speedster." He could hear the smirk in her voice. "Actually, you bought one of the shuttles, so if it breaks, no biggie."

Dean rolled his eyes. Probably better that she hadn't video called him.

"What else do you need," she asked, "before I enter this baby store with Mom and Patti?" Suddenly things were adding up. She must have taken an express tube down!

"Hello, Mrs. Lexso," Dean said loudly. Cassandra told him she said 'hi' back.

"Cassie, when are you going to be home?"

"Oh, well, apparently I have a bedtime set for about ten hours from now," he heard Patti snicker in the background, "so before then, I guess."

Dean rolled his eyes again.

"What was the last thing?" Cassandra wondered.

"I'll have to dance around it.... It's actually good, though." Dean took a moment to figure out how he could tell her without just blurting it out.

"So...," he took a deep breath, "remember how there was the sudden appearance by our bed when you and I first... enjoyed the view in our new suite? Well, deep down, I sometimes wondered if I was really the cause of the crops blooming out of that wonderful view." He prayed Cassie could decipher what he was trying to say. "Basically," he rushed to tell her, "my fear of not planting the crops has been washed away, completely, if that makes any sense at all."

"Love you, too, Babe," Cassie said softly into the phone. "How long do you think you'll be gone?"

"I'll try to make it home fairly quickly, after our first visit, once I get a feel for the new adventuring spot," Dean adlibbed.

The phone was then passed around, with her mom taking a few minutes to congratulate him. Patti did the same and mentioned how excited she was to come visit.

Dean was chipper and cordial, even though internally, he was a bit miffed. He should have realized what buying a tavern would mean—when the family came visit, they stayed with you. At least it was a big place.

With the phone conversation over, Dean waited for Felna to finish chewing. "Quincy and I have survival suits we can wear, will that be a problem?" he asked.

"Yes and no. To the gateway, not a problem, and on this trapped-souls of a planet," she snorted, "I highly recommend it. The deal with Mixonia, though, is that it provides a common denominator. A super high-tech planet with dematerializers, for example, would go into the games and run roughshod through the floors, without any competition."

"The old adage of bringing a gun to a knife fight," Quincy quipped.

She raised an eyebrow, while otherwise ignoring his comment.

"Magic using species would also have an unfair advantage," she explained. She gave Quincy a look and smirked, "Kind of like bringing a fireball to a knife fight."

He grinned and conceded her victory with a bow.

"You'll be given an outfit suitable to your species, upon first arriving." She frowned, tapping her chin. "I think humans get a toga, to start. You'll find out soon enough, however, when Sable takes you in. Then, once inside, you'll learn all about how the 'great game of the gods' works."

Dean sighed and realized a great factor in learning was experiencing. He could ask a million questions, but still be clueless as to the reality of the situation.

Dean also had a sneaky feeling, that when a god showed up and gave you advice, you should heed it.

"Grab a to-go salad, Felna. Quincy and I are going to get into suits and will be back shortly," Dean guided his friend towards the suits in his suite upstairs.

When they left the kitchen, Dean asked Quincy for his thoughts.

"So, I'm nervous. Apparently, there is a war on for Oakley, and we don't know about it. Why do the demon things care for the surface, anyhow?" Quincy asked as the elevator closed behind them.

"Ah, yeah. I'd have to go with 'fickle gods and their trivial competitive nature' for three-hundred, Alex." Dean shrugged. "How the hell should I know? Zued," he called out, "any input here? At all? Will we be safe inside Mixonia?" Dean asked. Quincy shook his head, half expecting for the god to suddenly appear inside the riding carriage.

When the elevator *dinged*, however, Zued waited for them on the third floor.

"Look, teleporting costs me vital power I tend to cherish. I've got children to run normal errands..." Zued grumped, "but you're not a normal case."

He folded his arms and stared at his nails as if they were suddenly the most interesting thing in the world.

"The core species live in a utopia that involves heat and a craggy landscape with trees akin to flowers. It's really weird, but it's important you understand that they can't live on the surface, unless they win the contest for that planet."

Dean nodded.

"If either side wins," Zued explained, "Magical energy swaps the planet to a full planet of the winner's choice. Basically, if humans win Oakley, they'll get to convert the core to a new biome, suitable for human expansion. Would people actually live there?" He chuckled mirthlessly, "Probably not. Would it piss off the Core gods?" His wide smile was genuine. "Oh yeah! And that's what we're going to try to do."

"Why anger them?" Quincy wondered and Zued flared with irritation.

He calmed with a few deep breaths. They'd reached Dean's room by now, and the trio went in. While Zued kept talking, the two men got into the spacesuits.

"There's some really bad blood and old resentment between the two sides. Sable comes from a planet known as Konbi. Konbi is no longer home to her mother's species. It was a rare defeat of the Suca. Her mother perished, unable to get off the world in time before the transition."

Zued rubbed the back of nick, and gruffly admitted, "Stubbornness may have also played a role."

Dean groaned. What the hell had he gotten roped into?

"A few things to help bring clarity to the situation," Zued ticked them off on his fingers. "One: Humans don't travel the stars. They wormhole through space. Two: Core species wormhole through cores. Three: You'll actually travel via an inter-planar wormhole from Oakley to Mixonia. Four: There are a lot of rules on Mixonia to protect champions before they compete."

The god stopped and waggled his thumb at Dean. "Five: The most important thing to remember, and almost everyone forgets it at some point, is that you're all on the same side when in Mixonia. Got it?"

The god folded his arms again with a huff. "You'll never go to where the Core species gather to compete. They'll never come here. Just understand that Wixomia exists, and that once you leave from there into a competitive floor in the labyrinth, you'll likely face a Demon or a Snarling trying for the same goal as you are."

"With that said, get into armor immediately. You should be fine with Sable, but don't ever drop your guard, thinking your friends are friendly—present company excluded, he waved down Quincy rebuttal before he could protest. I know this is a lot to take in, but stay with me here, Dean. Are you listening?"

"Yeah, everything seems fairly basic, so far," Dean said as his suit sealed. "Two sides vie for planets. Oakley is the latest in a long series of contests. If I do well, I can banish the Core dwellers and force them out of Oakley's core. This is done primarily for spite, revenge, and because if I don't do it, then they can or will do it to us."

Quincy got Cassandra's suit working and said, "Damn, I'm with him on this. Fook those demons, I say. That's about what I got so far—not that my opinion matters."

Zued was smiling widely.

"Quincy, we're a team. Understand that. Now, I need team Oakley to reset the scale and then dump it heavily in our favor. I want to banish those demonic assholes from this planet." He smacked a mighty fist into his other hand.

"So how is that done? You might ask," he grinned wickedly, "It starts by getting a floor lead. You go into competitions and there are tracker boards all throughout Mixonia that you can check to see how every planet is doing. So, that challenge you won against the Demon on the water was a boon opportunity for the Core gods, after their team had reached a hundred combined floors."

Dean zoned out with all this talk of floors.

"Okay, your eyes are glazing over," the god huffed, "not good. Let me rephrase it, then. They scored a hundred points—easier to wrap your mind around? Sable will cover earning points later. Just know that a hundred-point lead grants the leader a bonus challenge. Every time you win one of the bonus challenges, a magical disaster befalls your enemies."

Quincy patted Dean on the back proudly.

"On Earth," the god continued, "this might be a plague or a blitz of hurricanes. Here on Oakley it would probably be a tsunami that would crash through half of Ola. Your victory saved a lot of lives, Dean, not just your own. Your mission is to keep the enemy from winning; doing so, will save many, many more."

"It's imperative," he emphasized, "you never let them get another lead that big, ever again. Then there is the thousand-point lead. This will increase the number of entrances to Mixonia from four to sixteen, to give the defenders a chance to cycle in a proper defender. You hit ten thousand points, however, and *boom!* —the magic converts the core into a surface utopia—the Core dwellers' version of hell."

Dean was waiting for the elevator button, but Zued stood in his way.

"Got it," Dean said sternly, "Bug Sable on how to compete." He was taking this seriously, but the context was sorely lacking, at the moment. He desperately needed context before all this 'contest of the gods' would make any sense.

"Get ten thousand points to rid Oakley of the Core species. If I don't, they could rid the surface of all of us or unleash disasters. If I get a hundred points, I can challenge their champion to an uneven fight in order to rain destruction down on their home."

"Ah, so Felna mentioned something and it was a full truth. It's exceedingly rare for one side to even get a hundred points lead, let alone ten thousand. There are six events you can compete in and each has a ceiling of a thousand floors," Zued said.

Dean sighed. "You're losing me. What is a floor?"

"A level in essence. Think of a game inside a tower. You do floor one, easy-peasy. It's level one or floor one. You go up, the difficulty goes up. Just so we're clear, though, there is no actual tower. There is a portal which resets to a floor's level and sets you loose into a labyrinth. Clear?"

"Clear as mud," Dean grumped, "But I'll be clear before I compete."

"Perfect. The record, by the way, is 293 levels on solo. And 271 on the team events. So, assuming you do amazingly well and reach level two hundred on each of them without ever getting trapped, there will only be roughly a thousand points you accrue. If each of the four gate masters for the Core Demons—the species that live on this planet—earn a quarter of what you do, then the score is even. You'll need to find the other three portals, by the way, and recruit other champions to help you hold back the tide."

"I'm good at math," Quincy said, "and that math is off."

Zued clapped proudly. "Cycle gate masters. You can only have one in Mixonia at a time. Dean goes in and wins a level, then leaves. Leroy Jenkins is waiting to sprint right in after him and wins a level. After him, you, Quincy, go in for a level. It becomes a pile of work itself, organizing teams to win the whole thing." He muttered under his breath, "Why winning is so rare."

They both gave long "*Ah's!*" of understanding.

Dean went to the nearest wall and banged his head against it. Quincy patted his suit-covered back and said, "Dean, what this fook wants and what we need to do are two different things. If we want to prevent disasters, we do what's needed. If we want to win a war of the gods, we go overboard." He glared at the pointy-eared god, "Evening the score sounds good enough to me."

Zued grunted angrily, but his voice remained even toned when he admitted, "Quincy is right. I'll happily settle for evening the scales. If you go full tilt and try to win the planet, it'll make a lot of gods take notice and start blessing this world. While you may think that is trivial, trust me, it's not. There is an incentive to Oakley gaining traction." He beamed at them.

"This should be more than enough information to properly motivate you. Just know that you saved millions of people by defeating that demonic team, Dean, and reset the scoreboard. I'll be watching."

There was a *poof* and Zued vanished.

Dean groaned and Quincy sighed.

"No pressure, right?" Quincy snickered. "And I wonder if he really is supposed to be Zeus, but lost some trademark infringement battle?"

"Names are close enough..." Dean scrubbed his hands through his hair and reached for his helmet, "And yeah, since there are portals on Earth, how much of this is legend versus fact? I'm sorely tempted to just stay here and avoid this Mixonia bullshit. Screw the millions, next time I'll just—" Dean raged, then suddenly paused, throwing his head back and exhaling loudly.

Who was he kidding? "Okay, pity party for Dean is over. I'm ready to go claim my reward. Let's grab Felna and see what clunker of an air shuttle Cassie bought us. Time to go visit the city of the gods."

"Right! That's more like the Dean we all know and love!" Quincy exulted, "Let's get rich, bitch!"

They reached the main floor quickly and found Felna waiting next to the door with another helping of salad.

"Ya ready?" Dean asked.

She nodded, still eating.

"I can bring you more salad, if you'd like," he offered.

"I'd love that. Is there an auto navigate option on this flying contraption?" Felna asked as they clomped together across the tiled barroom floor.

The exterior landscape revealed a setting sun and Dean realized he was probably going to have to adjust to yet a third planet's time zone. Instead of pestering Felna, he decided to just soak up all the details he received and spend his time more productively on processing a few things he found to be most important.

"Oh wow," Quincy said with a smirk through his helmet when he saw the shuttle. "I need to get me a sugar momma."

Dean scoffed, "You've already got a sugar great-grandpa. And this shuttle is only middle-of-the-line."

He walked up to the box van, with a flatbed on the back half. The vehicle had lots of windows and extra rotors to lift it.

When they entered the vehicle through the passenger compartment, Dean pulled up a map of the area on the control panel.

Felna handed Quincy her salad and tapped an area on the map, called 'Deathly Caverns'.

"What if I want to go to the other portal?" Dean asked and Felna chortled and wagged a finger at him.

She otherwise ignored his question, snorting an 'as-if' and leaving Dean to figure out he was SOL—shit out of luck—when it came to tricking her into revealing any of the other entrances.

He entered the destination into the autopilot, and they lifted off the ground and jetted away towards this Deathly Caverns.

THIRTEEN

DEAN

Deathly Caverns

They'd flown into a cavernous pit that leveled out at the bottom. There was ample space here for their shuttle and some evidence of previous explorers. At least one set of boot prints from a heavy explorer's suit could be seen clearly in the mud. Felna said they'd have to leave the shuttle behind up ahead, where she noted the way would become too narrow.

The setting reminded him, somehow, of a movie set. Maybe it was how someone had removed all the clasts, stalagmites, and other obtrusions to make a nice, clear path. The journey involved only a half hour of walking across the bottom of the pit, with minimal twists and turns. It turned out to be pretty straight forward—simply take the left pit exit and walk for half an hour. This alleviated one of Dean's fears, at least, of becoming super lost and not being able to find his way back to their shuttle.

Quincy, unfortunately, had complained continuously about how much he hated caves. By the time Dean and the others suddenly shimmered through a magical wall, he was quite irritated with his friend and was glad the trip was almost over. Their actual transition through the portal was fine, it was when Felna morphed into a nine-foot tall, hideous cow woman in a kilt, however, that set him on edge. Hideous may have been a bit harsh, but still fairly accurate.

The duo followed the Minotaur as she led them past an alcove that must serve as her room. Inside, Dean noted some hay bedding and few trinkets to help pass the time—no wonder Felna had been so excited about the bed in her hotel room. Eventually they ended up in a cavern tinted blue from in which Sable waited.

Her angelic wings, impatience, and sour attitude were on full display. Sable was clad in bits and pieces of golden armor that didn't leave much to the imagination. Golden plates of scale mail armor and bustier covered her shoulder, hips, and midriff, with a nearly see-through white linen body suit underneath that covered her supple breasts and between her legs. It accentuated, more than hid, her sexiest parts. Dean could clearly see Sable's nipples; the bodysuit was so tight that he was fairly sure that the angelic beauty was clean shaven below the belt. Dean's eyes much preferred the sexy human with the wings over their Minotaur companion.

"By Min's saggy tits!" Sable exploded, "It's about damn time you returned from your mission, Felna. I was expecting you to fail again." The angel walked forward, cursing the entire way. "What a waste of time this has been. Hurry up you two," she snapped, waving Dean and Quincy forward.

They couldn't help but stare.

"What?" the beauty narrowed her eyes at them, "Haven't you ever seen a female body before?"

"Uh… yeah… sure, b-but… you're naked," Quincy stammered.

Sable scoffed, "You should see the orgies if this little old outfit is getting you all hot and bothered."

Dean laughed at the dumbstruck look on his friend's face.

"Did you cover the contract requirements?" Sable turned back to Felna, her words tumbling out at such a rapid pace, they nearly blurred together.

"Yeah, ya daft Demi," Felna grumbled. "Doesn't mean they listened, though."

"Make a deal you both agree with," Sable ordered. "With one of you being in charge."

He disliked their current attitude and snippy tones between Sable and Felna. These ladies obviously had bad blood.

Dean spread his hands wide, palms up, clueless as to what she expected him to do.

The angel pinched the bridge of her nose. "You," she pointed at Dean, "ask him" she waved at Quincy, "to do something for you, for a stated period of time. You can promise him something in return, or he can just do it out of the kindness of his heart or in desperation—I don't really care, but it's a rule, so you have to do it."

"Uh… Okay. Quincy," Dean said, half-assed, "I offer you a contract to follow me around for a week of Earth time for the pay of one Galactic coin."

"I agree," Quincy shrugged.

Sable clapped her hands together.

"Glad we finally got that taken care of, else Mixonia would soon become over-crowded with people entering to compete," Sable said, waving her hand forward to hurry them along. "In this case, Dean is the Gate Master and you're the sidekick."

"I'm not his sidekick," Quincy objected, but was ignored.

"Follow me, Dean first," Sable said, walking quickly to the back wall. She huffed, throwing her hands in the air. "Anytime today, Felna, if you would be so kind."

"So not going to miss our lovely chats," the Minotaur rumbled dryly.

The bovine hybrid's furry arms traced a pattern into the air. Magic coalesced around her hands in cascading tendrils of pink. She deftly swirled the gathering power into a design. When something akin to a ying-yang glimmered in the air, she blasted the magic at the back of the cavern wall. A crackling yellow portal spread before them on the wall into a wide hexagon.

"Fook me," Quincy and Dean exclaimed together.

Sable didn't waste any time and stepped on through.

"It's safe," Felna chuckled. "There'll be hell to pay if you two don't get a move on."

Dean ducked his head, mustered up his courage, and stepped into the dull yellow light.

☺☺☺

Dean was lost in the transition. Confusion washed over him as he held a small fishing rod while standing in lush green grass. He realized this was one of his earliest memories of fishing, with his fathers, at a lake preserve. One of only a few good memories of those early, forgotten times. As suddenly as the recollection arrived, though, it was snatched away.

Dean's eyes adjusted to a cloudless, sunny, blue sky with a moderately bright light —though there didn't appear to be a sun. The horizon contained banks of rolling clouds that stacked slowly on top of each other. To his side he noted rocky ledges that transitioned into fluffy nothingness.

Ahead of him there was a grand city, its skyline soaring high into the air; it stretched for a few miles with almost every building towering higher than most of Ola's skyscrapers. Quincy stumbled into his back, forcing Dean to shuffle forward.

They found themselves on a cobble stone road. Directly to either side of the road stood hundreds, if not thousands, of statues. Dean inspected himself and Quincy.

Both wore simple, white togas, their armored spacesuits had disappeared, as if by magic.

A sign embedded in a boulder just off the road read:

'Welcome to Mixonia, Home of the Gods Above."

Below it was a map he inspected closely. It wasn't perfectly to scale and more of a representation than a map, but from it, Dean was able to get a feel for the layout of the town. It also seemed to be somewhat dated, as the area where it indicated there were private homes, had obviously been converted into high rises.

After he'd studied the representation of Mixonia for a while, it was the statues that caught his attention next, more so than the buildings, the ominous clouds, or the fact that there was sunshine without a sun.

Only a few humans dotted the decorative pieces. Dean saw a snake man, a busty unicorn woman, a tree hybrid with leafy hair, a siren, and a Dwarf. Those were just a few of the hundreds of species on display. The myriad and variety of monster humanoids was intense—in all his life, Dean had never imagined he'd first see aliens under the surface of his planet.

For all of Sable's earlier irritation and impatience, she now let them soak in their surroundings.

Dean approached a statue of a human. There was no name or indication of what this statue was for, nor was there a name to go with it, just the image etched in stone for eternity. To Dean he appeared to be an explorer. His boonie hat, compass around his neck, and a machete on his hip painted a picture of a late 18th century adventure seeker.

"A random collection of competitors displayed here for inspiration. Your defeat of the Demonic team on Oakley will probably earn you immortalization in a similar statue. Not many solo defenders take down an entire team of opponents."

Quincy grinned and clapped him on the back.

"You only won, though, because they weren't prepared," Sable sniffed nonchalantly, and Dean scoffed.

"I mean it. You'll learn. He was nerfed to your level, which was level zero. A master mage of his skill level suddenly flinging tiny magic missiles instead of massive fireballs tends to be a nasty shock."

Is that what happened? Dean tried to remember the fight. *That's right, he was angry at the big Minotaur god for some reason.*

"Ah, that actually makes sense. He did have puny spells; and, the Demon was screaming at the referee like something wasn't fair. His animals hurt me, but a lot less than I'd expected. I thought they'd kill me with a single bite," Dean mused.

He continued to inspect the statues and was drawn to a sexy bunny girl with a delicious figure and a cute little tail. "So many species."

"You think this is a lot, wait until you get into the city," Sable smirked down her nose at him. She was pretty and she knew it, why else flaunt her body so openly? She was one of the types of women Dean would gladly fook but had never cried about being tossed aside afterwards.

"What happens if I step on the clouds?" Quincy asked breaking them of their studying one another.

"Don't do it," Sable snapped, shoving them to the side as five lizardmen exited the portal, "or do so, but don't complain when you fall until you become a trapped soul; eagerly waiting eons for someone to free you with twenty five of their oh so valuable tokens."

The lizard team walked confidently towards the heart of the city, geared up as if expecting to fight the Roman legions of old, with kilts, shields, short swords, daggers, and light armor that *clanged* with every step they took.

No laser rifles, no spacesuits. Brutal weapons from forgotten times. Where am I?

"When you go home," their guide continued, "the gear you're wearing gets tucked away into trans dimensional storage. When you come back, though, you'll find yourself once again in the gear you left with. Just like if you exited the other side of this portal for Oakley, you'd be back in your spacesuits." The angel pulled them further off to the side of the path.

"How much did Felna tell you?" Sable asked, holding them back as a single Halfling stepped past them and out through the portal.

When Dean glanced around for an exit, he noted a path that wrapped around to the other side of the sparkling dull yellow gate. It seemed that there was both an entrance, and an exit side to the portal, in addition to a relatively clearly marked 'out of bounds' border to the city that they should avoid and the many statues here by the portal to 'inspire' them.

"Your father told us a bit more, actually, though both said nothing about how Mixonia actually operates," Dean reported.

"Follow me, then," Sable instructed. "We're going to pass the dual towering structures of Min—Min being the final arbitrator of all things regarding the games. He, or she, as an intermediary, is as neutral as any can get; though it remains a complete mystery as to whether Min is actually male, or female, or both... or neither. Hence the two-hundred-foot tall statues we'll pass of both sexes."

"Yeah, I had no idea what their sex was when I went dealt with them, either," Dean muttered, and Sable hushed him.

"Speak not of the Minotaur god that graced your presence. You're beyond rare. Almost always there is a champion to select from for a challenge due to planetary points. But not for you, my guess is Felna, that lazy bitch, is the reason," Sable said with resentment.

"What did she do?" Quincy asked with his neck craning back to ingest the epicness of the Minotaur god's statues.

Sable pulled them to the side under the male Minotaur statue's towering frame. She led them around the base until they were in the shadows out of sight.

She spoke in a very low tone. "Minotaurs are supposed to be neutral. They're also supposed to lure champions to their gates. Imagine our surprise when we learned that Oakley is not only in play, but is rapidly losing, with four Core portals allowing demonic champions entry, and no Suca champions. Could it happen? Sure," Sable said leaving it at that.

"Wait, you're intimating that not all Minotaurs are neutral? Bit paranoid, isn't that?" Dean snort, wholly unaffected by her reddening face. "I mean humans have been on Oakley for only a few hundred years. I have to assume these Core Demons have been here a lot longer, right?"

"Irrelevant," Sable retorted with a sassy sharpness, "we've validated our suspicions, before, and this game has been played far longer than humans have been an upright species." The beauty narrowed her eyes at them. "The Minotaurs and their labyrinths are revered by the Core species—much less so by surface dwellers. Which can lead to... problems."

They stood there awkwardly for a moment waiting to be told what to do next. Sable huffed, glared once more, and finally pointed upward.

"Min is cherished in both Mixonia and Wixomia. Whatever you do, do not be crass or brazen about seeing them. Follow me," Sable commanded, leaving their side to approach a huge water fountain.

At the top of the cascading falls of water, there was a crashing battle of vibrant blue liquid. Two statues squirted the cerulean liquid at each other, locked in eternal battle. A Demon and an Angel blasted torrents of water into a middle point where there hung a balance of scales. The water *roared* as it then filled and overflowed the scales to fall hundreds of feet and crash into the pool below.

Dozens of benches were arrayed to view the pool and the fountain; every one of them was occupied. Families sat enjoying the view. This surprised Dean. He grunted in curiosity, noticing that these people weren't champions, eager to compete. This was all just... normal. Well, beside the fact all the people were very alien, if humanoid.

Dean wondered how the water was sucked back up into the two-hundred-foot tall decoration.

Magic, he thought, *it has to be magic.*

"The city is broken down into districts," Sable continued, "And yes, other things exist within districts. And yes, they do expand suddenly, when enough new planets arrive, and their champions enter the games." She paused, briefly. "Though there are some things that have never expanded," Sable noted, "like Crystal Lake, out to our left."

The moment they were around the fountain, a myriad of aliens was revealed. Dean froze. There were so many two-eyed, two-armed, two-legged humanoid combinations that Dean was in shock.

"Keep moving," Sable prodded them along, somewhat politely. "We're heading out to Crystal Lake."

They soaked in their surroundings while searching for an empty bench. Alien-looking children frolicked in the water; a triple tailed boy with blue skin splashed water at a brown, spiky porcupine girl.

"This is a leisure location and serves no purpose, other than to provide a place to relax and find your center. On the opposite of this lake, you will find the Gardens of the Gods." Sable pointed in the other direction. "Further along that edge, is Min's Vault of Treasures. There are several vendors next to the lake over that way, that we'll be visiting next."

"Why are all the aliens we've seen about the same height, build, and have only two legs," Quincy asked.

Dean leaned in close to hear Sable's answer.

"The creator created all Suca life to resemble a certain frame—following a certain template, if you will. The diversity that you see is based on what the creator wanted. You'll see a few variations and the odd deviation, here and there, from the standard model, but most fit it rather closely." She rolled her eyes and took a couple of deep breaths. "I have nothing more to say about it, really because the reality is... that is the best answer," Sable said irritably.

She stood up from the bench and headed for the market and they were forced to pick up the pace to follow closely behind her. It was clear she was in a hurry.

The roads were busy with pedestrian traffic. There were a few flying species following the cobbled roads as flightpaths. Every so often, small carts with two wheels were strategically placed. Vendors shouting out their wares for sale—mostly food and drink. A little girl, with slithering cables of hair that wasn't snakes, but instead vines, pulled on her father's wrist and pointed at Sable.

Dean wave to them with a warm smile and the girl turned her head to look at him curiously. They kept moving and soon entered the city proper. Here, the skyline was no longer visible, lost in the very midst of the towering buildings that had composed it. Maybe Sable was leading them to some three-hundred-foot tall market, thirty or more floors above the ground.

Worst idea ever, Dean thought. *I've seen those shows where the stores are hundreds of feet up, and for some reason, I doubt they have elevators here. That would make my calves ache like a mother if I needed to buy something up on the top floor.*

Sable cut left, darting between the immense stone structures. Dean noted a few squatters, sitting outside some temporary wooden lean-tos they must use for their homes. The streets were clean and though the garbage may have been missing, the stench of the poor wafted off them, nonetheless. Their guide led them around the big building and turned down a number of narrow alley ways.

At the end of one of these passages, Dean spotted a unique structure. Sable led them up to the outskirts of a six-story market. The numerous booths reminded Dean of an odd combination of parking garage, mall, and flea market, all commingled together. It was much easier to navigate within the immensely wide bazaar. Dean glanced around in wonder, noting a wide variety of weapons, staffs, bottles of potions, statues, armor, boots, pieces of armor, and more for sale. It was overwhelming, really, how quickly the crowded marketplace simply swallowed them up.

"Dean," Quincy nudged him with an elbow, "what are you thinking?"

"That there is a lot of business here and I've no idea why," Dean replied.

Sable scoffed at their incredulity with a burst of light laughter. "This city houses thousands of residents," she explained. "Some planetary leaders don't hide their portal locations, like Earth does." She snorted. "Belmont has no idea your portal even exists, but on other planets, competing brings in big money, with lots of incentives."

"Are things fairly priced, here?" Quincy wondered.

"When fearful planets pour resources into their champions and contracted teams, prices tend to become inflated rather quickly," Sable admitted, sounding more than a little bored. "Okay," she snapped her fingers to get their attention, "that was the market, you can visit it on your own time. I'm only obligated to get you to Min's Vault. This short side-tour is because I'm in a good mood. You can spend your tokens here, though I'd recommend, for most transactions, you shop around and take your time doing so. This society is full of beings eager to take your tokens— and there are not that many tokens to go around."

"What are all these items for?" Dean wondered, unable to contain his questions any longer as they left the market.

"A varied mix of items to help one compete or survive," the angel shrugged. "Tokens are the ultimate exchange. For everything else, gems and coins named after the gems, are the staple currency. It gets more confusing because they fluctuate frequently as to which holds the highest value. Gems were the only thing that was supposed to be allowed in when the gods agreed to build this place. Well, then came food issues, raw material issues, and whatnot. So those were all allowed in to sustain life," Sable said, looking back at us over her shoulder while continually moving forward.

Sable may have felt right at home, walking crowded streets filled with tiger people, dragon folk, and even a hopping frog woman, but Dean kept getting distracted by every new and wondrous detail around them. He realized they would have time to take an in depth look at the market later, and hopefully learn more about its intricacies. As for the aliens... well, he was not sure he'd ever grow accustomed to them.

They left the market district for a set of wider buildings that still were just as tall. Dean read a sign one of the buildings that had several guards stationed out front: 'Lithe Eliminators'.

Huh? Is that a shop? He wondered. *All I see is guards.*

"The guilds live here, need a team, this is the place to go." Sable pointed at the guild building. "That one specifically you're looking at with a dumb expression focuses on team combat climbing"

"Will I need a guild?" Dean asked and she shrugged.

"Moving along. Here is a sad fact about Mixonia. There are champions here who have infinite contracts with four people; they legit lockdown the gate from letting fresh competitors come in because they never leave or compete. That is why the portals expand from four to sixteen after a thousand-point deficit is accrued. It's too easy for slouches to hide in here and not care about those who remain out there."

Quincy accidentally bumped into a boar man and Sable paused to rescue him from the confrontation. "Stay out of trouble," she snapped.

"What did I do?" Quincy said irritably.

Dean moved the conversation along, before the two started in on one another and asked, "And the children born here?"

Sable sighed. "A problem that nearly brought about a fresh war and why Mixonia is no longer a training camp, like it was supposed to be. The original concept was simple. You arrived, realized what was at stake, and trained hard before entering the great games. But no, men and women couldn't focus on what's most important; couldn't keep their hands of one another. The problem was the children. Every time a female team member pops out a baby, that's breaking the rules, technically. Only one master plus four helpers.

"So, children were allowed to remain, as residents, for eternity. Since there is no real danger here and immortality, in a sense..." She waved a hand at the huge buildings around them. "Hence the towering buildings. All because of a loophole in the whole agreement that is endlessly exploited. Both sides let it be, though, because it feeds souls to the system; which in turn expands the city." Sable grunted, looked about them, and shrugged.

"Next over," she continued, "is inns, taverns, and bars. Then crafting and housing is the next district after that. Across the street, there," she pointed, "are immense dwellings that continue on up into the sky. And there," another pointed finger, "is more housing, and finally" another vague gesture, "across from here are the training grounds which are filled with trainers."

"All this runs off gems?" Quincy asked, tucking his chin in confusion, his brows drawn down.

"Yes," Sable nodded, "and if I were you, one of the first things I'd do is add a dealer to your team. Not your adventuring team, mind, but at least to the roster of retainers you hire. Because if you take them home with you, you can really get some good exchange rates. You'll notice Earth already has plenty of people here swapping diamonds they get here for rubies and sapphires from back home."

That sounded backwards, to Dean.

"Diamonds are relatively cheap here," their guide explained, "and the other two worth more." She rolled her eyes at their bewilderment. "Which is backwards, I know, and a boon for humans. Knowing stuff like that helps immensely. Assuming you've got gems to make gems, of course, which further fuels the soul collections."

Dean was getting aggravated by this point with Sable's cursory overview of the city, interspersed with invaluable nuggets of information. He grabbed her elbow.

Sable's eyes flared and Dean caught her other fist as she tried to hit him. His mass and strength were too much for her to overcome. Or so Dean thought. She smirked and power flared down her arm and into her trapped fist, knocking Dean to the ground a dozen feet further down the walkway.

"You're strong and stubborn. I get why my father chose you. You're also naïve," she growled, "I can use powers to supplement my natural abilities. That was quite foolish of you." Sable stated this matter-of-factly, not appearing like she'd been upset, not in the slightest.

"Your father said he needed us to establish a base, to help Oakley succeed. I can't do that in a half-as rushed tour through the city," Dean snapped, picking himself up.

The flow of pedestrians circumvented them as their tense postures spoke of violence. Most were hesitant of Sable's flared wings.

"I'm weak right now. That bitch died on purpose; I know it. The longer I remain out of demi-purgatory, the more pathetic I become. Nothing worse than slowly weakening with time. Demi-gods have a very shitty existence. We spend our entire lives trying to either become the one in a thousand to rise to become new gods or the one in a thousand who find a permanent home,"

"Huh?" Quincy blurted.

"Trust me when I say being born a half-god has many perks, but far more downfalls. We're our parents' errand boys and girls and regulated to a long existence of mediocrity. Our souls ever for sale," she admitted bitterly, "to limit our usefulness to our parents. Both sides suffer this."

"I'll get you a guide so eager to hear your endless questions, she'll never tire of them. Mixonia is ruthless and vile to most, all but the gods and a few lucky champions. There are lives shattered in here, every second." She pulled them back into the moving crowd. "We're going back to the beggars, Min's Vault, and then I'm going home."

"What are the beggars?" Quincy asked.

"Glad you asked, let me show you," Sable said with a winning smile. "The sooner I do, the sooner I can pawn you off on someone else and return home to regenerate my exhausted power."

The pace she set was brisk, at one point she leaped up and flew over a crabby Dwarf. The Dwarf was just like what he had come to expect from the movies, making Dean wonder how many authors and movie directors had drawn upon this sea of humanoid races for their inspiration, after having set foot in this place.

The drinking district was not exactly limited only to taverns, bars, and inns. The bottom floors had many of those establishments, though, with the vast majority being restaurants.

Above the bottom floors were apartments with wide alleyway ramps leading up to a lobby of sorts on the third floor. Judging by how tightly packed the windows were, the places were either tiny, or meant for smaller species. A few of the bigger structures had massive balconies and expansive views, meaning not every dwelling was a tenement for the poor.

While Dean walked down the busy street, he noticed there were only a few hand carts parked in front of shops. Most side alleys lead up ramps to stairwells that continued on up to the housing. He kept looking around, trying to find where all the pack animals must be kept, but couldn't figure it out.

He may have snickered, slightly, when he saw a centaur hauling bags labeled flour. When he overheard conversations, though, he immediately recognized what people were saying. Everyone was speaking in English. Everything was written in English. Either this was factual or a magical adaptation. Dean strongly suspected magic was at play.

The city felt congested, loud, and small, when in the very heart of it. Even with the cluttered collection of aliens cohabitating in such a confined space, there was little garbage or waste to be seen. Dean hadn't seen any cleaning crews or even signs for, or the actual presence of, garbage bins. Another question for their next guide, he supposed.

From Dean's understanding in school, if shit didn't get flushed, he and everyone else would soon know about it, from the stench if nothing else. But the air smelled crisp and pure, despite his being in a busy city, with thousands of creatures packed on top of one another all around him. Bemused, he watched thousands upon thousands of Mixonia's residents go about their day. Shaking his thoughts away, he jogged to keep up with Sable.

Quincy was actually flowing behind in her wake quite well. Dean caught him checking out her shapely hips. That woman was a firecracker, no doubt, but Dean already had his hands full. More power to Quincy, if he were brave enough to attempt to tap that. After seeing all the half-naked women here, he dreaded the eventual conversation with Cassandra; he'd have to be honest about this place.

He was getting a lot of interested eyes eagerly devouring his body. There were far more females than males, he noticed. A woman with bunny ears pushed up her cleavage when she caught him staring, just to tease him with. She winked as he passed by.

His attention diverted as the city ended and The Garden of the Gods sprouted over the crowds. Dean had expecting some lush meadows and vibrant flowers, and to be fair, there were some of those. Mostly, though, it was the impressive trees, each stretching hundreds of feet into the sky, that captured his attention. He craned his neck back to see another mini city, high up in the branches. Down low, at the ground level, tunnels stretched through massive trunks, with streams of residents flowing through them.

They entered a tunnel, burrowed through a massive tree, and walked out the other side into a meadow where a dryad played the flute on a stage. Dean was unimpressed by the tune, but the gathering of forest creatures seemed to be enjoying it. He realized it was much less frantic here, than it had been on the main road.

Ha! He chuckled to himself, *the hippies created a shortcut to get away from the crowds— and the crowds let them, because of their bad music. Some things transcended species.*

Dean had no problem stepping over roots or lazy horned people with goat legs as the bright light illuminated the forest floor magically, despite the thick canopy of branches overhead. There were no electrical sockets or power lines. Dean was starting to put together a more complete picture of what appeared to be taken for granted around him—Mixonia was magical. Defying logic was its forte.

Beyond the trees was another parking garage type structure. This one was just as massive as the previous market had been but appeared to have fewer stalls. A sign hung from the pavilion type opening.

Hiring, Recruiting, and More

Dean wanted to ask Sable what was going on, but the demigod ducked quickly into a stairway before he could begin to form his question. The cheater used her wings to flap quickly up to the sixth floor. Dean was breathing heavily, and Quincy was still on the fourth floor, when he ascended the final flight of stairs. There was a sign here, embedded in the concrete type wall.

Pandering - Desperate families trying to free the souls of those they care about. All deals are bound by Min—enter into an agreement at your own risk. The exploitation of the vulnerable, while discouraged, is allowed. Support team Suca, save a life.

Dean only had only a single thought after reading the sign: *Savage.*

"Hey, wait up!" Dean shouted to Sable who finally paused. "I get you're in a hurry to get home," he huffed and puffed, "but I can't let us get separated from Quincy." He looked around them. "Where the fook are we, anyways, this is depressing."

Dean saw people sitting behind portraits or signs. Sometimes there wasn't even an advertisement, just some poor soul seeking help. Dean studied a few of the faces on the placards or paintings, etched lovingly from memory by desperate loved ones, and grew sad. Signs indicated who their significant other was, briefly told their sob story, and why they needed saving.

"You're aware of how trapped souls work, aren't you?" Sable huffed.

Dean shook his head, no, waiting for Quincy to catch up to them.

148

"You compete in the Game of the Gods. There are variations for solo and team. You finish a floor by securing the prize, a locket, and placing it in its intended slot," Sable explained. "You lose," she frowned at the sad evidence of loss around them, "by dying. When you die, your soul becomes a figurine, and is displayed in Min's Vault of Treasures."

Dean frowned.

"If you fail a labyrinth, Dean, and this weakling has twenty-five tokens, he can cash those in for riches or he can honor your friendship and free your soul. We're talking, potentially, millions of Galactic coins or your soul being freed from limbo—all depending on how the tokens are spent."

"So," Quincy sought, between deep breaths, to summarize the salient facts, "you compete in the labyrinth and get rewards if you win. Great. If you fail, however, your soul fuels the magic which runs the city, and which keeps the peace. Your soul's figurine is preserved in Min's Vault and available for a princely sum of Tokens. If someone is willing to bail your dead soul out of hock, you are resurrected and get to try again? A rather ingenious idea, actually." The shorter man frowned, rubbing at his sore quads, "Is exercise harder here for some reason?"

"Yes," was all that Sable said. "Tempting to believe your friends will do what is right, isn't it? Only guaranteed if you get it in contract." Sable leaned towards him, urgently. "Don't be an idiot, Dean, contract a professional to free your soul if you are ever defeated. If, however, Quincy has only twenty-three tokens..."

"He competes for two more and is likely to become another potential casualty," Dean muttered. "I like the idea less and less the more I hear about it."

"Dean, the initial planets lost more lives a few times over from out of control wara than Min's Vault has ever captured. The process is not even that bad. The mind goes into hibernation until aroused to agree to a contract of release. The buyer holds all the power."

She tapped his locket, with its bold 'One Hundred' etched onto the face. "You could unlock a full team of experts with that necklace. Instead, though, we'll want something slightly different," Sable murmured, running a hand through her hair.

A few desperate, pleading aliens tried to approach their group, but Sable shooed them away.

"What do you mean, different?" Dean asked.

"We've built teams for champions before, and they never work. The contract holder always ends up burdened unduly with strife they never bargained for, for one reason or another. Honestly, we've deduced it best simply to let you build your own team, with as little undue influence as possible." She rolled her eyes. "Let you do... you."

Dean nodded in agreement. Hard to argue with the option to run his own operation the way he wanted to.

"You still need an expert on Mixonia, however, and that expert is not me. You will need to first train on how the labyrinths work—which means finding a trainer down on their luck, but with lots of skill and know-how." The whole time she talked, Sable kept peering at the hundreds of faces around them. Suddenly, she smiled.

"And I know just who to approach to help you out. Over this way." Sable pulled him down one wall and over to the other side of the open floor. "Best part is, she's in such a pathetic state you can hire her without promising anything. She'll probably help you, for the mere opportunity of her daughter being freed."

Dean was about to comment on how fooking wrong it was to play upon another's fears, when she spun back around and darted deeper through the crowd of pandering aliens. There were endless sob stories all around; Dean was feeling pretty shitty about them being here. Although he wasn't poor, he had been; he wasn't the kind of man to exploit.

One thing was certain, though. Dean was interested in meeting a trainer whose misfortune promised such an opportunity, that even demigods were excited about it.

FOURTEEN

DEAN

Mixonia

"Hello Anoka, you've looked better," Sable said with disdain.

Anoka groaned at hearing Sable's voice. "Hasper went back to Lixkus, exactly like I'd said he would. I tried Sable. I tried. Don't rub it in that we failed."

"I'm here for something else," Sable said, sorrow tingeing her tone. Dean saw her face reflect pain, for the first time.

Dean didn't think it was because of how battered Anoka was, though, and Anoka was indeed in a sorry state. She lay crumpled in the corner and looked pitiful.

A sign rested beside her. It showed an image of a defiant young woman with a staff and sword. A short story about Kambry was etched onto sign. It said enough to tell him she was probably never going to be freed by Anoka and a warrior with bad luck.

The hope of life had fled her. Dean had seen this before in the desolate poor of Ola. You give up at some point.

Dean studied her body.

Tragic really. She was a dragon woman. Older, fit, and yet broken. One eye was swollen shut. Her arm was in a dirty sling and her shattered leg poorly splinted.

Quincy gagged at the sight of a jagged tip of bone protruding from a wad of dirty bandages.

Dean paused to nudge Sable.

"Why isn't she healed?"

"They keep beating me," Anoka said, looking up at him with her one good eye. "After months I'm finally out of debt. Only twenty-five more tokens worth of ass-kickings left. When my work shift ends, I get a few gems to take a beating from Thero. His tiny cock gets hard when he swells my eyes shut. He offers to fill my ass for extra but—"

"So," Dean ground out, "when can I kick the shit out of this Thero guy?"

Quincy's eyes widened.

"You'd get caught," Sable snorted. "Min sees all. Normally such beatings would not be allowed inside the city, but Anoka has agreed to her torture, in order to raise money for her daughter's freedom."

Dean rolled his eyes. She'd fucking agreed to this?

"The problem is," Sable continued, "gems are but a pittance compared to what she needs: twenty-five tokens to—"

Dean held up a hand to interrupt Sable. "Get up Anoka," Dean commanded.

She weakly flipped him the bird.

Interesting.

Dean kneeled down to her level. Willing his necklace into existence, he covered it so only she could get a glimpse of it. Just as quickly, away it went, but her uninjured eye flared with hope.

"Get. Up. Anoka!" Each word was clear and concise.

His voice was growling with fury. She obeyed this time but stumbled and nearly fell. Dean was lightning quick and caught her. It was hard not to crush her wings or cause further damage to her injuries in the princess hold that he scooped her weakened body into, yet Dean managed.

He seethed. His stomach burned and roiled with rage. It was with difficulty that he held his temper in check, his desire for violence trembled eagerly at the precipice, impatient to be unleashed.

Dean had known shitty parenting. This was the opposite. All around him, emotionally battered mothers and father humbled themselves to beg help for the ones they loved. Maybe, eventually, he could help them all. For now, though, he'd start with this one.

Sable went to protest, reaching a hand out, as if she could stop him. Quincy knew Dean's temper was white hot with a raging fire and in no mood to be interrupted and stepped between them.

Sable understood perfectly. She poofed out of existence. Dean could honestly admit he was not sad to see her go.

"Why?" Anoka asked.

A few deep breaths later and they were trotting down the stairs.

"Why what?"

"Why help me?" the battered dragon woman asked.

"You're the right kind of person to help," Dean muttered. "You're the right kind of person to train me."

"You don't know me," she replied with a cough.

Dean had to lift her over to his shoulder when a group of Orak refused to let him by. Both sides glared as if they were offended.

"I'll disclose more when you're in your new home," he grunted. "Tell me, should I unlock Kambry for training, or have you train me first?"

"Free her, part of her torment is that she is awoken to reject attempts to contract her from Thero. He sends a new pawn each day to tease her with the possibility of release. Even paid me to try a few times," Anoka said.

They arrived in the busy job market and Dean made a bee-line for the exit, Quincy hot on his heels.

"Where is she?" Dean asked and Anoka pointed down a long cobblestone road decorated with pink blossoming trees. "Can you walk?"

"They went further than allowed to this last time. I had to be carried to my perch for pandering. Serves them right. Technically, they should be carrying me," Anoka said, and Dean grunted.

"You weight no more than a feather," he lied, and she smiled.

Quincy chuckled. "What did your daughter, Kambry was it? What did she do?"

"She went into a combat floor expecting it to be empty. There was a big event going on, and she hoped that would distract the higher-level competitors," she sighed, "but that is when the wealthy pick on the poor the most."

"What happened to her?" Dean asked.

"She was ambushed and reaped for tokens. Twenty tokens are rewarded for every kill. It takes twenty-five to unlock a reaped soul," Anoka replied. "This is the second time she has lost, too. The first time was reckless abandon. The most recent failure was just poor judgement and bad luck," the dragon woman said sadly, "she isn't even on her third floor yet."

"Well, we can work on that," Dean said, trying to be positive and it worked.

Sort of. She sniffled back a few happy tears; at that moment, Dean knew he was doing the right thing.

"Not to complain but you don't need me if you've got a golden necklace with a hundred on it," Anoka muttered after collecting her emotions.

"Sharp eye for a lady only able to use one," Quincy quipped.

"I was instructed to wait to tell you the story, in private," Dean reminded her, settling the matter.

They walked down the road at a normal pace. While Dean was ripped and built for endurance, he had lied; Anoka was not as light as a feather. She was heavy and tiresome to haul. He found a bench to set her carefully down on to take a break.

She groaned and mumbled at being set down.

"How much further?" Dean asked, stretching his muscles as they recovered. It was a long walk home and he had no gems to buy a cart ride with.

"Five more minutes' walk, if we keep going. Please, she needs to be free." Her rambling was a bit incoherent.

"Do not worry," Dean eased her fears. "We are going to go get her, I just need to catch my breath."

"Thero was such a nice mage for so long. I considered him a fine employer, worthy of respect. He knew her floor limit and, somehow, he knew she was going into the combat zone." She shook her head bitterly. "He followed her in."

I should have never told her of my debts," Anoka said.

"While we rest, tell me about your problems because I need to understand them before I can help," Dean said clearly.

A sudden wind whipped her long black hair and flared her left reddish black wing. She tucked them in tight and grimaced from the pain.

"When Kambry was locked up the first time, I thought it wasn't such a big deal—the young being reckless. When I started to convert everything I owned to release her, however, I found myself woefully short of twenty five tokens. I went back over the beginning levels until I was so tired of it, I almost quit. I borrowed—"

"Hold up," Quincy said, butting in, "sorry, but how does acquiring tokens work?"

"Trade is the easiest. If not that way, then you go into one of six portals. You start at level one and work your way up through increasing levels of difficulty. You can do solo, no combat, or combat, but don't let the name fool you, there is always a foe to keep you from completing the maze."

Quincy frowned, trying to keep up.

"The difference between combat and no combat, is that other competitors can try to end you or get to the reward first. Solo non-combat pays out one Token per level. Combat, on the other hand, pays five tokens per level of the competition, one per level if you go in with a party, or three tokens per level you luck out and there is no competition."

"Are all competitions against Core species, then?" Dean asked.

"No, it may be Core or Suca that you compete against. In competition mode, it's more about Min reaping souls to increase her power, than letting one side get an advantage over the other."

Quincy grunted at this and asked, "So, a level three solo is worth three tokens?" Anoka nodded. "And if you run it a second time, is that another three?"

"I wish it were that simple," Anoka said with a sigh. "The same reward is only given every factor of eight. So, though you get three tokens the first time you beat a level three solo, you don't get another three tokens until the eighth time you conquer that level three solo. You get three more tokens the sixty-fourth time. And yes, not until your 512th victory will you get another three. I never went beyond that. Though low, there is always a risk that a level three trash mob may kill me if I have terrible luck and slip on a leaf or something. Besides," she snorted, "Eight times 512 is a really big number."

Dean offered to pick her up again, and she nodded. He princess carried her again.

"Thank you for explaining that to us." He grinned, "I look forward to learning much more and competing."

She raised the eyebrow of her one working eye and said, "Why're you lying to me... Unless... You don't know do you?"

"Know what?" Dean asked, confused by her question.

"How did you get that locket? You have no idea how the great Game of the Gods works—at least not for a planet in trouble," Anoka deduced.

"I was told to discuss it later," Dean admitted, bouncing her with a shrug, "by Sable no less."

She grumbled but held her tongue.

They reached a building that reminded Dean of an overpriced university, one determined to awe you with its lavish displays of wealth. The patterned red bricks and black marble broke up an otherwise overly bright building, which flashed gaudy gold trim everywhere you looked.

The main section was nearly half a kilometer in length, and nearly half that as wide. Further on, there was a second section, capped with a large dome, attached to the first. To say the building was expansive was a gross understatement.

Even the massive, deluxe WalKays on Oakley paled in comparison. At the entrance stood statues of a male and female version of Min, though little bigger than Dean.

A set of Minotaurs trooped past him as they patrolled the fence surrounding the Vaults of Min. There were more guards even closer to the building and these Minotaurs made Dean look and feel like he had skipped too many sessions in the gym, especially arm day. He saw a few more Minotaurs by the front entrance, checking for lockets. There must be hundreds of them guarding the building.

They entered a queue and when Dean finally made it up to the front of the line, he flashed his necklace.

"Halt," the guard said, without the slightest hint of allowance for any backtalk, "you are only allowed to bring one other with you inside."

Quincy pointed to a waiting area, where some very cute bunny girls sat and chatted.

"Stay close," Dean smirked.

"Uh, mate," Quincy replied, "I'll try, but if they go hopping off, no promises..."

"Yeah, yeah... just be here when I'm done," Dean said with a chuckle.

Dean carried Anoka beyond the brutes, down the long walkway, and up the stairs into Min's Vaults of Treasures.

"Fook me," Dean exclaimed the moment he was inside.

He saw a shopping cart to one side and carefully deposited Anoka in it. A guard came to complain—Dean figured it was probably about some rule violation or another—when an unseen hand stopped him. That was enough to let Dean push Anoka around, instead of having to carry her.

No longer encumbered with the muscular dragon woman, he took a moment to absorb the shocking scene before him.

There were isles and isles of gems in the center in clear jewelry displays. These rows of precious stones continued deep into the structure. To his left, there were shorter rows of weapons and a lot of them—every medieval creation a warrior could possibly dream of.

He started towards the left side of the store.

Was it really a store?

Dean grunted at his random thoughts. Here he was, in a vault of the gods, and was getting hung up on semantics.

"Everything in this section can be crafted for much cheaper than you can find it for here. Min's Vault is not the place to get gear. Most folks come here to exchange their tokens for warriors and occasionally for gems—mostly for warriors, though." Anoka winced in pain. "Then you take the warriors you contracted to go back into the labyrinth and earn more tokens... to trade in for more gems or warriors."

She pointed a sword and Dean hefted the weapon awkwardly. "Take this sword, for example." He had no idea how to use a sword and it showed.

The price was 1.118 tokens. Um... alright... sure.

"You'd get something close to a hundred carats, or 200 grams, of sapphires for a single token," Anoka continued, "And—"

"Hold on," Dean interrupted her, "I can get sapphires for cheap. You're saying that I can bring sapphires in bulk into Mixonia and exchange a hundred carats or 200 grams of sapphires for a token?" Dean asked.

"Yes and no. First, there is a difference between trading in Min's vault, versus buying here. A piece of advice," Anoka smirked, "Never, ever trade in here—not if you can help it. The general market is the best place to get the most gems for your tokens, or tokens for your gems."

Dean nodded.

"You'll have daily limits on your imports and Min sets them to something equal for everyone, based primarily on your species market. This is to attempt to make the valuation stable. As to what that is for your kind, your gate guard should know," Anoka said.

"Half-truths indeed," Dean muttered. "So, I can swap raw gems for tokens, though?"

"Yes, but not at a twenty to one rate, either. More like a forty to one rate. The goal is to force competitors into the games, where they risk becoming an energy source, not to use this as a market. Go forth and win," Anoka groused, sarcastically pumping a fist. "Again, trade elsewhere for everything besides statuettes, or really big gem purchases. And find a broker. A healthy, handsome man like you should have no trouble getting a side piece to work for him."

"I've got enough woman troubles," he grunted. "We'll talk about that later, though, because the abundance of females undressing me with their eyes did not escape my attention. I've been tempted by some of what I've seen, too," Dean admitted. "I hear ya about this place, though. Don't plan on shopping here for much of anything —shop at the city market."

"For everything besides statuettes, and collection pieces," Anoka clarified. "Statuettes tied to souls are only sold here, through Min's Vault of Treasures, directly."

"Why didn't you say that at the start?" he snorted.

"Well, would it have had the same effect as it does after my explanations?" Anoka quipped.

Dean kept his mouth shut. She had a point. Somethings were best learned on their own.

"I'm not insanely wealthy. Humans value diamonds more than rubies or sapphires and we dig them out of the ground, easily. I'm guessing I'll be fairly limited in what I can import. If I don't rush it, though, I should be able to shift a decent amount of wealth into here. Remind me to check the scoreboard when we—"

"Turn right there," Anoka instructed, pointing to a blank chalkboard next to a ruby gem case. "Ask for your planet with primary species governing. If it's a coalition, say the governing coalition's name."

"Human planet Oakley." The board scribbled a score. *Core Lead - 37.*

"When it gets to a hundred there will be another battle for a disaster," Dean whispered just loud enough for her to hear.

"Fairly safe to speak in here. Min is the god of secrets," she smirked. "It's kinda what the Minotaur species are known for. Now," she continued, "ask to see your champion card. This is called many things. You can even touch the board while thinking of it, and the board will retrieve it for you."

"Champion card," Dean repeated with a shrug.

Champion Information
Name: Dean Forrester Gender: Male
Level: 0 Tokens: 100
Race: Human Alignment: Suca - Mixonia
Luck: 14 Charisma: 41

Health: 346 / 346 H-Regen: 1.0 / Sec
Stamina: 296 / 296 M-Regen: 1.0 / Sec
Mana: 322 / 322 S-Regen: 1.0 / Sec

Strength: 214 Vitality: 132
Dexterity: 107 Endurance: 189
Intelligence: 94 Willpower: 218
Magic: Electrical

"Am I in a video game?" Dean asked in confusion.

"What?" Anoka chuckled. "No, we don't have those here—but on my home planet, we do. This is the Game of the Gods. It is all extremely real, with terrible consequences. Do you have a way of remembering this information so we can go over it later?" Anoka asked and Dean shrugged.

His phone was in his spacesuit. He tried to memorize it but failed. Anoka muttered something about men never being prepared and pulled a pen out of her sling. She wrote the details on the cloth, before the pen disappeared once again.

"I promise to cover this in more detail, later, when were not inside here and I'm healed," Anoka explained, motioning for Dean to proceed.

"Anoka. Before we go over to that wall and find Kambry. What items are worth checking out in here? I mean, besides statuettes. There have to be some exceptions," Dean noted.

"Statuettes mainly," she shook her head. "I went over this already, and while I understand your being cautious, you're getting a bit tedious. Besides soul statuettes, collection items—like legendary weapons, big gems, or armor—are the only thing worth buying here. There is much to go over and no need for me to saturate you in one sitting. If you're not hurting for funds inside or outside of Mixonia, at the moment, then ignore everything here besides Kambry."

"I'll train you and then you adjust based on what you learn that you need. No sense buying a fancy sword when you use a mace. Or buying a pet parrot when you really want a mount. I'll need some gems to buy training supplies as I sold all mine. And Dean?"

"Ya Anoka."

"Don't trust anyone. Get a contract. I'd not do that to you. I'm not that kind of warrior. So, let's go ahead and settle up, since I can put in my contract that it's contingent on you freeing Kambry. You'll have to work out your own contract with her.

"Min binds the words we weave and then we can trust each other to fully fulfill our end or face a collected soul. So careful about what you promise too. Last thing you need is failing to meet obligations and you end up here in the vault on that wall," Anoka said, pointing to a far section of Min's Vault.

"Okay. I want you to go back to my home world and train me until we both *feel* I'm ready. When you're not training me, you'll help maintain my estate during off hours, within reason. You'll be given proper free time to maintain yourself and your needs, and you'll be paid at your going rate for any training you provide me the same as you would have received here," Dean said, feeling confident that was fair.

"I agree to those terms on the condition you strike a deal with Kambry to return her to the living," Anoka said.

"I agree, do we sign –"

Anoka grunted an, "I agree."

A woman with Minotaur horns, who was actually kind of cute, spawned beside them. Dean realized she was probably half human or maybe half Elf, and other half

Minotaur. Except her dominant traits were surely from the human or elf side—if there were Elves in the Universe, though Dean figured there had to be, because Zued had looked part Elf himself.

"Can I help you?" Dean asked.

"Thumb here," the Minotaur babe in the short skirt and cropped top said. She held out a chalkboard with the terms of their contract on it out to him.

"I forgot to include a time frame," Dean noted, and turned to Anoka. "What are you comfortable with?"

"Until 'you're ready' could mean forever, and I understand and accept that. You have to feel the same way, though, for the contract to be binding. If I die of old age in a distant world as your trainer, then I've done what was necessary to free my little girl," Anoka said, almost causing Dean to tear up.

He pressed his thumb to the tablet, as did Anoka.

"Go easy on him Anoka, this one's cute," the contract confirmer said with a wink.

"You're fairly easy on the eyes yourself," Dean said and eyes around him widened in shock. "What's your name?"

Gasps this time.

A male guard approached Dean with stomping footsteps. "Still your slanderous tongue, you pathetic human. That half breed abomination is—"

"Can we like, duel or something?" Dean asked with a shrug.

Sure, the Minotaur had reach on him, but Dean didn't care. He tended to pick fights with assholes every chance he got.

The Minotaur spat at Dean, the large green mass of phlegm splatting right onto his chest. Dean raced to close the distance between them, his fist cocked back to land a blow. That would normally make him the aggressor, in accordance with human law, but he wasn't where human laws applied, though. His body froze mid-stride when a ten-foot tall version of Min suddenly stood between him and the Minotaur guard.

"Explain yourself," Min demanded of Dean.

He relaxed, fists loose at his sides. "I was telling this lovely lady, that she was... well, lovely. I'm not looking for another mate, just stating the obvious. She is very attractive. This big guy came over in a huff and called her an abomination. I then challenged him, and he spat on me. When I went to crush his skull you—"

The male vanished. Just like that... poof! Same with the ugly snot stain on his toga.

"Can I get my twenty tokens?" Dean asked.

There was a deathly silence.

"This is a sacred place. You're on notice. Never speak to me, unless I speak to you first, ever again. I may only be an arbitrator, but I still can make your life heaven or hell," Min ground out. She gestured to the young hybrid woman, who stood there in shock. "Carry on with your conversation. The others have been put on notice."

"Thank you, Min," Dean saw with a bow.

A pink burst of magic shot from Min into Anoka. She instantly went from battered to healed and fell on her ass when the cart vanished out from underneath her.

Dean watched as Min vanished and, as instructed, carried on.

"I'm Dean," he smiled. "Your name?"

"Dean, you play with fire. I'm Lexis. Can I help you with something?" Lexis asked with a curious glare. Or was that longing?

"I need some gems that will sell well on a human world. Rare diamonds should work. I need to spend less than seventy-five tokens," Dean said, and wondered why Lexis fidgeted so.

"You're being rude," Anoka butted in, removing both her sling and splint, before setting them in a nearby cart. "Thank you for getting me healed, that beating sucked."

Dean shrugged. He had intended to have a doctor heal her, back on Oakley.

Dean said, "I need some gems. Why is asking this pretty woman with kind eyes and a friendly smile for help rude?"

"Because she is an outcast demi. One of the first, and longest stuck in purgatory," Anoka said. "You not only drain her of energy by keeping her here, but by throwing around such a large number of tokens, you unnecessarily raise her hopes for freedom."

"Freedom shouldn't have to be hoped for," Dean snorted. "This system is so fooking broken. Sable only danced around the plight of demis."

Anoka rolled her eyes.

"My apologies for not being better informed," he turned back to Lexis, "would you care to elaborate, though?"

Dean watched her head turn briefly as she conversed with an invisible being.

After a few nods, Lexis focused once again on Dean.

"I'll never become a full god," she admitted, "due to my half Mino, half Suca roots. My freedom will likely never be purchased, leaving me eternally in purgatory, because I'm hideous to all. A demi has no purpose in Mixonia or Wixomia, other than to carry out the will of their parents. A Demi's freedom is a vanity purchase, of little utility to a perspective champion."

"Sable would be an exception as she is a warrior demi and could train you. She also will likely be a full god, one day. She improves in the trials often enough to legitimately aspire to godhood. I, on the other hand, am regulated to cleaning up after the gods in heaven, for lack of a better term."

Dean listened intently and started to understand. Half gods were downtrodden, both by the rules and by their parents. He hated this place. Though, to be fair, he'd been told repeatedly that it was vile and merciless.

"Thank you for sharing that information, Lexis. I find your candor as welcoming as your smile," Dean said laying it on thick. He could be a fool at times, but he'd figured out whose daughter this was, and saw no harm in being as charming as he could.

Lexis beamed happily at him before spinning around. "This way, please."

"I take it a Demi's freedom is expensive?" Dean asked once Lexis had moved ahead of them a few steps.

"Thirty tokens." Anoka winced. "I've been in Mixonia for a very, very long time. Only a handful of demis have escaped purgatory by the grace of a champion's good nature or their foolishness."

"Do the gods have real children—" he started to ask.

Both women spun quickly and shushed him. Under their watchful glares, he kept his mouth shut and followed behind the duo. Lexis led them by gems he'd never seen before with dazzling colors.

They passed sparkling rubies that shimmered intensely. Then moved through a row of diamonds, of all sizes, some in truly massive carat sizes, with similarly large prices to go with them.

When they reached a case that gleamed with pink, Lexis slid her hand through what looked like a plate of glass but must have been a magical barrier, to clutch a massive pink diamond. Dean focused more on how her hand passed through the glass and less on the gem.

"Neat trick," he smiled. His eyes focused on the gem.

"Dean this gem is seventy-five tokens and will fetch a lot of Galactic coins. I'm showing no reference on Oakley. If I use Earth's data points, this will auction for upwards of twelve million G-coins," Lexis handed Dean the gem.

"I love it, would make a perfect gift. You'd recommend this?" Dean asked.

She fidgeted and batted her eyelashes. Dean knew what was coming. Lexis reached into the same display and pulled out a slightly smaller gem.

"This slightly smaller gem is only forty-five tokens and should go for around ten million," Lexis said shyly.

Dean handed the bigger gem back. When it was tucked away, he said, "Put that one back to, at least for now." He paused for a moment, pressing his palms to his eyes. It was a bit of a gamble, but somehow, he knew he was right—and it was the right thing to do.

"If I free you," he asked, "how does it work? Contracted as a demi, or are you just a mortal suddenly?"

"Both and I am banished from Mixonia and Wixomia," Lexis said and then angrily shushed an invisible being beside her.

"Would you be interested in helping run a hotel and raising snot dripping babies filled with infinite questions about why everything is the way it is? You'd be a maid and nanny, accepted as an equal member of society, but still an employee," Dean asked, seeing a win-win here; including a hot-nanny dream coming to fruition.

Anoka tugged on his arm.

He spun on her. "Do not do that again, Anoka! Consider that your one and only warning. I have a firm grasp of the situation, even if you feel I don't."

"Yes, master," Anoka said and curtsied.

"Will I have to call you master?" Lexis asked worriedly.

Dean frowned. "Uh, no. She doesn't even need to. She's just worried about her daughter, Kambry, and about me too, I guess. Her heart is in the right place, though," Dean said with a shrug. "So, a lifetime of caring for babies, cleaning, and living in a nice home full of loving people, surrounded by a dangerous desert. You'd be just like everyone else, I think, if I understood the transformation rules—a full human."

"Please don't tease me, I'd do –"

"I, Dean Forrester," he stated loudly, "offer thirty tokens to free Lexis, the demigod, from purgatory. In exchange, she will be a sworn caretaker of my estate, and will do everything in her power to help my family prosper. Upon my demise, which she can't aid or cause, she will have free will and may do as she pleases," Dean finished, waiting for it.

Min appeared, female this time, and it looked as if she'd started crying. Lexis suddenly vanished. Dean hadn't seen that part coming.

"Yes," the Minotaur goddess clarified, "she accepted the moment you started talking. Press your thumb here to sign the contract, she'll be waiting for you in the guard's cave on Oakley. Tell no one of what you've done. Ever. Not even Sable or

Zued. I even erased her memory," Min said pointing to Anoka. "Lexis is just a nanny you hired to help you run your estate."

He nodded and pressed his thumb to the contract.

"Your contract with Lexis was finalized for a single token, after the purchase of this gem."

Min picked up the larger of the two gems.

"This gem cost you seventy-four tokens, so Lexis and the gem both for 75 tokens. Cross me, though, and you'll burn a horrible death, understood? I can't help you or aid you in the games. I'm truly powerless to assist you, other than to ensure your compliance with the rules, inside those portals. Mixonia is different, though. Just know that I can ruin Oakley, as well as all of humanity, with a slip of my hand... Or help them, as you'll learn. Tread extra carefully Dean Forrester and be good to my little girl."

He nodded, solemnly.

"And Dean," the minotaur goddess said, "Thank you."

There was a poof, and suddenly Dean had the massive pink gem in his hand. He found he was standing back by where he had first met Lexis.

Anoka stifled a short laugh. "I'd have taken no pay and no time off. But I appreciate you giving me such a fair deal."

"What?" Dean asked, confused.

Anoka patted her repaired body and gave an *'ah'* in recognizing what happened.

"You just signed a contract to help me free my daughter. Oh, you're holding a gem. Those transactions are normally private from other parties. I've been frozen, I guess, while you did the deal. Thank you for making my healing part of your deal. I was in a tremendous amount of pain."

Dean grunted a "You're welcome."

"I like that diamond," Anoka said pointing to the pink rock. "Put it in your locket for now, though. Did you get anything else?"

"A maid for a token. A lifetime contract to help with babies and cleaning," Dean said nonchalantly.

"Score, that should help. You ready for the big moment? When you first meet Kambry, you'll need to bend her to your will."

"Speaking of that," Dean asked, "what do I hook her into?" He scratched at the back of his neck. He needed Anoka, not a wild young woman. He hadn't the vaguest idea how to handle her. "Where to?"

Anoka pointed to one section of the back wall and Dean walked to where she indicated.

"Dean, what I'm about to tell you almost needs its own contract of secrecy, except I've nothing left to bind you to it," Anoka sighed, and Dean frowned.

"I'll keep my word, as long as it's fair to do so," Dean grumbled. There was more than a little irony in his next statement. "Not big on secrets, personally."

"I understand and well..." She took a deep breath but pushed ahead. "Kambry can be an idiotic hot head. She is doomed to spend eternity in a semi-conscious state of torment unless you or someone like you saves her. Every time Thero sends a minion to negotiate for her contract, she is forced to recall her mistakes, along with how much time has passed since she made them. Thero will not age and he will not tire. Eventually, if you were not here to save her, he would wear her down."

Anoka paused and looked to make sure no one could overhear their conversation.

Dean's brows pulled down. This next bit was important, though he wasn't quite sure yet how.

Anoka took another deep breath. "It's best just to rip the scab off," she muttered. "My daughter is... not really my actual daughter. She is the daughter of a fallen queen—a princess of our race, hidden here under my protection. Even Thero doesn't know this. I only tell you this, so you have a full grasp of the situation, not to lead you into thinking she has a throne to return to or some hidden wealth to exploit. None of exists, not anymore; the throne is far beyond retaking."

"Why tell me this now?" he asked.

"While Kambry's beauty is divine, her attitude is entitled and reckless." She shook her head. "You need to make her your bitch."

His head snapped up, shocked.

"You have to understand there is some language auto translation happening here," Anoka frowned, "so if I sound crazy, please reinterpret the words you hear. You gave me my freedom to do whatever I wish outside of work hours, without your explicit approval. Whatever you do, don't give her that. You can always alter your agreement as a reward for good behavior, later. Force her to agree not to go into any floors without your approval. Make her get approval for everything beyond going to the toilet."

Damn, that was harsh.

"Force her to work, constantly, even when she has free time. We require six hours of sleep, normally. Otherwise, she should be working. Don't break her completely, but she must be humbled. Make her live humbly while paying for her mistakes. Do you have a mistress for your home?"

Dean frowned, winced, and groaned at what she wanted him to do to her own daughter. "How old is she?"

"A few years over twenty, but don't tell her I told you that. She likes to hide her true age, because she knows what she is—a fallen princess, who powerful foes would kill without hesitation. As sad as it makes me to say this, she is more of a liability than an asset. But I love her."

"Great. I had to get stuck with a dragon princess," he groaned, "just my fooking luck. And yes, there is a mistress of the estate—Cassandra."

"Dragona is our species' name. Left here," Anoka said, pointing them toward a doorway nearby.

Dean led them into a new section of Min's Vault and his jaw dropped. Millions upon millions of four-inch statuettes were stacked neatly on seemingly infinite rows of shelves. There were signs between the rows, indicating each species. Man, oh man, were there a lot of trapped Suca souls. She guided him to the 'D' section.

"Okay, she is not far. Remember, she is in a really bad spot, so really twist her titties on this deal. That sounded..." Anoka grimaced, "really, really weird." She pinched the bridge of her nose. "Make her pay for her mistake and be firm. You can always go soft later. She is a Dragona princess. The odds of you taking away any of her freedoms, outside of this moment, are zero. Trust me, I'd know, I'm her mother. Make her obey your mistress, too, or else your house will be a dumpster fire." She groaned. "Dumpster fire? I don't even know what that is... why are human analogies so strange?"

"Got it, be firm, and make her suffer. I'll do my best," Dean promised.

The formerly broken woman gave him a long, stern glare. She ensured Dean understood the gravity of the situation when she simply replied, "Your best likely won't be good enough; do better."

Dean titled his head in confusion when he picked up the four-inch statue of a fierce looking Dragona woman holding a staff and a medium sized sword. He pressed his thumb to the button at the base of the statuette, and it synced to his locket, first ensuring he had enough tokens to negotiate.

There was a blinding light and then blackness.

"Am I in a video game?" Dean asked in confusion.

"What?" Anoka chuckled. "No, we don't have those here—but on my home planet, we do. This is the Game of the Gods. It is all extremely real, with terrible consequences. Do you have a way of remembering this information so we can go over it later?" Anoka asked and Dean shrugged.

His phone was in his spacesuit. He tried to memorize it but failed. Anoka muttered something about men never being prepared and pulled a pen out of her sling. She wrote the details on the cloth, before the pen disappeared once again.

"I promise to cover this in more detail, later, when were not inside here and I'm healed," Anoka explained, motioning for Dean to proceed.

"Anoka. Before we go over to that wall and find Kambry. What items are worth checking out in here? I mean, besides statuettes. There have to be some exceptions," Dean noted.

"Statuettes mainly," she shook her head. "I went over this already, and while I understand your being cautious, you're getting a bit tedious. Besides soul statuettes, collection items—like legendary weapons, big gems, or armor—are the only thing worth buying here. There is much to go over and no need for me to saturate you in one sitting. If you're not hurting for funds inside or outside of Mixonia, at the moment, then ignore everything here besides Kambry."

"I'll train you and then you adjust based on what you learn that you need. No sense buying a fancy sword when you use a mace. Or buying a pet parrot when you really want a mount. I'll need some gems to buy training supplies as I sold all mine. And Dean?"

"Ya Anoka."

"Don't trust anyone. Get a contract. I'd not do that to you. I'm not that kind of warrior. So, let's go ahead and settle up, since I can put in my contract that it's contingent on you freeing Kambry. You'll have to work out your own contract with her.

"Min binds the words we weave and then we can trust each other to fully fulfill our end or face a collected soul. So careful about what you promise too. Last thing you need is failing to meet obligations and you end up here in the vault on that wall," Anoka said, pointing to a far section of Min's Vault.

"Okay. I want you to go back to my home world and train me until we both *feel* I'm ready. When you're not training me, you'll help maintain my estate during off hours, within reason. You'll be given proper free time to maintain yourself and your needs, and you'll be paid at your going rate for any training you provide me the same as you would have received here," Dean said, feeling confident that was fair.

"I agree to those terms on the condition you strike a deal with Kambry to return her to the living," Anoka said.

"I agree, do we sign –"

Anoka grunted an, "I agree."

A woman with Minotaur horns, who was actually kind of cute, spawned beside them. Dean realized she was probably half human or maybe half Elf, and other half

Minotaur. Except her dominant traits were surely from the human or elf side—if there were Elves in the Universe, though Dean figured there had to be, because Zued had looked part Elf himself.

"Can I help you?" Dean asked.

"Thumb here," the Minotaur babe in the short skirt and cropped top said. She held out a chalkboard with the terms of their contract on it out to him.

"I forgot to include a time frame," Dean noted, and turned to Anoka. "What are you comfortable with?"

"Until 'you're ready' could mean forever, and I understand and accept that. You have to feel the same way, though, for the contract to be binding. If I die of old age in a distant world as your trainer, then I've done what was necessary to free my little girl," Anoka said, almost causing Dean to tear up.

He pressed his thumb to the tablet, as did Anoka.

"Go easy on him Anoka, this one's cute," the contract confirmer said with a wink.

"You're fairly easy on the eyes yourself," Dean said and eyes around him widened in shock. "What's your name?"

Gasps this time.

A male guard approached Dean with stomping footsteps. "Still your slanderous tongue, you pathetic human. That half breed abomination is—"

"Can we like, duel or something?" Dean asked with a shrug.

Sure, the Minotaur had reach on him, but Dean didn't care. He tended to pick fights with assholes every chance he got.

The Minotaur spat at Dean, the large green mass of phlegm splatting right onto his chest. Dean raced to close the distance between them, his fist cocked back to land a blow. That would normally make him the aggressor, in accordance with human law, but he wasn't where human laws applied, though. His body froze mid-stride when a ten-foot tall version of Min suddenly stood between him and the Minotaur guard.

"Explain yourself," Min demanded of Dean.

He relaxed, fists loose at his sides. "I was telling this lovely lady, that she was... well, lovely. I'm not looking for another mate, just stating the obvious. She is very attractive. This big guy came over in a huff and called her an abomination. I then challenged him, and he spat on me. When I went to crush his skull you—"

The male vanished. Just like that... poof! Same with the ugly snot stain on his toga.

"Can I get my twenty tokens?" Dean asked.

There was a deathly silence.

"This is a sacred place. You're on notice. Never speak to me, unless I speak to you first, ever again. I may only be an arbitrator, but I still can make your life heaven or hell," Min ground out. She gestured to the young hybrid woman, who stood there in shock. "Carry on with your conversation. The others have been put on notice."

"Thank you, Min," Dean saw with a bow.

A pink burst of magic shot from Min into Anoka. She instantly went from battered to healed and fell on her ass when the cart vanished out from underneath her.

Dean watched as Min vanished and, as instructed, carried on.

"I'm Dean," he smiled. "Your name?"

"Dean, you play with fire. I'm Lexis. Can I help you with something?" Lexis asked with a curious glare. Or was that longing?

"I need some gems that will sell well on a human world. Rare diamonds should work. I need to spend less than seventy-five tokens," Dean said, and wondered why Lexis fidgeted so.

"You're being rude," Anoka butted in, removing both her sling and splint, before setting them in a nearby cart. "Thank you for getting me healed, that beating sucked."

Dean shrugged. He had intended to have a doctor heal her, back on Oakley.

Dean said, "I need some gems. Why is asking this pretty woman with kind eyes and a friendly smile for help rude?"

"Because she is an outcast demi. One of the first, and longest stuck in purgatory," Anoka said. "You not only drain her of energy by keeping her here, but by throwing around such a large number of tokens, you unnecessarily raise her hopes for freedom."

"Freedom shouldn't have to be hoped for," Dean snorted. "This system is so fooking broken. Sable only danced around the plight of demis."

Anoka rolled her eyes.

"My apologies for not being better informed," he turned back to Lexis, "would you care to elaborate, though?"

Dean watched her head turn briefly as she conversed with an invisible being.

After a few nods, Lexis focused once again on Dean.

"I'll never become a full god," she admitted, "due to my half Mino, half Suca roots. My freedom will likely never be purchased, leaving me eternally in purgatory, because I'm hideous to all. A demi has no purpose in Mixonia or Wixomia, other

169

than to carry out the will of their parents. A Demi's freedom is a vanity purchase, of little utility to a perspective champion."

"Sable would be an exception as she is a warrior demi and could train you. She also will likely be a full god, one day. She improves in the trials often enough to legitimately aspire to godhood. I, on the other hand, am regulated to cleaning up after the gods in heaven, for lack of a better term."

Dean listened intently and started to understand. Half gods were downtrodden, both by the rules and by their parents. He hated this place. Though, to be fair, he'd been told repeatedly that it was vile and merciless.

"Thank you for sharing that information, Lexis. I find your candor as welcoming as your smile," Dean said laying it on thick. He could be a fool at times, but he'd figured out whose daughter this was, and saw no harm in being as charming as he could.

Lexis beamed happily at him before spinning around. "This way, please."

"I take it a Demi's freedom is expensive?" Dean asked once Lexis had moved ahead of them a few steps.

"Thirty tokens." Anoka winced. "I've been in Mixonia for a very, very long time. Only a handful of demis have escaped purgatory by the grace of a champion's good nature or their foolishness."

"Do the gods have real children—" he started to ask.

Both women spun quickly and shushed him. Under their watchful glares, he kept his mouth shut and followed behind the duo. Lexis led them by gems he'd never seen before with dazzling colors.

They passed sparkling rubies that shimmered intensely. Then moved through a row of diamonds, of all sizes, some in truly massive carat sizes, with similarly large prices to go with them.

When they reached a case that gleamed with pink, Lexis slid her hand through what looked like a plate of glass but must have been a magical barrier, to clutch a massive pink diamond. Dean focused more on how her hand passed through the glass and less on the gem.

"Neat trick," he smiled. His eyes focused on the gem.

"Dean this gem is seventy-five tokens and will fetch a lot of Galactic coins. I'm showing no reference on Oakley. If I use Earth's data points, this will auction for upwards of twelve million G-coins," Lexis handed Dean the gem.

"I love it, would make a perfect gift. You'd recommend this?" Dean asked.

She fidgeted and batted her eyelashes. Dean knew what was coming. Lexis reached into the same display and pulled out a slightly smaller gem.

"This slightly smaller gem is only forty-five tokens and should go for around ten million," Lexis said shyly.

Dean handed the bigger gem back. When it was tucked away, he said, "Put that one back to, at least for now." He paused for a moment, pressing his palms to his eyes. It was a bit of a gamble, but somehow, he knew he was right—and it was the right thing to do.

"If I free you," he asked, "how does it work? Contracted as a demi, or are you just a mortal suddenly?"

"Both and I am banished from Mixonia and Wixomia," Lexis said and then angrily shushed an invisible being beside her.

"Would you be interested in helping run a hotel and raising snot dripping babies filled with infinite questions about why everything is the way it is? You'd be a maid and nanny, accepted as an equal member of society, but still an employee," Dean asked, seeing a win-win here; including a hot-nanny dream coming to fruition.

Anoka tugged on his arm.

He spun on her. "Do not do that again, Anoka! Consider that your one and only warning. I have a firm grasp of the situation, even if you feel I don't."

"Yes, master," Anoka said and curtsied.

"Will I have to call you master?" Lexis asked worriedly.

Dean frowned. "Uh, no. She doesn't even need to. She's just worried about her daughter, Kambry, and about me too, I guess. Her heart is in the right place, though," Dean said with a shrug. "So, a lifetime of caring for babies, cleaning, and living in a nice home full of loving people, surrounded by a dangerous desert. You'd be just like everyone else, I think, if I understood the transformation rules—a full human."

"Please don't tease me, I'd do —"

"I, Dean Forrester," he stated loudly, "offer thirty tokens to free Lexis, the demigod, from purgatory. In exchange, she will be a sworn caretaker of my estate, and will do everything in her power to help my family prosper. Upon my demise, which she can't aid or cause, she will have free will and may do as she pleases," Dean finished, waiting for it.

Min appeared, female this time, and it looked as if she'd started crying. Lexis suddenly vanished. Dean hadn't seen that part coming.

"Yes," the Minotaur goddess clarified, "she accepted the moment you started talking. Press your thumb here to sign the contract, she'll be waiting for you in the guard's cave on Oakley. Tell no one of what you've done. Ever. Not even Sable or

Zued. I even erased her memory," Min said pointing to Anoka. "Lexis is just a nanny you hired to help you run your estate."

He nodded and pressed his thumb to the contract.

"Your contract with Lexis was finalized for a single token, after the purchase of this gem."

Min picked up the larger of the two gems.

"This gem cost you seventy-four tokens, so Lexis and the gem both for 75 tokens. Cross me, though, and you'll burn a horrible death, understood? I can't help you or aid you in the games. I'm truly powerless to assist you, other than to ensure your compliance with the rules, inside those portals. Mixonia is different, though. Just know that I can ruin Oakley, as well as all of humanity, with a slip of my hand... Or help them, as you'll learn. Tread extra carefully Dean Forrester and be good to my little girl."

He nodded, solemnly.

"And Dean," the minotaur goddess said, "Thank you."

There was a poof, and suddenly Dean had the massive pink gem in his hand. He found he was standing back by where he had first met Lexis.

Anoka stifled a short laugh. "I'd have taken no pay and no time off. But I appreciate you giving me such a fair deal."

"What?" Dean asked, confused.

Anoka patted her repaired body and gave an *'ah'* in recognizing what happened.

"You just signed a contract to help me free my daughter. Oh, you're holding a gem. Those transactions are normally private from other parties. I've been frozen, I guess, while you did the deal. Thank you for making my healing part of your deal. I was in a tremendous amount of pain."

Dean grunted a "You're welcome."

"I like that diamond," Anoka said pointing to the pink rock. "Put it in your locket for now, though. Did you get anything else?"

"A maid for a token. A lifetime contract to help with babies and cleaning," Dean said nonchalantly.

"Score, that should help. You ready for the big moment? When you first meet Kambry, you'll need to bend her to your will."

"Speaking of that," Dean asked, "what do I hook her into?" He scratched at the back of his neck. He needed Anoka, not a wild young woman. He hadn't the vaguest idea how to handle her. "Where to?"

Anoka pointed to one section of the back wall and Dean walked to where she indicated.

"Dean, what I'm about to tell you almost needs its own contract of secrecy, except I've nothing left to bind you to it," Anoka sighed, and Dean frowned.

"I'll keep my word, as long as it's fair to do so," Dean grumbled. There was more than a little irony in his next statement. "Not big on secrets, personally."

"I understand and well..." She took a deep breath but pushed ahead. "Kambry can be an idiotic hot head. She is doomed to spend eternity in a semi-conscious state of torment unless you or someone like you saves her. Every time Thero sends a minion to negotiate for her contract, she is forced to recall her mistakes, along with how much time has passed since she made them. Thero will not age and he will not tire. Eventually, if you were not here to save her, he would wear her down."

Anoka paused and looked to make sure no one could overhear their conversation.

Dean's brows pulled down. This next bit was important, though he wasn't quite sure yet how.

Anoka took another deep breath. "It's best just to rip the scab off," she muttered. "My daughter is... not really my actual daughter. She is the daughter of a fallen queen—a princess of our race, hidden here under my protection. Even Thero doesn't know this. I only tell you this, so you have a full grasp of the situation, not to lead you into thinking she has a throne to return to or some hidden wealth to exploit. None of exists, not anymore; the throne is far beyond retaking."

"Why tell me this now?" he asked.

"While Kambry's beauty is divine, her attitude is entitled and reckless." She shook her head. "You need to make her your bitch."

His head snapped up, shocked.

"You have to understand there is some language auto translation happening here," Anoka frowned, "so if I sound crazy, please reinterpret the words you hear. You gave me my freedom to do whatever I wish outside of work hours, without your explicit approval. Whatever you do, don't give her that. You can always alter your agreement as a reward for good behavior, later. Force her to agree not to go into any floors without your approval. Make her get approval for everything beyond going to the toilet."

Damn, that was harsh.

"Force her to work, constantly, even when she has free time. We require six hours of sleep, normally. Otherwise, she should be working. Don't break her completely, but she must be humbled. Make her live humbly while paying for her mistakes. Do you have a mistress for your home?"

Dean frowned, winced, and groaned at what she wanted him to do to her own daughter. "How old is she?"

"A few years over twenty, but don't tell her I told you that. She likes to hide her true age, because she knows what she is—a fallen princess, who powerful foes would kill without hesitation. As sad as it makes me to say this, she is more of a liability than an asset. But I love her."

"Great. I had to get stuck with a dragon princess," he groaned, "just my fooking luck. And yes, there is a mistress of the estate—Cassandra."

"Dragona is our species' name. Left here," Anoka said, pointing them toward a doorway nearby.

Dean led them into a new section of Min's Vault and his jaw dropped. Millions upon millions of four-inch statuettes were stacked neatly on seemingly infinite rows of shelves. There were signs between the rows, indicating each species. Man, oh man, were there a lot of trapped Suca souls. She guided him to the 'D' section.

"Okay, she is not far. Remember, she is in a really bad spot, so really twist her titties on this deal. That sounded..." Anoka grimaced, "really, really weird." She pinched the bridge of her nose. "Make her pay for her mistake and be firm. You can always go soft later. She is a Dragona princess. The odds of you taking away any of her freedoms, outside of this moment, are zero. Trust me, I'd know, I'm her mother. Make her obey your mistress, too, or else your house will be a dumpster fire." She groaned. "Dumpster fire? I don't even know what that is... why are human analogies so strange?"

"Got it, be firm, and make her suffer. I'll do my best," Dean promised.

The formerly broken woman gave him a long, stern glare. She ensured Dean understood the gravity of the situation when she simply replied, "Your best likely won't be good enough; do better."

Dean titled his head in confusion when he picked up the four-inch statue of a fierce looking Dragona woman holding a staff and a medium sized sword. He pressed his thumb to the button at the base of the statuette, and it synced to his locket, first ensuring he had enough tokens to negotiate.

There was a blinding light and then blackness.

CHAPTER

FIFTEEN

KAMBRY

The Soul Pit

There was no sense of time in the soul pit. Only numbness. When her activation triggered, she was yanked out for a meeting. A passage of understanding washed over her and morphed into a concept of time once again.

Only a few hours since the last visit. A henchman named Innor had said her mother was beaten severely for her yesterday's refusal. Unfortunately, that had become commonplace these last few months. What was uncommon, though, was a second visit in such a short span.

There were timers in place to prevent the torture of those trapped inside the Soul Pit. After all, how could Min power anything, if everyone was pulled into side-bar negotiations every ten minutes?

She was being hailed by a Dean Forrester, a level 0 human who somehow had enough tokens to tempt her with an offer. A most unusual set of circumstances, indeed.

Kambry decided to create a throne room she'd seen in pictures once, to set the appropriate tone for their meeting. It was a huge dwarven construct, populated with a host of brooding dwarves. Kambry occupied a massive stone chair in which she sat regally.

This was certainly a bold strategy. Most trapped souls would hovel, beg, and plead while in something more suiting for their needs. Kambry was not most beings, she was getting harder in her resolve from spurning Thero and his attempts to trap her in a contract as a Kubas breeder.

While Kambry was fine with having children, never with that vile thing. This human, though, was certainly another henchmen to throw her off her game.

He suddenly appeared walking in circles trying to fathom his situation.

The man wore a toga draped over his right shoulder, lost in the abyss of the meeting room. He stood at or near six and a half feet tall, with sandy brown hair and hazel eyes. His muscles bulged as his bare arms were exposed. A specimen of regimen and training. His brawn was surely how he he'd won the tokens to afford her presence.

He must have a strength of at least two hundred.

She saw his eyes roaming the dwarven hall until they zeroed in on Kambry.

"Can I get a mead?" He asked with a charming smile and open arms.

Ah, yes, the mage had sent a handsome man to woo her to Thero's side. "You daft idiot. There is no finery in this place. Your tease is refreshing, though, and your tactics new. At least I'll give you that."

"How should I have known that? Name's Dean. I recently contracted one Anoka, the Dragona trainer of battle. Well, almost. All I need to seal the deal, now, is you," Dean said nonchalantly with a wink that went with a finger gun click.

"It's been done before," she snorted. "I'll not fall for your trickery."

"No trickery," Dean replied in irritation.

"Regardless. I'm moderately content," Kambry said waving him away. She certainly didn't believe him.

"Look, I'm not into being an asshole for no reason. How about I let your mother convince you?" Dean said with a shrug. "How do I send for her in here?"

Kambry laughed, not falling for his trick. "Think no deal and then you'll–"

Dean vanished. She gulped.

Oh no. He'd been the real deal. What had she done? Calm, he had to have been a plant, to rile her up this much.

Back to the numb she went. A blistering sucking sound accompanied the consumption of any energy her soul had accumulated during the brief visit. As her power was siphoned away, she wanted to protest or scream. Instead she cried.

Time melded, melted, and became rigid as she lost contact with it, once again.

A pulling force yanked for her the pit. After understanding of the universe returned, she saw something unexpected, again.

It was her mother and her mother alone. The tokens were hers. At first, she thought hundreds of years had passed. And then she realized it had only been minutes.

She formed the hovel of a home she grew up in with Anoka in her mind. A dirty tiny apartment cascaded into creation with magic. Kambry sat at the two seated rickety table they shared meals on.

Her crying was in racking sobs now. A month of torment from Thero and his goons had torn on her soul for what felt like an eternity. That idiot Dean Forrester had given her mother a fortune in tokens. She was so happy when her mother plopped into the seat across from her.

For the first time since her trapped soul had been pulled out for a meeting, Anoka was unblemished. Seeing Anoka again in her prime, almost made Kambry's heart burst with happiness.

That is, until her mother crashed her hand into the table with an ear-splitting *crack* of power.

"I told you! I warned you! And I raised you better than this," her mother scolded her with barely controlled rage.

Shit! Dean had been the real deal.

Her mother would never show this kind of emotion if around Thero.

"I'm so sorry," Kambry said drying her eyes.

Another *crack* as Anoka's palm slapped the wooden surface. "Silence!"

And there was silence as precious time ticked away. Kambry was starting to understand. Her mind was processing what was happening. Her mother was not here to save her.

"Who is he?" she mumbled.

"By the lucky stars, he's your savior. My savior. Sable tossed us a lifeline. He defeated a challenge against a Core team, all by himself. With zero training," Anoka said sternly.

"A worthy man then," Kambry said. Ashamed that she couldn't even beat two sneaks. "Why'd Sable help us?"

"She knew I tried with Hasper. The Dragona wasn't interested in spending a fortune on a useless sex toy. He was fully trained. Love wasn't worth the thirty tokens. Yet, I tried. Funny thing is, she ignored all my requests for help until I was at my absolute rock bottom. Today was the first day I was ready to jump the edge," Anoka admitted.

"The edge?" Kambry said and slumped at the statement.

"That bad. You've broken my heart. I'm training the man, regardless of whether or not you accept," Anoka said with a grimace.

"But you –"

Crack. Her mother's hand smashed into the table, once again cutting off her words.

"Before I present your contract offer. I'll only say this once so nod if you're ready," Anoka said and Kambry nodded. "If you decline, I promise you we'll not offer once a day like the minimum allows. More like once a month, if that. You can rot here while Thero torments you with his asinine ways. I'm free of his oppression. Are we clear?"

"Crystal," Kambry replied.

"Good. You're in hot water with me. I'm free of you as of this moment. You're an adult. Scolding you or bailing you out is no longer my prerogative anymore. If I'm not there to catch you when you fall, who will be?" her mother asked.

Kambry stared defiantly at her mother. She saw it at that moment. She'd lost her mother's faith and knew her purpose in life had shifted. The saddest part was she not only understood but respected her decision. Kambry knew she'd been rash and immature.

"No one," Kambry grumbled.

"Wrong," her mother informed her, "Dean will be there."

"Pfft. As if some human will protect me, nurture, and care for my stupid... Wait?" Kambry said seeing a smirk crossing her mother's face.

Her wings flared in happiness and Kambry became confused. A slate was pressed across the table. She picked up the tablet and read slowly, methodically, and very intently.

"I'm confused," Kambry muttered catching a number of things in the contract she had not expected.

Anoka scoffed. "Not hard to do. Sign that, and you leave with us to go to his estate, today, to begin your new life on a planet called Oakley."

"This is too much, Mother. It has your crafting all over it. I'd need approval to even go to the market," Kambry said. "Wait... Kubra?"

"Yup," Anoka said with a hard lip smack on the p.

"I'm not ready," Kambry grumbled.

"It's obvious you are not ready. Exactly why we're sneaking that in."

"Mother, are you serious? This says he already has a mate who I must obey, and you want me to... but, if she forces me away, though, I'm free. Oh, you're as sly as a

Kitsune," Kambry said with a smirk that faded back to a frown as she kept reading. "This is a lot, Mother."

Anoka gave her daughter a long, stern glare. "It's less than you deserve and the best you'll get. I actually don't want her to push you away. You've got three months before he has to even try. You need a nice home to transition out of, so I can continue being me."

"Take the offer or stay here. If you accept, work on making the situation with Dean better. He is hungry to fight Kambry, you'll like him. Not that I know that much about him, but he seems to be connected. I blanked out during a trade in the Vaults," her mother said and Kambry's jaw dropped.

"Min! The Demi's could handle anything less than a major deal. There are about a hundred of them, but if you're missing... and Sable too. I'm assuming he isn't poor?" Kambry asked.

"He flipped the rest of his tokens into a massive gem and I think he intends to play the daily swap game while we train," Anoka said.

Kambry fake vomited. "You'd love him simply for making the smart, rational, and safe play. You're just pulling me from one prison into another with this contract," she sneered. "You just want to dote on the Kubas."

Her Mother shrugged guiltily. Kambry stared some more at the tablet, which had already been signed by one Dean Forrester.

It had everything she hated in it. A Master, hard work, a Mistress, no freedoms, and absolutely no control over her own life. Yet, it had Kubas and no Soul Pit. She'd have to become a human.

Kambry was extremely beautiful as a Dragona and had to mask her appearance.

At least as a human she could be a new her. An estate meant there'd be other help. Kambry saw she was expected to treat the other contracted help 'with diligence and professionalism'. Whatever that meant.

The scene around her *crackled*. Her time with her mother was ending. With a groan, she slammed her thumb heavily to the tablet and signed her life away.

CHAPTER
SIXTEEN
DEAN

Planet Oakley

They rode the entire trip back from the Deathly Caverns in silence. Quincy was stunned when Dean had mentioned they'd be bringing three women home with them. He may just have been upset about having to leave his new friends—the bunny girls—who had been very interested in Quincy.

Dean had been ready to leave Mixonia and get home. He had things to manage at home, if he expected to gain any ground on the demons' score, which had started climbing again. He also needed to flip diamonds for rubies and sapphires to acquire some spending gems for the general market. Anoka had emphasized her lack of training gear enough times that Dean finally had to ask her to stop bringing it up.

His first question to Felna, when they got back to her cave, had been how many gems he could bring in with him each visit. It turns out the limit was not on what could be brought in, just what could be sold—a single token's worth in the market, per day, per portal, not per person. So, it was basically fine to bring extra; what he wasn't allowed to sell, would go into the storage when he entered Mixonia and returned when he came back out.

Dean remembered freezing, and Quincy stumbling in shock when they first saw Lexis and Kambry.

Lexis was a plus-sized woman in her early twenties with her bountiful curves hidden under a monk's robe, baggy and humble. Her black hair and brown eyes complimented her features, of Asian descent. The smile on her plump, rosy cheeks was the polar opposite of the woman she sat beside.

Kambry frowned with all the grumpiness she could scrape together, but Dean gave exactly zero shits.

Why? Because Dean was worried. He could explain away Lexis and her mild cuteness. He could explain the four duffle type bags of clothing he had to lug to the bed of the shuttle. There was no confusion with the gear, this was everything Anoka and Kambry owned. And he certainly could talk his way through bringing back a middle-aged woman wearing worn leathers with features scarred from years of training.

Kambry, though, was not something Dean was going to be able to easily explain to Cassandra. She had long wavy black hair, piercing green eyes, and plush lips he already wanted to kiss. Her face was gorgeous, and Dean knew that was only the beginning.

She had long legs like a runner, but tits that belonged on a stripper, with hips that curved out and a waist that tucked in flat. In simpler terms, she was an absolute bombshell. Kambry was also wearing a see-through toga that did nothing to hide her pert, swollen tits or large, puffy nipples. The fact that others could see that she was naked seemed a trivial thing of no consequence to the young woman.

The worst part of it all, was that Dean couldn't come up with a good reason to have saved her, beyond the basic truth—contracting Anoka to help him train. He did have his pink gem to try to soothe things over, though, and Cassandra was a very forgiving and understanding kind of gal.

But when your girlfriend says she's open to threesomes, you don't start out by bringing home someone like Kambry right off the bat. His baby momma was not going to be happy being anything less than the brightest star in Dean's constellation.

He kept his eyes off of her during their flight home by dealing with a host of emails and work offers that demanded his personal attention. There were quite a few, even though Cassandra had screened most of them. Some she'd had let through because she wasn't certain Dean would reject them, depending on how things went in Mixonia.

It was safe to say, though, that Dean would be not working for anyone else, besides the gods, that is. After all he had seen, he now had a clear and driven purpose—to kick some labyrinth ass while saving his planet. He'd first have to expand his headquarters and train, while consolidating his power base.

This was not a sprint for him. He needed to tell himself that, a lot. Over and over, actually, because even if he wanted to dive straight into the lower non-combat or PvE floors, he still needed to train.

Rain *thrummed* down onto the shuttle's metal roof; it was loud and soothing in its constant repetition. Quincy was tired of the quiet as he patted his leg with impatience. His zombie stare at the desert below shifted to Lexis.

"So, Lexis, were you a bunny girl?" Quincy asked.

Lexis wasn't dissuaded by the direct question and replied with a smile, "I was half-elven. That is not the true name, but the magic translates my verbiage to account for how you would classify my species. My mother's background was not known." She frowned, "Sorry, I wish I knew, myself."

Dean checked the forecast and blurted out irritably, "Fook me, it's gonna be straight rain for the next fourteen days."

"It's almost like someone wants you to train indoors," Anoka muttered, looking outside the shuttle.

Lexis rubbed her hands together excitedly and said, "This much rain might change the dangerous nature of Master's estate."

Kambry rolled her eyes at the other woman, "Why're you so happy to change diapers and clean up sex stains?"

Insert problem two. Kambry was allowed to be full of piss and vinegar. You'd think literally saving her from being the Energizer bunny, or freeing her soul from purgatory, would cheer a girl up. Not this one. A hard look from Anoka, though, and she softened.

"I mean, I'm here because my soul was saved from purgatory, for which I am grateful. Thank you, Dean," Kambry nodded to him and Dean smiled. *That was better.* "But why are you here?"

"I was in desperate need of work, and Dean gave me an opportunity I couldn't pass up. I'm excited to start my new life," Lexis admitted with just a bit too much zip.

Everyone besides Dean stared at her with curiosity. Dean bit at his nail, dragging his eyes off Kambry's fine form. He'd sent Cassandra a warning. Kinda. Well, not really.

His message has stated he was 'bringing back three guests to help run the estate'.

Her reply had been 'okay, see you soon'.

Dean figured she'd be busy. There was no doubt in his mind she'd been slammed with stuff because there were a number of massive tarps over what had once been Bob's Tavern. Dean knew he'd need to rename the place, but that was the least of his worries for today. He stuck it at the bottom of a growing 'to-do' list, for later.

Dean gasped when he saw an orbital shuttle behind the tarps. Those were almost always prohibited and if allowed on the surface there were costs beyond even what Cassandra could afford.

That must mean... Mr. Lexso was here. The man oozed money. Dean was no dummy. You didn't get into the only 'Ivy League' school on the planet and get a high paying, cushy, county job without connections.

Dean had yet to meet Cassandra's father, who'd always been absent from events. Suddenly he was far more nervous. The ace in his pocket may be less of an ace and closer to a time bomb.

"You okay?" Quincy asked, noticing that Dean had started hyperventilating. The shuttle descended through a trap entryway. "Fook me," he muttered with a grumble. "Everyone's here. You're so screwed."

"I might have a party trick to woo them with," Dean tried to stay optimistic, with a final chomp on his poor nail before the shuttle finally touched down.

"Do I need to be aggressive?" Anoka said.

Quincy chuckled. "I love her attitude. Need more of her sort around here—not that there's anything wrong with you other ladies—just that Dean here is usually a punch first, ask questions later, kind of guy."

"Pfft," Anoka grunted. "I'm asking for trouble, bringing this wild... Oh wait," her grin grew into a full-blown smirk, "she can't do dumb shit without Dean's express permission."

"How's that work if she breaks the rules?" Dean asked over his shoulder, as he exited the shuttle.

They'd arrived in front of the tavern, unnoticed, as far as he could tell.

Construction crews were hard at work. Apparently, the expensive exterior remodel was getting done, anyway. Dean swore under his breath when he noticed Marty's car here, along with many, many more.

"She breaks the contract and into a timeout, she goes. You can get a partial refund on her, if necessary, for five lost tokens—twenty tokens back. She is forced to stay awake during her punishments, though those should be rather limited. A mind breaks infinitely quicker that way. A three-day timeout costs you nothing, and Kambry everything.

"But if you violate your end of the contract enough times, it will void the contract and free her." Anoka finished with, "that almost never happens though."

"Dean, look," Quincy said excitedly, pointing to a trio of air cars in a much larger parking area than Dean remembered there being there before. "Scotty, Dave, and Lonny are all here. What's going on?"

Dean indeed saw his friends' vehicles. "Whatever it is, we're not in the loop, because I got zero messages. Which either means surprises to trump our surprises, or Cassie was busy. Patti say anything?"

Quincy shook his head. Dean tossed a duffle to Quincy and made for home. The construction noises were loud and annoying. He checked his phone one last time, just in case Cassie had sent him last minute warnings. Nothing.

He noticed it was only a few hours before bedtime. A laser zap lit up the area under the construction tarps that *drummed* from the rain. Someone was busy in the death pit, doing Dean's favorite task. Somehow, he figured shooting laser pistols was not going to be in his training regimen. A random construction worker rushed forward to get the door for the small group.

The doors parted to reveal a barroom stuffed with friends and families. They mostly had turned to greet them.

"Surprise!" Erupted from a gathered crowd.

All Dean's worry faded instantly when he saw his friendly faces. Even Uncle G was here. Champagne bottles popped, confetti pops burst, and congratulations were shouted his way between enthusiastic claps on the back.

He hurriedly set the duffle in his hands to the side to man hug his Uncle. He went to clasp Marty's hand next and exchanged cheek kisses with Orlith. His drinking buddies jumped him on his way to give Cassandra a hug and a warning. He first had to unlock the bar for them, though, in the middle of back pats and big smiles.

Of course, they were thrilled about the free drinks and seemed to ignore the fact that they were losing a drinking buddy and wingman extraordinaire.

Quincy dragged their new recruits over to meet Patti and the Kendricks while Dean nervously sought out Cassandra.

Cassandra stood without her father. She wore a comfy pair of slacks and a flower printed sweater. Lydia, her mother, was in a somewhat fancy, though mostly casual, dress. It screamed of money, unlike most of the other guests' attire, which was either utilitarian or comfortable.

"Thanks, Cassie, this is amazing," Dean nearly had to shout. Fortunately, the speakers masked most of his nervousness. "Hello, Mrs. Lexso," he smiled.

"Lydia, please, Dean," Cassandra's mother said. "I'm going to go mingle, I don't get to get planet side often, or woo college boys."

She was gone, darting for the bar, and surfaced a moment later with a drink in her hand.

Cassandra rolled her eyes and smiled up at him. If he'd expected her to grill him immediately with a ton of questions about the new arrivals, he was wrong.

"We need to go see my Dad," Cassandra said. "He is up in our suite, handling a business call."

"How did baby shopping go?" Dean asked, feeling a heavy weight lift off his shoulders. Suddenly he was a lot less nervous. Business, he could deal with.

He followed behind her as she led them to the elevator and waited patiently as she jammed the up button. Cassandra was about to speak when Lexis ran up to join them. The elevator doors opened and the three stepped in.

"Baby shopping was exhausting. There is a ton of stuff you buy, when you really should just stick your baby in cryo until age four. Against my better judgment, Mom and Patti talked me into most of it. Of course, nothing here matched with the items, so we had to redecorate to match all the baby stuff."

Dean chuckled; glad that he had been busy in Mixonia as the pre-natal hurricane settled around their new home.

"I'm Cassandra," Cassandra suddenly said, extending a hand to Lexis.

Lexis avoided the handshake to curtsy instead. She said, "Mistress Forrester, it's an honor to meet you. I'll be your maid and nanny for the foreseeable future."

"Excellent news. Where is your cell phone so I can give you codes to run an –"

The elevator jolted in place with a slight rattle.

Poof, Zued appeared.

"Welcome to Oakley, Lexis," Zued said, handing Lexis a box. "This is all the proper documents you'll need going forward. Even has an iPhonie46s in there," he grinned at Dean. "I went cheap, because it was Dean's money."

"Thanks for the baby," Cassandra said to the sudden arrival.

Zued's jaw dropped and he replied, "You see that Dean, manners maketh the man. Or the woman in this case. Congrats on your baby, Cassandra, and you on your new home, Lexis. I applaud this move, Dean. Sable? Not so much. But I applaud what was obviously a wise move."

A poof, and he was gone.

"Uh... Can we tell her?" Dean asked Lexis.

"She is the Mistress," Lexis said, staying in the elevator when they exited. "We're going to need to have a very thorough and long conversation about my expectations and job requirements. I'll ease her into my back story, though, and how you saved me, in private. Enjoy your evening, Master, Mistress. I've got some stuff to hand out and I'm mighty hungry."

The door *dinged* closed and they left for the suite.

"Well done, Dean," Cassandra chuckled, "looks like you saved *another* woman and got me a real servant. If my father wasn't beyond that door, I'd let you know just how much I appreciate you," Cassandra pouted.

Dean flipped a U-turn for the other suite.

"Where you going? Ah, I applaud the spontaneity," she laughed, "but that room is occupied."

Dean threw a cross jab at the wall and muttered, "Dammit!" at his failed attempt for a quickie.

"What's your Dad want?" Dean asked, honestly curious.

"The usual things all Dads want. To make sure you understand the gravity of the situation. If you weren't you," she grimaced, "I'd probably be worried."

Dean chuckled as they entered their room and said, "Your confidence is inspiring."

Cassandra tucked her hair back behind her ears and stuck a finger to her mouth to shush Dean. He could hear Mr. Lexso on the phone.

The man was sitting in their living room, of sorts, drinking a soda with the business channel stock ticker flashing across the screen. He was in the kind of power suit only a wealthy businessman could afford. Standing an average five-foot-eleven with a thin build, the early signs of age-reduction enhancement were starting to become noticeable.

Dean realized Cassandra's father must have been much older than Lydia—at least a decade or two. The old adage that wealth makes a man younger had definitely played out here.

Cassandra sat by her father, as Dean went into his closet to get changed. His closet was packed with stuff, none of it his, besides a tiny corner. He jerked a long-sleeved dress shirt off a hanger and found a pair of jeans he could fit into.

Normally he'd simply don a logo'd t-shirt and workout shorts. Not tonight, not for Cassie's big night. Honestly, he was just glad she was happy. The whole ride home, he'd worried she'd be a stressed-out mess.

He released the seals on the power suit and left it standing upright in a corner of the closet; it would be easy enough to move later. He doubted Cassandra would complain. After quickly sliding into his clothes, he secured his cherished loot.

Dean left the bedroom to see Cassandra and Mr. Lexso discussing some company's earnings reports. They smiled, and both stood.

"Father, this is Dean," Cassandra began. "Future husband, I'd like to introduce you to my father, Ravi Lexso."

Both men shot a startled look at Cassandra, who snorted a laugh at their shocked expressions.

"A pleasure to meet you, Sir," Dean said.

"Going to marry my daughter, are you?" Ravi asked, eyebrow raised.

"One day, Sir, yes. Yes, I will."

Ravi growled with a grumble and said, "The hell you will, you can't even provide—"

Dean fished the gem out of his pocket and tossed it to Ravi. The man fumbled it, hand-eye-coordination, obviously, not his forte. The gem fell to the, thankfully, long shag carpet. While Cassandra and her Dad retrieved the massive stone and gaped at the pink diamond, Dean went to the fridge for a soda.

"Dean, where'd you get this?" Ravi asked, confused by the gem he held. His eyes remained laser focused on the pink diamond as he studied it.

"What the hell, Dean?!" Cassandra added, amazed.

"The Vault of a Minotaur god," Dean admitted, and shrugged as casually as possible.

Her father pulled his phone out to use some app on the gem. "It's fooking real. By Odin's stanky armpits it's real. My phone is estimating this gem should sell at auction, at least, for seventeen million Galactic coins," Ravi exclaimed.

"Yup," Dean said, adding extra pucker to the p.

Cassandra walked over and kissed him sweetly on the lips. Her eyes burst with pride. The blues sparkling with a hunger that he couldn't wait to satisfy. She whispered a single word softly in his ear from her tippy toes. "Showoff."

"You know it, wanna kick your dad out and ravage me!" Dean murmured, bouncing his eyebrows.

Ravi cleared his throat that was followed by a grunt of displeasure.

"I'm afraid you only leave me two options, Mr. Forrester," the businessman frowned, "Either I underestimate you and fight a losing battle with my daughter over you. Or give credit where it's due, and respect how happy you've made my daughter," Ravi admitted. Dean held up a finger for Ravi to pause as he walked quickly to the balcony.

The sliding glass door opened automatically, and Dean looked around to ensure no work crews were between him and the open air under the tarp. A hot burning sensation cascaded through his body.

Dean recognized and finally had full control over the nauseous feeling that roiled his gut. He extended a hand and fired a small electrical sphere, about the size of a baseball, over the edge of the balcony and out into the rain.

He rotated slowly to show them how his hand crackled, a candle of electricity lighting up his palm.

Father and daughter stood quietly, in shock.

"Mr. Lexso. I'd love to be friends. I really would. Just know the danger you'll be getting into, though I could use help protecting your baby girl and your grandbaby," Dean confessed.

"Are you a god?" Ravi asked.

"No, but probably the closest thing to it on Oakley, besides an actual god. And if I somehow pissed one off with that comment, I'm sure they'd show up. I unlocked electrical magic somehow," Dean shrugged.

Cassandra's Dad just stared at him.

"The rest is not important, Ravi, and the less you know, probably the better. Helping us succeed in converting this place into a fortress will be a big boon. I know we can do it on our own, but I'd like to invite you to assist with the effort."

Cassandra kissed Dean deeper this time. "When'd you learn to shoot electric balls of white light? I knew you'd been augmenting the laser pistol, but this... this was amazing!"

"I figured it was high time I tried. Now," Dean continued, "there is a party downstairs and lots of people for us to mingle with." Dean hefted Cassandra into a twirl. He set her down and gave Ravi his attention. "Did this satisfy your father, son in law conversation?"

"Uh... No. I was hoping you'd say you were going to be a stay at home dad and stop taking risks. That way I could ensure you were happy and your life boring. When you needed help, we'd gladly help out, while keeping things simple. This is not bad, just far more complex than I'd bargained on. I thrive on a challenge, though." The man chuckled nervously, "Welcome to the Lexso family, Dean."

"Thanks, Dad," Dean grinned, and they had their first awkward man hug.

"Okay, while adorable I have a burning question for you Dean. Why is there a premium escort downstairs barely clothed?"

"About that..." Dean took a deep breath and launched into the best explanation he'd been able to come up with.

There was not much he could do, really, besides pray the two women got along. The contract was pretty much airtight—Kambry was going to be working a lot, helping him train, and staying out of trouble.

Or so Dean thought.

CHAPTER

SEVENTEEN

DEAN

Forrester-Lexso Estate

*C*lang.

Dean raised his shield in time to catch Anoka's wooden sword. He rolled, trying to escape the pressure she was applying. Her fighting style was so fluid it left him defenseless with every different weapon he tested. He stopped his tumble sideways to find her wooden sword inches from his eyes.

Defeated again, he sighed in frustration. The mace had actually jabbed into the leather armor covering his stomach as he rolled. He didn't like the ball on the end of a stick. Even if it was useful for breaking bones, it was too clunky for him.

"Not your worst," Anoka admitted, never scolding or correcting at this early stage.

She flipped her wooden sword onto her shoulder while walking toward the training weapon storage rack. Dean picked himself off the rough, dry desert terrain, *scraping* the sand and grit from his leather armor.

"I felt clunky with this thing," Dean grunted. He decided the mace was not for him and walked to store the weapon back in the rack. "I was so natural with my trident, I flowed with it in my hands."

"It's day one Dean. I can have a wooden trident made; though it'd need guards above where your hands rest. If not, any sword could simply carve down the shaft and remove your arm," Anoka said, handing him a spear. "I hate training new champions on two handed weapons. Maybe a half size trident and a light shield will be better for you."

They were going through most basic of motions right now, at half speed or less, inside the covered parking space that stood in front of The Forrester-Lexso Estate. The renaming had been made official this morning, after a very long night of entertaining guests.

Before Dean retired last evening, though, he'd ensured Anoka had his powered suit, his shuttle codes—with instructions on how to use them—and a few tokens worth of gems to open an account. That was going to be Anoka's morning task, for the next... forever. Get up, go to Mixonia, deposit gems, and come back with needed supplies.

She had purchased a few sets of simple weighted leathers to mimic armor and a wide selection of wooden weapons to test Dean's reflexes and natural prowess. Dean was wearing leather leggings and a long sleeve tunic that, while not too heavy, made him sweat. The outfit simply was not breathable.

An insanely tight belt wrapped above his hips and squeezed on his stomach. He'd grumbled about the fact that it was crushing his guts, but Anoka promised him a loose belt would be deadly.

"Why do I feel like we've regressed, like a thousand years?" Dean muttered to himself disparagingly.

"You know the common denominator among all species and worlds is swords and basic science, less magic. Well, metal, leather, staffs, and basic magic from your core. You cannot bring weapons or material in from outside, other than specifically approved exceptions," Anoka lectured. "Even then, exceptions are all limited and must be specially forged in Mixonia by a crafter. Your metal trident, for example, will take a week or two to be forged. I may just pick up a metal short spear for you in the interim."

"I'd like that," Dean nodded, "and a sword please."

"Come, sit with me while we watch my daughter beat on your friends," Anoka gestured him over.

The clash of wooden weapons rang over the area. A simple bench had been brought out from storage to provide a place to rest alongside the makeshift training yard. Dean plopped down heavily next to Anoka to watch both Dave and Lonny cross swords with Kambry.

Dave was another hazel-eyed stud who Dean would routinely bar hop with. The man was a decent insurance salesman. His sparse frame and gut were mostly due to his easy life, and probably too much alcohol. His swings to best Kambry were horrid. Kambry timed his movements with ease and dealt fluid counterattacks that pushed his friend back. Dave's big, red faced smile told Dean he was loving getting thrashed by a pretty girl.

Where Dave was a lanky pale white guy with blonde hair. Lonny was shorter and stockier, with short curly hair and light brown skin. Lonny had played Zball during his college years. Now that the fun school life was over, though, he worked as a drone operator. Lonny was less of a drinking buddy and closer to a fellow gym rat and workout friend.

The two of them had been excited about the opportunity Mixonia presented. Lonny, Dave, and a third friend, Scotty, had all promised to train and possibly team up—at least once Anoka approved of their skills and conditioning. Both of the friends he watched now were reliable compared to Scotty, though.

Scotty had left last night with one of Cassandra's friends. He'd promised to stick around. That was about average for Scotty and Dean had expected it. He didn't mind. He knew better than to rely on the man.

When it had come up last night that today was going to involve medieval battle training, Dean was shocked. The mere mention that he hired a professional trainer had ignited a spark of interest from just about everyone. Even Marty had wanted in on the action. Patti's father now crossed swords with his daughter, both beaming smiles.

Cassandra's lawyer friend and one-time lover, Tiffany, was in a spear and shield fight with Quincy. A few others watched, waiting for their turn to poke, prod, slash, and spar with the wooden weapons.

Dean knew the new purpose of the Forrester-Lexso Estate had found its mark. Anoka shooed him out of the way as she got up to coach and instruct instead of simply watching the sparring. He got up and followed along with her, hoping to pick up some pointers from others' mistakes—he found it hurt a lot less than the hard-earned lessons he picked up from Anoka, usually those lessons cost him a bruise or three.

"Less strength, more finesse," Anoka shouted at Lonny. "He shows some natural talent," she noted to Dean. Then she pointed at Dave. The man was smirking and in heaven. "Dave just keeps ogling Kambry's hips and ass. She's used to having to cover up her beauty. When it's out in the open like this it sure does sway a man. We covered her up to protect her. I'm glad she can be more open here."

"Hiding her whole origin thing?" Dean asked, watching her fight. "I bet she loves being a human, then."

Kambry had left her thick black hair free flowing. The tennis sized skirt she'd picked from Cassandra's closet looked great on her. Every swirl, twirl, and deflection resulted in her skintight volleyball shorts revealing her shapely ass.

"If you got it," Dean snorted, "why not flaunt it?"

"What would you like to learn about?" Anoka asked as they watched. Indicating her daughter's eyes, she continued her coaching. "See how she watches their hips and shoulders. That's a good habit for you to get into."

"I've got a lot to learn," Dean admitted, having to tear his eyes from Cassandra's busty top. No wonder his friends had stuck around, there was a lot of soft skin on display amid the dust and heat. "I remember hearing something about pets, though it seems like cheating, if you can have a team member and others can't."

"No pets are permitted in team portals, at all—no excuses, deviations, or allowances. Pets aren't simply pets, if that makes any sense," Anoka said, and Dean chuckled at the statement. About how he figured it might be. Mysterious rules abounded, though with executed with the flare of the gods.

She continued. "A pet is a statue, well, more like a figurine, that you take into solo portals. To build off your 'Is this a game question, from last night'... I was informed you have gaming on electrical devices here in human society. Last night I was able to pick up a lot from your family and friends. I can cross reference those systems to better explain your experience in Mixonia."

Dean vaguely remembered an extended conversation with his friends about virtual reality and other immersion type role-playing-games (RPGs).

"There are six portals in Mixonia. Three are PvP (Player versus Player), with the other three being PvE (Player versus Environment). You probably saw this on the map. Environmental combat portals are on one side, with Champion combat on the other. Solo play always allows pets. Generally speaking, if you're going for a stealth build or strategy, no one takes a pet into PvP. There are events that allow pets, but they are solo as well."

Dean thought about what he understood of the intelligent pets. "Aren't pets just an extension of each Champion, through their telepathic link?" he asked.

"Pets are not an extension of the mind of a champion," Anoka shook her head. "They're animals and will do what you train them to do. The downside for pets, again, is that they break stealth. If you're a resident of Mixonia, they can't normally be summoned inside the cavern—besides at a specific training hall or inside a solo floor of the labyrinth. There is a caveat, though, which you can exploit."

She smiled grimly. "You can train a pet here and bring it into Mixonia. It'll be transformed into a figurine during the portal hop."

"Ah, that explains why I never saw any animals while I was there," Dean said and she bobbed her head in agreement. "What would you recommend?"

"There are few tight labyrinths, where maneuvering a big pet around would become a problem, but those are not often enough to deter using something like a horse. The ceiling inside the maze would prevent using too large of a pet, like..." Anoka frowned as she tried to recall a large animal that humans would be familiar with, "an elephant, as the ceiling is only twelve-feet tall. A warhorse is probably the best all-around pet in the games. You could get something like a predator, but don't be surprised if it suddenly turns on you and sends you to Min's Vault to become a statuette."

Dean was searching for how to buy a New Texas warhorse when he heard his name being called softly from behind.

"Dean," Cassandra repeated, and Dean turned to see her and Lexis. Cassandra had her arms folded tightly across her chest and a scowl on her face.

Though Dean wasn't the best at reading body language, even he knew an approaching storm when he saw one.

"I was reading over the contract you offered Kambry." Her eyebrows rose dangerously. "What's a Kubra?"

Dean shrugged and flipped a thumb at Anoka. "Anoka said it was like a pet," he shrugged, "something to help with Kambry's long term stability."

Those eyebrows came together sharply "And you didn't ask for more information?" Cassandra demanded with a stern tone, arms unfolding and fists coming to rest on her hips. Altogether, her posture and resting bitch face indicated he'd better reef sail and batten down the hatches. It looked like things were going to get rough.

Dean shook his head, returning to his search for a pet.

Maybe if I pretend I'm busy, I'll stay out of trouble.

Lexis patted Cassandra's shoulder and sympathized, "I told you he wouldn't have a clue. This one is Kambry's fault." The Minotaur hybrid in human guise looked thoughtful for a moment, "or... actually, probably a well-intentioned mother's interference."

"Dean Forrester," Cassandra ground out, controlling her volume through clenched teeth, "that is the last time you extend a contract without letting your lawyer review it first." She pulled him down to where she could hiss in his, "A Kubra is a baby, Dean. You've got three months to stick a baby in her, or she goes free and you wasted the equivalent of four million Gs on freeing her fine ass."

Dean opened his mouth and promptly closed it. There were times when the less you said, especially when you were guilty as charged, the better off you were. Fortunately for Dean, Kambry decided to take a break at this point and trotted over.

"Lexis," Cassandra all but snarled, "take Kambry and show her the tasks I assigned to her. Then come back out here and help me make plans for a proper training ground, with Anoka."

Lexis curtsied and Kambry bowed before the two left for the interior. Dave and Lonny walked for the bench to take a break, jostling each other about how awesome this was.

Dean remained mute, in denial of the whole situation. He studied the loose layer of dirt in front of him like it was suddenly the most interesting thing in the world, he used his boot to play with a clod.

"Walk with me, Anoka," Cassandra decreed in a regal tone, "you and I need to talk."

Anoka gave a firm nod and walked off at Cassandra's side. Dean had somehow come out of that shit-storm unscathed. He almost wanted to check his body for puncture holes.

Am I bleeding? Nope... amazingly, no dagger sticking out of my back. Penis still attached. Ha!

He'd been warned numerous times to not be so trusting. Yet, here he was, again, in a situation where a simple misunderstood word might upend his future plans.

Instead of fretting about what punishments Cassandra come up with for his egregious lack of judgement, he went back to horse shopping. A horse dealer with a money back guarantee popped up immediately at the top of his search feed. Dean dialed the number while excusing himself from the bench as his friends sat down.

"Gilligan's Horse Dealer, Nathanael speaking."

"Hi, Nathanael. Dean Forrester here. I'm starting one of those renaissance retreats and want to do jousting and that kind of thing," Dean said, and he heard the man groan. "I was –"

"Well, before we go much further, you're talkin expensive horses—both to buy and maintain. Most people call me, thinking they can get two draft horses for cheap and then let them forage on their expansive lands. Nope, these animals aren't cheap and come with high vet bills and large food uptake," Nathanael paused in his tirade.

Dean sighed, knowing this was important. "For now, let's assume money isn't an issue. Not going to let you gouge me, mind, but I can afford the horses and the hay."

"Not to be rude, and I know this will sound like it. But the typical food, wenches, brew, and battle restaurants don't earn enough to support a decent sized stable. Hell," the man snorted, "I got four Ardennais sitting in my stables, right now, waiting on a new home. They're relatively cheap, due to a desperate seller who failed to make a go of the same path you're wanting to tread. However, he didn't realize they eat three percent their weight in a –"

"How cheap?"

"Uh, you comfy meeting on the orbital? I can let you see the horses in person," Nathanael asked.

"I just happen to be standing beside a shuttle," Dean said. "Let me call you back after I talk it over with our pilot."

"Wait," Nathanael blurted out.

Dean paused before hanging up.

"You're serious. I can tell by how you're not blinking when I'm trying to dissuade you. I'd have to pay to haul the whole stable down to deposit your purchases there anyway. I'll bring the animals straight to you for ten thousand coins. If you buy, half of that goes towards the purchase price."

Dean knew he was being tested. "I only want big horses that want to fight."

"Not how it works," Nathanael said with a laugh. "My ship is literally a massive horse farm and cow barn; I travel across the Galaxy and land where my buyers are. You get to see them all, and yes, I'll try to sell your kids ponies, too."

"Fine, send me the invoice and I'll see you soon," Dean said, hanging up the phone.

He trotted to where Anoka and Cassandra walked, along the edge of the overhead cover. The rain was still crashing down beyond them, and the desert landscape was thick with mud. Weeks of rain following a drought season would definitely alter the landscape. Dean felt this was likely more nefarious interference by the gods.

"Cassie, got a second?" Dean asked when he got near.

She scowled but dipped her head. "We aren't done with this, Anoka," she dismissed the trainer.

"I'm frustrated with you Dean," Cassandra admitted, after Anoka walked off. "Luckily there is IVF, as I was just explaining to Anoka."

Dean again held his tongue and handed his phone over. Cassandra studied the invoice, and then looked up the seller.

"Huh," she looked thoughtful, "this is good Dean. You did the right thing. Hired a specialist for a specialty item. I'd love to get into horse riding with you." Cassandra hit the approve button and kissed his cheek. "Thank you for consulting me before jumping in with both feet. This is a step in the right direction."

I couldn't help the impish grin that stole onto my face.

Her eyes still said I was in trouble, though.

"I mean it, Dean," she groused, "use me for contracts. I'll forgive this transgression because you were trying to do something good, and I wasn't around to give you expert advice. Fortunately, we can still fix this."

"Watch me gallop away," Dean said riding a fake horse, exactly like in the Monty Python skits.

He trotted his goofy butt over to the weapons rack. He deposited his phone there and retrieved a short sword and small spear. Testing their balance and weight with a few test swings, he walked over to a training dummy.

The wooden man never saw Dean's wrath coming. The resounding smack of the sword and spear on the innocent dummy *cracked* through the makeshift training grounds. Dean tried to find a rhythm but failed. He felt like a blind octopus who suddenly found himself out of water. The wooden man was actually a clever agent in disguise, and Dean cursed him as such, each time he foiled Dean's attempts at victory.

Even though Dean was ambidextrous, he struggled with two weapons. It never flowed or felt right. When he two handed the sword, or two handed the spear, it felt natural; but, never fighting with one in each hand.

Stepping back from his latest failed combination, Dean found Lexis standing at his shoulder with a large shield, when he finally gave up two handing the weapons.

"Master," she instructed, "try this."

"Dean, please," Dean said, pant lightly from his exertions. "Not really your master," he smiled, "more like a friendly caretaker."

"I can accept that, thank you," Lexis said.

He traded the spear for the shield. With his left arm locked into the brackets of the shield, his right hand cinched down on the leather grip of the wooden sword. A few jabs and stabs against the training dummy, and he felt much better.

This felt more natural to him. His left arm hefted the wooden shield that resembled a narrow half door. If he wasn't such a brute, Dean might struggle with this. It wasn't the weight that concerned him, though, but the bulk. He decided to go smaller. The tower shield was just too bulky to tuck and roll with, and Dean already knew his fighting style depended on maneuverability and agility.

Cassandra and Anoka waited by the rack.

"Anoka, when would I need to use something like this?" Dean hefted the tower shield.

"When you get into team fights. You will want to build a front line and a back line. The reason for the bulky shield is simply to absorb incoming damage while dishing your own." She shrugged, indicating his broad shoulders, "You'll always be in the front."

He grunted. That made sense.

"On a side note, I left your stats behind on my sling, when you had me healed. I do remember strength and willpower being your highest attributes, though," Anoka said, and Dean nodded.

A curious Lonny trotted over. "Can I see my attributes? Is there an app you have that lets you display such information?" he asked.

Dean smirked and patted Lonny's back. "Tomorrow morning, we're going to where you can get your stats checked, if you'd like to join us," Dean offered.

"Sure," Lonny replied, "But I can't stick around for more than a few hours. I have to work tomorrow night."

Cassandra butted in at this point, "I'd love to go this time. Anoka assures me it is safe. I'd like to be there with you to help you pick out your armor."

Lonny whistled jealously. "You're really getting into this whole medieval thing, aren't you?"

"Yeah, I think you might too, when you see it all for yourself," Dean said with a shrug. He turned back to Cassandra. "The horse guy is going to be here in twenty minutes. I need to go grab a shower and make myself presentable if he's ever going to believe I'm willing to spend millions on war horses."

Cassandra held out her hand that Dean accepted, after stowing his training gear. Lonny bounced his eyebrows as Dean was led away.

When they entered the bottom floor barroom, Tiffany was eating with Candace and Cassandra's mom, Lydia. They exchanged waves on the way to the elevator.

The elevator doors *dinged* open and when they shut, Cassandra clung to Dean.

"I talked with Anoka. I've got a better understanding of what the fook is going on," she admitted. "Slightly. It's a bit crazy, but I'm coping."

Dean kissed her forehead lightly, and apologized, "Sorry."

"You're a softie. Love it about you, though," she sighed. "We'll knock her up at the end of the frame. Either in a steamy threesome or via IVF. If she wasn't so damn sexy, I'd be less jealous," Cassandra grumbled.

Dean gulped at the thought.

"Ha! I get it," his lover smirked up at him. "I mention being comfortable with other women in our relationship and you bring home someone like Kambry. Basically, she's a wild one and the time for that is over now. She is cleaning the gym, the showers, and the shitters, by the way."

"Did she bitch and moan about it?" Dean asked.

The elevator *dinged* and they walked into their suite. Cassandra's dad was taking a meeting in the other suite, which meant they finally had some alone time, together.

Lydia had crashed in the guest room last night to avoid interrupting the hours of scheming her husband was up to. Riva had even had business partners flown down from the orbital. Marty had mentioned how badly he wanted to be a fly on the wall for that meeting.

Dean greened the door code and walked straight through the entryway for the shower in the master bath. Cassandra talked loudly as he separated from her side.

"Kambry apologized. Said the contract had been prepared by her mother. She'd prefer to be free," Cassandra snorted, loudly, "even asked if I'd consider it. I asked her why she'd been forced into having kids—it's in our contract she has to be honest with us—at least Kambry didn't hold anything back. She thinks Anoka is trying to ground her in reality, one that matters. One in which her actions have profound consequences," Cassandra said.

Dean stripped out of his sweaty work-out leathers once the water steamed.

"Well, I'm not exactly the grounding type," Dean noted from inside the bathroom.

"You actually are—I like to think I've talked you into settling down—what with this fancy home, staff to help, and your long-term plans," Cassandra quipped. She entered the bathroom wearing only her cat tail plugin and Dean smirked.

He lunged for her and she eeked out a *squeak.*

Cassandra was light in his arms as he propped her up onto the bathroom counter-top. He dropped to his knees and buried his face in her little pussy. His tongue twirled around her pearl and in no time at all, he'd plunged two fingers into her.

Her cat tail slunk down to wrap around his cock to tease it while he pleased her. She grabbed Dean's short hair as he masterfully licked her clit. Her moaning increased as Dean teased her into a fervor.

This was the easiest way to make her cum quick, and she was loving it. The lapping of his tongue spurred her on. Her hips twisted on the countertop as she shifted on his fingers to ensure he hit all her most sensitive spots with the perfect rotation.

She arched her back as her tunnel pulsed around his fingers. She bit her lip as she orgasmed. She pushed weakly at his head, but Dean only licked her pussy harder; she shuddered from the over stimulus.

"Fook me Dean, you're too good with that tongue of yours," Cassandra pouted, pointing at the shower. "Get in there, you sweaty brute. I want you to pound this pussy," she purred.

Dean was certainly not going to complain about this request. He scooped her taut ass off the countertop and carried her into the shower before setting her back on her feet. She spun around and ground her ass against his stiff cock. There was a shower seat in the corner of the shower that she propped her elbows upon.

With her face down and ass up, in no time he had his girth balls deep in her hot, wet slit. Her tail wrapped around his waist, pulling him tighter into her every time he pulled back. Dean smacked his hips into her firm ass, slowly at first.

"So fucking big!" She exclaimed, between moans.

"So fucking tight," he replied, between grunts.

For five glorious minutes he slammed into Cassandra as he neared completion. She'd climaxed a third time already, and was begging for his cum.

"You ready to feel my seed dripping out of you?" Dean asked, knowing her teasing ways.

She shot forward to get off his cock. "Not this time," Cassandra said with a wink.

Her blue eyes twinkled with passion as she kneeled before him. "Oh," was all Dean could manage, as the blowjob started.

She twirled her tongue around his tip and stroked his girth. She worked his cock expertly, alternately sucking and pumping his length. Swiftly, he approached ecstasy. "I'm going to cum," Dean warned her; it was the polite thing to do.

She gagged on his cock, burying it deep in her throat. He exploded into her, then, grunting as he released his load. She moaned with pleasure, all while gulping down his jizz. Cassandra savored the release, and even cleaned him lovingly as he softened. With a few finishing head bobs, the last of his seed dribbled out. She licked the last glob seductively off his tip.

"I need to do that more often," Cassandra murmured, a sparkle in her eyes. "I see you really loved that."

Dean nodded. "Yes, yes you do. That was amazing. I'd go for round two in a few minutes, because I'm so turned on, if this horse seller wasn't going to show up soon."

"Well, let me clean up, my champion," she grinned, "then we'll do some horse shopping."

He pulled her up to kiss those sweet lips and hold her tight.

"Dean, even with all the craziness, I want you to know that I love you. I've wanted to be your wife for a long time," Cassandra said.

"Cassie, I don't keep a journal," he smiled into her wet hair, "but if I did. You'd see your name in it a lot, and the plans I had of the two of us, in our forties, on vacation together. We've simply moved the timetable up on getting married and settling down," Dean admitted. He kissed her deeply. She went to respond, but he never gave her a chance—round two happened after all, on its own.

CHAPTER
EIGHTEEN

DEAN

Lexso-Forrester Estate

D ean parried a sword strike from Kambry. Her movements were all emotion and raw passion. He could almost feel the frustration coming off her as he turned aside another blow. Her eagerness to defeat him was palpable, it drove her forward relentlessly—making her next movements and strikes almost ridiculously easy to read.

He frowned from behind his shield, knowing she was about to expose her legs. She used an empowered swipe with her wooden sword, which he deflected with his shield. Capitalizing on her overextension he executed a leg sweep that flung her off her feet.

"Damn you, and damn this human body!" Kambry shouted from where she sprawled in the dirt.

Clearly, he had gotten under her skin. She grunted as she sat up and stared at her boots, as if it was their fault she was on her plump ass.

"I've bested all the others," she growled, "But you... somehow, you can sense what I'm going to do before I do it."

He frowned at her, feeling a pang of guilt.

"Kambry, I get it. You've been eager to smash me down and show me how great ya are. I already know you're great," Dean said extending a hand down to help her up.

She scowled at him, but accepted his hand.

"By great, do you mean my looks? You human males can't keep your eyes off my big tits and thick hips," Kambry sneered, but her eyes told him a different story. He had caught her smiling from the attention a few times.

This outburst caused Dean to chuckle.

She dusted off her juicy booty, smacking the dirt off her yoga pants. He couldn't help but eye the way her taut ass jiggled.

"What?" She glared at him. "Are you mocking me now?"

"Kambry," he sighed, "you asked for this training session. We're up three hours before the others are even scratching their asses and brushing their teeth."

He pinched the bridge of his nose before saying, "Why are we out here, other than for you to try and prove something?"

Her request last night to meet him before dawn in the training arena had left him perplexed. He had kind of expected her to disclose some big secret or have a stern talk with him about the nature of their contract.

Dean knew things between them were complicated.

The contract Anoka had given him to rescue Kambry from Min's shelf had been a goof of epic proportions on his part. He should have read it more closely and pushed back on any parts he hadn't understood.

But he'd agreed with her mother that tough love and strict rules were what the headstrong young Dragona needed—even though he thought it was a mistake. Their predicament seemed to affect Kambry the most.

Honestly, things between him and Cassandra, were at an all-time high. Dean was very happy in his love life.

Maybe that was what was bugging Kambry.

"I'm supposed to be beating you. I've got all the training. I've spent a decade plus under the expert tutelage of Anoka.

"And yet, you refuse to stare at my tits. You watch my hips and my shoulders. You time my moves with skill and knock me on my ass with ease," Kambry ground out from between clenched teeth.

Dean noticed her fists were clenched tightly at her side and the crease on her brow was growing. There was a blazing fire in her eyes that grew by the second.

"Ease off on the anger. I get it. You're in a new body. And no, I'm not mocking you," Dean held his hands up defensively. He hoped the open palms would placate and calm her. "I'm going to sit here on this bench and we're going to talk this out. Us sparring is only fueling some fire that threatens to burn whatever this is between 'me and you' to a crisp." Dean shook his head. "I want to strengthen our bond instead of widening this bridge between us..." He looked up at her honestly, "it's a relationship that I'd like to improve."

"For a brute of a man, you have a way with words. Most Dragona, well, they are either lithe and wise, or big and dumb," Kambry said as she sat beside him.

Dean didn't even try to hold back a long peel of laughter at her backhanded compliment.

"What?" she asked, confused by his reaction.

"Well," he chuckled, "it's just that, I appreciate the flattery. You said I'm a big brute, and a wise one at that." He let his giggling calm. "I don't believe I'm much more than a simple fisherman. A man destined for great things?" He waved his hand back and forth to express his doubts. "Whatever it is I'm supposed to become, I'd like for ya to be at my side, helping me become it, instead of fighting against me every step of the way."

Kambry's stern glare softened. She took his hand in hers. Dean raised an eyebrow but didn't pull his hand back.

"I know I'm stubborn. I also know that I owe you a lot. You could be a right asshole to me, instead... you've be nothing but nice. I see how hard you work at pleasing Cassandra. I see how happy you make her... and it hurts. I want that," Kambry finally admitted with a long sigh.

"Kambry," he said gently, "we all have our own demons and challenges we must face. For whatever reason, fate has pulled us together. I've focused on Cassandra first and foremost, not just because you and I have time, but... well, because I love her."

He smirked. "That being said, I was more than happy to wake up a bit early this morning and plant that sexy ass of yours in the training dirt." Dean gave her a winning smile. "We can sneak away during our free time to work on us, if that is what you want. Maybe I can be that man, for you, too."

He frowned at her, "I'm not sure if I can live up to whatever hero image you've dreamed up over the years, because I have to be true to myself, but I'm more than happy to try."

"Well, I think I'm ready to let you..." Kambry kicked shyly at the dirt. "For all the brutes to get contracted to, you're the perfect mix of strength and weakness—hard when you need to be, but soft where I least expect it." She shook her head. "I'm conflicted as to the why, up here," Kambry pointed to her head. "Here, surprisingly..." she pointed to her heart and took a deep breath. "Here, is open to you and Cassandra. It's not every day that I find a male who is so loving, but also able to dominate me so thoroughly." She grinned at him. "Whatever else it is, it certainly won't be dull."

Dean kissed the back of her hand and she blushed. He stood up and stretched, then started heading for the exit. Without looking back he said, "I eagerly await our next sparring session. And when the time comes... sheet wrestling with you. I bet you're a ten in bed."

"Ha!" she yelled out in a boisterous tone. "Make that a fifteen and you're closer to the mark."

As he left to get cleaned up, Dean knew he'd made more than an initial connection. He hoped Kambry and Cassandra would do the same. A long, low whistle escaped his lips at the thought of a potential threesome.

∞∞∞∞

Dean left his suite after a shower to restart the day, only to find unwelcome visitors at the door—ones that he had been expecting for a while. He honestly was surprised the bureaucrats had left him alone this long. Really, there was no excuse for the government not to poke and prod at him. He'd caused quite the sensation, first about his near-death survival, and second his 'discovery' of the gem that suddenly made him worth millions. Granted, millions were nothing on Oakley, but it was enough, surely, for the government to at least want to investigate.

When Dean arrived downstairs, eager to meet the horse dealer, he ran into two governmental groups waiting patiently in the lobby barroom. The first group was a bunch of tax collectors—and they were actually the easiest to handle.

They had arrived to get a thumbprint signature along with to administer a lie detector test to verify that he'd received his gem from a cave. They were even cool with everything happening in a back room, without drones and without saying exactly where the cave was. Dean merely had to swear that the gem was found, not stolen, and that all appropriate taxes for treasure finding were applicable and would be paid forthwith.

Eighteen million became twelve in the blink of an eye, and Dean now better understood the numbers Lexis had given him in Mixonia. He also understood why they were so easy to deal with. He didn't put up a fight with them and the representatives, after a few bureaucratic formalities, left with oodles of money. Lame, but a rule he couldn't avoid. When they were done, Nathanael arrived eager to show off his horses. Unfortunately, he had to be told to wait.

Dean had medical doctors demanding a physical. It was not that they hadn't been demanding to inspect him. There were rules and laws in place that Cassandra, his lawyer girlfriend, had sheltered him behind. It seems the doctors had their own lawyers, who'd found some shitty loophole to try to haul him away to be poked and prodded.

Except that Dean refused, which had led to a standoff. That was until something unique happened that shouldn't have surprised him.

"Dean Forrester, your refusal to come with us will result in every one of these people getting physicals. We'll be so thorough that you'd wish you'd simply–"

Time froze suddenly, for only the doctors and their team. Even the horse guy waiting inside the main doors was stunned. Dean was not amused by the situation.

"Nathanael, this is my lovely partner, Cassandra," Dean said, waving him over.

The man was fixated on the frozen people.

"What'd ya do to them?" Nathanael asked, his eyes wide and his jaw still on the floor.

Dean shrugged and said, "They're messing with something even I wouldn't mess with. Come give me a tour of your stables. I'm eager to have a look at–"

"Dean Forrester," the doctor said suddenly, as time suddenly resumed for the science team. "Thank you so much for your cooperation. We'll take these findings home immediately. It's rare we get a patient so willing to submit fully to our full barrage of tests. Come on team, time to go."

Dean and Cassandra shook the same idiots' hands they'd been about to forcefully kick out of their house, exchanged faked pleasantries, and flipped the fooks off as soon as the door shut behind them.

Nathanael gulped and said, "Don't mind wash me, please. My wife and kids would be homeless if you rob me."

"Do you believe in gods?" Dean asked with a single brow raised as he looked down upon the man. "Not one as in the creator, but gods as in the many?"

The poor businessman shook his head no.

"Then you should," Cassandra grinned, "and they believe in you, it seems. Trust me when I tell you that you'll be fine, our G-coins are good, and that we really want to spend some money on the fine horses you brought to show us."

He blew out a long, relieved sigh and tipped his hat. "Your deposit cleared, so let's have a walk."

Lexis ran up beside Dean to join him. She was wearing a shirt of Cassandra's that was at least a size too small on a large bust, making her nipples clearly visible under the taut fabric.

"Lady Anoka wanted to inform you that she left the estate, to go get your trident made in numerous sizes. Lonny went with her," Lexis reported.

Dean's eyebrows shot up. "Excellent. I hope we can start to rebalance the scales if he competes. We just need to set up a recovery fund for each of us," Dean said thinking the idea was good. He needed to develop a team to help balance the score.

Dave hadn't gone with them to Mixonia, he was following Kambry around like a lost puppy dog while she worked.

Dave took in the Minotaur hybrid in human guise's outfit. "Have you done any clothes shopping yet, Lexis?"

Cassandra laughed and shook her head, no. "I've added G-coins to her account but haven't had a chance to go over digital shopping with our nanny, yet. I like her in my clothes. I now understand better why a man digs seeing a woman in his shirt."

Dean gave her a brief look of confusion, and when she winked with a sly smile, Dean grew even more confused. He pointed a discrete thumb at his chest, then at Cassandra, and then pointed at Lexis. Cassandra responded from behind the horse dealer by splitting her fingers and sticking her tongue between them. Dean's jaw popped open in shock.

Score! Gotta be cool, though.

Nathanael, fumbling on his phone for some security code he needed to allow them into his ship, missed the finger gestures and looked up to see Dean grinning goofily at Cassandra and then Lexis. He looked momentarily lost.

Dean figured he was probably super concerned with what he just saw. If Dean had to guess, that was probably just Min zonking out his memory of a bunch of meddling government officials.

"So," Dean said as they exited the building Nathanael, "tell me a little bit more about your home."

A medium sized shuttle stood waiting under the covered area for them. The rain still pelted down from the gray bank of clouds, with its unrelenting task of converting the desert into a paradise.

"My grandfather finally retired, after breeding horses for almost a hundred and fifty years. When his body grew too frail to keep up, he left this world for a virtual one. My Pa was not a fan of animals, always complained of the stink," Nathanael chuckled. "Turns out, they don't smell too bad in a spaceship, with all the air scrubbers."

Dean laughed at that as Cassandra linked her arm in his.

"Anyway, I love space farming. It's farming with the ability to sell direct to clients all over the galaxy. So, at only twenty-two, with a good reserve, I took over the family business. Times were different, thirty years ago," he sighed wistfully. "Now, humanity has over-expanded. People are having fewer children and that means fewer families willing to risk it all purchasing expansive lands on the frontier. Getting a horse has always been more of a want than a need, but for a long time, folks busting sod on the frontier could justify the purchase."

"I've got some friends and family who'd like to go, if that's alright," Cassandra interrupted. Looking at the size of the shuttle, she frowned, "We might need to make two trips."

When Nathanael beamed, "the more the merrier!", Cassandra typed some information into her phone and sent a proximity text. Dean read the invite she sent to all the guests still around. She told everyone that the shuttle would be leaving in five minutes.

"Thank you," Cassandra smiled, "I told everyone who wanted to come to meet us here in the next five minutes. Please continue with your story."

"Even twenty years ago," the horse trader continued, "most folks thought bigger than just a pony for the little one. Why only buy one, we'd tell them, and instead focused on selling breeding stock. Well," he grinned, "if everyone's breeding, then prices for stud fees go up. But we never got into that mess too much—and good thing too, 'cause about ten years ago, prices fell like a rock. The horse bubble, as some called it, burst."

"Were you okay?" Cassandra asked sincerely. Her empathy was evident, and one of the things Dean loved about his little blonde firecracker.

"We had to tighten things down a bit," Nathanael admitted, "but we managed to survive—only 'cause we were able to bring our horses to the clients, though. A lot of Mom-and-Pop breeders went under."

A crowd of folks spilled out of the house at the same time as another group came around the corner of the house. A waving Lydia and Ravi were the most eager and got there first, immediately followed by the entire Kendricks family. Visiting a horse trader was a rare treat. The two groups stepped into the shuttle.

They all crammed in, with still plenty of space for Kambry, Dave, Tiffany, and three more of Cassandra's lady friends who Dean had met the night before, but for the life of him, couldn't remember what their names were. When people stopped pouring out the entrance to The Forrester-Lexso Estate, Nathanael took off for his spaceship.

The man raised his voice so all could hear him clearly and said, "We just covered the recent downturn in horse prices. When the ballooning horse market bubble burst. Gilligan's Horse Trading, fortunately, was in prime shape to weather the storm. We never bred many horses; mostly only traded them. Business was good, stock was low, and our accounts fluffy."

Dean heard bits and pieces of Marty and Ravi's sidebar conversation about getting into the horse business. One was a titan of space, the other a titan of Ola.

"Well, as you can imagine, when no one is buying horses, then getting a commission on selling horses tends to be harder to come by. I swapped to selling horse feed and stopped taking on horses to sell for new clients."

"I shifted from all our eggs in one basket to integrating more cows and other animals that have multiple purposes." He shrugged. "Everyone loves milk and steak. Eating a horse is a delicacy to some, sacrilege to others. A horse breeder I've been friends with for years who'd shoot me for trying to sell him horse meat will eat a cow, with no problem. I guess that's my point. Ya just always gotta be ready to adjust to the market," he said to bobbing heads of agreement.

"And how did selling hay, barley, and oats work out for you?" Marty wanted to know.

Nathanael scoffed and said, "Very well, then not so well, and then back to the middle. Like I said, I adjusted quickly. People who stuck with horses wanted cheaper feed, and I undercut the big boys. They undercut me and we cycled into a no profit lose-lose scenario. I stopped selling hay and switched back to trading horses or cows. Not trying to make ya cry, but the horse market recovered. Between government incentives, tax credits for expanding, and the instant cash for babies born to revitalize a once booming part of the economy, the market has found some new life. Shoot, I'm heading to New Alamo next. They really went all-in on the whole cash for kids thing a decade or so ago—got a bunch of horses to sell 'em as people are expanding out of the cities again. Can only stay in momma's house for so long, ya know."

Cassandra bumped an elbow into Dean's ribs and murmured in his ear, "Twenty thousand in G-coins for a baby. A whole year's worth of an average fishermen's pay. Some planets are offering more."

"Here she be," Nathanael said as their shuttle approached a massive freight hauler out in the middle of the desert, ten times the size of the old mega shipping tankers on Earth.

The exterior was a shiny gray and shaped oddly. This mighty spaceship had random T-sections, oddly place towers with boxes strapped in odd configurations, and connectors tying it all together. It almost resembled your typical farm-house—with new sections continually being added to the original frame over generations. The layout was so disjointed with its protruding extensions and elevated towers, Dean was surprised it had survived a trip through Oakley's atmosphere. Getting her down to the surface must have taken some immense shielding.

"Gilligan's Farm," Nathanael held out his arms and gestured to the ship, "houses thousands of horses comfortably and no less than ten thousand milkers. I got all the milk you'd ever want. Organic too. Sells great on the Oakley Orbital. Which is why I stay parked outside of it, for months at a time."

The shuttle descended gently until it slipped inside a massive hangar bay with hundreds of mooing cows, enjoying some fresh air. The shuttle touched down gently in one corner, and all eyes eagerly soaked up the sights. Dean saw the bay doors were open and the animals, in their large pens, roamed around the fencing closest to the bay doors, wanting to explore the muddy desert.

"These here cattle are from the great state of Wyoming," Nathanael said.

Dean shook his head, impressed. Earth was a stickler for releasing animals to the great spaceships that cycled the Galaxy's solar systems. Even Dean knew that meant Nathanael had friends in high places.

"Before you get too excited, though, I'm not allowed to sell these and the black and whites over there," he pointed to a smaller pen, "are show cows. They're meant to wow you with their awesome coloration and perfect moo's," he laughed. "I got some better-quality cows from New Texas further in that go for a fraction of the price. Not that you need cows," Nathanael sighed, setting the bait Dean knew someone was sure to fall for.

Quincy asked, "But the cows are like ya said. They produce milk, can be bred, and if things turn sour, you can always sell the meat."

"We're in a bull market for cows for a reason, son," the horse trader grinned, "I got some for sale, and I'll happily sell you some. Hell, even got the feed to sell you cheap, too. But I expect prices will go down before they go back up again," Nathanael said and Marty clapped, appreciating how well the trader was working this crowd.

Dean's mentor smirked and turned on the young man. "Quincy," he asked, "if I said I'd manage six cows for you, would ya buy some?"

"A few, sure," Quincy nodded, and Marty shook his head.

"What?" his friend protested.

Nathanael laughed while everyone waited for Marty's answer.

"Buy low, sell high," Nathanael chuckled. "Yer friend has it right, though. I swear I sell more animals when I try not to sell animals. It's like telling a child to not play with matches. Eh," he scratched his chin, "bad analogy. Basically, though, if I told you it was a great time to get into horses, you'd shy away. If I say it's meh, you'll bite."

Marty grinned like the cat who'd got the cream.

"If I say it's a horrid time for cows and the prices are going crazy, that they've doubled recently, you'll see coins in your dreams filling your treasury with riches,"

Nathanael explained, stepping off the shuttle first with the group trailing after him. "If they doubled once, you'll tell yerself, why not twice?"

"How are all these animals cleaned up after?" Tiffany asked from the back of the group.

A younger version of Nathanael showed up from a room overlooking the hangar. The younger man was fit, like Dean, and Cassandra's girlfriends leaped into hushed side conversation with the handsome farm hand.

"The flooring had machines. Name's Barthemou, but people call me Bart. I'm here to give most of y'all a guided tour while those of you with deeper pockets continue on with yer shopping. If you want to learn about the ship and see the sights, though, just follow me. If you want to talk shop and unload yer bank accounts, follow my Pa," Bart said stepping over to the side of the cow pen.

Kambry went to join the others, until Dean spoke up. "Kambry, you'll be staying with me. Lexis, go have fun with the others; if you see something you want. I'll get it for you."

"You spoil me, Master," she grinned and curtsied, and then hurried over to catch up to Dave, who was already chatting with Cassandra's friends.

That left Dean, Cassandra, Kambry, Marty, Ravi, and Lydia. Nathanael managed a tablet while frowning.

"You guys buying horses suddenly?" Dean asked, his eyebrow raised, curious.

"She's important, isn't she?" Ravi said, nodding his head at Lexis.

"Lexis is beyond important. She's... family. I'll leave it at that. A family member I should spoil. Does that clear the waters?" Dean asked.

"After a long talk with Anoka, last night, and your gem, well, I'm invested in this planet." He turned to his wife. "Honey, ensure she is cared for, and I promise to buy you three gorgeous horses," Ravi said to his wife, and Nathanael held a finger up. Ravi rolled his wrist for him to speak.

"Mr. Forrester paid for me to be on the ground for a full Oakley day, so I'm not in a rush. The fresh atmosphere helps the air recyclers recover, anyway, and it was a five-thousand-coin fee just to land. I've got more clients coming to check on some cows." The trader shrugged, "shocker, I know, that I'd want to make hay while the sun shines, since Mr. Forrester was kind enough to pay my landing fee. If she wants–"

"Very well, thank you, Nathanael," Lydia smiled, "I'll gladly take a private tour afterwards. The air purifiers do wonders in these space farms. Your home is lovely." She kissed her husband's cheek before walking over to the other group. "See you later, dear."

"Follow me," Nathanael said, taking charge once more and leading them to an elevator.

The group shuffled in and easily fit. Dean waited until the doors had closed and addressed the others. "I take it, I'll be stabling your horses? I want to use mine to take into battle."

Ravi sighed and handed an NDA tablet to Nathanael that he quickly signed. "Thank the Gods. This makes me feel so much better," Nathanael muttered.

"Yeah Dean, like he said. We spoke at length last night with Anoka," Marty said. "Ravi and I are going to finance finding the other three portals."

Dean let out a long whistle. "That's a mighty big task."

"Dean, I've already laid claim to your Deathly Caverns with Lexso Mining and More. It's officially off-limits from further competition and the necessary inspections have already been completed," Cassandra said with a proud smile. "That cavern is off-limits to the public and our private property."

"We'll want to secure the other three," Ravi nodded. "If you're cycling diamonds for cheaper gems, we want to start doing the same. The competitor stuff we'll need to learn more about, but I've got some men and women I trust with my life that should do well in the competition."

Dean nodded and grinned. "I guess a family business, it is, then. I take it I'll play host and primary training academy, then?" Dean asked.

"Yes, Master," Kambry spoke up.

Dean rolled his eyes at her.

She frowned at his expression. "Not like they know how to fight... yet. Plus, it's what Anoka recommended," the pretty dragon-woman in human guise finished.

Ravi and Marty bobbed their heads, confirming her words.

"So, you both want to help and to profit from things. I've only got a problem with that, if it affects the scoring. Not like you two need more money," he snorted. "Why didn't you visit Mixonia with Anoka?" Dean asked with a smirk.

"We can go at any time. After your dazzling display last night," Cassandra's father admitted, "I believe ya. I've even got some business partners I want to go in with—they'll be sub-contracted to me—so when the last one arrives, I plan on going in today," Ravi explained. "Then, when we've got the rest of the board... 'onboard', so to speak, Marty will go in next. So," he smiled, "don't worry that it's not going to happen. Just not this instant."

"I was going to go in with Lonny. Going to make him an employee. Orlith liked the idea of a riding barn, and you know how wives can be," Marty smirked at Cassandra, "or you will, soon enough." He shrugged, "We've got big plans to build a large barn in the coming weeks." Marty cracked his knuckles and grinned. "Mixing pleasure and business is good for the soul."

That was something Dean could agree with.

"Now that we're in an NDA, Nathanael, I need combat horses," Dean turned to Nathanael. "And not the fake combat kind."

The big man frowned, "What you're asking for... doesn't really exist. That will always depend on the horse, it's always there, inside the right breed, but it takes a special someone to bring it out. If I don't have it already, though, I can get it... but you won't need to special order. The excuse for ranchers buying larger horses always won out over endurance breeds. There are some beefy species on this ship. Some custom, some from Earth, even. The New Texas stallions get awful big." He thought for a moment. "Got a height limit?"

"Ceilings are a dozen feet minimum on most floors," Kambry interjected as the elevator pinged and opened to let them out on another floor. The nickering of horses immediately reached their ears. "The labyrinth will appear wide open, with no roof. But pets over a certain size will not be allowed out of their statuette forms."

"Whatever that means." The trader shook his head. "That only cuts out a few of the biggest breeds. Leaves plenty of mean SOBs to pick from. Ya got a color preference?" Nathanael asked, leading them past some ponies.

"Black," Kambry said confidently. "The mazes sometimes are so dark, even my Dragona eyes, need additional light. Not that a horse is a stealthy creature, but every little bit helps. Hobgoblins have shit hearing anyways, and they are common enough on the lower levels."

"Shucks, I had the perfect mare for you too, Dean. She's not black, though" Nathanael admitted.

Dean shrugged. "I'm limited on my cash flow in Mixonia. Not on my purchases out here. I'm more interested in ensuring we get the right breed, than the right color."

The ponies transitioned into small unicorns and Cassandra couldn't help herself.

"What're these?"

"Unicorns," the trader smiled, "in the traditional sense, natives to planet Klovia. Great for little girls, but they didn't get big enough for an adult to ride, and cross breeding has failed. If you want to wow a single sugar momma, with a daughter, that right there's the best way to do it," he chuckled.

Dean smirked at Cassandra's deflated sigh, and drooping shoulders. Evidently, even big girls wanted a unicorn. "Back to war horses," he said.

"The Ardennais are a fantastic breed. Started in Roman times, mainstay of many armies through the time of Napoleon. Died off after World War one as a fighting breed. Still bred across Earth, though, as draft animals. Fifteen to seventeen hands high at the shoulder on the bigger blokes, about a meter and a half plus, measured between the shoulder blades.

"For a while, everything was about size, then health issues peculiar to the bigger breeds brought some sense back to breeders, and over the last few hundred years, horse breeds in most controlled breeding programs, by and large, have gotten smaller. Though it's not uncommon to find healthier, finer animals, when you let them breed naturally."

Nathanael paused to get a carrot for a lovely white stallion. The two were clearly friends, the horse was eager for the carrot and all the scratches it could get.

"Six-and-a-half-foot tall man, even standing in the saddle should still be under eleven feet. But we can test, to be sure. High upkeep, and I wouldn't take them on a long journey. But a joust, hell yea. Even woo the crowds with these ones. Good temperament too. I got the four, and then a few other variations that would breed just fine with them. Great part of doing business with Gilligan's is we process your paperwork."

"What kind of paperwork is involved?" Cassandra wanted to know.

"When you birth a foal, or baby horse. Simply send me a blood sample and into the Galactic database, it goes. It'll cost you a few coins, mostly the shipping fee. We're always happy to help with quick stuff like that."

They were walking past mostly riding horses, beasts that seemed a lot less bulky and more refined. As if they were to be ridden by a lady. Cassandra trailed the group, falling further behind, which caused Nathanael to pause. He darted to a box, popped open the lid, and scooped out a trio of carrots to give to her.

"I want a riding horse, not a battle horse," Cassandra notified them, and turned back to look at to the long line of smaller horses. Nathanael continued their tour, without her.

The draft horses started alphabetically. Of course, this made the four Ardennais easy to locate. Dean walked over to the box Nathanael had gone to earlier, to pilfer a carrot.

"These Ardennais aren't supposed to come in black. At least for a while the color was rare and fell into unregistrable conditions for the breed. Bay is the breed's primary color, with a darker roan thrown in occasionally."

Dean patted the neck of one of the big fellas while he fed him a carrot.

"I'm going to be honest with you. I see this species traded a lot for the jousting dinner type places. Not much else for them, really, without farm work to do–

besides, there are bigger horses now, too, in other breeds. But they are showy, with their fancy manes."

Dean saw a big bloke poking his head out the next stall over. The animal was wary, its striking eyes watching him closely as he approached. The horse pulled its head back sharply, even when Dean offered him a treat. Dean noticed he was a tad skinny. When he shifted past the big fellow, though, to the mare next door, the stallion nickered and thudded a hoof against his stall door, demanding their attention.

"What?" Dean asked, and the animal smacked its lips in a hearty whicker. Kambry snatched a carrot from Dean and stepped into the stall. The two were immediately best friends, causing Dean to laugh. He had a lot to learn about animals, apparently.

"They're tricky animals. None of these lot seem interested in you. Hmm... Follow me, you ladies and gents keep on looking. Dean, I've got a special horse for you. Even if you end up buying half my stock, I'd still recommend this stud, merely for his looks. He's a sweetie to humans, no idea what nonsense you have going on though—"

"Taking horses into combat," Dean said, "to fight magical monsters."

Nathanael didn't know how to respond.

"Uh... this is Apache. He's a variation of a Clydesdale."

They went to a stall at the end of the row. Inside stood an eager horse. Unlike the others he'd seen so far, Apache was jet black. The lad was a very handsome horse, with a presence about him that spoke of charisma. Dean instinctively wanted to be around the horse.

He walked up to the horse who snatched at the carrot. "Wait," Dean commanded.

Surprisingly, the horse fumed, pawed at the ground, but listened. Its emerald green eyes contrasted sharply with its midnight coloration. He fed the carrot to the well-behaved Apache, once the animal had calmed down. He was gently nudged to go get more and let out a quiet laugh.

Nathanael went to the door and thumbed the code to let the stallion out. "This one, is a dream to be around. He also is ten times the price of the Ardennais. He's on retainer for a downtrodden breeder. Been so for the last year, though. Owner refuses to—"

"Full price is fine," Dean said, feeding his new best friend another carrot. "You want to make a bunch of babies, big guy?"

The horse responded with a happy nicker and a gum flap.

"I'll get you your own harem of lovelies, my friend, if you'll help kill the bad guys with me," Dean murmured next to his head and Apache stomped his hoof. Eager for blood, or to fuck. Probably the latter, he laughed, but Dean couldn't fault the stallion.

"Just like that?" Nathanael said with a head shake. "He costs three hundred thousand coins. This is the part where people tend to retract their love."

"I paid eight million for a woman, give or take. This one will be worth every penny. Plus, didn't you hear?" Dean said with a snicker, "the horse market is on the rebound."

"Aye, it is. It is indeed. I got some saddles I'll throw in too. He'll need a special ride home, but you can let him pick out some ladies. They connect pretty easily," Nathanael said.

Dean was lost in admiring the animal, scratching the horse behind its ear.

"I need to see about Cassie. While his price is worth it, if the others are only the price of a shuttle, and not a house, we should get extras," Dean said, then frowned. "Looks like hiring a knowledgeable stable master just became a top priority."

"Well, you can store 'em here for the next few days, but when I leave, your purchases are your responsibility. Based on the crews I saw at your estate, you'll have no problem sticking a horse tent up until a barn is ready," Nathanael said, reassuring Dean.

Cassandra raced for Apache. "He's fabulous. Jet black with white fur over his hooves. Your foes will fixate. I love him," she beamed.

Apache nuzzled her blonde hair.

"Oh," she laughed, "thank you for the kisses you big lug."

The big stallion butted his head into her, smelling her hands and nibbling at her hair.

"Are there more like him?"

"Females and males, yes," Nathanael admitted. "This gorgeous or striking," he shook his head, "no. He's one of a kind. Three hundred thousand coins," Nathanael mentioned Apache's steep price tag, and Cassandra moaned sadly.

"Fret not," Nathanael grinned, "Dean didn't hesitate."

"Really. What's with that?" Cassandra asked with a frown. "We haven't been paid for your gem yet, the sale is in tax transaction verification. I'd have to loan you the money–"

"I can weather two weeks of financial bureaucracy," Marty said, pulling out his phone. "If Anoka didn't mention you could die in there and be trapped for eternity, I'd be less forthcoming with the cost of a nice Ola apartment. However, she was very convincing and I'm eager to visit Mixonia."

Riva patted Marty's back in a friendly manner. "All the Ardennais, the Clydesdales, and the mares that'd breed well with this guy. He's fantastic."

The cat got Nathanael's tongue for a moment. He shook his head and said, "That'd be sixty-something horses. At least three million coins, with feed, saddles, and supplies. Why don't we head on over to my office and draft up the paperwork?"

"Let's," Riva replied. Marty joined them as they left.

Dean smirked with a slight chortle. "What's so funny?" Kambry asked, coming out of the big Ardennais' stall. "My pick is that one, named Arrow. We're going to do great. I'd have maybe beaten Thero with Arrow." Kambry scratched Apache with Cassandra. "This black beauty is too nice and polite."

"Sure, but I need a trained horse," Dean snickered. "I've already got my hands full of too many wild things."

"Your hands wouldn't know how to handle something as fine as me," Kambry sneered, full of sassy confidence, before running to catch up with the men already starting to talk business.

"Her ass is divine," Cassandra admitted and sighed, watching the tennis skirt flap up teasingly.

"Easy Cassie," Dean grunted with a wink, "slow and steady. I know I want to get in the ring and fight, already. Patience will win us the day, though, in all our battles." He smirked, "Besides, I thought you wanted Lexis?"

"I want them both," Cassandra growled, grabbing a hunk of Dean's ass. "I've been repressed. I like a woman's touch," she smiled, "you know that–you just haven't seen it, yet."

Dean couldn't help the cheesy grin on his face.

"You're married to her, more than me at the moment," Cassandra winced, "with that damn contract."

"We can change that easily enough," Dean said, folding his arms.

Cassandra pulled them open and then snuggled into his chest to get a hug. "No," she sighed, "you need the trainer, I'll just–"

Dean started laughing, and couldn't stop, especially after Cassie poked him.

"... Oh, you were talking about me."

He didn't respond, other than to keep grinning down at her.

"How long until we get married?" she asked.

Dean shrugged. "Ah, I concede to the lady's wishes, there. As early as tomorrow, if you'd like."

"But you haven't even proposed, yet," Cassandra pouted.

Dean grinned, walking Apache back to his stall as he fed the stallion another carrot. "Neither have you," he shot back over his shoulder.

Cassandra jogged to catch up to and walk with Dean. Together, they returned the handsome stud to his stall.

"Dean Forrester," Cassandra said, once he'd shut and locked the Clydesdale into his stall, "will you marry me?"

"What," Dean smirked, "not going to get down on one knee for me?" He laughed and then pulled her close as she made to kneel. "I'll forgive you, though, the shower floor has rough tile and ya knees probably still hurting from earlier," Dean smiled.

Cassie thumped him in the arm with a teasing punch. Still holding her close, Dean went down to one on a hay bale in front of the stallion's stall. Taking her hand, he lifted her knuckles to his lips and kissed them. "Cassandra Lexso," he began, then got choked up. "Cassie Lexso, Will you please be my wife?"

She beamed down at him, "Yes, you big daft fool. Now get up." Her smile stretched ear to ear. "All it took was promising him some threesomes, and I scored the man of my dreams for life! Didn't realize it'd be so easy," she giggled, with a sexy wink and a long kiss.

Dean was not sure what the future held, but he did know one thing for certain. His Cassie needed to be in it with him.

CHAPTER

NINETEEN

DEAN

Forrester-Lexso Estate

They spent another two hours with Nathanael in Gilligan's Farm. An hour of nothing but paperwork and then Dean shopping for cows for an extra hour. Lexis wanted some fresh milk for the estate. Secretly, he was fairly certain she was crushing on Nathanael's son, Bart, the space farmer.

When Dean finally arrived home, he realized it already past midday. He hit the gym for an hour, utilizing a few of the newer workout machines. His ability to be and stay in such great shape came only with commitment and dedication–something he refused to let slip.

Dean had Quincy and Dave join him for the rigorous exercise. He needed to keep his endurance and strength up, even if he wasn't training for a planetary competition. After lifting on the machines, he dove into the pool to swim some laps. He was on his twentieth minute of doing laps, when Lonny showed up with an ear to ear grin.

"Lonny," Dean teased from the edge of the pool, "ya get laid or something?" He pulled himself out and hopped up onto the pool deck to let the water cascade of him into the drain.

"Check it out," Lonny said, proudly producing a necklace with a locket. The locket held a number three on it.

Dean was dismayed. He tried to grab the locket, only to have his hand pass through it. "But what about the training?"

"Yeah, well..." Lonny started to say, when Anoka arrived.

"A rare and most prosperous water event has started. One that none should avoid. It's almost as if there is a blessing in progress," Anoka said with raised eyebrows.

"How do events work?" Dean asked, not wanting to get into whether or not Min was rewarding him.

"The event portals have two sides. PvP and PvE, just like the solo and team competitions. Easy enough to figure out, because they're on opposite ends of the city. They can vary a lot, depending on what the event encompasses and how it works. Events are usually something to help high-level people still compete, once they plateau and stagnate in their progression."

Dean retrieved a towel, drying himself off as she explained.

"Probably a good time for me to finally explain about the portals themselves. For example, you enter a PvE solo portal and compete your way to a locket. Touch the locket to the exit slot, and you're done–Poof, you're back outside the portal where you prepare and check stats. If, however, you see the threat is too great, you can always turn around and head back out the way you came."

Dean grumbled and said, "Sure. I get it. On a regular level one floor, objective is to find the locket and apply it to the keyhole or exit slot. Nothing else matters. If you get scared, flip a bitch and head back out the entrance. Sounds easy enough."

"Fair assessment," Anoka grinned. "Different way of putting it, yet a fair assessment."

"I take it events are different, though," Dean grunted.

"Event portals rotate colors. Blue for water, red for no magic, black for magic, and on a rare occasion, there will be a pink portal, which means weaponless," Anoka explained, following him into the showers. Lonny trailed after them, listening intently. "Ninety percent of the time, however, they're black."

Anoka continued, "They also don't have the same kind of exit, nor are they structured the same. Let me start by noting that in all events, contenders' levels are all baselined at zero. Your core stats are what matter."

Lonny cleared his throat and offered, "We're level zeros. I'm still a zero. The event is a blue–a water event–and all of Mixonia is in a fervor. Even I caught onto the hype. I was dropped into clear, deep water. There was a podium at the bottom. I swam down, grabbed the locket and stuck it in its slot. When I finished the level, two buttons appeared. One said exit, the other said next level."

Anoka halted him with a raised finger, "And there is the problem or boon, depending on how you look at it, with events. You can only run it once per event cycle and the event cycles last for two weeks, on average. Greed traps champions who otherwise feel too comfortable. I put Lonny here to the test. Get three tokens and exit. He's not marred by greed and will be training with you. Quincy and you will go here in a minute."

Dean furled his brows in confusion and said, "Shouldn't I train first?"

"The PvE solo water event has no foes until level four. You go in, do three levels, and get three tokens. Nothing fancy. If you attempt a fourth level, you'll have risked your life, before starting your training. Which you need. But two weeks of training with me will not make you deadly in the water. This event is a boon to some species," Anoka admitted with a shrug.

"What about the Core species," Dean asked. "You think they'd die in water?"

"They get a version of Core water, and when they compete in PvP, what they see is different. I'm not telling you to stop after three levels. It's not my place as your trainer, to give you orders. But I am telling you that we should all go and get three tokens while the event is open."

Dean nodded, it sounded like easy money.

"The second and third floors are only marginally harder than the first. If you can swim decently, there's a fairly low chance of drowning," Anoka said. She showed him her locket with a four on it. "This is what the cash in this morning got me. A token with a few leftover tiny gems. Shocker," she snorted with a smirk. "The token price went down, even in the short time I was there. Plus, I went ahead and did the first three levels."

"Whoa, even you went in?" Dean asked, a little surprised.

"Yup," she grinned. "Kambry can't go in without your permission, but I can. Here," Anoka handed Dean a curved dagger on a thigh belt. "It's like the filet knife you used in the combat video I saw. You're a natural in the water. Head to the blue portal and do six levels. There are approved flippers in the shuttle. If you somehow become a figurine, which I doubt with your magic, swimming strength, and willpower; then after a few more of your friends run through the first three levels, they can bail you out."

"What am I showering for then?" Dean snorted, stepping past the shower he was waiting to use.

"Exactly. Mr. Lexso and Mr. Kendricks are already back. Take Quincy, Cassandra, Kambry, and one more with you. I went so earlier, so I suggest taking that Patti girl. She seems capable," Anoka said.

Dean turned to his friend. "Did you talk to the businessmen about a job?" Dean asked.

"What I'm about to do right now. I got to see the Vaults of Min. These three tokens I earned in nine minutes would pay for my annual salary. So... I'm in," Lonny grinned. "Good luck, the first level is really easy."

"Can I bring Apache into a water portal?" Dean asked and Anoka stared at him, incredulous.

"Of course, you can. And he can kick you into a statue," she said with a roaring laugh.

Dean left the two of them chuckling over his dumb question. On the way to his suite he started to get excited. He'd had some minor regrets, spending all his tokens to free Lexis. Sure, he kept those feelings well hidden, while not doubting the value such a good will gesture may bring in the long haul; the issue was, it had left him without a reserve.

He stopped moping about his lack of a safety net when he entered his room. Cassandra was gearing up in a diver's one-piece swimsuit. Dean didn't bother to tell her their clothes would be transformed into togas. It'd just mean another outfit change, which didn't matter, really, since she'd be wearing her spacesuit for the trip there.

"You're coming too?" Dean asked and her face said everything he needed to know. He held his hands up in mock surrender at her glare. "Any objections to Patti, Quincy, and Kambry joining us?"

"No," Cassandra admitted, snapping her suit's butt to cling to her sculpted ass. Apparently, everyone around here is catching Mixonia fever, and our fathers... yes," she smirked, "I know Marty is not your real father. Our fathers are NDA-ing everyone they see and convincing them to come see the cave of wonders. If there wasn't serious money on the line, they'd be organizing a second trip. Right now, the portal is open for us."

"Then what are we waiting for?" Dean grinned, "Let's go show you Mixonia. It's different. Vast, yet confined. Actually, I'll let Mixonia speak for itself. Oh, and you'll get to see what Kambry looks like, in her natural form."

"Should I get in my spacesuit?" Cassandra asked and Dean nodded.

"I'm not going to. Mainly because we don't have enough and there is a really low risk. Plus, I think your Dad still has it," Dean said, as she went to gear up in her suit.

"Hey Cassie. If I fail, you pick me off that shelf, okay?"

"How is that working? Are we loot piling for the socialistic greater good or what?" Cassie said and Dean frowned.

He'd not considered that. There was a big reality here that was sinking into Dean. Especially with Lonny having a locket around his neck. The math would never mean that everything was up to him. This needed to be a planet-wide Oakley group effort.

"I get Kambry's three tokens, by contract, she forfeits all tokens earned forever until I release her from her contract. Savage, but I didn't write the thing. Hence my mistake about the Kubras, earlier.

"Lonny is already his own champion, with the ability to lock the portal as a gate master. Any of us are, really, if we go in alone. Key thing is, there can only be one gate master at a time," Dean said. "I guess we shouldn't just trust anyone, though, because if they never come out, we'll be fooked until we find the other portals."

"Well, everyone understands taxes–and that overhead costs need to be covered. Maybe institute a twenty percent tax that goes to two things? Ten percent into a communal fund to free others, and ten percent that goes to the upkeep of training grounds, supplies, materials, spacesuit, shuttles, and everything."

Dean called Anoka, who surprisingly, picked up on the first ring. "What are taxes like in the guilds?"

Dean placed her on speaker.

"Thirty percent. Ten percent automatically goes into a recovery fund, the other twenty to be used at the guild's discretion. Why? If you're going to implement a tax, I completely understand. Just know, however, that it's common practice to let new members earn twenty-five tokens for their own recovery, first, before implementing the tax," Anoka said.

Cassandra came back in with the suit on. "Sounds fair," she said, "You deposit your tokens into a contracted token bank. First twenty-five tokens are never taxed. Tax kicks in automatically after that. Not amazing for those of us shouldering the upfront costs. However, we are talking about lives here."

"Exactly. Even the soulless guilds understand you can't tax statues who are not producing. The guild will kick out members who earn their twenty-five, become a figure, and then repeat that cycle too often." The experienced trainer sighed, heavily. "Of course, I'm not perfect. I trained Kambry to know better; her double deaths are a huge no-no."

Dean thanked her and hung up the phone. When he texted Quincy, Kambry, and Patti, they all said they were already on the shuttle. Perfect.

Cassandra was ready to go and the two of them rode the elevator down with excited small talk. When they entered the shuttle, Dean was nervous. He had no problem admitting he felt unprepared. Kambry scoffed at this and noted that Lonny had already finished the trial.

During the half hour flight, they reviewed a video of Lonny explaining the scenario. It was very basic, and by the time they were ready to land, Dean was feeling much better about the first three levels.

What happened on the fourth floor was still a big concern, however. Yet, if he lost, he knew he'd be rescued. He was sure of it—until self-doubt's insidious tentacles wormed their way back in again. He was mostly sure.

The five of them trooped down the tunnels with Cassandra's suit in front of them, her headlights illuminating the way. Dean promised himself he'd buy a whole locker room full of suits. With the constant rain, he expected critters to occupy the caves at some point. Then again, he'd yet to see any life down here, so maybe the magic of this place kept it free of monsters topside—so that Oakley's champions could face the monsters below.

He was fairly certain Riva would do exactly that. Dean was fairly confident the board members and desk jockeys would all be using suits to transition.

Which led to the problem of figuring out a rotation, as to who was inside and during what times. They were avoiding each other, for now, and coordinating the few folks who entered Mixonia was fairly simple. Dean was reminded, however, that this needed to become a planetary operation. He was just a simple fisherman, a single competitor among what should be hundreds of champions, to share the risk and win the game.

When they reached Felna, Dean stopped by her alcove, to make a brief delivery.

"Felna," Dean said with a warm smile. "Here's your salad."

The Minotaur licked her bovine lips. "Thank you, Dean. Always busy on event days. I actually miss the interaction. So... I've got no way to pay, but ..." Felna hesitated.

"Just ask," Cassandra smiled.

Dean was surprised Cassandra and Patti were unaffected by the Minotaur.

"Would a screen and some movies be a possibility?"

"Without a doubt," Dean grinned. "Make a list while we're gone, and I'll get your items delivered. Just because some Suca mistreat Minotaurs, that's not us."

She said thank you almost a dozen times before spawning the portal. When they finally stepped through, Dean was still a mix of excitement and nerves.

∞∞∞∞

Patti squeaked when she stumbled into Kambry's wings. Finally, a reaction Dean was expecting. Cassandra cursed the fact that she was suddenly in a toga. There were grumbles, shocked expressions, and sounds you'd generally hear from a gaggle of excited kids.

Dean let them have their moment and went to check out the map again.

Kambry was explaining how she had been born here and rarely used this portal. She mentioned the entryway platform and the statues were a great spot to start. Dean noticed she was in a frumpy robe with her hood drawn up. She was not going to be a distraction, for this trip at least.

"Come on over and take a look at the map. It's not perfect, and it's out of date, but it'll help," Dean said, shaking them out of their awed 'ohs'.

"This is amazing," Cassandra smiled. "So, we need to go to Event PvE, correct?"

"Yup," Kambry said. "It's imperative you don't go beyond floor three. I'd even recommend Dean not do that, but he is the Master, and you're his Mistress," Kambry said from beneath her hood. "This event happens only once a year, sometimes less. Apparently, Dean has the luck of the gods, because this opportunity was not expected for several more months."

Dean grinned and couldn't resist giving Kambry a wink.

"See this chalkboard tablet?" she continued, "You get your information here. There'll be another at the Event PvE Portal."

Dean went to the display board she'd pointed at to pull up Oakley's score. *Core – 58*

Kambry saw and said, "Relax, everyone is doing events. This is a long, long game. Even if a disaster happens in your preparation phase, you'll recover. They'll find the other portals. Riva and Marty are the right humans for the task. Also, events don't count for the planetary tally."

"Huh, why not?" Cassandra asked.

"Basically, events are not evenly matched whereas the non-events are. For example, a level on solo PvE will put you in a randomly generated labyrinth that is at the same difficulty for any Core or Suca species."

Kambry frowned. "Events are different, though. Events can be swimming, climbing, fighting, and so on. If the event is flying, can Dean fly? No. So adding an event that they may, or may not, be able to participate fairly in competitions that may spell a planet's demise isn't just. Events are primarily for luring in retired champions, thirsty for sweet, sweet tokens."

"Okay, that alleviates my fears to some extent. I'm still worried that the next event, it won't be me defending Oakley. Go over the stats for everyone, please," Dean said, pulling up his own stats.

Champion Information
Name: Dean Forrester Gender: Male
Level: 0 Tokens: 0
Race: Human Alignment: Suca
Luck: 14 Charisma: 41

Health: 346 / 346 H-Regen: 1.0 / Sec
Stamina: 296 / 296 M-Regen: 1.0 / Sec
Mana: 312 / 312 S-Regen: 1.0 / Sec

Strength: 214 Vitality: 132
Dexterity: 107 Endurance: 189
Intelligence: 94 Willpower: 218
Magic: Electrical

Kambry continued, "As you'll note, Dean right now is middle of the road. With his superior strength you'd think he'd only be fit to stand on the front line, but the man has immense willpower and endurance–those round him out.

"Patti pull up yours. I bet we see something different."

Champion Information
Name: Patti Kendricks Gender: Female
Level: 0 Tokens: 0
Race: Human Alignment: Suca

Luck: -3 Charisma: 21

Health: 191 / 191 H-Regen: 1.0 / Sec
Stamina: 226 / 226 M-Regen: 1.0 / Sec
Mana: 194 / 194 S-Regen: 1.0 / Sec

Strength: 87 Vitality: 104
Dexterity: 121 Endurance: 105
Intelligence: 111 Willpower: 83

"Ugh! What's this mean? Negative luck?" Patti asked, her face twisted in confusion. "Ain't that the truth? Why am I so much lower than Dean?"

"Let's walk and talk," Kambry said, stepping down the ramp. "You add your strength and vitality to get your health. Your endurance and dexterity together give you your stamina. Your willpower and intelligence together equal your mana. If you score especially high on any single section, you tend to gravitate to a particular slot in a party–be that melee, ranged, or mage," she explained.

"Now, as to why your stats are so much lower than Dean's," she shrugged. He works out a lot. His work over the years has improved his hand eye coordination and he has the willpower of an ox. For you, stamina is your highest score. If you start running every day, that stat will continue to increase."

"Okay," Patti said, examining her stats and excitedly tapping her finger, "so I'd probably be best suited to become a ranger. Running is easier than trying to slam weights. Being an archer with a tank pet would be awesome. Assuming I can get one."

Dean knew from experience that she was a closet gamer. She was probably already designing her build.

"Um... Sure. I'd still go with a horse, though. Because they're smart, nimble, and deadly themselves. However, don't let my opinion deter you. The market has some interesting pets that are comparatively cheap," Kambry admitted.

Patti beamed.

"But Patti," Kambry warned, resting a hand on her arm, "for all that is holy, realize that your pet can and will kill you. Or those you have around you, when you bring it home. So, choose very, very carefully."

Quincy stuck a finger up. "I checked my Champion state. I've got decent luck and charisma. What're those stats for and what are the regens all about?"

"Luck is random," Kambry shrugged, "you'll never figure it out. Charisma is how others will probably receive you, based on your looks and attitude. Dean, for example, is easy on the eyes and pretty good with his tongue, or so I heard from Cassandra when I was scrubbing a toilet one room over."

Cassandra burst into a laugh that they all joined in on. Dean blushed.

Kambry let everyone calm before bypassing Min's statues and leading them around the waterfall to reveal the city of Mixonia. Patti and Cassandra gasped at all the aliens and the sky soaring stone structures. Dean now understood why Sable had paused with him here, too, the view tended to be overwhelming.

"Stay close to me," Kambry instructed, "the streets are going to get crowded." The dragon woman stepped out onto the main road that separated the districts. "To answer your other question, Quincy, 'Regen' is short for regeneration. Regen rates are dictated by consumption: food for strength, drink for stamina, and potions for mana. Mana potions are crafted here, though you should only buy them from the market."

"Inside the portals you'll notice you can die. Which means you can get hurt, too. It's a game world inside the labyrinths, not a real one, though. So, if you take an arrow to the knee, pull the arrow out, and retreat. With time it will heal, assuming your foes don't end you while you're wounded. And that sums up your character sheet."

Cassandra tapped her shoulder and asked, "How do we improve our stats?"

"Training. Lots and lots of training. While intelligence is the hardest to increase, it can be done. Willpower is pretty much withstanding shitty situations with ease. For strength, you can lift weights. For dexterity, focus on your hand eye coordination. Endurance is increased by exercising for extended periods. Vitality is a mix of the others, factoring in your age, and your overall health. All that can be done at the estate," Kambry said leading them into the crowd.

She slowed their advance into the city and pointed out each district, calmly explaining one at a time, unlike Sable's half-assed tour. Dean commented on how quiet it was, and Kambry mentioned that was because most citizens were competing in the event to get tokens.

He found this a bit farfetched until they passed Min's Vault, and he saw that the queue for the PvE portal wrapped around a whole section of the city. They got in line. He was pleased to note that the queue was moving quickly.

A lot of aliens came right out of the portal and headed straight for the market, leaving a trail of dripping water behind them. Dean realized he had a really pressing question he'd meant to ask Sable, but had forgotten to.

"So Kambry," Dean asked, "what happens when a baby poops in a diaper? Same with trash... there doesn't seem to be much litter around."

The Dragona snickered and shrugged, "Magical toilets and trash bins. Pee into a toilet and it just vanishes. To where, I'd rather not know. For diapers, you simply hold it in the trash for a few seconds, and when you remove it, it magically comes back clean. There are still ground crews, however, who go about cleaning up the litter."

Quincy started trying to find the garbage collectors.

Kambry smiled. "They're there, just harder to spot."

"Oh," she continued, "before you ask, you'll never see it become nighttime down here. If you want it dark, you have to go somewhere private."

Patti started to raise a hand.

"Before you ask the obvious," the Dragona grinned, "why? Legends say there was an unexplained crime spike during those times. Go figure."

Dean elbowed Quincy when he noticed the bunny girls. His friend blushed. Patti noticed their exchange and frowned.

"They're pretty. Why are there so many more women than men?" Patti asked.

Kambry pointed to the portals. "Sure, there are some women with hot heads, like me. But think about it rationally. A mother of two isn't going to race into a PvP portal. She'll likely do this event, because even the old grandpas do this one. But generally speaking, women tend to be more levelheaded."

"Exactly," Cassandra said with a big grin. "And now you're one of us."

"In three months, I'll either be free, or indeed just like you," Kambry admitted, "with a 'bun in the oven' as I heard it called. Not a fan of the needles, though." The pretty Dragona shuddered.

Dean blushed.

Cassandra kissed his cheek, slipping her hand into his. He reddened further from the public display of affection. Cassandra gave him a smile, squeezed his hand, and leaned into him. The line moved quickly, and soon they were nearing the portal entrance.

"Should I get a weapon and go beyond level three?" Quincy asked.

"Please don't," everyone said, with varying levels of concern, at slightly different times.

Quincy grumbled at this. "But Dean is," he muttered.

"I may not, and we both know," Dean said with a shrug, "I'm part fish."

A merman in front of him spun around, eyed him from head to toe, and scoffed.

"Figure of speech," Dean admitted, chagrined.

The portal loomed twenty feet high above. The line was thin enough at this point for Dean to see the entry process. Everyone placed a hand on a pedestal, said something, and then went in. He was still nervous when Kambry paused right before she was due to go next.

"Permission to—"

"Granted to level three," Dean snapped, and received a death glare in return. She clearly wanted to do more and was disappointed in him. He could live with that, though.

"Okay before I go in, one last thing," Kambry said, pointing to the regular portals. "Events stack rewards, unlike over there. There, they add on top of each other. Here you keep going until you decide to exit, and the final floor is your reward. Not cumulative. Got it?"

We nodded and she waved goodbye.

She placed her hand on the pedestal, stated her name, said she understood the consequences of her action, and then walked into the shimmering blue.

Dean was next. Before he stepped up to the pedestal, he handed Cassandra the flippers that were tied to his waist. "I don't say it much to anyone. I love you and I'll be angry if you don't take these."

Cassandra accepted, graciously, and Quincy bounced his eyebrows at the rare display. Before she could thank him, or get into a longwinded reply, he walked up to the Minotaur guard who stood by the pedestal.

"I love you too, you big lug," Cassandra shouted. "Now bring home the bacon! Mama needs a new pair of shoes."

Dean shook his head and chuckled.

The hulking Minotaur guard was unfazed by the outburst. "Place your hand on the pedestal, state your name, and confirm you're here to compete with an understanding that if you fail, your soul is forfeit," the guard said.

If Dean had a newb sign over his head, he never saw it. He placed his hand on the pedestal and said, "I, Dean Forrester, am here to compete and understand I will become a statue if I fail."

"Close enough," the Minotaur grunted. "Hit the exit when you're ready to leave. Only one entry per event."

Dean walked into the blue watery portal.

CHAPTER

TWENTY

DEAN

Water Event – Floor One

Dean experienced a falling sensation when his senses returned. His eyes rapidly absorbed his surroundings. He tucked his arms in a twirl to see the horizon held an endless bright blue ocean.

He gulped a lungful of air before his feet dove into the crystal-clear water. Opening his eyes under the water, he saw a pedestal about ten feet down. He rotated to reorient his frame in a downward posture and swam for the shiny golden locket.

A second or two later, he removed the locket from the pedestal. He studied the magical item and judged its weight in his hand. On top of the pedestal there was an indicator and a sign. 'Insert locket here'.

Lonny wasn't kidding. This is a breeze.

Dean stuck the locket in and found himself magically transported to a dry room. Excess water dripped from him. He was shocked at how easy it was. He was no longer in an ocean. The magic had been so smooth and seamless it caught him by surprise.

No wonder the whole damn city is doing this event. That was less than a minute of work for a token. Holy shit. Score.

The room held no windows or doors. Two pedestals stood before him, each with a button.

One was labeled (Exit), the other labeled (Next Level). Dean smacked the next level button and the room vanished.

He was above the surface of the water again, falling from twenty feet up. He rotated around into a dive. Dean did exactly as his swim coach from middle school had taught him: body tight, hands flat, and slim your profile.

The water welcomed him as he dove in. There was a T shaped structure of rocks where the pedestal had been before. Dean kicked and stroked until he entered the only large opening.

Once inside the tunnel, he was surprised to find it wasn't dark. The clear water was bright with magic. He swam to the intersection and saw an air pocket here.

Oh man, this is easy mode. I'm not even close to being out of air.

Dean decided to test the air bubble and went up for air, while treading water. He may have relaxed and let a pee go he'd been holding in. The air pocket was only at the intersection, though, so he dove back down and went to the right. When he entered that room, though, there was no podium and no golden locket.

He scanned the room thoroughly before turning around to head back to the air pocket. Pausing briefly to grab another breath, and he went left. There rested the gleaming beauty of a token. Dean quickly grabbed the item and quickly stuck it in the indicated slot.

Teleportation to the dry room was swift. He parked his butt down for a bit to see if anyone or anything would rush his next decision. When nothing had happened after ten minutes of waiting, he mashed the (Next Level) button for another easy token.

Dean reappeared once more about twenty feet above the water. He tucked into a dive, splashed down, and went for the cavern mouth. There were six rooms, now. The T into additional T-junctions, off the original. Dean bypassed the first intersection with plenty of air in his lungs.

He turned right with some rapid strokes and entered a room with two tunnels. He went right again and came up empty. There was an air pocket here, though, so he stopped for some fresh air.

A quick trip back down and he swam left this time. His strokes were calm, the water was nice, and he was enjoying the event. Soon enough, he found the locket.

No wonder the city had a line stretching so far back. He stuck the locket into the slotted groove and poof, he was dry again.

Now came his first real test, though. The big moment. Anoka had faith in him. After those basic levels, Dean had more faith in himself, too. The tingling in his mind warned him this was a setup. An obvious con in the works. Three simple wins, he thought, why not go for a fourth, fifth, and sixth? At what point did it switch from easy mode to hard?

He was certain it would.

Dean walked up and hovered over the exit button. He wore a necklace again, with a locket that said it had three tokens. That was good money. Maybe another chance of freeing some other desperate soul or stockpiling in case he got stuck on a shelf. Yet... There was a moment of self-doubt that he buried deep.

His left hand left its temporary hover and smashed the Next Level button like a boss.

Poof.

He was twenty feet up once more. Dean tucked neatly into a dive. A single shark, about six feet long, circled the pedestal. Dean suddenly wanted to belly flop, instead of plunging in deep, but he was committed. He slipped into the water cleanly.

He yanked the knife out of the sheath with a swift movement. The flow of water tried to rip the weapon from his grasp. He clenched onto it and kicked hard, speeding for his target. The shark was oblivious until the very last moment.

The shark's eye rolled back to notice the predator trying to kill it and bolted.

Huh, fook. I guess he didn't want to die.

Dean had no idea what level of realism there was here or if the generated monsters in your path were not realistic at all. In most virtual games, they'd go bonkers and attack immediately... Ah, Dean saw the shark regroup from its startled flight.

Dean grabbed the locket and pressed it into the indent before it could return.

He arrived back to the dry room dripping water with his knife sheathed at this thigh. *Hmm...* He immediately paced, trying to come to a resolution.

"It's a shark. Small, but still a shark," he reasoned. "Fighting a shark in the water is dumb." Dean bit a nail, deep in thought. "If I avoid its detection, though, can I stealth past it? Is the goal here to kill or simply dodge? Will killing it bring others?"

Dean knew some might consider him crazy for talking to himself, but he was hoping Min might pop up and save him with some inside, in-depth vital information, but that never happened. Something else did occur, though.

When Dean hovered his hand over the Next Level button, a spark from his palm linked to the round device and indented it for him.

Poof.

Well, shit, Dean thought. He wasn't mentally ready. He also knew it simply was what it was, no use worrying about it. When he plummeted the twenty feet into the water, he did so at a slight angle and pulled his feet up quickly to stop his descent. He spied a single shark circling the underwater caverns. He knew there was no rush or a timer, so he watched.

"Are there more of you?" Dean wondered, treading water.

An idea crossed his mind of cutting himself to free blood into the ocean. He passed, knowing better. He swam away from the cavern below him and thumped into an invisible wall.

Right, just like there was a hidden roof. This barrier felt exactly the same as the one he'd encountered during his fight with that Demon. He concluded there'd be no hidden shark snacking him from behind. The real question was, were there two sharks below or merely the loner, doing laps.

At this point, Dean wished he still had his flippers. Cassie would've been fine without them, and now he found he needed them. That was probably exactly why the Events section prohibited reentry. He couldn't see any other sharks.

There was no point in waiting any longer. Dean gulped some air and shot down into the water when the shark was around the back end of the cavern. His breast-strokes were fluid and within seconds he was in the cavern's mouth. He darted down the short tunnel, unopposed. He immediately went left at the T-junction without stopping. No locket. He turned around without taking another breath and went into the room to the right. While he sought his treasure, he was pleased to find that there were, thankfully, no extra sharks.

The second room held the golden locket. When he placed the locket in the indent, he reappeared in the dry room.

His necklace showed a five now. He allowed himself a celebratory grin and fist pump.

Dean was starting to pick up on a pattern. If this went all the way to a thousand, and each step was a little higher than the one before, then there was a long way to go before it should get tough. At this point his apprehension at the situation was fading, his worries unfounded. The next floor should have six rooms and one shark.

He smashed the button for the next level.

He fell from above the ocean with another feet first insertion. He treaded water until the shark was on the far side of the extra-large caverns. His race to the bottom was swift.

Into the tunnel he went, once again unopposed. This time he picked wrong at every single turn, until the last room finally rewarded him with a victory. He placed the locket into the indent and was magicked away.

Inside the dry room he was about to do something crazy and go for level seven. His gut said hell yeah, while his mind screamed no. Seeing as how he'd pissed off his gut lately, having starkly limited the amount of booze he'd allowed himself, it won the fight. His hand smacked the 'Next Level' button.

Fook me.

Dean didn't fall from the sky. He found himself on a circular platform, fifteen feet off the ground. There were only about two broad arms lengths of space to pace up here.

He inspected the labyrinth before him. There were jumping pedestals arrayed in varying height differences. He scowled at the sight because at the very end was a pedestal with a shiny golden glint on it.

To get from the platform he was on to the one over would be a ten-foot jump. Craggy rocks separating the two spots below. Meaning a fall would either kill him or maim him. Dean knew he could regenerate health, whatever that meant. He was in no hurry to break a bone to find out.

What am I missing? Dean scanned around and saw behind him was water. Barely deep enough to jump into. He noticed the distant platform had a roundabout way to it with what looked like handholds. Sure, it'd be slower going to take the outside water path instead of the jumping shortcut...

Yup fook risky jumps. This was a water portal anyway. Dean lowered himself until his fingertips left him dangling over the water below and let go. The plummet was shorter than he expected, though; the shallow water barely slowed his descent.

"Argg..." Dean cried out, twisting his ankle.

So much for not testing out health regeneration. He started the long walk around the exterior but found the trek through waist deep water with a hurt ankle was slow going. Dean was not in a rush, though, and wanted to ensure his ankle felt better before he had to climb.

Dean found a nice spot on a rock to wait before the water started to get much deeper. A few minutes on his perch allowed him to roll his ankle with ease. *Alright, that answers that question. If I get hurt, I do feel better with a bit of time, assuming I have time to heal.*

When he was nearing a deeper spot, he noticed movement in the depths. Dean was in no hurry, so he waited patiently for the movement again. After five minutes he could see a vague outline of the beast. There was a crab, the size of an elephant, below him. A back-leg twitching in its sleep gave away its position.

Dean pondered how best to handle this new obstacle. There were some rocks over on the right that he could crawl over, or he could race for the other side. Dean picked the rocks. He gingerly and carefully navigated their slimy surfaces to get around to the other side of the deep pit.

Five minutes of this resulted in a host of scrapes and cuts, as his soft moist skin collided with slippery as well as jagged edges. The moment he was clear of the deep pool, Dean hopped back into the chest deep water. He swam for the final pedestal.

Blinding pain shot through his left calf causing Dean to cry out. His whipped his knife out instinctively as he spun to defend himself. The king crab had pincered his leg into mush; the tibia and fibula were both shattered. Dean thrust his dagger at his foe's pincher, barely visible beyond the stars in his eyes.

He was picked up out of the water as the vile beast twisted to dodge his thrust. A flick of its wrist sent Dean flying for the rocks. His body crashed into the large stones with a painful snap. His left arm was broken behind his back. Punctured ribs screamed at him telling him they were shattered. He laid there, broken but unbeaten.

Dean knew a dagger was never going to kill this monster. That left Dean with only one option.

As the crab *clacked* up onto the rocks in a sideways skittering crawl, Dean raised his one good arm until his right palm aimed at the huge crab. The black monster hurried to finish off its prey.

A surge of heat coursed through his body, along with the nauseas sensation of needing to spill his stomach contents. He poured that feeling into his palm. When it felt like he might explode, Dean unleashed the power gathered there.

The blast of intensely bright light cascading out of his hand literally blinded him. Dean didn't hesitate or celebrate at the *crash* of hard shell smacking into the rocks. He blasted electrical magic at the beast, and kept blasting it with magic, until there was nothing left to eject from his hand.

Broken, battered, and probably out of mana, he tried to get comfortable while his body healed. That simply was not going to be possible. He shrieked in agony as his injuries screamed at him for attention. Without a way to see, down an arm, and his leg a crushed ruin of flesh, he was forced to suffer.

It felt like an hour of pure misery before his eyesight suddenly returned. He looked down to see that his crushed leg was mostly healed. His arm popped back into place five minutes later. His scream drowned out the loud thump as it went back into its socket. Ten painful minutes later, and he was able to wiggle his toes.

Fook floor eight. Fook floor eight and fook this labyrinth. I need ten drinks to forget this ever happened.

He gingerly limped over to his destroyed foe. There was a hole the size of a basket-ball clean through the main shell. Golf ball-sized holes littered the rest of the body, from his follow-on desperation shots. Dean learned a few things in the next moments.

Most importantly, that his electrical magical ability was devastating. He also realized he couldn't eat the crab, no matter how hard he tried. A bit disappointing really. Crabs were near impossible to catch on Oakley. Dean grumbled when he left the corpse for the last podium. He scaled the tower once he felt almost back to normal.

The magic of this place was amazing. Everything was just a touch too real, though, to be a video game though. He'd known and faced death before—this felt no different. The pain had been unbearable and the memory of it still ached in his mind. He was almost done, though, and a drink would be waiting from him soon.

When Dean reached that pinnacle spot, he felt so proud and so glad to be done with this level that he cried out for joy. Only to scream in rage when he saw what stood atop the pedestal. It was a golden coin. Not a locket.

"Curse you!" Dean shouted to the empty arena. His attempts to pick up the coin were about the same as how they went with the Demon's loot. The coin always returned to the point at which it started. Even when he chucked it into the water it returned to its resting spot.

There was a locket in here, and it wasn't on the pedestal. Down he went from the tall pillar to start his hunt for the locket. The next three hours were spent searching between rocks. He almost drowned hunting for the locket in the big crab's lair. The cave was filled with skeletal bones and hard to see in. That part sucked double because it was just a colossal waste of time.

At the very end he returned to the shallow water he had initially jumped into. Right there, in that pillar, was a cutout.

A locket and an indent rested right there.

Dean screamed in rage until his voice was scratchy and broken.

Duh, it was only level seven. He snatched the locket and touched it to the indent for a trip to the dry room. Without hesitation he lunged and pressed the exit button.

Seven was better than six and good enough for Dean.

TWENTY-ONE

DEAN

Mixonia

Dean exited the portal on the other side of jammed Mixonians eager to go in. Immediately he learned a lesson when he found out he was alone. Set a rallying point to regroup at, or even rent a shitty bedroom to stage gear in. Something besides going home to Oakley and the estate.

He was lost in the sea of people with seven fresh tokens to his name and a burning desire to have a drink.

He knew he was an idiot for almost dying to a crab he could have avoided by inspecting the base of the very first rock. And now this. He didn't need anything from Min's vault. He knew what he needed, though, to find a bar.

Sobriety blew and after pretty much dying, some throat burning belches seemed like a grand idea. That meant he'd need some local currency. Probably everyone and their mother was selling gems for tokens right now.

In the distance he saw a massive line for Min's Vault of Treasures. He sure hoped Cassandra wasn't waiting for him in front of a human shelf. With a shrug he walked for the distant market. The mood of the many Suca aliens crammed in this dense city was joyous.

This was a monumental day. A day where hope filled a city filled with tragedies. A wave of noise assaulted him as vendors hawked their food, the poor peddled, and the joyful skipped with glee. Dean took it all in. He was overwhelmed and yet, simply another soul among the crowd.

His aimless wandering came to halt when he spotted a long line in the middle of a housing district. The snaking wait appeared to be for a bank.

Perfect. Dean knew there were swindlers on the street eager to trade him gems for a token. He also expected to get hit with a fee from this business. He didn't care, just like losing six million to taxes didn't faze him. Sure, it bothered him. But he refused to cry over taxes or fees–they were unavoidable.

He set a leisurely walk to the line that was long. Further down he saw a bank's line that was almost empty. That told him all he needed to know.

Dean joined the queue, the last body in the trailing snake. He adjusted his mostly wet toga and wished he'd thought to have another set of clothes handy. Probably for the best that they did get an apartment in the city, or at least rent a storage room.

While he fiddled with his outfit, searching in vain for a dry bit of cloth to cover his crotch, he saw a full team of warrior cat men flirting with what looked like a bunch of shy raccoon girls in front of him. Dean wanted to name this city Monstertopia, but figured the name was probably trademarked by Chrysler-Pixar entertainment.

Dean was drifting in his focus when he heard a throat clear behind him. Ah, no longer the last sucker in the long line, he turned to see a woman with fluffy bear ears.

She had hair on the back of her palms, a flat nose, and accentuated canines. Other than that, she appeared human. Her body was mostly covered in a barmaid's outfit, a shawl draped over and hiding her bust.

Since, Dean couldn't see her rear, he automatically wondered if she had a tail. The inner man-child in him desperately wanted to know. The bearish woman was almost six feet tall and smiling at him. Her inspection of his mostly see through toga ended with a brief curtsy and a 'hello'.

"A human. Don't see your kind around much. I'd a drinking buddy, eons ago, from a place called Alaska. Charles, good man, bad drunk. Charles disappeared one day, though, and he never showed up in the vault," she said passively. Not shy, yet with a hint of caution. As if her confidence was down and recent events perked her up.

"I'm Dean, from a new planet to the... this," Dean grinned, making a mild all-encompassing gesture.

"Scarla," she smiled back at him, "nice to meet you Dean. How'd you find your way in? Me, I waz born 'ere." Her proper talk was quickly slipping, as she grew more comfortable.

"Well met, Scarla. A Demon firecaster and his four hounds met me while I was at work. I slew them and was led to my treasure," Dean said honestly, and not sure why.

"Ah, already back for more bounties out of the vault are ya. I went and got three myself today. Between work and the few easy events, I get by. Not a big strong adventurer like you, though." Scarla's eyes lingered on Dean's frame hungrily. "Surprised you haven't been scooped up by one of those bunny girls. Charles loved to talk about how their tits squeaked."

"Like a dog toy?" Dean asked with a raised brow.

This was one thing he'd certainly have to test... for science, of course.

"Afraid ya lost me. Squeak like a noise. Anywho. What's your plans in Mixonia?"

"Ah," Dean guiltily scruffed the back of his neck, "Seems I lost my party. I went to the seventh floor in the event, after being told not to go past the sixth." He shuddered. "Needless to say, it sucked, and I spent far more time there than I had intended. Barely survived, actually, and now I want a drink. I can't get a drink with tokens, though, and I've been meaning to open an account."

"Bearclays Banking is a fair place. They work on volume. Better rates and lower fees. No one of import comes here, though, mostly just locals. Not everyone can waste their time in line," she pointed to the shifting line and nudged him forward so Dean could close the gap. They weren't even halfway there, yet, but Dean was okay with that. "Mind you, it's extra busy at the moment. As more people come out of the portal, it'll get even busier. You want to know a sad truth?"

Dean didn't, so he shook his head, no.

"Aye, I can understand that. I, myself, should focus on the positives. Work's steady, pay is shit but enough, and my roommate is setting me up on a nice date with another Brooza. That's my species. I'm almost five hundred years old, hiding away in this place," Scarla admitted.

"I take it my need to find employees for outside of Mixonia will be tough if I tried to hire from within? I happen to be needing a bartender for my estate," Dean said with a charming smile.

His charisma check failed.

"Not me, love, I'd not leave here, no matter what. How much ya paying though? I got some lady friends who'd love to shack up with a champion like you. Assuming you're willing to give some assurances, bound by Min," Scarla said pleasantly.

"What would entice them to the point they'd be content?" Dean wondered. He noticed the two Oruk moms with well-behaved kids nudging closer to eavesdrop on their conversation.

"You've got work?" the first mom asked and Scarla rolled her eyes.

"You'll find that a lot, Mr. Dean. Mixonia is expensive. Wives be needing to work, to get up enough tokens to free their husbands. Or simply leave them and start anew, sorry kids," Scarla said with a fake smile. "So be mindful. If you're paying well, the job market'll empty out for you.

"But no need to pay well. They're those who'd lick your toilets clean to stay alive inside here, out of self-preservation. And then there are those who'd let you pack their back doors to save their siblings or children. The wives have it the worst, of course. They're desperate with morals, which more often than not, leads to them having to leave."

The first mom stepped forward beside Scarla and nodded, "She's right. I'm saying goodbye to Larkner today. It's simply too expensive to live in this city. If I leave, I'll grow old, and Oruk men have no use for old women. His daughter will get a chance to compete, one day, mayhap to free him. Or if I find the proper setup, I'll return for easy events like today while I age. Five years should see him free. He'd not leave me then." She shifted her little girl over to her other hip.

"I smell wolfman all over you," Scarla said, flaring her nose with a long sniff.

"Uncle Rarmer's a wolfman," the little girl giggled, "he howls in mommy's room when they wrestle."

Just like that, the two moms left for the back of the line. Kids say the darndest things.

"Probably pleasing him for money. It's really hard to survive here with kids," Scarla admitted with a sigh.

Dean shrugged. "The whole point of life is to have a challenge. I hope she finds happiness. I guess I'll limit myself to a single drink, and then try to find a bartender and maybe some stable hands to shovel horse shit."

"You ain't got help for common chores on your estate? There were two single mommas back there that'd do it for room and board if you'd let them use the portal when events were up," Scarla said and Dean rolled his eyes.

"Ah," she laughed, "you want pretty ones. Can't fault ya for that. Charles was into those bunny girls. They tend to breed quickly, hence why you see them around here so often."

That wasn't what he wanted, but he wasn't going to argue semantics. Sexy babes on the estate were better than ugly ones.

"Downsides?" Dean asked.

"Dumb, which is fine. They'll never be master scientists." She laughed.

"Hell, Narma, my boss, he never lets the bunny-lasses handle any transactions. They can write up the bill, but when it comes time to pay, that's handled by someone else."

Dean smiled. Sounded like some girls he'd gone to high school with.

"They don't like to leave Mixonia, though, which you'll find is beyond common. Also, they're real bitches when they get knocked up. Which is super easy to do. The males are hotheads and either get tossed onto the shelves for law violations or they enter portals and lose quickly, because they're idiots."

"Ah, what would you recommend?" Dean asked and Scarla pointed a thumb to her chest and then at the raccoon girls. "Both easy on the eyes and plump. Probably make great humans."

"What'd it cost me," he wondered, "for say, five years labor with portal access?"

"Including room n' board?" Scarla raised an eyebrow.

Dean nodded.

"Can they fuck for money?" she wanted to know, and Dean winced.

He jostled his head left and right as he thought about it. "Start with no, dance for tips, sure. Brothels are legal, but then I've got to deal with the proverbial howling wolfman. I got some single friends that'll be competing in here. And others too. I'd rather just pay them more, so they are happy."

"Wholesome," she nodded. "Let me be honest with you, Dean, a woman rarely sells her flesh if she has extra funds to live freely. How about I take you to Tammy's Tavern after you set up your account and introduce you to some of my friends?"

Dean frowned, and again shook his head, no. His previously burning desire to get wasted was replaced by a heartache for his love. Deep down, he knew he was changing. Sure, he still planned on squeezing a bunny girl's tits, to find out if they squeaked, but he also wanted to hold his Cassie tightly.

"I'll find you next time I come back," he promised. "We normally do morning runs into Mixonia and now I know where to find ya." He blushed. "I appreciate the offer, really I do, but I kinda got a drinking problem," Dean admitted with a guilty shrug.

Scarla nodded with a frown and said, "That's what I think happened to Charles. I'd like to imagine so, anyways. He went back to Alaska with his favorite bunny girl, had a bunch of babies, grew old, and forgot this place existed."

They had shuffled with the line as it moved forward. Their conversation filling both the time and wait in line.

"Next," a commanding voice said from in front of the bank.

"That's me, Scarla. Thanks for helping me understand the city, better. I'll see you at Tammy's Tavern in the future," Dean nodded to her before heading into the bank.

She waved without another word.

The teller was a Merman of some sort, with flashy jagged teeth, tiger shark lines on his light green skin, and gills on his neck.

"What can I do for you?" the teller asked.

"Here are my winnings from today," Dean said, handing over his locket. "I need to open a new account please."

"The locket I'm going to give you, will be your master device for this account. If you need a second one, or want to close the account, you'll need to come back to the bank. When you get more tokens, simply add them to this by applying them with a focused thought. They'll sync to your account, by the power of Min. How many tokens would you like to deposit–be mindful that it's at least a full token to start," the teller said in a dry tone.

Dean deposited his entire seven tokens after imprinting his hand on a chalkboard pad. While the teller created his account, Dean pulled up his stats.

Champion Information
Name: Dean Forrester Gender: Male
Level: 0 Tokens: 7
Race: Human Alignment: Suca
Luck: 14 Charisma: 41

Health: 347 / 347 H-Regen: 1.0 / Sec
Stamina: 296 / 296 M-Regen: 1.0 / Sec
Mana: 315 / 315 S-Regen: 1.0 / Sec

Strength: 214 Vitality: 133
Dexterity: 107 Endurance: 189
Intelligence: 95 Willpower: 220
Magic: Electrical

After staring at it for a while, he noticed he'd gained some willpower, and maybe a point in vitality, he wasn't sure. But it did give him seven tokens. Nice.

The bank teller flung a marker at Dean. He tried to catch it to no avail. A new silver necklace went around his neck with the number six point nine engraved on it.

"A full tenth of a token fee?" Dean protested.

"Fraction of that going forward. When you return your silver necklace, even that is returned. Anything else?" The teller asked.

Dean shook his head and walked for home. He sure hoped Cassandra had done okay. He'd find out soon enough.

CHAPTER

TWENTY-TWO

DEAN

Deathly Caverns – Felna's Cove

Dean arrived in Felna's cavern to the sound of gunfire.

The fook.

He ducked, scrambling for cover until he realized it was a movie playing.

I hope no one saw me do that.

While Dean was thrilled to be back on Oakley this was not what he expected. His party from either was gone and the cavern had been upgraded.

Marty had four stout men with him. Mercenary types. All prior military or damn sure wanted to look like it. They were lounging in what was a haphazard living room of sorts with a battery generator giving a light hum.

Dean saw a video screen playing a guy flick on the wall to his left, which explained the fake bullet spray from earlier. Two men escorted a fridge in with a clear door, setting it up right next to the power source.

On his left, a dozen space suits hung, with changing stations in place. Well, more like one section of lockers and two benches, but the concept was clear. This was converted, all without Dean lifting a finger. *Nice, this is better for those stuck outside when the gateway is locked.*

He noticed Felna was sunk down in the middle of a big couch, munching a salad with glee. She was so interested in her food, she never glanced up at his arrival.

243

"Dean!" Marty shouted at seeing him. "About time. You've been gone for twelve hours. You musta gotten thirty tokens. How'd ya do?"

The soldiers paused the movie and peeled out of their comfy spots, eager to hear the tale. Dean waited for them to assemble. A curious Anoka joined them from a side room, a book tucked under her arm.

"So," he began, "levels one through three are a breeze. I bet Apache the horse could do them. Four through six had a single shark. Avoid the shark, claim the prize. Again, nothing complicated and exactly as expected. I think floor seven deviates into a challenge geared for individuals but–"

"Technically they all are," Anoka interrupted. "I've done four before. I didn't have a shark for mine. I got a chomping sea hare, alien creature about this big," Anoka held her hands up slightly wider than her shoulders. "So, the first three are only the common levels for everyone. After that, these guys might get dolphins instead of sharks."

"Okay, good to know. Seventh floor broke the pattern, though," Dean sighed as he spoke. "There were high platforms on pillars to leap across, or a long route through shallow water. I took the long way through the water, fought a twenty-foot crab and almost died. An hour later, after a very painful recovery, I reached the platform to find it was only a ruse. After hours more of searching, I finally found the locket, right under the very first pillar. A very hard lesson learned. I banked my seven coins at Bearclaws Banking and came home."

Anoka cleared her throat to get attention and said, "Bearclays Banking. Well respected and often busy."

"We'll there ya have it," he cracked his neck. "Long wait and only seven tokens to show for it. Sorry I made you guys wait. I pretty much had to sit and wait on a rock for an arm and leg to grow back," Dean admitted patting Marty on the shoulder in passing. He went for a spacesuit on the wall. "I take it, these are free for all?"

"Yeah," Marty agreed, "there's another dozen at the estate. We're heading in, Dean. See you in the morning."

Felna spun up their entrance, now that Dean was out, and they hopped in. To see them wobble through the portal as they plunged in and vanished was a neat treat. He donned the spacesuit, with Anoka doing the same.

"Said not to go past six," Anoka said with a grumble. "Thoughts?"

Dean sighed as the suit sealed around him, "Almost failing helped, actually. A lot. I was on a winning high. Nearly dying really made me want to get a drink. I've gotten past the shakes, though. Well... mostly. Coming that close to dying also knocked some sense into me." He stretched in the suit. "Don't get me wrong, though. I want to compete some more before we get into really hardcore training."

He thought back through the day's highs and lows. "I found the early levels surprisingly easy, and I bet the other early levels are too."

"They are, but still proceed with caution. Let me at least drill the basics into you," Anoka grunted, and he didn't argue.

He waved bye to Felna who had restarted her movie. When Anoka was ready, they walked up the tunnel to the shuttle. They mostly handled the half hour trek back to the ship in silence. About three quarters of the way there, Dean started to hear the sound of jackhammers, auto-nailers, and other construction machines.

"Ah," Dean said, "I wondered how long before they'd want to remove this long walk."

Anoka just grunted, in reply. "I need to talk to you about something, Dean."

"You don't want to grow old outside Mixonia?" Dean asked, taking a guess.

"I'm ancient. The Dragona are truly an ancient species to humans, and we have a far different life cycle than humans. I was born inside Mixonia before Roman times Dean, and I made my bed to save Kambry.

"While I believe we should all be training inside Mixonia, that's simply not possible. I can return the moment we're done, and I don't count for that portal. Neither does Kambry. Children born in Mixonia have free reign in and out.

"I'm worried about Lexis. Or Lexi as her nickname is starting to stick," Anoka said, and Dean shrugged. "She is wanting to play the field, have some fun, and live her life."

"All good things, especially since she was trapped in purgatory. I don't see—"

"If her mother finds out she went on a space farmer's ship and fucked a cow herder she won't care. If she takes off on that ship out of puppy love, you're as fooked as can be. Your Oakley sayings are growing on me. Think Dean about what can happens. She could flee. Or if she gets hurt. Or if she dies mysteriously. Or just about every scenario you can think of."

"But my contract with her—"

"Is extremely vague. I cornered her and found out the truth. I know who and what she is. She has to help your estate and your family. You've got no kids and your estate can technically be managed if she hires people to do her job," Anoka's eyes bulged as she said this. "Don't tell her that."

"Okay, I can adjust the contract, right?" Dean asked.

"The person approving it won't want it changed. Nor will Lexis," Anoka said in a stern tone. "Just hire a bodyguard for her. Have him or her or they follow her everywhere. Trust me on this."

"A human or someone from in there?" Dean said, tossing a thumb over his shoulder back the way they had come.

"Human, please. Another issue. I'm a grown woman who recently removed herself from having to provide for a little snotling. Thanks, by the way. I'm also going to carefully play the field and don't want you to get upset," Anoka said, and Dean raised an eyebrow.

"Got it. Have fun, and I'll get a guard on Lexis. She already slept with Bart?" Dean asked.

"Yeah he is in one of your rooms with her right now. He tried to get her to come with him onto the ship, but Ravi convinced her to stay–that man is about three levels smarter than the others," Anoka said with a blushing smile. Her tell was tucking her hair behind her ear. Dean pieced it together quickly.

"No drama Anoka. I don't care who you choose to knock the dust off your vagina with, as long as it doesn't cause me problems," Dean smirked.

"Ouch, but not entirely inaccurate, and I've since learned about this consent thing. Speaking of which, Cassandra was crying, last I saw her. Kambry was comforting her. She was ensuring Cassandra, that because the contract with you was still active, you were still alive," Anoka said with a shrug that Dean almost missed.

"Ah, there waiting for me, then. Excellent," Dean said with a pep in his step that matched his smirk.

His smile was contagious, and Anoka winked in reply.

What was with the wink? Did 'comforting' mean something more than what he thought it did? While he caught the odd longing glance in Kambry's eyes, he'd never seen her looking at a woman that way–only him, and it was closer to leering, really, more than longing.

The roar of construction demanded his attention as the soon discovered the landing cavern was being greatly expanded. Crews were carving out sections to give the area a boxy feel, so more shuttles could fit. Hauling drones with massive flat beds carried loose rock out in a steady stream. Dean estimated there were at least a hundred workers fixing up the area.

"Whoa, the landing spot is improving," Dean noted, as they arrived at the shuttles. There was a two-seater small speedster waiting for them that unlocked with his code when they approached. It beeped green and blinked its lights at them, so he popped open the door and squeezed on in. Dean entered his estate as their destination and noted the flight time. "Only five minutes, nice."

"I got one of your tridents specially made, in wood. In the morning, you can find me out in the training yard, after I swap your daily allotment of gems into a token. I'll need you to go with me, at some point, to Bearclays to get me added onto the account with deposit permissions, only," Anoka said.

Dean nodded. He checked on the news to see the latest forecasts. The rain still poured on. Dean knew this was not natural, though, and the poor weather forecaster had all sorts of theories. He laughed at some of their wildly inaccurate guesses. He knew at some point the rain had to stop, to let the vegetation grow. But then again, when gods played with a planet, who knew how it worked.

The five-minute flight went by quickly. He saw the estate had additional tarps surrounding it, to the point that the area appeared to be closer to a tent city. When they neared the area, their shuttle had to wait for a flight of construction parts arriving. Dean gulped at the sight.

He knew a barn was going up, but this was a mountain of supplies.

He remembered Cassie mentioning a training area—what else could there be?

A long yawn forced him to drop the thought as the autopilot brought them in for a landing. His phone showed it was well past midnight, Zulu Earth time. That'd explain his tiredness. Anoka excused herself with a final congratulation on learning his lesson—albeit the hard way—she seemed to think that was much more important than his picking up a spare token. She went to a side building that was being erected from prefabricated parts.

Dean went straight to his third-floor suite. The barroom was empty, except for two security guards, who watched over the elevator and the stairs. *Uh, that made sense.* Security was probably needed, and he'd never even considered it. Nor would he have hired a medical team, or built a med bay, which he heard the guards talking about.

He wasn't stopped or questioned, though, and they continued chatting, as if he didn't exist. Whoever these new guys were, they knew he was allowed. He rode the elevator up in silence, priding himself on skipping the bar. When he coded his door, it pinged green.

Dean gently ensured it latched closed behind him quietly. He doffed the spacesuit, right there to the side of the elevator. When he started to tiptoe forward, he learned he needn't have bothered with the stealth approach. The sound of a cheesy romantic comedy blared loudly in the background.

The door to his room was open, but the closer sound of snoring in the living room caused him to pause. Kambry was asleep on the couch, smothered in blankets. Her long black hair spilled over a pillow, as she peacefully rested.

He entered his room to see Cassandra racked out on one side of the bed, with Tiffany on the other. A few pillows separated them; the situation clearly indicated she was getting some girlfriend support. Dean went straight to the shower in the master bath to rinse the salt off his body.

247

Cassandra joined him, right before he shut the water off. They held each other for a good ten minutes in a tender embrace. He stroked her hair under the warm torrent of water while she buried her head into his hairy chest. Eventually, Dean turned off the shower.

They dried off and a hand pulled Dean into bed after he tugged on some boxer shorts. Cassandra removed the pillows and Dean carefully slid in. Tiffany snored lightly, somehow undisturbed by him jostling into position. Her long blonde hair spooled in a mess around her face. Her small tits lifted with each breath, showing off her pert nipples under a frilly nighty.

Dean got comfortable on his side so that Cassandra could be his little spoon. She crawled into the bed and pushed him onto his back. When Tiffany sneaked a peek, he realized she wasn't sleeping. He opened his other arm for her to snuggle into.

Dean knew better than to talk at that moment. After threesome consent signatures were passed around, he played the 'this is perfectly normal' card.

The girls had probably already discussed this, because when they eyed each other, it was with confidence. There was neither hesitation nor trepidation. His Cassie had hungry eyes and Tiffany was amused.

Cassandra peeled back the covers and slid between his legs. His rising erection was pulled out of his boxers, slowly. Sweet kisses caressed his hardening shaft with a teasing delight. She was having fun, smooching on his lengthening girth. Her eyes exuded lust.

Tiffany bit her lip at the sight. Cassandra slurped his cock eagerly, getting him fully erect. Her wrist twisted as she lightly gripped his shaft. The up and down warmth from her hand wrapping around him, mixed with her lapping tongue, spurred Dean on.

His hands pushed her head down, plunging his cock deep in her throat. She gagged, giving him an evil eye. He knew better, though, she deep throated him all on her own.

He stopped the blowjob to tug lightly on Cassandra's brown hair until she was back on top of him. She teased his cock with her moist, swollen pussy. Dean wanted to flip her onto her back, and Tiffany tried to scoot out of the way, to give them space.

That's when Cassandra pounced on her. While they kissed, hands groping, and tongues tangling, her hips swayed back and forth, enticing him to enter her. Dean bent his head sideways to lick her slit. He needn't have bothered; she was dripping with anticipation. He readied himself behind her, his tip teasing her entry, a fact he reveled in. Her pink slit pulsed eagerly for him.

He stuck the tip in, only to ride it over her clit. She tired of the tease, pushing back against him, welcoming his girth into her wet warmth. Her ass bounced in circles, enveloping him deeper with each twirl, this time leaving him wanting more.

He plunged his cock into her until he could go no further. The teasing was over. He slammed into her roughly.

He saw fingers working Tiffany's clit as the girls kissed. His thrusts into Cassandra were interrupted when Tiffany broke her kiss to wave at the door.

Kambry stood there in underwear and one of Dean's shirts. Her nipples erect with tense excitement sparkling in her green eyes.

"Care to join us?" Cassandra asked.

Kambry shook her head no and said, "Not sure if I'm into girls. If you want to watch, though, sure," she nodded at Dean, "because I want to play with that."

"Next time then," Cassandra pouted. "I missed my champion."

Kambry shrugged and closed their bedroom door. Tiffany leaned up and pulled Cassandra's face down into her pussy. Dean pumped just a bit too hard and all action paused as he found himself facing two sets of 'ease up cowboy' stares.

His cock went back into his Cassie, deep and slow, so she could enjoy devouring Tiffany's swollen lips. Their rhythm was gentle, with long steady thrusts, followed by him flexing his cock inside of her. He knew that would send her over the edge, and her little pussy clenched at him as she came on his cock. Her moans were loud, which caused Tiffany to giggle.

Tiffany left her spot at the head of the bed and climbed onto Cassandra's back. Dean was confused at first, until she leaned forward and spread her thighs as Cassandra handed him a condom. He pulled out of his woman and slapped the rubber on in a hurry. Two wet, pink slits were stacked, one on top of the other, for his pleasure.

His alternating thrusts into first one then the other slick channel were fun but weren't going to bring him to a climax. Tiffany rotated over onto her back and waved for Cassandra to sit on her face. Dean thrust into Tiffany's quim while lifting her thighs. Cassandra ground her clit on the blonde's face even as she reached back and diddled her friend's clit. The intense nature of the duo sent Tiffany overboard after only a few minutes of action.

Tiffany squealed and surrendered to a shuddering orgasm.

"Did you cum?" Cassandra asked and Dean squeezed the end of the empty condom. "We'll clean up in the shower. Come back in Kambry, I see your shadow from under the door. Have fun making Kubras."

"That was amazing. What's a Ku-" Tiffany started to ask, but Cassandra stuck a finger to her mouth. The duo left as Kambry walked in.

Dean waited on his knees awkwardly while Tiffany closed the bathroom door behind them. The spurt of the shower told him they'd be busy for a while.

"If you want this, I'm all for it, if not–" Dean started to say, when she gave her answer by ripping off her shirt and shimmying out of her panties.

"I love sex, but it's always been hard for me to find a worthy man, or the time once I do," Kambry sighed, sliding into the bed and opening her legs wide. "You're a bit big for this body, so go easy, please."

Dean hovered over her and they kissed. It started slowly at first but built quickly into a burning hunger. Dean reached down between them to find her dripping and swollen with desire.

Kambry was so wet, he knew he'd be in for a slippery ride. He ripped the condom off and buried his rock hard, raging boner deep inside of her. Kambry groaned in pleasure, arching her back to take more of him, her big, plump tits bouncing in Dean's face.

Those juicy boobies were perfect in their roundness. These weren't stiff, fake rocks, though; these were what every man craved in a woman's tits. Dean's lips locked onto her nipple, lashing it with his tongue.

Kambry shimmied down to get his cock deeper inside of her. Hot passionate kisses landed on his neck as they entwined. He thrust down, timing his diving hips with her upward thrusts. Her moans kept getting louder. Dean caught sight of the bathroom door opening silently and two sets of wide eyes watching the show.

With powerful jabs, he rocked the bed. The frame slammed into the wall in time with his stabs. Things turned animalistic as they screwed with gusto. She ground her clit into his crotch while he hilted himself balls deep in her. A few minutes of being pounded by his well-timed thrusts, and she crested into a back-arching, lip biting orgasm.

Kambry's juices soaked the bed as she squirted around his cock. That did it for Dean. He joined her in ecstasy, spurting into her with a cry of release. He tried to pump a million little Kubras into her belly as he emptied all he had into her, his balls pumping spurt after spurt of cum into her womb.

Cassandra brought a towel to lay down, before dragging them both into the shower. For Dean, the suffering he'd endured earlier that day was replaced with a night of amazing sex. Kambry even loosened up around the ladies, once they got in the shower together.

The best part for Dean, though, was that because he skipped the bar, he remembered every exquisite moment of their four amazing rounds of sex. They were at each other, all over the suite, for hours.

Exhausted and unable to go a fifth round, Dean fell asleep, tangled in a ball of beautiful women.

TWENTY-THREE

DEAN

Forrester-Lexso Estate

"Shield arm up!" Anoka bellowed across the training field.

Lonny beat on Dean's shield that he clearly had up. The smashing *crash* of the wood on his shield rang his ears. Dean's brain fired a signal telling him his shield was fine. Lonny was getting yelled at.

An overhand cross swing of his short sword slid through Lonny's guard and smashed into his collar bone. His friend cried out and Dean lunged forward. His shoulder lowered, bracing for the impact as the shield slammed into his opponent. Lonny's feet left the dirt as his back crashed into it.

Finally free of hiding behind his hefty shield he lowered his sword to his defeated sparring partner's face.

"I concede," Lonny grumbled from his back. The man was not sneering or resentful. His baggy eyes told Dean he'd been studying more than sleeping. He grunted from his back and turned his head to an approaching Anoka. "Thanks for helping him."

Anoka snickered with a confident walk. "And you should have heeded my advice. The shout was for both of you and only one listened, right?"

"Aye," Dean agreed. He held his hand out to his friend. They clasped leathered forearms that leaked sweat. With a mighty heave, he hauled his friend back to his feet.

"Again, Dean. Krasken, get your ass over here," Anoka hollered to the gathered spectators. "Take ten Lonny."

Awe not Krasken.

"Yes, Arena Mistress," Lonny said with a bob of his head as a salute.

Anoka sighed, "Lexi has been riding him when he should be sleeping."

"Huh, wouldn't have—"

"She is having lots of fun. Safely. Which means we should keep our noses out of it. Unlike you," Anoka said with a scoff backing off Dean.

He squared against his opponent instead of letting her bantering jabs land.

Seven days had passed since he had a night of epicness. Things had fallen into a routine since then, with minimal hiccups.

One thing had blown up in his face, though. So... maybe Tiffany had a boyfriend. And there may have been a consent check that resulted in a very angry man threatening to sue Dean and Cassandra. It'd never work, and his angry tirade fell on deaf ears. Shortly after Tiffany fled into hiding in Ola. Dean was just starting to get to know her, which was rare for him.

Every night he'd slept in a cozy bed of warm bodies. The tangle of limbs was bliss, both his sleep and the sex were legendary. The rest of his week, however, was less divine. Hard to compare brutal training to sleek lustful bodies that drained him nightly.

Anoka clapped to signal the start of the fight, bringing Dean's daydreams of his mini harem to a close.

Krasken had no mercy, the asshole was known to break his opponent's bones, even in training. It wasn't out of spite, though, the man merely lacked a half-measured approach. Dean knew better than to give him an inch.

A wooden short sword lanced forward with precision. Dean parried and rotated his body to prepare for the next round of smacks. With his shield up he kept his feet back. Krasken stomped, hoping to catch overextended toes.

Dean crashed forward. The one advantage he had on Krasken, was his size. The man's stomp wasn't a feint, he'd put Dean's foot in an auto-cast twice already. He was going for the win and Dean had finally managed to avoid it.

Krasken was trained in mat fighting. The moment he felt himself flying backwards from Dean's assault, he tried to bring Dean down with him. A sweeping leg kick cracked into his right knee. Dean hacked down hard enough to break his sword and probably Krasken's leg.

That didn't stop the two human titans though.

Dean dove onto his opponent, raining blows into forearms expertly raised to deflect his attempts to subdue the man. Krasken's grin told Dean everything he needed to know.

He rolled off the smaller man towards his abandoned sword. His hand gripped the leather covered handle. Dean tried to get more distance between them, but it was pointless. Krasken still had a good leg. Dean was wrapped up, until they tumbled about in a ball of fury.

A few jabs of the wooden sword into the ribs were enough for Anoka to call the fight. The two of them fought until they were pulled apart.

Krasken smiled, a set of white teeth marred with blood. Dean could tell the gesture was genuine. The man's hobble to congratulate him was real, pain merely a step in the right direction for a soldier like him.

"Good fight brother."

"Aye, you fookin hurt me. I need to go to Mixonia and get some sexy magical healing. I'm tired of these old men patching up my wounds," Dean said with a wince. He prodded gently at his ribs, yup, at'least two of them fractured from the hard-hitting Krasken's punches. "Good fight."

He hobbled for a bench, each awkward step bringing additional pain. He almost arrived at the seat when suddenly a boom echoed over the arena.

There was a flaring white light that *crackled* with power. Dean cover his eyes from the brightness. When it cleared, he was somewhat surprised to see the Minotaur god.

Min stood tall, hunched over under the ceiling. The Minotaur god's ears flapped, and it snorted in irritation. The displeasure of the god eased into a neutral face as they shrank to a more accommodating dozen feet tall.

"Your planet requires a champion. You have an hour to select," Min bellowed, then stomped into the middle of the arena. A circle was drawn in that odd yin-yang symbol Felna traced out for the portal to Mixonia. "Have your champion ready here, else a random citizen will be drawn."

A crack of lightning, a blinding light, a whoosh of air, and then the god was gone. It was a bit dramatic, but Dean was learning that was how the gods tended to operate.

Bull cocks and bollocks. We'll lose another hundred points.

Dean loaded himself onto a drone cart that settled heavily, its motors *whirring* intensely to support his weight. Once he was stable, the medical carrier gently flew him off to the medical bay. He grumbled and groaned. Stupid Krasken had just ruined his chances of competing to save Oakley. As far as Dean knew, he wasn't the most powerful of the trainees, but he still wanted to be a contender for the defense.

A few of Ravi's mercenaries had already hit level ten in solo combat. Something Dean had been dead set against, though, was competing before they were ready. This is where the Forrester-Lexso estate's teams disagreed, and rightfully so.

Dean had no problem sharing the portal for the water event. Over the past seven days, Riva and Marty cycled people non-stop through the event portal for the easy tokens.

Honestly, he agreed wholeheartedly with this part. Stick an NDA on your space-ship's janitor. Escort him via blindfold to a blue portal and toss him in. Three tokens later, give them a five thousand G-coin bonus in exchange for their tokens. Rinse and repeat. This was a no brainer, really, because unless you couldn't swim, the three trials were almost impossible to fail.

The businessmen promised the moment a second gate was found, there'd be less crowding at the initial entryway. New bases would come to fruition with time.

Riva had his teams amassing a mighty war chest of tokens and trying to help even the score for team Suca. He was taking big risks, though, calculating the lives which may be lost against the danger of another hundred-point discrepancy trial, as his justification.

Marty was less productive and ran his own team, a team that achieved a lot and risked only a little. Team Marty had far less infrastructure behind it to get things done, though, so Dean understood and agreed with his measured approach.

Finally, there was team Dean, the smallest of the bunch. He'd recruited friends of friends and recruited about a dozen people into his group. Dean had contemplated taking Marty's route. The problem being, his custom gear had just arrived this morning, and most of it was shit quality.

His team was trivial in comparison and it reflected. Technically each group had an eight-hour slot per day. Dean's team was really only using four of their hours, until he finished the water event and ran out of friends to send in.

While Dean was training. Riva was trying to tip the scales with his pile of tokens. The enemy Core team had started upping their game, though. As Riva's soldiers went in and gained levels, they learned from a host of mistakes—like don't bring an ostrich in as your pet, even if it was super chill on Oakley.

The worst was when a soldier who was killed by a Ratkin. After he'd already defeated the monster, he noticed it was leaking a green gas. He stuck his nose in the gas, took a sniff, and died.

How did everyone else find out what was going on? After-Action-Reviews (AARs), daily meetings, and a concentrated effort at disseminating information. That and because Riva's war chest from the easy event was dwindling as he pulled people off the shelves. He was going backwards fast, literally bleeding fortunes to try to prevent what Sable had said was unavoidable.

The score would reset after this event; the most important thing was finding more portals.

The problem was how vast the landmass on Oakley was. Because there was so much ground to cover, their efforts at finding those other portals had been unsuccessful. They had thousands of drones diving into every cavern they could find.

Sable visited one evening, to ask why Dean wasn't scouring the planet for the other portal entries. He may have gotten a bit defensive over their efforts; by that point, even Dean was sinking money into the project. The fact she was prudish about him freeing Lexis didn't help the situation, which quickly devolved into lots of shouting.

When they stopped their catfight, Dean learned you had to send a resident of the planet to get the lure of the Minotaur guards. A drone would see a blank wall, and nothing more. They'd never see past the magic with a million types of cameras and Sable was furious that they'd had no one physically checking every cavern. She even said an orbital visitor wouldn't get the welcoming luring signals–it had to be a planetary citizen.

That turd in the punchbowl completely reset their massive hunt for the other portals and jammed a major kink into their timeline for balancing the bleeding score card. With only one portal, minimal teams, and limited training time–Sable had said a challenge was unavoidable.

Dean's needling questions resulted in Sable saying this would likely happen a few times–things were bound to get worse before they got better. The appropriate counter was to find more portals, figure out better rotations, and grow their teams. She did say, as their point discrepancy edged closer to a thousand, the lures would increase. At a thousand, when sixteen portals spawned, which she felt highly unlikely, the portals would all but glow.

All this led back to the point of Dean moaning on the cart while clutching his ribs. He was the only mage they had, besides Kambry. He also was injured. The top Riva guy was currently inside the portal, going for level fourteen solo which meant Kambry was the best choice to send as their champion.

The next best, was a level ten archer with a four hundred stamina. Kind of hard to kill an entire team of five, though, with just a bow and arrow. Those were the rules Sable had told him about. And to add insult to injury, the Core team Dean had beat, back on the ocean, those Core scum didn't even go on shelves like he'd have done.

Quincy ran over to Dean as he headed for the medical ward. "Dean! Staff meeting."

Dean groaned. Mostly in actual pain, though some was also because of the upcoming pain. Thank god he'd had his training injury to hide behind. He'd be tucked safe inside a medical bay for this one.

Dean's desire to work with Apache was effectively squashed, which was too bad really, the duo was finally starting to find a grove in their training.

"Get over here," Dean beckoned to Quincy. "Hand me your phone."

His friend handed his phone over. "Wait don't unlock..." Quincy blurted out, urgently.

"Ugh. Dick picks. You suck," Dean grumbled, swiping away the image.

"Sorry bro. I was texting Patti."

Dean found Cassandra's number and called it.

"Hurry up!" Cassandra hissed.

"It's me," Dean said.

Her voice softened. "Oh, are you coming?"

"Infirmary," he admitted, "what's the situation looking like?"

Cassandra huffed into the phone and said, "Everyone wants you or Kambry. If you're in the infirmary, though, I'm nominating Kambry. And before you ask, it's because you're both capable of magic. Sable is here, so there is at least a calm voice among the generals."

"Okay, love you, and keep up the good work. I'll hurry here, get in battle gear just in case and—"

"No gear. I'm scanning your vitals. You're probably going to get slated for four hours of bed rest, even with bone injections," she sighed, "eight without."

Dean ignored her. "Gotta go."

Dean handed the phone back. He reprogrammed the drone to take him to the locker room.

"Where ya goin?" Quincy worried, his eyebrows drawn low. He huffed and scanned around them. "Even Marty will complain if you don't get to the medical bay, Dean. There's no going into a statue, if you die in training."

"Ya, ya, ya. Get the door for me. Kambry will be in there," Dean muttered. The door auto opened without Quincy's help. "Okay off ya go."

Dean limped in on the leg Krasken had kicked. That guy was a worthy sparring partner. While Dean was proud to finally win, he sure as fook had paid for the privilege. He reached the women's section and punched his code in with his face scan. The yellow light indicated it was waiting for authorization, since there was someone inside.

"Yes," Kambry asked over the intercom. She must have recognized the code. "Oh, allow entry."

The door slid open, allowing Dean to hobble in. Anoka was snapping clips together on Kambry's chest piece. Dean saw how tight Anoka was ratcheting those clips, which meant Kambry's tits must be sore.

Her outfit was old school Roman soldier gear. Her breastplate was a jet black, with a Dragona etched into it. A male and a female were depicted, back to back and weapons at the ready, prepared to face any foe.

Her skirt was free flowing chunks of thick leather that overlapped to help turn sword parries and thrusts. Underneath the pteruges war skirt, her thighs were protected by steel cuisses—which matched the black metal bracers protecting her forearms and the greaves that defended her shins. Shoulder pauldrons and a gorget protected her neck, but tucked are to provide minimal bicep covering, leaving exposed skin on her upper arms.

Thin leather gloves and thick boots covered her digits. The final piece was a roman helmet, no plum or peacock feature, and again all black. It was dark outside, so this was fitting.

"You look fierce," Dean said leaning on her for support. "I want you to know Kambry, I approve of you fighting for Oakley. Fighting for our home. You make waking up in the morning worth it. Even with your stinky breath." He chuckled and then grunted in pain as she whacked him in the side. "You may never be a queen on your home of Laxris, but you're a queen of Oakley," Dean said with pride.

Kambry smirked, though her eyes shone tenderly. "It's Lixkus, Master, but that is the sweetest thing a man has ever said to me. I will strive to bring honor to this family and do my best. Now, handsome lover of mine, get your busted-up ass to the medical bay. I need to finish arming myself, and then go sit in a meeting, apparently."

Dean clasped the sides of her helmet and kissed her tenderly. "Wait for me if you fall. I'll head to Mixonia the moment my ribs are mended; I'll even do the injections to make our time apart less."

She said nothing, instead just lightly kissed his cheek. Lexis helped Dean to exit the locker room. He'd just signed up for an hour of painful bone injectors. The worst part was, if he was sedated that'd mean a full day of recovery. He'd just have to grin and bear it, to keep the promises he'd just made.

That was the moment he knew he loved Kambry. His only regret was that he was going to miss seeing her epic fight.

CHAPTER
TWENTY-FOUR
KAMBRY

Forrester-Lexso Estate

"What did I tell you?" Anoka smiled at her as Dean limped out of the locker room.

"That I'd have someone else to rescue me. I actually thought he was going to be an idiot after you slipped the Kubra into my contract. He's big, misses things, and isn't perfect; but to me," she smiled back, "he's exactly what I need."

"My favorite part of the day is watching movies with him and Cassie," Kambry admitted with a long exhale, wanting nothing more than to be doing just that, right now. She winced from how tight her armor was. "I need to focus," she muttered, "not long to get mentally prepared."

Anoka shrugged, handing her the belt. She hated this part. Her mother lifted her breastplate and she sucked in her gut. The belt quickly wrapped around her midsection, the loose end finding the loop. She cinched down as tightly as she could, locking the belt in place.

"Suck in again," Anoka said wiggling her fingers under the leather. She grabbed the tail of the belt and yanked again, with all her might. "Good, that's not going anywhere now. And I disagree," she shook her head. "Remembering what you are fighting for is incredibly important. How's it feel?"

"The belt crushing my intestines or this sudden, overwhelming sense of a family?"

Anoka rolled her eyes.

"Oh... the family. I love it. Before, there was always only you. I'd sneak away sometimes to find my inner self. Now I don't have to." She got lost for a moment remembering their time together the night before.

"We're growing and I'm happy. I'd like to be free, but I'm getting to know Dean and understand my contract is to help me learn from my errors–as much to keep me grounded, as to repay my debts. He plans on setting me free, once he knows I'm pregnant," Kambry admitted with a sigh.

"You should start trying harder," Anoka frowned, "if you want to stick around, that is. You can do a lot worse than Dean and Cassandra. I know, remember–"

"Mexxman the Crosna, he'd purr at you and wink at me. I was fourteen. Ugh..." She shuddered at the memory. "We're both without inhibitors and trying," she grinned at her Mom. "How's pregnancy work with becoming a statuette?"

"No idea, I know a lot, but not that one–at least as far as planetary contests go. Ready for your staff?" Anoka asked.

"Mom," Kambry softened, as much as she could in full armor, "thank you. For all of this. I'm the happiest I've ever been, and not just because I'm free of the soul pit."

Anoka wrapped her in a quick hug.

"Dean inspired me," she smiled, "just enough to get butterflies about potentially being his queen."

Anoka couldn't help but roll her eyes at her daughter. "You've got that boy right where you want him, wrapped around your tail–well, if you had a tail in this body." She grunted with a sour smile, "Don't get me wrong, human forms are nice and all. I certainly don't miss the leather itch or the problems with simply sitting down, but I do miss the–"

"Flying!" they both said at the same time, followed by chuckling together.

Kambry went to the closest mirror to inspect her outfit. "When do you want to start teaching these humans magic?" she asked, knowing she was about as ready as she was going to get.

"I relied too much on Thero and his crew for magic. I know it's going to be a painful, expensive, and a time-consuming endeavor. Riva and Marty are shopping for instructors now," Anoka said as they left the locker room. A loose strap clanked and Kambry paused. Dexterous fingers fixed the missed hook. "Speaking of which," the older Dragona noted, "your skills are at a level I can no longer teach."

"Oh. Oh!" Kambry said, slowly coming to a realization. "You want me to run the team with Dean? You're a better mage, though."

"This place is expanding and someday soon, there will be other bases. I'll be living in Riva's estate before long, and no, not just because Lydia and I share his bed. I'm going there to give nightly classes for fire magic. It's the only field I'm even half decent at," Anoka admitted, crossing the training grounds in the direction of the Sleipnir. "But mostly, though, because Riva is more my style–whereas Dean is more yours. Combat wise that is."

Kambry replied by patting her mom on the back. It was true that Dean didn't love injuries during training whereas Anoka did. She'd have to find him one of those naga healers, expensive but worth every coin in a place like this.

Sleipnir was a fancy spaceship which Riva kept parked outside of the Forrester-Lexso estate. The thousand-foot-long and five-hundred-foot-wide vessel was Riva's corporate headquarters and where they held their meetings. Kambry had never been on a spaceship, until recently. She'd yet to experience weightlessness. The best way Anoka had to describe it to her, was flying in water. Which was, apparently, something you just had to experience.

The guards let them pass without a second look. The two of them stomped up the metal ramp, the extra weight of her gear causing extra loud *bangs*. The moment they were inside, though, lush carpet killed the sounds of their footsteps in the corridor. Blue indicator lights guided them to the designated meeting room.

A few minutes of passing historical art pieces that showed images of labyrinths and they arrived at a green door.

Riva was fooling no one. The man had been deeply converted into a warrior for the Suca. He'd even set up a prayer room, for the true gods, as he called them. While this was totally normal in most of the rest of the universe. Among humans, Kambry noticed it occasioned a lot of frowns.

When they entered the meeting room, the side chatter abated. Sable eyed Kambry as if she were an ant. Even without a tail, she didn't bother to sit down. There were two other hulking men standing behind the far side of the table in flashy armor. Unlike her, they carried shields and one-handed swords; probably because they lacked any casting ability.

"Listen up," Sable said, pacing at the head of the table. "You may think it's common for one of mine to grace your meetings, but it is not. I warned you and I told you this was happening."

"And we've bought gear that will actually be viable," Ravi retorted, pointing at each of the potential champions. "We listened, as well, as tried to slow the score creep."

"Which I..." Sable tucked her chin suddenly, her ear tilted slightly to the side. "We're impressed. Yet. Your two best champions are either still in the game or hurt. No offense to you three, we're talking raw stats. Kambry has trained in this style of fighting for years. Raw talent can and will beat you, sometimes."

She shrugged when numerous sets of eyes turned to study her. A few wanted her to say something, but a stern glare was all they got.

Cassandra stood to get everyone's attention. "We understand. Actually, I tried to go into the portal today to get my champion's new weapons custom ordered." She turned to her father. "Your Tucker soldier has the entrance to Mixonia locked. I had to send Anoka, who should've been training."

Ravi grunted, sitting forward, "Tucker is due out any minute now. We picked up water magic for him. He even won some PvP levels and is my primary earner. Probably duking it out in a close fight," Ravi said with a pause. Kambry noticed his worry lines deepen when he turned to Sable. "You're right, though, Sable. We're new to this. I hope to be unlocking other portals soon, while having a larger and better-trained team."

"You're going to keep losing a hundred points until you find those other portals and ramp up champions in those locations. I can tell you now, they're going to be spread out." Sable rubbed at her temples. "I've got to go," she said, with a tired sigh, "good luck."

"Wait," Ravi stopped her, "who should we send?"

With a finger pointed at the Dragona, Sable groaned, "Kambry. Even with our sour history, send her." Then she poofed away into nothing.

As Cassandra walked up to her, to guide her over to the training grounds, Kambry shifted out of the meeting room early, so they could get in lockstep.

"Cassie, what armor was Ravi talking about?" Kambry asked. Together they passed the paintings of battle that adorned the walls of the corridor.

"Ha! You just don't want me asking why Sable is sour with you," Cassandra quipped.

She looked down at Cassandra and waited for their eyes to meet. The taller woman gave a sad harrumph.

"Fine," Kambry roller her eyes, "but this is confidential. Hasper was a Dragona from my home world, Lixkus. Where Dean is charming and leads with both his heart and his actions, Hasper was smooth with his tongue, his words magical, and his looks dashing. His tongue had other amazing qualities, if you were lucky enough to get him to use it."

The Dragona smirked. "Hasper knew he was handsome. His attitude was always bright while he playacted his way through training. He was only in Mixonia for a few months and it took me much too long to learn that his smile and charm had no depth. In Mixonia, a dashing man can be very... charismatic? Yes, charismatic works."

"I'd have to disagree," Cassandra snorted, "I tried to get Tiffany to come back and–"

"You did?" Kambry said with a raised eyebrow. "I'm surprised."

"Yeah, she's all alone, not that she'll stay that way, though, and I thought we meshed well," Cassandra said with a frown.

"She'll never be a queen like you or I ... maybe she realized that. She was your friend first, and a plaything for us second. I don't think she was ever more than a plaything to Dean," Kambry noted. Together, they descended the Sleipnir's ramp, their boots echoing loudly on the metal plates.

"Well, you're right on that bit. She craves what Dean gives us and never gave her." Cassandra shook her head sadly. "The excuse she used to spurn my advances was that we're all tied up in some mega-big drama and that Dean will vanish on us one day. She wants the type of commitment that I have."

Suddenly the woman looked small and lost. "Honestly," she sighed, "there was a frightening amount of truth behind her words. Mixonia lacks men. I don't think it is hard to figure out the why," Cassandra ground out in an even, emotionless tone.

"Dean... I hope he doesn't get addicted. The rush is something else. The fact that he is out here training, though, and not in that portal, tells me I signed on with the right savior. If you take smaller risks and always have a backup plan, people don't vanish. It's the reckless, stupid, and desperate who vanish," Kambry comforted her friend and lover, patting Cassandra on back with a gentle smile.

"Funny how we went from talking about a handsome Dragona to our lover boy," Cassandra said, walking through the single door to the training arena first. Her hair flipped as she talked over her shoulder to Kambry. "Spill the details, girl."

Kambry groaned, she'd hoped she'd dodged this question. "Hasper was training with Thero. Hasper went a bit overboard, and a Demi was sent down to issue a fine–Mixonia has to keep the peace somehow. Sable was the one they sent. The problem was, Hasper talked her out of the fine. She erased the fine–even angered Min by doing so–another story for another day," Kambry said as they walked towards the center of the arena where Min's symbol rested.

"Oh, yeah, I bet that'd make a good one," the smaller woman chuckled.

"Cassie, Hasper lacked a backbone outside of battle, and he said things to get women to sleep with him. Things that often led to rather one-sided disappointments. He promised to take me home, that we were going to reconquer my mother's province, one small settlement at a time," Kambry noted grimly. Cassandra leaned into her to give her a hug. She kissed her smaller lover's forehead for the kindness. "Hasper was a less honorable man than our Dean. He made promises to free Sable and led her down a flower strewn path, making her think he was going to take her to Lixkus."

Cassie looked up, her blue eyes full of concern and gasped, "Wait, what about his promises to you?"

"Indeed. Hasper dumped me for Sable–the moment they entwined, I was spurned. Sable loved Hasper, like an inseparable amount–and I don't mean just a love to get away from purgatory. Sable is a top contender for godhood; she'll become one someday." Kambry pinched the bridge of her nose. "Pestilence and fleas," she growled, "I still get angry about it all."

Cassandra rubbed her back.

"Hasper stopped courting me soon after Sable arrived. Those promises of conquering a home together were dashed when Sable's moans first came from his room. That initial jealousy grew into anger and me disliking a Demi for stealing my man–though I think he genuinely saw himself with her."

Cassandra fidgeted and said, "The ruins are activating, we can finish this conversation later."

"That's a five-minute warning, silly, we have enough time to finish this sordid tale. There's always a downside to dating a Demi, though. Sable had to go home to regain energy after staying almost a month at his side. She was so frail by then. Probably didn't help things between Sable and I, that Hasper was crashing in our small apartment during his training."

Kambry shook her head. "Anyway, Hasper and I grew very distant. When Sable didn't return for more than a day. He grew bored. He ran five straight low-level PvP events and racked up a huge bounty of tokens. That night I heard the squeaking of bunny tits from their room–a lot of squeaking and orgasms. It was awful. That next morning, he was gone. Sable came back two days later to an empty room; her wrath was mighty."

"Oh, wow," Cassandra murmured, rocking from heel to toe, imagining how awkward it must have been for Kambry to have to explain the situation to the Demi.

"Dean made a promise to me earlier–he is coming to free me, if I should lose. I doubt they'll send an easy team for this challenge, though, after their last loss. I'm more than likely going to die for you both tonight."

Cassandra shook her head in denial, her eyes wide.

"My point is, Dean is everything Hasper never was. He is a worthy mate and a man I trust. I love spending my nights with you both and just..." She blew out a breath. "Just being us. I'm coming around to the fact I've finally found a home of my own."

Cassandra gave her a hug.

"Don't you dare tell him I got all sappy, Cassie."

Cassandra chuckled, kissed her cheek, and stepped back. Kambry noted the pride in her eyes. "You're going to win. I know it. And if not, rest assured that nothing will stop us from bringing you home."

The ground flared white, the runes gleamed an eye shutting bright yellow, and a moment later Kambry was transported to the challenge.

∞∞∞

Kambry felt a minor disorientation wash over her. This was different than any other teleportation she experienced before–it hurt.

She stretched the pain out, noticing that it was more of an ache. An overhead arm stretch allowed her to survey her surroundings. Min, or a variation of them, stood off to the side, tall and imposing in their grandiose figure.

Across the field, two Golems stood in front of three Succubi. Kambry cursed her luck. It looked like they'd sent an actual demonic team, with proper tanks and damage dealers. She'd never fought either before, though her schooling in Mixonia gave her some insight into what these were.

The golems were eight feet tall, with bulging muscles. Crafted armor, that appeared rocklike, covered their fairly thick hides. They carried clubs and shields. Everything Kambry knew about them said it was best to get them alone and apply damage over time to wear them out. They were slower than average and if you could stay a step or three ahead of them, time was on your side.

With three Succubi behind them, though, she doubted she'd ever get a chance to employ such tactics.

Succubi were hideous soul drinkers, though nothing like the stories of them on Earth. Those, she'd scoffed at, when Dean told her about them. The reality was that they'd steal enough of your soul to warp your mind, making their victims think they were with a bombshell date. Then they'd fuck you until they attained the essence of your soul–your seed. At least the Earth humans got the thirsting for sex part right. The fact they'd melt your dick off before killing you was an odd part to leave out of the stories. Quite charming and useful, though, if you fed them your ex-lovers.

Their savagery was why Core species weren't supposed to get on the surface and were forced to get past layers of labyrinths to do so. Besides being soul drainers, Succubi were also excellent mages. Based on the three Succubi's staff colorations of white, red, and yellow, Kambry was facing a wind mage, a fire mage, and an energy mage.

Those staffs could also be used to deceive. Kambry, herself, held a red staff–but she could also fling a decent water spell. She'd read plenty of reports where, as battles unfolded, a blue mage arced a powerful lighting ball into their opponent to suddenly win the battle–her relatively harmless blue 'water' magic luring the enemy into a false sense of security.

Kambry sighed, knowing her preparation time was about to come to an end. Based on the power before her, she was confident in a few minutes she was going to be a statuette once more.

If she defeated none of these ugly bastards, then their next point would be a hundred and one. If she killed two of them, their tally would be dropped to sixty-one, with another two hundred points' differential required until the next challenge.

She'd get no reward for losing, besides the fact that the new tally would help Oakley. That was her ultimate goal here. Dean's team, which was her team, had forty-seven tokens saved up for emergencies like this. He'd free her, of that she had no doubt.

There was only one thing left to do. Kill as many of these ugly Core scum as she could, before she went down.

Quick short jumps helped her psyche herself up. She raised her arms up to give a final stretch, causing her back to pop. A few final knee pumps and she felt ready.

Min clapped so violently that air washed over her, bowing the shin high grass down in a wave.

Kambry clenched her weapons tighter. The enemy stayed where they were for the moment. No heedless charges from either side, resulting in a quick, reckless death. The arena would shrink gradually, meaning these foes knew more than the idiots Dean had fought.

Her eyes flicked to her new staff. This magic enhancement tool was far weaker than the one she'd detonated against Thero. It was a single step above a training staff; she knew she'd be having to try a new technique.

A slow trot brought her forward.

The air itself twisted as a fireball the size of a horse swirled towards her in a twirling arc. Kambry used a few simple side steps to dodge the overloaded spell. The searing heat of its creation singed the ends of her hair.

Good. They lack discipline.

Kambry saw the fire mage getting scolded by the rest of her team. With their attention diverted she sprinted forward, only to shift directions randomly, expecting a trick attack. She spun twice and slowed to brace herself for an attack.

There was no sudden lightning strike or gust of air to fling her into the group, though. That fireball had not been a staged event. The overcasting was real–she was just being overly cautious.

Disgruntled by the fact she hadn't properly capitalized on their mistake, she grunted.

The foes who bickered with each other with a lot of finger pointing were sent a present. Kambry rocketed four mini fireballs their way in rapid succession. The red gem in her staff dimmed from the minor consumption.

The fist sized bolts spiraled tightly with her expertly cast spells. Fire magic was by far her strongest spell type. The two Golems in the front rank were prepared, though, and the one bolt that didn't crash into a shield was dodged by the Succubi.

"Cowards!" she bellowed across the field. One of the Golem's faces twisted with a snarl, its body tense with the threat of violence.

"Core species, five versus one," she sneered, "and yet you cower like Munak!" A Munak was a variation of a worm that fled from everything. It was supposed to be the most insulting thing you could say to–

The agitated Golem lost his composure with a petulant, stomping fit one might normally expect from a child.

Finally, he's close to breaking.

"You'll never find a mate being this scared of a single foe," she taunted them. "Maybe you can make baby Munaks together!"

That did the trick. The enraged Golem broke ranks, despite the warning cries of its allies. Even a single Golem charging Kambry wasn't a great situation, but it was better than having to deal with all five of them at once.

Her hopes of the four separating piecemeal to join their brethren were dashed–the others remained locked in place. She'd planned on circumventing the two big brutes to hit their backline, but such was not to be, not this time.

She retreated to drag the lone golem back away from his friends. Not too fast to have him halt his thundering run, just enough to keep him fixated on his target. Her back made the most appealing of targets, and her foe continued to lumber towards her as she spun and danced backwards.

A new fireball was sent out toward the fleeing duo, but it missed. Kambry barely had time to risk a glance back at the other four, but there definitely was a definite lack of cohesion with that crowd, as the fire Succubus stomped her clawed feet in defiance of her allies warnings.

Kambry figured it was time to turn and face the Golem, before she ran headlong into an invisible wall. This one versus one play really was the best option she could have hoped for.

She dug a foot into the soft grass to spin to face the Golem. Eager eyes thirsting for her blood, the stampeding enemy was far closer than she'd have preferred.

Pestilence, he's faster than I thought.

The Golem's club cocked back with a speed she envied. The rotund weapon came surging forward with blistering speed.

Kambry tucked forward into a roll her dragon wings would have prohibited. Her blade blindly swiped at the Golem's calf. When it met resistance with a tug, she knew she'd at least managed to wound the brute.

Her roll carried her directly into the path, though, of a gale force wind.

Kambry was picked up and slung back a dozen yards, her back slamming into the grass. Her air fled her lungs from the impact.

Knowing seconds mattered, she tucked into a roll just in time. A lightning bolt competed with the Golem's club to end her life. The two collided, the jolting energy shocking the Golem, who thought he'd gained the upper hand.

Kambry leaped forward. Her body swiftly closed the distance to her foe, who impotently rage as his body violently shook from his own team's electrocution. She used her sword as a lance.

The blade sunk into the neck, parting the golem thick hide with a loud *ripping* sound. Electricity coursed up the blade and into her body. She fought against her locked muscles to release the grip.

A gust of wind sent her into another tumble, minus her weapon. The blade clattered in the grass against a rock not far from her hand. The golem's hands were locked onto its neck. It glared daggers, not at Kambry, but at the energy mage on its own team.

She scurried across the grass, desperate to retrieve her weapon. Kambry was worried the Golem would end her now that its muscles were its own to control again. Fortunately, though, it darted for the energy mage, blood spurting from its neck and calf.

The rest of the Core team had no qualms about blasting their former ally with fire, energy, and wind thrown rocks.

With her foes distracted, this was her best opportunity. Kambry charged her spell while fully depleting the mana in her staff. Her body coursed with tendrils of raw power. Her hands exuded heat. Flames licking her fingers, the magic pleaded to be freed.

When there was a chance she'd succumb to the power that all but overwhelmed her, she unleashed everything she could.

A dozen fireballs rapidly darted from the end of her staff. The burning infernos scorched the grass as the head-sized orbs sought her foes. Too late did her foe notice she'd expended all her mana in a last-ditch strike.

The remaining Golem kneeled behind his shield, unfazed, and unafraid of her magic.

The fire mage, however, never saw the three balls of fire that blew her into bits. Gore splattered her allies as her own flammable spells detonated in the midst of her own team.

The wind mage dove to escape the wrath Kambry had unleashed, but the Succubus' slow reaction time was not enough. A fireball consumed her chest and her eyes glazed over in death before her body smacked down into its final resting pose.

I can do this. Only two left.

Her positive thoughts were not echoed by her opponents. The remaining Golem shook the ground with his thunderous stomps as he charged at her. The snarl, the spittle, and the burning hatred in his eyes told Kambry he'd gone into a battle frenzy.

She flung a spell at the Golem that never materialized. She was out of mana. Her hopes of a miracle save were dashed. Without many options left, she sprinted away, fleeing from her massive enemy.

A dozen strides into her run she pivoted to dodge an electric orb. The downed fire mage's staff beckoned to her and she diverted for the weapon; a potential way to live through this crazy battle leaped into her mind.

Yes! The staff is holding a charge. I just need–

She stumbled, twisting her ankle in a gouge in the earth. An arc of electricity froze her muscles, and she crashed to the grass, her muscles no longer responding to her commands.

Teeth broke in her mouth as she vibrated and cooked from the jarring voltage. Her body bounced as the golem's heavy footfalls signaled its rapid approach.

If only I'd reach that staff.

Kambry never felt the blow to the back of her skull. She did feel, however, her soul being sucked into the pit. This time she went, knowing she'd be freed.

∞∞∞

Time was stripped from her understanding, her energy was siphoned, and once again, she became another body-less being trapped in and one with the pool of fuel for all things magical in Mixonia and Wixomia.

She had no thoughts or even chains of emotions as she simply .... Was. She drifted in the vast sea of energy as just another energy source. Her last fleeting thought had been a feeling of serenity, that all would be well.

A tugging pulled her from the depths of the soul draining container, reeled her in like a fish on a line. Time washed over her, and an understanding of who and what she was crashed back into her mind; everything suddenly made sense again.

She was being summoned to negotiate with Anoka. Disappointment flared into anger as she shook with disbelief.

Dean better have one hell of an amazing excuse, or she was going to flay him alive.

When she generated the hovel she'd grown up in for their meeting, her Mom stepped into existence to sit at the table.

"Daughter, I'm so proud of your performance. You goaded those Demon fools–"

"Where's Dean," Kambry demanded, her arms folding and her fingers gripping her biceps tightly.

She put her bitchy face on full display, and for good reason. *Where was the bootlicker?*

Anoka frowned, gestured for her to take the seat across from here, and said, "Manners, Kambry," she frowned, eyebrows drawing down.

"Try not to interrupt me again. You did marvelously. While they won the challenge, they now have to get a hundred and sixty points ahead of Oakley's Suca to get a new event. Which could mean thousands of lives saved–the others are singing your praises."

"And Dean?" Kambry gritted out, between clenched teeth.

"Stuck on Oakley. As are all the humans eager to try to keep another event from happening."

Her mother's words hit her like a club to the back of the head. Her popped elbows folded down to become pillows as she pressed her head to the table and processed the news.

Of all the shitty luck, she groaned. *My luck stat must be negative by now.*

"That human who was late, Tucker, he's still in Mixonia isn't he?" Kambry asked sadly. Her question was answered with a tender pat on her arm.

"I tracked him to Labyrinth's Honey Hole of Awesomeness," Anoka said and Kambry groaned.

She dramatically raised her head and banged her forehead against the table, several times.

"Oh no," she moaned, "that means he'll be hiding in there until he's out of credits. Their protection is the best. What's Dean doing?"

"Raging at Ravi." Her Mom chuckled, "he got so mad at his future father-in-law, he had to be forcefully escorted out of the Sleipnir by Ravi's guards. He left in a speedster shuttle with Quincy and Patti, while Cassandra tries to patch up the bad blood between them."

"He's a stubborn one," Kambry said, nodding against her arm.

"They're going to the other side of Oakley as we speak," Anoka admitted, tucking Kambry's hair behind her ear. "I told you he'd be your new champion. The one who'd endure hell to get you home." She smiled, "I'm sad you're stuck here, but glad it's not me suffering to get you home, for once."

"I can free you," Anoka began, but Kambry shook her head no.

"Why not?" her Mother demanded.

"I want his contract, not yours. If he's willing to scour a planet to free me, then Dean is a worthy mate to bind myself to. But visit, please, and send me their messages." She perked up a bit. "Did they leave any for me?"

A note was pulled out of Anoka's bodice. "I couldn't bring the recording in, so I jotted this down:

'From your Cassie. I'm heartbroken by the turn of events. We beat at the portal, pleaded with Felna, and screamed at father. He's manfully taking the blame, but that helps no one. I'm emptying my accounts to find a new way to get to you. We'll never give up; I'm sorry my family trusted someone they shouldn't have.'

"She's so emotionless, normally, but this felt like it had a lot to it. Cassie doesn't take loss well, with everything being handed to her. I bet she's a wreck," Kambry muttered.

Anoka nodded in confirmation.

"And from Dean?" Kambry asked.

'Dear Kambry, I'll never rest until I free you. You've made me the proudest man alive with your prowess and sacrifice. I'll sunder heaven, I'll rip apart Oakley, and I'll cool the core to get you home, your home. Our home. Your family. Our family. A city hidden by the god shall not restrain me from getting to you. Love, Dean.'

Kambry tried to hold back her emotions but couldn't help it and sat upright with boundless joy. She tapped her fingers excitedly, trying to put together the perfect reply. "How about we start simple?... Tell him 'his princess awaits'. Just those two words."

"You mean three words," her Mother snorted. "Just, 'his princess awaits'?" She paused as Kambry rolled her eyes and bobbed her head in agreement.

"I'll do exactly that, then. We have about ten minutes left before I have to go. I want to know every little detail of your fight. All we got was a simple overview from Zued—A god commended your actions! Share, so I can generate a report."

Kambry smirked. She knew somewhere out there, Dean was coming for her. His message had sent her heart crashing against her chest. Kambry knew some things were worth the wait and the butterflies in her stomach told her, this was one of them.

TWENTY-FIVE

DEAN

Planet Oakley – Pandorima Continent

"Dean how about this one?" Quincy asked, pointing a finger at the screen. Dean caught the movement in his peripheral vision. He'd been watching outside as the shuttle zoomed over the forested landscape. Dean gave the screen with a quick look. They were in endless forest preserve, without any nearby settlements. "I feel so lonely out here, mate."

"You're going to confuse the Mixonians by calling your friend 'mate'," Patti noted with a raised eyebrow.

Dean's gaze lingered on the shuttle map and he sighed. They were randomly picking cavern openings–no true rhyme or reason to their choices, other than it being big enough to walk into. They were inspecting only a few in each area, while bypassing most. There were tens of millions of caves on a planet this vast; the task left the three of them overwhelmed.

Their plans and hopes depended on a lure from a guard catching ahold of one of them. They had no idea as to proximity required to activate the lures, but when you were covering this much area, hitting every single cavern seemed unwise. They hoped a desire to look in this or that cavern would catch the guard's attention. When that hadn't happened, Dean had asked for help.

Dean's incessant pleading for aid from the gods had gone unanswered. At this point, though, Dean was fairly confident it was not a personal vendetta against humans or against him, directly, that withheld their aid. There had to be some unspoken rule about finding the portal caverns that was so hidden, even the gods had been banned from discussing it. Nothing else made sense.

"Aye, let's try there. It's my turn I think?" Dean asked, tapping a larger cave opening that Quincy then highlighted as their destination for the shuttle's autopilot.

They'd been rotating through who went down to check out each cavern, to avoid the chance of all three of them getting trapped. They'd been relatively safe from the caverns themselves—only Patti had gotten stuck, and only once. They did know that outside of the deserts and the oceans, Oakley was supposedly tame. Tame that is, until you went spelunking.

Bear bats were a thing. Mole bears were too. Apparently, the big furries were frequent hibernators in Oakley's larger caverns. Not that Dean cared.

Dean had upgraded the fancy spacesuit he wore with a heat sensing laser rifle so large, he had to haul around a large power cell in a backpack to energize the weapon. Dean had named it 'Beamza'. While it'd never replace Kambry, Beamza had earned a fond place in his heart, because of its immense power that swiftly killed the cavern beasts he disturbed in his search for a new portal.

Beamza was the length of an old-style assault rifle, except just a bit bulkier, with its boxy frame. There was no precision scope needed for this laser emitting device; it was a point and shoot, then guide the beam to, and then through your target. Its beam was far bigger than what one normally required. The weapon was built on the planet New Texas, though, where you went big or went home—rationality be dammed. In this case, Dean went big, pulling down Beamza from an overhead rack with smirking confidence.

His admiration of the weapon was interrupted when Dean felt the ship jerk slightly. The shuttle's rotors rotated them into a dive to hug the tippy tops of the trees. This meant they were close, so he unsealed the back door from the crew compartment to the shuttle's cargo bed. The wind whipped around the shuttle's reinforced frame, tugging at his spacesuit. The *whining* of the tilted rotors decreased as they approached the next hole to inspect. He closed his eyes, trying to sense something and came up empty.

Of course.

The same as for the last hundred caverns. The moment they'd realized that asshat Tucker was not coming out, they'd left on the grand hunt for another portal. Dean wanted to sulk in defeat. He really did. Not only had he lost Kambry, the portal, his wealth, and his mission in life, but Oakley Orbital had been hit with a plague.

A Belmont resident got sick with a new type of flu, went to the orbital, and boom— Black petulance. Thousands were sick, hundreds were dying or dead. The quarantine at the orbital essentially left families confined to their living quarters.

Thankfully Belmont had been spared. A cure was in development and the disease was being contained, at least for now anyway.

This string of defeats put Dean in a dark place. His only means to act, to vent his mounting fear and frustration, was to systematically dismember Oakley's cavern dwellers. He stared down at the various colors of sticky blood liberally coating the arms of his suit. At first, the killing had been a welcome outlet for his rage, fear, and frustration. Soon, though, Dean had become disenchanted with the killing.

After the first dozen or so brutal massacres, he had tried to leave the residents alone. He'd have gladly done so, if only they'd let him. A human in a spacesuit invading their homes, regardless of peaceful intentions, always provoked the most intense aggression. After dozens of grisly encounters, he was succumbing to the savagery of it all–not completely, though, not yet–just enough to feel numb.

The shuttle hovered next to a steep hill, over a five-foot wide opening that gradually disappeared into the depths. Dean wondered if there was some giant spider down here, maybe even a spider bear. That'd be epic. A legendary discovery, since they were supposedly extinct. If there was something waiting for him down there, he hoped it was something new. Anything but the 'fookin moles, they were the worst.

The sound their claws made, dragging across his suit like nails on a chalkboard was grating. The moles always got in close before he noticed them and required him to use his blade or bare hands instead of Beamza. Thank the gods there were never more than a couple of them. With a sigh, he let go of his downward spiraling thoughts.

This was for Kambry, the Dragona in human guise who always smiled. The woman who never said turned down a challenge–the lover he dearly missed. Her sacrifice would not be forgotten. Dean sure as fook wasn't going to quit on her.

For the last forty-eight hours, he'd slept in the shuttle with Patti and Quincy while they explored Oakley's wilds. Their suit's rations were running low, Quincy's determination was fading, and Patti had started grumbling about eating some real food and wanting to sleep in a real bed. Dean knew this was their last run, at least for this trip. They'd be heading home for a breather and resupply after this cave.

"Hover stable," Quincy reported in a monotone, his tone betraying his exhaustion. "Dean, you in there?"

Dean grumbled an incoherent reply before he scrambled down the back ladder to the loose rubble at the entrance.

His feet slammed into a rocky section of the scree on the hill, surrounded by yellow-wood trees with minimal underbrush. Nothing special about this place stuck out to Dean. The few trees there were, were all tall, reaching thin fingers a hundred feet or more into the air. Their thin trunks and stringy leaves in their upper branches let plenty of sunlight through.

Variations of Oakley's forest critters made themselves scarce as he tried to identify what was around him. Dean noticed a viney strangler plant not far from the mouth of the cavern–a good indicator that were no moles nearby. The moles loved to eat those troublesome weeds.

His inspection of the rubble showed no tracks, the loose dirt and scree contained no divots from travel and the muddy sections were clear of print. Another boring cave that was probably too small to house a portal. Dean stepped into the cave, Beamza on active, the hum of the weapon's power cell loud in his pack.

The suit's lights pierced the darkness beyond the opening. The rockwork here was an ashen gray, a weathered trail downward eroded in the stone from water weaving its way into the depths. A dozen paces in, Dean slowed his pace. He'd come to a steep drop off, so steep that his light couldn't hit the bottom.

Thank the gods I noticed this in time.

They were taking precautions, like the upgraded suits, to mitigate the risk of injury or getting trapped. It was always a risk, though, your suit couldn't save you from a thousand-foot fall.

He activated his HUD and requested Quincy send him a drone from the shuttle. His weapon scanned the hole for signs of heat with its infrared beam. This was the reality of most of these tucked in holes. They were short, tight, and a waste of time.

Deathly Caverns, where the first portal was, might have led one to expect all portal entries to be in an easily found, big cavern–one you could explore and get lost in. Those were not common. Even though he'd wanted to only explore the big ones, something in his gut told him not to ignore the medium openings.

The drone zipped by with Quincy at the controls. Dean waited patiently at the cliff's edge as the *buzzing* device descended into the depths, the noise of its rotors fading quickly. He flipped a display from the drone's camera on in a corner of his HUD. The light from the drone finally picked up the floor of the cavern, amidst a pile of sharp rocks Dean spotted the white bones of some long dead explorer.

"You seeing this?" Quincy asked. "Fook me, Dean."

"Phrasing, Quincy," Patti snickered over the audio feed. "Oh shit! That's a Minotaur skull, isn't it? You feel anything, Dean?"

"No," he replied, peering over the edge. "How far down is the drop?"

"Don't bother," Min said, suddenly beside him.

Dean jumped with a shriek and flailed his arms about to keep from losing his balance and going over the edge.

What the fook!?

"Min?" Dean asked, with uncertainty as he caught his breath.

"Dean... you're break... up," he heard Quincy say through a wave a static. "What... going on ..."

"One of my kind escaped their home," Min said without a trace of emotion in her voice, though Dean could see the pain in her eyes. "This youngling died of starvation, its demise from heading to the surface either forgotten or missed. A sad thing. At least we are alerted when a body like this is found and allowed to return the remains back home."

"You want to talk about it?" Dean asked, moving to sit on the edge of the cliff.

Min's hand rested on his shoulder. Without notice, sensation, or any warning, he suddenly found himself outside the cavern, back in the sunshine. The shuttle rotors were frozen motionless, his friends inside unmoving. A flapping bird was stuck in the air mid-flight. Everything, besides the two of them, was frozen in time. Min walked for a sunny knoll in between the yellowwoods.

"We... we rarely die. Minotaurs are special," Min said as Dean hurried to catch up.

He glanced up at the slightly taller god and winced, "Losing someone close always hurts. How are you taking losing Lexis?"

The Minotaur god snorted, a big smile revealing lots of molars.

"That girl is in heaven right now. Partly why I'm here, talking to you. The other part is we're grieving," Min said, and Dean didn't miss the plural. "And finally, we're righting a wrong."

"You're not just one Minotaur, are you," he stated more than asked.

The bovine figure shook its head. Dean watched as the face morphed into dozens of slight variations for the next minute or two. There must be hundreds of Minotaurs managing Min. He was shocked by the implications.

"I've heard it referred to as the Great Sacrifice. Would you be willing to share?" Dean asked, stepping over a root.

"I'm surprised those vain Suca gods haven't poured out their version of what happened to you already," Min sneered, snapping a branch in their way with a loud *crack*.

"Uh... will that make a noise when time resumes?" he wondered.

The god chortled. "This is why we need to get out among the common folks more often. You amuse us, Dean. You jumped on the Lexi grenade without hesitation, making us all proud of a Suca. Quite the rare occurrence, we assure you."

"I'm different," Dean admitted, flicking a number of light-colored leaves up from the ground with his foot. A bit of a sap, really."

Min smiled.

"I really believed her," he shrugged, "and Cassandra and I needed a nanny. So, rescuing her was a win-win, I guess. Though she's been pawning off her chores," he grumbled, "while making a mess of beds instead of fixing them."

This comment incited a burst of knee-slapping laughter from the Minotaur god. A deep rumbling so loud it echoed across the landscape. The Minotaur god kept laughing for longer than Dean thought the joke had been worth. *Who was he to judge though?*

"And now you understand why I'm here. To answer your earlier question, yes, there will be a sudden wave of noise all at once, when time resumes." The large horns shook side to side. "Oh, that girl. She is so very much like us—We found a male, long ago, not too different from you actually. Maybe you carry his genes?"

The Minotaur snorted. "Yeah, I'd recommend you stay away from Lexi, I see it more clearly now. We made a deal and soiled ourselves with his... ugh." The goddess, now, paused, embarrassed.

"My apologies," Min said, arriving at the meadow of bluegrass, "I started in the middle of the tale."

Dean was trying to follow the twists, loops, and turns of their conversation and getting more than a little bit lost.

"Umm... Okay, I've been good to Lexis, but we've kept things cordial. I've had a full bed as of late, same with her. Fun fact," Dean announced, finger in the air dramatically, like he'd stumbled across a great clue. "I've noticed that a lot more people are calling her Lexi these days."

"We used that nickname in private. We were never that close, though. When we'd freeze time to have our private talks, she would revert—as I'm sure you will soon find out as a new parent—to a never-ending list of 'why?!' questions that inevitably led to a petulant 'it's not fair!'. Which was understandable, given her situation, I guess," Min said with a grunt.

"I guess we'll chat about Lexis first," the Minotaur smirked. "She's planning on fleeing for an around the galaxy vacation and coming back in time for Cassandra's birthing."

"That's not really fleeing," Dean said with a shrug, "and I'd be powerless to stop her. Her contract is so vague that you could fly shuttles through the loopholes in it."

The Minotaur's face changed to that of a smirking male. Wearing the kind of look only a father gives when he's won an argument about his daughter or kept the bad things at bay. Or was he simply smirking at Dean's plight?

"Lexi will be staying put." The smirk changed to a glare. "Having an all-powerful god as a parent tends to result in random things happening," Min's vagueness left Dean clueless as to whether that might be a good thing or a bad thing.

"I'd struggle to monitor her when she's in the void," the Minotaur explained. "Even if we were never close, she is our daughter. Your estate is perfectly suited to fulfill her needs and maintain her happiness."

"Sure, not going to complain. Lexis is awesome to have around."

"You might when you get home," Min said, "though this is for the best. I'm limited in what I can do to help you. Consider my transgression a trade."

"Transgression?" Dean frowned, looking up at a still smirking Minotaur. "And a trade for what? You're losing me again. Are all gods riddle masters?"

Min sputtered their lips in a raspberry. "Zued has been downright straightforward with you. Some of what I hide in vague wording is due to the rules I am bound by. You'll adjust. Just know that I... we, appreciate the efforts you have made to ensure Lexis' happiness. We have a few more younglings who now pester us constantly for similar deals." Again, the horns shook ruefully.

So much for a god's apparent omniscience, Dean thought.

"Lexi grabbed life by the horns. She shot you some cleavage and a sad story and worked out her freedom on her own. As it has to be."

"Ah, I can only imagine the problems of a lifetime of parenting when your children are immortal. Though purgatory seems to be–at least from how the Demis describe it–pretty awful," Dean said.

"You want to see it?" Min asked in a chipper tone. "They'd be frozen, it would be a nice backdrop for when I tell you about the Great Sacrifice. Better than this meadow."

Dean fidgeted, picking a handful of long blue grass stems and letting the blades drop in the windless air.

"I get to come home, right?" Dean asked hesitantly.

"Onto the shuttle, no less," Min assured him. They were the god of contracts and trustworthiness, after all. If he couldn't trust Min, who could he trust? He nodded in acceptance.

His eyes stopped working and Dean left the plane of mortal existence.

TWENTY-SIX

DEAN

Purgatory

Dean arrived in what could be summed up best as a university quad, surrounded by three mighty dorm buildings. Vaguely gothic in architectural style, with domes and steeples soaring into the skyline, the large buildings loomed over the small quad. The main structure was white, with ashy gray accents.

The layout had the buildings backed up against a cloudy edge, with the majority of the space between the buildings simply grass. On the other side of the buildings, the same rocky edge and puffy clouds that bordered Mixonia encompassed the much smaller space. This place was so basic, it made him feel like purgatory had been lazily thrown together and only partially completed.

Dean spun around to get a full picture. The sidewalk scraped beneath the soles of his dragging boots. He gazed down to see slate stone, the coloration a mixture of dull red and brown hues. Only a few such walkways graced the area, allowing a large number of Demis to lounge about on the plush grass.

As he took in his surroundings, which contained a lot more Demis than he had expected to see, there was a disturbance beside him. The air shimmered and Min appeared in a form that he only had to look up at slightly.

The duo arrived at the only attraction besides the surrounding fields. In the center of the quad, there was a simple water fountain with no design other than being a circular pool with a single jet of water. The water was frozen in time, as was the rest of the area with its overcrowded Demi residents.

Myriads of aliens, hybrids, and the rare human were everywhere. Dean was miffed and confused. Something was so wrong about this picture; he was left speechless. Min noticed his confusion. Instead of addressing it, they led him into the main building.

He caught up quickly to the Minotaur's long strides. "The creation of this... half-assed realm, if you can call it that, came after what some have termed the 'Great Sacrifice'. I, we, fought vehemently against it. There was a time before humans that gods meddled in planetary affairs. Even humanity understands, with great power, comes great caution of exercising that power," Min said pausing at the doors.

"I have heard some of this," Dean admitted.

"I have the best knowledge about it. I was there. Gods are a species. The Suca, Minotaur, and even the Core gods—we all fall under the same species, just different branches of it. When a species is born, generally new gods are born. I, we that is, figure how many are needed based on the creator's whims."

Dean's eyebrows climbed skyward.

"Basically, the first human god was born when a random elf's belly swelled. Zued's mother was an elf. His father, the seed from the creator. Zued uses a miniscule amount of the energy he stores up to give himself the appearance of an elf," the Minotaur snorted. "His ears are as human as yours, though, you didn't hear that secret from me."

Dean grinned with the god.

"Your stories of both heaven and hell are born from a mythology, based on fact. Core is hell. Heaven is where the Suca gods roam, at the pleasure of the almighty creator. Take from that what you will, but know those are the facts as I, we, know them."

Dean nodded. While he desired much more detail, he figured it was best simply to listen, for now.

Min entered the building. Dean wormed his way through the mass of Demi bodies in the hallway, barely managing to keep up.

"During the first age, a god named Evimicus stewed in his hatred. His lover, a Merman—yes, you heard me right—fell prey to a Succubus god's snare. Out of spite Evimicus destroyed the core of the planet they entwined in. A billion souls were consumed, in an instant. The gods didn't die, however, instead they suffered in agony as they moved to a new planet. This resulted in war between the Suca and the Core gods, as the Succubi had lured their victim in unwitting. The galaxy, the first galaxy from eons ago, was torn asunder. Trillions perished until the gods were regulated to worlds without life."

They arrived at a dark room, crammed full of Demigods reading books. A Minotaur-Bunny Hybrid male was reading a thick tome. Min lovingly stroked the full-grown creature's hair.

"Gods don't need people. They need gravity. If you think living on an asteroid is boring, then you are correct, it is. If you imagine living on a planet with no life would be grating, well, yes—it's also tedious. Life is the greatest gift of the creator and the gods were denied it. Suddenly, as if a flip had switched, the violence stopped, and we entered the second age." Min found them an open table in the poorly lit library.

They seated themselves and Dean said, "The creator must have intervened."

"I'd say so," Min shrugged, tapping nubby fingers against the table, "common sense does too. Vain gods would say they came to their senses, suddenly, after blowing apart thousands of planets in a war that gained nothing. It was petty. With most of our homes destroyed, we, the Minotaur gods, relocated to empty planets and built our labyrinths, in peace."

"While the Suca and Core gods debated how best to continue their conflict, this time without destroying galaxies or the universe itself, life found new footholds. The fragile peace lasted long enough that new gods were born. A first in eons. When that life matured, it was cherished by both sides."

The Minotaur sighed, remembering.

"That is, until an elven god—Karlithen—went mad. The only way for a god to die, is for them to enter into a sun or go into a black hole. Which as you can imagine, for a species who automatically gravitate to the nearest planetary body, is very tough to do. You'd need to capture your opponent, entomb them in an asteroid and then propel that asteroid beyond the event horizon into a vortex or a sun. Karlithen did this to a trusting Jenica, a humanoid demon with spikes and horns."

Dean grunted figuring that probably hadn't gone over well.

"We Minotaur gods were sent in to officiate Karlithen's trial. The other Suca gods apprehended Karlithen and confined him, until justice could be served. The Core gods stayed their vengeance. For once, since the creation of the universe, there was due process and stability. I, we, sentenced Karlithen to death. His mind was already gone, anyway. His ramblings were almost impossible to understand, so deeply had he'd delved into insanity."

The massive head bowed briefly.

"The Core, Suca, and Minotaur gods, in time, realized why he'd gone mad. Mainly because the original enmity between Suca and Core remained unresolved. It was a festering grief that had no outlet. Gods on both sides felt an unsatisfied yearning for perpetual violence. Thus, the third age was born, when the first iteration of the game of the gods began on actual planets."

Two massive elbows leaned on the table. "The original games were not in Mixonia, like it is now ... Or Wixomia, if you're from the Core. Those games were a joke, compared to what we have today. We Minotaurs could not enforce any rules and madness still consumed both Core and Suca—the gods continued to be little better plotting villains, on either side."

The Minotaur god fixed him with their unflinching gaze. "The planet Linotha was the final straw. A full planet of Elves and Grancin, a golem with four arms was destroyed—billions of immortal souls extinguished when two gods fought over the outcome of a wager. The creator was fed up, His patience withered and gone. Gods from all three sides were consumed, in order to create what you know as Mixonia— as well as Wixomia—without so much as a by your leave."

"There was no voluntary sacrifice, just a reaping of immortal souls to power the creation. The vast sacrifice required a god's soul, on both sides. They are the orig- inal power source—more than enough power, actually, for us to manage the games in perpetuity."

"The portals spawned, and hesitant champions entered into what is known as the middle realm, and the fourth age was born. I, we, became custodians of the middle realm—unfortunate immortal souls, committed to managing the games for an eter- nity. Back then, none would have volunteered," the god snorted. "Eons later, if you asked me now, I'd regret nothing and volunteer willingly. The peace the middle realm has facilitated has been divine. Life has prospered and wonton death has been avoided."

Dean sat there in stunned silence. "I didn't know where the initial power had come from to create the games. I guess I had this image of gods leading unending lines of mortal souls to an altar, there to be consigned to an eternal nothing. Now I know it was the gods, themselves, who had to pay the price for their sins."

His voice faded away, staring at nothing. A thought suddenly occurred to him and he lifted his gaze to the being across from him. "If it fixed the problem, these games, with all the scheming to win a planet, then these Demi-gods—"

"The Demis came later. I, we, created this hell hole. Half gods were zooming through the game's floors without issue or repercussion, causing massive imbal- ances to the early, quite fragile, system. There was no police force, either." The god rolled its eyes.

"Breeding was prolific and there were no measures in place to prevent gods from seducing mortals. When the Demi purgatory was enacted, a new war almost erupted. Yet, it didn't."

"You said 'almost' and that it 'didn't' ..." Dean wondered, "why not?"

"Mainly because we soiled our mutual body and birthed two children from each side. The gods were henceforth limited to two pawns and two pawns only–so it has been ever since. This constraint, to only have two Demis, along with this unfortunate creation," Min gestured around them, "brought about the fifth age."

Dean wanted to move on, so he scooted back his chair and stood. "Could I get a brief tour? If you'd be so kind, there is a certain Demi–Sable–who I'd like to see."

"You are sure?" the god grunted with a sigh. Their snort caused him to hesitate, briefly.

Dean reviewed his reasoning with a grimace but nodded. "Yes, I need to understand the basis for her anger."

As they walked toward the exit, weaving through the many occupied tables of time-frozen Demis, Dean thought of another question. "Why do I not see elves in Mixonia?"

"The creator favored that species, or maybe they were in the void and recolonized, like we Minotaurs, after the first age. Out of all the species destroyed in the first galaxy, they were the only ones to return to it. You don't see the elves in Mixonia because they are immortals. They won their contests and evicted their core neighbors below them–on... Every. Single. Planet. The war against the Core is their pride, their purpose. Even I am scared by the lengths they are prepared to go to," Min shuddered.

Dean frowned. "Impressive. I take it the Core species have something similar?" Dean asked, exiting the library.

"Denacids, a spider lower half, demon top half, with eyes capable of seeing in every direction. They're the Core's counter to elves; and you might well see them. If you do, I urge you to run. The games were altered after both the Elves' and the Denacids' figured out how to exploit a loophole in the games. This triggered the sixth age, and we're now into the seventh." The Minotaur gave him a nod. "Smart, to guess there was a counter," Min said with a smirk.

Dean realized something at this point. Min was being nice, and when the most powerful of the gods, besides the creator, was nice to you, there had to be a reason for it.

"Can I ask what happened?" he asked.

Min frowned at him.

"Sorry, let me clarify. Earlier you said you were righting a wrong," Dean began.

"Later," Min said, pausing before a wide staircase. A statue of an elven god rested on the banister. "Give me your hand."

Dean extended his hand, which she promptly flipped over. Dean figured her face was representing a female Minotaur at the moment. Deciphering expressions on the combined form did get complicated, at times. Her stubby finger ran down the seam of the scar in his palm.

"This is not from one of us," she murmured, "yet it reeks of magic. Rarely am I surprised by anything. This is either the creator's work... or the soul of the creature you killed resides in your spirit, funneling your magic. You will be quite the powerful warlock, eventually," Min frowned and then let loose a violent huff of air. Dean felt a tingling along his palm.

The god's neutral face returned, and they scowled at his unchanging scar.

"Ah, it's just a simple battle wound," Dean said, shrugging it off.

"One it seems I cannot mend," Min said irritably. "Not your fault, though, and I'd rather leave Lexi with a powerful family. Follow me."

They stepped around dozens of frozen Demi-gods. Some were reading in the stairwell, no intention of moving.

"So, Min ... why force the Demis to stay in purgatory? Why not just move them onto a vacant planet where–"

"Ha! Exactly what I recommended. The two sides, however, came to a different compromise." The Minotaur frowned at the Demis all around them. "There is no purgatory for the Core's Demis and the Core gods' halflings may roam about Core worlds freely, but they are forever prohibited from entering Wixomia. Suca gods, however, wanted their children to handle mundane tasks in Mixonia as well as on the surface, for them. This is the result." Min snorted, "If it keeps the peace, I'm happy."

Min paused on a third-floor landing, "Let me warn you now, freeing Sable will infuriate Zued."

"Because of the trial of Demis to get godhood?" Dean guessed.

"Ah, so... I'm bound not to say anything specific about those matters. What I can recommend, is that you ask Sable how many champions she's seen return as gods," Min said cryptically.

Dean tilted his head in thought and mulled this over.

Min mentioning this specifically, probably meant the answer was next to none, or simply zero.

"If you... then you..." He stopped eyes wide. "They must free them. The best of the best warriors are... what, breeding stock?"

Min shrugged nonchalantly, abruptly shutting down further conversation on that topic.

Dean grunted, "Now you've properly hooked me, like a silly fish, with such bait as that."

"Yes," Min nodded sadly.

"Thank you for showing me all this, and talking with me," Dean said sincerely.

"You're going to love and hate me soon enough," Min sighed ominously, leading them down a hall. Min bypassed numerous doors, all no further than six feet apart. A door on the left was ajar and they squeezed beyond it.

Dean noted another narrow hallway, this one barely wide enough for two Demis to barely squeeze past each other. Horizontal stacks of doors were mostly closed. The interior living space each Demi apparently was allotted was almost like a coffin—roughly ten-feet-long by three-feet-wide and only four feet tall. Dean tilted studied one such space and admitted the coffin was a poor comparison—more like a berth on a starship, for the crew's quarters. Tiny, yet enough to live in. Min flipped open one of the hatches to reveal Sable, sitting against one wall and jotting down notes on what Dean guessed was magic.

One stubby finger tapped Sable on the shoulder, and she jerked back in response, suddenly included in their little time bubble.

"Is my presence required?" Sable asked, not lifting her eyes from her notebook. She continued her notations. "Min, you only—"

"Hi Sable," Dean said calmly.

Sable's head whipped up and she flew against the back wall, a spell readied in her hand. She grunted as one wing smashed into the corner. When her eyes frantically settled on the two of them, calmly watching her freak out in her mini compartment, she stilled.

"You shouldn't be here," Sable grumbled. "Why him? Never in all of purgatory have you brought a mortal into—"

"He is our daughter's caretaker. Understanding this place ensures she is properly maintained. And he wanted to ask you something," Min said.

"I did?" Dean replied, his face scrunching up in confusion. Min rolled their wrists, indicating he should continue. All the while, Sable stared daggers at him. "Sorry. I'm afraid ya lost me there, Min."

"Demis competed to become..." Min hissed under her breath, just loud enough for him to hear.

Dean's eyes lit up in understanding. "Yes, yes. Got it." He turned to the beautiful Demi, still huddled in the corner. "Sable," he began, "you're never going to become a god. If I'm telling you this, that means my sappy butt is going to free you. At least, I'm fairly certain Min wants me to, so ..."

"So, you can get some proper magic training," Sable finished for him. "Dad would lose his marbles, though." Her brows came down sharply. "I'll think about it, though I'd require a loose contract like what Lexis has." She frowned. "Min, we know we all don't become gods. We still want to be the best, though, and the one selected to be doted on. That does happen, right?"

"I suppose you've left me enough room with that question that I can safely tiptoe around the rules. If Dean were a Demi, which he is not, he's a blessed," Min admitted and Sable startled, smacking her head against the low ceiling in shock.

"Wait, he... is a blessed?" Sable asked and Dean, guessing correctly, showed her his hand. Sable's eyes flicked back and forth rapidly as she studied the seam in his palm, her mind deep in thought. "Maybe," she finally concluded, "maybe not. It does explain Dad's fascination with him, though. I do love hearing reasons to escape this place, though. Please," she smiled at Min, "continue with your hypothetical."

"If Dean is a Demi, he wins the championship to become a god. Which has judges, to pick exactly who is needed. Then Dean is offered a plush retirement. The only downside is that Dean becomes a mortal and has to entwine with the god Hamine, who made a deal with Jued to fill his missing Demi slot. Afterwards, Dean would live a life of luxury until he died of old age, doing whatever Dean wants to do because–"

"Whoa, bad analogy," Dean interrupted defensively, "Although a strong supporter of open sexuality, Dean is not into dudes."

Sable rolled her eyes. "Dean is me, Hamine is Damien the Siren god, and Jued is my father, plotting to send me to birth a Demi. I actually like everything about this, minus becoming a Siren. I hate getting water on my wings. Or would I be an Angelina. Argh... Father will never tell me."

Min tapped her shoulder with a frown. "Hmm. Didn't see that one coming."

"One baby, escape prison, and be a queen for the rest of your life. I'm not a woman, but I can see the appeal. I wonder if they ever refuse," Dean mused with a shrug.

"Champions are known to return, unable to make the ascension, having no memory or knowledge of the attempt," Min admitted, an ironic eyebrow raised.

"Ah, the mind wipe and return to sender. Ouch. I take it when a Demi is done living here, they just walk over the edge to become a soul battery?" Dean asked and Min nodded.

"Time for me to repay the wrong done to you," Min sighed, touching Dean's shoulder.

∞∞∞

286

Dean appeared back in the shuttle next to a human sized Min. His friends were still frozen, looking at the screen of Quincy's drone feed. Min walked towards the shuttle's navigation station and expanded the map.

"I had a talk with Felna. She did her job, when Sable approached her to bring you to my vault. The others were not asked because they were simply too far from your estate. Zued officially complained this planet was not properly bringing champions into the portals."

Dean looked up at that.

"He was both wrong and right." The god grimaced. "A Mixonia portal cavern will have no obstacles to its entrance," they continued. "It'd be dumb to lure in a champion and then let a cave dweller consume them. That said, caves are spooky. Felna has had two potential champions turn back before getting far enough in, since humans settled this planet years ago.

"Lonnar, had the same thing happen to him. Some humans heard his call of riches, their minds felt the pull, but they weren't champion material and turned back. Kordin and Edith," the god glared at the map, "well, they never sent out a lure, not once. They'd been reading Core philosophy and will be punished for failing their duties."

The Minotaur god winced. "Their personal belongings were littered with gifts from their time guarding Core portals. We Minotaurs pride ourselves on our neutrality. Since we've apparently slighted Suca of two portals, here are the locations."

Min reached down and touched two spots on the digital map—neither location was anywhere nearby. Dean did a fist-pump the air, his grin stretching ear to ear. About 'fookin time.

Before he could thank Min, they said, "We will not see each other again soon. I'd recommend a Siren or a Naga for healing. A Banshee for electrical magical training. I'd expect Sable to spurn your offer but there are trainers who will come to you. Thank you for being so understanding."

"Understanding of what?" Dean asked and she vanished.

Time resumed and his friends shrieked at his sudden appearance behind them. "What the fook!" Quincy exclaimed. "Dean, how'd you get in here?"

His fingers worked the controls on a drone that was flying inside the cavern. He lifted a hand off the joystick to poke at Dean. He tapped his suit twice, to ensure what he was seeing was real.

"How?" Patti said with wide eyes.

"I had a visitor," Dean said, and sighed. "A divine visitor."

"You fooking think!" Quincy muttered, his red eyes droopy. "Damn, fookin gods freak me out."

"Quincy, I get it, you're tired. I'm tired. But I've got amazing news! I know where two of the remaining three portals are!" Dean pumped his fists excitedly.

Patti shrieked for joy. "Oh, I can't wait to get home and take a shower... A bubble bath, too. A pedicure because my toes are all fugly from this suit. Oh, and a daiquiri, too, because I deserve one. This has been–"

"I'm going to free Kambry," Dean said.

I feel so relieved. Finally, I can keep my promise to her. I can compete again and try to save Oakley.

Dean's phone suddenly rang, causing him to tune Patti's chatter out for a moment.

Lexis was calling him. *Hmm.*

"This is Dean," Dean said hesitantly.

"Mistress needs you here, for the birth," Lexis began.

Part of their horse purchase had included a mare who was due, any day. It was a four-hour flight home from where they were–with the shuttle pushing its limits. He checked the remaining charge. Five hours, unless he diverted energy from Beamza's power cell to the shuttle. He groaned.

"Is Cassie sure she can't handle birthing the foal herself?" Dean asked, not wanting to get caught up in an argument of who to help first. He fumed internally, while waiting for her to answer. There sure was a lot of yelling in the background about sending for a doctor. He knew he needed to get a healing mage. It'd been on his list of things to do, but training had been going so well, he hadn't made it a top priority. "Ya there Lexis?" he finally prodded.

"Sorry, I'm getting pulled a dozen directions. Get home, Dean. Rush–like the gods themselves are hounding you," Lexis said, and closed the connection.

Dean's stomach dropped. He rushed to the controls and entered the estate as their destination. A few taps later, and the shuttle returned a five-hour estimated travel time. 'Like the gods themselves are hounding you' Lexis had said–that was an emergency, if ever he'd heard one.

He stripped out of his suit and carried it to the back of the shuttle. The charging port auto connected to the device. His HUD gave him an option to take Beamza's battery pack off for re-charging. He selected yes and the device detached from his pack and hovered above the floor.

"Dean!" Quincy shouted at him, to get his attention. Quickly selecting different options in his HUD, he soon reversed the charging flow, sending power from both the power cell and his suit to the shuttle. The suit hissed open and he stumbled out of it.

"What's the fookin emergency?" Quincy wanted to know. "Kambry is going to be so pissed..."

Patti cleared her throat, getting their attention. "No. Dean won't hesitate to make her wait another day for him in a cozy soul pit. She will understand. Dean," she waited for him to focus, "look at me."

He did.

"Cassandra's gone into labor. As in some god apparently swelled her belly and her water just broke."

Dean's smacked his hand to his forehead. He stumbled into a chair, everything suddenly making sense.

"No wonder they were so nice," Dean muttered. "This changes everything ..."

Quincy waved Patti over to the wall and they both exited their suits.

They all tried to ignore the stench of them being inside the devices for too long, but soon, all three of them were breathing through their mouths.

"Mate, we've got four hours. How about you tell us everything that happened in that cave, alright?" Quincy said slowly. "Try to remember it all, every fooking word."

This is how you plan to keep Lexis from traveling the stars. You sly god. I get it. I'm sad Kambry won't be here for the birth, but I understand why you did it.

Dean calmed himself by taking several deep breaths. He waited until his mind had wrapped around all that was happening, and then he told them everything.

TWENTY-SEVEN

DEAN

Forrester-Lexso Estate

D ean's grin was frozen on his face. He'd arrived at Cassandra's side just in the nick of time. His daughter, unnamed for now, popped right out as Cassandra crushed his hand. There was a surreal feeling; it was almost like his timing was divine.

When he'd quipped in a witty tone, "That was easy!" it did not go over well.

That evening, after Dean had managed to freshen up, he snuggled in the bed with mother and child. Their slumber was only interrupted by the baby's cries of hunger twice that night. With his fatherly duties only partially fulfilled, he was sent by Cassandra to retrieve Kambry. She was safe, she was happy, and she wanted her friend and lover, Kambry, home. Dean fought her a bit, but learned the hard way that Cassie was more than prepared to practice her new magic, a mother's scolding, on him.

On his way out, there was a slight hiccough, though. A dastardly meeting stood between him and Kambry's freedom.

A large oval table with inlaid carvings of stars stood in the meeting room aboard Sleipnir. Riva sat at the head of the table. Marty at the foot. Dean sat on one edge with Anoka on the other. They'd exchange family greetings, congratulations, and friendly paternal advice before sitting down.

The burned bridge between Dean and Riva had been repaired, to a large degree. Portals had been found, Riva had apologized, and a new grandbaby brought a sense of unity of purpose to the two of them. Dean was happy his outburst had been forgiven; he'd gotten a tad heated. Riva appreciated that they'd restored some decorum amongst the leaders of Oakley's war against the Core.

Dean was surprised there were no guards, advisors, or lawyers present. Just the four of them.

"We have a golden opportunity here," Riva began, starting the meeting. "I erred. We both erred."

Marty nodded, accepting Riva's statement as an indicator that he should speak. This meeting was clearly staged for Dean to adjust to the new situation.

Marty sighed while tapping the table. Finally, he said, "I'm guilty of not following my own advice Dean. I was the one who drafted the original contracts–contracts not bound by Min. That is changing. As of yesterday, every single person in training was let go."

"Umm..." Dean furled his brows. "Why? There were some really solid soldiers in training and competing."

"Min," Anoka said with a determined, if stern, grimace. "I also am partially to blame for this failure as well, by not stepping forward to give you better advice. I advised you how the guild handled their champions, not how planetary forces do."

"Sooooo... okay. I'm glad we're burying the hatchet and making peace, but what exactly went wrong... and how do we fix it?" Dean asked.

Riva grumbled and said, "Before, we implemented a tax. We said that if you competed, you would get the lion's share of what you earned. The tax was set at thirty percent, primarily to keep the ball rolling. Yea." He shook his head. "That was dumb, in retrospect. Now, Tucker is buried away, hiding for who knows how long, in Mixonia." He blew out a breath.

"As one of our best competitors, he was lavishly supported, and went through ten levels of PvP, amassing a fortune in winnings. His contract didn't have enough protections for us, or for the portal." He paused and frowned, "Well, it did, just none that were bound by Min. Technically, he'll be fired for breaking at least seven rules. Problem is, we can't enforce them."

Dean nodded his understanding. "Okay. Mixonia is expensive. Around the clock protection can't be cheap, he'd–"

"A few years Dean. He'll have a few years of squeezing squeaky tits in a back room that we can never drag him out of," Anoka admitted, and Marty rolled his eyes while shaking his head. "Mixonia has very strict laws. Even if we catch him in the open, we aren't allowed to kill him or forcibly drag him to the portal."

Marty scowled. "The only chance we have is either A) he runs low on money, and fails in a competition; B) he sees the error of his way and comes out voluntarily; Or C) he is bribed to return home with a Min guaranteed contract, filled to the brim with amazing incentives."

"Rest assured," Marty said, resting his elbows on the table, "we're taking all options seriously and this will never happen again."

Dean snorted, "Nothing we can bribe him with is better than immortality and pleasure servants."

"We feel Tucker should come out at some point, though, and we are prepared to negotiate with him in good faith." Marty winced, causing Dean to realize Riva'd had him say that. "He also can go into solo PvE, though, and use those winning to extend his time in Mixonia." His old friend and mentor shook his head. "As you noted, though, there is very little we can do. Which is why there are four portals, in the first place."

Dean nodded thoughtfully. Finally, he looked between Riva and Marty. "So, what's the plan going forward and how is the search for the final portal going?"

"With three caverns to study and pull data from, we have narrowed down the likely openings to a few hundred that will have to be investigated," Riva reported. "I've got men and women heading to every single one of them. This meeting is to tell you ..." he paused and grinned ruefully, "to admit to you that we've learned our lesson, and–hopefully–to get you back on board," Riva said.

Dean waved his wrist for him to keep going.

"I want you to contract your team," the older man said.

"Here is the new plan. You'll pay your team Galactic coins for work performed on a salary. The moment they finish a competition all tokens go to Bearclays Bank. They will never be given tokens, allowing–"

"You want me to tell Lonny that his trials in the game of the gods will be rewarded with a mere fraction of what he has earned?" Dean asked, stunned. He controlled his rising anger by softly setting his hands on the tabletop, instead of slamming them down.

"Yes," Marty admitted, "and here is the caveat. There will be given a pot of gold at the end of the rainbow. When they finish, you give them a portion of winning, but... Big but here... They can't retire in Mixonia or ever go back. We're sticking heavy security into the caverns and only authorized personnel are allowed to go in. For my team, I'm assigning handlers for each of the competitors, too."

"Basically," Riva continued, "for our teams, they'll go in blindfolded and compete. They'll do so for a healthy salary that is much better than they were earning before–and the honor of fighting for their planet. They'll never know exactly how much they're giving up. Which means ..." Riva shrugged at Dean.

He nodded. "I'll need my guys and girls to stay mum on the topic. Aye, I hear ya. Contract them in the caverns, bind them to our purpose, and then work together on preventing tragedies like the pestilence on the Orbital. Learn from our lessons. Going on a limb here," Dean asked, scratching at his scruffy four day's growth of beard, "ya got contracts ready for me to agree to with my team?"

Anoka slid a paper across the table to him. Dean read the verbiage and mostly understood this was–

"Cassie has approved this contract?" Dean asked, not surprised when nodding heads confirmed it. No way would they lie about that. Dean knew they'd learned a hard lesson with Tucker's betrayal. This contract avoided the risk of that ever happening. He accepted the paper and folded his hands overtop it. "What else?"

"I'd like to leave, if you'll allow it," Anoka admitted.

Dean raised an eyebrow at the request.

"I'd like to train the other fresh champions," she shrugged. "Your group is the smallest one. Riva has hundreds of new champions testing out."

"The greater good," Dean muttered.

"The greater good," Marty and Riva repeated. "We could really use Anoka. Is her coming with us going to be a problem?"

Dean shook his head, staring briefly at the ceiling. "Consider it done, I take it you're wanting to split portal times still? I need to get Kambry and I've got people to add to here to build a better team. Unfortunately, I'll need to compete, now, to afford them," he said.

"Well, yes and no. Once, there are three open portals, it should flow better. But for now, since you're running a militia type team and we're running military operations, we feel it's better not to encroach on you," Riva said populating a hologram on the desk and pointing to a spot to the east. Dean saw a set of mountains he didn't recognize, a cavern vibrantly highlighted. "So, you get Spelunkers Delight. That is the next closest portal, after the Deathly Caverns, at a two-hour flight by speedster ... Or six via a regular shuttle."

"I'm taking Team Riva and building a city on my portal. Marty will get portal four, once we've located it. If Tucker comes out, you'll switch back to Deathly Caverns, and we'll bring in a fourth manager. We need you and your employees all to agree to a contract–bound by Min–not to live in Mixonia. You okay with that?"

Dean was upset, he had a right to feel hurt here. They were putting him on notice that he wasn't trusted.

"Are you taking the same oaths?" Dean asked and they both nodded. "Okay, I can live with it, I guess, so long as what's good for the goose is good for the gander and everything is equally fair. We have to keep the portals open to save Oakley."

He sat up straight, his smile grim. "To summarize... You're both leaving to open a training camp at the other new portal, on a massive scale. You want to take that portal, as well as the one currently being sought, and in return will give me complete autonomy of one portal and my own team. The caveat to me getting to run my own team the way that I want, is that I have to promise—via Min-bound contracts—that I'll never have a Tucker. Which will effectively mean that you will control security in the portal cavern, itself."

"We tried to make it fair Dean," Anoka said softly.

"Aye, it's fair. It cleans up the mess somewhat, too. Who's working on Tucker?" Dean asked and there was a lot of head shaking. *Ah, it was still an open item on the agenda.* "I'd like to have a shorter commute flight, and this base is nice." He turned to Riva. "How much do I owe you for the upgrades?"

"You sure you want to buy all the addons I installed here?" Riva asked and Dean nodded. "Best go get a few more big gems then. My daughter has the exact numbers and I'll sell you the permits and structures at cost. Heaven knows I need the money. Which leads to our last topic. Daily conversions."

"If Anoka trains at Snagglecrest City," Riva smirked, "yes, that's the name of the other portal, then she'll first be flying to the," he indicated the original portal, "Deathly Caverns portal every morning to cash in gems for tokens. Once we control all four portals, I'd like to claim two portals. Marty will use the fourth and you either get Delight to manage how you see fit or we can swap, Spelunker's Delight for Deathly Caverns. All we ask, is that if— for any reason at all—you should stop converting diamonds to sapphires or rubies, you let us use the daily allotment."

Dean grunted with a nod. That was fine with him. He stood up. "So, I take it this is goodbye? For now, at least?"

"Indeed. We'll be in touch. If you need to add to your team, we should have extras you can pick and choose from, since we're going mainstream, while you're staying tight knit," Marty said. "But Dean," he cautioned, "don't be surprised if we hand you our problem children, or those who need structure like you have here."

Dean grunted and chewed on the inside of his lip. "Fine, but I can fire them if they bother me too much."

They stood, shook hands, and Dean wished them both luck. He exited the ship in silence, mulling over the changes. They were the right things to do, in the long run. It bothered him, though, that he'd be stringing his friends along. Putting himself in their shoes, that was something Dean knew would rub him the wrong way. At least until you considered the cost of a closed portal entrance–that was just too important to jeopardize.

When he left the spaceship, he headed straight for the training arena. The inside of the arena was eerily quiet. Gone were the dozens of mercenaries training at all hours of the day with fervor. The only three people who were there now included: Quincy, smacking a training dummy, with sword and shield; Patti was shooting arrows at targets fifty feet away; and, Lonny, stabbing a spear at targets that spun wildly whenever he approached.

"On me!" Dean shouted to his friends. Quincy and Patti moved quickly in his direction. Lonny hadn't heard. He was wearing full battle armor and the *clang* of his spear striking the targets was loud.

"Lonny!" Dean's voice boomed across the training ground.

His friend heard him that time. Lonny removed his helmet and trotted over to the assembling group. Dean waited until he had their full attention.

"I've got good news and bad news," he admitted. "Bad news first. We're losing a ton of support. Anoka is leaving to go train Ravi and Marty's teams. We'll have to find a replacement. And we'll need to replace the medical teams they're taking with them."

Patti frowned.

"This next one is going to hurt your pride, more than anything else," he rubbed at the back of his neck. "We're shifting payouts in a big way–to cash lump sum salaries. You'll never actually possess tokens of your own. Cassie will manage our team's finances. This is being done by all the teams. So–"

"Wait, I won't get to keep these?" Patti asked, showing him the three tokens on her locket. "Even if I promise not to stay in Mixonia?"

"You can't live in Mixonia, if you don't have those. Look, I want to be fair. I'm not here to profit from you guys. You've all known me for years–if there's one thing you know about me, it's that I'm not about money, never have been."

They all nodded.

"This isn't about money. Hell, it isn't really about trust–though a part of me is worried that you'll see it that way." He frowned, trying to make sure he said this right. "What it is about, is Tucker, and the risk of losing another portal–not you. If none of us live in Mixonia, then all you need are sweet Gs, here, for Oakley. Right?"

He nodded to her locket. "What else would you need those for?" Dean asked and Patti deflated, her eyes flicking back and forth as she contemplated her reaction.

"I wanted some trophies. Maybe some gems for a collection or something. Would have liked to get a servant, like Lexis, of my own for when I have kids one day," Patti grumbled, "Or a maid to clean up after me."

"Patti, look at me," Dean said, and she did. "I promise to make it fair and to do right by you and this team. We can still make any and all of that happen. If you trust Cassie and me, then give 'em up and keep helping the cause. I made a deal with Marty and Riva that we'd behave the same as the other teams. I even promised never to lock down a portal."

"Fine, but I want spreadsheets tracking–"

Quincy busted into laughter. When she frowned at him, he smiled. "That's Cassandra's forte, love. She'll be professional about it–you know she will." He turned back to Dean. "I accept."

"I accept." Lonny and Patti both said.

Awesome. I kinda had a feeling they might bitch and moan some.

"Now for the good news. I've secured full autonomy for team Ola–that's us. We're team Ola now." He grinned mischievously, "Just made that up, too. Anyway. We're taking the training gloves off. Combined, we have fifty-nine tokens. Freeing Kambry will put us at thirty-three tokens and–"

"Thirty-four," Lonny snorted. "No wonder you quit accounting."

Dean snickered, "Right, so were going to do some very basic level one grinding. Maybe as many as sixty-four runs. We'll have our own cavern, that Riva is probably converting just like he did to the other one."

Dean knew he'd need to get confirmation from Riva on that assumption. "This should mean a crash pad outside of Mixonia and a place to rest. We're going to do some on the job training in the portal. That's right, after we free Kambry were going to group PvE. I want to get us back up to fifty tokens. If we can manage to do that, we can unlock a healer from Min's shelves."

"Why not just get one from the labor market?" Lonny asked. "Probably cheaper."

"Yeah, I'm with Lonny on this one," Patti said, and Quincy nodded.

"Fine, we can do that, too. Cassie will want to do up the contracts, either way. We're desperate, though, can I count on your help?"

There were bobbing heads all around that he could.

"Anoka pulled out the equipment Cassie bought us. Let's go ahead and gear up and head to Spelunkers Delight. We can debate what to do first after freeing Kambry, once we have her with us. Just know that I intend for us to start competing as soon as today," Dean said, gesturing for the armory door.

He wasn't sure if Kambry would agree to this team decision. Dean was also uncertain about how she'd react to his inability to keep his last promise to her–how long and hard he'd had to struggle to get to her.

He'd best put on his armor and his most charming smile. Hopefully, they could fix some of the problems Tucker had caused.

TWENTY-EIGHT

DEAN

Mixonia

D ean stood at the shelf for the Dragona species inside of Min's Vault. He was alone in the vault; the silence was eerie and made him think this was an instanced set up.

He saw Kambry stuck in an epic pose, her staff held high, and her sword at the ready. His heart jumped a beat seeing her statuette, his stomach tingled, and his palms sweat. After almost four days of missing her, here she was.

He indented the button of her statue and waited for the magic to happen. The twenty-five tokens from his Bearclays' silver necklace were sent into an escrow account. That part was simple, his locket number altered automatically. When his body faded by dematerializing everything around him, things got weird. His soul was pulled into whatever meeting place Kambry chose.

He materialized inside a hovel of an apartment, not the grand dwarven throne room where he had first met her, like he'd been expecting. Here there was only a small square table with initials carved into it, a small bed in an alcove, and two other rooms. The kitchen was little more than a sink and a cooking station. The table had seating for four and Dean waited to take a spot.

Kambry formed from particles in a flash so quick the transition was hard to follow. The two stood apart shocked for a moment.

"About time, Dean!" Kambry squealed, leaping into his arms. "Why didn't my mother visit yesterday?"

"About that. I've got some news. Can we sit, please?" Dean asked, gesturing to the table.

"That sounds pretty ominous," Kambry said hesitantly.

"I've got some news–both good news, and well, bad news... sorta–if you're willing to hear me out," Dean said.

"Of course, my dashing rescuer. I wish Cassie were here. Too bad you can't both enter at the same time. Is she in the vault with you?" Kambry wondered, then noticed Dean's frown. Her hand leaped to cover his as they sat beside each other. "Please tell me she's okay!"

"Well, yes," Dean shifted uncomfortably in his seat. "She and our daughter are doing great. I gave them both kisses before I left. They were still asleep," Dean winced.

Kambry tilted her head at his words. He could see her mind racing to piece together what he told her.

"Wait, that's not possible," she frowned, "unless..."

"Unless, indeed," Dean smirked. "Min wanted to keep Lexis from running off to tour the galaxy. This did that .... in spades–"

"Dean Forrester!" Kambry shouted with joy." Are you serious?"

"Yeah... yes."

"How big is she, what color are her eyes, and did you bring a drawing of her with you?" Kambry demanded to know, her feet bouncing off the floor. "Oh, my word, I'm so excited!"

"Eight pounds three ounces. She has my hazel eyes. Puffy little cheeks and doesn't do much. No drawing, sorry, but you'll see her soon, I promise," Dean said with his biggest smile.

Kambry stretched across the table and kissed him, deeply. "I missed you so, both of you. I'm thrilled by this. Please continue with your report of the outside situation, though."

"Min righted a wrong and gave us two portal locations that the guards were helping the Core to hide from the Suca. So... here I am. The first free moment I could get to you, I arrived," Dean said. He locked his hazel eyes with her sparkling greens. His hand instinctively squeezed hers.

"I missed you Kambry," he confessed. "I went to a pretty dark place in my hunt for another portal. There was nothing I wasn't willing to do to get to this moment. Well spider bears, they were a hard pass, but a man needs to know his limits."

She fake rolled her eyes, though her joyful smile told the true story. She kissed him, lovingly. "I missed you too, you big brute. I knew you'd come. Wow, how is Cassie taking this?"

"How do you mean?" Dean asked.

"Well, we were just starting to be a loose family, and now you two—"

"Are eagerly awaiting you to come home. Cassie was heartbroken over Tucker locking you out. Here is our offer. We love you and are giving you twenty-five tokens free. No commitment, no contract, no nothing. Come home to us," Dean said, getting a wee bit emotional. He wiped at his eyes. "Sorry," he said shakily, "it has been really hectic these past few days—I'm normally more in control of my emotions."

Kambry leaped across the table and tackled him. Her passionate kisses apologized for her rough handling. Things started to get heated with both of their hands roaming and caressing. Suddenly, they were no longer touching each other.

"Drat the damn vault rules. Stupid gods," Kambry grumped. Dean stared up at her from his back in confusion. "We can't do more than simple kisses," she explained. "Or else spouses with twenty-five tokens would just visit their loved ones and invest their tokens, instead of freeing them. Anyway, Dean Forrester," she batted her eyelashes at him, "I gladly accept your no-clauses attached offer of freedom. I take it from your armor, you want to earn some tokens?"

"Yup," Dean said, kissing her. "Do you go out into the cavern or come out here, in Mixonia? Your gear is already in the cavern." He smiled at her. "Our new base is supposed to be called 'Spelunkers Delight', but we're calling it the 'Delightful Caverns'."

"Cavern it is then. Just confirm this," Kambry said, sending him her contract, "and I'll meet you there."

Dean didn't hesitate and signed. A moment later they both left Min's plane of existence to be reunited in person.

When Dean returned to the vault, he stood for a moment staring at the shelf. Kambry's statuette was no longer a figurine among the others. He'd run a risk taking this route. The last thing Cassandra had said to him before he left, though, was, 'This is the right thing to do—regardless of the consequences or the cost'.

Dean left Min's Vault for the city's exit. Even if Kambry fled, he agreed fully with Cassandra. This was what he should have done in the first place. He walked down

Mixonia's busy streets, just another champion among a sea of aliens, eking out a living.

His long legs and a brisk pace enabled him to return to the Delightful Caverns after only twenty minutes of pushing through the crowds.

When he returned to Oakley, he did so in his Roman segmented lorica armor. That was the benefit of going back and forth in gear that Mixonia allowed. He found Kambry already suited up in her armor, with her staff and sword, ready to go.

"Were you worried I'd leave?" Kambry asked with a smirk. The twinkle in her eye begged Dean to drag her off to someplace private.

"Cut it out, you two. Save the cute stuff for later. I'm nervous, and rightfully so," Quincy admitted with a chuckle. He tried to look casual, leaning against the cavern wall and failing miserably. Dean wasn't especially worried, but Quincy seemed uneasy. "We've already welcomed her back. Now that we're all together, please explain why we're suddenly taking risks."

"I have to admit, I want to go see the baby. This rush to earn more tokens has me a bit perplexed, Dean," Kambry pouted, making a fake sad face with duck lips.

"Tucker made me realize something," Dean admitted, "and the plague aboard the orbital something else. We've got to get this score evened out. That means taking a few risks. We've all got a week of training or more under our belts. I know, not enough, really, and we still need a mage. But–"

"Why stick to PvE?" Lonny asked. "The good tokens are in PvP."

Dean sighed and nodded. "Baby steps, my friend. I want to do something where, if one of us struggles for any reason, the rest of us can help them out. This also lets us ease into the labyrinths and get a feel for how they operate. I really don't think we'll wipe. But if we do. I'm confident, that with time, we'll all be unlocked by all of our favorite sugar momma–the lady with the purse strings, Cassie."

That elicited a round of laughter.

Kambry tapped her staff on the ground. "I'm glad we're doing this. Let me explain how it works. Dean goes in first, which makes him the portal master. We do level one and get one token, just for him. If we do level one, eight more times, another token. Or we if decide to tackle a higher level, which I will go into later. When we reach a fatigue point on Dean's leveling, we come back out, and I go in first with a contract for you all to help me do level one nine times and boom, we make two more tokens. Rinse and repeat with each of you as portal master."

"What's inside the actual first floor?" Patti asked.

Kambry shrugged, "No idea. That's the joy of the games. They're unique and unpredictable. I can say that level ones of every type are always super easy. In solo PvP levels one and two, for example, there aren't even monsters to kill. You just have to find the locket and go. PvE solo levels one and two, each had a single monster."

"Alright, anyone wanting to back out now, say so. If not, let's perform some combat checks," Dean said walking first to inspect Lonny.

The man was wearing garb similar to his own. He had a no-frill, plain black helmet. A nose guard split between his eyes, darkening his sockets and making his dark brown eyes pop. A chain-link coif wrapped around his neck and covered his chin. A single horse adorned his dull gray breastplate. He wore a thick leather strap kilt, called a pteruge, and fully armor encased boots. Dean inspected his clamps, his belt, and tugged on each buckle of his armor.

Lonny did the same to Dean's gear. Dean had a Roman red mohawk on his helm splitting the middle. His face was open, his segmented lorica armor–composed of overlapping bands of metal–golden, and his black pteruge kilt, thick. The back of his shield, which he wore on his left arm had a quick attach and detach slot for his trident. When Lonny was satisfied with his inspection, he merely gave Dean a nod and grunted.

Quincy was the odd man out, because the ladies were busy inspecting each other. He wore another set of Roman armor, the difference here was he didn't have a large shield and a long weapon like the other two. He had a buckler shield, only slightly larger than his head, and a short sword. His job was to protect the ranged damage dealers in the backline. Mainly because Dean didn't know what else to do with him.

Patti was clad in a light chain dress. She'd be their most vulnerable team member. She needed the freedom to shoot her bow, so she and Cassandra had picked out this weird armor. It just seemed flimsy to Dean. He'd seen her get ready and it had looked quite painful, how tight Kambry had wrapped the chainmail around her chest. She wore a hooded light green leather cover over her chainmail, and he watched her spin her arms and test her range of motion. With a full range of motion verified, Patti adjusted the quiver stuffed with arrows that rested on her back. Her bow was unstrung in her left hand and a confident smile was on her face.

That left Kambry. She was back in a duplicate set of the armor she had worn in her close loss against a full demon team. Her mother had picked this new set up while they'd been busy searching for the portals. The gem on Kambry's long staff sparkled with energy and her eyes thirsted for battle... Or sex. Dean kept catching her winking at him and bouncing her eyebrows or batting her eyelashes. She wanted both, he finally decided... yeah, definitely both.

Dean sent out a contract for nine runs through the group PVE to each of his friends. They accepted and he led them into Mixonia.

When they arrived in Mixonia, it reminded him of when he'd seen the five lizardmen in a loose formation head into the city during his first visit. Except that, now, was them. One difference was Dean was pretty nervous, whereas they'd exuded confidence.

This was a big risk, and yet, also represented a new start. A new way to push forward. Dean took the lead, walking them through the city, when Sable suddenly arrived at his side, matching his stride.

"Father sent me. Said to tell you good luck, but that you won't need it. I've talked with him. We discussed you as a hypothetical example, but I'm on board with his plan, not yours," Sable said with a nonchalant shrug.

"Okay, I respect that, and I respect you," Dean said and though she didn't stumble, Sable's swagger faded a bit with this statement. "I'd appreciate your insight on a suitable replacement, if you don't mind."

"I have an Angelia or two I can introduce you to. A few that should fit your needs, and you, possibly, theirs."

They walked on together without saying anything for two more blocks.

"I'm glad you're not sour," Sable finally said, looking at him from the corner of her eye.

"I want the best for my friends, even if—" Dean stopped abruptly when Sable vanished.

"What was that about?" Kambry trotted up beside him.

"We need a new trainer," he shrugged, "Your mom has going over to Riva's teams. Ideally, we need to build three groups, inside team Ola. Your mom's leaving makes sense even if I'll miss her, because by going with Riva, she'll be training hundreds. Our team, team Ola ..." he shook his head, "well, it's just us for now. Unless we can convince more of my friends to compete or join a guild or mess around with finding mercenaries in Mixonia for hire," Dean grumbled, slipping his free hand into hers.

"The problem with the last option, is that they will help if you're the team leader, but not if they are. For Oakley's points anyway, unless they move out with all their stuff and hold no residence here." She gestured to the grand city in front of them. "I do like the idea of us forming our own teams. Lonny here would make a great team leader," Kambry said, sliding her hand free to pat Lonny on the shoulder.

He strutted for a step or three and grinned, "I'd like to think so, too. However, I want to learn magic first and get some experience. So, this is fine, for now. It's a good first start. I can't help but think of the water event, how easy it was."

"Won't always be like that, though, right?" Patti asked from behind Dean.

Dean angled the group through the Gardens of the Gods to take a shortcut.

Kambry shook her head, "That's a simple answer, no. There are some very complex events. The options are numerous. A few allow duets, trios, and even a ten-person group. Which can get into some very intricate dynamics, to say the least."

Dean snorted.

"For the standard portals," Kambry repeated, "it is generally accepted that the beginning floors are easy. The point is not to kill you at the start. It's to lure you into a false sense of confidence and for a champion to get defeated on a floor they had no business being on."

"What about finding us a mage trainer?" Dean asked.

"As far as magic goes, and I really hate to admit it, but Sable is a master. Thero runs the largest mage academy in Mixonia, but he's the one who killed me before you and I met. The hiring market will have plenty of mages–unfortunately, they'll likely be ones who I don't know." Kambry shook her head. "Training in magic is super expensive. I once spent my whole years' salary simply to pay rent and for two magic scrolls." She turned to Dean with a frown. "I do advise getting Sable's help–if you can."

"So... Kambry, how does learning magic work?" Patti asked.

"It's both incredibly complex and amazingly simple," Kambry frowned. "There are some species with naturally attuned magic in their home worlds. Dean is probably the only human on Oakley who naturally has magic. Which is stunning, by itself." She smiled at Dean.

"If you come here, to Mixonia, you got your stat sheet, right?"

Patti nodded.

"That unlocked Magic for you–in the sense that the moment you set foot in Mixonia, you're suddenly a champion capable of more than you were before. Simply coming here unlocks magic for you."

Patti frowned, "But my stat sheet didn't say anything in the 'Magic' column.'

"Oh bugger," the Dragona shook her head, frustrated, "that was a bad way to explain it." She closed her eyes tightly and rubbed her temples. "A human on Oakley can't learn magic from a scroll on Oakley, unless they've been to Mixonia first. Arriving here unlocks your ability to consume stored mana with magic." She smiled. "Although you have opened your pathways to mana, you still have to unlock the magic itself through a scroll. That clears it up, I hope."

Patti smiled at her.

"Now," Kambry continued, "there are seven main types of magic and thousands of minor ones. The ones that can be learned from a scroll are fire, water or ice, electrical or energy, earth, air or wind, healing, and finally Suca arcane. There is a Core arcane to balance the Suca arcane magic, but that is usually simply called void magic."

"Do Core mages have access to eight kinds, then?" Quincy wanted to know.

"Enemy mages have the main seven magical types also available. Be cognizant that you can see other types that come naturally to other species. A mage instructor would cover the process for unlocking and actually using the main types. Since we're here, though," Kambry gestured to the corner ahead of them, "I'd rather we focus on fighting without magic, for now."

Dean rounded that corner and saw the tall portals looming at the end of wide walkways, each on their own floating mini islands. A big sign indicated the way to go for *Group PvE*. He doubted it actually was written in English like that, but that was exactly what it showed him. The nervous butterflies in his stomach took flight again, as they approached the portal staging area.

The portal island, as he figured it should be called, was mildly busy. Nothing compared to the chaos of the water solo event, though. This island was bigger, since it was for groups. It was about three football fields wide. There were two beaches surrounding a row of single pedestals—probably a hundred group spots. Other teams looked to be talking strategy or were performing pre-combat checks. Dean even spied a male bunny-hybrid team. They were slamming their fists down on each other's shoulders, psyching themselves up.

"And there go five more figurines onto the shelves," Kambry sneered, scoffing at the display. "So many Bouncries have donated their energy to the soul pit, Min had to put them in their own section—separate from the normal alphabetically order rows. That's when you know you've got problems winning. A soul is a soul is a soul, though. Hopefully enough will enter the pits to expand the city again. With rent prices this high, Mixonia certainly needs it."

"New buildings just pop up?" Dean wondered, arriving at an empty pedestal spot.

Kambry shook her head. "Each district will grow by one building slot. So, eight plots would become available. A month-long bidding war then ensues for rights to the new space. The winner gets the building for life. So..."

Quincy let out a whistle. "I bet they go for tens of thousands of tokens," he exclaimed. There was a hunger in his eyes at the thought. Quincy was well of sure, and Dean had only rarely see him become enthralled in thoughts of more wealth.

"More like millions. There are slum lords and guilds here who are absolutely loaded. All those tokens cycle back to Min. It's a vicious place, Mixonia is. Alright, let's pull up our Champion Stats," Kambry said, showing them how it was done by going first.

Dean was not surprised at her stats.

Champion Information
Name: Kambry Gender: Female
Level: 2 Tokens: 0
Race: Dragona Alignment: Suca
Luck: -1 Charisma: 11

Health: 286 / 286 H-Regen: 1.0 / Sec
Stamina: 305 / 305 M-Regen: 1.0 / Sec
Mana: 282 / 282 S-Regen: 1.0 / Sec

Strength: 184 Vitality: 102
Dexterity: 156 Endurance: 149
Intelligence: 84 Willpower: 198
Magic: Fire Water

She was a fairly well-balanced all-around competitor. He was surprised her intelligence was so low, though. He pointed to that stat and quirked an eyebrow at her.

"Before you think I'm dumb," Kambry roll her eyes at Dean, "if you make bad decisions, it will reduce your score. Mine will recover with time. Before my first defeat, I had over a hundred and sixty Int or Intelligence. Which would put me in a mage category that I thrive at. Okay, your turn Dean."

Champion Information
Name: Dean Forrester Gender: Male
Level: 0 Tokens: 35
Race: Human Alignment: Suca
Luck: 16 Charisma: 41

Health: 344 / 344 H-Regen: 1.0 / Sec
Stamina: 294 / 294 M-Regen: 1.0 / Sec
Mana: 321 / 321 S-Regen: 1.0 / Sec

Strength: 212 Vitality: 132
Dexterity: 107 Endurance: 187
Intelligence: 92 Willpower: 229
Magic: Electrical

Dean noticed he'd gained some willpower while losing some strength. Probably from not working out as much as he usually did, during their hunt for another portal.

"Perfect front line stats. That is, until you see his insane willpower. A bruiser mage is rare, but these stats are always about what you put into it, while some are raw luck or skill, others bust their butts. Lonny your turn."

Champion Information
Name: Lonny Marx Gender: Male
Level: 0 Tokens: 0
Race: Human Alignment: Suca
Luck: 9 Charisma: 21

Health: 322 / 322 H-Regen: 1.0 / Sec
Stamina: 314 / 314 M-Regen: 1.0 / Sec
Mana: 270 / 270 S-Regen: 1.0 / Sec

Strength: 190 Vitality: 122
Dexterity: 117 Endurance: 197
Intelligence: 109 Willpower: 161

Lonny stuck his hand to the podium and his stats showed for the team to see. "Oh hey, this is awesome. Now I can track everything."

Champion Information
Name: Patti Kendricks Gender: Female
Level: 0 Tokens: 0
Race: Human Alignment: Suca
Luck: -1 Charisma: 21

Health: 193 / 193 H-Regen: 1.0 / Sec
Stamina: 238 / 238 M-Regen: 1.0 / Sec
Mana: 197 / 197 S-Regen: 1.0 / Sec

Strength: 87 Vitality: 106
Dexterity: 129 Endurance: 109
Intelligence: 111 Willpower: 86

Patti went next, as soon as his hand was off the podium. "Hey! I'm improving. Good, that makes the extra hours of training feel worth it. Your turn Quincy," Patti said, smacking his ass.

Quincy pulled up his stats and frowned.

Champion Information
Name: Quincy Hilton Gender: Male
Level: 0 Tokens: 0
Race: Human Alignment: Suca
Luck: 33 Charisma: 36

Health: 224 / 224 H-Regen: 1.0 / Sec
Stamina: 309 / 309 M-Regen: 1.0 / Sec
Mana: 222 / 222 S-Regen: 1.0 / Sec

Strength: 135 Vitality: 89
Dexterity: 204 Endurance: 105
Intelligence: 89 Willpower: 133

"This says I should be ranged," Quincy huffed.

"Quincy you're in a niche slot. I'd stick you on dual wielding, for close ranged flank attacks. These two are bruiser enough to protect our backline. We can always adjust as we go. For now, though, I think we're ready. The team leader just heads over the Minotaur guard," Kambry pointed, "Gives his oath, and the team is sucked in when he is. Or we can follow him in," Kambry said, pointing to the portal. "Which is why you really have to be careful about who you make deals with."

"Alright, here goes nothing," Dean said, walking up to the Minotaur guard. He looked up at the guard, waiting to be addressed.

"Place your hand on the pedestal. State your name and acknowledge that you understand the risks of spending an eternity as a soul inside Min's Vault," the guard rumbled.

"I, Dean Forrester of planet Oakley, wish to compete on floor one of the team event, without combat. If any or all of us are defeated, we understand we will become statues on Min's shelves," Dean said.

The Minotaur guard pointed to the portal. Dean squared his shoulders and, with a determined look on his face, stepped into the green shimmering light.

TWENTY-NINE

DEAN

PVE Group – Floor 1

Dean arrived in a tall grass that obscured his vision. He tensed, instinctively flexing into a defensive posture. Kambry, Quincy, Patti, and Lonny materialized around him. The only confident person about the whole situation was Kambry. Everyone else similarly took up a defensive battle posture.

"Easy, easy team. Okay, we're in. Here are the simple rules," Kambry said, pointing to the black portal that *hummed* behind them. "The four of us could leave, but if Dean stayed, he'd be in here until he also decided to leave, died, and or completed the floor. Basic, simple, and easy. We decide the floor is too hard, we turn around, and head home. Empty-handed but alive."

"And this tall grass?" Dean asked, looking up to see that it was at least a dozen feet tall.

"Same as the two PvE solo floors I did. Meant to help you escape, if you need to. Texts and journals say these safe zones go away, at higher levels, and turn into more or less a very small landing pad for the start of the labyrinth. Shall we proceed?" Kambry asked, pointing in the opposite direction of the portal.

"Lonny on my left," Dean ordered, locking his shield with Lonny's. "Girls in the middle, Quincy cover the rear. We'll take it nice and slow."

They stepped forward together, as a team. Dean peeled the tall grass to the side with his trident. The weapon was shorter than the one he'd had on his ship, but intentionally so. This baby was only five feet long so he could still tuck and roll with it. He'd tried the same maneuvers with longer tridents and it always resulted in painful failures. After putting significant thought into it, he'd decided that–with adjustments to the overall length to increase his maneuverability–the trident was his go-to weapon.

Dean even had another, longer one, getting crafted for when he soloed with Apache. That custom weapon resembled a lance and Dean was excited to ride Apache into battle with it. Heck, he was excited to finally train with the gentle stallion.

The group exited the tall grass to find themselves in a clearing that revealed more of the rocky black terrain; something akin to the hard surface left once magma cooled. Dean's boots crunched over the pebbly loose rocks. A few hundred feet in the open rested a pedestal. Two brown wolves slumbered under the glinting locket.

"Chances of the locket being fake?" Dean asked.

"Oh, that one is real, there are no mimic lockets. Sure, other golden things may mislead. But never a locket," Kambry said.

Quincy turned to face the front and said, "Wait, it's just two wolves. That's it?"

"It's the first floor," she shrugged.

Dean twirled his trident until it pointed down. He drove the triple spiked head down. When he was sure it was secure, he aimed his hand at the wolves.

"If you're smart and want to raise your intellect," Kambry muttered to herself under her breath, "you start here."

"On three, we all fire," Dean commanded.

Patti grumbled as she pulled out and knocked an arrow, "That's at least a hundred feet further than what I normally practice at."

Dean shrugged. "Three, two, one, and fire."

A magical ball of energy laced out of his palm. He adjusted quickly to the other target and sent another fist-sized orb racing forward. An arrow *whizzed* by Dean's ear and the uncomfortable heat of a fireball raced past his shoulder.

The wolves stayed restfully sleeping, completely oblivious to the oncoming attack. Dean watched his first orb smack into the resting wolf. There was enough force that the energy ball burst into the skin and sent the wolf tumbling. The second wolf jumped angrily to its feet, causing Dean's electrical orb to zip between the wolf's legs.

Patti unleashed her second arrow when her first fell about a dozen feet short. The standing wolf spotted the fireball, however, a touch too late. The animal tried to run, but the orb of fire consumed its face before it even managed to take a single step.

"Uh... is that it?" Lonny said, his eyes darting around them, waiting for a new foe to appear.

"Yes," Kambry grinned at him, "there are no respawns or suddenly generated monsters. There are, however, creatures that can emerge from stealth or drop from ceilings, and some that burrow or hide in crevices. Some of the labyrinths get really big--but not here. We just earned a token."

She slapped Patti on the back.

"Something to note. Killing your foe is not always the most prudent course of action... Or so I've been told many times by my mother. Lonny could have distracted the wolves, while Quincy retrieved and slotted the locket. We'd still have won, and all been portaled out," Kambry said motioning for the others to follow her, as she led the way forward.

"We don't have to kill more stuff?" Quincy said, dismayed.

Patti snickered beside him and punched him in the shoulder. "Nope. This is the easiest real-life game, ever. At least on these levels. No wonder people repeat them so often." Patti started hopping up and down to see better. "Did anyone see where my second arrow landed?"

"Your arrows will be returned automatically to your quiver upon completion of the level," Kambry explain, walk a bit slower to scoop an arrow up off the ground. "If they break or dull, though, that is the condition they are returned to you."

"That's good to know. Scouring for hours to recover my arrows would suck," Patti said.

Dean arrived at the pedestal. A neck shaped incline held the locket. Dean slid it up and off the holder and touched it to the slot that was the lock.

∞∞∞∞

There was no bright light or fancy transition like coming in. One minute they were in the labyrinth, the next they were outside the portal, standing by two benches and a podium.

"So..." Lonny said letting the sentence hang.

"We get two tokens at level two, right? What's your necklace say now," Quincy asked, and Dean flashed him a thirty-six. "Dean, that was cake. I mean we can do it eight more times. But..."

"Yes, each floor's rewards are equal to that floor number. So, floor two plus this floor would mean we'd have earned three tokens." She took a deep breath. "Keeping in mind that I'm not the right person to be saying this, given my past history, I agree with Quincy. Here is why, though. If we get in a jam later on, and have already flooded these early levels, we'll have nothing to grind on to pick up easy tokens," Kambry explained, twisting her fingers together nervously. She rocked from side to side, worried about Dean's response.

"Fret not my lovely Dragona. I, too, see the value in your logic. We'll go on to level two, unless anyone has reservations about doing so," Dean opened the floor for the team to comment.

"I just feel so useless," Quincy whined.

A burst of laughter escaped before Patti controlled her impulses. "Sorry, Quince." She gave him a kiss. "You're here and doing great."

Quincy scoffed.

"Protect the girls," Dean said with a tight-lipped smile. "Come on man, don't get down, we're helping keep plagues at bay and I promise there'll be riches at the end of the rainbow."

His troops followed him to the Minotaur guard this time, wanting to enter with him.

"Say the same thing as before, this time specifying which floor—one or two—you wish to compete on," the guard said in a gruff, uncaring voice.

"I, Dean Forrester and team, wish to compete in floor two. We understand that if we're defeated, we head to Min's vault to be statues on the shelves," Dean said.

The guard waved them forward. The green had changed subtly, a barely noticeable change. Dean entered their next challenge with the others right behind him.

∞∞∞

There was a stone wall ten feet tall this time that boxed them into a garden. A single arched doorway led to a lavish door that spoke of a wealthy interior. The team arrived right behind him while Dean shifted to peer out the front. It looked like they were going into a building.

"What do we have?" Kambry asked.

"A manor?" Dean said, questioning his own assumption. He slowly pried the door open. "At least I think it is."

"You ready?" Lonny asked and Dean shrugged. Lonny peered down the hallway to assess the situation.

Dean joined his side to see rows of candles illuminating the narrow corridor before them. A single door waited at the end. A lush rug, fancy paintings, and a high, arched ceiling were all there were to see. The two of them spent a little extra time, looking for traps or hidden foes, and came up empty.

"Alright. Quincy," Dean ordered, "You'll face the way we came. If some spider crawls out of a painting and you're facing forward–"

"Hey, so maybe sometime soon, I could get some scrolls and learn some spells. I'd feel a lot better about this," Quincy groused.

"Your stat sheet has you as fast ranged damage-per-second or DPS... so, bow or dual weapons, but that doesn't mean you have to stick with that. Obviously, I'm a mage with low mana... at the moment. It'll improve," Kambry said.

Dean paused and waited. Then waited some more. Finally, Quincy put his arms up with a shrug. "What?"

"Bro, watch our back. We're here to make tokens to get you and everyone else better gear or scrolls or whatever. Lonny and I have the front. If we come upon a threat," he explained the plan, "we'll duck and you two fire."

The girls nodded, Patti with an arrow nocked.

"Quincy," Dean grunted and said, "you do what?"

"Sorry." He turned back around and said, "Alright, Ready. I'm just nervous."

"All good. Okay, Lonny, we lock and walk. In hindsight. I'll want to replace you in the future with a lefty," Dean noted, and Lonny bobbed his head. "You're more than capable of managing your own team."

"Shall we?" Lonny said with a grin, locking shields.

The hallway was fifty feet to cross and Dean was fairly certain the challenge was on the other side of that door. They walked down the hallway, slowly, with Dean and Lonny ready to kneel and hide at a moment's notice. Heads stayed on a swivel, checking and rechecking every aspect of the corridor. The group kept quiet as they progressed, their steps cautious and filled with angst.

He held up his fingers to do a countdown for the door. Three, two, one, and he slowly turned the handle while opening the door.

A Dwarf charged Lonny's shield screaming.

"Begone you vile invaders. I'll cleave you in–"

Twang

The Dwarf's speech went silent mid-sentence. Dean heard a thud as the Dwarf fell over onto his back, stiff as a board. He peered over his shield hesitantly until he noted an arrow sticking out of his eye.

"Oh, my gods," Patti cried, shaking her hands in a panic, on the verge of tears. "I panicked. I-I just killed him. What did I do?"

Dean went further into the room to ensure there were no more threats, while the team went to comfort her.

She covered her face with her hands, crying as she kneeled beside the body. When she suddenly ripped her arrow out of the corpse and stood, Patti was smirking.

"Got ya, as if I'd care," Patti said, reveling in the fact that she'd fooled everyone.

"Oh, you got us good. I've got the locket," Kambry said, pressing the locket to the indent.

A moment later they were back outside the labyrinth.

∞∞∞∞

Dean and his group arrived at a staging station. A quick inspection revealed a thirty-eight on his locket.

Awesome. I wonder what the planetary score is.

His hand willed the information from the pedestal.

Planet Oakley

Core lead – 151

"Enemy is only up eleven points since you lost, Kambry. Very nice. Objections to floor three?" Dean asked.

"So... I'm hungry but we can take a break after next floor, might just be my nerves. Never survived a level three," Kambry said with a frown.

"Yeah, you just needed someone in your life to keep you from charging into PvP," Dean smirked. He realized that might have come out harsher than he intended, so he tried to smooth things over with a charming twist. "I mean, Cassie and I are both proud of the changes you're adapting to so wonderfully. Besides," he snorted, "you kick ass and its bull shit you died twice to campers."

"Better, and it is okay, I try to own my flaws. See," Kambry said flashing her stats.

Champion Information

Name: Kambry Gender: Female

Level: 2 Tokens: 0
Race: Dragona Alignment: Suca
Luck: -1 Charisma: 11

Health: 286 / 286 H-Regen: 1.0 / Sec
Stamina: 355 / 355 M-Regen: 1.0 / Sec
Mana: 286 / 286 S-Regen: 1.0 / Sec

Strength: 184 Vitality: 102
Dexterity: 156 Endurance: 199
Intelligence: 89 Willpower: 198
Magic: Fire Water

She'd already gone up five points in intelligence. "Come on back to momma. And Dean, the more I think about it, the worse I feel being here."

Patti slung an arm around Kambry and said, "Cassie would rather have another plague prevented than have you rush home this very second. She said so to me this morning, noting that I was to mention this if you two started guilt tripping yourselves. The bonus is, Lexi is there."

"Lexi?" Kambry said with a furled brow. "You mean Lexis?"

"Ask Lonny, I heard him screaming her—"

"Hey, why you dragging me into this," Lonny gave him an elbow to the ribs, though he did so with a big grin plastered on his face. "But... yes, she prefers Lexi over Lexis. Into the breach once more, dear friends, please. Before I have to start talking about how Quincy asked Patti to wear bunny ears."

Dean tried to contain his laughter, but it burst forth despite his best efforts. Quincy stole Patti from Kambry's side for a deep kiss.

"This lovely number gets me," Quincy said with bouncing eyebrows.

"Alright, level three, then a break," Dean admitted, his stomach grumbling. "I've been delinquent on eating enough protein and working out. Hopefully, this will help with my stats."

"Why not check them now?" Lonny asked.

He patted his belly. "When we're done and after I fill this beast."

Dean walked to Minotaur who had a team of Oruk waiting to go in. Their leader was a foot taller than the others in spiked armor. The big brute had light green skin, covered in scars. They all wore so many weapons the metal clanged and banged as they walked. This confounded Dean.

There was no way they could possibly fight like that.

When Dean saw two female Oruk in mage robes dragging a cart behind them, his interest was piqued. He tried to spy what was under the sheets of black cloth. draped over bulky items. His failure to glean any useful information made him grow curious. The leader had a quick chat with the Minotaur guard. The guard laughed, showing the first sign of emotion Dean had yet to see from one of them. With a quick wave, the Oruk group were through the checkpoint. The portal shimmied into a rosy red, and the team vanished.

"Couple of things to go over with what you just saw there," Kambry said. "From my schooling here... Ah, go ahead and get us in there first."

Dean saw a Siren team stacked up behind them, so he went to the guard and stuck his hand on the pedestal.

"I, Dean Forrester and his team understand all risks and request floor three," Dean said, and the Minotaur guard proudly gestured them towards the portal. The rosy red morphed into a lime green before he'd even neared. He smiled, knowing they were about to get Kambry a whole new level.

∞∞∞

Dean found himself on a gently declining mountain slope. There were big boulders around them and a black portal behind him in case he wanted to go home. The terrain was solid rock and when Dean peeked around one of the boulders, he noted three humanoid rat creatures a few hundred paces down the slope. There was a pedestal down the slope, though one with no glint of gold on it. Dean saw Lonny surveying the scene with a frown. Dean stepped past the protected rocks and out into the open.

"Where are you going," Quincy hissed.

"Follow me. We've yet to get a maze. I think... yup, there it is," Dean said waving his team over. "We're good to talk here, we'd range those ugly things down quickly, anyway. But..." he grinned cheekily, "guess what you ugly fookers, we don't need to go to them."

"I'm confused," Patti said, her hands coming wide as she shrugged, perplexed.

"The labyrinths are not about anything more than finding a locket and setting it into its slot. Got it? Never forget that the objective to every Minotaur Maze is simply to go in, get the key–which is always the locket–and get out when the key is touched to the lock," Kambry said, womansplaining to the max. She was slow and methodical with every word. "Proverbial key into the proverbial lock. Focus on that, always."

"Right, we all got that," he nodded down the hill. "I see an empty pedestal, so this is like, what? Dean's seventh water event floor?" Lonny asked and Dean pointed to a rock with a locket and locket slot on it that was just the other side of the protection ring of boulders. "Oh, three tokens for this. Epic. We can run this one five-hundred-and-twelve times–"

"Finish a floor and it resets into a new creation. All right, we're learning good things. That Oruk team? They were bringing in everything, including the kitchen sink, with them. Part of that was for comfort, another part was to be able to adjust to any scenario. If they all needed to break out archery gear, they can. Or mage staffs. Or whatever they need. They probably brought tools to enable them to build defenses and more," Kambry explained.

Quincy was heading for the locket and paused, "Wait, you mean some of these challenges can take days?"

"Ruby red is in the seventies, I think. Pause and think about that for a moment. If you complete floor seventy, you can almost free three souls in one go. That is crazy," Kambry exclaimed, her hands animated.

"Okay, I agree and it's making me want to train harder. Still. I'd like to know more about how the system works. So, will there always be a chance of this?" Lonny said, indicating the easy win.

"Once you finish a floor," she reminded him, "your next attempt is a clean creation. If you leave a floor without completing it, this all stays the same, except that foes you have killed will respawn. Which no one gripes about too much."

The Dragona turned to Quincy. "If you come in here without water, on a ten-day mission, you'll die. That wagon probably had tents, tools, weapons, cooking supplies, water, ale, and I noticed two of the party were females, so maybe even in a relationship. Kinda like us. Oh," she smirked, "almost forgot–without medical supplies you might die, so they had to have had that with them, too."

Patti paused before shouldering her bow. "I thought you regenerated health in the labyrinth."

"Sure," Kambry explained, "Dean broke some bones that healed. That is a great example of suffering through an injury and regenerating. Take an arrow in the knee? Just rip that sucker out and gripe about it to everyone you ever meet. If you take an arrow to an artery, though, you'd die from blood loss if you can't staunch the flow or regenerate health fast enough. Fail to stick all your guts back in and hold the wound closed–"

"Got it, why not use a healer, then?" Dean asked.

"Healing magic doesn't work inside the labyrinths. It's for Mixonia and performing miracles on your home world. Thankfully, Oakley technology is not far behind magic when it comes to the healing arts. Think of it this way. If we four were healers, and Dean weighed down in some slow, immense armor, he could just waltz past bad guys while we endlessly healed him." Kambry unfolded her arms to point first at the locket and then down the hill at the rat folk who were heading their way. "To be fair, though, ask Min. I don't have the perfect answer, but they will."

Quincy grabbed the locket and touched it to the slot.

∞∞∞

Champion Information
Name: Dean Forrester Gender: Male
Level: 3 Tokens: 39
Race: Human Alignment: Suca
Luck: 16 Charisma: 41

Health: 344 / 344 H-Regen: 1.0 / Sec
Stamina: 294 / 294 M-Regen: 1.0 / Sec
Mana: 325 / 325 S-Regen: 1.0 / Sec

Strength: 212 Vitality: 132
Dexterity: 107 Endurance: 187
Intelligence: 96 Willpower: 229
Magic: Electrical

Dean pulled up his information. His intelligence had gone up a few, but that was it. The team rotated through, pulling up their information sheets. There were only minor improvements, if any at all, resulting in a minor sigh of annoyance. When they finished checking their stats, he walked up to the Minotaur guard.

"No food?" Kambry asked and Dean shook his head, no.

"Dean Forrester and team. For floor four, and we understand the consequence," Dean said. The guard simply nodded. A yellow portal shimmied to green. Without answering Quincy's pleading cry for snacks, Dean stepped through.

∞∞∞

They weren't in an alcove or protected area this time, causing Dean to frown at what he saw. There were a series of tall plateaus, with suspension bridges that connected them to each other. The drops were deep enough that he couldn't see the bottom, between the raised shelfs. There was a mini maze, at the end of which was a pedestal with a golden glint coming from on top of it. Dean cursed because he was unable to see that far.

Need to add binoculars or a pirate scope thingy to my items that I carry around. Super need one of those. Oh, there's bad guys in here, too.

There were hooded mages on each of the suspension bridges, their species unknown to him. This caused Dean to grumble because he had no way to ascertain their abilities.

"The quickest way is left, right, left, then right," Lonny said, pointing out the obvious. "Only four foes to dispatch... Can Kambry just fly across?"

"They'd probably knock me out of the air," the Dragona admitted. "This is actually Patti's chance to shine and get us another victory. Would be a good time to have a cart with bows and arrows with us," Kambry gave Dean a finger wag, happy with her idea.

Dean smirked. "Let's give it a try. The portal is right behind us, and we can defend this spot, if we have to. If things start to go badly, then we'll leave and go get lunch, grab some bows with enough arrows for all of us, and come back when we're ready. But that's all heresy... Patti is a ruthless killing machine," Dean smirked, "carry us to victory."

Patti rolled her eyes at him before nocking an arrow and walking to the edge of the bridge. The mage never noticed her, his gaze trained downward. Patti released her breath, drew to her ear with great poise, and released.

The arrow launched of her string with a twang, moving so fast Dean had trouble tracking it. The twirling projectile sunk into the mage's neck, causing the hooded minion to tumble over the edge. In desperation, the mage spawned a golem, but as it was created in mid-air, it too fell into the trench below, along with its creator.

"Nice shot," Quincy congratulated her proudly.

"Earth mage. Good, we can rotate and let Dean and Patti do all the killing. I'll be useless—not a good idea using fire around rope and old wooded bridges," Kambry groaned. Her glum grimace signaled she was less than thrilled with not being able to contribute.

Dean gestured for Lonny to lead the way.

"I'm thinking multiple gear sets would be a nice thing to have. What if we have a jumping challenge? Doing that in a light robe would be so much easier than in bulky gear," Lonny mentioned stepping onto the bridge. "Or you know, decreasing your bulk while trying to cross a rickety old bridge."

"Cheer up," Dean said with a smirk, "at least there's no lava below us. We all have underclothes on. If we win, the stuff we leave behind comes back with us. Go ahead and remove your gear if—"

"Yeah, I'm going to do that," Lonny said, and quickly shifted to the middle of the platform. "Heights, I can somewhat handle, but this is freaking me out a bit."

Dean let him finish talking before stepping onto the bridge diligently. His foot placement was toward the outside of each of the planks; each step was cautious, yet certain. A minute later he reached the next plateau.

He saw Lonny shaking his head. Unfazed by Dean making the trip in full armor, he continued to get out of his gear. Quincy went next, casually walking in the middle of the bridge. Kambry simply flew to Dean, and Patti tiptoed her way across. Finally, Lonny attempted the suspension bridge a second time. He never shifted his gaze to anywhere other than the horizon. His steps were even and when he returned to solid ground, he breathed a long sigh of relief.

Dean handed Lonny his trident and crept to the edge of the next suspension bridge. Again, the mage was gazing down into the trench, oblivious to his surroundings. Dean built up his inner magic, letting the heat cascade through his body until it reached a boiling point.

His hand extended, locking onto his target. The power coursing through his body had a familiar tingle to it. The seam in his palm begged to be opened.

"Close your eyes," Dean said calmly, taking his own advice.

He gave them a second and then unleashed a beam of energy. His eyelids blazed white, and the heat fled his body. The nauseous feeling he was quickly growing accustomed to, faded.

"Fook me, I'm sitting down. I can't see shit. Please don't let me die," Quincy moaned from behind Dean. Obviously, he hadn't closed his eyes.

I warned him. Not sure I should keep him on the team. The problems are starting to add up.

Dean flicked his lids open to peer out. His foe was in two parts, obviously dead, on the bridge.

"Okay Patti, your turn. Lonny, guard Quincy and just wait for us to finish," Dean said, walking out onto the planks.

When he reached the body, he nudged it with his toe over the edge. He looked down to see what it was the mages were so entranced with and saw nothing. Whatever there was distracting the mages was for them, and them alone.

"So, Dean, you sure you don't want to just cut them in half. Seems hard to miss, you know, with your hand cannon and all," Patti grumbled.

"That's what she said," Dean quipped with a smirk. "White beams of body covering awesomeness."

"Ugh. Men. I guess I'll shoot this one," Patti growled.

She nocked an arrow while stealthily walking to the edge of the next bridge. Patti lined up her shot and fired. Twang. The arrow zoomed forward to take the mage in the gut.

The mage spun their direction, its hand shooting forward while it charged a spell. Crackles of brown magic shot forward summoning a three-foot tall mud golem.

The little creature waddled forward, eager to fight them. Dean crouched in front of Patti with his shield out, doing his job of protecting the ranged champion.

Pattie cursed, fumbling for another arrow. She ignored the one she'd dropped in favor of a new one out of her quiver. She took a deep breath and prepared to fire.

A shard of dirt, from the mage, cracked into Dean's shield. The golem came nearer, and Dean's trident lanced out, impaling the foe. Twang. The mage cried out. Dean saw a second arrow in sticking from its chest. The golem on Dean's trident collapsed, lifeless, as the mage died.

Dean used his boot to pry the golem's corpse off his weapon and walked quickly to the last junction. He didn't hesitate in dealing with the final mage. His hand came up and he unleashed five small orbs of electricity.

The mage, who remained transfixed by the awesome nothingness below them, was paralyzed by the five direct hits. These were slow lobs. Dean had figured out that he could shoot weaker or more powerful shots. In this case, he'd wanted to incapacitate the mage, not eliminate it. Mainly out of concern for accidentally damaging the bridge.

The body twitched under his boots when Dean finally reached the halfway point of the bridge. Dean gave the face a glance to see what he was fighting. An angelic face with long ears peered unblinking back at him. Not an elf, though, because of the fangs. A Vampire, maybe?

Dean was shocked the stunned foe was still alive. He left the body convulsing on the bridge and moved quickly to the pedestal. He snatched up the locket and touched it to the slot, freeing the team in a heartbeat. That was four more tokens to his tally. A challenge, but a simple one. If only they were always going to be this easy, he thought.

INTERMISSION

TUCKER

Mixonia

Tucker grumbled to himself as he slowly came awake with a jaw-cracking yawn. He awoke in the midst of a pile of bunny bodies, which were surprisingly hard to navigate around. His stupid contract with the well-endowed but brainless bunny women left him unable to harm them—he couldn't simply shove them out of his way. Unable to clamber over three girls stacked together in a heap, he clamped down on a big tit to rudely wake the others with a loud squeak.

"Out, the lot of ya," Tucker growled at the groaning group of bunny girls.

He watched them jiggle, shake, and bounce as they wriggled into silken robes before scurrying for the door. He needed to shit and hated doing so with an open door and guests.

A trip to the Mixonia shitter was the worst. The water was cold, unless you magically heated it, which he couldn't do. There was no shower, just a tub of cold water, and a bucket. The last of the bunny girls hovered over the extra big bucket. What the hell had these girls eaten last night? Ugh. The foul smell was almost better than the sharp spike of ammonia that everything had to be wiped down with. That was just the start of things he didn't like about this place.

At first, he'd been as amazed in wondrous disbelief as the rest of them, by this whole city of the Minotaur god. The problem was, though, that it certainly was real. And when he discovered that he was pretty damn good at this champion bullshit, that meant all his trials and tribulations of the past ten years had found a solution.

Tucker had grown up spoiled, privileged, and arrogant. That didn't make him a bad guy, just a lazy one. He'd dropped out of college, when they expected him to actually work for his grades, to live with his parents. His mother was the one he'd had the biggest problems with. This rift led him to distrust women.

When his girlfriend, at the time, broke up with him, Tucker confronted her soon after with a long angry rant. She slapped him, he punched her. This allowed him to press charges for assault, the same as it did for her. She went to get a tooth replaced and he had a sting on his face that faded long before the trial came around. That was a big wake up call, for what his mother had called her 'petulant' child.

His sentence was a stint in the military. Ten weeks of basic training on Oakley's Flagship Oracle did wonders for his 'petulance'. After that, he did his full year, as required, and his punishment was done. His career wasn't over, though. He really loved the military. It remade him. All the naysayers and assholes in his previous life suddenly vanished or became a lot friendlier.

Just under ten years in the service, and he decided to use his leave and take some time off. His position would be held open for him, if he returned within an Earth year. He decided to see what private security work was like. Megan, a friend of his from basic training all those years ago, blasted him on social media with a prime opportunity working for Lexso Corp.

He saw that the sign on bonus, for a month's worth of work, was at least a year's worth of wages; he leaped at the offer. Tucker's biggest disappointment with serving in his planet's military was the pay–hence why he was trying to tuck away some extra cash on a long leave. He'd never be able to afford an orbital home, or a spaceship of his own, if he stayed in the service. He'd be regulated to live on the planet with the other surfacers. Tucker still held tight to his spacer elitism, even though he knew it did him no good, other than to fuel his anger.

With Lexso Corp offering vast riches for little work with few potential risks, Tucker signed on. At first things were casual and simple. Go in, get a few tokens in some swimming event and huzzah, be celebrated as the good guy. Except on his second trip in, while earning a single token in solo PvE, everything had changed. He visited a bunny brothel to follow up on a squeaking titty rumor making the rounds among the training groups. When he stayed past his mandatory return time, he blamed the mission for taking too long. He quickly realized they had no way to verify his fibs–and that nothing was going to happen to him. He'd violated his contract and everything, but not a word from the group. He even received a bonus and a congratulations from the boss for earning a point for Team Oakley.

Without anyone to stop him, after his second solo floor, he went to the market. Knives were easy enough to buy, throwing knives less so. He eventually found the right vendor and geared up, as if he were a ninja on an assassination mission. The easy tokens from the water event and the solo PvE afforded him more than enough for his new gear.

It was dumb of Lexso to be so trusting. He'd only handed over a single token at that point. Ready to rumble, he went into the PvP solo portal.

You'd think a bunch of aliens trained for war would be able to handle a knife thrower. They were not. He wore a black outfit with sheathed throwing knives and used his military training to murder his foes. The fights played out differently each time, though the results were the same. Throwing knives were not something many expected, and he was very good with them. Up the ladder he climbed, until the number and strength of the defenders became a hassle.

He'd told his boss and the squeaking tits that he'd stopped on level ten. The reality was, he made it through level fourteen–nine opponents defeated. That added up to over five hundred tokens. Which was a staggering amount of wealth in this city, he quickly found out he could be a king here.

There was only one problem. He wanted to be a king up above Oakley or somewhere else in this Galaxy humanity called home. He could always replace pleasure girls. What he couldn't do, was turn this place into a swanky spaceship with a floor-to-ceiling view of Planet Oakley.

So, as Tucker shit into the never filling bucket of odd magic, he sighed. When he finished his business, he dressed for the day. His battle outfit was snug, and he was ready to kill. He thought briefly of competing some more, the PvE levels had more easy tokens but he didn't need them yet. His single trip after level fourteen to Min's Vault had left him loaded up with rare gems and he still had more than a hundred of them left to extort the bunny babes and pay the rent.

He left his large private room for the restaurant down in the lobby. Ah, the damn stairs. Not that he minded the exercise, but he missed technology. There literally was little else to do here besides fook, compete, drink, eat, and well... fook some more. He guessed he could read or train, but he inevitably replaced those boring options with squeaky tits, because what fookin idiot would rather read a book than squeeze some perky, soft flesh-colored squeaky toys?

A dozen flights of stairs later, he arrived at the posh diner. A flirty fox girl seated him at a table facing the busy street. A coffee was set down before him, his usual already known by a butler type. The male's species was a mystery to Tucker, not that he gave two fooks what race the help was. Two blue eggs and a full round of meat would be on its way, shortly. This, he could get used to.

The private room upstairs was shit. Service down here was cheaper anyways. The ability to live like a king was awesome–it almost made being stuck here in this disgusting city manageable. He grunted, watching the average citizens–desperately grubbing around for a single token–go about their day. A shuffling of feet made him aware of a guest standing next to his table, which he ignored. Security wouldn't let him be hassled, so he expected a groveling manager to show up any minute now.

He raised a single eyebrow when the new arrival–who had thick braids in his beard, was nigh five feet tall, and looked like he hadn't slept in weeks, with sunken eyes filled with blackness–slammed a meaty palm down on the table so hard Tucker's plate jumped.

A Dwarf. How amusing. What the?

Time froze around them. His plate, the meat and eggs, all hung suspended a few inches off the table. For Tucker, this was a first. A Minotaur appeared from nowhere and placed a restraining hand on the Dwarf's shoulder.

"Aye, master Minotaur. Favor redeemed. Won't be needin more than five minutes in private," the Dwarf grumbled, and the Minotaur vanished.

The bottomless black eyes met his. "Tucker, is it? I'm Havnier, a Dwarven god. You seem to like money and power."

Tucker sipped at his coffee and nodded. Obviously, he liked having nice things and the power that riches afforded. Morals were for the weak, and he tried to avoid being controlled by them.

Havnier smiled cruelly and said, "I've got limited time, so I'm gonna be blunt, direct, and to the point. Humans need to lose Oakley–I've nothing against the residents... just everything against my fellow gods. Were on our laurels, comfy in our heavens, and we haven't lost a planet in ages. Yours is the perfect scape goat, since it's new and already well behind on the scoreboard." The dwarf leered at him. "You're my perfect tool."

Tucker shrugged, "What's it worth to ya?"

"You don't care about the surface?" Havnier asked and, again, Tucker shrugged. He took another sip of his coffee.

"Good. You're going to get an offer to never come back here from the powers currently controlling the portals on Oakley. I want you to accept their offer and go on back home with your riches. Once back in their good graces, I need you to make them fail–with the power you've gained from here, from me, and from them. They'll be so worried about Mixonia, they won't notice the internal problems you sow."

Tucker frowned at Havnier and thought it over. "Okay, so I go home, get a fancy ship, and then what? Lobby the government to investigate Lexso Corp and shut them down?"

"No need to roll yer eyes at me lad. Yes, something like that. I just need this side to struggle. Struggle, that's it. Make it harder on them, and you've have fulfilled your end of the deal. If the Core wins Oakley, the gods will finally wake up." An impossibly large hand for such a small body tugged at his beard in frustration. "Even Zued has gone back to his retreat," Havnier muttered under his breath.

"And what's in it for me?" Tucker asked.

"Ten free unlocks in Min's vault," Havnier replied. "Yup. You'll go there after this and build yourself a team."

"I didn't sleep through orientation, you know," Tucker smirked. Havnier snorted through his squished short nose. "I know this planet will become a hotbed of disasters. Also, sixteen portals will mean the world will be impossible to contain."

"Lad yer dense, humans ain't wanting other humans knowing there's aliens–not yet. They'd rather say a plague is comin' up from the planet and force an evacuation of the Orbital. Or simply claim the planet is a hotbed of natural disasters–that it will be transformed by irregular unforeseen volcanic activity–which it will, when it loses." The short stout god snorted. "I need ya to agree to the terms and sow discord. If you fail, so be it," Havnier sneered. "You're just a long shot, hedge bet, of sorts. Any last questions?"

Tucker sat forward in his chair and set his coffee cup back on the saucer.

"For two hundred and fifty tokens upfront, I promise to try... keyword being 'try'... to cause problems for Lexso Corp and its friends managing the portals on this planet," Tucker offered.

The dwarf god stared at him with narrowed eyes, "That's a lot for a very vague promise."

"You made the offer, friend," Tucker smirked, "I was just enjoying my coffee."

A locket with *250* engraved on it slid across the table to *clink* against his saucer. "I'd advise you to extort them the best you can. If they see that you have over five hundred tokens left, without knowing you've got hundreds of tokens stashed away in gems, you'll spook em." Again, a cruel smile. "Ya spook em good, then you'll get a sweeter deal. And Tucker, last thing before we go. Don't accept any clauses that include no violence against them. A Min-enforced contract requires two sides for a deal to remain valid." Black eyes sparkled at him. "Remove the other side of the contract..."

"And I can come back here. Okay, I'm in. I get to transition into a filthy rich man with servants and near infinite wealth. All I have to do to hold up my end of the bargain, is to exploit some desperate fools and assist with their eventual demise. When they fall, I'll cycle my own champions in and pull as much cash out of this cow as I can until the planet falls."

Havnier smirked with a finger to the side of his nose and a nod. The Dwarf disappeared and time resumed. His waiter noticed him wiggling the empty coffee mug for a refill.

Tucker grinned and watched the hubbub outside his cafe. He was curious–what would he really want to take home with him? Technically, he could just contract a harem full of some dumb bunnies and use the tokens he'd just received for more wealth.

Vault shopping did sound like fun, though. The man Riva had watching the building would likely pester him, and that was exactly what he needed to set his plan in motion, before finding some muscle and babes worth taking home with him.

Time to have some fun. But first, breakfast.

THIRTY

DEAN

Mixonia

"Ah, I'm so stuffed," Kambry said, popping her belt open to let her bloat out. "Hate this damn thing. Going to need an hour before I can get it back on properly."

Dean chuckled at the sight of her hard abs converted into a round belly; the crazy woman had gone back for thirds.

"What's on your mind, Quincy?" Dean asked his friend. The man had grown despondent during their joyful lunch.

"I think I want to quit," Quincy said, turning to Patti with a meek shrug. "Before you guys scold me, hear me out. I'm a drinker and a partier. I've never been much of anything, really, besides ..." He paused, huffing with uncertainty. "I tried this out and just seem to be holding ya back ..."

"Where would you go?" Dean asked, snacking on a vegetable chip.

"I don't know. Maybe you'd hire me to tend bar at the mansion and I'd still be around for moral support. I don't fit readily into a lineup–I'm a lover, not a fighter," Quincy tried to joke, staring down at his food, ashamed to meet anyone's eyes.

Patti leaned back in her chair and eyed her boyfriend. She was patient and the rest of the table was silent.

"We'll miss you, but I understand," Patti said, and Quincy visibly let out the breath he'd been holding. "Things down here have real consequences. If you can't get your head in the right mindset, by all means, do something else."

"I wanted to hire a hot babe to tend the... ouch," Dean said when Kambry pinched the tender underside of his upper arm. "What?!" Dean scowled. "I guess he's handsome enough for the lady patrons. We're no longer running a military camp at the estate, so probably high time we find some regular staff and develop the place into a real business." He rubbed at his eyes. "Quincy, thank you for coming with us today. I take it you'd like to head on home, before we go any deeper into group PvE or even group PvP?"

"Pretty much, I thought about being a mage. Then I realized, even generated death doesn't sit well with me. I can't follow simple orders, and I almost pissed myself walking over a gorge. So ..." Dean's friend shook his head sadly. "This isn't for me. But, I'm still Team Ola, right?" Quincy asked with a lopsided smile and a cross jab at Dean's shoulder.

Patti snickered while covering her mouth. "And now Quincy's grand scheme becomes clear. Hence all those veiled hints about getting us a bunny maid. Right? Alright, let's head on over to this hiring market. I need to walk off this double mystery meat burger." She patted her tummy and Dean agreed, a walk would be nice.

"I'm heading home, too," Lonny said, pushing back his chair. "Have you got a problem with me building my own team, from here on?"

"No, it's a great idea," Dean admitted. "You need some tokens?"

"Uh... How is that going to work?" Lonny said grabbing onto the arms of his chair as he started to get up but halting himself briefly before sitting back down with a grunt.

Dean shrugged. "We're all contract bound to leave here in six hours, if we're not competing or shopping. I trust you fully, but even you can't build a team out of thin air."

"I was thinking of pulling from Riva's guys to start. Gear is cheap, right?" Lonny asked. Dean opened his mouth and shut it again. "Right, Anoka and Cassandra shopped for you before."

"Sorry, I know we're disorganized," Kambry said sincerely. "A few tokens should be enough to outfit a team with all the basics."

"Can I split this?" Dean asked, willing his necklace with the locket on it. He saw 45 engraved on the locket. He willed five tokens to become their own necklace for a trade. A second necklace spawned around his neck. "I, Dean Forrester, give Lonny–" he began.

"Just hand him the new locket," Kambry interrupted with a chuckle.

Dean lifted the new locket off his neck and handed it over to his friend. "So, we've got a lot of growing and learning to do. This should help. We'll need more tokens, but we'll figure it out soon enough. Obviously, a reserve would be nice to have–to rescue trapped souls from Min's shelves with, as needed. All in due time, though."

"Takes tokens to make tokens," Patti said with a chipper grin. "Dad loves saying that but usually with coins in place of tokens, of course... So, Quincy's quitting and Lonny's going to head up team B," she frowned, "Where does that leave me?"

"We can walk and talk, the manager is friendly but there are others wanting this nice table," Kambry said, tilting her head towards the green lizard-like aliens looking for a table to eat at.

Dean and his friends left the restaurant for the busy street. They parted ways with Lonny; Dean was sad to see him go. When Quincy said goodbye to catch a ride with Lonny, Dean was frustrated, but understood why his friend was leaving. He'd worried he might have to kick Quincy off the team, since things didn't seem to be working out. Quincy volunteering to go saved hurt feelings all around.

"So..." Patti said after a sad pause once Quincy was out of earshot. "I think I'm going to be replaced."

If Dean knew Quincy; she was probably right. The man was not into girlfriends, and unlike how Dean had accepted all these changes to his personal relationship status, it looked like Quincy was wanting to return to his old ways.

"What makes you say that?" Kambry asked.

She shrugged but Dean caught the sad glimmer in her eye and the hopeless tilt to her head, which was a tell that she was sad. "He won't stop talking about your relationship with Dean and goes on and on about bunny girls. It's–"

"Sorry," Kambry whipped her head around to make sure Patti hadn't been overheard, "be careful. They are Bouncries–not bunny anything in public. You'll get into a heated fight with any of them who hear you call them that and then they'll end up getting fined, ejected, or put in a soul pit." Kambry warned her friend with a hand on Patti's shoulder.

"Real quick," Dean asked, feeling bad about further interrupting their discussion, "what laws are there we really should know about that could get us into trouble?"

"Be civil, no violence in Mixonia. Pretty basic–just stay out of trouble. At least you'd think it would be basic," Kambry smirked and poked Dean in the arm. "Don't think I haven't heard from Anoka about you trying to challenge a Minotaur to a duel–in the middle of Min's Vault, no less." She turned back to Patti. "Please continue."

They walked towards the hiring market and Dean tried to keep the ladies at his side, but the street was just too busy. He glanced back to see Kambry's wings were tucked in tight to help her navigate through the congestion.

"Basically," Patti picked back up where she'd left off, "Quincy has stopped talking about me or even us. I'd get it, if we had more than us, like you two do, but we don't. I'm into the two-guy thing more than the two-girl thing, anyway," Patti sighed, "which Quincy is far too vain to ever go for."

"Hey, have you asked him?" Dean said, even though he knew the answer.

"Well no, I... We fought a couple of times during the hunt to find another portal. When you were in caverns, we would bicker and argue. I think part of him leaving the team is to give us space," Patti said.

Dean grimaced. He didn't want to see either of his friends get hurt.

"Some space... that might be what we need." Patti shook her head. "Or it's over and this was his way of saying goodbye, without saying goodbye–the non-goodbye."

"She brings up a good point," Kambry said with a mostly teasing tone. "I wasn't into girls until I met Cassie. What if I wanted to add another guy to our relationship?"

"We just had a baby, and I'm happy right now. I'd like to work on us. I understand men can be ugly or attractive. But ..." He stopped in the middle of the street and kicked at a loose stone. Meeting Kambry's gaze, he said, "it's just not my thing, nor will it ever be my thing. I was perfectly okay accepting you as you were–with just me, or with me and also with other girls," Dean admitted, hoping that was enough for now.

"I tease, Dean. Cassie and I have had this conversation already. We've both played the field. We know how men are. You're exactly what we want and we're both very happy–a family now, even." She reached up to stroke a finger along Dean's cheek. "Please don't interpret my joke as something it was not." She darted in on her toes to kiss Dean's cheek, causing him to blush.

Kambry turned back to their other friend. "Patti, I'm sorry about you and Quincy's rough patch. Do you think you'll want to fight with us, or with Lonny's team?" she asked.

They entered the Garden of the Gods, where there was much less traffic. They were able to walk, shoulder to shoulder, at a nice, easy pace. The sounds and smells of the Garden were soothing and calm. The tune of the music today wasn't bad; Dean found himself enjoying the stroll. Patti picked a pretty flower to pull the petals from as she walked.

"That was cute," she began, "see Dean go all red like that. PDA..."

Kambry frowned.

332

"Public Displays of Affection, PDA, is not his thing." Patti smiled at him, wistfully. "Dean and I tried to be lovers; it just didn't work out. Since then, though, we've been good friends," Patti said tossing the crumpled petals onto the walkway. "I say that because I know Dean, his ins and outs, to some extent. I mesh well with you guys, is what I'm trying to say, I guess." She shrugged. "If you don't mind, I'd like to stay on this team. Let Lonny build his team from the ground up."

"Well, that leaves two slots open if we want to climb, as a team. We can pick up other humans on Oakley, or build from Mixonia," Dean said.

Kambry nudged Dean to step around a bench in the middle of the garden path.

"So," she paused, "I may not count towards Oakley's score. I would have, before, because of our earlier contract, but..."

"We can add on to your new contract, where you state you'll live in Oakley instead of Mixonia right? Wouldn't that cover things?" Patti asked and Kambry fidgeted.

"Yeah, it would." She paused. "I just have to either be in a contract or live on Oakley for ten days in a row," Kambry admitted.

Dean frowned.

"Right now, as a Mixonian citizen, I can return to Mixonia whenever I want and therefore am not counted as an Oakley citizen, even though my stuff is up there. I'm at like ..." she tilted her head, counting days, "what... nine days, technically, so it's no big deal." She frowned at Dean, "Unless you want to contract me again, which I'd really prefer not to, no offense, it's... it's just... demeaning."

"I don't want to contract you again, but I want to free Oakley from further disasters. I feel like there are forces conspiring against us. Sable said the guards were most likely trying to help the Core, and it turned out that they were." He dug in the turf with his toe before looking up and meeting Kambry's gaze. "You can wait another day to do your own team or go solo, Kambry, I made our position clear. You were freed from the long list of requirements your mother said I should use in any contracts with you."

"Now you have our offer, if you wish to change it, you're welcome to, assuming Cassie agrees," Dean stopped, wishing she'd just drop the subject.

"Well, it's not that simple," Kambry grumbled. She gave her braid a hard yank.

"Don't fuck it up now, Kam," he heard her mutter to herself.

"However," she lifted her head and smiled at him, "thank you. We need a healer, both for training and everyone's health at home. We also need two new team members, preferably with contracts changing their residence to Oakley, and we'll need a–"

"Master Mage to train you," Sable said, arriving suddenly next to them to finish Kambry's sentence.

The three of them jumped back, alarmed.

"Don't look so shocked," the angelic snorted, "I keep my word. I'll help you, by helping a friend of mine." She turned to Dean, "I need to warn you, though, she can get... clingy."

"Oh..." Kambry said hesitantly. "Hi, Sable. We should probably clear the air or something."

"Like how you slept with my man when I went back to Purgatory to recover?" Sable said. She diverted the group over to a patch of grass to continue their conversation.

"Umm..." Dean could see Kambry struggling to hold her anger in check.

"Actually, I never slept with Hasper after he ditched me to cling to you. He did sleep around after you left but—and I'd happily enter into a contract to be honest with you—it wasn't with me. I'm sorry he left you like that," she blew out a breath and met Sable's gaze, "and I... I thank you for bringing Dean into my life." She closed her eyes and ground her teeth. "That said, you're also an absolute—"

"Charming woman," Sable said, cutting her off. Dean sighed, wishing she'd chosen to deescalate the situation. "I know. I believe you. I sent a Dragona agent to Hasper months after he left. He was surrounded by a harem, lavish in his spending and ways. He never suspected my agent at all... and for dropping his guard, he paid with his life."

Dean gasped and Patti snickered.

"Damn, if he'd have just stayed here ..." Kambry muttered.

"He'd have had a long life and been safe from my vengeance." Sable snorted. "The idiot didn't even have a healer in his home. Dean called me a friend with a straight face," she gave them a thin-lipped smile, "something I don't hear too often. I want to help. But... Angelina like me are essentially humans with wings."

She rubbed at her temples and flicked her wings out irritably. "Humans have so many... feelings, a lot of which I try to avoid. Dorthy, the friend I'm going to introduce you to, is seeking what Kambry pursued, long before she realized she wanted it. She wants what the majority of Mixonians and all Demis in Purgatory want," Sable said and Kambry nodded, slowly.

"A home? Friends? A boyfriend?" Dean wondered, giving Sable a shrug. "There happen to be a lot of good-looking guys in need of training, too. Not sure if she wants that kind of home, though, but Lexis has taken to Oakley rather well."

"So we hear," Sable snorted. "Lexis has been the talk of Purgatory ... So has your visit and the fact than only I can, somehow, directly come to your side anymore.

Father vanished after we made our deal, which is making me start to think someone is either putting some pressure on him to get me to help you, or for him to stop helping you. Gods, right? Fickle flighty things, they are."

Dean grimaced. Too damn true, that.

"Anyway, my friend Dorthy is over this way," Sable grinned, leading them over to the hiring market.

"Thanks, Sable," Patti said, stepping up to walk beside the Angelina. "Guy problems, right? Tell me all about your assassin friend."

Sable glance down at Patti with a glint in her eye and a smile tugging at the corner of her mouth. "I sent a younger Dragona, one with a tiny waist, but extra big butt. Small boobs, though–he was never into boobs. That back door, though, Hasper loved it. She slit his throat during a post-coital snooze. That was what she reported to me under an honesty contract and it was confirmed. His tokens–the ones he'd fled with–all went back to Min, and I sleep a lot easier since then."

"Wow, remind me not to get on your bad side," Patti muttered, jaw hanging agape.

"Darling, I'm the daughter of a god. I deserve respect, not to be abandoned for some squeaking titty of a quick lay. Hence why I'm here, now." She nodded at Dean. "It's this fisherman's soft heart and alluring smile–Makes a woman go weak in the knees," Sable rolled her eyes, "even if she doesn't want to be. He did right by Kambry and Lexis. Both are the happiest they've ever been. I doubt that will change–without someone else being the reason, so I'll introduce you to Dorthy." Sable gave a nonchalant shrug, though the quick tug on her blonde braid said it wasn't that simple.

"We've also got two slots left on our team," Dean noted, "any recommendations?"

"A set of Oruk twins, maybe? They messed up... I'll let Bamba tell their story. Good soldiers, though, well versed in the ways of war. Bamba is without a home, at the moment, and in a bind. Pamrii is in the vault. They'd be a huge boon to your team and your estate. Not as easy on the eyes as Dorthy, though–not like you should care," Sable smirked, pointing at the very sexy Kambry. "This one's a ten and probably is more than you can handle, already."

"Yeah, her human form is fun to play around with, I'd probably be in over my head with her Dragona form," Dean admitted, getting a swat on his arm from Kambry.

"I'd go easy on you," Kambry said with a wink, "and Sable... I do believe that was a compliment. Thank you."

"Dorthy can use an arcane spell on Oakley. Let her... be her," Sable said, leading them out the back of the Garden of the Gods and to the field next to the towering hiring market.

"Hold up," Dean said, shifting them over to an empty bench. "Before I get put on the spot and things get awkward... explain, please."

"There are technically eight types of magic. Really seven and only six per side allowed in the–" Sable rolled her eyes and started to lecture them.

"Not that. Dorthy can teach us magic," Dean growled. "The part about Kambry not being human on Oakley. I thought that was a Min mandated rule."

"Oh, yeah, it is. Cast a spell, though, and you can go back to what you were, for a while at least. How long depends on mana consumed by the affected person, the strength of spell, and the difficulty in conversion."

Dean gave her a blank stare.

"So, have you not noticed how all the fish type Suca in Mixonia have legs?"

Dean and Patti nodded. Kambry snickered.

"I assure you that they do not. They are given the ability to move on land in Mixonia so that they can compete." Sable shook her head. "I'm getting off topic. Just know that there are more than just hard-coded rules for every generic species on a planet. Kambry can be a Dragona on Oakley–it just takes a bit of effort and some magic," Sable finished with a huff, extending a hand to Dean to pull him up.

"Thank you. I appreciate the honesty," Dean said laying his hand in hers and letting her pull him up. *Those pink eyes are surprised. I bet she doesn't touch others much.*

Sable looked slightly flustered before releasing his hand. "So," he cleared his throat, "it will cost us twenty-five talents for the Oruk twins? Not a bad deal, really, for a duet."

"No, it's stupid good. Just be happy the guilds blacklisted them. Sure, Pamrii made a mistake and Bamba can be really stubborn. They'd be forgiven, though, over time, and snatched up in a heartbeat. Literally, they've spent fortunes buying legendary weapons... and now... this," Sable gestured to their relatively inexperienced team.

"Huh, guess I really need to go talk to Bamba, now," Dean said.

Patti snickered, "I fooking love that name. Perfect for a fierce warrior."

They entered the market and Sable cheated again when, with a flick of her wings, she flew up to the third floor. Dean bounded up the stairs with Kambry only cheating a little to keep up with him. Patti kept up no problem, surprisingly, and when they arrived on the third floor, Dean saw a sign.

Specialist hiring– You must qualify as a highly trained or skilled individual to offer yourself for hire here. If you are hiring, know that there are no cons on this floor. These experts are verified.

"Bonus," Dean mumbled under his breath. Sable raced forward, of course, not letting any of them take in their environment.

He decided she'd wait for them, since introducing him to Bamba was why they were here, and walked after her, instead of hustling through the crowd. He looked around. He saw small booths only shoulder-width apart, to allow for the maximum number of professionals in a small space. Unlike above this floor, where the market was a mix of chaos and haphazard organization, everything here was neat and tidy—almost rigid in its pragmatic functionality.

There were trainers, mages, healers, bartenders, pet tamers, pet trainers, warriors, and more. Dean frowned trying to see what quantified one to be considered a highly trained or skilled individual. There did not seem to be a set pattern he could find; their qualifications were all over the place.

A finger snapped next to his ear and he glanced up to see a frowning angelic face glaring at him.

"You okay?" Sable asked sharply.

And there goes the softer side. Gone in a flash. She is so pretty but filled with such inner turmoil.

Dean nodded and followed her through the loud space. "Why is it so crowded?" He had to raise his voice to be heard, "And what makes you eligible to get a booth here?"

"Well, they're free to use and highly desired. You see that line out there in the gardens?" Sable said, pointing to a short line out in the field. "You have to get in that line by proving to a guard you have a sought-after skill. Floors one and two are for generic hires, but it's a flip of the coin as to what you will find. The businesses who are looking for workers have booths set up down there to recruit from. This floor and the one above it are reserved for professionals. The fourth floor is relatively regulated," she nodded back to the line out in the field. "The fifth floor is a free for all, and floor six is for those trying to get help, freeing trapped loved ones."

"So, folks have to stay here the whole time to keep their booth?" he asked.

"When you leave a booth on this floor, for say... lunch, you have to get back in line and hope a spot opens up quickly." She stopped and looked around. "Dorthy is right over... here."

Dean looked in the direction Sable pointed and saw an angelic woman like Sable, who was almost a foot shorter than him. Dorthy was curvier than Sable, with a plumpness about her that screamed academic. Her puffy cheeks and rounded hips let him know she was not a warrior. Seeing her, with her wings wrapped around her tummy, was an odd look for an Angelina. Dorthy was busy studying a book and didn't notice them at first, allowing Dean to study her advertisement for a moment.

Dorthy Lorieli– Expert Mage, with all seven schools unlocked. Proficient even in arcane and healing magics. I will teach or instruct, ages ten and up, with conditions. If you're looking for mage training, no one is better. No scrolls provided. Bookings available for up to a year at a time. Wages must be paid in advance.

"Dorthy!" Sable shouted and the mousy looking Angelina jumped. "Always so skittish," Sable chuckled. "This is Dean and he needs your help."

"It's why I don't compete," Dorthy chided the statuesque blonde in a stern tone. "Been on a shelf before, never again. No thank you." She cocked her head to the side, studying them. "Hmm... Two humans and a Dragona with Sable." She wrinkled her nose at the blonde, "I thought you said you wanted to eradicate their species?" Dorthy pointed at Kambry.

Sable rolled her eyes. "You owe me, Dorthy."

"I do? Since when?" Dorthy responded in a snooty tone.

"Don't play games," Sable said and leveled a finger at the mage trainer. "I have friends who need help in all things magic. They've been honest and straightforward with me, so I'm cashing in a favor, in case I have to go."

"Go, as in going to be a Demi champion? Good for you. While I owe you for helping me get off the shelf, I can't quantify that Sable, and if you haven't noticed; a classroom mage is not exactly hard to find. Work has been spotty, lately," Dorthy said pointing around them at the half dozen mages in booths near hers, all seeking work.

"What's your rate for a year?" Dean asked.

"Does it include foot rubs from a hunky man like you?" Dorthy asked, teasingly biting her lower lip.

At the edge of each booth was a chalkboard for contracts. Dean could play that game, too. He jested, writing up a contract for a year of mage training, with 'foot rubs once a week by a hunky, muscled man'. Before looking up with a smile. "Start filling in the blanks, I've got two Oruk to hire, as well. Well," he frowned, "hire one and free the other one."

"Dean, was it?" Dorthy asked and he gave a terse bob of his head. "Please tell me about your situation."

"Uh... Okay," he began, "I have lightning magic, but that is it. No one else has–"

"Why didn't you–"

"Not here," Sable said a decisive chop with her hand between Dorthy and Dean, giving each of them a glare. "Discuss your unique magic elsewhere."

338

"Okay... so you have no magic and need to know everything. That means a library's worth of materials. I'd need to start a schoolroom and that means more supplies. Which would mean months, if not years of training, right?"

Kambry nodded.

"I'd need my own residence, guaranteed meals, and..." Dorthy paused because Dean was chuckling.

"What?" she grimaced.

Dean smirked and simply said, "Yes."

"I'm confused," Dorthy stammered, "Yes to which part?" Her eyes widened, "or... yes to all?"

"All," Kambry quipped.

"Surely you jest! Planets don't start magic schools, unless they're brand new, and there hasn't been a ..." She paused. "What kind of accommodations did you say they were, again?"

"I've got an open suite on the floor below ours, or a spare bedroom in my suite. Not sure exactly what you're looking for," Dean said pumping his eyebrows with an impish grin.

Kambry rolled her eyes.

Sable snorted to disguise a barely held in laugh. "It's super nice," she said, "and better than here. Movie nights involve books acted out on a screen, with good food and company. You'll probably adore it," Sable admitted, causing Dean to give her a questioning glance.

"What?" the blonde Angelina blushed. "I peek in on you guys... sometimes."

She then startled Dorthy by putting her hands on the shorter Angelina's shoulders. "Draft a contract, Dorthy. Make it a dream contract." She grinned. "One you could imagine yourself calling a forever home."

Dorthy gulped before sitting down, hard. She reached for her contract tablet and in less than a minute said, "Done."

"Already?" Dean asked looking over the contract. "Five tokens a month? That sounds pretty steep." He frowned. "A thirty-token budget? Living space for three, three meals a day, and an official title. You retain the right to cancel, with all recovered materials' value returning to us if you leave before the end of the contract. Contract to last for five years, exclusively to teach magic to Dean and those he finds worthy of learning magic."

Kambry pulled him aside while Sable interceded with Dorthy. "Three is fair, four is great, but five is extortion," she shook her head. "The rest is fine–though a bit sneaky on the room size–but it won't be a problem at the Forrester-Lexso estate. And Dean, I don't need to have Cassie here for you to know it's a good deal."

"Cassie is it, now?" Dean smirked and Kambry shrugged, not willing to say more about it.

Dean turned back to the mage. "I don't have thirty tokens to spare for scrolls, let alone instruction materials," Dean grumbled.

"Which is why there is no date set on when the budget is required. I'd be happy to accrue easy tokens and sit on my hands," Dorthy smiled.

"You have enough to teach the basics, though, for now?" Patti asked from the side.

"I do," Dorthy said and hurriedly added. "I forgot to mention," she added a few notes to the tablet, "no competitions, and while I do training, I don't battle instruct, other than from the sideline."

"If there is no rush on the extra stuff for training, I'll accept this. Heaven knows I can go do some PvE solo or events, and eventually PvP, to pay for this," Dean acknowledged and accepted her contract at a salary of three tokens a month. Assuming he kept the right to change gems for tokens going forward, otherwise he'd just eaten up ten percent of his total tokens. "Welcome to Team Ola, Dorthy."

"Thank you, Sable. Thank you, Dean," Dorthy beamed, hugging Dean. She shifted to Kambry "And you are?"

"Kambry."

The next hug went to Patti. Who introduced herself without being prompted?

"Mr. Dean. I'm going home to cancel my lease and pack my things. The portal will take me to your cavern. At that point, I could use some help."

"We'll go with you," Patti and Kambry both said.

"Meet you back at the cavern. This shouldn't take long," Dean said, hoping for the best. They parted ways to carry on with the mission. The vendor booth before them reset the moment Kambry picked up Dorthy's books for her.

A one eyed, one boobed cyclops appeared in the booth. He knew what would make a wonderful pillow, if he ever saw one.

THIRTY-ONE

DEAN

Mixonia

S able dragged Dean forward happily. The normally stern-faced Demi caused him to roll his eyes.

"I just realized something," Sable said, passing numerous booths with professionals.

"What's that?" Dean asked, smirking. Her smile was contagious.

"You're getting an all-female team. Not that the Oruk are all that feminine, really."

Dean shrugged following her to a booth further down the line. "Never been a sexist, it's more about skill and job capability. Gender be damned. There are some women who can out fish me, though it is rare, since most lack the requisite upper body strength, but it does happen," Dean admitted sincerely.

Sable paused and hesitantly asked, "Would you... would you be willing to take me fishing?"

"Uh... sure." He frowned, "I'd have to rent a boat and it'd have to be a private trip, which means we can't sell what we catch. Else I'd be due a physical, which really won't go over well." He shrugged. "We have a restaurant on the estate, so it's allowed. Wouldn't that drain ya though?" Dean wondered. He did miss fishing.

"Sure, I'd just have to save up enough energy and stop bugging you... Say in a week or so?"

Dean nodded, confusion washing over him, before he decided to go with it. "Sure, I'd love to."

"Thanks. Okay, I'm heading home. If this doesn't work out, there are other options. I'd advise this one, though, as the best deal you can get," Sable said with a friendly finger rolling wave goodbye.

She seemed like she was in a really good mood. Maybe she'd turned a positive corner in her life. Or maybe Sable really wanted to go fishing. Leave it to a woman to tell you to bugger off, not interested, and then be super nice afterwards.

Dean went up to an Oruk standing behind the counter that Sable had left him in front of.

She had very light green skin, a height Dean had to peer up at, and a jagged scar down her cheek. Her lithe, narrow frame had very little curve to it. She wore a leather shirt that left her chiseled midriff bare. A massive single headed axe sat in a sheath over her back and she exuded confidence. There was no doubt about it, this woman was a warrior.

I know she is an Oruk, but her eyes tell me she is indeed a woman. I wonder why all these species are so... human. I can't believe I forgot to ask Min about it when I had the chance.

A tap on the counter from one long, sharp looking nail pulled him out of his internal 'was this a woman or a monster girl' debate.

Wouldn't that just be a ripe prank if Sable had set him up with some random Oruk? "Bamba?" Dean asked hesitantly.

Bamba nodded.

"I need team members and warriors willing to help train a new planet."

"You losing to the Core?" Bamba asked in a gruff voice.

He nodded.

"Free my sister?"

"If I did, what would you offer?" Dean asked.

"The Demi sent you?"

Dean nodded, assuming she was referring to Sable, who had vanished moments ago.

Bamba grimaced and tapped her lip. "Important fight then, we do a year of fighting and training. You free us if we go into figurine, you house us, and feed us. The deal between you and Pamrii will have this as a minimum.

342

"Since I didn't make the mistake, you can make her contract include more. That is the best you'll do with me, though. And there is a caveat–for me at least–I'm booked for the next month. Pamrii is, obviously, free."

Dean saw the contract and grew confused, "What about your pay?"

"Huh?"

"How much do you wish to be paid?"

"Free my sister," the tall Oruk shrugged.

"And the pay?"

"You dense or just ignoring the subtle hints. Or are you soft? The Demi tells me you're connected, and this is for the cause. Believe it or not, some of us fight out of our hate for the Core. But I'll take one token a month... on one condition, I can keep any earnings from events."

"As long as you don't lock the portal then–"

"We were born here," Bamba said and Dean frowned. "Is that a problem?"

"I just had a baby, maybe should have rushed her to be born in here," Dean said in hindsight.

"Obviously. Accept my contract," Bamba said in a pleasant tone. Dean accepted her terms. "Oh, the guild is going to be so royally pissed we got a contract. Come, let's get Pamrii."

"What level are you?" Dean asked.

"Solo ninety-three, team seventy-four," she said in a gruff voice. "I look forward to working with you in a month." She looked him up and down. "Pamrii will eat you up," she chuckled.

"What's that supposed to mean?" Dean asked hesitantly.

Bamba removed herself from behind the vendor booth and it reset automatically. Dean followed in the wake of her fast pace for the exit.

"Oruk, like many other aliens, have needs... we lust. You're a big human. Biggest I've seen in a while. Since the guild put us into a timeout, our Oruk mates will have moved on. We're not exactly warming their beds on the missions," Bamba admitted.

"Ah, so what happened?" Dean asked, curiosity getting the better of him.

"Well, Pamrii will be mad that I told you, but it's best you know, going in. Last event was a team champion ordeal, ten-large team. Pamrii is an off tank. She pulled an entire side room, retreating from a leprechaun," Bamba said and Dean paused her, before navigating through a team of leopard humans.

Dean's shins got swatted by a flinging tail. A male catguy winked at him. *Umm, what?* They exited the hiring market and were soon on the main strip headed for the vault.

"Do I give off a gay vibe?" Dean grumbled. "And Leprechaun? As in short, little green dude?"

"Short yes. Green no. And you're a handsome human. Humans have substantial appeal, due to their adaptive battle behavior," Bamba said slamming a hand into his back with a stiff thump that knocked him forward a step or two. "Some are reckless, but most win enough to stop at the challenge. If you latch onto a human male, you might end up with a very rich mate, at the very least, you're in for a fun ride." She laughed. "I'm surprised you're alone."

"My wife... well, soon to be wife, just had a child. We're in this throuple thing with a wonderful Dragona." He smirked. "Honestly, I was pretty much a 'have sex and run' kind of guy for the longest time. Funny how life can change in a moment," Dean admitted, picking up the pace. "Speaking of which, I need to get home to see my little girl. So, let's speed things up. Tell me the rest of the story."

Dean weaved and dodged through the crowd and Bamba was all for speed walking and nudging folks out of her way.

"She pretty much got herself killed. She knew it, too. Pamrii had... failed and it was right there in her contract," Bamba said with a huff, slowing down briefly. "You can't reset in the middle of events. It's the one place where getting killed stupidly costs the entire team. We were only on the fifteenth floor, but it wasn't worth risking nine more deaths, so..."

"You left," Dean grunted, "ouch. She cost you more than fifteen tokens. Hundreds if you could have kept on going," Dean said.

Bamba nodded. "That's the rub. She is liable for a hundred tokens to the guild, as that's about how high we expected to go in the event. Pay that off, or we're out of our guild. Technically, I'm not, but I gave them my thirty-day notice. This will be a good change of pace for us. We love saving planets," Bamba said with a grin. "It's a noble cause."

"What?" Dean was startled.

"You'll see," Bamba grinned as they arrived at Min's Vault. "Alright, human, are you rich or poor?"

Dean showed her his necklace.

"Bearclays, nice place, and that's more than enough. So... don't let her take advantage of you. If we semi-retire, she'll want babies. We birth twins at a minimum of every six months, and she will want to birth them inside Mixonia--so at least you can say you were warned!" Bamba laughed.

"In a month, when I exit the city, I'll be on your planet, by your Minotaur guard. While I'm safe there, I really don't like hassles–and Dean..."

He looked up to meet her gaze.

"Waiting is a hassle."

Dean was about to give assurances that they'd be there to pick her up, when he spied someone lazily walking his way. Someone he shouldn't be seeing and someone who had caused him a great deal of grief. Dean saw Tucker strutting over to Min's Vault like he owned Mixonia.

"I'll see you in a month," Dean said, diverting for his confrontation to handle the situation alone, except Bamba followed him.

When he stood in Tucker's way the slightly shorter man smiled at him. "Do I know you?"

"I'm Dean, we haven't met. You kept me from my girlfriend when you locked the gate behind you when we needed it the most," Dean snarled. Tucker went to walk past him, but Dean sidestepped to stay in his way. Tucker obviously didn't care for him or the fact that Dean was in his face. "I can't force you out. But I can say you killed hundreds on board the Orbital."

"Bullshit," Tucker scoffed.

"I'm not lying."

"All the disasters are on the planet, we were told." He shrugged. "I get it. Dean, right? Look man, I got a little drunk, and had some fun. Hard not to do here. You can have your damn portal back, as soon as I make a deal with Riva. The guys all said you were the best one to work for–with that hot Lexis chick and that Kammy girl."

"Close enough, but yeah, Tucker. I'm being serious. If ya got family on the station, you might want to see if they're okay," Dean grumbled, his eyes finally softening.

"Okay, let's say I do believe you," Tucker said, folding his arms, "explain."

"Plague happened originally in Belmont, planet-side. Sole infected went up to the Orbital to visit a consent he got by swiping right on a girl from that app. The delivery that was supposed to be for the capital, we surmise, turned up instead on Oakley Orbital." Dean paused and saw Tucker grimace.

"And, the woman who defended Oakley was stuck in here for days because of you," Dean growled, and clenched his fist. "I've dreamed of kicking your ass for a week. Now... Now that I've met you in person... I see a bit of me in your eyes. Hell, I'm man enough to admit that a few years ago if I'd come into a sudden burst of wealth, I'd have partied, too."

"Dean," Tucker sneered, "this is all Riva's fault. He wasn't paying us the way you were paying your guys. But you're right, if I get the chance, I'll fix this. I appreciate the support," Tucker slapped Dean's arm in comradery, causing Dean to flinch.

"Tucker, just do the right thing. Compete, and then leave. As you've seen, not only the planet, but the orbital, too, can suffer," Dean called out to the man's back, who gave him a friendly wave.

Bamba had listened, nosily, without saying a word until she grimaced, "That was odd. I normally read reactions quite well. He grew even more resolved, not upset, over your peoples' deaths."

"We could have prevented the disaster if we were more aggressive. With three portals open we will be. The score is getting better and my teams will be doing solo competitions after we learn magic," Dean said.

"A cherry, what level?" Bamba asked.

"Four, just hit it today."

"Huh?" Bamba asked, confused. "How'd you get so many tokens?"

Dean pointed to the water portal. *Shit, I should go ahead and do the first six PvP events.*

"After he blocked our only way—"

"But there are four portals," Bamba mused and Dean plastered a fake smile on.

"We know this, now, but there was a mix up. Anyway, we're working to fix the situation. But Tucker could likely have prevented the event from happening. I heard he got fifty tokens for his tenth PvP run. You ever get that far in PvP?" Dean asked.

Bamba crossed her arms under her small chest. "Not quite how it works. And sure, when I was wealthy, I did PvP competitions. Level seven is the furthest I got, though. I died to an ogre, who chomped my head off. I was on the shelf for only a few hours, but I hated losing. It wasn't worth the risk, though, and facing those risks another eight times to get another payout was tough. You turn into a different being." The tall, lithe Oruk shook her head. "Group PvP Level twenty-six, though, made a fortune doing that. Ah..." She sighed longingly. "That was a few hundred years ago."

A few hundred years?!

"Alright, Dean," Bamba grinned at him. "Good talking with you. Go get my sister, please. See you in a month and we'll soon climb to fifty, under you and the others."

Bamba turned on her heel and left before he could say goodbye.

Dean gave a longing stare at the swirling blue portal as the flow of traffic passed him by. There was going to be a time for solo PvP, but now was not it.

He approached the line to get into the vault. Tucker was just entering, the quick glance the man shot his way was filled with squinted eyes, and a jaw held tight in determination. Dean sighed and waved. He didn't need to ruin their chances of him leaving voluntarily. Not that he thought the man would stay just to spite them.

Dean had properly set the hook. Tucker had said he would come out, if he told Riva to make it a new offer conditional on his exit. The line moved quickly, and Dean realized with a start that he had some tokens to spend. When he entered Min's Vaults of Treasures, before going to the shelves of statuettes along the back, he did some window shopping for weapons first. With a frustrated sigh, he gave up trying to understand their value vs market value. Another thing to add to the list of stuff he needed to learn or to do. A break just wasn't in the cards—not at the moment.

A roaming guard and a few patrons shopped around him. There was no sign of Tucker, though, not that Dean had an interest in further aggravating the situation. He went to the scrolls of magic, and found out that, sure enough, they were three tokens per. He decided he'd better let Dorthy deal with purchasing the scrolls. Maybe there was an aptitude test or something he should know about before spending their hard-earned tokens.

He left the scrolls behind and moved on to the gems. A Demi suddenly appeared before him; it was the male Bouncries-Minotaur hybrid. Min's son.

"Hello," Dean said.

"Why am I out of my studies?" the Demi said to the air around him.

"What do you study?" Dean asked. He was ignored. "Excuse me, I'd like to see that diamond please."

"Huh?" Min's son spun around and glared at him. "Be grateful I don't kill you for your insolence you pathetic—"

He vanished.

Poof, there was a new arrival. A yellow skinned, male alien, wearing a toga, scanned his surroundings. Dean saw a jade pair of eyes that peered around curiously. The alien's hand had only two fingers and an extra wide thumb.

"Been ages since I was sent to do vault transactions. Oh wow! They've changed the layout," the Demi muttered to himself.

"Hello, I'm Dean. I was interested in those small diamonds and the earring set. And then those rings, oh, not the pink ones... the green diamonds, please," Dean said pointing to the jewels to the left of the alien's shifting hands.

"Jaxon," the Demi said, "and it's a pleasure, Dean. You don't happen to be the same human named Dean whose visit is currently circulating in the rumor mill in Purgatory, are you?"

"Probably," Dean admitted, while Jaxon pulled out the jewelry.

"Ah, interesting. This will make me a gossip king for at least a day or two. Always nice. You don't happen to need an arcane mage, do you?" Jaxon asked in a pleasant tone.

Dean couldn't fault the guy for asking. "How good is your knowledge? And correct me if I'm wrong, but wouldn't the guild be snatching up you smart Demis and putting you on training planets?"

"Been studying arcane magic for eons. And they don't offer because I'd refuse and the cost is prohibitive, given that I'd die of old age in about forty or fifty years. So... Maybe thirty years of good training is all they could expect to get out of me. You can hire a well-rounded mage for a bit more and keep them in Mixonia, where training is easier," Jaxon sighed. "Assuming you have the space, which all the good guilds do."

"You ready to make a leap that big?" Dean stopped his inspection of the green diamonds to study the man.

"Technology would probably extend that life span; I don't know. You have to understand something, Dean. We philosophers rarely get to leave our prison. Especially if our parents forget about us. I do not..." He paused and looked around furtively. "I'll say this slowly. I'm here, in front of you, for a reason."

Dean tapped his chin in thought.

"That reason is probably something I shouldn't avoid. How about this? I'll have a talk with my current mage and see if she'd take a pay cut to help you get to Oakley. Well her, and the other portal team leaders. Right now, though, we're tight on tokens. While I do that, you have a good think about becoming mortal. How does that sound?"

"Like I should give it great consideration. Could I ask a favor?" Jaxon asked.

"Worst I can do is say no," Dean admitted with a shrug.

"Summon me to your home, that will... help. Yes. I've about a month of energy saved up, so at the very least, I can help–free of charge–for a bit, and we can see how well we mesh."

His eyes were very conflicted. Dean's eyes shifted his focus to the jewelry, and he decided he loved the rings. The earrings too. Dean saw the prices were mere fractions of a token. Combined, they amounted to less than half a token.

"Cheap due to the size, at the fact that the stones are very common–you're really just paying for the gold crafting process. These were custom crafted by the great Min–" He paused turning to face an invisible speaker. Dean knew this because he was bobbing his head. "These aren't for your nanny, are they?"

"No, my Nanny is, and always will be, my friend. A gift of jewelry would give her the wrong idea. This is for my Cassie and Kambry," Dean said, controlling his eye roll.

"Perfect answer. Simply hand me your Bearclays medallion," Jaxon said.

Dean did as he was asked.

39.53 showed on the locket as Dean returned it to its home under his shirt. Jaxon closed the boxes and handed them over. With the transactions complete, Jaxon stood there silently.

"I'll summon you when I'm back home. Dorthy will be the one to show you around, most likely. Thank you for this," Dean smiled, lifting the boxes.

"Min helps me get out on occasion; the least I can do is help them. Take care Dean. Even if we never see each other again, it was nice to meet you," Jaxon grinned and then vanished.

Dean fidgeted around, searching for a pocket. When you were in Roman armor there really was nowhere to stick three small boxes. He ended up stuffing them under his breastplate, where they rested uncomfortably.

When he left the jewelry section, he walked to the figurine vault. His pacing was regular up until the moment he crossed the line dividing the vault from the rest of the store. He felt the slight hiccup, as if time had shifted. Behind him he'd had all sorts of people, inside the statuette room, it was empty. Probably a simple way to deal with people crying or getting angry over a refused contract, or something.

He walked down the alphabetical rows of shelves, heading for the O section. He paused at the Elves. The shelf was empty, except for three figurines. Two males and a female. Dean frowned at the image. He concluded they must be here for a reason; his curiosity was certainly piqued. Yet, he didn't really want to contract anyone ...

Unable to resist, he lifted the statuette of the lithe elf, in her barely-there armor and triggered her indent. Twenty-five tokens automatically went into reserve and he was pulled into a waiting room, where he was kept waiting for much longer than he expected. Finally, a forest generated around him of immense whitewoods filled with hopping bunnies, the small animal kind.

"It has been a long time since I have answered a summons," the Elven maiden said, approaching Dean.

She wore a see-through gown that flowed about her as she walked towards him. The lingerie she wore underneath it enticed him with its seductive nature. Her large breasts transitioned to a smooth belly, and supple hips. He yanked his gaze up to meet her emerald eyes. Shoulder length brown hair was put into twin ponytails that she wore tucked behind her elongated ears.

In a polite, soothing tone she asked, "Why was I brought out of my sleep?"

Hmm... I expected her to be hostile or an elitist. She's testing me. Probably. Definitely.

"Curiosity. From my limited understanding, the elves won their contests, your race is gone from Mixonia, leaving behind only legends of prowess. I was figuring you'd have an interesting reason for being in here," Dean admitted with a shrug of indifference.

"I rest here until this prison is re-balanced. That was the quest I gave my father, I am Orabel. My mandate is non-negotiable," Orabel said in a boorish tone.

"Ah, got it, and the two men with you on the shelves?" Dean asked.

"My sworn guards," she replied.

Dean shrugged. He'd heard enough.

When he turned, about to leave, she stopped him. "Wait. Why are you here?"

"Save the world, protect my family. I sure hope my daughter has more common sense than you. I know what happened in the past. From the source. This prison, as you call it, is the most just thing in the universe. I may be an ant compared to a god, but I like it when the gods aren't allowed to arbitrarily blow up my anthill," Dean smirked, and she laughed.

"Fair assessment. Not incorrect. You exude something different. I'm drawn to you. Why?"

Dean snorted and said, "Probably because I must look pretty good if I'm the only man you've laid eyes on in eons."

She placed a hand on her belly, smirked, and then burst into a peal of laughter. Her emerald eyes teared up from laughing so hard and she calmed down only after several fits of giggling.

"No, not to discredit your self-worth, that would be beneath me. I... You're... Different. Something..."

Dean felt magic engulfing his body, her eyes flared open. "Oh, by the creator. You're blessed and don't even know it."

"This?" Dean questioned, showing his seam. "And yes, I know I am."

"Yes, fire it at that tree please," Orabel said and Dean shook his head no. "Please, I've waited so long. Shoot that tree."

He lined up his hand to the tree and the tree burst apart under a powerful torrent.

The princess giggled endlessly. Her delight was something that startled Dean. It was just a tree.

"Can you free me?" Orabel asked with wide eyes, batting her long lashes at him.

"Uh... no offense I came in here to satisfy my curiosity. I also have my hands quite full already, with a Dragona. And ..." Dean rubbed at the back of his neck, "I already promised to free an Oruk, named Pamrii." Dean frowned and gave the beautiful elf a 'forgive me' shrug. "And then there is the... yellow skinned, big thumb, and two fingers Demi."

"Ah, that species is called a Parnu, they're bad at the games and retreat into space to live on orbitals. Great students. So, it begins. The blessed champion will herald the eighth age and his wrath shall be unbridled. You'll need to build your team," Orabel said, tapping her fingers together eagerly. Her tucked eyebrow, wicked grin, and bubbly laugh were disconcerting.

"For Oakley?" Dean asked and she nodded.

"That and more, there is much I could tell you, but our time is up, at least for now. Just know that if you free me, I can guide you on your path," Orabel said and the image of the forest and her faded. "Come back for me..."

Dean returned to Min's vault.

In his hand, Orabel looked distraught. Dean frowned and tried to activate her statuette again. A timer appeared, telling him he'd have to wait until tomorrow. He grumbled a few choice swears and set her statuette down. He roiled with indecision. No. He knew what he had to do.

Stifling the rage that threatened to build within him, he found the O section.

Shit, what does she look like?

Then Dean remembered her name would be appear on her baseplate. He found the Ps and realized why Bamba had warned him about her sister. This Oruk was into slutty armor and had plenty of curves to show off. She wore the kind of armor that only provided protection because of its magic enhancements. No wonder she had died. He stepped back to look at the statuettes of other female Oruk. Yeah, she was certainly the only one he'd pick, if he was wanting an Oruk lover.

His hand went to pick up the figurine, only to have it vanish right before his hand got there. *Huh?* He waited for a moment, because the slot she had been in remained vacant. Bored, he went to look one shelf over. The figurines were Osamar, a unicorn species of humanoids. The ladies had a large curved horn jutting out of their foreheads, the males had a pointy one. They sure were built to be easy on the eyes.

He sighed in frustration, heading back to Pamrii's row, only to find her spot had closed. The figurines had reorganized themselves and her clay statuette was simply gone. He grunted.

So much for the Oruk twins, I guess.

A finger tapped him on his lower back, causing him to spin around in alarm. A little Dryad man in armor, barely half his size, waved up at him.

"Hello," Dean said.

"I'm a Demi, Torg. I have a contract offer for you. Twenty-five tokens to take over Bamba's contract. I am allowed to inform you that the offer is because Pamrii would like to be with her sister," Torg said and Dean gave a fist pump at his luck.

"How does it work?" Dean asked excitedly.

Torg offered him a chalkboard and Dean read the contract over. It was fairly cut and dry. Transfer his contract with Bamba over for twenty-five tokens.

"Can I make it thirty?" Dean asked.

"Yup, but careful. I'm not a bartering station. If you wish thirty, make it so, but you're not going to get a second chance," Torg cautioned.

"Thirty-five, and it's a deal." Dean said, thumbing the contract.

"They accepted. Congratulations Dean, it's rare to see something like this happen. Until next time," Torg said and vanished.

Dean felt on top of the world. Sure, he still needed to fill two slots on his team, but he'd just scored thirty-five tokens for nothing. As much as he wanted to mope and groan about losing a skilled warrior or two, there were plenty of them here in Mixonia.

For now, though, he was ready to go home, spend some time with family, and train to be the best Champion he could be. The coming days would be rough, with the trials and tribulations being fierce, and yet he knew the adventures would be grand.

Dean had no doubts that he would struggle to keep Oakley free from disasters and pulling down the Core's lead in the point count. He was worried, and yet excited about what the future held.

If only that damn Orabel wasn't stuck in his mind.

MINOTAUR'S MAZE OF MONSTER GIRLS 2

MAIDENS OF MIXONIA BOOK 2

CHAPTER
ONE
DEAN

Forrester-Lexso Estate

Dean woke to the sounds of a squalling baby. It was his turn and he'd only half slept, waiting for this very moment. He hurriedly exited the bed, retrieved a bottle from the fridge, set it in the bottle warmer, and went to get his sassy little Leena.

After leaving Mixonia last night, he had spent an hour on the phone, updating Riva on the Tucker situation. The man was already in negotiations to exit the portal, so that was good. When he'd come home to a droopy-eyed Cassandra, she'd had Dean simply hold her for at least ten minutes.

Leena Forrester, that was the name Cassandra had picked for their daughter. He had to approve, though, to make it official. He approved because he felt it fit the tiny darling. They signed some digital documents and the rest, as they say, was history.

Kambry and Cassandra went right to snuggling, happy to be reunited. They watched a movie while Dean had helped settle Dorthy in. Before he retired for the night, he remembered to invite the Demi he'd met at Min's, Jaxon, for a tour and let him roam the estate. He was exhausted from fighting and still recovering from his cave diving, so he let him do his own exploring. Needless to say, despite his groggy state and exhaustion, he was still put on father duty.

In what should have been the middle of his sleep cycle, he gently plucked his little girl out of her bassinet. He popped the warmed bottle of breast milk in her mouth while zombie walking for a rocker. The duo grew comfortable in the rhythmic, measured sway of the rocker. Both father and daughter had passed out before the bottle was emptied.

A soft nudge stirred him awake. Lexis held a freshly swaddled Leena and pointed him towards the bed. Dean ran a hand through his hair, rubbed the sleep from his eyes, and ignoring the tempting warmth of the bodies and blankets, instead decided to start his day early. A quick shower was followed by him heading downstairs to the kitchen. Lexis was on point, already having some coffee brewing, so he poured a large cup while deciding how he wanted to cook his eggs.

Of all the people to join him in his cooking, Jaxon was the last one he'd expected.

"Good morning, Dean," Jaxon said, slowly closing the door behind him.

"You didn't go home last night?" Dean asked, cracking an egg into the bowl.

"No, I got drawn into watching cat videos. Your internet is very amusing," Jaxon grinned, "Can I help?"

Dean chuckled. "Sure, there should be some sausage links in the fridge. Grab those and a pan from above the heating element. It will turn on automatically based on a scan of the contents. Eggs have still got to be stirred by a human, though—else you end up with an overcooked omelet instead of fluffy scrambled eggs. What did you think of the grounds?" Dean asked, cracking the final egg into the bowl, adding a splash of milk, and whipping it all together with a fork.

"Your human preservation has seen better days," Jaxon said and again, Dean laughed. *That's an understatement.* "It would make an excellent place to walk, though, if it had a proper gardener. Probably the most interesting thing about your estate is the work it will take to get it up and running properly." The three-fingered Demi sighed, "I happen to have been bored for a very long time."

Dean reached up and pulled a skillet down. He placed it on a separate burner and dumped the scrambled egg mixture in it. "Set that one there," he instructed, "And then just separate the links. Have you ever heard of an elf named Orabel?"

"Sure, the last maiden on the shelf. She has a tragic backstory, but who doesn't? Her father was a king on a mediocre planet. To Elves, you either thrive or you're replaced. His daughter, known as Sorceress Orabel, was part of the problem. She held walkouts, rallies, and protests. Her opinion was that Min was growing too powerful. Hopefully, Min doesn't smite me for saying this." He paused, wincing while looking around fearfully.

Dean snickered at his fear. Then again, he could understand the caution. Dean stirred the eggs when Jaxon continued.

"Orabel does have a point. Min is more powerful than all the other gods. Min has what they don't—a near instant source of almost limitless power at their fingertips.

When Orabel's father was recalled, he stepped down willingly. She threw a tantrum about the fact that there were more souls in the pit than were needed to keep the peace, and promptly lost an easy to win fight."

Dean listened while he added a dash of pepper. "So," he thought about this and said, "she wants Min brought down a peg or two. You think she's wrong?"

"Min is many things, but their defining characteristic is what makes them best suited to be an arbitrator. They are neutral, and completely dedicated to the cause of being fair. Of all the beings in the universe to give access to limitless power, the creator selected wisely." Jaxon paused and nodded to himself. "I say that based on evidence. Simply put, there are no cases of Min themselves ever being corrupt. The guards, the lackeys, the Demis, and the other gods, though? Most certainly corruptible."

Dean smirked.

"At the same time," Jaxon continued, "I do think Orabel was onto something. Why not fluctuate soul prices to more closely match the requirement? There are rumored to be over a million Bouncries inside the soul pit."

"Damn!" Dean whistled. He stopped stirring and looked at Jaxon. "That'd make a lot of sense. If the power available was more than adequate, why not thin the shelves? Why hold onto more souls than you need?"

Jaxon shrugged. "Of course, it was tens of thousands of years ago when Orabel railed against the system. There was too much power, back then. Think of how it is now, though."

Dean frowned, thinking of how Kambry had said more souls were needed to expand Mixonia.

"Orabel was something of a prophetess, she went on and on about how there would one day be a savior for the trapped souls," Jaxon said sadly. "The herald and his eight wives would come forth and right the imbalance, or some such nonsense."

Dean shrugged, not sure what Jaxon was talking about. "I told her myself that I thought Min was doing the right thing. I happened–"

"Whoa," Jaxon stared at him, wide-eyed. "You spoke with Orabel?"

"She didn't just mentally project into my mind," Dean snorted, and Jaxon waved a sneaky 'you got me' finger. "Yeah, she said I was blessed and wanted–"

Jaxon started to laugh, then hyperventilated a little. His eyes flared, first with panic, then acceptance, and finally understanding. Eventually, he calmed. Dean watched the three-fingered alien rotate the sausages, staring through the pan, deep in thought.

"It is starting to make more sense now. The soul pits were built with arcane magic. If you were to tear them, I could repair them," Jaxon muttered, scratching at his scalp.

"What?" Dean asked, not sure he'd heard the alien right.

"Ah, nothing. I'd very much like to live here. Hire me as your gardener, when you can," Jaxon said politely with a smile.

Dean recognized he wanted to change topics.

"I have about a month of energy stored up. May I stay for free, for now?"

"You keep cooking and helping," Dean shrugged, "of course."

Jaxon's grin stretched ear to ear.

Dean poked the taller Demi in the side. "Keep mumbling weird shit, though, and you'll have to go," Dean said teasingly. "As for gardening, sure. But Jaxon, I want to use my tokens to take some risks—If I fail, I may not be able to free ya."

"Dean, I wouldn't mind just having a month here. There are things at play, apparently, that will take time. Some may never come to fruition. That said," Jaxon warned, "I would be extremely cautious around Orabel. Even in the days of the Elves, she was a force to be reckoned with."

"I've got a baby girl, two wonderful women, and a house full of people I love. I'm not going to put myself in jeopardy. If she wants to help, it'll be done with plenty of strings attached. Now, you met Dorthy, what did you think?" Dean asked shifting the conversation.

Jaxon smiled, placing the sizzling sausages on a cooling slot. "She's wise, talented, and will make a great teacher. I can help her with that, assuming she doesn't get all territorial. She's new, so, probably will let me help. I have a huge collection of magical books I can bring down, if Min lets me." He paused. "I don't see why they wouldn't."

"Great, that would be a huge help. What'd ya think you'll need for gardening?" Dean asked. "I can start a fund for you with the local currency to set you up. Careful, though, don't go getting a bunch of cats until I can get you freed."

"A cat would make me complete," Jaxon said with a longing sigh. "There was a living area downstairs. I'd prefer that over—"

"It's awful dark down there," Dean grunted, shifting the steaming eggs to a bowl. He prepared two big plates and stole some sausages from the cooling rack.

"I'd like the west wing. Convert the right side of it into a school?" Jaxon asked.

"Nah, we'll custom build one. You and Dorthy can design one and we'll build you an academy big enough to meet the magical needs of a few hundred disciples." Dean snapped his fingers sharply, startling his new friend.

"Even more important than gardening, that will be your primary mission. We'll make you a custom building to teach in and if you want to include a residence for yourself in the basement or in a tower or something, put it in the designs. Human architecture is fairly advanced." He grinned. "I'm off for my suite. I've got some gifts to hand out, along with brekkie," Dean said, setting the plate on a carrying tray.

Forks, orange juice, and two ring boxes were added to the tray. Dean penned sweet loving notes that he tucked under the gift boxes. His morning's plan was coming out perfectly. He left a mumbling Jaxon in the kitchen and headed for the elevator. When he coded into his suite he tiptoed to his bedroom.

Arriving in the dark room, he paused to let his eyes adjust. It took a moment, but he finally was able to make out the silhouettes of his two slumbering babes. He left them a plate of breakfast, a gift box, and a note on their respective nightstands and tiptoed back out.

When he returned to the kitchen, Jaxon was gone and Dorthy was serving herself breakfast.

"I want to see the baby," Dorthy said, between bites.

Dean reached into the pantry to retrieve a big clump of carrots. "Sure, I'd work that through Cassie first." He paused. "Better call her Cassandra, though. So... any regrets?"

"No! Jaxon said you are going to build us a custom school, to our own design." She grinned. "Looks like I'll get a paid vacation while we wait for it to be completed. What is not to like? Sure, I may age a bit, but this place is awesome. What are those for?"

"The carrots?" Dean asked, surprised as much by the rapid flow of syllables that tumbled from Dorthy's mouth as by the question at the end. "The horses. Want to come?"

"Oh, I never get to use the stables in Mixonia. They're only for the rich."

"We're rich here, poor there. But we've got horses. I'd tell ya to hurry up and finish eating, but..." Dean chuckled as she rapidly scooped her food into her mouth.

"Whaa? These are so good."

In no time, she had finished her plate. Right as they were about to leave, though, Patti showed up.

"Morning. What happened with the Oruk?" Patti asked. He expected her to have bags under her eyes, but she looked fresh and chipper.

"Ah, I told the others, but you were... busy," Dean said. She'd broken up with Quincy last night, and it was kind of a big deal. Mostly because Quincy had asked if she would be leaving. Dean let Patti cry it out, while he told his best friend that Patti would be staying on Team Ola. Quincy left, instead, and Dean had dropped the conversation and the issue.

It'd resolve itself with time, at least he hoped so. "There's eggs."

"Let me snag a bowl to go, give me a moment and you can tell the story."

Dean nodded, giving her space to get to the food. "Basically, I hired one of them, and someone beat me to the second one, off Min's shelves. I may have taken a brief side-tour to check on an Elf and it cost me the duo. The good news, though, is that whoever got Pamrii, paid me thirty-five tokens to buy out my contract with Bamba."

"You're shittin me," Patti exclaimed around a mouth full of sausage.

"Nope. We're short two competitors... but I figure with the spare tokens we can afford to be picky and do some PvP or PvE solo events while we train as a team and get smart on magic–at least the starter levels," Dean said holding the door open for the two women while Patti scarfed down a bowl of eggs and sausage.

"I can get behind that. You wanting to go back in today?" Patti asked.

"Well, Dorthy needs to teach us about magic," Dean said and Dorthy shook her head.

"That's not how it works. I don't snap a finger and you're a mage," Dorthy said, snapping her fingers to prove a point.

Patti, talking with her mouth full, said, "Yeah it is. Dean shoots energy balls without training."

"He knows one spell," Dorthy snorted, while they left the bar and restaurant area of the estate.

Dean licked his lips, seeing the fully stocked bar and its glorious bottles of booze. He blocked it out and was able to keep walking past it, with ease. The chairs were stacked on the tables, the floor was clean, and the local news played on the big screen. The ticker said things were on the mend on the Oakley Orbital, but more deaths were expected. While he frowned at the mix of half-good and half-bad news, he knew the best thing he could do was to keep it from happening again.

Dorthy opened the front door for them and when Dean stepped out, a beautiful night sky welcomed them. The sparkling stars above could actually be seen; the near constant rain had stopped. In place of the previously empty desert landscape, lush green grass was popping up everywhere. They'd planted several kinds of trees, to help transform the area.

Riva had created a massive safe zone around the estate, while he was here. At least you could walk from building to building on their property without having to worry about being attacked by any of Oakley's dangerous flora or fauna.

"So Dorthy, I know energy balls and energy beams. What else is there?" Dean asked.

"Energy Ray, with which you can stun your target. Lightning Strike for enemies behind cover. Lighting Storm for area effect. Blinding Light... Hmm... I don't use energy much, though, it's a big mana hog. You'll need an alchemist, at some point, or you can just keep purchasing potions, but hiring one pays for itself over time," Dorthy said and Dean winced.

"Figures, I've honestly just been putting out one fire after another. It'll be nice to catch a breath. I take it you unlock spells, by just trying them until you succeed?" Dean asked.

"Sort of. Look, if you've had zero schooling, I'm impressed. Generally speaking, magic is a stubborn beast to be successful with. For instance, your average fire mage will spend days, if not weeks–and sometimes months–to get a simple flame onto their fingertips. Then the same amount of time and effort to turn it into a ball," Dorthy said, getting the barn door for him.

The moment the door was pried open they were assaulted with the earthy smell of horse manure.

"Got to love the smell of horseshit in the morning," Patti quipped, quickly finishing her food.

They walked into one of the stable runs, long strips of horse stalls connected by a corridor to the main riding arena. Dean grew confused by the stinky situation. Lexis' single cow mooed and there was barely any nickering from the horses.

"Ugh, who's cleaning this place out?" Dean asked, wanting to pinch his nose.

"How should I know?" Patti said and Dean huffed in annoyance.

They went to the stalls to find they were mostly empty. He was going to be pissed if his horse was gone. Wait... He saw Apache stick his head out sniffing for Dean.

"I guess we got a few left and when Riva's team pulled out their horses, they didn't clean up. Dorthy try to find a shovel. Poor Cassie," Dean said, realizing that with how swamped she must be with a newborn, the horses had probably become a very low priority.

"This the tool you wanted?" Dorthy asked, pointing at a shovel he was walking past.

"Of course," Dean muttered, "it would be right in front of my face."

"If it was a snake it would've bit ya," Patti snickered. "I'm surprised Dad let this slide, it's not like him to leave a mess behind."

"Can I let them out?" Dorthy asked. Dean pointed to the door that led to the riding arena. "Oh, he's gorgeous... needs brushing, but what a beauty."

"That's Arrow, he's a ladies' man. Here take some carrots, if the shit is piled up, I bet they're hungry," Dean said, handing her half a bushel of carrots. "Hey, Patti?"

When Dean turned to her, he saw she was on the phone. She held up a finger and he went to his stallion, instead. Apache was eager for some carrots. Dean coded his stall and was all but assaulted by the horse. They were starving. He dropped four carrots on the ground and stepped back to get some space, then continued down the walkway. Dorthy let out four of the animals and Dean three.

Only seven horses were left.

Are we hurting for money? Guess I need to talk with Cassie about our finances.

Dean continued to toss carrots onto the ground, mainly so the hungry buggers would leave him be. Within a few minutes, they had eaten the whole bushel and were eyeing Dean hungrily for more. Apache trotted by Dean for a supply shed and neighed. He pawed at it with his front hoof, scratching the door.

"I think there is food in there," Dorthy said, stating the obvious. "They're so big. I never expected this! I don't want to shovel shit, but brushing, feeding, and walking these guys is something I'd love to do."

"Apparently, I'm going to need all the help I can get," Dean muttered gruffly.

Dorthy opened the shed door and gave him a nudge to get by him to the feed. "Give me five tokens and I can have a dozen workers here in—"

"How long would they stay?" Dean wondered.

"Uh... just workers mind you, and you'd need to house and feed them. A few months. I'm skilled and working for three. Rent for an apartment that sleeps four is only a token," Dorthy said.

Dean thought about it. He didn't have much to compare relative value with. A diamond ring wasn't cheap, though, which probably meant a token was worth at least three months of wages. He'd never gone to the open market and had yet to get a feel for currency values, other than what he'd spent at Min's Vault. He'd have to trust Dorthy's numbers until the next time he went to compete and had a chance to visit the market.

Dorthy scooped out a bucket of feed and handed it to him.

"All the power goes to the competitors," Dean said, turning to meet the stares of seven hungry horses. "Do horses fight over food? Never mind I'll go into the arena.

There was a water trough in there I can drain. I'll dump the food in it and then refill it with water when they've finished eating."

Dean had to shoulder his way past the eager horses. The door responded to his code and the fancy new hinges didn't even squeak. Dean noted the riding arena was in excellent condition; it damn well better be—it was brand new. Suddenly the concept of him being nearly broke started to sink in. This building was huge, impressive, and probably quite expensive.

There were jousting training lanes, battle dummies, riding courses, and even sets of generic horse armor on stands in one corner. The arena was at least ten soccer fields in length. It was just overkill for how big it was.

Dean had been remiss, he should have spent more time in here, even if melee fighting was important. The shuffling of feet from behind him caught his attention.

"Okay, see you soon," Patti said, hanging up the phone. "That was Candace. She's on break from college and was just sitting at home since everyone left. She's going to help sort the mansion. I talked to Dad about this mess. What did Cassandra tell you last night?"

"About a million things regarding Leena. She is a very proud new momma. Said we'd talk shop today. Why? What's up?" Dean asked.

"You're out of money. Riva sank millions into building all these structures. Cassandra didn't want you in debt to others, so she drained the accounts or something like that," Patti said with a shrug.

"Even more reason to get back into the competitions," Dean grunted. "We've got Lonny at—"

"Lonny is training over at Riva's new camp with his guys. He needs to keep training there... until we're ready to bring his team back here. And we clearly need to work on a few things here, first. All in good time, let me," Patti said opening the water drain. "We got this. Maybe solo competitions are the best way to go, until we get things around here organized."

"We need to do a cost analysis..." He groaned, thinking of all the stupid paperwork that would be involved. No. He needed to take Cassie to Mixonia. She wanted to do the contracts, anyway. Really, that's all there is to it. "Hey," Dean hollered to Dorthy, who was giggling and talking in hushed tones to the horses, "what are you doing back there?"

"Nothing," she replied, a little too innocently.

Patti snickered and went to check. "They're eating out of her hand and she's making them give her kisses. It's kinda cute."

"Dorthy, can you heal Cassandra?" Dean asked, getting nudged by Apache.

"Already did, she said she wanted to have... a talk with you this morning. Yes, a talk. Easy you brute," Dorthy scolded, that had to be Arrow.

"I'm here you sly man!" Cassandra hollered from down the hall.

Dean's smile spread as he ran for his lover. "Good morning Cassie!"

"You foiled our surprise with your own surprise," Cassandra said with a huff, hands on her hips.

Dean drank her in. She was in a bathrobe, her hair in a tight ponytail. She tried to keep a straight face, but she failed when he ran to her with open arms. Her blue eyes shone, and her white teeth sparkled as her lips peeled back in a giant smile. Before he got to her, Cassandra's face scrunched up in disgust when Arrow plopped out a pile of... well, he guessed they called them horse-apples, for a reason.

"Hey, horse!" She growled, "This is my special moment." Cassandra turned to hold out her hand, like they were exchanging a baton in a relay. "Come lover. Your reward awaits," Cassandra said, deciding the stench of the barn was unfitting.

"Reward? And I need a meeting. I never thought I'd say that, but–"

"You have two options," Cassandra said, dragging him out of the stable. "Our bed and then a meeting... Or just the meeting?"

"Can we, like... bring strawberries?" Dean asked playfully.

"To the bed or to the meeting?" Cassandra asked, her interest piqued.

Dean chuckled and said, "Both. But we'd need to add how the estate has no straw-berries to the meeting's agenda."

"You're such a tease. We need more money. The fact that surprises you, means that I've been remiss. I thought everything was going so smoothly and that I had it handled, then poof... my belly swelled up and suddenly, I'm in labor. There was the challenge, you yelling at Dad, and Kambry in a pit of souls. When Dad vacated..."

"We'll be fine," Dean reassured her, pulling her into his chest and giving her a long kiss. Her palms slid up to the back of his neck, pulling him down to enjoy his lips for several minutes.

"Good morning," Dean finally managed, "How did you sleep?"

"Better. Apparently, Leena slept in your arms for a couple of hours last night. Lexis said that when it was her shift, she found the two of you zonked out in the rocker. Which is adorable, but I read that can lead to bad habits," Cassandra said, scolding him with a finger.

Dean rolled his eyes. "Cassie, are we going to be parenting by the book or by what we should be doing?"

Her glare made Dean want to run and hide.

364

"Mr. Forrester. Our daughter will not become some doted-upon princess. If you spoil her too much, don't cry to me when she cries for you in the middle of the night," Cassandra grumbled, bopping him on the nose. "Now come, lover, Kambry is waiting."

"For what?" Dean asked, a wide smirk on his face.

"Look at you, acting all pompous," she grinned. Cassandra led him into their home and made a bee-line for the elevator. "You make your ladies' breakfast, complete with love notes and gifts... what did you think would happen?"

Dean felt amazing as he was dragged into the elevator for a kiss. When their lips parted, he said, "You just gave birth, and that wouldn't be fair. I thought I was just being sweet."

"I know, the fact that Dorthy healed me up this morning was supposed to be a surprise." She smirked. "Surprise," she said with jazz hands. "I love my ring. Judging by the fact you came home with more tokens and fractions of one, I take it this was a splurge?"

"Uh... I'd call it an essential morale builder," Dean grinned, as the elevator dinged.

"Good answer, but Team Ola will be fair. More about that, later. For now," Cassandra said coding the door, "Lexi has Leena and your ladies await."

As the door clicked behind him, Cassandra raced away, the rapid patter of her feet as she sprinted for the bedroom absorbed by the thick carpet. Dean chuckled at her enthusiasm. He felt overwhelmed; there were a million things he needed to accomplish. A little fun, though, was something he could certainly allow.

He stripped his shirt off on the way to the bedroom and was not disappointed when he arrived to find two naked beauties kneeling at the foot of the bed.

"I like my ring, Dean. Jewelry is not normal... Well, it's just new to me. Here it means a binding of love and the best thing a woman can get from a man she seeks a commitment with. I accept and will plan appropriately –"

Dean bent down, silencing her with a kiss. She was somewhat nervous, and he aimed to fix that.

"I custom ordered a toy for when Tiffany was here, but it arrived late. Can I use it? Or did you want this to be sensual?" Cassandra asked, raising a single, curious eyebrow.

"As long as it's not going in my butt, you can do what you want, I'm not big on planning–not like you, my sexy little Cassie," Dean admitted, peeling off his pants.

Cassandra's small breasts were engorged with milk. Her nipples were pert and swollen. Her stomach was flat and her hips a tiny bit wider, but he couldn't tell that she'd just given birth.

"You look amazing," Dean said looking down at her.

She worked at the elastic of his boxers, gave up and yanked them down. His fully erect penis sprang back up. She glanced up him with a wink and grinned mischievously, "On to the bed, husband. I really want to try out this toy." She wrapped her fingers around his girth.

"We had this whole thing planned out where I was going to be a Dragona for this, but then you went and–" Kambry was saying.

"Wait, why is that not an option? I want to pull on a real tail, or some wings," Dean muttered, launching himself onto the bed with a bounce.

Kambry crawled towards him from the foot of the large bed, her eyes locked on his cock. Her bountiful breasts smacked each other as they dangled and swayed. Her hip snaps and supple curves were beyond enticing. Dean's cock bounced as he felt himself grow even harder. When she reached his penis, she kissed it lovingly, before sliding her lips around the head.

Her hand grasped his shaft to stroke him in tandem with a teasing blowjob. She kept her gaze locked on his, the entire time. Dean loved the sight. He raised an eyebrow when Cassandra hopped onto the bed with a strap on. She bent over and licked Kambry's pussy. Dean raised onto an elbow and smacked her ass.

"I didn't know you had a strap-on?" Dean rumbled, confused as to why she was so excited.

"Manulator," she giggled. "This is your penis," she stroked the length that jutted from her hips, "remember when I had you do a mold? This is the result. The sensors in the tip and along its length are attached to my pleasure zones." She gave him a wicked smile. "I get to feel like I'm fucking Kambry with your cock, and you get to see those big titties bounce while I'm doing so. While I think you can handle the two of us, this was mainly for when there were three vaginas to satisfy," Cassandra said.

"And I'll cum with it, just like if I were getting fucked by you," Kambry bounced her eyebrows. "The ads were very convincing."

She wiggled her hips for Cassandra to grab onto and popped Dean's cock out of her mouth. She licked his shaft seductively. His engorged member pulsed with the tantalizing sensation. Cassandra moved up behind Kambry and slid the fake cock into her. Dean's blowjob intensified as Kambry groaned around his shaft as she was fucked from behind. Dean was in a dreamy haze of ecstasy.

He watched two sets of tits as they bounced at different angles. Kambry's lips squeezed tight around him and she sucked hard on his head. She bobbed up and down. Each slurp was hungrier. Her moans were matched by Cassandra's pleasured panting behind her.

"Your pussy feels so fucking amazing," she gasped, squeezing her own tits. Tiny beads of milk formed on her nipples, then rolled down her breasts.

Kambry slammed back into Cassie, without losing her focus on Dean's cock. He clutched the pillow as she expertly worked him towards a climax. Her grin said it all. She smacked her luscious lips against his shaft, tickling his balls while teasing his head. She paused to grin at him with mischievous eyes, knowing he would enjoy the view. She wet his cock in a teasing manner, taking him in and out of her mouth playfully over the next five minutes. Kambry gave one final slurp, taking all of him deep in her mouth, before pulling off with a tender kiss for his purple, swollen head, before she lunged forward to bury his face in her soft tits.

Her big double-Ds grazed his cheeks as Kambry buried his face with her tits. He motor-boated her breasts in delight before turning his head and capturing a hardened nipple in his mouth. Her pussy juice dripped down from where she was poised over his throbbing cock, a trail of her wetness dripping from his shaft and down his balls.

Dean heard the clack of a bottle opening, the squirt of liquid, and then Kambry turned to look over her shoulder. "Go easy," she said.

He peered around the big titties in his face to see Cassandra setting a bottle of lube down. Kambry slowly eased her warm folds around his cock, bouncing a few times until he was firmly sheathed within her. She kissed him deeply, biting his lip.

She grunted, then moaned as Cassie eased the Manulator into her ass.

Dean felt the fake cock diving into her back door as he pulled back in the front. They entwined in their threesome. The rhythm increased as Kambry quickly adjusted to being filled. Dean just hung in for the ride, sucking on her huge tits while she clamped down on him every time he pulled back, trying to hold him with her vagina.

Time blurred as the passion intensified. When Kambry shifted the angle of her hips, taking both of them deeper inside of her, her moans reached a fever peak and she shuddered between them. The pleasure was euphoric, Kambry's orgasm tilting her partners over the edge; all three of them climaxed together. Dean's three days of pent-up jizz spurted into Kambry.

The pulsing releases of his cock was matched by her clenching orgasm. Dean heard a splash of wetness soak into the sheets as Cassandra cried out. Both Dean and Kambry shifted so that they could see Cassandra, her head tilted back as she shuddered, clutching at Kambry's hips.

Her lip was crushed between her teeth and her face was etched in bliss. She opened her eyes to look at the two of them.

"Ten times better than I expected. I've never squirted like that before. Thought the ad was a liar... for once, I'm thrilled to be proven wrong." She gasped, her chest heaving. "Shower or round two?"

"Shower," Dean chuckled. "As much as I'd love a second round, I've got a mountain of chores to do. This was amazing but a wee bit messy."

Kambry leaned forward, pulling off each of them, slowly. She kissed Dean first, then Cassandra. All three of them were flushed and sweaty. The shower was left on a lesser temp, to cool things down.

When they finished cleaning up and Dean was again ready for the day, he was ecstatic. A multitude of challenges lay before him. As a family, though, he knew they'd conquer whatever this amazing life threw at them.

He was excited to start training with Apache, hopefully the friendly horse would take quickly to combat. If he'd only known how it would go, though, he might just have stayed in bed.

CHAPTER

TWO

DEAN

Forrester-Lexso Estate

"Wait, we're not done. I understand you're excited to go galloping around," Cassandra said with her hands on her hips, "but you need to hear this."

They were sitting at two joined tables in the middle of the bar area on the main floor. The number of folks gathered for the meeting was a lot less than usual, at least compared to their previous meetings. Cassandra, Dean, Kambry, Patti, Dorthy, and Jaxon sat around the table—Jaxon with notes he was scribbling. Lexis sat a little behind Dean and Cassandra, with the baby in a bassinet next to her. Everyone else had gone with Riva to his new training city.

Dean had thought the meeting was over after Cassandra had admitted they were broke. Money was needed, so a shopping trip was planned for them to exchange tokens in the market.

"Huh? I just said we'd go shopping—to exchange some tokens—all four of us, after some drills. We can even do some solo competitions," he held his hands up, "only up to a level we're comfortable with, and then we'll come home. You, though, missy," Dean said pointing at Cassandra, "are going home after the hiring market."

Cassandra rubbed her temples in frustration. "This is not how a business operates," she growled. "You don't just cowboy in, buy whatever strikes your fancy on a whim, and then come home the hero." Dean's hands went up and he shrugged with a shit-

369

eating grin. Cassandra was not fazed. "No Dean. I'll go to the hiring market, while you train—just give me until tomorrow. Please? You'll need to help Lexis with Leena, though, she's not a slave."

"I'm actually doing really well and loving this a lot, my milkers even turned on. I need some cock though," Lexis said and Patti choked on her next breath. She turned her sputters into a giggle. "So does she," Lexi gestured at Patti. "No offense Jaxon, but you're off limits, seeing as how you're gay. With Jaxon out of bounds, that just leaves Dean and you two have him locked up." The buxom Minotress in human guise pouted, "I'm missing all the sexy lads who used to crowd into the communal shower. I just was always so dirty and needing to join them."

"What she said!" Patti laughed, and emphasized her input with a wink.

"Okay," Dean said with a shrug, combined with a friendly groan. "Although I get that you two have a history, try not to be so blunt around any humans you don't know. They can get pretty defensive quickly." He shook his head. "Look, we can't bring the muscle in here until we have support staff to handle all the day-to-day operations and chores. In order to afford the support staff, though, we need more muscle to compete, or else we have to shoulder the burden ourselves." Dean turned to Jaxon, who was still taking notes. "While I'm thinking about it, we'll need to stockpile some supplies, too."

"Which means every gem counts, literally," Kambry said. She turned to Cassandra. "So what's your plan—since it looks like you'll be running operations from here on the home front?"

"We need to organize living arrangements, first. The top floor has two suites and four rooms. All the bedrooms have balconies that we spared no expense to install. The second floor has eight rooms. The basement has a spare wing, if Jaxon is only taking up one. Before I start giving the help a suite, though, do you two girls want to share? Or you three?" Cassandra included Patti, Dorthy, and Lexis in her sweeping gaze.

"No thanks, I like my private space," Lexis said, adjusting her too-small bra. Her shirt showed some leak stains from the jostling motion. "Leena and I have a nice setup, right outside your master suite."

"My sister Candace should be here any minute. I'll take one of the suites and my sister can take the couch—that is, if you want the spare bedroom?" Patti asked Dorthy who shrugged. "We don't bite." Patti smiled at the Angelina.

"I'd like that," Dorthy said shyly, "either of the suites' guest bedrooms really. I'm not big on being alone."

"Okay, that frees up another room. The other three top floor rooms will be left open, the second floor will be for staff, and the basement wing will be considered a special place for a guest or important additions. Yes, Jaxon," Cassandra said when he raised a hand.

"This blueprint for a school that I'm working on will have student housing, and nice rooms for the faculty. I have no idea on the feasibility, but Dean seemed to think money wasn't a problem, at least at the time," Jaxon began earnestly.

Dean drummed his fingers on the table while biting a nail on his other hand. "So... getting money up here on Oakley is easy." He smirked, "Cassie don't roll your eyes at me. We now have seven million invested in structures we could leverage through refinanced mortgages if we needed to." Dean flashed his locket 74.53. "This is much more than I had when we bought the first gem. Not saying that the exchange rate for talents is the best one to go from, because I actually agree with Cassie."

"We should properly research the gem ratios to –" Patti began.

"Dad... Sorry, Mr. Lexso has a gem guy doing just that. He is on retainer and will be going with me... Put your hand down Lexi, he is an older gentleman who is happily married. Not your typical fit stud you like to shack up with."

Lexi pouted.

"Some of these issues are already being solved," Cassandra continued. "Some will require more work. Snagglecrest City is a good example of what a fully operational training organization will require."

"Require?" Dean raised an eyebrow. "What do you think we need to focus on, for here?"

"They have an alchemist, an armorer, a stable master –" Cassandra started reading off a list of support staff positions.

"Whoa, hold your horses, cowgirl! We don't need all that—not right off the bat, at least. We can buy potions, gear, and whatnot in the short term. I like horses, they're pretty and friendly, but I'd rather spend time in the gym than shoveling shit," Dean complained.

"Dean," Kambry stepped in, laying a hand on a frustrated Cassandra's arm, "Do you want to build up this place or streamline it?"

"For right now, until this locket has at least five hundred tokens on it, I'd rather streamline our operations. Why invest a ton of money into more infrastructure—no offense Jaxon— like a school? Teach them right here. Folks can go shoot magic out in the fields inside the safety lines. I'm worried we don't have enough in our reserves and I'm worried that if we don't hire some good workers, and soon, we're going to waste a lot of time that we could be training doing menial labor to keep up with the chores around here," Dean said to a grimacing Cassandra.

"You're right. I had all these grand plans when everyone was training here, and then everything shifted with the opening of the other portals. While I can ask Mr.

Lexso for help, we shouldn't rely on that. We should build this up as well as we can, knowing that it will likely take longer and that we will have to settle for practical, pragmatic things first and then move forward as funds become available." She blew out a breath. "Okay. With that said, I want a maid, I want a cook, and I want a stable master—and I want them sooner rather than later," Cassandra said.

Dean softly smacked the table and grinned at her.

"What?" Cassandra frowned at him.

"I fooking love you. You're the best, Cassie. Sorry to stress you out. How much money is left in the bank from the last gem sale?" Dean asked.

She snickered. "Zero. We still owe Mr. Lexso another two million coins. If converted properly, that should be between eight to ten tokens." She flipped her hand back and forth. "The mileage may vary, and our loan is only at five percent interest, so it doesn't all have to be paid off this month," Cassandra noted and Dean winced.

"Alright. This is what I'd like to do," Dean said and removed his tokens. He placed them on the table before sliding them over to Cassandra. "Get those three fine support staff folks you wanted, plus another nanny—take Kambry and Dorthy with you. Come back once that is done, ideally with at least fifty tokens. At a minimum I need to ensure we still have twenty five. I'll go train with Patti and we'll compete at the lower levels to earn enough to free that snooty Orabel."

Jaxon interceded, "Don't forget that she is dangerous. But... we have to assume she is only dangerous and deadly to those she wants to be. The Elves literally changed the games' difficulty level when they participated; after they left, the level leaderboards all had to reset. If she becomes an ally, you will have earned yourself something many have sought."

"You're saying she will help us win the point race?" Kambry asked skeptically, folding her arms and frowning. "Everything I have heard about elves is how they only serve their own vain needs." She tossed her hair back. "Dean, I agree with Jaxon here. Even if you free her—and I'm surprised she answered your summons—then we might have to deal with a lot of drama. The big issue, though, is one you don't know anything about. Can she even compete? Jaxon mentioned she may be barred from competing, due to some long forgotten rumor."

"My life is a dumpster fire of drama," Dean chuckled wryly, "but it drives, grounds, and completes me. We'll get through this—with or without Orabel. Lexi is going to watch Leena until we get her some backup; Jaxon can help if she is desperate."

Lexis went to talk but Dean held a palm out. "Save it. We need to keep these meetings shorter."

Dean pointed to each of them in turn. "Patti and I are going to go train, with Candace helping however she can. That leaves Dorthy, Kambry, and Cassie going to

Snaggletooth City to pick up the gem guy, before heading to the hiring market. Hopefully, they can buy some great gems to restore our Oakley funds."

Cassie smiled.

Dean grinned back at her. "Please ensure you get enough funds to run things here for a month, and include enough to buy a boat. Doesn't have to be anything grand, just a small, private one for pleasure fishing. The deep freeze can handle whatever we catch and my gear needs a new home, anyway."

"Uh... a boat?" Cassandra asked, clearly confused.

"I promised Sable to take her fishing. Figure it'd be a good change of pace, anyway, for all of us," Dean said. "Any other questions? Good, great, fantastic. Let's keep improving, Team Ola, one day at a time."

Dean kicked his wooden chair back and it screeched across the tile. He flipped it over and put it back up on the table. A quick kiss to his ladies had him heading for the barn to shovel shit. Patti tagged along as they walked to the stables in silence. Dean saw the rising of Oakley's sun and realized it was almost noon. That'd be nice, getting some real sunshine would help both him and the horses.

When he opened the big door Apache was waiting for him. Idly standing there, as if Dean would have more carrots or something. He scratched his stallion behind the ear and the brute nuzzled into him. He frowned at seeing him free roaming.

"Did they not get put up in their stalls?" Dean asked.

Patti snickered and said, "You try putting one of these beasts back in their shitty stalls."

Dean tilted his head to see all the other horse just hanging out in the central corridors of the main barn. "What're the mouth things called that we need to put on –?"

"Dean, I don't know horses. I'm just here to help you shovel the shit so we can start training quicker. The wheel barrows are over there. I can look it up and start figuring it out on my iPhonie if you want to shovel," Patti said and Dean nodded. "The barrow was in the other storage room—across from the feed."

Dean left her to go get the shovel. The tool had a large flat end and two cushioned grips. He suddenly had an idea.

"Patti, those Gilligan guys. They had bots that cleaned up shit, didn't they?" Dean said, trying to remember the name of the machines from the tour. "Probably some law against us having one."

"I'll look into it," Patti said sitting on a bench by the door. Apache decided to bug her for some attention, but Dean wasn't about to complain. He needed to get some work done.

A quick walk to the storage area and he opened the door to find a room with an in-floor drain. There were a few tools in here, including a wheelbarrow laying on its side with a hose nearby. It both smelled and looked like the cleanup had been abandoned halfway through, even if the shit was out of the wheelbarrow.

Dean cursed under his breath. There were gloves off to the side that he put on.

He righted the wheelbarrow and left the storage room. The first project was not the stalls, though, first he had to clean up all the horse shit in the middle of the walkway. In the first shovel full, Dean learned a valuable lesson--fresh manure was harder to clean up than old shit.

He grimaced, but was used to dissecting fish guts for a living. A little shit on a shovel was not an issue.

The first stall wasn't bad. The smell was probably from them having spent a full day in their confined stalls without a break. Jaxon showed up while Dean was working on the second stall with a big smile on his almost human face—his skin had just enough of a yellow tint that he didn't quite look human.

"Can I use this for the garden?" Jaxon asked energetically. "Not sure if it will work, but it's worth a try. Do you care?"

"Oh," Dean shrugged, "No, go right ahead. I'll get the other wheel barrow while you take this one. Thanks," Dean grinned.

"Eh, simple things calm me. Glad to see it's the same with you," Jaxon said, lifting the handles of the filled wheelbarrow and taking off with it. "Be back soon for more."

Dean left the shovel leaning against the wall and headed back to the storage room. His mood was oddly joyful. Shoveling dung was something he found he didn't really mind--not like he'd thought he would. Repetitive hard work tended to keep his mind occupied and happy. He entered the shed to find Patti handling some tack. She kept peering at her phone and then at the equipment.

"I need a bridle, that has a bit." She muttered to herself, not even noticing his arrival, at first. "Apache will probably let me put it on him, no problem. Then I'll need a saddle pad and a saddle... I think. I wish we could just go do the water event again," Patti grumbled.

"If we did PvP, maybe, but I've got an ace up my sleeve. Electric beams. Not saying you'd lose but you shoot a bow, and..."

"In water I'm shit," Patti finished for him. "Better add a crossbow to the list of equipment to buy," Patti said and Dean went to put his gloves away in the shed. She waved him down. "I'll text to find out if Kambry has any other recommendations on equipment we will need. At least another trident and spear gun. You really want to PvP?"

"Eh, I really want to train on these horses. Let me keep mucking out shit so we can breathe in here. When I'm done, if you can't figure it out, I'll help by just winging it," Dean said, and Patti rolled her eyes. "Good luck, if ya need me, holler."

When Dean finished the fourth stall, Candace arrived. She gave him an awkward wave and ran for Patti when he pointed to the riding barn.

Where Patti was a restless type, who skipped through jobs, apartments, and life's general choices, Candace was boring. She was the stable sister going to school for accounting and generally never upset anyone. She was also probably just as smart as Cassandra. Meaning those horses would be properly ready to ride soon enough.

Dean's work grew into a repetitive process. Shovel, fill, and repeat. Jaxon helped by rotating the wheel barrows and eventually Dean made his way down to their single cow. Her pen was neat and clean, there was feed in her bucket, and he had no shit to shovel. She'd even been brushed.

He let his resentment go, this was a personal pet. Lexis taking care of her outside of work was perfectly okay—it wasn't her job to maintain the whole stable. He was actually surprised she'd found the time to do this much.

With the task finally done, he wheeled the final wheelbarrow full of shit out to the preservation building. The caged preserve was barely visible from between the new buildings. Once Dean had stopped clearing out the critters in there, the pros had come in and finished the job. He could see the results from several hundred feet away. Six feet of dirt and clay had been stripped from inside the preserve. New concrete had been poured once the soil had been removed.

Inside, there was nothing but a smooth layer of concrete. Not a single thing lived within the preserve, because that was how you fixed the problem. Aringos were proficient burrowers, even after two full clears the young remained. So... they had simply removed their homes by extracting six feet of dirt and adding a thick concrete pad.

Dean found himself at the door with a wheelbarrow full of manure. They had added a new security inspection point to help keep the possibility of a new infestation down to next to zero. Dean and his haul were scanned. A laser suddenly fired into the steaming pile of shit, splattering a wet clump over his shirt. He clenched his fists in rage as an automated voice said, "Containment threats eliminated."

Dean chuckled and then laughed. A shit stain on his shirt was nothing, he was proud of himself that he wasn't covered in the stuff. When he'd entered the room, he'd noticed a single dirty tire trail leading deeper into the preservation. The smooth concrete was such a different feeling.

This was a blank canvas, it could become whatever someone imagined. Dean saw it as a great place to grow fresh vegetables. Dean especially loved those tiny cherry tomatoes that all the orbital walkways grew. They were best to just pop in your mouth and squish between your teeth, flooding your taste buds with their sharp, piquant taste. He suddenly had a craving that almost rivaled his desire for strawberries, earlier.

While he was lost in his thoughts of yummy cherry tomatoes, he came up to Jaxon. The ten minute walk had been soothing and gave Dean a chance to realize that things were good—even if they seemed bad.

"Ah, thanks Dean. I was thinking of planting something a little less exotic all the way here in the back. It's a decent walk this far, maybe some sort of vegetable," Jaxon said and Dean cracked a toothy smile.

"Aye, we'd love some fresh veggies. Don't know much about farming—other than that fish guts make great fertilizer. How about ya do some research and get a report on what we're going to need? Else I'm gonna be tempted to convert this place into something fun. This surface is great," Dean said scuffing a shoe on the smooth concrete surface.

"Right, I've been mulling a few things over. I'll get this gardening proposal to you first, though, and then we can see about doing something fun in the front half. I still want to design an academy, if it's alright with you?"

Dean lifted the wheelbarrow up and dumped the manure next to the pile Jaxon had already started. The old straw and crap was being mixed in with some dirt to form a bit of compost.

"Sounds great. I know the elitists collecting all our taxes in Belmont and the orbital would love some fresh veggies. We can sell them 'organically grown' veggies, produced in genuine horse shit and buy the cheaper chemically fertilized ones ourselves—though we're not hurting for money as much as Cassandra would have us believe, even if we are in debt," Dean said with a sigh.

Jaxon grabbed the shovel to sprinkle another layer of fertilizer on the dirt. When he finished, he tossed the shovel in the barrow, and started towards the entrance. Dean walked beside him with the other wheelbarrow.

"If you want security for your home," Jaxon said, changing the subject, "Orabel is your ticket. Assuming she can compete, that is, which only she would know. If so, then you can expect great things. Let me tell you more about the Elves," he started, but Dean stopped him.

"Trust me when I say this—I'd love to hear about them. But it's probably best if I go into negotiations with a blank slate; at least not all googly eyed with desire," Dean said hesitantly. "Some things I'd rather keep as a 'prove it to me' kind of deal. But I've got a feeling Cassie will pick her up anyway."

"You don't seem to be the greedy type."

"Are ya going to tell me she can do PvP above the current record?" Dean snorted.

"Not sure, they changed the entire games just to prevent another 'Elven disaster'. Back then, level three hundred used to be a thousand. A thousand now is rumored to have been more like thirty thousand. Min has sunk all bustling power into the games. If Orabel is able to compete, she's in for a rude awakening—literally and figuratively."

Dean frowned.

"You're going to do it, though, aren't you?" Jaxon asked.

"I almost feel like I have to... and I can see you think I should, despite your oft repeated warnings," Dean mused.

Jaxon nodded. "If nothing else, it will answer many question, and open up all new lines of inquiry. Of all the figurines on the shelves in Min's Vault, Orabel's is the most sought after," Jaxon stated with certainty.

They exited the preserve, sprayed down the wheelbarrows in the storage shed and parted ways. Jaxon went off to draft some plans for a magic academy and to see if Lexi needed help with Leena, while Dean walked back into the riding arena.

He passed a row of stalls full of whickering horses and the storage rooms to see two horses in the arena with beaming ladies on their backs. "You girls look fabulous," Dean said, seeing Patti and Candace trotting around the grounds with massive grins on their faces.

A black stallion with white fetlocks that nearly covered his hooves pranced over to Dean with a saddle on his back.

"He helped the best he could. We figured it out because he is so darn docile," Candace said happily. She walked over on a chestnut horse he didn't recognize.

"I'm going to mount up and then try to stab some little shields on the dummies from horseback," Dean grinned, sticking a foot in the stirrup.

When Dean pulled himself up to throw his leg over the tall horse's back, he did so rather awkwardly. He held onto the horn with one hand and gathered the reins in the other. Once he fumblingly managed to stick his far foot in the stirrup, he nudged Apache forward while pulling back on the reins.

Suddenly, the stallion reared up in the air, its front hooves lashing the air. Dean's eyes flared wide as the girth came loose and gravity dragged him from the massive stallion's back. He flew off the horse and landed ass-over-tea kettle with a *thud* in the hard, compact dirt. The air whooshed out of his lungs and he instinctively gasped and coughed. He laid there until Apache came over to nibble on his hair.

"We may... uh... have put your saddle on wrong," Patti snickered.

"Ya think!" Dean scrambled back to his feet. "I hope this gets better," he grumbled. Dean gave Apache a stern gaze. "You knew that was going to happen, didn't you?"

With wounded pride and a sore tailbone, Dean limped over to a bench, pulled out his phone, and started learning everything he could about a horse's tack—a fancy word for saddles, bridles, and all the other equipment you needed to ride.

Apache trailed after him. Leaving it to someone else would just lead to his smartass horse dumping his butt on the ground again. And so the next hour passed in relative quiet, with the gruff fisherman becoming a cavalryman while his horse looked on with what Dean swore was a cocky grin.

THREE

DEAN

Forrester-Lexso Estate

Dean cinched down on the saddle's girth to the point that his arms bulged. After watching all those dumb videos—fluffed up to add enough time to trigger a revenue transaction—he figured it out in a few minutes. A strap had been tucked in wrong. It was hard to believe things hadn't come undone when he pulled himself into the saddle. That must have loosened things just enough, that a quick jerk when Apache reared up, sent both saddle and rider heading for the ground. Not this time though, Dean was confident he'd put the saddle on right.

Sure he might fall off, but the saddle was on snug. He tucked a foot into the stirrup and pulled himself up onto the horse's back. Dean learned quickly that Apache was a prancer. Maybe it was because he'd been a show horse, or maybe it was his previous owner's riding style.

Dean led the horse over to a staging wall where wooden practice lances rested in a rack against the wall. Apache was quick to respond, eager to receive a scratch behind the ear or pat on the neck in praise. The handsome stallion made riding seem so easy. With the lance couched firmly under his arm, Dean sent Apache around the ring for a lap at a slow trot.

The horse caused him to jostle as they completed an easy trip around the very large ring. Patti and Candace were brushing their horses down. So it was just the two of

379

them riding around the arena. He regretted not wearing armor at this point, and he wanted to see what it was like. Of course, this was after he was already mounted, too. He decided to do this because he may have hated trying to get comfortable in armor the first time.

"You want to attack those dummy things?" Dean asked and Apache nickered. When Dean tried to direct him towards the target dummy, even at a nice, easy pace, the horse balked.

"I'm going to ask nicely, once." He paused until Apache's big ear rotated back towards him and he knew he had the big stallion's attention. "And only once."

Dean turned him for a slow trot at the target dummy. Going slow was fine by him. The end of the lance scored the target with a gong sound. Dean lifted his arms in victory and gave himself a fake cheer. Because... well, this was awesome. His morning had finally resulted in something meaningful.

Apache stopped and then with a light tap of the heel, went over to a mount and dismount station. There was a treat basket there that his face dove right into.

"Okay, I get it," Dean chuckled, reaching up to scratch the stallion behind his ear. "This was a very good start. I'm going to put you away, check on the baby, get myself some lunch, and grab you a snack." There were carrots in the basket that Apache happily munched on. Dean may as well have been talking to himself. "For now, let me get down." He hopped onto the elevated platform. "Let's strip off this addle and bridle."

The horse kept searching for more treats in the bottom of the basket as Dean messed with the bridle. Undoing a clasp, he slid the bridle over Apache's head and the bit came out of his horse's mouth, covered in orange slobber. A seating section became a temporary resting spot for it. He removed the saddle next. Looking around, Dean spotted a bar to rest the saddle over and a hook to leave the bridle on.

He pulled down a halter and lifted it over the big guy's ears. "I guess I can just leave it all here. You too? Or are you going to break stuff?"

Apache whickered.

The horse was being very cooperative and when Dean was finally finished, he ran a curry comb down Apache's sides, brushing him down. Apache was wanting a treat that Dean didn't have. The horse whickered for his attention, enough that he felt bad. Apache wanted human interaction and that meant more of his time. So did his daughter, though; at least that's what Dean told himself as Apache trailed after him when he turned to leave.

"I get it, I wouldn't want to be cooped up either," Dean said, opening a random stall. Thankfully, Apache stepped into the stall without a hassle. "I promise lots of treats when I come back."

Dean locked the horse in before leaving the barn for the tavern. The walk was short and the afternoon sun barely peeked over the horizon as it started its own day. He entered the main floor to see Patti, Candace, and Lexis sitting at a table watching the news.

"Where's Leena?" Dean asked, his eyebrows raised in curiosity.

Lexis wagged a baby monitor at him and said, "She's sleeping. But she's due to get up any moment. She'll want a bottle and then to be held. You want to take a shift?"

"Yeah sure, we've got everything in our room. There's momma milk in the fridge, right?" Dean asked and Lexis nodded, handing him the monitor.

"So," Dean began, "do you want to be called Lexis or Lexi? I hear it swapped around a lot lately."

"For family or friends, Lexi is fine. To everyone else, though, it's Lexis. So... Dean. I'd love an egg salad. I ordered some food while you were out playing with the horses. There's fresh greens and eggs in the kitchen," Lexis said with a hopeful look.

"Sure," he snickered, "I need to set out some treats for Apache, anyhow. The stallion is a ham for a snack." He shook his head. "I'm excited to get into armor and get beyond the slow training. Patti? Candace? You want some too?"

"Yes, please," they said in unison. The sisters smiled politely. Dean left for the kitchen, noticing the news was all about the recovery rate and containment of the plague. The latest reports gave Dean hope. More hope than they'd had that morning.

The kitchen had a bunch of supplies still out on counter and not yet stowed away. Dean placed the monitor down and went to work. The groceries weren't going to put themselves away, and the girls weren't his employees. Well, Lexis was, but he didn't mind doing some work. He first stuck a pot of water on the stove to boil.

Five minutes became ten, and before he knew it, the eggs were hard boiled. The food was stashed and he had washed the veggies. A sharp knife crashed against the board as he diced the greens. The cherry tomatoes he'd found were mostly gone by the time the salad was ready for them; someone was refusing to put them in the salad, and instead, kept popping them into his mouth. He sprinkled in diced cucumbers, fresh romaine lettuce, carrots, and even little bits of ham. He'd just added the last of the eggs when Leena cried out.

Dean washed his hands quickly and grabbed the monitor. When he exited the main room he said, "Salads ready, just in time, help yourselves."

They thanked him as he rushed for his little girl before she got up a full head of steam. It was like the baby's volume increased the longer he took, causing him to shuffle quicker and fuss about the slow elevator. Eventually, the elevator doors opened on the third floor and Dean ran. When he made it to his distraught daughter, she bawled at him.

Over to the changing station, she went. He unswaddled, wiped her clean, patted her dry, changed her diaper, and then bundled her back up again. He didn't think it was possible, but she was even angrier now than before. He went to the fridge. A digital notice on the bottle said 'simply shake to heat'. His hand jarred the milk inside the device and it warmed quickly to the right temperature.

Every attempt to soothe her, failed. He went into his room and adjusted the balcony door to dark. The room instantly dimmed as the windows blacked out. The bottle finally dinged at him, letting him know it was at the right temp, and not a moment too soon. He found his spot in the rocker, turned on the nearby noise machine, and stuck the bottle in her mouth.

Leena latched hungrily onto the nipple. The blissful silence was amazing. With her hunger abating, she kept slurping down the milk, even as her eyes closed. He yawned. With Leena snuggled securely into the crook of Dean's arm, he decided to catch up on the sleep he had missed that morning.

Dean woke up hours later, feeling rested. Leena was in her bassinet, sleeping. Lexis must have checked on him. His phone told him it had only been two hours. The lack of alerts, texts, and missed calls meant his life was stabilizing.

He left the bedroom to find Lexis on the couch, watching television with the baby monitor beside her. Dean gave her a thumbs up and she waved goodbye. Normally he'd ride the elevator but this time Dean trotted down the small stairwell that emptied into the kitchen.

At some point, either a guest or their pet must have pissed on the wall or carpet in the stairwell because it had a nasty ammonia odor. Another problem that Jaeger had probably ignored, due to the cost. Dean passed on a project he couldn't fix until later, and headed for the fridge, which soon transitioned into a hunt for a snack in the pantry.

With a big bag of jerky under his arm, a full sack of apples, and a smile on his face, he headed for the armory. Dean felt the estate was eerily quiet. With no other people around, it was somewhat spooky. The trip outside revealed a bright day with birds fluttering up from their perches as he approached. On the horizon, rolling clouds indicated that rain was likely later on. He sighed, they'd gotten enough rain for a while.

As much as he wanted to linger outside and bask in the warmth of the sun, he entered the armory building. The once fully stocked and busy room was nearly empty. Dean's gear was hanging over a wooden manikin, while Patti, and Kambry's gear rested nearby. This reminded him he needed to recruit more team members.

While he started gearing up, he snacked, eager to quell his hunger. The jerky he gnawed on was tough and delicious, it was some flavorful New Texas brand. He stuffed his face with the dried, spicy meat while preparing for battle.

His breastplate went on with a bit of a hassle. Getting the side clips on without any assistance was doable, but not easy. After a brief struggle, he finally had to leave a few of them undone. He grumbled to himself, noting that he should have brought someone to help him. The kilt wrapped around his running shorts, and when his warrior boots were laced up tight, he was almost done. The last bit he hated—the dreaded belt.

He sat for this part and it went on surprisingly well. *Maybe practice does make perfect,* he mused. With the belt securing the heavy leather straps of his war kilt, he attached two daggers to it—one on each hip. He got up and sought out both of his tridents—the lance sized one and the shorter one meant for melee.

"I'm forgetting something, I always do," Dean muttered to himself after grabbing his weapons and stuffing the extra gear into a large duffle bag formerly meant for hockey equipment. "Going to need to store some snacks for the horses in the barn," he grunted.

While he normally didn't talk to himself, he found it really odd that no one else was around. As if someone had read his mind, his phone suddenly rang.

"Ola," Dean answered.

"Like hello or answering for Team Ola?" Marty quipped, amused with his retort.

"Hello, how're you doing on your portal?" Dean snorted.

Marty paused and said, "Actually really well. Last I checked, the score was stabilizing, not swinging much in either direction. Their side is plus one-seventy. We also learned something interesting. A level fifteen solo only counts as a single point. We'd been expecting a big jump but... not how it works. How are things there?"

"Ah, quiet. Your girls are probably in the barn. I fell asleep in the rocker –"

"Ha!" Marty chuckled. "I used to do that with Patti, she became such a needy attention hog that I couldn't escape. You know, the books say –"

"Ugh," Dean groaned, "Not you too! Hard pass. If Leena wants to be held, I'll hold her. As far as Team Ola goes, things are slow. I'm about to go into solo PvE with Apache. Taking it slow today while I see what the estate needs. That and the girls are shopping. Anything new on your end?" Dean wondered.

"Snaggletooth City is swapping from tents to structures. That father-in-law of yours must have some friends in high places. Priority construction... and it's going up fast. I called for something else, though. Tucker came out. Said he was given a spaceship, to free up that portal, by you. He left with a full team to go asteroid mining or whatever it is those orbital junkies do."

Dean couldn't help himself. He growled at the mention of Tucker's name.

"It's in the contract that you can't attack him or try to harm him in any way, unless it's in self-defense." Marty sighed. "Not saying you would, just anyone associated with Mixonia is on that list. He wanted assurances and we wanted the portal. Still no fourth portal, but at least you're a short flight from your entry, now."

"And Lonny?" Dean asked.

"Busy, already built a team, and they're running team drills. He should be heading your way in a bit. We created a booking website for your portal. Best book your time now, or else your slots will get filled. Unless you want to lock in a standard slot, which..."

"You'd prefer I didn't," Dean finished for him, "so that it can always be in use. Do I at least get a bumping priority?" Dean asked, realizing what was going on.

"Yeah. We plan to have a standby team waiting to go, in case a team is late or a team cycles in and out quicker than expected. It's all about those single points, right now, more so than being about the tokens," Marty explained.

"I agree. I'm just about to do some more training, and then we'll head over to my portal. Have you rotated people there yet?" Dean wanted to know.

"No, we're behind on forming teams of trained recruits. We... may have overestimated the number of folks who wanted to kill monsters for salary. Some folks stayed... but most left. We're pulling from everywhere now, though. When you advertise asking for gaming experience... well, you tend to not get the fittest folks," Marty admitted.

Dean laughed. "Obviously, but that can be fixed. Dump them into the water event, and then –"

"We've got it well in hand, and Riva's team of lawyers is expertly CYA'ing everything with paperwork. Side note, your little Cassandra is a smart cookie, by the way. Riva and I are burning through Gs and messing with the gem market. Her father will ensure she gets her own lane to saturate," Marty said proudly.

"How's the missus?" Dean asked about the woman he'd teasingly called mom for years. Orlith had been there for him, for a long time. He was surprised she was actually there instead of here. "Is she still mad at me?"

"Huh? Why would you assume that?" Marty asked.

"Thought she'd be over here, doting on the baby," Dean said, heading for the barn.

There was a background scuffle for the phone and Orlith took over. "I tried," she growled. "Cassandra wanted to get in some prime mommy time before opening the floodgates to visitors. Even her mom was denied."

"I take it you'd like to—"

"Love to, on my way. Here's Marty. Thanks, son," Orlith squealed, handing the phone back to her husband.

Dean opened his mouth and closed it again. I hope Cassie doesn't get pissed. At least Orlith isn't mad about Candace anymore.

"So... that just happened. You should call Mrs. Lexso and extend the same offer," Marty said with a laugh. "Alright, I've got like a thousand things to do. Take care Dean."

"You too, and thanks for the call," Dean said, hanging up.

He called Cassandra, who answered on the first ring.

"About time," she said in a playful tone. "How is our baby girl? I was expecting an update at least an hour ago."

"You're heading home?" Dean asked, confused.

"What? No. Snaggletooth is a four hour flight. We just got here. We're prepping to head into Mixonia, now," Cassandra said and Dean counted with his fingers.

"So... I may have told Orlith that she could come and see Leena. Can you maybe call your Mom and–"

"Fine, fine. Grandmas are okay. I guess," Cassandra chuckled. "She is a de facto one. Even I know that," Cassandra said and Dean smiled. "Have you been training this whole time?"

"Ah, no. Princess and I had a little uh... naparoo. Before you ask, super guilty about it. We snuggled it up," Dean said and Cassandra scoffed over the phone, but in his mind, he imagined her smiling.

"We're about to hit checkpoint one, so let me get off the phone. But I'm jealous. I'll let mom know. Loves ya!" Cassandra shouted into the phone.

Dean shifted the phone from his ringing ear and cursed softly. "Love you too, be safe."

"Oh, one last question," Cassandra paused. "Do you want this Orabel lady on your team?"

"Um... Define team," ..." Dean let the sentence hang. "Are we talking team bedroom or team Ola? She was..."

"Right, so I've heard. Kambry here said she is about the best twenty-five tokens a man can buy. And... I'll be the one handling the contract," Cassandra said sternly.

"Oh, yeah, that is smart. I agree. I'll work with Patti on freeing or hiring our last two team-members, then. Something tanky, or an off-tank at least. I was –"

"Got to go, kiss our baby girl for me," Cassandra said and hung up on him.

Dean entered the barn with a wide smile on his face. The stench was down and the horses calmer than before. The clang of a gong echoed from down the hallway, reverberating its way to him. He smirked, looking forward to getting some practice in.

CHAPTER

FOUR

DEAN

Forrester-Lexso Estate

"Nice! Good job Apache," Dean said excitedly.

They were both in armor and working on hitting targets with a lance at a dead sprint. Dean had figured out Apache's weakness, though he didn't blame the stallion. The stallion was a sucker for treats, which was quite understandable. They'd spent three hours smacking gongs and the two had improved significantly, not only their pacing, but also with their accuracy.

Patti, who was riding a mare she'd named Betsy, was having some good success shooting her bow from horseback. That was what Dean wanted to implement in his training next—ranged combat. He felt he should be able to shoot a bow, regardless of whether or not he had magic, because of the mana limits. And of course, before he learned the bow, he'd need to get javelins to test. The amount of equipment he felt they lacked was piling up.

Apache slowly danced along the outside of the rail, eager to make another charge.

"Last one, Apache," Dean said as he ducked low over his horse's neck. "Let's kill this pretend ogre."

His trident spear was couched under his armpit, at the ready. The muscles in his arm burned from holding the weapon level. He settled into the saddle to absorb the blow, just so.

The duo came ripping off the outside track for an inside run. Apache's hooves flung clods of packed dirt behind them as he picked up speed. Loud snorts escaped his flared nostrils. Dean tensed, aimed, and gave a bellowing war cry.

The tip of his trident *clanged* against the round target, telling Dean he'd hit the bullseye again. He let out a loud whoop of joy while Apache pranced victoriously.

"Alright big guy. Time for a dismount and a break. I need to go ensure two rooms are clean and ready for our new staff while you catch your breath. You'll be staying in your saddle and bridle though. It's only a half hour flight in the big shuttle. Half an hour..." Dean hesitated before doing the right thing and stripping his friend of the saddle and bridle and rubbing him down. "Okay, you've got half an hour of freedom. Don't waste it." With a slap on his flank, Dean sent the stallion cantering off.

"We heading in?" Patti asked.

"Yeah, inside the estate, first, to ensure things are ready for our new staff, and then off to compete. What's Candace up to?" Dean asked.

A happy whinny echoed from one of the stalls. "In here, brushing these beauties down. I went over the supplies and found what they left behind—should be enough," Candace shouted from down the hall.

"You ready?" Dean asked and Patti trotted over to the dismount station.

She patted her horse's neck proudly. "I need to give this horse a better name at some point," Patti said fondly. "Betsy just doesn't suit her."

"I'm sure Cassie knows what it is, and if not, I can always send a blood sample to Nathanael. Personally, kinda happy ya found a friend," Dean smiled, removing the bridle while Patti worked the saddle.

"You talk to the ladies?" Patti asked.

"Yeah," he sighed, "We're going in one at a time. We both can't become statues. If we hit level seven each, we'll earn twenty-six tokens, and —"

Patti covered her mouth as she laughed. "You're adorable, Dean. No wonder you fish. One, three, six, ten, fifteen, twenty-one, and then twenty-eight," Patti chortled, patting his shoulder. "And I suck at math."

"Ha! Shows what you know," Dean said and then faltered as he checked his math. "Fine, it's twenty-eight." He blushed. "I'd appreciate it if ya didn't rub this one in."

"Not a chance, Deanie," Patti snickered, grabbing her bow. "These two will be okay loose in the arena, right?"

"There's feed out, water in the trough, and we just ran 'em. We're coming back in fifteen minutes, anyway. Assuming I can hook up the horse trailer to the shuttle," Dean said heading for the exit. "I bet that thing cost me a pretty penny."

"So," Patti began, "about the Elf... we going to add her to the team?"

Dean nodded.

"If we can, yeah, unless she won't take a fair deal." He frowned. "We need to figure out who or what, rather, we want for the last slot—if not two more," Dean said.

"Why two more?"

"Orabel may be stubborn, and again, Jaxon thinks she might be banned. Even if she can compete, what if Kambry becomes preggers, or needs to watch the baby?" Dean said.

Candace giggled at this, walking up just then.

"Who knows?" Dean grumbled. "With gods doing weird shit, even I could get a swollen belly."

"Not how it works Dean, mind if I join you on the trip? I haven't been to Mixonia since the water event," Candace asked with a hopeful look.

Patti shrugged and looked at Dean, who frowned. "Candace, you wanting to compete? We could use ya if you are, but I'd want you to train up first, though. Snarltooth would take you in and spit you out."

"I thought you needed me here, and I don't know. I'm the daughter who didn't bait the hook while Patti bit the worm in half," Candace said. She snickered with bouncing brows. "Though... getting all sweaty with those blokes is mighty enticing."

Dean and Patti both rolled their eyes as they walked out of the stables. Patti fielded this one and said, "Dad and Mr. Lexso are doing fine. You should focus on your schooling, when it resumes, and help out here while you can. I'm sure Cassie will pay you for your help, the estate needs it."

"Fine," Candace muttered as they entered the front entrance of the estate.

Not far from the bar, the baby rocker held a cooing Leena, who stared with rapt attention at the mobile that spun over her head. There was no Lexis in sight, but there was a monitor set up to watch her. Dean found Lexis in the kitchen, prepping dinner. She said she'd already fixed up the only room that was messy.

Dean kissed Leena on the cheek, said goodbye to Lexis and Candace, and went outside to hook up the horse trailer. It took him a moment, but he eventually realized that on the outside of the machine, there was a datapad with an intuitive touch display. He tapped on 'connect' before selecting the large shuttle. The horse trailer moved by itself to line up perfectly and the two flying devices latched together securely. *Technology sure could be helpful when trying to do complex things*, he thought.

Apache and the mare Patti referred to as "Betsy"—until she could come up with a better name—loaded up easily. Dean laid out the tack—saddles and bridles—inside the main shuttle. He checked again for everything he could think of. His armor was on him, his weapons were in the shuttle, and they'd even brought water sacks to go into his overfilled duffle bag. He wanted to bring a foldable ladder, or at least a step stool, but figured buying one at the market after earning an easy token made the most sense, since that would ensure it was allowed.

"You ready?" Patti called out from inside the shuttle. Dean dropped into the big bucket seat and Patti entered their destination.

"You heard from Quincy yet today?" Patti asked.

"Not a peep, sorry, Patti," Dean replied as the shuttle-trailer combo lifted off. The *whine* of the rotors whirling wasn't louder than a faint droning. "I feel bad about it, though," he grimaced. "I was the architect of your... whatever it was."

"It's okay, really Dean, I don't fault you at all. In a drunken stupor, you pushed us together. Reality pushed us apart. I don't know who the right man for me is. Maybe I'll find him... one day," Patti said wistfully. Then she giggled. "Never expected you to have two girlfriends, though, or a baby."

"Maybe three, soon," he smirked. "Actually, I better talk with Cassie and Kambry, first. I don't want to get into hot water, because I'm talking about family matters too openly." Dean shrugged. "I can say I'm happy. I still get the urge to drink, but..."

"You aren't, I'm proud of you Dean. That's not the easiest thing to turn off, either. Enough small talk. What're our goals for today?" Patti asked, propping her legs on the dash and folding her arms.

"I'd love for each of us to get to level seven and bank the profits. We need money and you need a servant. You know... basic stuff. Also, I've been remiss, not visiting the market. I really like Apache, but –"

Patti quirked an eyebrow, "Yeah, how does the pet thing work? If they die in a competition, do they... die?"

Dean scoffed and whistled, low, "I sure as fook hope not. Apache cost more than my house."

"He is one of a kind, though. Let me text Anoka," Patti said pulling out her phone.

Dean's eyes drifted out over the bleak landscape. They'd already passed over the area where the rains were returning life to the area. He watched the dry, cracked desert around them, thinking of how hostile and unfair the creator had made some life. He tried to catch a glimpse of a slithering snake, or a lumbering lizard, but came up empty.

Dean grew tired of the desolation and focused on the long trail of rain clouds coming for his estate from the Larvian Sea. This he smirked at. He was amused by the weather stations' constant confusion. As their flight dragged, with them going slower than usual towards the Deadly Caverns, he realize that building up a base right next to the portal was ultimately the way to go.

Dean entered a new name for the location—Ola Caverns. Give the team some pride in their portal.

"I've got the deets," Patti grinned at him. "There's good news and bad. The good first. Mounts regenerate health. Hurrah, so if your mount takes damage, simply wait and they'll heal—assuming they aren't mortally wounded. You can patch and heal them in the maze, but that requires specialty items. Same with cleansing a poison." She frowned. "If they die, though, they die. Yikes," Patti grunted and Dean fidgeted.

"Well shit, now... Never mind. If he dies, he dies." Dean blew out a breath. "We can't what-if everything, not when the world is counting on us. Okay, ask Anoka if we can take more than one pet figurine in with us?" Dean asked.

"Yes, but again, only one can ever spawn—per floor. You can't chain spawn pets during a level or lose a pet and spawn a new one, without first leaving and resetting the floor. Anoka said you simply set the pet figurines on the ground, step back, and let the magic happen," Patti said, reading from her phone.

"Alright, so a horse, a dolphin, and some sort of battle pet for when a horse isn't needed. Probably should sell Apache. I can literally ride any horse," Dean said in a huff.

"That line, I'll keep secret. Don't you ever say that to Apache, he loves working with you," Patti said, smiling.

Dean shook his head. "Again, this leads us back to visiting the market. Maybe we can buy ten mares for him to retire him with. Somehow, I bet horses are cheap as dirt on the Mixonia market. Especially if they are the preferred, go to mount. I'll get the stallion a nice harem of lovely ladies."

"Not all men want a harem, Dean," Patti said with a chuckle, "Just you."

Dean shrugged while ducking his head innocently. "I saw these unicorn girls who were damn cute. Well, they had guys, too. I thought Kambry was built for divinity."

"How about those Elf guys?" Patti asked, bouncing her eyebrows at him with a swat to her booty.

"Oh, they'd make me jealous, but so did the unicorn ones. I bet if I get Orabel, those two elven guards of hers are coming, too" Dean said to an amused Patti.

"Can we go say hi, if we do levels one to seven?" Patti asked.

"Yeah, sure. If we got to floor ten, I'd breathe a lot easier. But who knows. I fooking almost died on floor seven in single PvE," Dean said with a grunt. "Funny how things add up quickly. We go in, knock out some easy floors, and then go to the market. Then we can head back to do the rest of the floors. Our goal is floor seven, to increase our reserve against failing. If we get to ten, then great."

"Yeah, my contract states I have to give my tokens to either you or Cassandra, and then ask for an item in return. So, no buying an Elf boy for me, at least not today," Patti said, unfazed.

Dean reflected on the changes they'd made to the contracts; he'd already said it wasn't fair. Preventing another Tucker incident made sense, though, and they were on the right track. He knew that before going into the solo PvP matches, they'd need to earn some tokens and set up a healthy reserve.

Besides, he really wanted to PvP.

FIVE

DEAN

Mixonia

Dean pretended to gallop Apache's figurine across the table as he waited for Patti outside the solo PvE portal. The little figurine clomped against the wooden surface, drawing the stares of the other competitors. Not that Dean gave two fooks, he was having a blast using Apache to crush ants.

Did he bother to question how ants had entered a city of the gods? Nope, they were flipping ants, and ants bow to no god besides the food god. He added 'why ants?' to the list of questions to ask Mixonia's ultimate divinity, the next time he saw them.

"Hey, you bored? I was only gone for ten minutes," Patti said arriving from the portal.

Dean stood to give her a high five. She went to hand him the token and he said, "Sure, normally yes, but I'm going inside next. If I go in and wipe I think it locks the tokens to me. Or I lose them. Or else you'd never need to bank. Anyway, I'm ordering you to hold onto it for now."

"Sure boss, so... Wanna hear how it went?" She gave him a massive grin.

"Yeah Patti, lay it on me."

"I sat there waiting for ten minutes, then went to the locket and indented it," Patti said with a smug shrug. "There was no threat."

"Awesome, great to hear it. You ready for level two?" Dean asked.

Patti pointed to the portal for him to test the waters himself. He grinned, snatching up Apache's figurine off the table and hefted his duffle bag full of extra stuff. With a determined stride, he walked up to the portal guards. The guard eyed him skeptically with a frown. Dean knew he probably looked overly excited.

"Dean Forrester, floor one, and I understand the risks," Dean said with his hand on the Oath stone.

"Best one today. Into the green you go," the Minotaur guard said in a fake, chipper tone. Dean walked into the shimmering portal.

∞∞∞

Dean arrived inside a cave with a smooth floor. Behind him, the black portal lead back home, in front of him was an opening—to whatever challenge awaited. There was enough room to spawn Apache, so he set his friend's figurine down onto the rough, gritty ground.

After retreating a few steps, the figure shimmered as it grew. Tendrils of clear magic swirled about Apache until he stood there, full sized.

Epic, I was wondering how this would happen. It was slow, very magical, and he isn't spooked.

Dean patted his big friend on the shoulder, who looked around them, confused. He pulled an apple out of his bag and fed it to Apache. The horse calmed a bit and the two just relaxed for a moment by the portal. Dean wasn't in a rush as he emptied out his duffel. Apache was a slow eater, with his bit in. Next go around, he'd take the bit out, and just use the bridle as a hackamore. It'd probably be more than enough.

He picked up a short sword and clipped it to his belt on his left hip. The buckler went onto his left arm, and he strategically leaned the trident by the cave opening. He was ready to go, at least he thought so.

With his left foot in the stirrup, he tested the tightness of the girth with his weight. With a grunting leap, he launched himself up into the saddle. Apache munched contently while Dean got himself situated. A slight touch of his heels and the horse walked forward slowly until Dean was able to grab his lancing trident.

Dean smacked the trident against the small shield. This was a signal he'd been trying to engrain in Apache that he was ready for speed and violence, with a hint of momentum. They exited the cave at a lope to find themselves in a low, grassy field.

A few hundred feet ahead rested the locket on its pedestal, its shiny gleam reflecting the morning sunlight. There was a big turtle off in the far distance, munching on some grass. Dean spurred Apache forward, the horse trotted up with a bit of a prance. Dean rolled his eyes at the horse's showmanship.

"I guess it's just a simple grab and score. Makes sense, it's only level one," Dean said to Apache as he nudged the stallion out of his prance and into a trot.

Two minutes later, he had the locket with a *1* engraved on it, in his hand. The turtle stirred, sensing Dean and Apache and slowly lumbering their way. Without waiting to engage the beast, Dean indented the locket.

∞∞∞

Hell yes! Dean grinned at the single token on the locket around his neck. Just as importantly, was the fact that his duffel bag was bulging again. Which meant that he came out the same way he went in. He looked between the Minotaur guard and Patti, trying to decide between going on to level two, or checking in with her.

An Osamar pair flanked her, causing Dean to shift his decision from floor two to checking up on his friend. They seemed happy, with pleasant expressions, so it was mostly curiosity about the unicorn humanoids that triggered his interest. The normal commotion of the staging area was minimal, mostly single champions, or the odd duo, getting ready for their events.

Dean was surprised he'd remembered the name of the race of the mostly human-looking pair sitting with Patti. The Osamar were a unicorn species, with a small curved horn. These two were from the same species as the ones he'd seen on the shelf in Min's vault, near the Oruk.

He studied Patti's new friends as he walked up. These two looked to be in their mid-twenties. They wore matching leather outfits that accentuated their physiques. The male had a tanned skin tone, high cheekbones, brown hair, and handsome features. His blue eyes stared at Patti intently.

The female had blonde hair, a lighter pigment to her skin, and matching blue eyes. Where he was muscled and fit, she was firm and busty. That was one thing Mixonia got right—the monster girls. Unlike the buxom, airheaded Bouncries, this lady looked both sexy and deadly. Her eyes carried a weight behind them that spoke of more than a little experience, but little fear.

Patti waved at him as he approached and introduced him to her friends, "Guys, this is Dean. Dean, this is Zayra," Patti pointed first to the lady before shifting to point to the male, "And this is Wilfred. We're doing the same thing."

"Well, sort of," Wilfred said with a meek smile. "Zayra and I haven't started yet. Patti here gave a friendly wave that distracted us and called us over to sit at this waiting bench." He chuckled nervously. "We've waited a long time for this day, so we find ourselves a tad anxious."

Zayra frowned at him. "Worried is better. We did the right thing, though, saving up fifty tokens before attempting the individual events."

Dean set his bag under the table and placed Apache's figurine on the top. He dropped down beside Wilfred with a happy sigh. A moment later he pointed at the big blue swirl of the event portal.

"I take you did that one?" Dean asked.

Wilfred's eyes shot to the water event portal.

"Yes, we did that one a few days ago. It was –"

"We're going in while you boys talk," Patti said, grabbing her bag and mount. Zayra got up from the seat with her, the two ladies chatting as they walked away.

"What's with the bags?" Wilfred asked. "We were taught they were for advanced levels."

"Yeah, well, we're short on tokens. Figured there'd be less risk with the extra gear. I actually want to get a bigger bag, with additional things: potions, medical stuff, and whatnot." He shrugged. "So, you saved up, huh? Must have found your portal a while ago," Dean noted.

Wilfred shot him a strange look. "We were both born here in Mixonia. Her parents are currently figurines, while mine went home, and never came back. I think a trade must have gone wrong and they were murdered." A haunted look flashed across his features. "Not going to dive into that –"

Dean smiled gently and slowed him down. "We're not in a rush, here. By all means, don't let something so big define you, but at the same time, I have no problem with being a good listener."

"Thanks... It is uncommon to see humans here. They're known to be... well, ruffians. Not rude, just to the point and very direct. That is what drew us to Patti, we almost never see human females competing. It's exceedingly rare," Wilfred admitted.

Dean shrugged.

Humanity was indeed a male dominated society when it came to highly physical activities. Only in its recent history had that started to change.

"If both your parents went missing?" Dean wondered, letting the sentence hang.

Wilfred's eyes lit up and an easy smile crested his face. "You don't know about the orphanage?"

Dean shook his head.

"Let me explain, then," Wilfred continued. "Min has a program in place for kids who lose their parents. One of the mega buildings back towards the start of the market, over by the main portal entrance, is actually an orphanage."

"Oh," Dean muttered, "ya know... I hadn't really given it much thought. There must be desperate parents getting trapped on the shelf all the time." He frowned, deep in thought. "Exactly the kind of situation, where you'd think a single token from a kid to free their parent should be allowed."

Wilfred winced at Dean's statement. "Such is not the case. The orphanage is amazing, though. Zayra and I attended class together, grew close over the years, and set out on our own adventures when the time came. There are hosting programs, for those who don't want to chance the competitions, where planets will take Mixonia born refugees and help them stabilize. Since we can reenter the city without any portal issues, we have an advantage." Wilfred stared off into the distance, revisiting a memory.

"Yeah," Dean grinned, "my first trainer and one of my girlfriends was born here. Makes it so much easier. How long since you left the orphanage to get to this point?"

"Six years, and it wasn't easy. There was always something keeping us from getting to our goal of fifty tokens. Rent wasn't bad for our little one bedroom, planet side. Three months of rent will only get you one night here, though. Kinda crazy how expensive Mixonia is," Wilfred scoffed. "Feels good to have a soul retrieval specialist hired and to finally be trying our luck in the games. The only way to afford anything around here is to take risks."

Dean bobbed his head, pretending to understand, but decided to come clean. "I've not spent a gem in here, besides tokens in the vault. I have a big estate back home, and what I used to think was plenty of money." Hopefully they'd get their lack of funds situation fixed soon.

He looked back at his new friend. "What's your plan from here? Free her parents?"

"Yes, though technically we could unlock Zayra's folks already, but then we'd be broke and at risk of falling into the same situation they were in. After this, we were thinking about signing on with a guild." He frowned, "Maybe. Depends on how today goes."

"Why a guild?" Dean wondered.

"We've been training. We each unlocked a magic. I have water and a stun spell, and Zayra has fire. The years may have been tough, but they were anything but boring. We figured we're finally ready. Six years of building up our endurance, knowledge, and training. The problem is or was, rather, that we only have so much information about the maze. A guild can make us better. Get a few hundred tokens on our lockets and flee for the stars in luxury, with enough to raise a family." He shrugged, "a guild can help us do that."

Dean shook his head. "We'll beat their offer and give you a fair contract. But you'll need to reside on Oakley. That is, assuming you pass a background check, and are willing to sign a contract with Cassandra. We happen to be recruiting, but largely in the same boat as you guys—lower leveled and improving. We have mounts, trainers, and are building up our safety net."

"Well, that's mighty nice. I'm sure Zayra would like to at least give it a look," Wilfred said with a nod. "She and Patti seemed to be getting along."

"Since you're born here, it makes paying you easier too. We had a jam at our portal with a squatter. Fixed now," he grunted, "but left everyone on edge about being too trusting."

"What's your population control like there?"

"What? Like, can you have babies?"

"Yes. Joobi, the planet we saved up our tokens on, well, they had population controls in place. I take it from your reaction to mean that you don't. We'd need to study the local laws and rules. And there is -"

Dean paused him with a hand in the air, "By all means, take your time. We're planning on doing solo stuff for the next few days. But... Cassandra can guide you through all of that. Assuming the newborn is -"

"Newborn?" A chipper Zayra exclaimed, rushing over with a one on her token.

"This polite, and oddly kind human is offering us a position in his guild. Says he'll beat the other recruiting guilds' offers," Wilfred said.

Dean nodded to confirm.

"I think it's worth looking into something more niche."

"And there's a baby!" Zayra said and Wilfred gave a smug chuckle.

"You've doomed me. Doomed me, I tell you," the unicorn man groaned, leaving for the Minotaur guard.

"Patti seems nice. Looks great for just having had a baby," Zayra said with an 'I approve' nod.

Dean's eyes widened. "Oh, no, it's not Patti's baby. She just got out of a short term relationship. Leena is my little girl with my fiancé, Cassandra." Her eyes glazed over, not understanding who that was. "How was your first floor?"

"Five feet out from the starting area rested a locket. Years of schooling told us to be overly cautious. While I believe them, they were obviously not talking about the first floor," she snorted.

Dean grinned at her antics.

"A guild, huh? Why are you running a guild?" Zayra asked, scratching at the tight leather of her bodice.

"Well, to save our planet, for starters. Also, because we're trying to offer something different." He shrugged. "Mainly, I guess, because I'm different. Never been big on money or fancy things, happiness always came first," Dean said nonchalantly. "But there are organized operations that may offer more of a regimented operation, if that's what you're needing. We only have so much to offer; we're just starting out."

"As they say on Joobi, fancy me interested. That big lug over there is a sap for little ones. We've dreamed of three things: freeing my parents; starting a family; and, finding a worthy place to call home. Did you win the lottery to have your child –"

"Ah, no, it was much easier than that," he laughed. "We just had a baby. Actually, on Oakley, you get money from the government for having babies. They fuel the economy –"

"You get paid for having babies?!" She squeaked, biting her bottom lip while she considered it. "Oh, Wilfred is so going to get it. I told him to come over and meet Patti and he groaned, and now this. Yes!" Zayra fist pumped and smirked. "Going to win so many arguments with this ammunition."

Dean chuckled at her enthusiasm. Patti showed up with a winning smile and plopped down on the seat beside Zayra. "Oh, that was easy, killed some ugly looking thing—like a swamp hag or something. Didn't have to, but also didn't want to risk it casting some spell on me when I turned my back on it. An arrow to the neck did the trick, got her on the second shot. I'm getting better," Patti grinned, running her hands through her loose brown hair. "So what's new?"

Dean nodded at Zayra. "I offered them a room if they want to come home with us, as a potential long-term thing, even. Seems they're in-between places. Zayra will catch you up," Dean said over his shoulder after grabbing his duffel. He headed for the portal and the Minotaur guard. "I'm going to go continue on through level four, and then we can head over to the market. Make sure you figure out how they can visit our home."

Patti cheerfully extended a thumbs up. His horse figurine in his hand and his bag over his shoulder, Dean palmed the Oath stone.

"Dean Forrester, floor two, and I understand the consequences," Dean said. The portal shifted just a tiny shade of green.

Here we go, once more into the breach.

∞∞∞∞

. . .

Dean entered the second floor to find himself in a closet. *Hmm, okay.* He opened his duffel and pulled out a medium shield and his short trident. Those two he leaned against the wall while he dug around in the bag for his short sword. He attached the weapon with a leather clasp to his left hip, securing it tightly. He secured his shield on his left arm and picked up the short trident in his right hand. Apache's figurine went back in the bag, since he was a big horse, and wouldn't fit indoors.

I need to get a big dog, or some sort of indoor type pet. It was obvious that Apache would be useless in some scenarios. Dean walked forward carefully to the door.

His hand grasped the golden nob, giving it a twist. The hinges *creaked* with his slow inward pull. He peeked out through the opening to see a study. Books lined numerous shelves, their spines etched with titles in a foreign language. A large desk built for some massive creature occupied the main space.

The back of a chair faced him. He could hear a voice reading passages of text out loud in a guttural language. Dean couldn't see who owned this room, but it was clear that they were much larger than him. He spied no gleam or glint of gold. With a frown, he slipped from the closet to another door to his right. His steps were stealthily placed. He caught a glimpse of the reader's arm, enough to see volcanic black skin.

Without giving the scene another glance he crept out into the hallway. There, in the middle of the corridor, not three feet away, stood the locket on a statue of a demonic being. Dean slipped the locket off the creature's neck and pressed it to the indent.

∞∞∞

When he returned to Mixonia, he saw Patti and Wilfred joyfully chatting. Dean turned for the Minotaur guard before noticing he had a 3 on his locket. He trotted over to Patti, with Apache's figurine under his arm and the duffle on his back.

"Here ya go, be right back," Dean said, handing over his tokens. Patti merged them with those already on her locket.

"Well out with it," Patti said, clearly in a good mood.

"Was some boss level demon. Snuck past it and claimed the prize," Dean said with a smile.

"Wait. You're not going to believe this. A naga lady with big breasts came by," Patti said, rolling her eyes. "She claimed to be from the bank and offered to take our tokens back to Mixonia Banking Plus. Since Min doesn't allow deceitful practices for legitimate businesses, Wilfred called her out." She snorted. "There is no 'Mixonia Banking Plus'. I know how trusting you can be, especially when juicy boobs are involved—"

"Hey! I'm... okay, guilty as charged. But Cassie doesn't have massive rockets. Thanks. Maybe we can go to the market after this next level. Nine tokens is a lot," Dean said.

Patti small clapped for him having done the math correctly.

Wilfred showed Dean a 4 on his locket. "This is a lot, we can help you with the shopping, if you'd like. Zayra's little sister is a guide there. She'd be double thrilled to give us a tour. Costs a little bit, but well worth it. Or you could just use us as guides."

"You have a brother?" Patti asked with a raised brow.

Wilfred smirked and shook his head no. The Osamar started to reply when Dean interrupted. "Okay, this first, then the market next. Back in a bit."

That seemed to be enough and he trotted back for the Minotaur guard who ignored him. He stuck his hand on the swearing stone and said.

"Dean Forrester, floor three, and I understand the consequences," Dean said.

The portal was pink this time. The screen transitioned into a green that was closer to the last shade he remembered. He stepped into the portal, ready to face the next challenge.

☺☺☺

There was angry, hoarse chatter, not far away.

"Egam, I need the fish," the voice said.

Dean saw that he was on the edge of a five-foot cliff. The area surrounding him was a mix of rolling grass with clumps of trees that were segregated by a small, dirty river. The rocks were slime covered, the grass knee-high, and the trees big and red.

Two ugly creatures argued over a fish they'd caught in a net. They were thin, brown, and had wrinkled, gnarled faces—Goblin-like, but taller than a dwarf. Both wore a ratty cloth tucked between their legs that seemed oversized on their scrawny bodies.

Hobgoblins? Probably. Where's the locket? Hmm.

Dean scanned around for the telltale glint of gold, with no luck. The problem was that directly behind him was the portal, which cut off his ability to search to the sides. The only direction he could go, was toward the two creatures. Dean shrugged, leveled his right palm at one of his enemies, and waited. Things were about to escalate.

"Larnisssss... I neeedssss thisss," Egam said.

Larnis scoffed, clutching his trophy tighter. "Don't start talking like a baby Egam."

"That's why I need this fish. Think of my wife and kids," Egam moaned with a pout.

"You don't have any kids and I'm not giving this to you," Larnis said, stomping a foot.

This triggered Egam and he dove at Larnis. The two tumbled about in a flurry of legs and elbows. Dean knew this was the right moment. He leveled his right palm at the entangled targets and unleashed a dozen small energy orbs.

Two blasts would've been enough. The entangled bodies, fighting over a fish, were caught completely unawares. The initial energy bolts tore into Larnis, who was on top. His skin sucked in as the energy bolts tore through him. Bits of gore and bone tore forward, slashing into Egam. The bodies convulsed as the powerful blasts ripped them apart.

His barrage had been way too much, and Dean winced at the carnage. He hopped down off the ledge and turned around to check the sides of the portal.

Ah, that is why I didn't see you earlier. Tucked into the cliff itself, was the locket. Technically when they were busy fighting, he could have passed the floor with ease and avoided any conflict. He liked that the mazes were challenging, in more than a simple pew-pew kind of way.

A quick indent into the locket slot and he was ready to go to the market with easy tokens to spend.

CHAPTER

SIX

Mixonia

Patti was laughing hysterically at something Zayra had said. When Dean approached, she handed over the locket with a six on it. He combined the two lockets and tossed it around his neck where it vanished from sight.

The ladies kept chatting with crossed legs conducive to not having balls. Dean stuck his hand to the podium to see his latest stats.

Champion Information
Name: Dean Forrester Gender: Male
Level: 4 Tokens: 9
Race: Human Alignment: Suca – Mixonia
Luck: 16 Charisma: 41

Health: 344 / 344 H-Regen: 1.0 / Sec
Stamina: 294 / 294 M-Regen: 1.0 / Sec
Mana: 329 / 329 S-Regen: 1.0 / Sec

Strength: 212 Vitality: 132
Dexterity: 107 Endurance: 187
Intelligence: 99 Willpower: 230
Magic Electrical

.   .   .

Hmm... His intelligence had gone up a few points and his willpower increased by one. *I wonder if it's from using magic,* he mused.

"I take it Wilfred is still inside?" Dean asked.

Patti nodded and said, "We're going to run one more, right now, while you wait. Zayra has a freedom broker on standby to pop her out of Min's Vault. Since you're out here, mind if I go ahead and do level three?"

"Yeah I can wait, I would love to have a bit more leeway. Oh, on my third floor, I faced some combat. Nothing major. I killed two hobgoblins or something close to a tall goblin," Dean said, shrugging while dropping onto the bench with a *thud* and a sigh. "I should study up on the species the maze spawns."

"Green or brown?" Zayra asked.

He thought about it for a moment, "Brown."

"Mud Goblin probably, they have brittle bones and are horrid fighters. They tend to go for a tackle and then they'll punch you, but your face is stronger than their bones, so they render themselves useless," Zayra said, crooking her arm so Patti could link arms with her. "Jessabee will have some good tomes, filled with Min's creature descriptions she can show you in the market. It's a good idea to start learning about all the potential challenges you may face in the maze. Back in a moment." Zayra shifted to look at Patti. "You ready?"

"You bet I am," Patti said happily, accepting the offered arm.

The two would have skipped away if Patti hadn't been burdened with a bag of gear. Dean sat there waiting, watching his surroundings. A woman with fins under her elbow approached, gesturing at the spot on the bench beside Dean. He patted the seat letting her know that it was okay to sit down beside him.

Her breasts aren't that big, he thought. He realized this was probably the con artist Naga. Her legs had scales, but they were still legs.

"I'd asksss if you need any healingsss, but you seem okay. I'll just waitsss here for the next poor sap that needsss an emergency heal," the naga said politely, folding her hands in her lap.

Dean saw her forked tongue and understood that maybe this was a different lady. "I take it you're not here to fleece me of tokens for a fake bank?"

There was a hissing laugh and she replied, "Heavensss no. Just your tokensss to sssspare your life."

"Dean," Dean said, sticking a hand out in introduction. She pulled his hand up to her face and kissed his knuckles, like a knight would a lady.

"Ulinia, the pleasure's all mine, champion Dean."

Dean pulled his hand back to see a joyful Wilfred exit the portal.

"Where's the girls?" he wondered, "And hello Ulinia." He clearly recognized the Naga.

"Getting floor three done, and I just met Ulinia. She's a healer. Which we happen to be in need of. Charming lady," Dean smiled and she winked at him while getting up.

"A healer this time, really, interesting. Care to show your stats?" Wilfred said pointing at the stat podium.

Ulinia ignored him while walking away. Clearly, she realized it was time to move on. Dean grunted, confused by the interaction. That was life, not everything was clean and clear.

"Not sure what her play was, this time, but you were the con. Nagas get a bad rap, but they're literally snakes. I'll let you in on a secret since you've been a good talking partner and seem sincere; it's hard to lie to an Osamar," Wilfred grinned and pointed at his horn.

Dean looked at the horn in confusion. It was barely a full hand-length long and if you stared intently at it you could see a faint coloration in it, like a rainbow. Peering closely, he noticed thousands of tiny holes barely visible to the naked eye.

"Are those pores in your horn?" Dean asked, squinting a bit to see.

Were those some sort of lie detector? I guess that was what he was hinting at.

"Something like that. Anyway, I take it you need a healer?" the Osamar asked.

Dean nodded and said, "Eventually. I was told to look for either a Naga or a Siren."

"Did a lady recommend them?" Wilfred asked and Dean thought of Sable. He nodded.

"Then they must not want you getting tied to a Dryad. Better healers and gentler souls," Wilfred nodded. "And fantastic mothers. They only mate under contract and their contracts almost always have them stabilizing to be nannies or mommas."

"Ha! Cassie would love that," Dean said with a slightly grouchy tone. "She's probably already picked one up from the hiring market and is heading with her back to the house."

"Patti said you sent a friend away," Wilfred prodded, changing the subject.

Dean sighed, not really wanting to talk about Quincy.

"You okay?"

"Patti's ex is my best friend," Dean said, "It's just..."

"I take it you're upset at the situation. I get it," Wilfred paused, looking for the right words, "you're an alpha type—and don't like to lose. We can shift to talking about winning, if you'd like. If the girls both come out, we'll both be at twelve tokens. For us…" His grin was infectious, you could see the joy in his eyes as he thought about the rewards. "This will mean new beginnings. What's next for you?"

"I was thinking about trying the PvP event," Dean said, pointing over at the shimmering blue portal in the distance.

"You're not aquatic, most of us aren't, which is why that is the least used portal here. The payouts suck for the amount of time you put into it and the risks taken." Wilfred paused and pointed to the Solo PvP. "In there, if you level up to say, level eleven, you get paid for each floor. You go in for twelve, ace a competitor, and come out with eighty tokens. You'd have to beat twelve levels in a row in the event to get that, though," Wilfred explained and it clicked for Dean.

He groaned realizing why PvP Events were so much less rewarding—since they were chained, you couldn't come out after every level.

"Doing the first six levels would only get me thirty tokens, plus the rewards from those I defeat. Not as tempting as regular PvP," Dean groaned.

"Sure but… there is less of a chance you'd fight anyone. In theory anyway. Which would be eighteen easy tokens. Especially if you blitz the floors." He grimaced. "I'm not going to risk it, though. I'd maybe think about attempting it if we had hundreds of tokens saved up in a reserve, but not until then."

Dean nodded, that made sense.

Wilfred pointed to the team PvP portal, "Best to head there first. Actually, any and all of these competitions are great at our levels. It's easy money. Just need to have a rescue plan. Always have a rescue plan. That was drilled into us from a young age; hence why we saved for so long."

"I think that is the point of this place, get you hooked on the high life, live lavishly, and then crush you when you extend just a little too far. Ah! Here they come," Dean said standing for the girls. "So?"

"I had to jump over a wall with poisonous vines. My health regen was greater than the drain, but it got my heart pumping when a flying cat chased me," Patti said, frowning at her healed hands.

"Parrapurr," Zayra nodded, tapping on her chin in thought, "they're easy enough. I had to go through a basic maze and use my flame wall on a spider nest. It seems the challenges are no longer 'here's your free stuff'. They have some sort of… well, challenge."

"Shall we head to the Market? I'd like to meet this Jelonia lady," Dean said.

Patti rolled her eyes at him. "Jessabee," Wilfred grinned. "Good try, though. She's a looker, but it seems your heart is closed."

Patti scrunched her face up and snorted, "Dean? Nope. Man's always going to have a full bed. He just lost a babe.... Well, about a week ago. Wasn't exactly Dean's type, though. Probably Cassandra's."

"Ah, the ladies get to pick who comes and who goes, I like that... ouch," Wilfred grunted, getting slugged in the arm by Zayra. "Oh, Dean was getting conned. Not sure what sob story she was going to use this time, but Ulinia was setting him up to make her move. The lesson here is, no Nagas."

"Yeah, yeah, yeah," Dean said in a teasing manner. "Alright. Off to the market."

"So... What exactly are we looking for?" Zayra asked.

"I want to get a periscope," Dean said and Patti gave him a funny look. "You know, those eye thingies you use to see farther, kind of like binoculars, but with one lens —the kind that pirates used." When she nodded in understanding, he continued.

"I'd also like to get a dog, or something like a dog—an indoor combat type pet, some javelins, health and mana potions, medical kits, cheap horses, books, and whatever else strikes my fancy," Dean admitted, joining the others who were already on their feet.

"Spyglass is a much better term," Patti snickered, wagging a finger at Dean. "But it did remind me of water. We can't forget to look into spear guns and a crossbow, too,".

Wilfred led the way down the connector from the portal staging area back to Mixonia's mainland. He led the way, talking over his shoulder as he went. "Joobi is the planet we came from. There they had advanced technology—energy weapons, plasma generators, and virtual worlds you could dive into with the push of a button."

They followed after him.

"Here," the Osamar shrugged, "all that is gone. It's... well, weird is the best way to put it. Spear guns are okay and can be used in the maze, with a few caveats. The same caveats hold for crossbows, as well as dwarven blunderbusses. All of them have to be manually reloaded, which requires you have a strength level that matches the rarity of the weapon. More importantly though, they take a lot of time to reload."

Patti frowned, hearing this.

"Technically it's not fair, because a mage can fling ten fireballs in a matter of seconds, but those are the rules. One use, then slow reloads. If someone buys a crossbow, takes it back to their Mixonia home and tweaks it to auto fire. It reverts inside. At least, that's what we were taught. So tuck away your ideas of advanced weaponry."

"So just carry five crossbows around?" Patti wondered. She shrugged, which forced her to readjust her duffle on her shoulder.

"That is the best workaround we've heard about," Zayra replied, offering to help but Patti declined. "As for a dog pet," she grinned at Dean, "you're in for a rare treat."

Dean raised an eyebrow and took the bait, "Why's that?"

They had entered Mixonia's main thoroughfare. The street was crowded, the boisterous hubbub of aliens talking over each other making it hard to carry on with their conversation. Dean followed closely behind Wilfred, the group going single file for a bit since talking was so difficult. After Min's Vault, the crowd thinned out a bit, allowing a bit more space for them to walk in pairs.

Now that there was less congestion Dean noticed fewer street vendors, but more businesses had opened their doors. These were general stores with food, clothing, and other basic needs on display. Occasionally, he'd spot an adventuring specialty store, but they were rare—compared to the large numbers of service shops like bars, inns, banks, and such. The majority were packed with people.

Dean always felt a big city vibe down here. When one added in the towering city structures, Mixonia made him feel small. Unable to talk much, he tried to spot the street cleaners. After a bit of effort, he noticed small teams of young people, policing garbage into bins.

Overhead, the prostitutes were far easier to spot. They were regulated to balconies, many with colorful banners hanging down. Most brothels advertised 'a good time' for between ten to thirty ruby coins or between thirty to fifty sapphire chips.

Dean frowned, realizing he'd failed to spend any time in the city itself and was therefore unaccustomed to how it operated. There were notes posted on business fronts, hooker ads, and vendor carts. Many claimed to provide the best rates on direct token exchanges.

That made more sense to Dean than the ever changing gem rates. Why any society would elect to use three currencies, made no sense at all.

When his eyes finally stopped noticing everything around them, Zayra noticed. She'd been waiting to reply to his question about dogs.

"There are thousands of species here from thousands and thousands of planets. Think of all the animal choices you have on your planet, and multiply that by several hundred," Zayra said with a smile tugging at the corner of her mouth. "This will be an eye-opener for you. While growing up around here, I would often walk the market and dream of a day like today." She smiled at Wilfred and pulled him in for a hug. "Funny how when you set a goal and focus on it, your dreams can come true."

Wilfred happily hoisted his wife and twirled her expertly around, never missing a step forward. "I'm excited. So excited," he laughed, "What should we get?"

"Baby stuff!" Zayra cheered and Wilfred rolled his eyes. "I tease. We should save what we earned today. I'd love to unlock my parents."

"Well, these two are onto something. We'll need to be better prepared as we attempt higher levels." Wilfred frowned, "Maybe we should focus on the team stuff, for now, to get around that, but –"

Dean cleared his throat to interrupt, "Yeah, as for team gear, we probably already have a lot of the basic stuff. Anoka stockpiled a lot of things and the big Oakley managers will probably have gear we can borrow, with some proper planning. Eventually, we're wanting to establish a full gear set, you can roll into the portal on a cart."

"Ah, so the carts have to be spawned in the staging area, to prevent road blockage. Otherwise you have to use bags to get everything there. You can make multiple trips, but that usually means a storage locker. Storage lockers are... magical," Wilfred said, pausing to point out a sign that read 'Storage' in large block print. There was an entrance below the sign, with a staircase that led down.

"What my husband is saying is that below street level, there are instanced storage places. There is some kind of an annual fee that Min charges for their use. For us, it was not worth it. For a guild, though, with lots of items, it's almost always a necessity. It costs a few tokens, I think, but I'm not certain," Zayra said.

Dean grunted at this information, then glared as he was forced to dodge a trotting team of bird people running the opposite direction. As quick as they came, with all their squawking to get by, they were gone again. The crowd that had parted to make way for the flock went back to flowing normally in the street. Their group returned to walking four abreast.

"I was thinking of renting an apartment to store all our stuff and have as a rendezvous point. The problem is all our contracts state we can't stay inside Mixonia for more than six hours per trip, when not competing. So it'd be useless, besides for you two," Dean thought for a moment, "and a few others."

"Storage," they both said in unison. Wilfred gestured for Zayra to go ahead and she said, "Annual guild storage is only a couple of tokens. You'd eat that in a single month for an apartment. Min wants planet dwellers to stay outside of Mixonia, to help with congestion. Just use the storage location as a meeting point, if you get lost."

Wilfred nodded with more to input and said, "Although I love the place I was born and raised... I already miss technology. So if your home is advanced, we'd want to stay there anyway. Especially if it is peaceful, with stuff to do."

"We had to pacify the area, first, but we're good now," Dean said with a smile. He noticed they were approaching the business district.

Signs directed them to the most diverse market in the universe. Now that was something Dean could believe. Unlike with Sable's hurried initial tour, this time around he noticed the buildings had specific purposes.

Mixonia Armor Smithy, Weapons of Mix, Breeders United, Alchemy Mixonia.

The building signs continued on like this the length of the street. If Dean had to guess, there must be massive factories in place to produce what the market sold. *Breeders United* threw him for a loop, though, because that had to be done on planets. He didn't want to begin to contemplate how much of a headache cross breeding was.

If he wanted to breed Apache with a beautiful mare, he might have to go to different planets to do so; which probably meant using people born in Mixonia as intermediaries. While his mind chased down the rabbit hole of the logistics involved with pet farming, the massive market loomed in the distance.

A quick turn off the main street left Dean confused. Wilfred led them into the side entrance of a massive building. Above the arched doorway was a sign that read '*Market Guides R' Us*'. Wilfred grunted as he opened one of the two glass doors for them. They stepped into a lobby with dark granite flooring, a big reception desk, and a multitude of side doors.

Zayra walked up to the receptionist like she owned the place. An older lizard man in a black uniform smiled politely, and asked, "May I help you?"

"Private tour, for Jessabee Kilmead," Zayra said, flipping a thumb at the attendant. "Dean, hand him your Bearclays."

Dean hesitated. "How much for the guide?"

"How would you be paying, sir? And for how long?" the desk attendant asked politely.

"Token direct and four hours," Dean said, estimating the time.

The lizard man nodded and said, "Point zero three."

Dean was okay with that price. He handed over his necklace and the attendant returned his locket with *11.97* engraved on it. *Okay, that seemed fair.*

"If you could please wait over there," he said and pointed to a set of couches Dean had missed earlier, "she'll be down shortly."

Customers entered, went to the front desk, but generally asked for no one specific. A waiting tour guide agent, stationed behind the teller, would walk them out. There was, thankfully, no elevator music to cringe through as they waited, passing the time with small talk. A few minutes later, Jessabee entered the lobby from a side room.

Jessabee was shorter than her sister, with a bigger chest, flat stomach, and wide hips. Pretty much exactly how the rest of her species looked—curvy and sexy. She had fine brown hair, pulled back into dual ponytails. Her eyes were different, and only when she came closer did Dean notice they were rainbow colored. She caught him getting lost in the coloration.

"Ah, a newbie to Mixonia. I'm Jessabee, and these are what all Osamar eyes look like." She nodded at her sister and brother-in-law, "They're wearing contacts because our eyes tend to distract folks from our other features," Jessabee said running a hand down her exquisite body.

Of course, Dean followed her gesture with his eyes, seeing that she was in walking shoes, her long, toned legs leading up to a mid-thigh skirt. Her striped blazer was buttoned tightly—though it revealed her midriff, it struggled valiantly to hide her large breasts. It fooled no one and was probably a professional type look. Her horn was smaller than Wilfred's.

As beautiful as she was, Zayra was the less pretty of the sisters. Harsh, Dean thought, but true.

"You've got me for four hours, where to?" Jessabee asked and Dean bit back a sexual retort.

"I'm Dean. This is Patti. I was thinking about looking for some pets, first, and gauging the market. I can get a nice stallion for about 1.2 tokens at home. Show quality. I would expect the average mare is about, what? .08 tokens, I think?" Dean asked questioningly, turning to look at Patti.

"Uh, not bad, actually, but I'd wager Cassie has it down better," Patti smirked as Jessabee led them out the door.

"Follow me," she instructed. "Mares are about half that here, but the ultimate stallions can go for as much as ten tokens. You don't happen to have –"

Dean held up a finger to pause her while he dug Apache's figurine out of his bag. This kept the group from leaving. Jessabee didn't mind. She smiled, "Good, I can spawn him here, the building is coded to allow for interior spawns—for trades and such. Most prefer this way to the totem displays."

He handed over Apache's figurine, which Jessabee set on the ground. Everyone stepped back as the magic converted the figurine into the horse. Apache was confused, at first, until he saw Dean, which resulted in the big lug asking for a snack.

"He doesn't need this," Jessabee said, messing with the bridle. She kept the face harness on but undid the bit. "Also yes, a very, very fine stallion. This is... he is... unique. Did you want to stud him?"

"Uh... sure. We need the income and while I love competing with him, I –"

Her startled squawk gave him pause.

"No, no, and more no! Zayra, how could you let him do that? Dean, this is a prancer. Look at him. More importantly, look at them," Jessabee pointed to the group of onlookers that was steadily growing. "You can see their eyes flaring with thoughts of how many tokens he might cost. No," her gaze scolded him, "he is a pet. Sorry, one stab and he'll bolt. You're lucky you came to me."

Dean was conflicted. Deep down, he'd thought Apache was a warrior. Also, Anoka and Kambry had seen the stallion, and they never said a thing. Then again, they weren't that big on pets. Maybe he needed a pet advisor?

One he could oggle and drool over... that would be exactly what he needed.

"Uh... sure," Dean said, giving her a smirk and a shrug. Jessabee gave four light boops on Apache's nose and the horse returned to a figurine with a swirl of magic.

"Ah," Dean nodded, "so that's how that works."

"I have the power to do it here," Jessabee said, heading again for the door, "part of my employment contract. Anyway, his black coat and white fetlocks will mean he'll be highly sought after." The gorgeous Osamar sighed wistfully, "the good life, right sis?"

"Hey, don't be jealous, you keep trying to date males your age. I got lucky," Zayra quipped.

Wilfred rolled his eyes and held the door open for them. "Here we go," he muttered as Dean passed him.

Dean held a hand out for his stallion's figurine and instead received a contract. Jessabee kept walking away, Apache's figurine still tucked under her arm. The girls stuck sisterly noses up at each other, before wry smirks changed to a loving hug.

A slight chuckle escaped his lips, seeing their sibling rivalry in action.

"Standard agreement. I showcase the client—in this case, your horse—for a month. I'll take only a ten percent commission, since you came in with my sister. At the end of the month, you'll get your horse back, along with 90% of the profits he's made, minus any feed costs. There are no other boarding costs, and feed is super cheap here," Jessabee said quickly, leading them toward the expansive market.

Dean looked over the contract and sighed. "But I'll need a mount for competing with," he grumped.

"Dean, where do you think I'm taking you to? This horse is meant for breeding. Do you have more with a closeness to him?" she asked.

"Uh... Yeah, probably thousands could be purchased. You tell my guy what you want, he has a database you can select from," Dean said with a shrug. "Or I can show you."

"Advanced planet. Makes sense, surprised Zayra hasn't asked for a room, yet." Jessabee snickered, "She's always hunting for a nice place to call home with no baby restrictions."

"She's touring our place, soon," Dean admitted, seeing Zayra stick her tongue out at her sister. "Oakley has no breeding restrictions, and we'll pay them to fight for the planet. Won't be much, admittedly, but our taxes are low and our rules are few."

"Oh, really? No wonder she's beaming with that smile. Wait... Did you guys finally compete?" Jessabee asked, eyes wide.

Zayra's eyes lit up and she nodded with a wide grin. She flipped a thumb at the necklace Wilfred proudly displayed.

"Twelve! Today was the big day. Was going to take you to lunch to share the news... but we made some friends and got you some work, instead," Wilfred grinned, stepping out of the way of a large male with a rhino's horn.

"Whoa, I'm so proud of you! Did you visit Mom and Dad before handing off the tokens to the broker?" Jessabee asked, her upbeat tone dimming slightly.

"Yes, they're proud of us, and hope one day to find a quiet place, once we free them. Which all leads back to this Oakley planet that Patti has been telling us about. Lots of luxuries, lots of space, and twelve tokens would all but make us rich there!" Zayra beamed, barely containing her excitement.

"Easy babe, we've yet to see the place, need to review the contract, and will want to sleep on it. We're not irrational Osamar," Wilfred said, scooping her up in a hug and spinning her around again.

The younger sister smiled at their happiness. "You think Mom and Dad would retire there?" Jessabee wondered.

"They're young. Only a few years older than me at this point. Who knows?" Zayra shrugged. She squeezed her hubby. "Again, there are a lot of variables we'll need to get ahead of."

Jessabee nodded, deep in thought.

They finally arrived at the market's entry point. There was a bit of a line—a Minotaur guard let one person enter for every person who exited. The line went by fairly quickly, even though they had to wait for five visitors in-a-row to leave before being let in as a group.

The soft roar of chatter, negotiations, and a general swirl of activity greeted them as they started shopping. Dean's eyes shifted unconsciously to Jessabee's wide hips and juicy booty. Patti gave him an elbow him and he smirked.

"Finally," Dean said, soaking in the sights. "Time to find out what wonders the market holds."

CHAPTER

SEVEN

DEAN

Mixonia Market

"Get yer potions!"

"Famous Specter Canines! Two for one!"

"Need a training partner, we got ya covered. Dummy trainers right here!"

The vendors' callouts persisted with mighty shouts cresting the constant droning noise of the market. Jessabee snuggled up to Dean so he could hear her. "Sorry, it gets loud in here, stay close."

There was no way they'd be able to walk side-by-side in this environment. He wasn't sure if her sudden stops were to let him bump into her, or just her being overly cautious. At least she had a juicy booty, for impact support, of course. Dean gently grabbed her hand, pulling her back into him. She blushed at their proximity when he stared down into her rainbow eyes.

Damn, she's pretty. Losing focus here, quickly.

"I need to..." Dean said, sighing when he looked around. He'd already lost Patti and the others. When he caught sight of them, he dragged Jessabee by the hand and powered through the crowd to them. He split the necklace, giving Patti six tokens to spend.

"Thanks, Dean, I'll meet you at home," Patti said, loud enough for him to hear. "I'll be fine."

Dean nodded. This time, he was the one who was tugged away by the smirking unicorn girl. She weaved and snaked through the mass of bodies for almost five minutes. Her pace was fast, her destination certain. It was like she was on a mission.

Dean let her earn her fee as she kept them in the fast flowing walking section in the middle. He tried to spy on the vendors lined up along the sides of the lane, but soon gave up. It was partly due to the crowd. The other factor was that Dean was no longer a towering human among humans. A lot of these aliens were taller than him. He wasn't used to not being able to see over everyone's heads.

She led him to a central point, where there was an open food court. Hundreds, if not thousands, of tables populated an open section with no roofing. Large pillars supported the market's climb into the air. Dean noticed a railing that extended around the upper floors, which let people look down upon the large central fountain that a host of children frolicked in.

Between the outer edge of the market and the fountain, stood a long row of back to back food kiosks, preparing and selling everything Dean could imagine, from fish, to tofu and soy protein, to cheeses, even bugs. This was diversity at its finest. A sight that brought a smile to his face, seeing its uniqueness.

The crowd was a bit smaller here, and the din less intrusive. Dean's puzzled face gave away the fact that he was confused by the sudden change in noise levels.

"Food and drinks are seriously up charged here. You can sit down in a restaurant for cheaper than this vendor slop. Basically, most people come here to this place in the market for two reasons—a bit of quiet and the lifts," Jessabee pointed to a lift. "Follow me. Sorry. I normally do a scripted bit, where I explain everything and carefully listen to your needs. But I don't see Zayra too often. I broke up with my ex, Royer, who kinda kept us apart. He was controlling and hated traveling to Joobi."

She paused, waiting for Dean's response. He was focused on the sight of the kids having fun in the fountain. He missed his family at that moment. He'd love to bring Cassandra here, the scene was just so wholesome.

"You there, Dean?" she chuckled, waving a hand in front of his face.

"Just had a baby and really find myself missing her, that's all," Dean admitted with a shrug.

"Well, I'm glad you got an escape clause in place. My parents were dumb, not to have a backup plan, stranding us like they did. Your grumpy face is giving you away Dean," Jessabee snickered, and he frowned, patting her shoulder.

"I'm a softy, we'll free your parents. Assuming your sister and Wilfred sign on to Team Ola. Me, well, I have wealth-making conversions available on Oakley. Diamonds are worth five times rubies, give or take. That, and I already have two wives who have more determination than funds. It'd take less than twenty-five days. Hopefully," Dean admitted.

They approached one of the lifts—an elevator without walls. It descended to their level and aliens poured off the platform. They jammed in close, to go up.

"A harem man," Jessabee smirked, "that means you're a rare catch. Surprised you only have the two, if your planet is anything close to what you've teased my sister with. Mixonian women want stability. It's so flipping rare to find a hunky male worth pursuing." She tucked a loose hair behind her ear and stared intently at him.

Dean almost felt like he'd cast her under a spell or something. Sure, he had it easy with the ladies, but this was a tad different. Maybe Mixonia really was that bad for a single woman.

"I've noticed that you like what you see," she murmured, pressed in close against Dean on the lift, "and not once have you touched me back, or returned my subtle hints. Rare, indeed."

Her breath tickled against his neck.

"Also, it's not common for there to be a wide expansive planet with plenty of room on the other side of the portals. Most places are densely populated and space is super valuable, or the species are hideous, or the laws just suck," Jessabee rambled nervously. "Anyway, it's nice to see my sister so excited about the opportunity you are giving them. I can't remember when I've seen her so happy." She paused, peering up at him. "Safety and a place to raise a family, it's something I've craved for a long time."

The elevator stopped on the second floor. Jessabee didn't move so Dean stayed put.

"Oakley is amazing. I wouldn't leave it for anything, really—even for immortality. I guess I'd call it my ideal home. I just need a fishing vacation, every now and then, to retreat to." He sighed, longing for the familiar feel of a rod and reel in his hand.

He changed the topic back to their objective. "What floor are we going to?" Dean asked.

"I was afraid you'd say something like that. My parents and half the desperate folk struggling to afford Mixonia would flock to this Oakley. May I visit with my sister?" Jessabee asked, her chin tucked in, batting her eyelashes at him.

"To what end?" he wondered.

"I'd like to see where she might live; and more than simple envy. Who knows? I might want to rent a room or something. I can return here and work every day, and that'd mean more funds I could save up." She paused, looking thoughtful, "What does a token get you on Oakley?"

"A year of shitty wages, give or take," Dean said and she gulped. "Yeah, you'd be able to buy your own house in a few months. My house, which is an estate... well, it was a rundown tavern in a very undesirable area before we fixed it up. There are a bunch of desert dwellings in need of fixing up, the market is saturated with pioneers who abandoned their homes or died in the Outback. We paid about a token—give or take."

She fidgeted nervously while her eyes fluttered, making calculations. "You didn't answer my question. May I come to visit?"

He could see the timid excitement in her eyes. "Visit? Yeah, that's fine, I'm going home right after this. But you'll have to deal with my wife, Cassie, about your contract. Or Mistress Cassandra, if you want in on her good graces."

Jessabee beamed.

"What floor are we getting off at?" Dean asked again.

"Sixth, the Breeders Guild is mostly up there. Do you know the market rules?" the pretty guide asked.

Dean shook his head.

"Ages ago," Jessabee continued, "Min got tired of being an arbitrator for bad deals. Legend says it was awful," the unicorn girl shuddered. "I can only imagine the shady trading practices that probably went on before the rules were enforced."

She pointed to a sign in front of a display of casks as they went past. "You will find that there are three prices on display. The average price, Min magically calculates based on recent transactions for that type of item, along with a high and a low quote. Merchants can't ask you for more than the high quote, you can't ask for less than the low. If you see a sexy Catomi (a cat girl) and she offers to give you a back rub for a lower price, that won't work. You pay in the range and have to do side transactions separately. So..."

"I can go in fairly certain of what to expect, then. Should I be using tokens?" Dean asked and she gave him a thumbs up. He huffed and said, "You act like you've met a human or two before."

"A few that were in the orphanage," she nodded. "They got out before I did. From New Mexas, or something like that." She turned to look up a floor or two, and frowned.

"When you hire a guide, you normally do so to get in and out of the market as quickly as possible with a specific item. Well, that, and to understand how this place operates. There are thousands of vendors here and most champions want to buy what they need at the lowest price." She paused. "I'm going to take you to the most expensive place for what you want," she admitted.

"Umm... may I ask why?" Dean pursed his lips, as they finally rose above the fifth floor.

"Why I'm herding you to the expensive stuff?"

He smiled at her pun.

"Well, pet lives are important, but at the same time, when they die, they die forever —unlike champions. So, be prepared to spend a bit more to get a pet worth buying... but don't overspend. Anyhow, I know a guy who has a great selection and..." she wiggled Apache's figurine, "will absolutely drool all over this stud."

"Well, I'll need a damn good contract to ensure I get him back, along with a big, trained mount to replace him with," Dean said with a sour face.

He liked Apache. Then again, the likelihood of the big horse getting killed didn't sit well with Dean. *What was that old saying?* He mused, *if you love something, give it a harem and set it free? That's a motto I could get behind.* He chuckled to himself.

Jessabee turned to look up at him, quirking an eyebrow. He shook his head.

"I need javelins or short spears... oh, about this long." He held his hands about shoulder width apart—his broad shoulder width, that is. "As well as a tool to see further with, like a spy glass, medical supplies, potions, and then books to study up on the Maze's monsters."

"Well, when I leave you to haggle with Kriem, you can take your time. I can buy all that stuff for you. If you don't like what I get, we can always swap it out afterwards. I'm legally bound to handle your tokens responsibly, and cannot pilfer them or profit from any transaction by taking a cut or kickbacks from the merchant."

Dean nodded.

"A lot of my clients come in, check out my body, and then send me to come fetch stuff for them." She snorted disparagingly. "The market is beneath most of the elite folk who reside here."

"It's a nice body," Dean grinned at her. "I haven't seen an ugly Osamar, yet—almost as pretty as an Elf."

Jessabee pouted. "I do believe that is the first time a male has been not only direct but also honest—and then said that I'm second best. Follow me," she tugged on his hand with a twinkle in her eye. They had arrived on the sixth floor.

Dean was shocked by all the shoppers; he'd figured this high up, the market would be less congested. No, it was crammed full of aliens shuffling forward, shoulder to shoulder, occasionally peeling off from the flow to deal with the vendors. At the first series of booths he passed by, there was a scattering of vendors selling a host of general items.

Dean saw a spear vendor off to his right and tugged Jessabee behind him. The shop owner was waving bye to a customer as he approached.

The vendor was a mix of some forest creature and humanoid. Not like a Dryad, though, something more akin to a gnarled tree-person. They wore no shirt and a leaf barely covered its privates. Probably a nudist.

Dean shifted around to get a good look at the weapons. There were lances, spears, pikes, and even tridents. But no javelins, unfortunately.

"Hey, give a girl a warning before you divert like that. Hi, Grosca," Jessabee waved to the vendor. "This is Dean. Do you have any throwing spears?"

"One moment," Grosca said, reaching down to grab a box from under a table. "I keep them down here in a box, because I prefer to display the higher priced stuff. These are all a fraction of a token." He gestured at the box of javelins. "The sturdier ones won't break as easily, but I recommend sharpening the points, often."

"You have a spear gun or crossbow?" Dean asked, testing the weight of a sturdy looking trident.

"This trident here is good in water. Half a token, made with rare materials, so it should serve ya well—until you start to face harder creatures. Not challenging creatures, literally harder," Grosca noted, hefting the trident.

"Ah, got two of those already. I was hoping for a javelin set and a quiver," Dean admitted and Grosca frowned.

"Not sure if you've been in the games much, but throwing sharp sticks is less effective than fireballs. The only time I recommend it, is when you use the small dwarven powder-kegs attached to one end, to blow up bunkered enemies or reduce stalwart defenses. In those cases, you'd want a trash javelin, though it's probably better just to throw the powder-kegs from your hand."

"What you're saying equates to never using a bow," Dean frowned and Grosca shrugged. "Thank you for your time."

Dean left, sticking close to Jessabee. There wasn't much to say, really, so he kept quiet. Well, that, and it was really hard to carry on a conversation in the middle of the crowd. He followed close behind her as she darted ahead. She'd occasionally glance back over her shoulder, whipping her dual brown ponytails around, to see that he was still trailing her. The booths they passed displayed animal figurines of all sorts.

There were creatures on the shelves that left him mystified as to how they moved. The bloated two-legged giraffes instantly sent his mind spinning. He was starting to get overwhelmed when he ran into Jessabee's back. He grunted and started to apologize when she shimmied her rear against his crotch.

"This way," she said with a wink. He smirked. Deep down, he still thrived on the attention from a beautiful woman. "Okay," she continued, "do you still want javelins?"

"Yeah, I do. I've already been in at least one situation where I'd have used them. I want them uniform, though, and in a quiver that I can carry on my back," Dean said. "How much should I give you to pick up the other stuff we talked about?"

"A horse is cheaper here than on your planet, and Kriem will gladly negotiate on the side. For the books, a spyglass, and medical stuff, along with some mana potions..." She tapped her chin. "No more than two tokens are what I'll need," she said and Dean broke his locket in two—the one he kept still had 3.97 engraved on it.

"That's Kriem," she pointed, "the gnome with the goggles on his forehead. Good guy. Just waiting for him to notice me. And... we're good."

Kriem was two booths over and shifted their way. He wore a bomber jacket, everything below his waist was obscured by the table.

"Sorry, was covering down for Messa," the gnome started up in a nasal voice, "what can I—"

Jessabee handed over Apache's figurine to the stunned vendor. His eyes shot quickly from the horse to Dean.

"Thought you'd like to talk to this fine gentleman about this. I'll be back soon," Jessabee said. In less than ten seconds, she had disappeared into the crowd.

The gnome walked over to a station behind him, waving Dean into his booth. There was a totem pole at the station, with a flat platform on top, about two feet tall. The wooden wings of an eagle sprouted along its sides. The gnome placed Apache's figurine on the platform and crossed his arms.

A magical, lifelike rendering of his friend generated above the figurine. There were statistics, information boxes, and even his desired food types were listed here. Dean was blown away by the image.

"Ah," the gnome nodded, "you specifically bred for power, then went back to a healthy standard. Smart, and not common enough. Jessabee was correct. I do like your stallion. We don't get many, if any, humans here. I think your government must lock down your portals, or something, to keep out the traders and the general population." He snorted. "There used to be a bunch of humans who would come in. I traded often with them, then nothing." Kriem muttered to himself. "You're going to make a pretty penny flipping horses, I'd wager."

"Is there a daily import limit?" Dean asked.

"Yeah, a token." He snorted. "I see your eyes spinning calculations, so... Yes, that counts towards your portal limit. There is a limit increase, available if you run a booth, after eight days. Your portal limit goes from one up to five, but you have to reach at least six tokens in trade in that period. Basically, unless you're running a trading operation, you're limited to one token per portal—regardless of the medium of exchange." He grinned. "Figuring out the best ratios of what to trade can be tough."

Dean chewed on the inside of his cheek.

"On my planet," the gnome continued, "rubies and sapphires are expensive, along with horses. We produce ale quite cheaply, though, a stout draft that is savored here in Mixonia. So, I roll barrels of brew in by the five token load each day, once I'm stocked up on inventory." He paused. "Enough of my prattling, though, what did you want to sell the stud for?"

"Uh... I use him. In battle," Dean said flatly.

"This says he spooks easily," Kriem tapped on the display, incredulous. "Have you seen him fight?" He even popped his goggles against his forehead with a 'you're full of shit' look.

Dean scratched at the back of his neck before replying. "I work him up and off he goes. We haven't actually fought, yet. I like him, even if he's not a fighter, he's a damn good horse. What does Min say he's worth?"

"Low three to high three. What'd ya get him for?"

"One token and a half—give or take," Dean said. "So... double, huh? Well, damn. Do those totems work –?"

"Outside of Mixonia? Nope. Sorry." The gnome grinned at him. "Would make life a lot easier for traders, wouldn't it? This breed will sell well because of the hair on his fetlocks. It's rare to find, even among the breeders, and is a distinct trait. It also has far more applications at home. I can understand he's a friend. Let me contract him for a day. When I'm done, he'll show up in your portal waiting area on your planet."

Dean rubbed his chin.

"Rate is showing .1 to .2, so I'll offer ya .15 for a day of stud service... feed included. I'll return him as is, or in better condition. My magic sense is telling me how long one of your days is, so that should be plenty of time to get his samples frozen and return him to you."

Dean paced back and forth a few times. "He's family now. If he wasn't, I'd sell him for that price in a heartbeat. Tell you this, though," he shook his head. "Not getting close to any more horses. How would that work, anyway? Would the additional fund commitment reject my gem exchange over the next few days?"

"Min has magic tracking, so yeah. There are items that are always going to be worth more than one token. If you brought in a ten gem ruby, for example, it wouldn't break such a valuable gem into ten little chunks, it'd just count against your limit for ten days," the gnome shrugged and Dean nodded.

Kriem removed his goggles and set them on the bench while studying Apache with a handheld magnifying glass. Dean left him to his work while inspecting the shelves of pets he had on display for sale. His eyes hovered over the predators. Cats, the whole first section was cats.

Dean rolled his eyes. Cats were self-centered assholes. He could just imagine being pinned under a rock, desperate for help, and having the cat take off to give itself a bath. Maybe these monster sized ones were different. He doubted it, though.

He shifted further down the line to check out the dragons. Honest to god dragons! He picked a dragon's figurine up off the shelf and set it on an open totem.

Dwarf Dragon - Female. Age - 8 months. Weight - 192 pounds. Length - 7'. Height - 4'. Coloration - Green with Stripes of gold. Pros - Great eyesight and smell. Lethal predator with serrated teeth. Capable of ice magic. Cons - Temperamental. Horrible hearing. Prone to deviate or chase simple prey. Lacks restraint.

While Dean stood at the totem, fascinated with the information, Kriem cleared his throat.

"That is the best pet in the universe – some will say. I tend to think there are better ones available for much cheaper. It should include the cost, as a Con. That girl isn't fully grown, yet, she's got another five years before reaching maturity. She also is lime green and gold, so she all but glows in the dark. Oh," he chuckled, "temperamental means she's a right asshole. Despite all that, she's still a hundred and thirty-three tokens," Kriem said and Dean blanched and bit at his nail.

"But it has magic, and is a weapon unto itself," Dean muttered, enthralled.

"This stud is three tokens. A fine beast, not a fighter, but... I think you knew that going in. A good trainer, definitely. That dragon can sniff traps, detect things in the dark, and use magic to buy you some time. She'll also bite you, and might even eat you, if you become mortally wounded. At least at that age and without a bond."

"A bond?" Dean asked.

The gnome nodded. "Bond helps you control them—but it kills the pet when you die. Sad." He shook his head. "Oh, and you're done if she sees a rat running into the enemy position you're sneaking up on."

Dean put the figurine back with a sigh.

"I've got three perfect pets for you," Kriem continued. "Dolphin, it's cheap while also being reliable, and easily replaced. We're talking .1 to .2 tokens per figurine. It'll see you as the boss when it spawns next to you. It wants to please you, so it will get sent to a breeding farm—best reward you can give a pet that's served you well." He nodded to himself. "Well, that, or set it free before it succumbs to the games. Remember, if you die, it dies."

Dean nodded.

"Next, you've got your generic horse. Smaller, no frills, and faster. Also a great pet. I've got ten thousand of these back in storage. They're literally a use and forget. The only thing keeping them alive instead of becoming protein is Min's magic, which lets them sit in storage as a figurine, instead of getting diced up."

Dean was surprised to hear that.

"Finally," the gnome slapped his hands together, "the ankylosaurus. Its -"

Dean's eyes shot wide open. "Ankylosaurus? As in, the dinosaur?" he blurted out.

"Ah, Mins magic explains many things, and normally translates a lot better. I didn't know these categorical species were on your planet of origin. You will notice, after a while, that all life looks fairly similar. Well, there are some sentient creatures, such as house cats on my own planet—though I guess to you they would appear really fluffy, and more like a fox, sorry." Kriem chuckled. "Point is, you get used to seeing things repeatedly. Bears, for example, come in a thousand variations, but they..." the Gnome paused to emphasize his point, "are still bears."

"There are many creatures to use as pets. An ankylosaurus is loving, sweet, and compassionate to its owner. It's also a savage asshole to those it faces. Yet it'll respond well to commands, can be ridden in a pinch, but is partially blind and nearly deaf. It has no jumping skills whatsoever—just forget about taking it up the stairs. What else. Oh, yeah, decent reproduction, I guess, but at these prices... why bother? They're only .1 to .2 per.

"I'd recommend those three specific species for you. After all, they're so cheap. If they die down a gorge or are sacrificed so you can make it to the portal or locket, so be it."

"I can just keep them here in storage?" Dean asked.

"Long term, yea, but getting to know your pets helps. Sadder when they die on you, but it helps. That dwarf dragon, for example, would need a few days of being hand fed to not attack you. To do that there are a couple of options." He ticked them off on his stubby fingers. "The training ground here in Mixonia is one—you can just purchase rental time. It's not too expensive, but it adds up. Or two, you take them home with you. Just know that Min doesn't waste magic on transforming animals. You'll have a dinosaur in your yard, if you take one home with you. What do you think?" Kriem asked, finishing with a polite smile.

"That I want a fookin dragon," Dean smirked, "But... I'm a pragmatist. Since I'm not taking anything home tonight, though, I can sleep on it." He handed over the horse figurine. "That's a 'Yes' to renting out Apache for the stud fee. We need every bit we can earn. That doesn't count towards my daily token generation, does it?" Dean asked.

Kriem put his hands on his hips and shook his head no. "It counts when redeemed —in this case, when the animal is returned to you."

"Do you have a book on pets I could buy?" Dean asked and the gnome shifted around to dig into a bag behind him.

".1 token. Books are handwritten and never instant duplicated—so please treat this like the hidden treasure it is," Kriem said, handing over the book.

Dean gave him his locket and the number changed to *3.87* tokens. He felt good about the exchange, the book in his hands. "Thank you for this, and I'll talk it over with my other champions as to what pets I should pick."

"If I'm not here, Maxy will be, she's also a Gnome. Thanks for shopping with me, and I hope to see you again. Apache will be returned, safely, that I promise," Kriem said and they stood awkwardly.

"I'll... uh... just browse through the dragons while I wait for Jessabee to come back," Dean said, already heading back to that section.

He was jonesing for an awesome pet. An ankylosaur or ankylosaurus is a great idea. Though that means a no to bridges, gaps, stealth, and well... it wasn't a dragon. I just need to find a pet who doesn't cost me as much as six deaths.

None of the dwarf dragons called out to him though. He looked each of them over. It was one hundred tokens for some of the cheaper ones, and as much as four hundred for the breeding stock. Two hundred, on average, for the fighters. Three hundred tokens for excellent fighters. When Dean crunched the numbers, they were a worthy investment. If he did floors forty through forty-five... that was an above-average dragon.

Not to mention, pets weren't counted against their numbers and his whole team could utilize a roaming pet. Then there was dragon breeding, which was a serious business in its own right. He was just about to ask about their cycles, when Jessabee showed up, her arms loaded down with packages.

He rushed to help unburden her of the supplies. She dumped it all on the ground, so he could start stuffing things into his duffle. While he worked, she talked.

"Sorry," she stretched her arms out over her head, which did wonders for her amazing rack.

Dean couldn't help but stare.

"The local wizard is strutting his stuff on the bottom floor," Jessabee said with flustered red cheeks, "causing a jam. He's trying to find his lost lover or some such nonsense." She shook out her hair and redid her pony tails. "Only problem is, he has enough sway that he's not shooed off by the guards, or booed off by the locals."

Dean grabbed the quiver full of javelins and set them over his back, next to the duffel. "What was the mage saying?"

"It's Thero," she sighed, and Dean's eyes widened. "He's offering a reward for his lost love, Anoka, and her daughter."

"A reward you say?" Dean asked, a gleam in his eyes. "For what?"

"Just for information. You okay?" Jessabee asked, concerned.

He nodded and grinned cheekily. "Fair maiden, I've got an hour or two left. Take me to this Thero, if you would."

A plan had started to form in his brain that triggered an inner, evil cackle—though outwardly, he was calm and smooth as he followed Jessabee to go meet the villainous mage.

CHAPTER
EIGHT
DEAN

Mixonia Market

"Fair people of Mixonia, I seek Lady Anoka. One month of training for any -"

"No one wants your training old man, ya have our attention because there may be a token reward that will send us out hunting for Anoka," a white-haired, wrinkly old woman shouted up at the man on the stage.

Dean looked to the stage and saw a human man, who looked to be in his middle years. He had a cape dashingly draped over his shoulders and a black leather set of armor, tightly fitted to his average body. There was a gnarled old staff that he leaned on, as if he needed the support. He flashed the crowd a fake, condescending smile, which revealed he was not entirely human. His fangs were long, which led Dean to notice his clawed nails, and long, thin fingers.

Probably some species of vampire—a literal blood sucker. I so need to get my hands on a tome of species. It's stupid that I haven't at least seen a slide show overview, or something.

Dean nudged Jessabee. He had to shift his big, filled bag to get close enough to murmur in her ear. "Go tell him you have a client who will provide contract information about –"

"Wait you know the women he is talking about?"

"Yeah," Dean said. "Anoka is my friend, and her daughter, Kambry, is one of my wives. I thought I told you that?"

427

Jessabee's eyes widened before blurting out, "No, you only talked about a Mistress Cassandra. I know Kambry, we slung drinks together at the Tootsie Tails for a year. She'll cut your dick off if you betray her."

"Ugh, woman, the last thing I want to do is betray Kambry. I want to extort him." He ground his teeth. "I could kill him from here, but I don't think Min would like that." Dean muttered this last bit under his breath.

"Min never gets directly involved in anything. The Demis would keep your soul in timeout, though, and it'd take you forever to reach the shelves." She narrowed her eyes at him. "I need you to promise you're not going to kill Thero—Kambry would scalp me!" Jessabee leveled a finger at him until he nodded. She sighed and then continued, "This is my way in. Say nothing until I have him on the hook. We'll go to a private meeting room to deal with him—I need you to promise to stay cool."

"Like cool as in no expression? Or cool, like cool..." Dean said, going very casual.

She rolled her eyes, already pushing towards the front of the crowd. Her hand was scribbling a contract onto her tablet as she approached Thero.

"No tokens, if I said tokens, the lot of you would go crazy and then I'd have to waste even more time hashing things out. The goal of my being up here is for someone to hear me and..." Thero paused when Jessabee handed him a contract. "Now that," the mage grinned, "is how you get tokens. Thank you, fine folks of Mixonia, for your time and attention." There was a long exhale of happiness as traffic picked up once again.

Dean lugged the duffle behind Jessabee, wishing he'd simply tossed it in storage about an hour ago. They were heading for the market's exit, and he hurried to keep up—just another set of bodies on their way out of the chaos that was the market. If Dean had been claustrophobic, this city would drive him crazy. The moment they left the market, space opened up around them, mainly because the line kept folks in this area stacked neatly to the side.

While Dean was curious as to what the contract had said, he was also amused when five more mages joined the group. They surrounded Thero like a protection detail, as the group walked to the main road. Jessabee and Thero were talking quickly, ignoring the others. Occasionally, a glance over one of the mage's shoulders would be shot his way.

The way Dean understood the portals was that you had to be invited to go to a specific planet. Which made sense to him. Even if Thero could finagle his way to get to Oakley, he'd still have to hit Riva's checkpoints and safety nets. Dean had seen those auto turrets. You wouldn't be casting a fireball to melt those things in time. Technology would easily win the day.

I get some easy tokens out of him, he gets closure, and the girls can move on. Jessabee would've recommended a different course of action, if I was super off base.

He told himself all this as they walked between the looming buildings. Dean used the time to wave back at the brothel girls waving at him. A turquoise skinned woman with tentacle hair shot him a wink and he smirked. The ladies were mostly nude, and Dean saw there were ladders to get to their balconies.

I wonder why Min doesn't allow more lifts? Seems a shame to keep everything so archaic. Not like they are lacking for power.

When Dean bounced his eyebrows at a bunny babe who'd flashed him, he almost missed his turn. Not his fault, really! Okay, maybe just a little. He'd hoped she might squeak a tit at him. He detoured around a gaggle of Oruk to catch up, just as the group went into a massive gray building. A sign was etched into the stone above an entryway so big, it held four glass doors.

Mixonia Magic and More

When Dean crossed the threshold, he thought he'd gone to a wizardry school. Rows of pedestals supported busts of supposedly important mages, carved in stone. Plaques and staffs were attached to the sculptures, telling Dean stuff he didn't care to learn about. A group of youngsters, none of them older than fifteen, were clumped in a group, as if waiting for a tour. He struggled not to gape, as he saw the first human he didn't already recognize.

"Sir," an attendant said from beside Dean. He shifted his attention to a humanoid male, with furry goat legs and curved ram's horns. "May I take your bag? I promise it will be kept safe behind the counter."

"Those orphans?" Dean asked nodding at the group of soon to be adults. The goatman rolled his head, not his eyes.

"Hey... human," Thero growled, the moment Dean handed off his bag. "This way. For what I'm paying you, you shouldn't keep me waiting."

"Is that an orphanage class?" Dean asked again, not budging.

"How the flip should I know? This building houses hundreds of schools," Thero sneered, flashing his fangs. "Get over here."

Dean ignored Thero and went right up to the human kid. The other students parted for him as he came closer.

Right, I'm hulking around in battle armor. Best I take this off.

Dean popped his helmet off and stuffed it under his arm. "First other human I've seen," he said, "Name's Dean. Got a simple question for ya. You an orphan?"

The young man spun around and pointed to his chest. Dean nodded at the lad.

"No sir, my parents were born here. They work over at the training grounds, running a vendor's kiosk. Best milkshakes around," the lad said proudly.

"That was all, thanks for your time," Dean said, turning to see Thero impatiently waiting for him.

The Vampire scoffed, "A hero type, just my luck." Without another word, he stormed up a stairwell. Up they went for what felt like an eternity.

The only thing that made it worth it, was that Jessabee purposely gave him an up skirt booty snapshot. Dean wasn't stupid, he knew when a woman was interested in him.

He was confused, though. He'd openly admitted to having two wives already, and while he wasn't actually scorning her advances, he wasn't encouraging them, either. Then again, she did catch him checking out her amazing ass in a thong. He had yet to have the 'there are a ton of sexy babes in Mixonia' talk with Cassandra.

Not like she didn't know. He was sure Patti had given her an earful about bunny girls. Then there was Orabel, if she'd been to go see her, she'd find another hot bodied babe, just an elf instead of a unicorn girl. Not to mention, Kambry was super fine.

Yeah, he figured Cassandra knew about all the hot monster girls. Kambry had probably told her all about it, too.

His thoughts were interrupted when they finally exited onto what must have been floor three thousand.

If I had to climb those stairs every day, I might just jump out and take the 25 token respawn instead of tromping all the way back down. Fook me! Who has an office like this? The daily commute is ridiculous.

"What a view," Jessabee noted, walking up to a slightly tinted glass window at the end of a hall. All Dean could see was the drab gray building across from him. He gave a mental 'oh', realizing she was pandering to Thero's ego, more than being sincere.

"In here please," Thero said, opening a door to a meeting room. Inside, there was another Osamar, who immediately smiled at seeing Jessabee. "No flirting Hann, stay focused. Jessabee, so help me, this better be worth the thirty tokens I just spent."

Score! I'm so getting laid by Kambry tonight! She is going to give me, like, three babies for this. At least three. His grin stretched from ear to ear with these thoughts.

"Don't start bellyaching. The contract is clear. You will get your tokens back if my client doesn't –"

"Where is Anoka?" Thero demanded, before Dean could even sit.

The door closed and Dean dropped down into a chair. Pasting on a fake smile he replied, "On a human planet, helping the Suca defeat the Core."

"That's one," Jessabee noted, standing directly behind Dean. Her hot breath hit his right ear as she whispered, "He gets two more questions, unless he wants to pay more, for more information. If there is a follow on to a question, though, because your answer isn't true, then he is allowed to ask it."

"Which human planet?" Thero asked sadly. He'd deflated at this news.

"Oakley," Dean admitted. While he despised the Vampire across from him, he knew the way to win this situation was to stay calm.

"Is she happy?" Thero asked, tapping at the conference room table, his intense stare deflected off Dean without a care.

"Yes, she is doing what she loves. She is surrounded by those she cherishes and her life is advancing in a direction she wants."

Hann set a finger in the air. "Vague, but true. Why limited truths?" Thero started to speak but Hann let Dean answer first.

"Because that is the extent of my knowledge. I can only go off what I know. She smiles a lot, never complains, and is never upset. So, yes, I believe she is happy."

"Technically you asked three. Last question," Jessabee said.

"An extra five tokens to deliver this message?" Thero stuck a note on the table and Dean was handed a contract. He approved. "Good. Last question: who freed Kambry?"

"I did," Dean shrugged, sending Thero into a rage.

Thero snarled and squinted at Dean with eyes that had turned a deep red. The snarling and peeled back teeth were enough to tell him Thero had not been expecting this answer. A fireball blasted out of his hand with unbridled emotions and a scream of vengeance. The flying inferno froze halfway between them.

Dean expected a god to reveal themselves or some sort of explanation. Instead, as if a god had snapped a finger, everything vanished.

There was a whoosh of air and Dean found himself outside the PvP Solo gate. His duffle was on his back and his locket shined. There was *44.87* engraved on the surface.

Bonus! I bet I got paid the fine for his transgression. But why am I here?

When Thero spawned with shaking hate beside him, it made sense. If they wanted to fight, this was the place to do it. Jessabee arrived, along with Hann, though she shrieked from the transition.

"What in the unholy hells was that?" Jessabee hollered.

"You, me, inside. Ten tokens plus your respawn just to let me kill you," Thero seethed. Rage consumed him as his fingers danced between various magic spells.

Dean stayed calm, understanding that out here, he was protected.

"Twenty tokens plus the respawn, and you can try—I won't just lay down and let you kill me."

"Ha! Measly tokens, done," Thero said with a confident snarl. "What's your highest PvP floor?"

"Uh... zero."

Thero snickered in delight, his evil laugh lifting his cheeks and exposing his fangs. "You dense retard, there is no floor zero. Killing you will be the perfect way to sate my anger, I'll be on floor one."

Jessabee went to Dean's side. "You're probably going to lose and he'll kill you slowly—probably by draining your blood—but... Holy shit! Kambry is going to be ecstatic. You pumped him for a whole lot of tokens before dying. Sorry," she offered him a meek smile, "I'm sure you'll do fine."

"Jessabee, you're cute. Love the pink thong, by the way," Dean said with a confident wink. "Contract me to pop me free if I lose, and if not to return my tokens upon exit."

She tapped away at her tablet and added the remaining .34 from her earlier shopping spree back to his locket. It now read *65.21*. She handed him the contract.

"There is a lot to this," Dean grunted, confronted with nearly a full page of text. "Can't it be a simple contract?"

"I wish. You're going to house my sister... and me, I hope. And let us live lavish lives." She batted her eyelashes at him. "Trust me when I say, I'm popping your fine, handsome ass out from Min's Vault, and that I cannot steal from you." Jessabee said excitedly, "Kambry is going to give you a hundred Kubras for this. That girl is not one to let go of a grudge. Now hurry up and get in there, before he can set up too many traps."

"Traps?"

"Newb," Hann snorted, shaking his head. "At least I don't have to worry about you winning. If you did, Thero would lose his flipping mind and I'd need to find a new employer."

Dean dumped his duffle bag in the grass. Grabbing the smaller trident and a buckler, he trotted towards the Minotaur.

"Hand, give the oath, state your floor," the Minotaur said.

Dean shifted the weapon to his shield hand, to lay his hand on the Oath stone. "Floor one, I Dean Forrester assume and understand all risks," Dean said and the Minotaur thumbed the dark green portal. Dean jogged in, not sure what to expect.

∞∞∞

Dean materialized at the outer edge of a grassy field. In the center, rested a small mound with a pedestal at the tip. Dean couldn't see if there was a locket because Thero stood in the way. The Vampire spun around in circles, trying to see him arrive.

When his gaze slid right over Dean, he frowned. *He should have seen me.* Dean scanned around him, not finding anywhere to hide. There was only shin-high grass, everywhere he looked.

Out of the corner of his eye, he noticed that he was translucent, though shifting to become more solid, rapidly.

Must be a safety mechanism, probably to avoid spawn camping upon materialization. If it is, though, one thing is certain—my time is almost up.

Dean did the best thing he could think of. He leveled his palm at Thero, charging the magic inside himself. He instantly became visible, having begun his preparations for combat.

The budding energy begged to be set free. Dean's body coursed with power, the magic surging within him. He readied his spell with a wide, wicked grin on his face.

Thero saw him and spun around, his snarl turning to shock as a lance of energy burst out of Dean's palm. The mage panicked with a poorly timed dive. The energy beam caught Thero in the shoulder, with an impact so great that it sent the mage tumbling ass over apex, flipping him over the back side of the mound.

A tremendous scream ripped the air. "If you die after I exit, does that count?" Dean hollered as he approached. "Be great if it did."

"No mage..." There were grunts of pain from the far side of the mound. Above Dean, a storm swirled, dark clouds blocking out the sky. Icicles rained down from above, seeking his weak spots. He lifted his shield high to let the shards pelt into his protection. The clang and the bangs stopped quickly and the bright light blasted away the faltering spell. "No mage... Should..."

Thick wet coughs from the other side of the mound told Dean that Thero had a lung full of blood.

Dean crouch walked behind his shield, approaching the only cover available to hide behind. His peeking eyes noticed the pedestal was missing the locket. Dean sighed in frustration.

A glint of red and orange instinctively forced him to duck his face behind his shield. Thero's fireball spun towards his body, only to crash against the podium.

433

Dean heard more coughing—a body-racking, hacking cough that warmed his heart. The noise told him where his opponent suffered.

He readied his trident, walking slowly for Thero. When the coughing never slowed, he went for it. With the weapon cocked back he used a quick peek to aim. The trident lanced forward, crossing the distance in a fraction of a moment.

The triple barbs dug into the vampire's forearm and shoulder. Dean had caught him trying to cover his mouth to mute his cough.

"What..." Cough. "Are you?"

Dean saw Thero's chest starting to knit back together. He leveled his palm and lanced the other arm off. The way Dean understood magic, no arms meant no spells. Thero's scream was so loud, it made Dean's ears ring. The knife at his belt came out.

His victim squirmed, worming away from the pool of blood he had been resting in. His foe desperately kicked to put some distance between himself and Dean.

"You're so fooking pathetic," Dean snarled, letting his darker side out. "Now sit still, so I can enjoy this."

Tired of Thero getting away, he applied a knee to the side of his head, holding him still. The Vampire's eyes flared open when he saw the smooth curved knife in Dean's hand. With precision, Dean carved open Thero's cheek in a gruesome fashion. The side of the Vampire's face became a gore stricken mess. The exposed muscles bled freely, the bleached white of his teeth contrasting sharply with all that red.

This was nothing to Dean. When you've cleaned, gutted, and skinned over a thousand fish, cutting away some flesh was simple. With the cheek missing, he plunged the knife down between the teeth until the vampire propped his mouth open, to avoid the stabs. Dean slid his knife over the tongue, finally cutting off the strident screams.

"Gurgling is so much easier to put up with," Dean said, patting the mage on his forehead. He noticed that the regeneration had stopped. "I take it that when you stop healing, it means you're going to die?"

Thero whimpered. Dean ignored the armless mage.

"Kambry is family. Anoka is family. Ya... don't... fook... with my family." Dean punctuated each word with a stab of his knife into the mage. "I'm not some simpleton ya get to bully. In here?" Dean said, spreading his arms wide. "You are nothing to me."

He spit on the ground, right in front of Thero's face. "I'll make ya a fool's promise. I'll forget about you, if you forget about me and mine. Cross me again, though, and I'll make it so you never get –"

The sound of sizzling arrived a mere fraction before orange and red colors crashed against the side of Dean's face. Dean cried out in pain as his face melted. He rolled and put his shield up between himself and the direction the spell had come from.

"I'm coming!" Hann shouted, rushing in to protect Thero.

Dean opened his one working eye to see Hann holding a thick shield with golden inlay and black coverings. The Osamar was charging the mound. Dean leveled his palm, allowing crackling energy to dance between his fingertips before he sent two small orbs up high. Hann flung his shield up to deflect the attack.

With a smirk on his face, Dean sent a beam of energy lancing through the Osamar's exposed legs. The beam seared Hann's left leg clean off, and got halfway through the right before sizzling to a halt. Hann let out a cry of agony. His body slammed into the grass in a roll. The audible *snap* of his partially severed leg reverberated across the field.

"So much for one on one," Dean muttered.

He walked over to where Thero was still sputtering red flecks of foam, drowning in his own blood. The Vampire's vision was already glazing over. Dean leveled his palm at the arrogant prick. Energy crackled and he drilled a hole through his opponent's forehead.

A fireball arched his way from the downed Hann. It smashed ineffectively into Dean's shield.

"I'm disappointed, Hann. What ever happened to 'go team Suca'?" Dean called out, crouching behind his shield. *I wonder if I can loot his weapons.*

His other opponent only cried out in pain. Dean picked up the staff to study it. It stayed in his hand for only a few seconds before reverting back to the ground next to the dead body. *Well, shit.*

Dean searched the body while Hann continued to wail in agony. He didn't find the locket on Thero's corpse. When he finally saw the trinket, it was clasped firmly in the fist of the first arm he'd blown off. The fist was still closed firmly over its prize, so he heartlessly *broke* each of the fingers to get to the locket. The pops were loud enough that Hann noticed.

"D-don't k-kill him, please," the fool stammered. "He will terrorize us for ages."

Dean laughed cruelly. "Not my problem, asshole. Sounds like you need to find yourself a better employer. Now," Dean asked, unfazed by his foe's pleading sobs, "do you want a quick death or a slow one, like he had?"

The shield covering his opponent's torso was flung at Dean. It didn't even make it half way as a dozen small fireballs tried to catch him off guard. They soared low over the grass, eager to kill him. He caught the salvo on his shield, the force of the magic pushing him back. The smell of melting metal and wood assaulted his nostrils.

The heat overwhelmed his shield and he was forced to fling it aside. He leveled his palm at his opponent, who it appeared had had a change of heart and was surrendering, his hands up in the air. Without hesitating, Dean unleashed a full beam right in his face.

Hann closed his eyes with a smile, accepting his death as if it were a friend. His head exploded in a shower of gore across the grass behind him. Dean hurriedly scooped up the locket and went to indent before some new asshole tried to kill him. When he touched the locket to the indent, he realized something.

He probably was both special and blessed, which should make this competing thing far more interesting. His victorious laugh was cut short as he was pulled from the maze.

CHAPTER

NINE

DEAN

Oakley - Forrester-Lexso Estate

"I desperately want to see her reaction," Patti hopped on the balls of her feet with barely contained excitement.

Wilfred shook his head and spoke with dismay, "I can't believe you cut his tongue out. Actually—no offense—I'm still in shock that you won."

"Pfft, you should've seen all the lackeys berating him for another go. I'll give Thero one thing, he sure has loyal followers," Jessabee smirked, shaking her head.

The shuttle settled in for a smooth landing and Dean grinned at finally being home once again. He didn't have all that many notifications on his phone—despite the almost six hours he'd been gone—just a news alert that the plague was contained, and a message from Uncle G, saying that he was fine.

There certainly was a part of Dean that liked the quiet lifestyle without instant communication. He was relieved when he saw the shuttle Cassandra, Dorthy, and Kambry had used was parked next to them.

A quick summons revealed the *109.87* etched into his locket that Dean was so proud of. He liked to think of himself as a good guy, who'd just been helping out a family member... but things got a bit savage there at the end. Regardless, he knew this was partly about his survival as well as Team Ola's—there was no doubt these tokens would help, a lot.

Cassandra might have unlocked Orabel, but if not, he expected her to have fifty tokens left over. With this new amount, assuming Cassandra had enough to pay the bills, they could get ready to compete and start climbing the team ladder. Dean could even take a risk and do the water event. The idea of competing at the next level almost dwarfed his anxiety over how Kambry would react.

"Alright, everyone. We can put the stuff away in the morning. Let's go to the barroom. Cassie has a briefing waiting for us," Dean said, hefting his duffel over his shoulder to leave the shuttle. "Not a word, now. You all promised. Let Jessabee go –"

Jessabee was gone, she'd raced out the shuttle and into the tavern's main room. *Damn but that girl could run and that skirt defied gravity somehow.*

"She needs proper underwear," Zayra snorted and Dean snickered. Her older sister had a point, though. Jessabee's bare ass was on display her entire run, with only a pink slip of fabric tucked between her juicy butt cheeks.

He shook the image off as he adjusted his bag on his shoulder, remembering how he'd been hounded the whole way out of Mixonia about how easy it would have been to open a storage locker. He could open Team Ola's storage later.

He worried briefly about what this victory might mean for the future. There was very little Thero's goons could do besides toss obscenities at him in Mixonia. He'd just have to be extra careful about keeping tabs on the master mage's location before entering the PvP portal.

There was no doubt about it, though, Dean was happy to be home. His mini adventure had twisted into far more than he'd anticipated.

Patti started to ask, "How do you think –?" When the front door jumped with a loud *crash.*

"Stupid fookin door handle!" Kambry screamed from the other side. Dean decided it was probably best not to be on the small staircase when she finally got the door opened.

When Kambry bested the door handle, she burst forward, leaping over the four steps in her haste. Her sudden jump left her spread-eagled mid-flight, crashing directly into a wide-eyed Dean.

He managed to catch her, but her momentum sent the two of them tumbling across the rough dirt. She clung to him, wrapping him tightly in a hug.

Definitely not angry at me for instigating, extorting, and then killing her adversary. Score!

"You're amazing!" Kambry shrieked with joy. "I can't believe it. Oh, I've got to call mom. She is going to laugh for ages. Jessabee said you cut both his arms off, and his tongue out—that he drowned in his own blood! And you brought Jessabee, too, that woman is the best! Did she tell you how we were friends? Oh... I'm so happy right now." She positively beamed at him. "What was his face like when he realized he'd lost?"

"Frozen in disbelief," Dean chuckled. "Apparently, my level zero energy beam is more than should be possible. My first shot blew his arm off at the shoulder," Dean managed to get out between the barrages of kisses.

There was a long, evil peal of laughter from Kambry. Dean tried to escape her mad cackling but she locked their lips together in a deep kiss that promised a whole night of passion. Heated passion.

"Ugh... I want you so bad right now, I'm..." She bit her lip, struggling to control her desire. "We need to talk, but after... Oh, after we talk... you're all mine!" Kambry exulted with a twinkle in her green eyes.

"How did the shopping go?" Dean asked.

"You killed Mom's stalker... the guy who sent me to the pits, and you ask about shopping? Not about how I'm going to –"

Dean tilted his head at the others.

"Right. Sorry. Forgot you're shy in public. Fine, fine. Into the Forrester Estate we go, then." Kambry wiggled first her ring, then her ass, at Dean. "Since we're bound, now, we decided to make it just the Forrester Estate. Cassie has this whole spiel planned out. We've only been home for an hour, but we've been doting on Leena the whole time. Not that she noticed. Precious thing has been sound asleep, while being passed back and forth," Kambry said with a soft chuckle. "Did you know she coos in her sleep? I can't wait until we have more."

Dean patted her on the back to give her a cue to get off. She scraped off some dirt from her clothes, getting to her feet, then helped pull him up with a strong tug. When she tried to reach for the duffle, he slung it over his shoulder. They walked up the stairs to find Lexis, waiting just inside the door with her index finger up to her lips, indicating they needed to be quiet. The view screen on the right flashed the local news while on mute. In the center of the room, the tables were pulled together for a meeting.

Cassandra walked around the corner, rocking Leena. When she saw Dean, her eyes lit up. An awkward wave told Dean she was still scared of dropping their daughter. Dean tossed the gear off to the side and stripped out of his armor. He was in a plain brown shirt and undershorts once it was all off of him. He'd tried to leave the nastiest of the gear behind, and mostly succeeded. What didn't leave, though, was the stench of adrenaline soaked sweat from wearing all that armor. He walked over to Cassandra, his arms held open for his baby. When Cassandra handed him Leena, though, she promptly started to fuss.

Shucks, no daddy time, I guess—at least not right now—probably because I stink so bad. Lexis grabbed Leena from him and slipped with her into the elevator.

Dean turned to the table to greet the gathered crew. Lonny was back, the two exchanging that manly nod that men sometimes did. Jaxon sat in a chair to the side, scribbling notes or drawing a diagram. Dorthy studied a big book she had open on the table. Kambry sat, her elbows propped on the table, rapidly texting her Mom, no doubt. Patti helped Wilfred expand the table to add their Osamar guests.

There were three new strangers Dean did not recognize. A green haired woman with small curved horns that spun a half circle behind her head. Dean saw her eyes dart longingly for the elevator, which meant she must be the second Nanny. There was also a Naga male, patiently waiting for the meeting to begin. Finally, there was a male lizardman who wore coveralls and stunk of horses.

When the table was finally rearranged, he grabbed a seat at the head, while Cassandra sat at the foot.

"Pass your winnings over please," Cassandra said politely.

Dean handed Patti his locket and she combined hers with it, proudly flashing the 111.46 at Dean. That meant she'd spent a decent amount upgrading her gear. When Cassandra received the locket she studied the number and dropped back down in her chair with a huge sigh of relief.

"Oh, this is amazing Dean. We had no real backup. This is not nearly enough, but it's a great start. Let me give Lonny the floor first, since he needs to get going," Cassandra nodded to Lonny, who stood.

"My team is active and we reached floor five in Team PvE before pausing. I... We..." He let out a frustrated sigh and squeezed his eyes shut. "We had a mishap. One of my team members killed himself. On the fifth floor, we blew through a bunch of humans—not humanoids, actual humans. There were pirate variations with silly hats, awesome parrots, and thin swords. Pretty easy to eliminate, actually. Greg, the mage in the back, calmly walked away, charged up an unstable spell, and killed himself," Lonny reported sadly.

Dean grimaced, holding up a hand. "Did Riva –?"

"Said it's on you," Lonny replied pointing to Dean.

"Hmm... So how do we cover his loss if he doesn't come out? Call it a training accident, with no body to give to the family?" Dean asked, uncaring. "Super don't want to waste tokens on an idiot—or deal with any of this mess. Plus, he can refuse to leave death behind."

"Yeah, I get that. We've got some time, though, because his contract had a privacy clause built into it. Riva said his family was killed during the orbital plague. This opened up a whole new set of issues. Anyway," Lonny pinched the bridge of his nose, "it led to a rift between Riva and me. I got a tad upset because he had assigned Greg to my team, saying he could use the wins to boost his confidence..." Lonny stopped and Dean understood.

"I'm sorry you had to experience that," Dean said, moving the conversation along. "Also, welcome back. We will facilitate getting you a replacement on your team, or we can ask Marty for a spare, who'd be a better fit."

Kambry shifted from her chair to stand behind the Dryad. "This is Olivia, everyone, our new nanny. She came highly recommended by Anoka. Mom said she even helped raise me when I was a baby," Kambry mentioned with a smile and the Dryad nodded with a terse wave at the group. "Go ahead and say something, Olivia."

"I'm Olivia, very happy to be here. This is a grand opportunity for me. I will be helping with Leena while assisting Mistress Cassandra with tending to the estate. I am a gifted healer, more so than Dorthy, who is talented in her own way. If you need me, I'm staying in room two-three. Otherwise I'll be down here helping run the estate." Olivia gave them a crisp nod.

Kambry shifted to stand behind the male Naga. "This is Rew, everyone. He is our new cook and groundskeeper-slash-handyperson," she said.

"I'm Rew," the man nodded to them. "I cooksss, cleansss, and fixesss."

That was all he said as Kambry shifted next to stand behind the lizardman. "This is Yarka. Yarka will be our pet handler."

"Can you handle dwarf dragons?" Dean asked and Yarka nodded.

Kambry raised an eyebrow at Dean and Jessabee rolled her eyes.

"Indeed, they are fairly easy. The pretty mage would need to teach them magic, though," Yarka said pointing at Dorthy, who blushed. "They are very expensive and I've only managed them once. Easy enough to do, if you've got the right pen. Which I saw out there. Again, though, they cost more than Mistress has on her collar. At least the good ones do."

That left Dean wondering how the human preserve might work as a dragon home.

"Excellent. I guess it's my turn to do some introductions," Dean said, getting up as Kambry retook her seat. Dean stepped behind Jessabee. "This is Jessabee, she worked with Kambry at one point, and is a market guru. I'd like to hire her to replace Anoka to do our daily token runs as well as being responsible for acquiring our gear and such. She is looking for a family and a place to call home." He smiled down at the blushing unicorn girl, "I hope she likes it here."

He walked behind Zayra and Wilfred before placing a hand on each of their shoulders.

"This is Zayra and Wilfred. They'd saved up fifty tokens to compete, in order to earn fifty more to free Zayra's and Jessabee's parents from the Vault. They will be joining our team, Kambry, assuming they find Oakley suitable. I'm a sap and already promised to help free and welcome their parents here. Wilfred is a hybrid melee off-tank, and Zayra is a full mage." Dean turned to Patti. "Patti, please give our newest arrivals a full tour."

Patti gave him a mock salute and headed for the front door, while the others scuffed their chairs back to join her. She was already talking while the six new recruits joined her. Dean sat back down in his chair as Cassandra stood.

"I talked with Jaxon about Orabel. She won't let me free her—it seems that you'll have to do it. Jaxon verified that an old god, one named Karlithen, wrote a prophecy before he went mad that Orabel likely thinks may involve you. Go ahead Jaxon," Cassie nodded to the three-fingered demi before taking a seat.

Jaxon put his notepad aside and stole the book Dorthy was reading. He immediately flipped it to a predetermined page. His finger traced the words until he found the spot he was looking for.

"Here we go: I write this, knowing my actions will trigger the change we all need. For too long the battle has been waged without recourse. For too long the creator sat idle on their hands. My descent into madness is but a spark of what is to come if I do not take this leap forward," Jaxon read aloud. *He looked up and cleared his throat with a cough.* "This is where Karlithen kills a Core god by tricking them. It spiraled the third age into existence."

He ducked back into the book, his eyes picking up where he'd left off.

"The ages will find balance among the species, the gods included. Happiness will reign supreme over the seventh age. Like all things, though, the balance will be tipped with enough time. The power will go in one direction too heavily—to the point that maybe my sacrifice will never be worth it. Magic was not supposed to be limitless. In essence that is all the control the creator has over us playthings. His or her infinite abilities."

"This is the part where it gets good," Jaxon noted.

"There will be an eighth age or an end to all things which means that age is one of great import. A blessed champion, with eight wives of eight different species, will free the infinite souls fueling the game of the gods. When they do so, the creator will judge them for their actions, and even I know not what may happen then.

"It is my hope that there will be a semblance of balance and a change to the nature of the games. The eighth age shall be known as the age in desperate need of a guardian. All my meditation, contemplation, and prayer has led me to these conclusions. They could all be wrong, because I feel myself slipping into madness. My mind cackles in response to my endless questioning and my soul flees in terror. I can only hope my sacrifice will bring about the peace I've foretold."

Jaxon closed the book and stared at Dean, who shrugged.

"This is accurate, Dean," Dorthy confirmed, pointing to the book. "There's a lot more than just these passages. He has been right about everything, so far. Whatever madness twisted his mind was very prophetic."

"Uh, okay," Dean frowned. "I think Min said we were in the seventh age. And they called me blessed or a fooking soul stealer from the Eelraken."

Cassandra chuckled and said, "He read that because there is a certain Elven sorceress who believes you're the champion foretold, who will have eight wives of different species." Dean raised an eyebrow at her and she sighed. "I see you brought home another beauty, who eyes you incessantly, and Orabel said that she'd be freed when you agree to make her one of the eight."

"What?" Dean said in confusion.

"You're getting a harem," Kambry said, still all smiles from earlier. "Or a bigger harem, at least. Do you want to pout and moan about it? Or bring balance to the universe and create the eighth age?"

"Ah, do I get a choice in the matter?" Dean huffed and Cassandra rolled her eyes at him.

"No." Kambry teased with a wink.

Cassandra said, "We should all make decisions like that, together. I want a couple of days, at least, to digest the news. Moving on from how big our bed is becoming. We have been given the emerald route, but that is never going to garner as much tokens to Galactic coins as the pink diamond did. That earned us so much –"

"Have a conversation with Jessabee about it," Dean said and Cassandra nodded. "She knows that market better than any of Riva's people ever will. Hell, horses are a two to one ratio, I found out."

"That'd help tremendously. Her making the daily market runs and handling your gear needs will do wonders," Cassandra said with a sincere smile and warm tone for the blushing unicorn girl. "I have been wanting to stay home more, lately. It's a lot, expecting that I'd be able to go on a twelve hour adventure, so soon after having a baby."

Lonny raised a hand and spoke up, "My team has a list of supplies we need to get. Not much."

"We have a bit of breathing room, financially speaking, since Dean brought home over a hundred tokens. I paid off our debt with Mr. Lexso. We have enough operating cash to last us a few months and when I sell these emeralds, we'll have a few million coins in the bank," Cassie reported before stopping with a grunt when she heard Leena's cries coming from the baby monitor Lexis had left behind.

Dean leaned over and turned it off.

"We need a bigger reserve. You can afford to take some risks now, though—even a full team wipe could be restored. What were you thinking of doing next Dean?" Cassandra asked.

"Uh... Fishing has been pulling at me, but I know I need to help the score. Maybe after a six hour day of training, tomorrow. Aside from that? Probably Team PvE and maybe a single run at a PvP event." He scrubbed his hands through his hair. "Can we go back to this prophecy nonsense? If I'm this Champion of Eight. What is it I'm expected to do to restore balance? Wouldn't Min just smite me for stealing their power?"

Jaxon frowned and said, "Remember when you bought the rings these ladies are wearing?" Dean nodded and Jaxon continued with a head shake. "How many of them were there on display?"

"Aw, fook me," Dean groaned, "Eight."

"That is all we know. All Min knows. They wanted to ensure Lexis would not be receiving one of those rings. Think on that for a minute," Jaxon said. "I've only scratched the surface of Karlithen's work, pre-madness. There is a certain Orabel, waiting patiently for you on her shelf, who should have even more answers. We should also be cautious, though, she has been in the vault for eons. Who knows what that does to a soul?"

"Okay, I'll visit her at some point. Did you draft a contract for her?" Dean asked his first wife, who nodded.

"Yeah, she tweaked it a fair bit. She is able to compete, but the nerfs to elves were really drastic. She said you should count on her as more of an 'at home' magician than a ticket up the charts. She said she can do wonders to the nature around here, and for us moms. She wouldn't –"

Dorthy interrupted by raising a hand and clearing her throat. "Elves have nature magic unrivaled in its power. They used to be able to spawn creations so powerful, that the games became a joke. Min was limited by what the levels allowed. When the Suca and Core gods finally came to the table to usher in a new age the damage had been done. The Elves had raced away with over ten thousand points in every contest and dominated every single one of their planets, forcing billions of Core residents to find new homes."

"So nature magic has been banned by both sides?" Dean asked, and Jaxon nodded.

"Are Elves dexterous warriors?"

"Yes," the demi nodded, "and still extremely deadly."

"Are they master mages?"

"Orabel will undoubtedly be capable of magic that would astound today's master mages," their resident Arcanist smirked. "Will getting Orabel put me out of work? I doubt it. She'll be too proud to teach magic to the average student." He held up his hands pleadingly. "She may teach Dean or some of her fellow wives, but—no

444

offense—the average human is truly beneath her status. She also will remain an Elf when she leaves Mixonia. Min's magic is nothing for the Elves to bypass."

Dean nodded and thought it over, "I'll talk to her. For now, though, we need to train. Since I have a team of five again, I want to focus on training as a team for Team PvE. We'll monitor the score and go from there."

"Okay," Cassandra nodded, "we'll have another meeting after the three Team leads figure out what they're doing. It's been a long day."

Everyone started to get up. "Tomorrow afternoon, right here," Cassandra finished. "If you can't make it, don't worry, we'll draft minutes."

"Minutes?" Kambry asked, confused.

"Notes," Cassandra replied. "Now there is a wonderful movie I'd love to watch with my family. That is all."

Dean went to flip his chair over when Kambry pulled him away.

"That can wait, upstairs with you, now. You're getting your reward." Kambry shifted to wink at Dorthy. "Dragona me," she grinned.

A white glow enveloped Dorthy's hands and she cast a flow of magic that washed over Kambry. Her body shimmered from the effect until her form transitioned to include her wings and a tail. Kambry trotted happily for the stairwell, smacking Dean's ass on the way up.

Dean wasn't sure what to expect when he arrived in his room. He was dragged into the shower where he experienced a passionate, calm, and tender Kambry. She made love to him—sweet, romantic love. Dean didn't yank on her wings or pull on her tail. He ran a hand through her hair and traced all her curves while their lips remained locked together.

When they'd climaxed twice, Cassandra joined them in the bed for a night of blessed, solid sleep.

CHAPTER

TEN

DEAN

Forrester Estate

The next morning, Dean decided to wander around. His desire to roam had nothing to with a cranky baby no one could soothe. While he was on his way to do some training, he bumped into the Osamar couple, who were nothing but smiles. The two paused in their conversation to greet him warmly.

"We love it! There is a stable. I can ride all sorts of pets there; it's about a hundred times bigger than our old apartment. There is freedom to run around and someone said a kid's park and playground is on the agenda. I saw some amazing fishing videos of the ocean with no settlements on them. The best part, though," and here Zayra's grin stretched ear to ear as she all but bounced up and down in excitement, "We can have a dozen babies!"

Wilfred bobbed his head in agreement. "I have to admit, it's a bit less advanced than Joobi, but my goodness—the open spaces on this planet are insane, and the costs are fantastic. We found a spaceship with a fabulous interior for only thirty tokens or so. We could live in it now, and then travel the stars later," Wilfred said rubbing his hands together excitedly. "Even has room for kids. You simply cannot buy a spaceship for that rate on Joobi. Not even close."

"I'm glad you're liking what you're seeing," Dean smiled at the happy couple. "There's no rush in making a decision."

They both looked at each other and nodded. Wilfred smiled and said, "Dean... we love Oakley, human bodies are not really any different than what we are used to, and we love the fact that we can earn some tokens while living here. So we're going to find Cassandra and see what she'll offer for a contract."

"She got up an hour ago; you should be able to find her in our living room. Just give a knock on our suite door. What about—"

"Jessabee is grooming horses in the barn with a girl named Candace. Seemed to be a lovely young lady. How about we meet in the training yard in about an hour? Then we can head into Mixonia." Wilfred said and Dean nodded.

"You can't compete individually for –"

"Ten days," Zayra finished for him with a shrug, "but you, Patti, and Kambry can be the portal masters and we can grind some levels as a team."

"Let's do an hour together in the training room, first, so we can cover basic formations and then we'll start off with Patti as the portal master and begin at level one —we can try for level ten," Dean thought out loud, nodding at his own words. "Good luck with Cassandra," he winked at them, "I hope you get a good deal."

When they parted ways, Dean's boots crunched across the graveled dirt. The overcast black night of Oakley was actually early morning, Zulu-time, on Earth. There was a brisk wind and the heavy moisture in the air told him another set of storms were coming.

The exterior of the buildings had been designed to imitate daytime, even at night. They cast UV light brightly across the spaces between the structures, helping folks ensure they got enough vitamin D, but it didn't help with the chilly wind. Dean stuck his hands in his pockets, deep in thought. The lightning season near Ola Bay would be in full swing, so if he wanted to go fishing, he'd need to get out to the Parvian Sea.

He'd only fished there twice, and that was for white meat trolling. He'd always wanted to, but never got the chance to target the plump monsters of the deep. The thought of fishing new waters spurred him forward to find something to do.

The door to the stable was opened as he reached for it, breaking into his fishing daydreams. Jessabee walked out, arm in arm with Kambry. Dean knew she was going to be staying here, and figured Kambry would be overjoyed to catch up with her friend.

"We're off to see Cassie," Kambry said, pecking his cheek in passing without missing a step.

Dean stuck a finger up, but they were gone before he could say anything, two sets of yoga-pants clad yummy booties heading quickly for the estate.

Well, fook. What do I do now?

He shrugged and went to the armory to go ahead and get geared up. There was no mount for him to ready, since Apache was gone. He didn't even have chores to distract him, since Yarka shoveled the shit now. He decided to do the painful part of getting in armor.

While he had slept last night, Lonny had returned to Snaggletooth City and was pulling his team together. If he got a fifth team member, great, if not... well, maybe he could use Jessabee, or get a soldier on loan from Marty.

Dean sighed when he thought about helping Lonny with getting a few more Mixonians, instead. Even though he had over a hundred and fifty tokens on his locket, he needed that number to grow. It was never enough. Pets, damsels, and Demis all needed his help. Of course, there were also all the fine folks he might rescue from Min's, to start building out a third and fourth team.

The image of a dwarf dragon danced around in his head, but he knew he wanted to find the perfect one. Fortunately, he hadn't seen any yesterday to make the talents burn a hole in his pocket—not that he had enough yet to aim for the top-tier pet he knew he'd want to get. He cringed at the possibility of losing a three hundred token pet.

When his gaze fell on his gear, he was reminded of all the new costs maintaining additional teams would bring with them. These thoughts all swirled around in his head while he went about the task of getting into the Roman style armor. As he wrapped himself in the thin, soft metal armor, he couldn't shake the feeling that Min was indeed shafting the little guy.

Why not have a double payout day, or grant cheaper days once a month for freeing loved ones? Would that just lead to inflated prices for goods? Or to a shrinking Mixonia? Where did the homeless go who weren't invited to a planet's entry point?

Everything returned to the fact that he needed more tokens and more knowledge. He was midway through buckling the straps on his side when Kambry arrived.

"We're doing the communal dressing rooms again?" she asked, curious but otherwise indifferent.

Dean scoffed, "Just because one woman gets offended by leering eyes? People see each other in fewer clothes in the pool." Dean lightly laughed as Kambry laced up his chest armor for him. "Hell, Jessabee wears a skirt that floats, then flaunts a G-string thong."

She said nothing the entire time she helped him with his armor.

"You okay?" Dean asked, helping her into her chest piece. "Didn't you want to assist Cassie with the contracts?"

"My place is at your side," Kambry said, fire in her eyes. "I'd need years of training to do what Cassie does. She... makes me feel small. Not intentionally or negatively," Kambry frowned, "Just... she is very smart."

Dean shrugged while adjusting her side straps, "If it makes ya feel any better, I've always been scared of how smart she is. She operates on a different level. I'm not afraid anymore, though, we're family." He pulled back to look Kambry in the eye. "What's going on? I sense that you're brooding and anxious. Is there an issue I should know about?"

"Jessabee is direct. Too direct. She wants to take the most direct route –"

Dean took her hands in his. "Kambry, you're acting different than usual. Not saying that in any... Stop that scowl woman. Jessabee probably deserves your –"

Kambry stomped a foot and butted in, "Pestilence and plagues—of course she deserves my scorn. I'll get over it. She's nice, sweet, and pretty. Most importantly, she's loyal to a fault and trustworthy. She'll fit in fine. Honesty after Tiffany left, I thought we'd get her back. Then, I was content with just the two of you. But it's the –"

"Seven other women you'll be sharing me with? I get it. I feel ya. We have a loving family right now—one that I'm not opposed to opening up to new additions or locking down to its current size. It all depends on the women and how the rest of you feel about them. How about we take it one day at a time?"

She sighed, squeezed her eyes shut, and then nodded.

"I want to shift our daily training schedule to the gym first thing in the morning, for at least an hour. Then an hour to get geared up with a team warmup, followed by six hours of competing." He looked off in the distance. "Then I want to go fishing. Do you like fishing?" Dean asked

Kambry hesitated. "Uh, I'd be willing to try it... for you. I think I..." Kambry began uneasily, "I might get seasick, though. Not sure. Cassie said it's a real thing."

Dean tugged sharply on the final strap of her armor. A light laugh escaped his lips. "Oakley's waters are fairly calm, but I understand your concerns. Oh, and we should also do two hours of magic or other academic type studying—monster types or such—after we're done competing." He blew out a breath. "The rest of the day is free time. Seven days a week, ten hour days. Boom, done. Makes sense to me."

"And..." Kambry said with raised brows.

"Oh right, with the rest of your free-time, you can have Cassie teach you things... if that's what you'd like to do," Dean said, but she shook her head no. "Why not?"

"It's just not who I am. I'd rather read and watch Oakley news or work in the gardens with Jaxon. But," she said in a soft tone, placing a hand on his chest armor and her lips next to his ear. "I love that you care enough about my happiness to try. I know it may seem basic and simple to you. To me, it means a lot."

"Aw, shucks, Kambry... I literally cut out a man's tongue for you," Dean said with a chuckle, "the least I can do is ensure my lover is happy."

"We set a date. Six months from now, a big wedding. How big? Fate will tell," she said, eyeing his reaction.

He smirked and gave her a hug.

"I'm glad that you're glad. We will do this. We will save Oakley, improve our base, and face our challenges together. As a family."

"As a family. Now, my dear. I eagerly want to smash my spear into you!" Dean said with a fake evil cackle. Kambry rolled her eyes while jogging ahead of him towards the training arena.

The arena was way too big for what they needed. The grandstands, training dummies, and the massive training area was meant for hundreds, not two.

They began with a few laps around the oval interior, followed by some light stretching.

A few minutes into their first fight, Cassie arrived with Wilfred, Zayra, and Jessabee.

"So, we had to call Mr. Lexso. Seems there were no contracts in place for Mixonia born champions. There is your contract with Anoka, which is still valid even though you're excusing her of the required duties for the moment. This is what I got.

"Zayra's and Wilfred's retrieval broker will stay in place until they are sprung from Min's Vault. While it's not fair to Patti, you, Lonny, or any of the others from Oakley, I have to compete against the Mixonian guilds for Mixonian talent. Your deal, even with all this amazing stuff around it, is garbage," Cassandra said and Dean winced.

"Yeah, I didn't think of that. Patti will stomach this because we'd never —"

Cassandra handed Dean the proposed contract and said, "I pulled her in early, once I realized I was going to have to alter things. Team Ola has shifted a bit again. Lonny and his team understand the situation. From now on, though, we don't pull from Riva or Marty—we pull from Mixonia. They don't want to mix salary with our new system. That means we'll have to do custom contracts even better than the guilds'."

"The deal is great Kambry," Jessabee blurted out.

Kambry looked over Dean's shoulder to read the contract with him. Dean let out a whistle. "Ten percent tax on solo competitions, thirty percent on team competitions, and no salary. How is this amazing? Aren't the guilds doing this but thirty or twenty? Oh, ten year contracts too. Wait, what?"

"Yeah, ten years is bit steep, but there are caveats. It's mainly to keep us from getting rich and running, just when the planet needs us most. Also, the big guilds do not have this to go with it," Wilfred said, gesturing at everything around them. "Oakley adds so much, on its own. The big thing is solo is never taxed at ten percent. Ever, by any of the guilds. This will cause competitors to flock to you. But there is a stipulation."

"We have to meet the ten day threshold of living on Oakley before we can do solo competitions," Zayra nodded and shrugged.

"I hit my ten-day threshold today." Kambry looked at Cassandra, "Is this what I'll be going off of, too? If not, I'm fine with what everyone else on Team Ola is getting, and hurray for planet Oakley," Kambry chuckled.

Cassandra frowned. "You'll be able to pick whichever contract you want. As your employer, I'm hoping you'll take the salary and help us build up our token reserves. As your lover, I recommend you take the special resident contract and stockpile your tokens. With the special resident contract, you'll be responsible for your own bailout. If you take the salary, we'll manage it," Cassandra said, handing one of each contract to Kambry.

The dragona gave her a kiss before taking the contracts to look over them.

Cassandra turned to Dean. "I'm also here to get your approval, as Team Ola leader, Dean, on the new contract type."

"Uh... Yeah... looks great," Dean smirked and Cassandra rolled her eyes.

"What?" he held his hands up, "It does. If I didn't trust you, I'd have issues."

"True. Okay. Sign your contracts, then, and welcome to Team Ola!" Cassandra said, handing paperwork to the others.

A few signatures later and Cassandra was walking back to the mansion with the paperwork tucked under her arm, after a quick kiss from both Dean and Kambry.

"The rest of you gear up. You're on backup," Dean said, pointing to Jessabee.

Jessabee laughed so hard, she snorted. A few calming breaths later, her laughter died down. "Oh, you're serious. Um... I'm not a fighter. I can easily get you a few backup soldiers, though. How about I go get Patti and help her gear up, for now?"

"Fine, and yeah, we will start looking for folks to hire out on a daily basis, unless you have people you know who are wanting a home –"

"Yes," they all said at once.

"Awesome. We're going to do team PvE with Patti as the portal master, from levels one to ten and then come back home. While we do that, you can get Cassie some interviews," Dean said, pointing to Jessabee, who winced. "What now?"

"I've got to give a week's notice at work before I can focus on Team Ola full time. I have an evening shift, tonight. But... I'll sleep here and help out where I can. I happen to have the codes to a very nice Mercedes-Tesla that is so fast, it's only five minutes from here to the cavern entrance," Jessabee said with a happy twirl.

"Ugh. Fine, go get Patti already," Dean said with a teasing smirk, "I want to go kill things."

ELEVEN

TUCKER

Orbiting Oakley

"What do you mean there is nothing you can do?" Tucker growled with a frustrated sigh. This was the fourth Belmont official he had called, trying to get a legal claim on the caverns Riva operated portals from.

"I'm sorry, Sir," the operator said "you can submit a written request for an appeal that will be looked at within twelve months."

Tucker hung up the call, in frustration. Pamrii sat beside him on the bridge of Tucker's lavish starship.

"This Riva human, he sure knew how to handle you," Pamrii smirked.

Tucker clenched his fists.

"Not my fault you were outmaneuvered," she said.

"Right, I thought all the nonsense not related to Mixonia was... unimportant. He's frozen me out of every possible avenue for claiming rights to the caves he has already found," Tucker said running a hand through his growing hair. "I can at least say I tried. Hey, Havnier, you busy?"

The Dwarven god appeared and Pamrii grunted. The Dwarf pointed at the ugly woman and shooed her out, flicking his wrist toward the door.

When the door had sealed shut and they were alone, Havnier said, "If you want to see us without having us expend colossal amounts of energy, you should summon us. I've been meaning to talk with you. That shit, Dean, ruined our plans. Like that," the surly Dwarven god snapped his finger to emphasize how quickly things had changed, "my favor with Min wasted, your tokens, mostly wasted, and now I have to adjust."

"I have no idea what you're rambling about. I thought you gods were all powerful?" Tucker grumbled.

"Ha! I wish. Apparently only madness lets us understand the future. My very reliable agent —"

"You can't hear all and see all?" Tucker asked, tilting his head in confusion.

"Huh? No. And be grateful I said that much. My agent told me that Dean Forrester saw some random human kid and asked him about his parents. The kid lied," Havnier said and Tucker chuckled.

"Right," the god sneered, "good for the kid. His parents are important Mixonia managers for Earth. While human space is expanding, their base of operations is stretched thin. It won't take them long to notice Oakley is finally in play. Once they do, though, any chance we have of losing here is gone."

Tucker shrugged and said, "After seeing what happened on the orbital, I think your cause is not only stupid but —"

"Careful," the god warned, "I can and will smite you, if I feel like it. I understand that bleeding-heart mortals hate making sacrifices for change. The Suca gods have lost interest in the games, but that is bad for all of us. A few thousand, or even hundreds-of-thousands of fleeting mortal lives is a small price to pay to change that."

Tucker scoffed and replied, "You asked me to mess with their operations, and I tried. What do you want me to do now?"

"Kill Dean Forrester—not you, yourself—Min would find out I was involved if you did it. Take your time planning it all out. Oh, and the location of the fourth portal is yours if you accept my offer. Claim it before anyone else can. Unlike before, I won't be paying you everything up front. Here are a hundred tokens; finish the job properly, and you'll get three hundred more," Havnier sneered as he paced the ship's bridge.

"You want me to kill the one guy I don't hate?" Tucker asked with a furled brow.

Havnier gave a disgruntled sigh and rubbed at his forehead. "It's not about your liking or disliking someone. There are things at play you do not comprehend, nor ever will. Dean has been studied. There are too many loopholes in what little I can discover, and even Zued is in hiding, now." The Dwarf god winced. "Something big is going on, and if I'm right... if he survives, he'll do more than wake up the gods. I'll say no more because even that was too much. Have we a deal?" Havnier asked, extending a locket with 100 engraved on it.

Tucker's eyes lingered on the prize while he thought about it. It wasn't the locket he wanted. He craved the portal. His control of the fourth gateway into Mixonia would infuriate Riva. Tucker's spy in Riva's camp was barely reporting anything at all these days. One thing was certain, though, Riva was hunting for the fourth portal and spending millions to find it.

"I want to prevent further problems on Oakley," Tucker countered.

"Compete, win the planet, I don't care," Havnier grunted. "Just kill Dean Forrester."

"And if I send a team or a professional, and they fail?" Tucker asked, chewing on the inside of his cheek.

"I move onto a different option and you get another fifty tokens for having tried. I honestly can't have you linked to this, so ensure you do all your plotting up here, in the void. Min's influence doesn't reach this far up," Havnier noted.

The god's eyes lit up with a sudden inspiration. "There is Thero. He's been praying for a way to get to Dean. If you use him, then I'll never be suspected."

"Got it. You'll give me a hundred tokens now, and I can claim the fourth portal— today. Within a year, I'll try to have Dean Forrester killed," Tucker stated. "I'll send an agent to find this Thero guy in Mixonia and grant him access to Oakley, when he's ready."

"Kill Forrester in three months, not twelve, but yes." The god waved the golden prize temptingly back and forth before Tucker's eyes. "Take the locket, we both know you will."

Tucker snatched up the locket. This binding contract was different than the others that he had seen. At the bottom of the tablet Havnier handed him, instead of 'enforced by Min', it said 'enforced by a Suca god', with no specific god's name given. He signed his name and Havnier vanished.

Tucker's holo-display illuminated a map of Oakley. A location on the planet pinged red, over and over. Tucker smirked, knowing it was time to go back to Mixonia.

CHAPTER

TWELVE

DEAN

Oakley - Felna's Cavern

"I thought it was impossible for us to spend more than six hours inside?" Patti said with a scoff. She fidgeted, agitated, pacing around in a fit of boredom stewed in anxiety.

Dean sighed as a movie blared in the background. Felna munched on a salad completely uncaring about their delay. Dean was miffed, because the rules were clear. He'd even pulled up his contract to reread the exact verbiage when the previous time slot hit his six-hour limit. Now, it was hours since that suspense had passed and the portal master, Larshank, was still inside Mixonia, locking them out.

"We sent Kambry in. Nothing more we can do. Last thing we need is for him to come out and then we're stuck trying to find a missing member because we sent in Zayra or Wilfred," Dean said, pacing behind the couch Felna reclined on.

"You realize this could happen to us, too, right?" Wilfred said. Dean's questioning look encouraged him to continue. "We're going to climb to ten today. That means we'll enter actual mazes—places you can get lost in or trapped. If we all fall down a ravine, for example, without climbing gear –"

"Brought it," Patti interrupted with a smirk, gesturing at their massive bag of gear.

"The point remains, this six-hour limitation is only for when you're not in the mazes. I bet Min wouldn't enforce it, if you go to drop your gear off in storage after an eight-hour ordeal in a maze. Or if you stop on the way out to go pee, or whatever," Zayra said with a bob of her head.

"Yeah, I guess we just need to expect for competitions to run –" A sudden commotion halted Dean mid-sentence.

The blank flat wall blared to yellow life as a portal leaped into creation with a static hiss. Kambry stepped out and behind her followed a maternal woman, supporting a crying man. The two left with a rapid walk for the exit above.

There was a stunned silence that Felna broke by saying, "You guys want me to close that or leave it open?"

"I'll catch them up on the walk through Mixonia," Kambry said to Felna, before pointing to Dean and nodding at the portal.

He stopped pacing to get his gear bag. The damn thing weighed a ton, but he managed to heft it up onto his back with a grunt. He wanted to groan or complain, but instead hunkered down and stepped through the portal for Mixonia.

∞∞∞

The first thing Dean did upon arriving was to check the planetary score. *Planet Oakley - Team Suca 219*. There was minor grumbling from behind him and he ground his teeth in frustration. There wasn't much else he could do, though, other than to keep at it.

He decided to check his stats. After the fight with Thero and Hann, there hadn't been much else besides his workout this morning. Yup, he saw a few points of intelligence and one in willpower. While the rest stayed the same.

Champion Information
Name: Dean Forrester Gender: Male
Level: 4 Tokens: 0
Race: Human Alignment: Suca – Mixonia
Luck: 16 Charisma: 41

Health: 344 / 344 H-Regen: 1.0 / Sec
Stamina: 294 / 294 M-Regen: 1.0 / Sec
Mana: 332 / 332 S-Regen: 1.0 / Sec

Strength: 212 Vitality: 132
Dexterity: 107 Endurance: 187

Intelligence: 101 Willpower: 231
Magic: Electrical

"Apparently my workouts are at least slowing my strength and endurance losses," Dean muttered as the others arrived.

"What was that?" Patti asked. Dean shrugged and she frowned until she checked her stats. Dean missed seeing what the card said, but his friend shot a proud fist into the air. "I went up five endurance. Not having Quincy holding me back, means I can run a lot more."

"So... You guys want to hear what happened while we walk and talk?" Kambry began and they all nodded excitedly. "I went to Min's Vault first. The human storage had no Larshank so I went over to the solo PvE marshalling area where I found his handler."

"Oh... Are we doing that?" Wilfred asked and Dean shook his head, no. "Not the worst idea, if you've got the spare crew."

"Sure," Kambry nodded, "and it might be a good idea for us to end up doing something like that—just save it for the riskier runs to have less vault time and release time. Larshank goes by Ben. Ben's handler told me he was a stellar candidate for the maze." There was a pause as they passed under the statues in tribute to the male and female forms of Min. "So stellar he is on level twenty-three, solo. Quite an impressive score, for a new competitor."

They passed around the massive entry fountain and slid into the congested crowds. Dean decided to create a hole for the rest of his team to flow behind, as Kambry yelled over the noise from the front. The thick press of bodies flowing in opposite directions was worse than normal, though still ordinary for Mixonia. Dean was forced to slide his bag directly over his back after he accidentally clipped a Fairy's wings.

"So, Ben went into solo PvE floor twenty-four," Kambry hollered, loud enough for him to hear. "Get this, he ended up in a cavern maze. No biggie, he'd brought chalk, and yes Patti, we know you packed some, too. He hit a dead end. Not surprised, he went back the way his chalk marks took him, to a big cavern intersection."

"He'd cleared this room already and went in not suspecting the twenty-foot spider that leaped down. With no option besides to take a path he'd never been down before, he fled right into a massive web. Fights it so bad, the spider didn't even wrap him up. Into his guts, the spider's fangs went."

Dean gulped at the thought. Now he understood the man's tears.

"He was a sliver of health away from Min's Vault, when there was a noise from a direction he hadn't explored yet. The spider found another monster warrior, defending the locket. This variation of a troll was tossed into the web beside him. The spider's young came out and feasted on the new catch, a few of them digging their fangs into Ben, too."

Kambry shuddered. "Ben remained awake this whole time, struggling. His regen was too slow to repair the constant damage but was fast enough that he didn't die."

Dean found a shortcut through the Garden of the Gods and diverted their route to avoid the worst of the crowds. There was no music this time around; it seemed the majority of the party goers were elsewhere, allowing him to increase their pace.

"Ben regenerated over hours, in agony the whole time, his withered frame slowly restoring as new blood renewed his tissue. Mind you, this is why most champions boost their regen rates. We, as a team, aren't there yet, but soon we will need to consider it. Maybe after we hit level fifteen, is my guess, but I'm deviating from Ben's story. He survived this torture, only to be drained a few more times. After hours of unrelenting work, his nail clipped a path to free his hand of the web and he ripped his way to the troll's sword."

Patti cheered.

"He freed himself from the web and ran from chalk mark to chalk mark the whole way back to the black portal. He exited, the same way he'd come in. If, and this is a big if... if he ever goes back in, it'll be the exact same floor—just respawned."

Fook me. I could only imagine the horror.

The rest of the team walked along in a somber silence of thought. Dean picked up the pace. Just because Ben had come out late, though, didn't mean there wasn't another slot waiting behind theirs. He'd set a stretch goal today of reaching Team PvE level fifteen—even if stopping after level ten was more realistic.

When they stomped up the ramp to the PvE Group staging area, Dean reached into his vest and set the five-inch long figurine of a wagon down on the rough stone floor. Instantly the figurine converted into a wagon.

"Finally," Patti groaned, slinging her heavy bag of gear back into the cart bed. "Easy with yours, Kambry."

"I know, I know. I've got all the potions, drinks, and food in my bag. The bottles are thick, though; I think it'd take a fair bit of effort to break them," Kambry said, gently setting her bag down in the cart.

Dean picked up the wagon's handles, pulling the cart forward towards the gate. While they'd been trapped, waiting for Ben to exit, the team had done what felt like a hundred combat checks. Unless something crazy happened, they were more than ready. Dean arrived at the Minotaur guard and placed his hand on the oath stone.

"I, Dean Forrester and team, are requesting floor five, and we understand all the risks involved," Dean said.

The uncaring guard gestured for them to enter with a mild snort of amusement at their cart, piled high with equipment they most likely wouldn't need for such a low level. The purple shimmer before them converted to a lime green color and he stepped through it.

∞∞∞

Dean released the cart's handles, bracing for the incoming damage. A spell was pelting him with rocks from above. His raised his shield overhead, protecting his body.

"Get under me. Wilfred, grab a shield," Dean ordered, surprised there was no initial grace period.

The bulky Osamar grabbed a blocky shield from off the side of the cart. The situation became clearer to Dean, as he got a better look at his surroundings. "Ah! We're not under attack."

"Hail?" Zayra wondered, "Oh..." also realizing they'd arrived in the middle of a storm.

The howling wind around them was interrupted by the crack of lightning, somewhere off in the distance. The flashing light illuminated a dark, overcast sky. Dean's feet were on a dry riverbed of loose gravel and there were towering mountains all around him.

Kambry pointed to their front, indicating a dry cave Dean could barely see.

Wilfred warned the group, "Careful, there are deep ravines along both sides of us. The maze is telling us which way to go."

Dean was sick of the rain and hail already, so he manhandled the cart over the rocky terrain to the cavern's entry. Loose rock skittered out from under the cart's wheels, the rough terrain threatening to overturn the heavy cart twice. Dean didn't stop, powering ahead through sheer strength and stubborn determination.

Patti raced ahead, her bow drawn, posture tense.

With a whole mountain overhead to keep the rain at bay, Dean slowed his mad dash with the cart to a halt. "Alright, what do you see Patti?" Dean asked, wiping the rain from his face.

Patti trotted forward quickly, returning just as hastily. "Three tunnels. Each with its own cavernous mouth leading to a flat area about the size of the estate. Two of the caverns have pedestals with no glint—the one that does is the left entrance. There is a single yeti in each cavern—it's a white furred monster, probably double my height and three times my weight. Not sure –"

"Fire," Zayra and Kambry said in unison. Their eyes ablaze with excitement.

Kambry continued. "May we?"

"Yes."

Both mages grinned.

"Patti," Dean instructed, "you're only goal is to get to the locket and touch it to the indent. I'll run in, pull the Yeti, the fire girls will DPS while Wilfred covers our butts. I want this fooking cold rain off of me," Dean said, shivering a bit in the chill of the cave as he grabbed his trident off the cart.

There was a table of sorts to the side of the cave, where everyone locked eyes for a few moments. When there were no questions, and no hesitation from the others, Dean trotted towards the corridor to their left.

The opening was big enough for them all to walk through it abreast. Dean shifted his gaze to see the big monster waiting for them by the pedestal. A tingle in the back of his mind told him the eerie light illuminating the cave had to be from a magical source.

Dean slowed to a modest walk, shifting his trident into his shield hand. Energy danced across his fingertips, eager for release. Instead of yelling for attention, he launched a few stun balls.

The Yeti noticed instantly, leaping out of the way of his attack. The beast bellowed an ear ringing war cry before it charged Dean. His legs pumped into action as he kited the monster away from the group.

The sound of sizzling heat spurred him to increase his pace. The girls had unleashed their magic.

He expected to hear his foe cry out in pain. Nope.

When he glanced over his shoulder, he was forced to twist around and look up in order to see the snarling Yeti closing on him rapidly. The beast swung the spiked club that it carried dangerously close, almost catching Dean in the back.

Fook me he is fast! I gotta turn or something.

Dean skidded to a halt, his feet sliding across the slick stone of the cavern floor. The steely blue gaze of his foe, eager for a kill as it seethed in rage, burned down into his.

A roar escaped the beast's lips, sending spittle flying and revealing a mouth full of fangs. Dean lifted his shield and braced for impact. His arm tensed and he winced as the club crashed in from his left. He flinched, expecting to be sent flying.

∞∞∞

The noise around him faded from the creature's roar to the idle chatter of groups staging themselves for a maze run. Dean was immediately dry, once again, and thrilled to be out of the way of the Yeti's club. *Score! Not dying is always a plus.* When he saw everyone else was waiting on him, he hefted the cart and walked back to the Minotaur guard.

The ladies wanted to talk, but Dean was on a mission. Victory. The guard shifted so he could place his hand on the oath stone. "I, Dean Forrester, and team, understand the consequences and want floor six."

The green was a shade lighter this time. He walked straight in.

∞∞∞

Dean almost stepped over a cliff, his feet suddenly teetering on the edge. The damn cart pushed him from behind. "Not cool," Dean muttered, scampering back over the cart and onto the solid platform.

Safe, he took in his surroundings. They were above an expansive green valley, which lay hundreds of feet below the edge of the cliff. Triple suns illuminated a fractured skyline in competing shades of red, yellow, and orange.

He looked to the left and saw three narrow stairways leading down; to the right, there were three stairways continuing on up. None of the stone steps had a railing or any means to prevent a fall. At most, they were only four feet wide. There was an instant realization that the wagon was staying here.

"Can we do a debrief after next time?" Kambry grumbled, crossing her arms.

Dean frowned and said, "Yeah sure. I figured we could do it here where it's quiet and serene."

"The view is pretty. Still, smartass, it could be raining," Patti said with a smirk. "Just be happy I got you out of there. Apparently, the *fire* girls both missed the Yeti with their spells."

Zayra fidgeted, pretending to peer over the edge of the platform. She was tense without being closer than five feet from the edge. She stuck a finger up and said, "I want to apologize. That Yeti was insanely fast and my spell didn't account for his ability to jump. If you had brought him at us, though, he'd have been easier to hit. I think."

"Basically, the strategy worked, but..." Kambry sighed. "We almost ended up going the longer and more dangerous route, fighting the Yeti."

"We can troubleshoot problems later. First, we need to scout the area of this next competition from the entry point," Dean said. He gestured all around them. "For example, who else is afraid of heights?"

Only Zayra held her hand up. Defensively she said, "It's not so much the heights..."

Wilfred smirked at her and shook his head.

"Okay, maybe a little." She punched her husband in the arm. "I'm afraid of falling to my death. If there was a rope or something here to hold on to, I'd walk up to the edge. Maybe."

He bit back his laughter. "Patti?" Dean asked.

"Yeah?"

"Can you handle the heights and figure out where these stairs go?" Dean asked.

"Sheesh," his friend rolled her eyes. "Why not have Kambry fly off the platform and then –"

Kambry ran and jumped off the platform. Rapid beats of her wings brought her to a hover. She gave Dean a quick wink and then dove down below. There was a twang of bows and Dean saw a couple of arrows arc up into the sky from the valley. When the crackle of Kambry's spells reached his ears, he ran to back her up.

Dean had to take the human way—down the stairs—which was painfully slow. The angsty feeling he got, like each step might be his last, wrapped itself around his heart like a vice as he clung to the wall. He reached the first intersection, his quick peek showed him Kambry was further down and to his left. Her fireballs had stopped and her battle cry roared triumphantly.

He was about a quarter of the way down when she flew to join him.

Fook me! I shoulda just stayed put.

He turned around carefully and started his way back up. Kambry was waiting at the midway landing point with a smile on her face.

"Killed them all. Six simple ratkin. The poisonous kind who were dispelling billowing clouds of yellow gas into the air. Not the same as the bulbous Molekin or

Ratgobbies. In a few minutes, I'll fly back down and indent the locket. You look a little green," she frowned at Dean, "you okay?"

Dean sat down next to where she stood. "So... not really afraid of heights, but –"

"An edge, hundreds of feet up can be nerve wracking. Yeah, I'm sorta surprised by this map. I suppose you can do it without flying." She paused and pointed down to the left. "You get a big platform to fight on, once you've made the trek down. So I guess this ledge is kind of like a bridge, with no edges. So... I guess, it's actually pretty fair," Kambry mused, changing her mind halfway through her thought, then agreeing with herself.

"Glad ya find it fair," Dean snorted, with a dry chuckle. "Good job killing them."

"Pfft, they have worse aim than Quincy did," she sneered.

Dean pinched her cheek, under her armor, right next to her tail.

"Ouch!" she blushed. "Sorry. Have you talked to him at all?"

Dean shook his head, "Not a peep, it's like my best friend just up and vanished. To be fair, though, he's done this before. Quincy can be pretty self-centered, when he wants to be. At the same time, I do think that we all are built to seek what's best for us. Giving him space is probably the best thing right now—I'm sure he'll come around, eventually."

"Wow, I thought I loved you for your hulking muscles, turns out you can have profound thoughts too," Kambry gave him a teasing smirk.

"You guys okay down there?" Wilfred hollered out.

Kambry cupped her hands around her mouth and yelled, "On my way up." She patted Dean on the shoulder, her gauntlet *clanging* against his pauldron. "Going to tell them we're good, then head back down and indent the locket."

Dean watched her black and red wings propel her higher up the trail, her tail providing a counter-balance to her body. *Impressive.*

∞∞∞

They all sat around a table as Dean admired the eleven etched into the locket. He sighed and relaxed. No one had much to say. They'd waited for Kambry to indent the locket and did nothing to contribute towards earning six easy tokens completed by a single member of their team.

"Umm... Next time we need to make a slower, more controlled entry. Push the cart in," Zayra said and the others nodded their heads, "don't pull it. We did well, assessing the situation, though."

"I concur." He met each of their gazes. "We ready to move on?" Dean asked.

"Yuppers," Patti hopped to her feet with a smile.

The others merely stood and followed him to the cart.

He pulled it behind him right up to the guard. In front of Dean, for the first time that he could remember, was a non-species driven team—probably a guild team. They all wore capes with a golden compass on it and matching, black gear. There was a wolfman, a turtle guy, a duckgirl, and two aliens who reminded him of those green big-headed kind from the movies. The team was professional and short with the guard.

The coloration of the portal flickered from teal to a ruby red. A voice from behind Dean's group shouted, "Good luck Yen Guild. Come home safe!" The group at the portal spun around and waved goodbye to a small crowd of cheering family and friends.

Then it was Dean's turn. He paused a moment, watching them shimmer into nothing as they walked into the portal and vanished. His hand resting on the Oath stone, Dean said, "Team Ola, floor seven, we understand."

The guard raised an eyebrow at him, but gestured them towards the portal, allowing it. The coloration shifted to a lime green and Dean rotated the cart around to push it through first.

∞∞∞

Dean cracked his knuckles and popped his neck. They'd arrived in a field of pink rice stalks, with a blue sun overhead. Alien cows with three legs and a head in the middle of their spine brayed at them from a few hundred feet away. To say that they were odd, was an understatement.

Patti was fascinated with the cows, her eyes bulging slightly as she peered at them intently. "I want to take one home."

"Nope," Dean chuckled. As awesome as these mini-creations were, they stayed where they should—in Min's magical realm. "I wished we could take stuff we find here," he smirked. "I wanted the fancy staff Thero was carrying. I'm pretty sure that cost him a lot more than it did for his followers to recover him from Min's shelf."

"Oh, don't remind her," Wilfred groaned as Kambry sauntered over to give Dean a kiss.

Kambry teased him with a light peck before flapping her wings to propel her straight up in the air to get a view of their surroundings. Dean's eyes lingered on the amazing view she gave him up her skirt. She had such an amazing ass. He loved those fine leggings. He snickered at her tease; he'd actually wanted that kiss.

"Wings are like... cheating," Patti grumbled, a smile tugging at the corners of her mouth. "So, no rain, and no cliffs. Hurray."

Wilfred and Zayra spun around, seeing about the same amount of nothing. Soggy ground stretched before them for miles, except for in one direction. A mile in the distance there was a small village. The homes were one story, the design circular, and the roofing thatch.

Kambry settled back down to the ground beside the cart and retrieved a spyglass. A moment later, she was back up in the air again. There was not much for the rest of them to do, besides inspect the cart while they waited for the pretty Dragona to report on what she saw.

When they had prepared for today's delve, they had found the cart figurine on a shelf in the armory. Dean had thought the cart was simply a decoration. Apparently, teams were permitted to spawn and despawn carts and wagons just before the competition portals. A cart or team pulled wagon was the closest thing to a mount allowed in group adventuring.

Dean and the team had loaded the cart full of spare shields, javelins, bows with quivers, and extra swords. They'd even strapped two long pikes to the outside of the cart. The interior held their bags and other loose paraphernalia—that apparently had to be carried to the portal by the team. If not attached by a permanent latch to the cart itself, other materials did not transform with the figurine.

He'd rushed them here from the estate, though, and that had turned out to be a bit of a mistake. Going forward, their bags would get secured to the cart, instead of carried.

Dean found a water container latched to the front wall of the cart. The container was thankfully a fancily crafted wooden jug from the market, and not some animal bladder. He was on his third deep draught, when Kambry finally landed next to the cart.

"Alright, the locket is in the village. It was hard to see, until I went really high. There are probably twenty minions scattered throughout the village," Kambry reported and everyone grew confused. "Three foot tall hooded mages. Minions are a caster type. They have wands about a foot in length, with gems embedded into them."

"Thoughts on how to get the locket?" Zayra asked.

Kambry held a finger up while pulling a spear out of the cart. She found a nice level spot in the dirt and drew a map, as best she could.

"A dozen buildings in," she pointed to a point near the middle of the village, "between these two larger structures on the right side, is where the locket is located. Stealth will be hard. I recommend we fight it out," Kambry said and Dean frowned. "With a twist..." She smirked at the odd looks they gave her, rubbing her hands together excitedly.

"Turn that frown upside down," she bopped Dean on the nose. "You four, get into a formation and get ready to start a slow approach towards the village." She frowned, "Patti is going to hate me for this, but we'll need to kill these animals to lure the minions out of the village."

"While you engage the cows, I'll fly off to the side. The minions will either have to split up to protect both the locket and their herd, or they will try to swarm you. If they leave it unguarded, I'll swoop in and we get out quick with seven more easy tokens. If they don't –"

"We'll cut our way through a divided enemy," Dean finished for her, grabbing a quiver of javelins from the wagon. "Patti, drop one of the three legged things, please. Zayra, use your mana sparingly. Let's clear the field."

There was a twang from Patti's bow and an arrow zoomed across the field. It made a wet smacking sound when it drove into the animal. The noise the animal made, though, was more akin to a howler monkey. The field of three-legged herbivores darted away in just about every direction. Dean hurled a javelin after a fleeing target that was nearly out of range. The tip didn't even land right, though, because the damn thing was off balance.

He watched the wounded animal be put out of its misery with a fireball. "Okay, these need to be resold and replaced," Dean muttered, picking up another javelin and noticing the weight was off on that one too.

"They sure can run, for only having three legs," Patti chuckled darkly. "We ready to go?"

"I need to know if you want me on tank or damage," Wilfred said.

Dean spied the village in the distance, his eyes darting over soggy terrain. There were paths outside of the farm fields. None were big enough for the cart, however, which meant his decision mattered, now.

"Grab an extra shield," Dean said, tossing his buckler back into the cart. "I'll do the same. We'll form a shield wall and hide behind it."

Dean slung his trident across his back as the two men grabbed a couple of sturdy shields, each the size of half doors. He grunted at the weight when the wooden slats were locked to each arm. Taking point, he stepped off the small landing pad onto the elevated trail.

Patti was close on his heels, her bow at the ready. Zayra stayed close behind her, and Wilfred covered their rear. It was going to be at least a ten minute trek to get into position. Dean kept scanning the area and watching for traps. Kambry flapped high into the air, flying lazy circles over the group as they marched forward.

The trip was fairly quiet and they made steady progress, stepping occasionally around fields to stay out of the muck. Dean noticed a few, small triple-tailed fish in the fields of pink rice. Where there was prey, there were normally predators. He checked for snake holes or creatures buried in the sludge.

His searches came up empty, though, as they made their way to the outskirts of the village. The team followed his lead up to the leading edge of the hovels. Where the fields ended, there was a slight incline. He kept walking with both shields in front of him expecting to have to slam the wooden armor into the soft dirt below him; except no enemy rushed for them and no cry was given to alert others they were near.

He made it all the way to where the ground in the village leveled off; the nearest hut was only twenty feet away. Dean slammed his left shield into the squishy ground with a wet *slop*. He buried his right shield next to the left one. Wilfred proceeded to give their impromptu shield wall covering on the flanks, pulling back their barrier at a forty-five degree angle on either side.

They nodded to each other while the team prepared to fight.

"I'll go bring the party to you and then split," Kambry snickered.

Dean grunted with an approving smile.

She gained altitude until it was clear from the reaction of the agitated mages inside the village that they had seen her. Red, mixed with orange, rained down from the tip of her staff. A half-dozen inferno balls arched into the village, beyond a couple of the buildings that obstructed his view. As soon as clumps of ice were sent her way in retaliation, Kambry whirled around and made a slow dive for the shield wall.

"Here we go," Dean said with a grin.

He stood with his hand leveled, his palm out. A half dozen little mages ran with a wobbly gate around the structures and right into their ambush. The *twang, sizzle,* and *crackle* of the team's first volley assaulted his ears. Those sounds faded out, but were dwarfed moments later by the horrific wailing of the wounded.

The enemy had remained solely focused on the sky. Dean rapid fired energy bolts into Min's hooded, midget employees. His bolts stopped after three minions went down—he'd over charged his shots again. Wilfred froze the feet of two more of the little mages. Patti placed a perfect shot through a minion's open mouth with glee. Zayra smashed those frozen in place with fire. Their cries, along with their twitching bodies, eventually died.

When the first wave ceased to twitch and moan, Dean inspected them. They were odd creatures. Their lower half consisted of a bug-like undercarriage, with four legs. They had a humanoid torso, though Dean could see but a single arm and only spied a single eye under the creatures' hoods. Dean had to assume these creatures existed somewhere, unless Min had custom created these hooded, midget employees. He snickered at the thought.

A battle cry sounded from inside the town. "They left the locket unguarded," Kambry cried happily from above. She soared low around the side of the village.

Dean could only watch her for a moment, though, because a flood of minions came from between the buildings. His palm laced a couple of bolts of energy into the mass of minions, until he stumbled from the sudden mana drain. His spells killed at least a dozen of the creatures, though, cutting them in half with searing, blinding white light. When he tried to shoot once more, he realized he must be out of mana.

With his right hand, he wrenched his trident out of the soft turf where he had stuck it, and waited on the right flank. A firewall erupted right in the middle of the charging minions, causing wails of despair to pierce the air. Dean had trouble focusing, as the sounds of spells and arrows being unleashed nearby distracted him.

With a thrusting jab, he skewered the first minion who tried to get around their shield wall. He pried the body off the tines with the shield and was stabbing out once again when time slowed.

He twirled around to see his team ceasing hostilities and canceling their spells. *Ah, the game of the gods is warning us we're about to return to Mixonia.*

When Patti dropped her arrow into her quiver, Dean's vision went black.

∞∞∞∞

"That was a first," Patti blurted out, staring at her hands.

Wilfred nodded and said, "When you're aggressively fighting, there is a brief cool down period. There has to be. If not, every time a team came home during a fight, they might end up flinging spells who knows where. The staging area would be madness."

Heads nodded agreement at this statement.

"How did it go?" Dean asked, turning to Kambry.

She shook her head agitatedly. Her arm was bleeding from a decent sized gash. "They ambushed me," Kambry finally admitted and Dean noticed the hastily concealed anguish on her face. "I... I'll need to go back in, to heal," she muttered.

He scooped up the cart's handles and went to the Minotaur guard. There was no line, so he was able to place his hand on the Oath stone, quickly.

"Team Ola, floor eight, understanding the consequences," Dean rattled off quickly.

The yellow portal before them shimmered a light green color. Dean rotated the cart around and pushed it in.

∞∞∞

They were inside a cinder block building, in what appeared to be an underground room. The staging area was barely large enough to fit the cart. Dean spun around to see a broiler belching out heat, not far from him. *Okay, so we're indoors. I'll need my small trident and buckler, and we're leaving the cart behind.*

The others adjusted quickly to the limited space as each of them arrived. Kambry went right to her bag and grabbed a specific sandwich. She took a large bite of the food and sighed in relief.

"Thanks for hurrying," Kambry said between great mouthfuls of her snack. "This will increase my regen. I take it we're inside a building? What's the plan?"

"First we'll wait for you to regenerate your health. The locket is already at eighteen tokens; we'll be at twenty-six, after this level—these missions really start to add up. They're a lot more fun than I'd thought they'd be," Dean said in a chipper tone. "Excited to do them all over again, next time with Patti as the portal lead. The solo missions are always so tense."

The others bobbed their heads in agreement. "I know, I'm loving this far more than the individual challenges. It's far more exhilarating than being on roller skates, handing out food to families," Patti smirked with a snarky tone.

"You quit that a while ago, right?" Dean asked with furled brows.

"Dean," Patti sighed, "we all have our secrets."

He chuckled.

"I never got that desk job Dad wanted me to. I kept working at BunnyHop. It was... well..." she slapped her bum. "A tight butt like mine in skates earned me more in tips than pushing paper around a desk ever did."

Dean chuckled and patted her shoulder.

470

"Yes, your butt is very nice," Zayra agreed, raising her eyebrows when Dean winced. "What? Is that rude to say in Oakley's culture?"

"Not rude, just means you might want to see it naked," Patti chuckled with a single eyebrow bounce.

"I already saw it naked..." Her brows furled. "When we geared up, remember?" Zayra replied, still confused.

Wilfred rolled his eyes and corrected his wife. "Naked, dear heart of mine, as in sex. See, you're both blushing now. Too cute. How's the arm doing Kambry?" he changed the subject.

"Mending, we should talk a bit more before proceeding. What's the plan this time?" Kambry asked, holding the edges of her wound together as it slowly healed.

"Uh... I'd like for us to unlock healing magic—for at least one of us. That'd be nice to have, so we can get out and heal quickly, instead of rushing back in to do this. Then, I need to go talk to Orabel. Only floor five was quick, so that means we're probably eating up a lot of time. Maybe call it a day after this level?" Dean frowned. "What do you think?"

Wilfred found a wall to sit against. "I want to compete... solo, again." He pinched the bridge of his nose, "like a lot, but it can wait I guess. Would you be okay with us freeing Zayra's parents sooner, rather than later?"

"As in, using Team Ola's reserves to spring you, if you get trapped?" Dean responded to Wilfred's question with a question of his own, to which he received a nod.

"They're people," he frowned, "important people. I'll approve it, since we do have excess tokens right now, enough for a team wipe. However, talk to Cassie because —"

"She might be investing the tokens or adding more team members with Jessabee. I know," Wilfred said, slinging an arm around his wife as she dropped down beside him. "Figured the best place to start was with you."

"Fair enough. What kind of spaceship were you thinking about getting?" Kambry asked, showing them that her arm was mostly healed.

"We didn't know you were allowed to buy community ships as an individual. That is now our ultimate goal—the ecosystem ones. Joobi was really over regulated, so many rules and so much red tape that only the privileged got to avoid. On Oakley, we could free hundreds and start our own refuge that travels the stars as it grows. After our contract is done, of course," Zayra nodded at Dean, then let out a longing sigh.

"A mix of space farming and a tight knit community? Those are expensive to buy. I don't think Oakley produces any, do they?" Patti asked and Dean shrugged.

"We did the exchange ratios. It'll cost us a few hundred tokens—so it's a long-term goal. We can buy a nice atmospheric ship to start with, though, one that would suit our needs in the near-term and fit into the big behemoth, if we ever save up enough for it."

Patti quirked an eyebrow at him.

"What? We need a lot of space for our big family," Wilfred said in a jovial tone. "Honestly. Kinda why I want to do solo. If I make it to level thirty-one, solo, that'd be over three hundred tokens. Even with your tax."

Dean nodded at this and then watched Kambry spring to her feet with a smile and a healed arm.

"Okay I'm ready to go," Kambry said, rotating her arm back and forth. "Tight corridors like this will probably be a hindrance to a Dragona. So I won't be able to save the day on this one... probably."

"I'll take the lead," Dean chuckled at his lover, waiting at the door for everyone to get into formation. "I'm proud of this team," he said as his large hand clutched a pulldown knob. "Ready?"

When he heard the others affirm that they were ready, he opened the door.

"Fook me!" Dean screamed as the door burst wide open, flinging him backwards. Water gushed into the boiler room. Steam cascaded into the air as the cold water smacked into the heating device.

Dean's movement stopped when he reached the back wall with a *clang,* his metal armor scraping against the concrete.

"There's a dry stairwell!" Patti said, swimming against the rapidly rising water.

Dean recovered from the shock and powered forward. His body protested against this burst of energy, the chill of the water that drenched him soaking into his muscles. He grunted, kicked, pulled, grimaced, and finally, trudged through the water on his way to the stairwell. Any hope of a reprieve from the chilling cold was immediately dashed. A busted-out window further on up the stairs allowed in gusts of frigid air.

"We're going to get hypothermia if we're not careful," Patti's teeth chattered together and her lips were already blue. "We can either build a fire here and dry out or make a rush for the end."

Dean looked where Patti pointed, to a landing just past the busted out window.

Kambry was the last to leave the water and Dean saw she'd broken a wing. He groaned and started stripping out of his gear.

"Sorry," Kambry said, with a wince and a nod at Patti. "Told you my wings were shit in small spaces. Not cheating this time."

472

Patti frowned, stripping out of her chainmail and leather armor. "What do we burn?"

"The wooden shields and javelins should work," Dean said, shivering violently as his teeth started to chatter.

"Sorry, I was in a daze of shock. Don't bother with an actual fire, here," Zayra informed them. "We should go up and find a room without cold air pouring in, where Kambry and I can heat the air itself without adverse effects, like a fire."

Dean wanted to get out of his armor. Instead, he bounded up to the next floor. A shaking peek to the left and right showed him a few doors in each direction; the stairs continued on, higher. Dean peered left down the hallway. He walked forward to pop open the first door on his right.

There was a large classroom inside, desks littered the floors with paper strewn about.

A zombie's moans caught his attention and it slowly began to walk his way. Dean shut the door, quietly yet quickly. The room was expansive and the numerous windows meant it'd be hard to heat. Not to mention there'd been a freaking zombie in it.

The door behind him was labeled *Superintendent*. Dean twisted the knob with his left hand, his magic at the ready.

The zombie that groaned from inside was still seated at a desk. A lance of crackling white energy erupted from Dean's palm, splattering zombie brains against the back wall. The chair crashed to the ground as the body slumped to the floor with a wet *thump*.

"Get up here," Dean hissed back down the hallway.

He was careful not to shout but was still loud enough for his voice to carry. He grabbed the dead body from behind the desk and laid it out in the hallway. The team shivered their way into the confined space.

Kambry and Zayra's hands flared red as they poured energy into fire spells. The clean sidewall was lit up with fireballs, until the concrete started to *sizzle*. The room heated quickly while everyone huddled together for warmth.

They stayed in the tiny room, stripped down to their small clothes, their hands held out toward the heat for at least an hour.

Halfway through, their shivering abated. Towards the end, their underclothing dried out. Dean *snapped* Kambry's wing back into place, with her biting down on the leather grip of a dagger handle to keep from crying out. When they were finally dry and geared up once more, the cold chill of the frigid air was no longer in danger of causing hypothermia.

"Ready?" Dean asked, stacking up next to the door.

Patti put a hand on his shoulder, "What's the plan?"

"Well, we'll have to clear one room after another. Quietly, I hope. Then we go up to the next floor. I'm not going to rush to the end, only to only have to backtrack," Dean muttered.

They nodded that they were ready and Dean stepped out. The first dead body lay in the corridor, right where he'd left it. *Awesome. Last thing we need is headless zombies surviving a decapitation.*

There was an eerie silence, as he backtracked to the first classroom. Patti readied her bow, knocking an arrow without drawing it back. When Dean's fingers finished counting down from three, her bow was leveled and drawn. On one, he silently opened the door. *Twang.* An arrow zoomed by his ear and into the forehead of a waiting zombie with a sickening *splat*. Patti smirked, her shot had sent the zombie tumbling backwards. There were a few twitches, then the rotten corpse stilled.

Dean let Zayra in, who quickly scanned the room. She soon exited, though, her head shaking a negative.

The next room was empty of both zombies and a pedestal. Dean frowned but continued on to a door labeled *Janitor's Closet*. Patti was next to him, her bow at the ready. He counted down once more and pulled the door open.

"Fallback!" Dean shouted. The tiny closet was jammed packed full of zombies. At least a dozen spilled out of the small space, eager for their brains.

Dean felt fireballs pass over his shield as the surge of rotting bodies pushed him back. He struck with his trident, landing a brain shot. His weapon was pried from his hand, though, as the zombie fell backwards. His palm crackled with energy and the sensation of magic coursed through his being. He unleashed a powerful beam that he swept across the hallway at head height against the mindless walkers.

The five of them continued to backpedal from the pressure of bodies against the shields. Patti's arrows thinned the enemy's ranks with precise shots while the backrow mages lit the dead on fire. After what felt like minutes, but was probably only a dozen seconds, there were less than three zombies still standing. Dean bored small holes into each of their foreheads with condensed energy orbs.

Wilfred walked over to the rotting corpses, stabbing down into each skull. Dean heard the sound of moaning from above, which told him their fight had attracted more foes. Dean walked back towards the closet to confirm it was cleared and saw the locket, sitting on a pedestal next to a mop.

It was time to get out of this frozen zombie school. He smirked as he indented the locket and they finished the eighth level.

He had enough to talk to Orabel.

THIRTEEN

DEAN

Mixonia - Min's Vault

K ambry leaned into his shoulder supportively. The pair gazed down at the lone female figurine on the shelf. Patti, Zayra, and Wilfred had gone back to the estate for the rest of the day, to study magic. Dean and his lover went to talk to Orabel.

On his way in, Kambry had him deviate to the jewelry section to view the rings. All remaining six rings in the set were marked reserved. Behind them was another band of thick, woven white gold. The smooth surface had divot lettering, filled in with pink diamond dust that spelled *Dean*, which was about as obvious as could be.

Min seemed to be supporting, rather than fighting, the prophecy. This caused Dean to walk from the general shop to the vault. With Kambry by his side, he touched the figurine, lost in thought.

"I have to wonder. If it was so easy to talk to me before, why the silence now?" he muttered, running his thumb over the Orabel figurine's hair. "You okay in there?"

Kambry picked up the figurine gingerly. "I still believe her soul is in this indestructible vessel, but it's not—not really. I... am conflicted. I dreamed of being with a powerful male who'd sweep me off my feet and whisk me away to our paradise." She shook her head, sadly. "Life had dealt me some hard realities."

Dean kissed her forehead, pulling her in for a hug. "Yeah, well, life does what it wants... not what you want. I learned long ago with Uncle G that you have to make the most of what you've got. You can always cut ties and run, but family is all about sticking it out." He sighed, "When you push family away, then you're all alone."

"That is the crux of the matter, isn't it? I can pout like a baby or be inclusive. I shut Sable out, when she didn't even know Hasper and me had a thing before she showed up." Kambry let out a shaky breath. "I literally called her a bitch, behind her back, for no fault of hers—it was just jealousy."

Dean held her close.

"It's odd. I'm happy with Cassie and you. Our bed is big, our hearts are filled with love, and our family is growing. You know I'm going to get pregnant soon, right? If I'm not pregnant, already. It's not some giant surprise, given what we're doing on an almost nightly basis," Kambry said, reaching up and pulling his lips down to meet hers.

He was supportively listening. There wasn't really much he could say. "I love you. If it's what ya want, she goes back onto the shelf and I'll forget about her."

Kambry let out a deep sigh, though there was a gleam of pure joy in her eyes. "No," she said finally, "free her. It has been hundreds of thousands of years since she was locked up in there, if not more. She should have answers for us—and if not, she's still an Elf. They aren't legendary just for shits and giggles. They possess insane fighting skills and magic that makes a girl like me all wet just thinking about it." She pulled him in for another kiss and then tilted her head to whisper in his ear, "Plus, I can lord this very moment over her whenever I want."

"Kambry!" Dean pulled back and gave her a shocked expression. She smirked and they shared a chuckle. "You wouldn't, would you?"

"Bet your fine ass I would. This is about much more than freeing a pitiful soul from the shelves. This is maybe freeing another woman into my bed. Which..." a blush crept up her neck and heated her cheeks, "I can't believe I'm saying this, but I might be okay with."

Dean snickered. "And Jessabee?"

This earned him a light punch on the arm.

"She is different. I've never kissed her, but I've seen her naked several times while we were getting ready for work. She'll, quite literally, fit right in. If there are seven others tied into this crazy family with us, I'm sure we'll have cliques. I know I get along with Jessabee and Cassie. Her?" Kambry said, pointing at Orabel's figurine. "Who knows?"

"Kinda my point. I'd hate to free her only to have it drive you –"

"Pfft, Dean read her contract. It's bru," she paused, smacking her lips, "tal. If you think this sorceress has any room in that contract to make our lives hell, think again. Cassie wrote the contract airtight. Her only allowance was for a baby. Remind you of anyone?"

Dean smirked at her wink, stroking her wing lovingly. "Got it, no contract changes allowed," Dean nodded, building up his confidence. "Anything else?"

Kambry shook her head. "Cassie said for you to trust your instincts. So, although you are free to change whatever you want, just know that Cassie and I built this," Kambry said handing over the contract slate from a pouch on her hip. "Good luck, Dean."

With a sigh, he pressed the button on Orabel's statuette. His body dematerialized as it was sucked into the figurine.

∞∞∞

Dean drifted for only a few moments before a forest spawned around him, complete with hopping bunnies and a very seductive looking elf, who showed up in a nightie.

Her piercing green eyes twinkled in the soft moonlight that filtered down from above. Her ripe, full breasts displayed erect nipples. *Yum...* Orabel sauntered over, putting one step in front of the next in a way that caused her Elven body to sway rhythmically side to side.

"Got it," Dean snorted, "you're sexy. I have that at home in spades. A Dragona and potentially an Osamar. Seduction is not what I need. What I -"

She rolled her eyes, stopping him to say, "Min is meddling again. I agreed to Cassandra's terms already. Did you bring the contract?"

Dean twisted his face up in confusion. "You what?"

"After the sixth age, there were limits and sanctions placed on the Elven race. Why? It's shameful. The Emperor of the Elves caved to Min's outrageous demands so that they could finish out the games and free the last of my kind's trapped souls. For a full millennium, I rejected offers," she smirked, "in the thousands. Now, even after all this time, I think I am only allowed five minutes per offer, not fifteen," Orabel admitted and Dean winced. "I am more than just a battle sorceress. I am worth every damn token you have. I'll even sign your ridiculous contract."

She was getting angry, her foot stomps caused her tits to bounce and Dean bit back a smirk.

"I want you to look into my eyes, Orabel. I'm freeing you because you're a soul Min shouldn't have," he began, "and I want answers. If you –"

"Daft man did you not read –" she snapped at him.

Dean's face reddened and he lost his normal composure. "I'm not a tool for you to berate. You will not rule over us. When the moment calls for it, you will refer to both Cassie and Kambry as Mistress, and you'll abide by your contract," he all but snarled at her. He took a deep breath.

"The moment you sign this, though, you're part of our family. I need to be clear about this—you don't rule me or our family—you are a *member* of that family. Keep your elitist, sassy ass comments in check and try not to lord it over the hired help. Are we clear?" Dean handed over the tablet, having already signed it.

She curtsied, accepted the tablet, and nodded. "Excellent, my King. These rules will not bind us, the love our family develops will."

"Good answer, I don't like to yell. And no, in case you were wondering, I didn't even read the contract," Dean said with a shrug. "Cassie and Kambry came up with it and I trust them completely."

"I know, Cassandra is a Queen of a higher order—she just doesn't know it yet. I accept, Dean Forrester. Thank you for freeing me. My history is a bit rusty and being in here for so long will require me to relearn a few things. I will await you at your portal exit," Orabel said and lifted the tablet. Dean put a hand on the pad, not letting her sign. "Yes?"

"What about your guards?" Dean asked.

"Karixin and Noorsta are mine to free. They're more than simple guards. I'll free them by doing a few solo quests. I'll need my first fifty tokens and not a single one more, to do it. Which I can only spend on freeing the boys, too," She said, eying him speculatively. "Anything else, my lord?"

"The boys? Are they your sons?" Dean asked and she nodded. He removed his hand. "Should make for an interesting dynamic at home."

"They won't go with us. They will return to their home world and be proclaimed heroes for their dedication to their foolish mother," Orabel sighed, signing the tablet.

She gave Dean a tender kiss on the cheek before she dematerialized. He faded back from this plane of existence to his real body.

∞∞∞∞

"So how did it go?" Kambry asked, holding up the two male Elves. "They look so alike."

478

Dean shook the proverbial cobwebs out of his head. He gently took the male Elven figurines from her hands. They went back onto the shelf—for now.

"They look alike," Dean said with a frown, "because she is their mother."

Kambry's eyes widened. "Whoa, that's huge. Lexis and Patti will positively devour them," she snickered.

Dean rolled his eyes so hard, his head went with it.

"Honey, I know." He snorted. "Bless your heart, too, I'd hardly trust you around them. But... they're going home. Apparently, there is a reason we don't ever see Elves helping other races. They were banished after the sixth, or maybe it was the fifth age." Dean shrugged, "So... She can compete to free them, but then after that, she is done with Mixonia."

Kambry laughed. "There are going to be more than enough hunks around, that we don't need these pretty boys constantly distracting us on the estate. I didn't know they couldn't compete."

"I don't think many do," Dean said with a grunt. "Might be a secret, or might just be that it's been so long that everyone has forgotten." He frowned at his locket. "I'm down to my last token. You want to go do a solo PvP run?"

"Tomorrow? I really want to get an ice spell—"

"Kambry," he held a finger to her lips, "I want to pressure you to get a victory on level two, but it can wait. How about we go home, then? We can welcome our newest addition and see how Cassie's and Leena's day went," Dean said with a smile.

A gong sounded in the vault so loudly, that it shook the building's foundation. Dean's hands instinctively shot to his ears a moment too late. There were five echoing *gongs* and by the time the last echoes died, he was confused. When Kambry acted so naturally, as if this wasn't a complete surprise to her, he became puzzled.

"Is that it? Is that the eighth age?" Dean asked quickly, scanning quickly around the vault. "Why aren't the shelves emptying?"

"That signal means the portals are dark—that everyone has exited or died," Kambry said and Dean went full-on defensive. He whipped his short sword out of its sheath and he readied himself to be attacked.

"Whoa, whoa, whoa. Err... sorry," she pulled his arm down and tried to soothe him. "The event portals are dark, meaning the event is over. The guards probably stopped letting people in hours ago."

"Aw, dammit, I wanted to do that event in the PvP. The tokens are so good." Dean slid his sword back home. "What event follows water?"

Kambry gave Dean a flat stare. "We'll find out what the new event spawn is in a half-day earth time, give or take. You looked ridiculous." She shook her head. "Let's get going. There is a certain ancient lady with a..." she frowned, "What did Mom tell me you called it? Oh yeah... a dusty vagina."

"Ha! Yeah, guilty. I hope Orabel doesn't stir the pot too much. I'm a tad overwhelmed as it is. I feel like everything has been ripped apart in my life. I'm glad it's finally starting to come back together," Dean said, leading the way out of Min's Vault. "I'm excited to learn some crowd control magic."

Kambry nodded and pulled on his arm. "I've been dying to learn more magic than just fire and water. Honestly, though, the lessons were crazy expensive. My water magic theoretical knowledge is non-existent. I may have relied too much on the fact that I can twirl a mean fireball. Never really thought that much about locking an opponent down with ice, or an earthen spike. Thero killed me after doing just that—it's a lesson we should all learn from."

Dean mumbled a few choice curses under his breath as her sad voice trailed off to a whisper, at the end. "We all need to improve," he shrugged, "all there is to it."

"So... Who are the rest of the eight?" Kambry wondered, suddenly chipper once again.

Dean chuckled, holding the door open for her, so she could leave first. She performed a slight curtsy in thanks. "Hey, before we launch into speculation about the rest of our growing family..." Dean tilted his head to the side. "What makes a king a king or a princess... well, a princess? Is it all a fairy-tale until people believe it, like a corporation?"

"Uh... I guess. I'm Kambry, the Dragona, of house Forrester. If I'm ever anything more than that, it will be because my family becomes more. Why?" Kambry asked, fluttering lightly down the stairs.

"Orabel called me a King," Dean mumbled, blushing bright red.

Kambry nodded.

The crowds had started to pick up, outside Min's Vault, as people returned from the portal staging area. There were people wailing in abject horror, having realized their loved ones had been killed. The hope these distraught folks had held onto all day, that those they missed would come home, was gone. Dean was seeing the reality of hopelessness and it was worse than the cries of anguish. There were a lot of citizens, too hurt to even cry. He realized something at that point, you don't get to check the vault, unless you had twenty-five tokens, which meant that most friends and family had to wait for the portals to close.

Dean let his Dragona lead him away from the sad sight. The Garden of the Gods was not far away and they walked side-by-side, holding hands, once they had the space.

"I hate that," Dean muttered, not letting go of Kambry's hand.

She eyed him questioningly.

"Fine. Getting back to our conversation..." he shrugged, "Um... well, it takes eight species. So that rules Patti out. Right now, it's Cassie, you, me, and now Orabel."

"Jessabee will probably join us." Kambry snickered, "What do you think of Dorthy?"

Dean shrugged, "Been too busy lately to really think much about her at all. I like Sable, personally, but I don't think she'd go for being in a harem. And –"

Sable appeared in front of them, suddenly. The Demi wore human clothes, a blazer without a bra, and yoga pants. Modest, for her at least, and yet still, very, very sexy. Kambry bit her lip at the sight and Dean raised an eyebrow. *I think she is starting to find women just as appealing as I do.* Sable fell into step with the couple.

Kambry waved and said, "Hi Sable, I take it the mere mention of your name –"

"Yup, you have to mention a god or a Demi, at least in passing, to get their attention. It's different, a bit like a ping with a shimmering window showing who is discussing you. When I saw it was the two of you, I dove into the image."

"As far as the rest of the eight goes, don't be so hasty, Dean," Sable smiled gently. "There is no mad rush, Kambry, Dean is doing things correctly. He is learning the system, as he should." She shook her blonde curls. "Anyway, Father can hear my calls, but is not answering them. None of the gods are answering their children's calls," Sable said with a sour tone, her face tightening into a grimace.

"What does that mean?" Dean wondered, leading them out of the Garden of the Gods. "Are we still going fishing?"

"Give me a few more days to follow a couple of leads, and yes I'd love to go fishing."

For some reason, Kambry smiled at that.

"There is something different about the groups the gods form," Sable continued, "they can step into a speeded up time—where a single party that would feel like it lasted a single night on Oakley, lasts for a hundred or even a thousand years. There have been times when these have occurred before, and I've been ignored for what felt like ages."

Dean nodded, wondering how the time dilation worked.

"As for your wives, Dean, I recommend patience. Keep competing. Grow your estate, your skills, and your family through your trials. You're on the right path and I dare not say more on the subject," she said, tucking herself between them. Taking Kambry and Dean's hands into hers, she proceeded. "I've been thinking about my father's offer."

Sable sighed. "I'd be completely at his whim. On your estate, I could flee to the stars if I got upset, or we could go as a family. Also," she blushed guiltily, "I may have peeked in on all of you a time or three—your family is adorable. You are attentive to one other, and none are treated like servants. And yet, there are still servants. It is kind of like what the gods have."

"What?" Dean stopped, confused.

"I've never been to the proverbial 'heaven'. The theory is that the gods form groups to cohabitate with. Some have harems, some groups are mixed. Each of those groups crafted a master plane of existence, tied to a planet they love. They live in an isolated heaven, occasionally venturing down to the surface of the planet. If it is confusing to you, then please understand that it is to us, as well." She sighed. "Yet, we still aspire to have our own covens, our own cliques of those we enjoy spending time with."

"Do the gods always stay in these master planes of existence?" Dean asked.

"Father has moved twice, since I was born. It's not unheard of that immortals eventually tire of one another and move on." She smirked, "I'll never live long enough, seeing as I'll become a mortal, to get to the point that I tire of my family."

"My family?" Kambry said with a smile. "That has a much better ring to it, than my servants."

"Please," Sable released Dean's hand to fling her hair over her shoulder. "I'll have those too. Yet, I concur. I'm an alpha girl. We don't have manulators in purgatory," Sable said with a double brow bounce and a wink at Kambry.

She jumped slightly when Kambry pinched her ass in reply. Dean chuckled. "Sorry, Dorthy," he said with a laugh.

"Probably best that way, she's falling in love with one of Lonny's team members. If you haven't noticed, love is pretty scarce here. It's hard to find a family or even a partner. When you do? You go for it. You gave her a bit of a cold shoulder at first, and she's already moved on. Same with Lexis," Sable said as they passed under Min's statues.

"So... why don't you draft up a contract?" Dean asked.

Sable paused them before they reached the exit portal. "Next bedroom adventure, please invite me. If fishing gets pushed back –"

Kambry suddenly kissed Sable, causing Dean to smirk.

"Okay, off with you both," Sable said, desire flaring in her eyes. "Fishing later, sex first, and then I'll draft a contract."

Sable vanished.

"I think her father gave her a super shitty offer, and she pretended it was good," Dean said in a sad voice.

"Dean," Kambry squirmed beside him. "I'm super horny, right now. Take me home, please," Kambry begged.

Dean did the best thing he could—still holding hands, they ran the rest of the way home.

∞∞∞

When he crossed the portal into Felna's cavern, he saw Orabel chatting with a soldier and his handler.

"Dean!" Orabel said, running up to him. The clank of the chainmail she wore threw him off.

"Hey, you're in armor already?" Dean said, confused.

Orabel smirked. "I caught Patti before she left. She said I could use her gear to free my boys. I'm heading on in with Carl. He is the portal master, now that you're out. I'll be at the estate in no more than a few hours. An Elf like me with a bow like this will wreck the solo PvP ladder."

"Okay," Dean chuckled. "Good luck and see you when you get home. I'll talk with Cassie about where you'll be staying. There are spare shuttles to fly you home up at the top of the cavern. There's a tram that will give you a ride to that point. Used to be a half-hour walk," Dean trailed off, he could see her mind was elsewhere.

She kissed his cheek and fled to the portal once Carl ducked in.

"She seems nice," Kambry said. "We need to get a shower down here."

Felna paused her movie and turned around. "It's in the works. Getting water down to this point either meant hauling it down that long tunnel or constructing plumbing. Now that the tram is here, though, we're good to go. 'Soonish'... is what the construction guys said. I've got a magic shit bucket, but a shower would be amazing."

"Thanks, Felna," Kambry said, shaking her head at the Minotaur's forwardness. They removed their gear into the expanded armory. Kambry pinched Dean's butt when he removed his leather kilt. "Quicky in the shuttle on the way home or a group thing with the manulator once we get there?"

"Both sounds great," Dean laughed, hurrying to get out of his gear.

Kambry smirked and gave a nod. They stowed their armor, hustling for the tram. The new system shot them up to the main cavern with a return enclosed cart passing them coming back the other way. The entire three-minute ride, Kambry kissed him and nuzzled into his neck, sliding a hand back and forth over the growing bulge in his shorts.

When they finally entered the shuttle and it left the construction crews behind, Kambry ripped off her top. He buried his face in her big, plump breasts when she straddled his lap. Dean pulled his shorts down to his knees, while Kambry lifted her up skirt and pushed her panties to the side. She teased his tip with her dripping vagina.

"Do you want this little pussy or my tight ass? And Dean." He looked up from her breasts. "Both is not an option this time," she giggled, teasing his cock with her wetness.

"I'll save your ass for in the shower, later. This will do, for now," he grunted, holding her hips still and thrusting up into her slick heat.

She arched her back and moaned. When Kambry focused on Dean her eyes were hungry as she rubbed her clit in circles against his body. His shaft was hilted and her desire dripped down. Her hands clasped onto the back of the seat so she could grind him in deeper.

The swivels turned to aggressive snaps. Dean sucked on her nipples, squeezing her large tits to hold them steady while she rocked. He playfully bit her swollen tits, just enough she enjoyed the pain. His girth was enveloped and he felt her pulses of pleasure.

After only a few minutes of his cock hitting her G-spot and her finding the rhythm she wanted she climaxed at a very loud level. Her hands clenched his hair as she shuddered in orgasm. Dean grunted, his grin ear to ear. He was nearing the same point when she suddenly hopped off.

"Hey," he said and she wagged her finger, darting away.

She pretended to hide behind the seat a row up. "Your turn," she said playfully.

He leaped out of the chair to catch her. Kambry peeled out a joyful squeal. Her face squished against the side window of the shuttle when he bent her over. He had two options. Without lube, he passed on her ass.

His palm rushed down to *crack* against her butt cheek. Kambry's long black hair flipped over her shoulders and she said, "Harder Daddy."

Crack, her ass glowed red. After the third ass smack, he buried his cock in her dripping slit. Dean yanked her away from the window so he could relentlessly pound into her. The slap of his hips into her juicy booty echoed in the cabin. He added an occasional smack, a hard hair pull, and at one point, a slight chokehold.

Kambry loved every minute of it and Dean grew frustrated that he couldn't finish.

His frustration turned to shock when the shuttle started to descend towards the estate. They tried to adjust their clothing, as best they could, trying to appear relatively decent. Not a chance—her plain white shirt clearly highlighted her wet nipples, while his engorged cock was pitching a massive tent in his shorts.

There were people waiting for them, too, which meant getting out of the shuttle would be awkward. He saw Patti and Zayra talking with Jessabee and Cassandra. He sent a quick text to his other wife, asking her to come into the shuttle. She read her phone message, tilted her head to the side in confusion, and excused herself for the shuttle. Jessabee followed after her, while Patti and Zayra went inside.

The moment Cassandra entered the shuttle cabin she snorted, "Ugh, it wreaks of sex in here."

Jessabee flushed, "Should I go?" She looked around shyly. "I'd like to stay."

"Where are we going?" Cassandra asked with a raised brow. When she noticed their appearance and flushed faces, she grinned in anticipation.

"Our balcony," Kambry chuckled, sealing the door and inputting their suite's balcony as the destination before Jessabee could get out, or even get an answer to her question.

"Quick catchup. Orabel is free but competing to free her sons. We're going to pull out the manulators and fuck in the shower with a surprise guest."

Cassandra started to respond when Dean lunged for her and pulled her into his lap. They kissed passionately. She smirked, breaking the kiss and put a finger to his lips. "Jessabee," she called over his shoulder, "you in or out? Oh!"

Dean's attentions had distracted Cassandra, and she'd missed that Jessabee and Kambry were making out. Their smiles were wide and their hands were roaming all over each other's curves. The shuttle docked at their suite and the four of them ran inside. Cassandra dove into the closet; she was on a mission.

He followed after her. "Uh... Grab two... Sable said she wanted to join in the fun if –"

"Ooooh... kinky, she is always peering in the window with her wings. Yeah, I figured she'd be a strap it on kind of gal," Cassandra said with a devious smile.

When Dean walked out of the room and into the shower, Sable was already sprawled naked across the bench. Her blonde hair spilled down her body, wet and dark from the water. Her thick hips curved over the edge of the bench, and she twirled a finger around her clit while watching Kambry and Jessabee kissing. Her pink petals were unfurled and her pussy lips already flushed a deep pink when Dean looked. The gorgeous woman squeezed a supple boob with her other hand.

She blew him a kiss.

Dean smirked, he wasn't one to walk blindly past the sight of a woman strumming her clit. He had been going to lick her sweet, little pussy, but saw it was already leaking with desire. The one thing that concerned him about bringing Sable into his family was her habit of asserting dominance. Better to nip that issue in the bud.

He walked confidently towards her, his swagger swinging his cock side to side.

She reached for his penis, only to have her wrist snatched up by him. A yank on her arm ripped the Angelina off her bench. With a few rapid, aggressive moves, he spun her around and bent her over. She shivered in anticipation, looking back at him over her shoulder.

He teased her briefly with the tip, lining himself up inside her inner lips. She tensed and then relaxed, pushing back at him in earnest. Without warning, Dean slammed his cock to the hilt into her wet slit, while leaving a pink handprint on her taut ass. She gasped and suddenly came with a scream.

Shit! How long had she been here, playing with herself while waiting for his cock? With a grin, he twisted her long, blonde hair in a bunch so that a slight tug had her arching her back, pulling him inside her even deeper. He ground his hips into her plump cheeks. In the side glass, he watched her swollen tits bounce after each hard thrust.

She started whimpering. He could feel her pussy reflexively grabbing at his girth; he knew she must be close, once again. Holding her hip tight against him, he eased her overbalanced torso up until she was flush against his chest. She lifted one leg onto the bench, ensuring he stayed inside her the entire time. He let go of her hair and reached up and around her throat with his large hand.

They ground together. The more she pushed back against him, the tighter he squeezed. Her whimpers became moans; those moans became screams of pleasure. She came hard on his cock, a rush of fluids squirting out of her pussy and coating his balls and thighs. She slumped against him, having nearly passed out, she came so hard.

There was no question in his mind. Dean had conquered Sable. He decided to let her have her own fun, since there were extra ladies around. He let his cock slip out of her pulsing pink pussy and gently set her back onto the bench.

He went out of the shower to get Sable a manulator when Cassandra arrived, her dildo flopping lewdly from her hips. Dean let her get in the shower, trailing her tight ass. He watched the four women get into a mini orgy in the shower. *I'm the luckiest man alive!*

He watched Sable's wings pull Cassandra in close. Cassandra removed the manulator to attach the strap on to the taller angelic woman, before dropping down to her knees.

"Oh my, this is different and amazing!" Sable squealed a bit in shock, as Cassandra sucked on her manulator. Sable pulled Kambry over, pushed her head down to join Cassie's and placed a hand to the back of both ladies' heads as they pleased her.

That left Dean alone with a very seductive Jessabee in the shower. Her rainbow eyes hadn't transitioned with her human body and they devoured his naked form. Her teeth pinched her bottom lip while she groped her big tits, playfully. He couldn't take his eyes off her smooth hips and flat stomach. The vision of loveliness before him was divine as he watched the water flow down her hourglass figure. She, too, dropped to her knees and then waved him forward.

His cock swayed briefly before her, on his journey to her side. She took him into her mouth and gagged on his penis, trying to deep throat it and failing. She switched quickly to a pleasing, talented blowjob. The swirling of her tongue was in tandem with her head bobs and two-handed strokes. Her rainbow eyes kept stealing glances up at his face, while he enjoyed the sensation.

Out of the corner of his eye, he caught sight of Kambry fully doubled over. Her hands clasped her own ankles while Sable fucked her with rapid pumps of her hips. Cassandra watched with a smirk, her eyes alight with a smoldering desire, sitting back on the shower bench. Dean folded Jessabee's hair into a ponytail, gently pulled her off his cock and walked her mouth onto Cassandra's strap-on.

Dean mounted Jessabee from behind, his bulging cock sliding smoothly into her welcoming vagina. There were a lot of moans all around and very little talking. Dean slammed into Jessabee over and over. He felt her pulsing around his cock, her slick walls squeezing his girth felt amazing.

After a few minutes of nothing but grunts and moans, Sable cried out again in orgasm. Hearing her go, Dean set off soon after. In only a few more minutes of rapid thrusting, whatever he'd held back on the shuttle, earlier, now released as he pumped his jizz into Jessabee with a shudder. He felt Kambry's big tits press into his back. Her hands reached around him to pull Jessabee's hips back into his, locking his cock in place while he filled the unicorn girl up.

His seed pulsed into her womb while she continued to please Cassandra. Kambry walked around Dean to gently pull Jessabee from Cassie. The Dragona straddled Cassandra and slid down onto the manulator; Cassandra fucked her just the way she liked it. Dean slid his cock from Jessabee and watched his cum drip out of her still clenching vagina.

"Welcome to the family," Cassandra said, and grinned at a flushed Jessabee. "Sable had so much fun, she left to go calm down."

Kambry snickered and said, "She's a squirter, alright. Showered us all when she came—even with that manulator on." She wriggled her soft pillows against his back, her hands groping and teasing his still half-hard cock. "When I asked her how

Dean was," Kambry chuckled wickedly, "she was almost speechless, could only say she'd never cum so hard in her long, immortal life."

Jessabee pulled Dean's lips down to hers. When their kiss finally parted she said, "Sit down, Dean. It's my turn to please you."

The next half hour was an orgy the four of them would not soon forget. Dean loved every minute of it.

CHAPTER

FOURTEEN

DEAN

Forrester Estate

"The seven major magics are?" Dorthy asked the assembled class.

The view screen behind her read the exact question she had asked. In front of her sat the ten active members of Team Ola. Dean and his troops occupied a row and behind them was Lonny with his full team.

When no one answered at first, Patti cleared her throat and said, "Fire, lightning, air, water, earth, healing, arcane or is it light?"

"Arcane and very good," Dorthy said and the screen changed over to one word— limitations. The word was gigantic and looming on the display. "All master mages meditate, study, and seek new knowledge. Why?"

Nick, the newest member of Lonny's team, said, "To increase their mana pool."

"Exactly. Now, what I'm about to get into is considered controversial. My job is to provide the information, your job is to properly utilize it. Dean brought up a good talking point when he asked me a question earlier. He'd had a conversation with a vendor that left him conflicted."

Dean snorted, remembering how quickly Grosca had dismissed the value of his javelins.

"In this example, the said vendor, in my opinion, was not only wrong, but dumb. Mazes grow in strength. They become more challenging as you progress with more length and monsters inside. When all this adds up, it's commonsense that a level seventy floor is riskier than a seven.

"I want you to think about something," Dorthy continued. "When flinging a rock with air magic, you can get it up to such a speed that it will cause a sonic boom. That noise reverberates throughout the maze."

She clapped her hands for effect. Leena cried out from the kitchen, and an angry momma Cassandra popped her head out to glare daggers at Dorthy, who covered her mouth apologetically.

"Sorry, Cassandra. And this is exactly what I mean. I pulled aggro, in video game terms." She frowned and ducked her head, "and in real life, apparently, my ruckus caused a commotion. The cause had an effect. More monsters or mobs further in the chain become aware that you're in the area. Your battle line falters, and you wipe or scramble back to the black portal of defeat—suffering the most ignominious of deaths."

Kambry tilted her head to the side in confusion.

"Perfect, Kambry is frowning. She hasn't lived through this type of death yet—death from embarrassment, or survivor's guilt. I have," Dorthy said and tucked her chin down, wiping at her eyes. Her pause was reflective as she took a couple of deep breaths to regain her composure.

"It's okay if you —" Dean began.

"No Dean," Dorthy sighed, "let my lesson be your gain. Limitations is on this screen for a very good reason. The question you should focus on, though, should not be why mages are limited, but instead... how. How are mages limited? And how was that vendor oh so very wrong? I was on floor sixty-eight. Our team of five spawned outside of a city. The city itself was the maze, assuming we could get in.

"I was a backline mage. We brought three mages, a tank, and a mix-build dual wielder. Our lineup was fantastic—for most mazes. Most being the key word here. We knew at some point, our composition would cause us problems, but we'd only lost one maze, too, up to that point. In that one... Rigo, well, he held the tunnel up so we could escape."

She shook off the memory. "Back to outside the marbled city. We saw bears, not the humanoid kind, and came to a conclusion. The plan was simple: buildup a defense, lure in our foes, and kill them off by sections. When you get into the upper levels of the maze, this is a common strategy. We elevated our perimeter to the point that we were comfy and confident of being able to hold our defensive position. Then we pulled the first section of bears.

"We knew they'd roar and growl; they most certainly did so, making a great racket. I expended spell after spell into the bears. Despite my heavy mana consumption, my spells were thinning the herd, and victory appeared certain.

"Suddenly harpies, so many..." Dorthy shook off the memory, looking up with tears in her eyes. "Harpies flew out in droves, a flock so big it blotted out the fake sky. The trick with harpies is that they are useless in a corridor or inside a building. In the open, though, they are... deadly.

"I ran out of mana well before the swarm was defeated. When Rigo called out the retreat, it was too late. I was dragged to a roost and feasted on for days... alive."

Cassandra covered Leena's ears from the side of the room where she hung on every word.

"Patti, if she learns magic, will be a powerful champion. More powerful than me, Thero, or Kambry. Why?" Dorthy asked with a somber tone.

Lonny raised his hand and said, "She will be using all the three bars, instead of two. Her arrows will rain down on her foes, using her stamina. She can pause to let her stamina bar refill and cast spells, draining her mana bar, until she needs to return to ranged damage. Where a mage has only health and mana. Running in a fight is sometimes an option that uses up stamina, but it won't kill more foes. Kambry has a good combination, with melee potentially draining her health, and magic, but the perfect scenario is using all three bars."

Dorthy smiled and said, "A vendor told Dean 'Why use static weapons like javelins or arrows when you can fling a fireball'. There is part of the answer. The other is Patti's high overall stats, which also means she has more health. She will be more flexible in a fight, and suitable for additional situations that a basic mage will not be able to contribute to.

"When you tell a mage, don't use your mana to kill, it's offensive to them—understandably so. I never learned archery. I wish I had." She shook her head, sadly.

"A mage's limitations are offset by increasing their intelligence and willpower to improve both the size and reconstitution of their mana pool. Then again, they can also drink fancy potions for mana regen.

"I like to think of all the ways I could have avoided that death. We would have needed to build our defense next to the portal in order to escape the harpies. I could have rained arrows down on the bears. Ice stormed from the sky. The list goes on and on, but is irrelevant.

"I never went back in after that. The guild was slow to free me and I was resentful we didn't build a cover."

The double doors at the front entrance cracked open, letting in the sounds of the downpour outside, the rain smacking into taut canvas and pouring over rocks. Orabel, in human guise, entered with a smiling Jessabee. Dean saw they were in casual, dry clothes, not a drop of water on them. He figured the auto tarps had kept them and their satchels dry.

"Perfect timing. So... what is it?" Dorthy asked

Jessabee handed her a bag.

"The event is duets," Jessabee said, rubbing her hands together, teasing the big reveal. "It's black for magic allowed. Oh, and I got Apache back, only to send him back out again. Hurray, free token fractions."

"Thank you, Jessabee. If you and this new woman want to go –" Dorthy began.

Dean held a finger up. Dorthy stopped for him.

"Welcome home, I hope things went well? I'm curious as to why you're in human form?" he asked Orabel, tilting his head to the side to admire her new look.

"You disapprove?" Orabel asked. Her green eyes and brown hair gave her a unique, human look.

Dean shook his head and blew a raspberry. "Not in the slightest. Come, sit here at my side. You can brief me after the lesson is done."

Orabel found a chair and placed it on Dean's right. Dean gestured for Dorthy to please continue.

"With Mistress Cassandra's permission, I had Jessabee purchase ten scrolls: two healing, three water, and three earth."

Dean's and Lonny's eyes lit up.

"Designate a healer per team. The rest of the spells are primarily to control your opponent's movements. Once you pick out your scroll, everyone is to go to a quiet place. Alone." She grinned at Dean before including the rest of the class in her sweeping gaze. "I'm looking at you all regarding this one—not just Dean."

"Forrester Estate needs to be quiet for the next few hours. You'll digest your scroll. Focus on the magic that you now have access to, and try to summon the element into your palm." Her grin blossomed into a smile. "Don't worry if you pass out from the exertion, simply take a nap and try again." Her expression turned serious once more. "Any questions?" Dorthy asked, this time with a stern tone and serious, high eyebrows. She nailed the stern teacher vibe.

"What do we do if we bring the element to our hand?" Gerald, from Lonny's team, asked.

"Hold it there until you pass out. This is a willpower exercise that will be part of your training routine, going forward. The longer you hold onto the element, the more you drain your mana pool completely, the more willpower you will gain. Be mindful, though. Focus too long on developing your magic, and you'll get muscle atrophy—becoming a glass cannon."

Dean stood up and looked them over. "We all still need to hit the gym, swim, run, sword fight, play catch, shoot bows while riding, and well... you get the idea." He smirked. "It is amazing and new and you'll want to invest heavily in your magic, but that is exactly why I want you to limit your time on this," he said.

Dorthy walked over to Dean and handed him five scrolls before passing the rest to Lonny. Dean handed Kambry the healing spell. He snagged a water spell and passed the rest down the line. He saw Wilfred trade with Patti.

Dorthy broke up their side-bar chatter by saying, "I know you want to know how to effectively use these spells, and you will—in due time. Focus, for now, on learning your new magic and growing your mana pool. And... Mistress Cassandra has the floor."

"Thank you for your insight, Dorthy. With this major purchase for both Lonny's team, and Dean's team, we didn't have to drop below a hundred and fifty tokens. That is my threshold for our reserve, ensuring we have enough to free a wiped team. As we just heard, it happens."

She looked at everyone, eagerly clutching their new spells, and smiled. "You earn, you get rewarded. Jessabee just whispered the score to me. Team Core is at 279," she said to a chorus of groans.

"Do we have a champion selected?" Lonny asked.

Cassandra nodded. "Last time, it was Team Ola who represented Oakley. This time, Team Snaggletooth has a champion ready to go. All we can do is continue to compete and keep growing. Which means more tokens. Have fun with your scrolls."

Dean unraveled the scroll. The top line read. *I _____ want to learn water magic.*

He grunted and said, "I, Dean, want to learn water magic."

The paper scroll shriveled up until it was nothing but a fat drop of water in his hand. *Magic was amazing!* He stared in fascination at the transformation. That is... until the water split into three streams that flew up his nose and into his ears.

He jumped in surprise, coughing furiously. Orabel failed to hold in her giggles from his side. The ingestion was for but a second, and he recovered quickly from the shock.

"Fook me," Dean muttered, "didn't see that coming." He glanced around to see the others going through a similar process. He grinned at the still giggling Orabel. "Come, walk the human preserve with Cassie and me."

Dean scooted his chair back, offering Orabel a hand. She daintily placed a palm in his and he guided her over to his wife and daughter. Leena was swaddled into a snuggle sack against Cassandra's chest, sleeping peacefully. Dean crooked an elbow for her to latch on to and led them outside.

The sun tried to peek through the overcast skies, despite the heavy rain. He knew it was daytime, and yet, it felt like a gray beast had occupied the skies. Orabel splayed her fingers out and danced them in an odd pattern. A green aura shot from her digits to the dead garden in front of the estate.

Big beautiful sunflowers sprouted from the ground. A full dozen of the creations reached Dean's height, with bright yellow petals. Dean tensed when the heads of the flowers swiveled to follow them.

"What the fook did ya do?" Dean asked, stepping in front of Cassandra to get between her and the animated plants.

"I told you that I was worth far more out here than simply as a sorceress in the games. Those will defend our family now," Orabel said, removing her hand that held Dean's to sprout a bulbous plant next to the walkway. "This will explode if a foe is detected."

Cassandra rolled her eyes. Her hands came free of the baby, the snug wrap holding Leena up. "Why do we need this and how does it determine friend from foe?"

"My goal over the coming days includes a few things. And I'd like to get some potions to hurry along the development of our defenses. I was –" Orabel continued.

"Why?" Dean interrupted her, stopping suddenly.

She frowned. Her finger pointed up to the rain clouds and she said, "I was going to get to the point. Elves are patient and social creatures. Do not rush me if you wish for my happiness. With that said I'll get to the point. Min won't always be protecting you. She drove off the deadly desert creations and –"

"Because of Lexis?" Cassandra asked, her interested piqued.

"Who's that?" Orabel asked, tilting her head at the unfamiliar name.

"Um... our nanny. Never mind," Cassandra blushed furiously as Dean gave her a pointed stare.

"Ah, her secret is safe with me." Orabel held up a hand to forestall Cassie's denial. "I know you didn't tell me who Lexis is, but Min wouldn't go to these lengths for someone simple. I will keep it in mind, and treat Lexis with the utmost respect."

Cassandra nodded, settling down.

Orabel frowned. "I'm surprised Min let someone so important to them close to the Vault Breaker."

"Vault Breaker?" Dean frowned.

"Yes, it's a title of yours in the prophecy. I think I said it right." The ancient elf shook her head, "My mind is so foggy from the soul pit."

"Wait, I'm supposed to like... break the vault with a mighty hammer or something?" Dean asked as Orabel cast another patch of sunflowers before they entered the preserve.

"I... I don't remember. I need to dig back into the books and I will, soon. I promise to tell you everything I can, once I know or remember more. My storage was ejected, with the release of my sons, and my books are waiting in the shuttle, to be placed in my accommodations. My boys were the trigger, the final straw. As of today, for who knows how far into the Elven future, no Elf may return to Mixonia."

"How do you like your new home?" Cassandra asked cheerfully, trying to shift the topic away from a mother's loss.

"I thought you'd be worse. You actually care, which is not only surprising, but heartening. It is kind of you to be so considerate. As for this estate..." she shrugged, "this is my home, now. At least until Dean passes of old age." Dean shot her a look of 'hey, easy' that she ignored. "For now, though, I will improve upon it. You need to make this place impervious to sight—from the stars and other spying eyes."

Orabel gestured at the grounds around them. "I have magic that can disable drones, trees that will block infrared sensors, and plants that will keep us alive by defending us. Call me paranoid, but this newfound life is one I want to protect—in accordance with the terms of our contract."

Cassandra nodded.

"As for how the plants tell friend from foe, well they can tell who lives here, and then gauge who is hostile. It's part instinct and part magic. Look. My guess is rumors are already spreading. The moment my figurine was gone from that shelf, some very powerful people likely began to put in place plans they have hoarded for eons against such a contingency. This new home will become a target, if it is not one already."

"Can you elaborate?" Cassandra asked, turning them around.

Orabel shook her head, no.

"What can I do to ensure my... our baby is safe."

She playfully swatted Dean's bum causing him to skip an extra step with a smirk.

"My books need to be brought in." She paused, clenching her fists in frustration. Her soft eyes hardening with her deepening worry lines, she admitted "I need to study the text all over again. Which will take time. To give myself a break, I want to build a big forest around us. That means potions—probably twenty medium potions. They will be worth every token. When I'm done with that, I can bring in animals to help defend our forest," Orabel stated.

Dean snapped his fingers, because he finally understood. "You're our protector queen. You can manage animals?" Dean asked.

"Like the horses in the stable I sense?" Orabel replied and he nodded. "Yes, they could be set free now. No stable needed. They will even drop dung in designated compost areas. And it's not me casting spells on them. It's me simply explaining to them how things work here. Animals are smart, if you can talk to them on their level. Though, to be honest, that is tough."

"Dinosaurs?" Dean asked.

Orabel tilted her head and then her eyes lit up in understanding. "Yes, my mind associates something different with that word, but I believe I understand what you mean. Hint, I'm not an Elf to blend in and to adapt. I would be lost without Min's ability to translate and extrapolate."

"Okay, you and I are going to hand off this little girl to Olivia or Lexis. They are her Nannies. Oh," Cassandra stopped and pulled back the snuggle wrap's cover, "this is Leena. She's actually been a very chill baby, so far. Sleeps a ton."

Dean snorted, recalling a few not-so-chill sleepless nights.

Orabel gave a slight laugh and said, "Wait until she cuts a tooth."

"The books I read –"

"Will never do as well as you can," Dean quipped, quickly dodging an ear flick attempt. "Oh, real quick, how did your competition go?"

"I sat on floor one and killed two people while perched high in a tree. I killed the third literally turning them into an ice cube. My willpower is in the thousands from stubbornly staying in the pit. Anyway, Min auto ejected me."

"It took that long?" Dean asked.

Orabel shrugged. "I never shot the bow from my perch, unless it was a kill shot. And, yes, I can craft bows and arrows. If you would have read the contract –"

Cassandra snickered and stuck out her tongue before saying, "Let's leave the brute to stew in an empty horse stall while he tries to summon water to his fingertips."

Dean snorted and rolled his eyes.

"You, though, my dear," Cassandra hooked an arm through Orabel's, leading her back towards the mansion, "we need to figure out where all your stuff is going to go. Do you want a spare suite, attached to our room, or would you prefer your room be separate from ours? You get to pick because Jessabee hasn't moved in yet. Is that all your stuff?"

Dean shifted around to where he could see the back of the shuttle; it was loaded with bookshelves and chests—not totes or cardboard. Finely crafted wooden boxes, with nice curves and intricate clasps, lay waiting in the shuttle. Even the handles appeared to be inlaid with silver. Those looked awful heavy, so Dean quietly started backpedaling. Cassandra frowned at Dean before shaking her head, no.

"We have hired help from Mixonia, dear. I will send Rew and Yarka to collect Orabel's things after this. Do you want to live by a baby or in solitude?" Cassandra asked, pulling the elf away, while giving Dean a wink.

Orabel stretched, drawing Dean's eyes like a magnet, before turning a nearby sapling that had been only a foot tall into a small tree. Dean decided he should get on with his studies. While Orabel thought about Cassandra's offer, he went to the riding arena, searching for a quiet spot.

"Couldn't we share the suite?" Orabel began. "We can build a bigger estate, where the top floor is a communal area –"

Dean bit back a giggle when Cassandra huffed and said, "Yes, how about we discuss this more when Leena is with a nanny and there are people moving your stuff."

"Deal," Orabel said.

Dean heard them fade into background noise as he entered the fresh-hay-smelling stable. While he was excited to practice magic. He was even more excited to compete in the two versus two event.

He just had to figure out who he should be teamed with.

CHAPTER

FIFTEEN

DEAN

Forrester Estate

A week. Dean spent an entire week mastering his ability to draw water to his hand. There was no magical moment for him. The proverbial, I focused harder and it worked, didn't happen either. While he was attempting the feat of creating magic, Dean soon realized that he had much more mana than the others.

While he was working out, swimming, and running, he'd try to generate ice. Maybe it was the fact that he was skipping a few steps—that he didn't want just water—that made the process so challenging. The irony was, he froze his hand to a treadmill, didn't understand what was happening, and flung himself off the treadmill when he tore his hand free. That stunt resulted in a broken collar bone.

Orabel healed his wound, but pride be damned, he was ecstatic to finally be able to control ice.

That was on day three. By day seven, he could create an ice slick or encase a target's feet in ice—which is what he'd been waiting for. Life had pushed him so hard lately, he'd decided to take a breather. There were still competitions, but it was only to get him beyond the basic levels of solo PvE.

Well, that and they cycled through as a team with Patti and Kambry as portal leads from levels one to ten. While there was an excitement to those floors, since they built on each other, it wasn't nearly as thrilling as their first time through.

For Dean, it was a week of smashing basic mazes. He was starting to get really excited about the next stage of competing. As a whole, though, their efforts were productive and positive. No one died and got locked into a figurine. Everyone was progressing, with both their stats and their magic, while continuing to work on both melee and ranged combat.

Dean had finally stomached the high cost and had Jessabee pick him up some expertly crafted javelins. Testing these well-balanced weapons, he learned a few things. From ten yards back, he could hit the center of the target almost every time. From thirty yards back, maybe two out of three times he could hit a man-sized or larger target. From fifty yards back, he could only hit the target—if he was lucky— once every two or three throws.

He learned hurling a stick was not ideal for ranged fighting, unless you were facing a massed formation. Even with his poor aim, at least to start out with, he practiced it often. He wanted to get good with hurling javelins before picking up a bow— which would certainly come next.

Jessabee moved in with Orabel. That was a bit of a surprise to Dean. With her work as a market guide finished, she spent her spare time training. She'd never be a huge competitor, but without the massive fear of getting locked away forever, she could afford to take a few risks. Like him, she wanted to properly train first, though.

Orabel, on the other hand, had gone crazy with her magic and mana potions. When Dean left his home or glanced out a window, there was nothing around them but forest. Intense, dense forest—with trees soaring to unbelievable heights. There was a myriad of life in the foliage and vines that were either bought from the human markets or exported from Mixonia.

The Elf had literally transformed the Forrester Estate, to the point that environmental agencies showed up. Min didn't care about this intrusion and left Dean and Cassandra on their own to handle these pencil pushers. The hundred acre forest sprouting around their home, was growing bigger and taller every minute. The rains fueled Orabel's magical creations to new heights. The billowing overhead cover grew so dense, that they had to install new lighting outside the mansion.

They had to deal with government geeks prodding around the property. These ones had zero backbone, though, and little actual power. Cassandra told them there was nothing she could do, because this was simply how nature worked with the crazy amounts of rain that had fallen lately and alien plant life. She apologized, without offering much else by way of explanation. The agents all swore that this wasn't natural... and it wasn't. But, they couldn't prove it was magic, either. Which meant they took a number of samples and eventually let them be.

Cassandra was kept busy, trying to balance the finances. She purchased an atmospheric shuttle, so she could start getting the most Galactic-coins for their tokens. Since they were stuck mostly doing lower levels, their talent reserves were mediocre, at best. But even that meant big money on Oakley, if she traded properly. After a lot of talks with the family, their mid-term objective became to fund a community ship.

Dean had been hesitant at first, and still was, actually. But... They had no plan to leave Oakley, long term. It was, more or less, a safety net, a vacation tool, and a means to visit Orabel's home, one day. She dropped a hint or two that Dean might live much longer than a normal human, if they did so. Of course, that warmed everyone up to the idea.

Plus if they poured their extra funds into a bigger mansion, it would be really hard to sell—being in the middle of a forest that sat in the middle of a desert. If they bought a mega mansion that could fly, on the other hand, not only was there no inconvenience as it was constructed, they could resell it if need be, and tailor it to their specific needs. Ultimately, those were all things he could agree with.

Kambry learned to heal. She'd actually gotten that spell down in the first two days after reading her scroll and was surprisingly proficient at it. Her water magic, though, refused to cooperate.

No ice. Nothing. She'd throw fits and tantrums in her frustration, though it did no good. That was just one frustrating aspect of her life, lately. Dean had caught Kambry vomiting in the mornings—twice. Since she had no medical chip, there was no automatic alert. Although her tests kept coming back negative, her body was clearly telling her that she was pregnant. This left them all confused. The only answer was to wait and see, to give it more time.

Zayra and Wilfred soon hit their ten-day mark, and they were really excited to free Zayra's parents. Dean had offered them the equivalent of fifty tokens, guaranteeing that Team Ola would free the duo, if they got trapped on the shelves. In a stubborn show of 'we did it on our own'—the proper way, they refused his assistance. Her parents, it seemed, could wait a few more days.

Jaxon was freed from purgatory. The arcane mage quit gardening and continued his studies. He locked himself away with Orabel, the two of them trying to decipher everything they could about the coming eighth age from the prophecies. He asked Dean to buy a number of arcane scrolls in passing, and it was added to the never-ending list of items to get. Arcane spells would be everyone's next magic, because they were the hardest to learn and the most efficient in their mana usage.

Quincy never responded, though Dean had sent a few messages asking him to come by and visit. Getting nothing back from his best friend frustrated him to no end. Quincy's breakup with Patti was a stupid reason to stay away, and Dean was starting to worry he had fallen into a deep depression or something.

Uncle G was doing great, frequently sending photos of himself eating or drinking with older sugar mommas. In a photo of him next to a slot machine, he proudly displayed some measly jackpot he'd won. In another picture, he cast a line into a river—trying to catch some local delicacy fish. Those messages made Dean's day and he was happy for his uncle.

He'd never told his uncle that magic was real. He was one of the few who was out of that loop and because of that, Dean couldn't share with him that Leena was out of the womb... eight months early.

Anoka would stop in occasionally for a quick training session, and then poof, she would run back to Snaggletooth city. She thanked him for defeating Thero, but warned him that the mage did not let grudges go—ever.

Patti was learning water magic, but she could barely draw liquid to her hand by day six. It frustrated her, but she was persistent, if not patient, in her diligent practice. Her archery was improving and she started to pick up sword and shield occasionally during training to improve her melee abilities. That was a common theme among everyone on Team Ola; they all cross trained to be the best they could at magical, ranged, and melee combat.

All in all, Dean's world was slowly improving. His decision to wait to attempt tougher mazes came at a cost, though. Not all the news was good during the preparation time.

The three hundred point challenge from the Core arrived mid-week. Whomever Riva sent, well, they failed. To be fair. It was still five against one. Not until five hundred points did the odds change—to five against five. The poor sap they sent, got crowd control chained, then slowly mauled. In a way, his death was a message.

The disaster that followed was an out of season hurricane—the largest the planet had ever seen. A port city on the other side of Oakley, Helmuth, was smashed. Scientists were baffled, the death toll ran into the thousands—continually climbing as the list of people who were missing shrank, with their names then appearing among the dead. The economic damage the hurricane inflicted was in the billions.

Things got worse, when Marty asked to borrow some tokens. He'd had two teams wipe—in a row. Riva went on a tirade—furious that neither of the other portals were earning as many points as his. Then there was the shocker that set everyone, besides Dean, on edge.

Tucker found the fourth portal. Not only that, he had all the legal stuff organized and ready to go before making his claim, to the point that Riva was powerless to stop him. Dean listened in on the meeting and saw that his father-in-law was losing control of his passionate anger. The man was blaming himself, as if the hurricane had been his fault.

Which left Dean with few options. He was ready to take on bigger challenges. His portal needed more champions and he needed more tokens—always more tokens. He still desperately wanted to get a dwarf dragon for a combat pet.

Cassandra's clap brought him out of his dour reflections and back to the here and now—another one of Cassie's staff meetings.

"Okay," she started again, "we're down to our minimum reserve of a hundred and fifty tokens again. I'm about a few bazillion G-s short of our dream community ship, and we need to improve our gear and pets, as well as a general resupply—which includes restocking our potion inventory."

She blew out a harsh breath. "Then, there is also the fact that we should be freeing new team members." She looked up from her notes. "Tomorrow we shift to doing solos, at least according to Dean's notes from last week. Comments?"

Dean tapped his fingers on the table. He huffed in frustration and asked, "What's the latest score?"

Jessabee cleared her throat and said, "Team Core is at 332."

The ten fighters and all gathered support staff winced as one.

"Alright. We've spent a week getting ready, it's time we tackle the duet event." He frowned, scratching the back of his neck. "I've been putting it off. There are only ten of us. And honestly, I want even our support staff doing the first three levels of all events—except..." Dean met the gaze of everyone around the table, "PvP. Stick to PvE. We're not that desperate for tokens. Today will be all about tokens, tokens, and more tokens. Tomorrow we will start climbing the solo ranks, if we get enough today to purchase some pets."

Cassandra frowned. "We've learned that if a duet reaches level twenty and one of you dies, the team can still get a payout. So –"

"Complete the floors, regardless if one of us dies, or flee out the exit," Patti finished for her, and Dean nodded.

"No," Wilfred said cutting them off, "that is factually wrong. Events have no exits—other than completions or Min's Vault. There is a reason both Mixonians, and Wixomians, avoid event PvP. It sucks. It's meant to suck. A champion who grinds to a level one hundred on regular portals, eventually hits a ceiling. They are now stuck and useless—their only remaining ability is to compete in events."

"Which are biased, in the grand scheme of things, towards the negative," Dean said. "Let's be honest, even if we get a hundred levels done in the event today, we give nothing to Oakley. We add zero to the planet's point score. Overall, today may even hurt the planetary score—the whole reason behind the games."

"While Zayra and I grew up in the orphanage," Wilfred continued, "We were taught that the event portals were an afterthought. They were added some time after the sixth age. The three sides—Minotaur, Core, and Suca—agreed to have something special. The way it was explained to us, was that champions who had reached their ceiling wanted to still be able to support their planet's teams, financially, by earning tokens. They wanted to free someone or help fund the next generation."

Dean frowned, wondering whether it was altruism or washed up champions' need for funds that drove the events.

"The sides came to a resolution, which included that events would vary, events would be cumulative, and that they'd carry additional risk, for less reward. Hence, you go and win, you then have to decide to keep going or get out. That's it. There is no retreat. There is only victory or the shelf. If you go to, say, the seventh floor, when you should have stopped at the sixth. Well..."

Dean's frown converted into a wry smile as he remembered his own time in the water event on level seven. Wilfred was right. There'd been no exit once he'd decided to continue, other than the locket. His only opportunity to leave had been in the dry white room, when presented with two buttons.

Kambry piped up in a chipper voice, "Wouldn't it be better to focus on PvP?"

There were a few chuckles from the group.

"Here is my thought," Dean said with a sigh. "If we get to level twenty in PvE and someone dies on that level, we're at a big fat negative five tokens. If any of us get to the point where in PvP, you get kill bonuses and a hundred tokens. One winning team can cover the ten of us. Not saying don't head in and get ten easy tokens. Actually, let's do that. Go to floor ten dual PvE, and then swap to PvP."

Orabel raised a hand to give her input. "If you say you're going for an event competition, you're allowed more as the portal master. Else you'd never be able to get your ten competitors inside Mixonia. Any event that is not solo allows –"

"Are you kidding me? Those fooking Minotaurs," Cassandra cursed while stepping away from the table. Her phone went to her ear as it connected. "Felna, what's our portal limit, if we say we're doing the event." A pause. "If the event is five person?" Another pause. "Ten champion events? And how often do events change, so I don't have to speculate?"

She talked for a few more minutes and then returned to the meeting.

"Okay, I knew some of this. Event rotations are roughly ten days to twenty days. The good news is that Min actually opens up the limits on portals for specific events. I need to tell the other team leaders this information... Including Tucker, can you call him?" Cassandra asked Dean, who nodded.

"Great," she tapped her chin with a finger, "we're up to ten competitors per portal for the duration of this event. For five man events, the limit goes to thirty competitors, with the same increase for ten person, er... champion events. Ugh! You get my point. Sorry for the slip up."

"This is great news," Lonny said happily, his team all smiles. "How about we gear up and head to the entry point? We can spend a full day competing, now that the contracts state our six hour limitation only counts against time outside of events."

Cassandra bobbed her head and said, "Meeting adjourned. Have fun in the duets. Report back to us when you're burned out, and I'll try to run the first three floors with Candace. Assuming I can get her to take an evening off from school. Good luck, Team Ola."

Dean picked up his phone and selected Tucker from his contacts. He'd never called the man before, but had been given the man's contact information by Riva.

"Ola," Tucker said right away.

"Hey, just wanted to let you know that you can add ten to the portal as of –"

"The event, I know. All you had to do was ask the fat cow man. Is that all?" Tucker chuckled.

"Yup, good luck," Dean said and the line disconnected.

He wasn't going to give it a second thought. If Tucker was helping to reduce disasters, great. There was only one thing on his mind right now. Who did he partner with?

Lonny's team had already left the barroom floor, while Dean's team stayed at the table.

Wilfred went first. "I'd like to team with Patti." Everyone, besides Zayra, was surprised. "We talked it over. If one of us was dying... well, I don't think I could abandon Zayra, even if I knew we'd rescue her."

Dean was given a kiss by Cassandra who was on her way to the spaceship to handle the finances. He tugged on her shirt to make her pause. "Ask Felna if we can bring pets. I know they normally aren't allowed in events, but it's better to hear it from the source," Dean said. He shifted his attention back to the table. "Okay so, I'm overpowered and can carry whoever I get stuck with." He flexed with a smirk. "So I was thinking I'd probably be the odd man out. Zayra and Kambry can work as a duo."

"I..." Kambry gave him a pout. "I guess I can understand that logic. We can always see, during the next event, if this setup works better in reverse. Use your partners. But we really, really need the tokens."

"All my gear is in Felna's cavern. I don't need anything from the armory. Do you guys?" Zayra asked and Dean saw everyone shake their heads no.

"Everything should already be in Felna's cavern. I have plans to convert the armory into a play room or something. Maybe a classroom," Dean mused.

Cassandra tapped him on the shoulder and rapidly bobbed her head yes, her eyes shining brightly.

"Alright. Let's head to the shuttle," Dean said, standing up from his seat.

He went out the door to find Lonny's team under the forest canopy casually joking. Dean approached his friend who gave him a terse nod.

"I'm the odd man out," Lonny said as his fellow team leader walked up.

Dean smirked, "Oh Hell. Looks like we're going to do some work, then."

"That's the hope, anyway," Lonny agreed.

"I figure we can start PvP and then do the basic stuff after. We'll probably get to level twenty," Dean said confidently with a bit of a swagger.

"Bet your ass we will," Lonny grinned.

Kambry rolled her eyes, "Your bromance is making me sick. Get in the choppa!"

"Whoa, cowgirl! When did you start watching the classics?" Dean asked Kambry.

"Sheesh, when your daughter was up at three a.m., with gassy farts. There was no 'get in the shuttle' quote. I surfed for an hour trying to find a killer meme and failed," Kambry muttered darkly and Patti chuckled.

The ten of them loaded up in their normal clothes. The showers, changing stations, and training equipment had been installed and were operational in Felna's cavern. Even their wagons had a home, where they could prep them.

The moment the door sealed tight, Patti pointed at a tree limb up high. "Is that a fooking jaguar?"

"Uh... it's... just relaxing. Cassie would flip her shit if Orabel didn't give us guarantees that none of the creatures would ever harm us," Kambry scoffed. The large cat with black spots watched them while licking a paw. Its tail swayed off the tree limb, casually.

"Oh, by thunder," Dean cursed. He called Jessabee who failed to answer. When the message beeped he said, "I wanted to go creature shopping. Get a list from Orabel and meet me outside the event PvP gate."

"You still hung up on a dwarf dragon?" Lonny asked, curious.

Dean sighed and waved his hand back and forth. "Yes and no," he said. "I went to the market two more times. I think I'm going to try a different floor. The vendors up on the sixth that sell pets are identical. That special something hasn't jumped out at me."

"So... Just a thought. Orabel can talk to dragons, right?" Wilfred said and Dean groaned. "Why not just get a cheap one and have her train it for you."

Dean called Jessabee back. She answered this time. "I'm getting ready to go to bed," she yawned. "Cassie had me selling titanium on Earth and I barely made it back in time for the meeting. What can I help you with?"

"Hand the phone to Orabel," Dean said, the frustration in his voice evident. There was some grumbling in the background. Dean heard Jessabee telling Orabel to get a damn phone, some curses were traded back and forth between the two roommates. Finally, the elven sorceress was on the line. "I'm pet shopping today give –"

"She already has a list of creatures I want to add."

"Orabel, why is there a baby eating cat staring into my living room?"

"Oh, you mean Omena? Super awesome lady jaguar. She is jealous and wants a litter of her own. And she finds you humans... amusing," Orabel said it as if everyone should already know how jaguars felt about people. "Anything else?"

"If I get a hostile dragon can –"

"Fook no... As you like to say. If you go animal shopping, these are the negative attributes I need you to avoid, regardless of species: bad temperament or overly stupid. Got it? I can work with everything else. Easy to displease is okay, but it'd be better to find something with an average or good temperament," Orabel said.

"Thanks for clarifying. And Orabel, the forest is fantastic," Dean said as the shuttle cleared the canopy, "thank you. Good luck with your studies."

"I should have something soon to brief you on," Orabel said, hanging up the phone.

A silence settled over the group before the small talk resumed. The flight was a short one and Dean was really excited to compete in some PvP.

CHAPTER

SIXTEEN

DEAN

Mixonia - Outside Black PvP Event Gate

Champion Information
Name: Dean Forrester Gender: Male
Level: 10 Tokens: 0
Race: Human Alignment: Suca – Mixonia
Luck: 16 Charisma: 41

Health: 348 / 348 H-Regen: 1.0 / Sec
Stamina: 302 / 302 M-Regen: 1.0 / Sec
Mana: 336 / 336 S-Regen: 1.0 / Sec

Strength: 214 Vitality: 134
Dexterity: 107 Endurance: 195
Intelligence: 105 Willpower: 232
Magic: Electrical Water

"Bottoms up," Dean said after clinking his potion's glass vial against Lonny's container.

They were slurping down blue goop. It was thick, tingly, and not refreshing. Still, he didn't want to vomit, so... small win. When that was done, they uncorked what appeared to be sodas and downed those.

"Those grub burritos were awful," Lonny said, scraping his tongue with his front teeth.

"Right, the goo killed the taste, at least. Ha! Those were the cheap smalls, thank you Snaggletooth alchemists. Should last a few hours with minimal boosts. Better than letting them sit on a shelf. Time to go," Dean said, using a few short jumps to pump himself up.

"How do events work without running into others? It's not exactly busy here." Lonny looked around.

Dean shrugged. They were the only ones on the entire platform. The event's freshness had faded, and champions hated PvP events. So it was not a huge surprise that they had the platform to themselves. Team Ola's goal had been to stagger their groups of two. Dean and Lonny would go first in the PvP, while Zayra and Kambry started PvE until level two.

"Let's go ask," Dean said, walking up to the bored female Minotaur guard at the Oath stone. "Hello. We were curious how this works with competitors. Does another team have to enter behind us? Or are there time bending tricks that –"

"Can't say. Give an oath and go in, or go back and wait in staging," she said with what he guessed was a frown. Her snout tilted up as she snorted.

Dean's hand went to the Oath stone. He said, "Lonny, and I, want to compete and understand the consequences."

The guard tossed a massive thumb at the portal, which stayed black. Dean gave Lonny one last inspection.

The man was geared up in Roman armor, painted a black hue that blended with his brown skin tone. He wore a single handed sword on his left hip, a shield on his left forearm, and carried a short spear in his right hand. There was no plume on his helm, but there was a long nose bridge protector. His bag on his back had medical bandages, hooks, a pillow with a blanket, a mini shovel, water containers, and snacks.

Dean knew he was similarly kitted out, except that he had his trident instead of a spear, a quiver of javelins on his right hip, and his armor was golden. They had duplicate bags that had become pretty much standard issue.

The two gave terse nods to each other and stepped in the portal.

∞∞∞∞

They arrived translucent; Dean realized this because he could see through his friend. Instead of posturing defensively he relaxed, and soaked in the view.

There were walls slightly taller than him around them in an oval. Stadium seating style benches were staggered along an incline. Huge overhead tarps shaded the rough grainy surface. The view told him they were in an arena about the size of a hockey rink.

Right in the center was a pedestal with a locket on it. Lonny tensed defensively raising his shield and instantly materialized. Dean stayed calm and patient. Lonny trotted to the locket and buried it in the key hole.

∞∞∞

They arrived in the decision room. Dean had a necklace with a locket at the bottom. A 3 was etched into its silvery appearance. There were the two buttons with 'exit' or 'next'—just like there had been for the solo water event.

"Well that was easy. Good that you stayed translucent the whole time. Does it fade after a bit?"

"Yeah, I think it lasts for a minute or so, or until you make a move indicating you are prepping for combat. Well that was an easy three tokens. I guess if we fight someone later, it becomes five. You ready?" Dean asked.

Lonny hit the next button and when nothing happened Dean put his hand on top of it, too. That did the trick, and they faded onto floor 2.

∞∞∞

A light rain crashed against a jungle canopy far above them. Alien insects called out in an annoying pattern. There was no pedestal in sight and Dean scanned around them in the dim light, trying to find any sign of their opponents. The fact that Orabel had said she sat in a tree for hours was unsettling, and caused him to glance up at every shifting motion of the leaves above.

Lonny stepped forward coming out of hiding as he spawned completely.

Whistling sounds were their only warning. Dean raised his shield hastily with quick reflexes. Without being able to see his attacker he crouched, backpedaling for a nearby tree. *Thunk. Thunk. Ping.*

The sound of projectiles rapidly landing told him whomever was firing was skilled.

The moment he was behind the tree he saw they were arrows. Okay maybe his fear of an archer waiting to ambush competitors was not unjustified.

"You okay?" Dean asked just loud enough for Lonny to hear.

The man removed his helmet and stuck it out from behind the cover he crouched behind. An arrow whizzed forward. Dean finally saw their target, a tigerman with black head fur and green stripes. His armor was black as the night and he had the drop on them. He was confidently sidestepping to get a better angle on Lonny.

"Take the locket and move on," Dean called out. "When it respawns, we'll wait for you to get ahead of us."

An arrow slammed into the tree between them with a crack. It was an answer, though not one Dean was hoping for, but an answer nonetheless. Dean pulled out a javelin and tossed it out to the side into the underbrush, not five feet away.

Dean had his energy beam crackling in his palm the moment he let go of the stick. Sure enough, his opponent unleashed an arrow at the rustling noise. Dean's eyes clamped closed as his body unleashed a powerful beam. He swept his hand left to right in an attempt to slice his opponent in half; if they dived out of the way in time, though, it would be a costly waste of mana.

There was a cry of pain to his left, not twenty feet away. Startled by the proximity of a new foe, Dean's shield went up to address the threat. He shifted his trident into his right hand.

The foolish opponent blurted out, "I'm falling back, cover me... ouch!" The *smack* of a body running into a tree echoed over the *thrumming* rain. That just made the situation worse for the enemy.

Lonny crashed through the underbrush towards the voice. Dean flanked left to help spread the noise. The original tigerman archer had gone silent, leaving Dean to think he had killed him. The sound of someone stumbling around was right ahead of Dean.

"I surrender!" the voice clamored as Lonny and Dean came up to their prey. A green Leprinix held her open palms up. Her eyes were open, but the way her face shifted towards any noise led Dean to believe she'd been blinded by his energy beam.

Dean was about to make her an offer when Lonny drove a spear toward the blinded Lerinix's face. The weapon cracked her cheekbone as it entered her skull with a *snap* and a *squish*. She died instantly, her body shitting itself upon death. *That was a first. Probably time to go before I smell that.*

"So... I was going to strike a deal. We could use fighters..."

Lonny chuckled, his spear making a sickening slurping noise as it came out of his victim's skull. "Dean, while it is true that we can share the floor and be the good guys, as in the pedestal would respawn a locket if we let her go..." Lonny smirked and shook his head. "It takes half a day or new foes arriving to do so, though. Which is why we might get fooked when we enter, find no one, and discover the locket is gone." He chuckled again until he caught a whiff of the nastiness she'd fouled herself with and gagged.

They both stepped off towards the middle of the jungle. "You really should attend more meetings."

"Hey," Dean said defensively, following him. "What meetings did I miss?"

"The ones in Snaggletooth. Walk and talk. Riva even sent a large speedster for us," Lonny said, trudging through the underbrush. "In here, there can't be another team behind us for at least half a day—nothing changes for that long, unless one team is removed or eliminated. No two versus one battles like you had in PvP—though here that would be three versus two, I guess. I thought you knew all these rules and your team not attending was just Patti avoiding Quincy."

"Wait, Quincy is at those meetings?" Dean asked with a raised brow. "He doesn't compete."

"He weaseled up to Mr. Lexso. He's a briefer sometimes... Again, Dean, my bad. I thought you knew all this," Lonny shrugged, finding the first body. He kicked the corpse over to see the dead eyes staring wide open. "If you really want to hire them, we know what they look like. She was stealthy as fook."

"Yeah, got lucky when I blinded her. Can only imagine how bad that hurt. These two were set for night vision. Look at his face," Dean said, staring at the corpse.

The male's expression was twisted in a snarl, his eyes full of shock. Almost as if his eyes realized what was happening first. Dean's beam had cut their foe across the chest and sliced apart his heart. There was no healing that kind of damage—clearly evident from his victim's stiff, final pose.

Lonny sighed, kept walking, and said, "So the briefings went over all this. If we'd wanted to spare her, it would have cost us twelve hours. Honestly? Not worth it. For numerous reasons. She came in here to fight. You gave them a chance to call it—"

"I did tell them to give up the fight." Dean frowned, "I wasn't exactly inspiring in my attempt to talk them down, though. She was probably about to kill me. Indent the locket, I want to be dry while we talk," Dean said when they found the golden trinket on top of a rock.

Lonny stuck the locket in the slot and they vanished.

∞∞∞∞

"That is my point Dean, who cares if she was surrendering. I mean –"

Dean placed a hand up halting him before he went to a corner of the small white room and dropped down. "The morality talk. I don't want to get too far down the rabbit hole. But... we could have let her live and moved on ourselves."

"And if she got killed by the next team? Then we lose twenty tokens for nothing. They were playing a dangerous game. They were watching for spawns to appear. Dean, that's not something you forgive," Lonny said seriously.

"Aye. I know. I've no problem admitting they were hostile and in the wrong. She had her hands up and was blind. That –"

"In a game where you don't go in without a backup plan, he was a decent shot and she was silent. They weren't newbies," Lonny snapped, his temper rising. "And Dean. What if she got lucky? We almost fell into a trap they set and the next thing you know, we're both statues and they win. If it's them or us, I'm picking us."

"Fine, I just..." Dean paused, not sure what to say.

"Becomes a lot harder when the people you're killing aren't people you resent," Lonny said trying to understand.

"Sure, and I'm a big softie. I want to free people, not entomb them. Although," Dean said flashing Lonny his locket. "We have fifty tokens. We could hop out and free them or two others."

"Or keep going. If no one is in the next one, it's an easy five tokens. You're call," Lonny admitted with a hand hovering over the next level's button.

"Fook it, count me in," Dean said, smashing his hand down on top of his friends.

∞∞∞∞

They spawned amongst a series of sand dunes with whipping winds violently flinging the vile particles at them. Visibility was next to zero and the environment passed through them by means that had to be magical. Dean tensed, propping his shield up. *Ugh. Talk about a shitty environment.* Lonny noticed his actions and joined his shield wall.

"This is brutal," Lonny muttered in a tone that was barely audible over the screaming winds. The particles crashed into their armor and their shields with a drumming sound that continued without pause.

Dean felt sand getting in every crevice imaginable. The bright sun tried to peek through the swirling clouds of dusty brown, but it was almost impossible to see anything.

"Arggg! Help!" Lonny cried out as he was ripped from Dean's side.

All Dean could see was a black claw dragging his friend away. He lunged for Lonny, thrusting his trident at the claw. Lonny yanked his leg back, pulling the face of the scorpion into the trident's barbs. There was a loud crack as the triple tines drove into the creature's brain.

Dean released his weapon, aimed his palm down, and severed the arm of the five foot long scorpion with a beam of energy.

"Never saw it. My leg is busted. Sorta. Clean break in the middle of the smaller bone on the outside. Famibila, I think?"

"Fibula, broke mine dirt biking," Dean grunted with a nonchalant shrug. He slammed a boot onto the scorpion and used both his hands to wrench his weapon free of the dead creature.

"Shitty place to get hurt," Lonny said as they were battered by the sandy winds. "You want to just go for the win?"

Dean frowned with a grimace. "Yeah, fook this. I'll carry you. If I get attacked I'll toss —"

"Ha! No," he said with a scream as his bone cracked back into place. "Fook me, it's still broken, but I can probably hobble. Let me lean on your left arm."

Hoisting Lonny out of the sand was tough. It was tougher fighting a headwind of blasting particles with another man limping along at his side. A few minutes later and they'd found the podium in the eye of the sand storm. Dean hastily picked up the locket and slammed it home.

∞∞∞

"Thank the creator. My leg is still busted. But... at least the sand is gone," Lonny said with a sigh of relief. The man had instinctively tried to shake out sand that was no longer there.

Dean patted his friend with an empathetic smile. "We need to keep ahead of the girls."

"Well, I think the potion is helping. I broke an ankle on solo eight. Stupid horse died sniffing gas, trapping my leg underneath him when he toppled over. That healing took a bit longer than this, so we do have that going for us," Lonny snickered, hobbling over to the next level button. They jammed the button down and in they went.

∞∞∞

Floor four was a home. They appeared in a hovel of a home with a single living room. The ceiling was low, to the point that Dean had to crouch. He noticed they were in a kitchen. From the friendly banter out in the living room, Dean realized that there were three Gnomes playing a game of cards. Behind them, above the fireplace, rested the locket.

Lonny glanced at Dean and indicated with a tilt of his head that they should stack up against the wall.

Lonny ducked behind the kitchen wall, just before the living room, and Dean followed his lead. Lonny gave him a finger countdown from three, two, and then one. Dean hopped sideways on one and lanced an arc of energy from left to right across the unsuspecting Gnomes.

Cards and chips went flying as the raw energy tore through the space. The back wall was splattered with bits of gore. Blood pumped out in squirts that hit the ceiling. The violent spurts slowed until the red fluid just oozed from the severed bodies.

"Gnarly," Lonny said. He had a victorious smile etched on his face as he pointed under the table. "Hey did you even see their feet?"

"Oh, no, missed that... but good job. I see you can use Earth magic." He patted Lonny on the shoulder. "Can you do the golem thing yet?" Dean asked, peering under the table.

His inspection of the Gnomes lower halves revealed clumps of dried mud had locked down their feet. The thickness was minimal, but Lonny had managed to snare all three at once. "This is better than my ice spell."

"Thanks, I've been working on it a lot lately—whenever I can, actually. My archery is shit, but my magic is improving. I plan to get a little crossbow and strap it to the back of this," Lonny said, smacking his shield. "Anyway, my leg is feeling better. Onto level five?"

Dean grinned as he fed the locket into its slot, causing them to leave the messy hovel.

∞∞∞

"I'm conflicted. I wonder if we'd asked nicely for the locket if they would have handed it over?" Dean mused, more to himself than to Lonny.

"Who knows? Basically, they're not fookin real, so I don't care."

"It was gross, they gushed so much blood. I can still hear the stickiness of it on my boots," Dean said, grimacing at the thought. "Keep going?"

Lonny grunted and slammed his hand onto the button. Dean's hand joined his and they vanished from the white room.

∞∞∞

The sounds of battle rang out loud around them. Dean gazed around, seeing that they had spawned in a dark alleyway. Brutish, guttural voices cried out in anger. Dean glanced back over his shoulder and saw the stained mossy wall of a dead end. *Only one way to go.*

His feet rested in a puddle of shit and piss that pooled above a clogged sewer grate. Large rodents scurried between piles of rotting cloth. Dean scrunched up his nose, focused on breathing shallowly through his mouth, and readied his trident.

"Can you run?" Dean hissed quietly.

Lonny nodded. *I love our manly conversations.* Having had enough of the stench, Dean trotted warily towards the din of battle.

"Plan?" Lonny whispered over the sound of them running.

The fighting was not far away. Dean grunted softly while saying, "My most powerful weapon is my magic. When we round the corner, I'll blast the foe and win the day."

A smile was all the reply that was needed. The duo slipped out of the alleyway and along the edge of a cobbled street. Dwarves cowered behind stacks of crates. A vendor ran his cart away from the noise and citizens, in ones and twos, followed after him.

Dean saw more of the city, but no fighting yet. He turned up the road and the fleeing residents gave them a wide berth. The panic on these people's faces said it all. Something big and scary was up ahead, and it was killing Dwarves.

515

There was more cursing in what Dean had to assume was a Core dialect. The street was lined with residential homes, concerned bearded faces peering tentatively out the windows from behind thick curtains. Dean knew the fighting was ahead at the next intersection, due to the noise.

When a heavily armored Dwarf maiden ran past them, having come from that direction, while lit on fire, Dean confirmed that was indeed where the fighting was. The poor, wee lass succumbed to the flames and collapsed in death. Her helmet skittered across the cobbles with a metallic clang as it rolled away from her corpse.

The loud clash of metal on metal was diminishing, spurring Dean forward.

His boots slapped against the stone cobbles and his armor rattled from the full run. He charged up his energy into a crackling ball in his hand.

The moment he turned the corner he was in for a shock.

A demon ogre with curling horns like a ram's crouched in the square, trading blows with Dwarves a third of his size. A carrion bird with four legs and four arms spewed magic into the dozen or so defenders. The fight was grossly one sided. Dean watched the Demogre's axe split a dwarf right down the middle. The weapon sliced right through the dwarf's armor and smashed his torso in twain.

The strike left the Demogre exposed, resulting in a number of Dwarves hacking at the armored Demogre's legs. Their blows were ineffective; the only results were more loud clangs. The Crixon supporting the Demogre swirled flames out from its primed staff in a long whiplash of flame, snapping it right into the middle of the crowd of Dwarves attacking the Demogre's legs.

Dean's hand crackled with energy. He felt his body heat rising, his ability to contain the flood of power was quickly diminishing, so he unleashed a tight beam at the four-armed Crixon. With his eyes tightly shut and Lonny hiding behind his shield, Dean released the blinding light from his palm.

When the spell completed and Dean opened his eyes once again, he was horrified.

The Crixon stood without any damage. A black bubble of energy vibrated before it angrily before the protective barrier flickered out with a loud *pop*.

The beast stumbled and Lonny was on top of it in a heartbeat. His spear went into the beast's neck with a precise thrust. With his immense strength, Lonny twirled the Core being around in a spin before flinging it into the nearest wall, where it landed with a sickening *splat*. The twitching body stilled as its neck poured out a river of black blood.

Dwarves cheered with renewed strength. The Demogre went into a berserk rage at his partner's death. Dean unleashed bolts of energy at the nasty creature's face until his hand quit emitting the beams and he staggered from mana exhaustion.

Dean cursed when his entire volley was absorbed by another magical shield. Just like that, he'd carelessly expended his mana.

"Kite!" Dean yelled as both he and Lonny burst into a run.

The lumbering giant roared in anger at the pair of humans, his fight with the Dwarves abandoned in favor of vengeance. Dean cursed when his run slowed as he felt a magical resistance going that direction. Three large arachnids scurried out of a sewer grate in front of them.

"Fook me. Put the bugs between us," Dean shouted and they raced for the new threat.

The Demogre was slow, but determined. A mighty roar was released to remind them he was coming. *Yeah, yeah, you're big and ugly and want to smash, we get it.*

The bugs were about the same height as the Dwarves, meaning they were too tall to simply jump over.

Dean pulled a javelin out of the quiver on his hip. He awkwardly threw it with his full power while running. He aimed for the middle bug charging at them. The javelin cracked the front right quarter of the beast's shell, crippling the bug, and causing it to tumble.

"Jump it!" panting "You first!" Dean shouted.

Thankfully, Lonny understood. He burst forward and jumped up and over the closing ranks of the remaining, upright arachnids. Dean, following closely behind him, just missed being stabbed with a pincer. They continued to flee, resulting in another magical wall willing them in a different direction. The duo was heading back into shit alley.

"Fook me," Dean groaned, seeing a foot high pedestal with the locket next to where they had spawned. "We raced past the treasure."

"Fight or flee?"

"I've got enough mana for a slick. But I blew –"

The arachnids were on them as they dropped from above to land mere feet from Dean. A trident and a spear lashed out, their tips crashing through shells, causing the bugs to *shriek* a horrible wail of pain. Two more foes skittered around the corner. *What the fook was this floor?*

Their shields held the arrivals at bay while the garbage danced around them from the heavy footfalls impacting the cobblestone road. The Demogre was closing on them fast. Dean readied a javelin, while bashing a bug with his shield. The noise of the footsteps of the giant were easy to track with each crack of his heavy frame impacting the ground.

Dean flung the javelin blindly. He shifted his trident into his empty hand and stabbed at an arachnid. His eyes flicked up to watch his projectile arc up towards the end of the alley. The Demogre ran around the corner and right into his weapon.

The tip carved through the cheek on their foe's right side and exited out the left. This slowed the brute's advance. Lonny shot brown magic in a huge torrent of mana focused on encasing the massive creature's feet in mud. Dean added a slick layer of ice, improvising as best he could before the situation deteriorated even further.

The Demogre went from trying to wrench the weapon out of its mouth to slipping and stumbling into the wall. The sheer power of the monster burst through Lonny's spell but when it reached the ice, its feet went horizontal and the creature shot into the air. In a panic, it reached two arms behind itself at horrible angles to grab onto something, anything really, and catch its fall.

The alleyway reverberated with two *snaps* so loud that Dean's ears rang. The beast's arms had not softened its fall and instead had broken under the massive creature's sheer momentum and weight. The Demogre groaned with twisting motions of immense pain.

Lonny and Dean jumped on their downed foe. Dean's shield partially absorbed an armored kick, but Lonny made it to the Demogre's injured face, unimpeded.

Dean had to give it to their foe. It spat at Lonny, but the Demogre had to stop squirming to do so. With a quick rapid thrust, Lonny drove his spear point into the enemy's eye; it burst with a sickly *squelch*.

There were death twitches for only a few seconds. "I got eyeball juice in my mouth..." Lonny groaned, spitting into the garbage over and over.

"Nice spell!" Dean exclaimed.

There was the clamor of pounding Dwarven footsteps. Dean grabbed the locket and held it over the indent. He paused. This was different. He wanted to know. So he waited and said, "We won. We mean you no harm." He hissed to Lonny. "Get next to me."

The pitter patter of Dwarven feet neared until a scout peered cautiously around the corner. Dean yelled out again, "We mean no harm. Tell me what happened, please. No more deaths."

A Dwarf with extra braids in his beard and a shiny golden helmet stepped forward. His warhammer was slung over his shoulder. His armor clacked with every step and his confidence was supreme.

"We were magicked here, though I've no idea by whom. We fought arachnids further down the road from where you found us. Those two Core demons watched their minions die without a care while they picked through the garbage and trash.

518

They grew tired of watching us slaughter the bugs and engaged us in a fight. I started with thirty dwarves in my patrol and killed over twenty bugs. These four probably mean –"

"This was an evenish fight, they could easily have turned the tide to their side. This was a Core versus Suca scenario," Dean muttered. He glanced back at the Captain. "Do you want to harm us?"

"If you are peaceful, no, if you linger, though... yes. There are rules in Ornsfeld. And I can't be having –"

Dean had heard enough to understand what he'd wanted to learn and indented the locket.

∞∞∞∞

They returned to the white room. A 105 was engraved on the locket around his neck and Dean let out a whistle.

"We need to rest. I blew all my mana and a lot of my stamina running from that beast. What's the count?" Lonny asked, dropping down in the corner. Dean started to answer but Lonny groaned, hawking a gob of spit onto the white floor. "I still taste eyeball juice, somehow."

"Gross," Dean chuckled. "Here, look," Dean showed him the necklace.

Lonny let out a long whistle. "That is nice to see. Whatcha thinkin?"

Dean relaxed in the opposite corner. "Time for a nap?"

"Indeed. A nap sounds lovely."

Dean's yawn triggered a yawn in return from Lonny. His eyes fluttered. He pulled his bag off his shoulder with a grunt, sliding it under his head to use as a pillow. The moment his eyes slid shut, he was out.

CHAPTER
SEVENTEEN
DEAN

Minotaur's Maze - Duo Event

Someone was shaking his arm. Dean stirred from the motion to peek up at a grinning Lonny. He was offered a jerky snack and a water jug. With a quick head shake, he told Lonny no and he dug into his bag for his own rations.

"Why'd ya wake me?" Dean asked, propping himself up to eat. He felt great.

Lonny snorted and said, "Bro, you've been sleeping for a couple more hours than I could. I figure you have to be close to recharged, and we still want to keep climbing. Right?"

"Well, yeah. I mean we can hit the 105 pay day and call it, or climb some more. I wonder if we had left from mana exhaustion would we have returned to Mixonia fully charged?" Dean mused.

"People come out hurt and tired all the time. But... we wouldn't have been clogging up the city as the portal master," Lonny said with a chuckle.

"I told the others what our intentions were. We're talking ten people trying to earn tokens in a slow burn event. Shit, PvE ten levels go by decently fast, but they still take up a lot of time," Dean said tossing the jug back into his bag. He got up off the white room's floor and stretched with a post-nap yawn. "So much for staying ahead of the others."

Lonny slung his bag over his shoulder before inspecting his gear. Dean checked his own side straps and connection points.

"You slept in your helmet?" Lonny smirked.

"Yeah," Dean snorted. "Regen actually has me feeling great. Ya ready?"

Lonny nodded and they pressed the button for the next level.

∞∞∞

The next three floors were all jungles: day, night, and dawn; lush, thin, and dense. The creatures they encountered were a variety of big monsters—primarily cats, deadly plants, and a really big snake. The duo moved slowly and methodically. By the end of the eighth floor, Dean swore he'd happily do anything—as long as it wasn't in another jungle setting.

They spawned on floor nine to a bright sunny day with two moons visible in the clear blue skyline. In the distance, there stood a wooden eighteen-hundred style farmhouse. They arrived on a knoll, with five Gnolls between them and the building. Knee high fields of oats littered the farm, with no farm animals in sight. There wasn't even fencing.

There were, however, four sets of cackling Gnolls, each one wielding spear and shield; their clumped formations boxed the farmhouse in. Dean scoured the area around them, trying to find a pedestal. He knew there was a chance the hyena looking humanoids might be only a distraction and the victory was behind them. He walked back, away from the Gnolls, until he felt the magic telling him he'd hit a boundary wall.

"Hey, look at that," Lonny said, pointing to the farmhouse. His friend held his spyglass to his eye. The smile spreading across his face said he saw something interesting.

All Dean caught was a glint of metal from the sunny day. "This place looks lovely, minus the mad humanoids laughing at each other with deadly intent. Of course, those fooks need to die."

"Right, so this fancy pirate tool gave me a bit of a surprise when I inspected the home. Looks like Zayra and Kambry are in the farmhouse," Lonny said with a smile. "Shall we go greet them?"

"We shall."

Dean lumbered down the hill with Lonny at his side. He swapped his trident to his shield hand and yanked out a javelin. Overusing his mana had left him jaded. Dorthy's story had not been enough for the lesson truly to sink in about just how bad mana fatigue could be. He wanted to be cautious.

"How would we even shoot a bow in all this armor?" Dean grumbled during the walk.

"Surprised that these things haven't reacted. And we can't," Lonny smirked, "that's why Patti wears a thinner mail vest. She doesn't even wear padding. Nick does the same thing, which is why he is so slow leveling, a single blow and there is damage. But–"

"They can move. Speaking of which, let's slow down." They slowed.

From beyond the Gnolls, Kambry and Zayra approached. Three twirling fireballs raced for the enemy.

"Throwing." Dean hurled his javelin. While he grabbed for a second one, Lonny trotted to his right side to grab one to try.

Their three javelins all missed. The Gnolls never even notice the two men. Kambry downed two with her initial salvo of fireballs and a third ran around on fire. Dean watched the other groups of Gnolls—either they didn't notice the fight, couldn't hear it, or simply didn't care.

When they arrived at the bodies, Dean noted the other two dead Gnolls had broken arrows in them. Zayra had been doing really well with a bow over the past week.

"Howdy ladies, y'all lost?" Dean asked, strutting over to give his lady a kiss. Kambry lightly frolicked in a silly manner towards him, until she met his lips with hers.

"Hey Dean, hey Lonny," Zayra said with a wave.

Lonny tipped the end of a cowboy hat he wasn't wearing.

Kambry smirked and said, "Fancy seein you gents here. Come, there is a table in the farmhouse where we can regale you with our tale." She kissed his cheek, her eyes sparkling genuinely with her love. "Floors one through eight there was nothing— not a thing. Besides the bunny duo."

"Ugh, we tried so hard to talk them down. The male went full berserk, though, with a hatchet and no armor. And –"

Kambry continued. "We're team Suca, we will wait," She said in a distant voice as if pretending she was yelling while using a level tone. "Nope, nothing reached his big, dumb ears. Worst part is, Zayra missed."

"Ouch," Dean said. "Ya killed him with Fire?"

"I'm getting better with a bow, but I'm nowhere near as good as Patti," Zayra grumbled defensively.

"Yeah," Kambry said, leading them into the farmhouse. "He melted in the wall of fire trap that Zayra set. It was... his screams were haunting." There was a park bench of a sorts inside. Dean dropped into a seat with the others. "The poor girl he was with, she had her hands up defensively and she was crying a lot. She was truly sobbing, you know—the kind that results in your whole body shaking? This wasn't some fake con."

"I thought you couldn't go unwillingly into the games," Lonny said and Dean pointed at Kambry that he had a good point.

"Yeah, well. Bunny girls are a dime a dozen. They almost always become little more than sex toys. Their preferred mate, at least how I understand it, is their own kind... But... Anyway, he said he'd marry her if they could earn twenty tokens. It'd be enough for them to flee Mixonia and be rich on some world," Zayra said.

"What's the maturity rate on these Bouncries?" Dean asked, internally scolding himself for wondering if they really did repopulate like bunnies.

"You're biting your nail Dean," Kambry pointed out to him. It was a habit she disliked. "It's because you should know this answer and you don't study enough on the treadmill."

"Maybe," Dean admitted with a grunt. "I tend to focus on Core species."

Zayra rolled her eyes. Lonny waited for the silence to say, "Fourteen. The bunny people reproduce at fourteen. Ms. Squeaky tits is fully grown and popping out babies well before humans. But don't think you're boinking a little girl. They never get any bigger or any more mature. Humans can have babies at fourteen and up but we don't stop growing and reach full maturity until around age twenty five."

"Is that in the book? The bit about humans?" Dean asked and Lonny nodded. "So, the girl?"

"We let her go. She'd gotten ten tokens to her name and that will change her life. We told her that if she wants a good home, she could help us, but that was hours ago. Nick and Gerald relieved us. Since we let her go, we did the whole back up thing. They let us push forward. We cleansed the floors without much of a struggle. When we got here, though, the pedestal was empty and the timer had started. Been about six hours or so since then," Kambry said. "How about you guys?"

"Killed cat people, then fought demons. Napped. Then some jungle bullshit, and now we get to set up an ambush—assuming the next team is not friendly." Dean grunted, got up from the bench, and stretched. "You going to go free the bunny hero you killed?"

"Um... no. Selina said she would be harassed if we did it right away. If we ever do free him, it's because we're rich and I can afford to remove the guilt," Kambry said with a shrug.

Zayra chuckled. "Okay, good luck boys. There is nothing else interesting here. We just swapped girl stories to pass the time. I think we're ready to head on home."

"See you in a bit. I'd say wait up, but it could be another half-a-day," Dean said getting a goodbye kiss.

Kambry led them to the master bedroom. The pedestal was in the spot where a bed should be.

Zayra stretched before saying, "Sixty-five tokens. Pretty nice. If all five teams come out with at least fifty tokens, that's a small community ship," Zayra said, bouncing her eyebrows.

"You girls got Cassie so fired up, it's funny. She's looking at the ones that cost a smooth billion. Exchange rate is like 250k a token right now. There are plenty of ships that we could get in the fifty million range but..."

"Pfft. Four thousand tokens is nothing. Just go into PvP and become a soulless villain," Kambry said, flicking his ear. "That has to be how Thero's been living so lavishly. Anyway. See you boys in a bit. Oh, when those Gnolls respawn, it means you have company. And you can sneak by them."

Kambry set the locket into its slot and vanished.

Dean sighed at his friend. "We could have come in and slept in here in rotations. Good news is, at least we'll be fully recharged for this next fight."

"Right. I'm going to figure out the best way to set a trap in here," Lonny said, leaving the bedroom. He muttered, "If at all."

Dean proceeded to study the interior of the room. Other than the pedestal, all there was in here, was a closet. *We'd die trapped and confined.* He left the room in search of something better.

The small hallway spilled out into the main living area. Beyond that, there was a kitchen. There was nothing special about this place and the only thing Dean noticed that might come in handy, was that the kitchen had jutting walls. He could use that as a better ambush point than the closet. A sweep would find them though.

"So... Lonny," Dean began, "Mister 'I go to all the briefings'. What was the black shield that Crixon had?"

Lonny snorted, heading out the back door. Over his shoulder he yelled, "Dean can recognize a Crixon, but doesn't know what a void shield is."

"Yeah, I do crack open the books. I tend to study the Core species, though, mostly to learn their strengths and weaknesses," Dean said.

Lonny laughed. "Makes sense to me."

Dean followed him out the back of the farmhouse in time to see his friend's foot vanishing as he scampered up onto the roof. Dean used the wood pile on the side of the house to get himself up there as well. At the top, on the ridge, sat Lonny.

"You face that way," he directed, "and I'll face this way. We could set an ambush, but if it's Patti and Wilfred, we could end up killing them and then really goof our numbers up. Best to take the best spot by the trinket with good vision. If we see something we want to fight, we do so... but if we see double Demogres, we haul ass inside and move on right quick," Lonny snickered, remembering how tough that fight had been.

"Those fooks are scary! I wonder what the best way is to solo them." Dean grunted as he sat on the ridge facing two sets of Gnolls. Behind the Gnolls were two other spawn points. "And the black shield thing?"

"Void magic. Just as hard to master as arcane. The fact that he stopped your spell means he was really powerful. His lack of armor and the staffs attached to his back meant he was a master Core mage, who probably had mana to spare. We –"

"Got lucky, yeah," Dean interrupted, finishing his friend's sentence. "I guess I need to learn arcane magic."

"We need to learn a lot, my friend. This..." Lonny gestured around them. "This is borderline reckless. Sure, it's not male Bouncry reckless, but I think we should take this win and head home afterwards. Or maybe earn an easy twenty tokens in the PvE. Assuming we don't fight anyone else, that is still a whole lot of tokens for a single day's labor."

Lonny grimaced and Dean nodded.

"Is there anything your team needs?" Dean asked.

Lonny drummed his fingers on his shield. "Yeah, pets to bond, scrolls of all magic types... Dean. Did you know that Marvin tried to open a capped soda with his armor and couldn't do it?"

Dean frowned.

"Sorry," Lonny chuckled, "that came out oddly. There was a soda bottle, with a metal cap that required a can opener. Marvin tried to use the edge of his breastplate to open the soda and the metal dented." Lonny snorted at the memory. "We have trash gear, no offense, though it's supposed to be easy to replace." He sighed, "If we die, at least our gear goes with us."

"It just goes to show you how crazy Mixonia is. I walked into a horse hitching post, got this dent right here," Dean pointed to his pauldron, causing his buddy to inspect the dent over his shoulder.

"Riva's got a –"

"Riva has a smithy, and I know. I'm stubborn. The question I keep asking myself is why build up an armorer station, or blacksmith, an alchemy station, a bowyer, a tanner, and all the crafting stuff when I'm likely to max out at one-fifty," Dean grumbled.

"It's not just for you, though. Cassandra seems to have caught on to the bigger picture lately."

Dean frowned, not sure where this conversation was heading; he indicated for Lonny to continue.

"She absolutely loves your estate, right?" Lonny asked and Dean bobbed his head in agreement. "Then why is she suddenly shopping for a ship that can tour the galaxy?"

"Ya know, I've not given it much thought. I guess because when I'm done, we sell the place to Riva or some other managing team. The tavern becomes a backup training point and... I'll just move on," Dean admitted with a sigh.

"Got a way to go before then, boyo. But the system is geared to cycle thousands of people through at the early stages. Shit, I bet Earth tells their new recruits they are going through some training simulation and cycles all of them through for at least the first ten levels. They probably let them PvP and have the tokens to revive them because all it takes is one guy getting through level ten in PvE and his risk in PvP is mitigated—especially if a handler cashes his tokens after every level," Lonny said, theory crafting.

"I bet Riva is rolling in the tokens. I just don't have it in me to start open recruiting kids out of college or high school or wherever. And then conning them into competing and then kicking them back out with a bonus. It'd take –"

"A corporate mindset and lots of power. Yeah, you don't have that Dean. Even Cassandra doesn't," Lonny said and Dean furled his eyebrows. "You could develop that mindset, with time and determination. But if you don't, you should sell the tavern to someone who can—for Oakley's sake."

Dean nodded thoughtfully.

"Right now, though. The other teams are begging to come over to live with us." Lonny smirked, "Did you know that Riva is offering any of his teams that reach level fifty, your estate?"

"Think about it. A fifty and up team is a slow grind. Completing floor fifty-one can take a day. Which means..."

"No rapid in and out. Which Riva needs to do, to keep his score points going. So... my portal becomes the slow portal, focused more on tokens and less on points for Oakley. Makes sense. I bet he planned to use the fourth portal for that," Dean said with a scoff.

Lonny let out a long whistle. "That Tucker gets Riva heated. And yeah. The theory was the fourth portal would be mostly for big token competitors and events. Mainly, I guess." He shrugged. "It'd be less about the Oakley score and more about funding operations. Since they made the deal with you, though –"

"Team Ola gets to clog up Felna's portal. I mean us being in here isn't helping Oakley in the short term. Does Riva have a plan for when the Core hits five hundred on the planetary score?" Dean asked.

"The five on five? Yeah. You'll face the four hundred challenge. He has a team with all magics unlocked but they're still learning it. He calls them his defense squad." Lonny rolled his eyes. "Anyway, I think they'll win the five hundred challenge, if you or whoever loses the four hundred. It'll reset the score to zero and we won't be facing any more five versus one."

Dean was about to comment that everything would be fine, in time, when Lonny unbuckled his spyglass. "The Gnoll squad we killed just respawned," Lonny said in a loud whisper.

Wahoo! I didn't want to wait for twelve fooking hours, anyhow.

He decided to not adjust much. If he laid down, he'd be seen. If he ran to get down, he'd lose the high ground. So, he simply sat, slowly sliding his bag off his shoulder. He reached in to get his spyglass and immediately learned he needn't have bothered.

The Succubi spawned behind the Gnolls and immediately took to the sky. "So much for having the high ground," Dean grumbled, getting to his feet, his shield at the ready and right palm unhindered.

The duo of flying soul stealers flew close enough to the first group of Gnolls to pull aggro. The first group of Gnolls followed the two flying bitches to the second group.

Dean groan as he realized their strategy.

"Uh... I can weigh them down when they get close. The void shields are weaker when they are moving," Lonny said, then frowned. "The twenty Gnolls are going to be a problem, though."

"Fight or flee?" Dean asked as they watched the Succubi kite the ten Gnolls over to the next group, making it fifteen. His voice picked up a sense of urgency. "We're running out of time to flee."

"They'll have to get close to drag the Gnolls our way. That will be their downfall. Literally. We can fight them," Lonny said confidently.

Dean handed him a javelin and they both lined up their shots, waiting for the gaggle of twenty Gnolls to be led towards the house. The lead Succubus diverted, to hover a moderate distance away. He guessed they understood the danger of coming close, and decided to only risk one of them, in the hopes the Gnolls would do the heavy lifting for them.

The hideous red eyed creature flapped low as it neared them. Dean could make out the gnarled crusty black skin covered in pus blisters as it drew closer. The trailing Gnolls tried to stab at the flying demons and a few tried to grab their target.

"Ready, steady, THROW!" Dean called out. "Close your eyes."

With a whoosh of air their mini-spears spiraled rapidly for the single target. The flying beast started a barrel roll to the left. Dean lined up his palm for the spot where the Succubus would come out of her dodge, his fingers crackling in anticipation. The blast of energy laced out in an instant.

When Dean's eyes peered open there were a few noticeable things. His target had a massive hole in her torso and lay crumpled next to the house. The Gnolls were beating the shit out of each other, now that they were blind. Apparently, they thought that whoever was making noise near them, was a threat. The remaining Succubus was just hovering where she had been, unmoving.

"Probably afraid of flying while trying to regain her vision," Dean noted with a grunt. "She's scared of crashing."

He lined up his second shot, squeezed his eyes shut, and unleashed a powerful torrent of energy. When he opened his eyes again, he saw the second Succubus was twitching in her death throes, down among the oats.

"You can open your eyes," Dean said.

"I fookin already did—I'm blind, you dick," Lonny cursed, "Go jam the fookin locket."

Dean hopped off the roof, noting idly that two Gnolls were trailing him. Instead of fighting, though, he rushed inside and went directly for the locket. Into the slot it went, dematerializing both champions.

∞∞∞

"Ugh, so what happened? I opened my eyes after your first shot, only to be blinded," Lonny grumbled. Dean helped him find a seat. "Another break? Or head out and hope that Kambry can heal me?"

Dean glanced at the 185 on his locket and knew right away, that another five points wasn't worth the risk. "I have enough mana to keep going, but I'd like to take a break. We'll need to wait about half-an-hour for your eyes to heal. Or we can risk it and hope someone is outside who can heal you."

"We can wait," Lonny said.

The two of them chatted for half-an-hour about life before Lonny started blinking with a painful grunt. When his vision had returned, Dean smashed the exit button.

∞∞∞∞

Dean grumbled when he couldn't find anyone he recognized outside the event portal. He did see one portal over, the PvP regular gate, was changing colors as people went in. *Hmm. The only thing better than 185 tokens is more tokens!*

"Lonny, what do you want to do?"

"I want to go to the market, if that's okay with you?" Lonny rumbled.

"Sure, you care if I do a few quick solo PvP runs? Just to level five. We've got almost two hundred tokens and I want to push us over that mark. Here, stick these around your neck, please."

Lonny held his hand out until Dean put the necklace into it. He put the precious tokens around his neck. "I'm going to just sit here for a while and think about how we could improve, then. If you don't come out in an hour, though, I'm going to Min's Vault to bust you out."

"Half hour, maybe a little more than that, at most. There's an exit. So, if I get in a jam I'll either jump out or win. I shouldn't be too long. I'm going to run a PvP floor two, then come back with the tokens," Dean said, watching Lonny settle into a semi-comfy position. He patted him on the shoulder as his friend inspected his gear.

"Floor two is cursed," Lonny said. "You know that, right?"

"I'll be back in a minute or before you can count to a thousand," Dean chuckled, leaving for the PvP. His hand fished around in his bag to find another mana potion. It was his last one. He gulped it down while walking over to the staging area next to theirs.

There was a small line that he ducked into, one that went quickly. A female Naga in mage robes and a short sword was in front of him. She flipped around to see Dean and winked at him. When she finished the oath, the screen went yellow, leaving Dean to wonder what level that was.

When it was his turn, he placed a hand on the Oath stone. "I want floor two and understand the consequences."

The guard grunted but thumbed the portal. Dean snickered at the Minotaur and went in.

∞∞∞∞

He materialized in a forest. Crunchy leaves surrounded him. A squirrel foraged, and a light wind whipped the air. He saw the pedestal, no more than five hundred feet away in the middle of a clearing. He ran at it in a full sprint, his legs pumping.

Snow fell from above and blasts of his frosted breath enveloped his face.

His crashing through the leaves sounded thunderous to his ears, while his heart slammed against his chest. Dean could feel his pulse quickening. He expected an attack from above that never came. When he left the tree line, there were only a few dozen feet left between him and victory.

His crashing had not gone unnoticed, though. The *whizz* of an arrow caused him to raise his shield and lower his head. The projectile glanced off his shield.

He was moving so fast he reached the locket before he could spin to fight. He indented the trinket and left with ten tokens.

∞∞∞∞

Lonny was still content in his thoughts after he added his tokens to the growing stack. *195... holy hell! Cassie is going to want more babies.* His friend wished him luck on the next level after a quick retelling.

Dean trotted back over to the PvP area and entered the fast-moving line again. This time, a female Vampire was in front of him. She stopped as he approached to spin on him.

"Dean?" she asked.

Dean looked behind him to see a man with a beak and a turtle shell. "Who's Dean?" Dean asked.

She shrugged. "Figured I'd try. Thero is searching for some human named Dean. Paying five tokens for any information about a human named Dean—white skin, brown hair, your height. All humans look the same to me though," she said as if offended to talk to him. He heard her whisper under her breath, "Like food."

"Huh, good to know. Charles," Dean said, sticking a hand out that she refused to shake.

He watched her go to the Oath stone. She also stated 'I', instead of giving her name —something Dean would be cautious about doing, going forward. When it was his turn, he smacked a hand to the stone and said, "I request floor three and understand the consequences."

The portal shimmered and changed to a lime green, from the red that the Vampire had entered. He trotted in to see what awaited.

∞∞∞

He appeared on a rocky ledge outside of a cavern an elephant could fit in. The opposite side of the ledge, at the other end of the mouth of the cavern, was empty. The fall beyond the ledge was steep; he didn't bother glancing down for more than a fraction of a second.

Dean decided speed was his ally here. He raced off the edge and into the opening. Inside the cavern rested a sleeping, mini dragon. The monster was tiny, only three or four feet long with no front legs. Dean slowed his approach, trying to be stealthy, but it was pointless.

His heavy footfalls had roused the creature and Dean was shocked when his feet slid out from under him. *The fook! It used a slick spell.* His mind caught up to the situation even as he went down.

He crashed and tumbled towards the pedestal. The moment he came to a stop, he reoriented himself and tried to find the little dragon to blast it. The only part he saw, was the tip of the tail as it rounded the bend outside the cavern. He slipped again, trying to pursue the creature.

His clumsy maneuver, accidentally falling again, was enough to prevent his death. A Spidetaur dropped down from the cavern's ceiling, its spear landing right where Dean would have been. Dean cursed and rolled to the side. He tried to scramble to his feet, only to feel mud coalescing around his torso and legs.

The dragon with no front legs returned. The smile on its toothy face said it all. Although Dean was entombed in a thick earth spell, his face was left exposed; his eyes widened.

When the Spidetaur jammed its spear through the back of his neck, he never felt more than a pinch. He could see out of the corner of his eye, how his ruined neck erupted with a spray of gore. The metal tip of the weapon was caked with his blood and he grew confused.

He tried to suck in a breath and failed. He tried to move and failed. The tiny dragon hovered within inches of his fading vision. The fire it spewed in his face brought unbearable pain and eventual release.

Dean died on floor three.

CHAPTER

EIGHTEEN

THERO

Mixonia

T hero grunted at the blue-eyed, blonde-haired human across from him. They sat in his meeting room, just the two of them at the big table.

"Master Mage Thero," the man began, "I represent a party who shares a mutual goal of yours—removing Dean Forrester from the equation."

"I'm listening," Thero said. This was the fourth person to come to him with information on Dean Forrester. The first three had all been let downs. This was also the first human, though. "What did you have in mind?" Thero asked.

"You come to planet Oakley. You kidnap Dean. You haul him away where you do whatever it is vengeful people like you... do. However... You must agree to release him, after five years," the man said, fidgeting nervously.

They'd sent him a meek human. He could hear the pathetic pounding of this man's heart. His nervousness brought joy to Thero's shriveled core. Hann, the idiot who was still in debt to him, had sworn this human was telling the truth in the pre-interview.

"What was your name again?" Thero sneered.

"Fred works for this occasion. Anonymity is important—both for me and the people I represent," the man simpered.

Thero tapped his clawed fingertips on the table's surface before saying, "The fact you mentioned Oakley, gives me hope that you are serious. What is your official offer?"

"No reward is asked. You'll get a private entrance onto Oakley that will expire in two months. Who invited you, will never be disclosed. You're allowed to bring a hundred souls with you from Mixonia to Oakley. You are to capture Dean at his home."

The man paused and wet his lips. "Look. This is not a kill operation. You can keep him in a prison and taunt him or whatever. That is our offer, it doesn't get more violent than imprisonment, though, with eventual release and full health upon release."

Thero frowned, his brow lowering ominously.

"We are pleasing powers greater than ourselves," the man stammered, "you must understand. The bottom line is easy, agreeing to the contract will earn you one hundred souls and access onto planet Oakley. This fulfills our end of the bargain and you get what you want—Dean Forrester."

"And if he dies, trying to resist capture?" Thero asked, tapping his chin with a finger.

The man, who clearly was not named Fred, gave a heavy sigh. "Then he dies, I guess. We can only try so hard on our end. We fear if he is not removed by us, through you, then someone else will come along who won't spare him."

Thero's finger tapping stopped. "Just so we are clear. I won't spare him in my dungeons—in there, he will suffer. I will learn what I need to know. Five years is a delightful time to feed on someone so powerful, though. I assume if you're giving me access to Oakley, you'll also give me his location?"

"Yes, there will be a contested event on Oakley, soon. We estimate Dean will not be the Champion selected for the challenge. While the others will be occupied, your window to attack will be open. Be warned though, we recently lost all access and vision into his camp," Fred noted.

"Why?"

"They bought trees and have been using rain magic." The man shrugged. "That's just a guess. The weather there on Oakley has been crazy with rain, lately, and there is all sorts of blooming vegetation around the estate," Fred waved this fact away with his hand.

"How many guards are there? What kind of defenses?" Thero wanted to know.

"None—well, at the last check when we had eyes on the estate, there were none. Oakley is a non-aggression planet. He keeps a dozen fighters on site, but again, most of these should be busy at that time," Fred repeated. "He lives on a private plot of land with only a few buildings and no neighbors."

Thero smirked at this news. "Excellent. When is this event expected to happen?"

"In a few days, the Core's score is climbing. When you see it nearing four hundred for planet Oakley, just let you and your team in. This contract will grant you entry to Oakley once, and allows you entry back to Mixonia through our portal afterwards. Any attempt to enter a different way simply won't work," Fred said.

Thero scoffed and replied, "I understand planetary politics. I'm ancient. This seems too easy, though... there has to be a catch."

"We think he's important. To what level, though, even we don't comprehend. Still, the pay to remove him from the board is good, and this way is relatively humane," Fred said sadly. He straightened his back before sliding a contract across the table to Thero.

"This says that the rest of the estate is to be left intact. Minus one Kambry..." Thero smirked, piecing it together. "You know me and my history with Mr. Forrester?" Thero asked, one eyebrow arched.

"Indeed, you get both Dean and Kambry."

"I want Anoka," Thero growled in frustration.

"We can give you her location, but that -"

Thero leaped to his feet, his eyes radiating violence. "Please do not mistake my eagerness for hostility," he hissed. "Anoka will be at my side. What of her?"

"Protected, heavily. I can attest. I see her often enough and know that you'd have to fight your way through automated turrets, aircraft, and a thousand recruits." Fred shrugged. "I can't promise you Anoka, nor would I even advise you try for her."

"Which is why Kambry is on this," Thero said with a defeated sigh, slowly retaking his seat. "I may have to make my run after the event. Is that agreeable?"

"The contract gives you two months to use the portal. After this, I will vanish, and we will never see each other again," Fred said with a fake smile, "and you either give it a try or you don't. Consider yourself the hired professional, in this scenario."

"You offer this contract for free?! You should be paying me much more than a hundred tokens," Thero snarled, but signed the contract. "This is too good to pass up, though. The best part of all is that you didn't require a release for Kambry. I'll take her to a private planet to do with as I please." Thero smiled cruelly. "Yes, this is fitting. Out with you, pathetic human. Your frightened heartbeat is making me thirsty."

Thero pondered on who to bring with him as the pathetic Fred departed. While he wanted this opportunity, and in some respects had dreamed of it, he knew Dean was powerful—extremely powerful. Thero also knew his magic wasn't limited by a floor on a planet. He'd have the full range of his eons of practice at his wrath's disposal.

With room for a hundred souls, he thought again about who would be best to bring with him and then sighed. He knew he had time to plan. He'd go in overly cautious, with the intent of drawing out a fight. Yes... it would be a messy fight—after which he would drag two bodies home with him. One he would play with, and another he would bury.

The Vampire Lord laughed. He'd have Kambry and kill Dean. Thero would get his revenge and Dean would never know what hit him.

CHAPTER

NINETEEN

DEAN

Mixonia Market

Darr's shop on the third floor was easy to find. Darr's Pet Emporium was stenciled on a taut banner between two tall poles. He controlled three vendor booths. Each booth had multiple tables, with shelving to hold thousands of figurines. There were workers in matching robes helping customers, as if they weren't in a market and instead were in a store. When Dean and Lonny approached, they went to the middle booth.

If he did have to sum up the figurines that were the first to greet him, well, it'd have to be the expensive listings. There was a small war elephant, listed for two hundred tokens. This was new and something he'd yet to see—even after three days of perusing the wares of the sixth-floor vendors. There was a dinosaur, the raptor kind all the movies were made out of. Dean saw the stand the figurine rested on; displaying that this dinosaur cost three thousand tokens.

"Sheesh," Lonny said, bent over inspecting a land turtle. "Two thousand tokens."

Dean scoffed but Darr himself stepped forward and tisked at them. Darr was a Parrov, or a parrot-human hybrid, who wore a robe with his name on it. He had two arms, a human mouth, and a large build, similar to Dean's. He had neck feathers in vibrant colors, and feathered wings that hung down from his triceps and connected to his torso. Barr had two deep, sunken eyes, black hair and a sharp nose.

"That turtle is unique. A legend of Okrixi, and since I cannot deceive you on the prices Min sets, try to fathom why. Think of that turtle as a collector's item for an endangered species. A worthy animal to add to your zoo or breeding program. The price is set so high, because only an enlightened individual would respect its worth," Darr said.

Dean frowned, walking further into the display section. There were tiered rows of figurines of various animals. No two were alike and as he dove deeper into the booth, the prices came down. There were so many animals here, more than just battle pets, that he'd never seen during his visits to the other pet shops. Meaning Darr was a collector.

"I'm Dean, I was recommended to visit here. While I may not be a wealthy zoo owner, I am in search of basic pets as well as something more exquisite," Dean said seeing a dwarf dragon for three hundred tokens.

"Ah, a dragon man are you?" Darr asked.

Dean tried to contain his true feelings, but his nod naturally came out. It's not like there was too much haggling to be done here.

"I fought today and lost. To a dragon with no front legs; it could -"

Darr held a hand up pausing Dean. "Incorrect. A wyvern is the term you were looking for. A dragon has four legs, a wyvern has two or none in some cultures. Now, before I show you wyverns, I need you to understand something. There are about a dozen species. The common ones that are typically available are not meant for home defense and only have two core variations. Tell me, for home defense or for competing?"

"How do I get you to keep a secret?" Dean asked and Darr handed him a contract. "Oh, a Non-Disclosure Agreement. Nice." He signed it. "I have an Elf building a forest. She said -"

"Flipping Dwarven rum and hooker snot!" Darr exclaimed and pinched his beak of a nose. "Newly acquired?"

Dean nodded.

"Oh boy. Stupid Min contracts. That news is worth more than my shops. Don't tell anyone else. You're blessed by that hellish contract."

Dean could see that Darr was visibly upset, but calming. The Parrov waved Dean to follow after him.

"She wants those you pick to be of mild temperament, correct?" Darr asked. When Dean nodded, Darr headed to a stand over on the left side. "Figures," he snorted, "most hate the ornery ones."

Dean opened his mouth and closed it. This Parrov had already figured out who his newest resident was. He knew there were ways around an NDA, though, and frowned. Dean realized he'd have to be more guarded and cautious than he was used to.

"Color of jungle?" Darr asked. If Dean hadn't been in a blue and yellow jungle earlier in the maze, he would have thought the question silly.

"Green."

"What is your budget?"

"We want to buy an excess of pets for the games. A few for defense, and still have a little in reserve for new gear—I did lose my set today," Dean muttered, picking at his Toga.

"We talking a few, dozen, hundreds, or thousands?"

"Dozens, please," Dean decided.

Darr nodded. The birdman deviated to wrap around a table of horned dragons. He led them for a back table on the far-left exhibit. Dean passed the cheap array of horses, cats, dolphins, dogs, and even hellhounds. The dinosaurs, oddly, were notably absent.

"You in there?" Darr said, catching Dean's eyes glazing over, soaking in all the images of animals around him.

"Uh... sorry, why?"

Darr held up a dragon before setting it on a totem. A rendering populated and Dean read over the stats. Forest Dragon - Female. Age - 22 years. Weight - 15,121 pounds. Length - 27'. Height - 12'. Coloration - Green with stripes of black. Pros - Great eyesight and smell. Lethal predators with serrated teeth. Capable of arcane magic. Temperament - Docile to host. Cons - Horrible hearing. Needs a mate or will go mad. Requires substantial amounts of food. Must have forest to shelter in.

Lonny let out a whistle and said, "Sheesh, that's a beautiful sight. What would her mate be? Wait what does she cost?"

"Quarter token," Darr grumped with a sad face that was further emphasized by his arms folding as he frowned down at the mighty forest dragon. "These dragons need space. Most of the planets attached to Min's gates don't have space. Then there is the upkeep. If you've got space for a beauty like this, you probably can buy chucks of fish, they -"

"Shit," Lonny grumbled, "you just said the magic word."

Dean actually jumped up and down with glee before running in place and pumping his fists in the air. "

He's a big game fisherman," Lonny snickered. "Our planet has mighty leviathans of the deep."

"I've got a water dragon that would be helpful. If your missy friend," Darr looked around to meekly wave another customer on to one of his assistants. "Passes the word to the water dragon to catch fish... Then you could have one dragon catch all the food for the others. Granted, the water types would need to have a lake built, but you'd have sustainment issues taken care of."

Dean's eyes glazed over in thought. His mind spun a mile a minute while processing the options.

"How fast do they reproduce?" Dean asked with a concerned frown. "Our planet is huge. Not sure how the EPA would take to dragons suddenly showing up. Oakley would love it for tourism, as long as they're not... well, eating people."

Darr handed Dean a water dragon to hold. "Both would need mates, and they'd reproduce only once a year. If you want to breed them, which would be insane with just four, then it'll be harder to find many more with these great traits. Sad truth, these prices are set low. The species is a pain to maintain and they... well, we struggle to find them homes.

"When Min has them near a cavern they can't fit in, she shrinks them down, which is what a lot of planets do instead of slaughtering them. There are only a few mazes big enough that you can spawn them in. Most have a ceiling cap, but some have flying creatures that need the space."

Lonny clapped his hands, rubbing them together and said, "Wait so there are PvP scenarios where -?"

Dean certainly loved the idea of cheap dragons. The concept of competing against a PvP opponent with a full-sized dragon seemed silly, though. Until he realized the chances were slim that the dragon would fit in most PvP mazes. He'd have to fight, hauling the statue around for ages before he could use it. He wondered if they were allowed in planetary challenges.

"Indeed," Darr continued, answering Lonny's question, "though there are not many of those scenarios, that is why some master competitors still buy these. Their bags are stuffed with situational pets. Solo events tend to let the big monsters out, too. I think Min has a soft spot for the big guys."

"If you have the space, I've got two water dragons and two forest dragons that would cohabitate and make great additions to your Mistress's forest. Lowest I can go is three-quarters of a token for the four. And... if things don't work out, I'll take them back at half cost. Otherwise, you'd need to try to locate buyers on your own. Min permits lower upfront costs with unequal return rates."

"We'll take the four," Lonny said when Dean hesitated.

"Hold. Please. The four have to be, -" Dean started to say.

"Temperaments are labeled wonderful," Darr interrupted. "Besides the forest female. Most dragons want to be left alone and get cagey when they don't have a home. Her temperament will go from docile to wonderful in a few minor steps."

"You sure know a lot about these dragons," Dean said.

"I'm old. Old enough to have heard that new friend of yours rattling her gospel in the food court back when this building only had two floors," Darr admitted and Dean's brows raised.

"Wow, I could only imagine the costs of living here for so long," Dean said

Darr looked at him as if he were crazy.

"I don't live in Mixonia, lad, our technology has achieved cell regeneration. Most have, my great fortune is that I was born here, and my planet lets me go back and forth as I wish. I don't do this," he gestured at all the figures, "for the money, kind of why I spurn Marco," Darr said pointing above him.

Lonny took the bait, "And Marco is?"

"The Breeding Guildmaster. We go back a long time. Anyway," the Parov snorted, "We're not here to get into times I try not to remember. These four will serve you amazingly. You won't regret the purchase one bit. Can I consider them sold at .8?"

Dean sighed but nodded. He'd been tested by Darr on his pitiful haggling skills and Dean let him win this round.

"Okay," the Parov smiled, rubbing his large hands together, "your mainstays for combat. The flipping vendors up top will tell you to use a horse. Ha! Idiots, the lot of them. Follow me," Darr said bringing them around to the front of his booth. There were water creatures here. "Let me guess, for a water pet, you were told to get a dolphin?"

Lonny grunted and said, "That one made a lot more sense than the anklyorex thing."

"Ha! Again, poor Ora-. Your poor friend would skin me alive if I conned you. Look, the horse is actually not a bad choice. I got better pets for double the price, though, and I guarantee they will be worth the added cost. The dolphin is shit. How far did you get into the water event and did you fight anything?"

"Seven and a crab like this," Dean said, seeing the crab he'd faced before. "Yeah, I was wondering how a dolphin would fight."

"They don't. My wife does the water event one through three. She uses a dolphin to aid her in swimming. Okay, there it makes sense. I recommend this."

A kraken was lifted onto the totem.

Ursun Kraken - Male. Age - 2 years. Weight - 3,329 pounds. Length - 11'. Width - 5'. Coloration - Blue. Pros - Great eyesight, hearing, and smell. Lethal predator with serrated teeth. Capable of earth magic. Temperament - Asshole. Cons - Violent. Needs unlimited space or will go mad. Requires substantial amounts of food. Must have natural habitat to flourish in.

"I'm afraid you lost me," Lonny said, his face twisted in displeasure.

Darr smirked at them while wagging a finger. "You can slime yourself in kraken repellent. It stinks and doesn't persist beyond each level, so each time you'll need to reapply it. Lube that stuff on, release the kraken, and -"

"The little devil clears the entire floor for you," Dean whispered in astonishment. "Could you imagine being the guy who tested that theory out?"

Lonny and Dean whistled.

"Best part is, this is food. They're farm raised in massive vats in space, cost .02 tokens per. The repellent costs a fraction of a fraction. Now, some will avoid them because if you do a poor job on applying the repellent or get the asshole who doesn't care that you're his master, because you shot him..." Darr said, letting the sentence fade.

"Okay, table those for now. No water events on the horizon -"

Dean was interrupted again by Darr. "Follow me for your ideal mount slash pet combo. And, sure, put the small kraken on a shelf in storage, but know this, you will find water monsters in a lake that you have to cross or mazes with water. Sure, you're not in an ocean, doesn't mean you don't need to bring a water pet along. You think about it, the prices are right to have as a backup."

Darr led the pair to another display section beyond the cheap horses. Darr held up a boar figurine, mighty tusks jutting from the front of its face. There was even a saddle mounted on its back.

"Only half a token. A Varidian boar is sturdy, reliable, thick skinned, and a killer. Fights twice as well, is twice as durable, and only costs a fraction more than a horse. How many will you need?" Darr asked.

"Do they come in fancy versions?" Dean asked, inspecting the mount.

"Sure. But you want this one. Trust me, your friend will verify my claims. If I deceived you, they still have a low price, and these sell well. Not up top, though, because there is less of a profit margin from rearing these than the horses," Darr said, convincing Dean.

"They don't bond?" Dean asked.

"Yes and no, should they be given time to get to know their rider, then yes, they will bond. Can you buy this, go right into PvE floor four and ride them. Yes. Give them a try. I'll rebuy these at cost if you don't like them. I sell at least five of these a day, so it's not a big loss if I resell them," Darr said, twisting Dean's arm with his sales tactics.

"Ten then and I may come back for more if my other partners like them," Dean said with a smile.

An attendant was waved over and told to grab a basket. Ten boar figurines with saddles were placed inside the basket, next to the four dragons Darr carefully set down. The attendant ducked under a table to add new figurines to the shelf. Darr walked on until they were in the dinosaur section. Dean saw mostly smaller dinosaurs, here, with a special row of the bigger ones.

"Don't get these for your home. At least not the toothy kind. You'll run into fights. Now, for these, my recommendation is that you go a bit smaller than a standard ankylosaurus. Pick a spiklyosaurus—the ones with a club tail full of spikes. They are a little smaller, cost a little more, but also weigh less, are deadlier, and have increased agility. Only .2 tokens per. Oh and these will be fine with the dragons. Say five?"

Dean nodded and the helper ran over while Darr carefully selected five specific figurines from the shelf.

"Why those?" Lonny asked, curious.

"These have the best temperaments. They are decent dwarf dragon counters, too. Not that there is a true counter for a dwarf dragon. You spawn these to buy yourself time to get away. The spikylosaurus will lose every time against a dwarf dragon, but it will occupy the dragon for a time. Just like other heavily armored animals. They do fine. You want to use these when you're facing bigger monsters or foes. The boar is great for speed and running down ranged, this is for melee. Then dwarf dragon for air."

Dean nodded and said, "We'll take the five. So why is there no counter and can you tell me about the wyverns?"

"The dwarf dragon gets its value from the fact it is airborne, magical, and lethal. Dwarf dragons are the kings and queens of the air pets. That little war elephant is the same for the mounts at two to three hundred talents. For tank pets, the expensive model is a rolling turtle with poisonous spikes," Darr said and Dean caught on.

"So then, there is a cheaper, readily available version for air, that is decent but -" Dean started to guess but was cut off.

"There are falcons, eagles, and even... I hate even saying this, parrots. Parrots are fantastic scouts and can even learn to talk, if you spend enough time with them. Still, the balance in the air is lopsided. A wyvern will kill everything smaller than it is. The next step up from a wyvern is a dwarf dragon," Darr said and then paused.

He scuffed his chin in thought. "Baxter, get over here." A young-looking dwarf trotted over. "Get me the battle appendix volume seven."

Dean watched the dwarf run off. "What's that for?"

"If you really want to compete, you'll want the battle appendix. Battle appendix seven costs a full two tokens."

Dean and Lonny both whistled.

"Yup. A book costs more than your dragons, boars, or dinosaurs. It will cover each pet in exquisite detail, though, with the greatest value being the pages on battle applications. You see a full-grown mammoth in your event. What do you spawn in an arctic tundra? You throw snow into the air and you realize you have a thirty-foot ceiling. You exit and go get which pet?" Darr asked.

Baxter returned with a heavy tome that must have weighed at least twenty pounds. He'd been listening and in a gruff voice said, "Arctic Mammoths are prey to Crystalline Yetis. They will handle a whole herd by themselves, with their ice magic. Page 4327. I transcribe these damn books between customers. Takes about a year for a tome."

Dean was shocked and then said, "Ah, for a side hustle that adds up quickly on an off planet. Two tokens gets you a nice home, where I'm from."

"Where's that?" Baxter asked and Dean almost said it.

"A planet far away. When things are more secure, I'll be happy to comeback and share that information," Dean replied. Baxter grumbled under his breath about humans and their arrogance as he trundled off to help a new customer.

Dean accepted the tome and Darr opened it and sifted through a few random pages. "I have a pet book—Common Mixonia Pets volume eleven," he said. "It is missing about ninety percent of these and doesn't cover battle applications."

"Find the wyvern please," Darr said patiently.

Dean dug into the table of contents, found the wyvern listing and started hunting for the actual pages. There were six pages of entries on wyverns alone.

"Wyvern - the worm dragon. A wyvern is a mage of the sky. They are fragile, sensitive beings with very few defenses. They were an adaptation on their origin planets and have since been bred for magical properties. Their magic is terrifying when combined with a damage dealer. Introduced in the fifth age, before the dwarf dragons, they were so desired a bubble in value was created. When dwarf dragons arrived, wyverns were replaced. A wyvern breeds slowly, with but a single hatching every forty-three moon cycles," Dean read with a frown, halting his reading.

"There is a ton to read here," Lonny noted, reading over his shoulder. "Even Riva doesn't have something this nice. I bet he'd buy it off you to digitalize it. Or you could put it on the net and sell it as fiction."

Dean snickered at the thought. He browsed over their breeding habits. Then stopped and pointed a finger at a section. Socialization. He looked up at Darr.

"I occasionally get a buyer interested in the wyverns, who only buys one or two, then they don't understand why the wyverns get sick. They need a community. A spot to call their own or some bigger dragons to bond to. The other option, of course, is to simply keep them in Mixonia, in their current form, as is. I'd recommend that, if you weren't getting a flock. Now you ready to see some prices?"

"Ya know it," Dean nodded, following Darr while still reading out of the book. A dozen were recommended for a flock, at a minimum. He didn't even have a dozen fighters. The figurines they were walking past shifted from the dinosaurs into smaller dragon types. They passed the dwarf dragons, with Lonny pausing to inspect a few.

"I will always recommend dwarf dragons. When you can afford them, you should get a few. They even make great livestock to breed, assuming you have access to Mixonia. They've been costly for generations. I don't have any doubt they'll be expensive next generation, too. You're not at that point, though, I get it. When you are, just be sure to keep the wyverns and the dwarf dragons segregated. The wyverns will do fabulous with the bigger dragons in the forest," Darr said, as they passed the last of the dwarf dragons.

Arriving at the wyverns, Dean saw there were only seven on display. Only seven. "Wait," Dean turned to Darr in confusion.

Darr flipped the table cloth up and dragged out a box from below. While he did that, Dean gave a sigh in relief. The cost of the wyverns was between a single token, and five tokens. Well within their budget to get a full dozen.

"Four tokens or more means they are prime breeding age, with excellent characteristics. If that's all you want, I got more in storage. If you want some older or younger with those qualities, I have the dozen," Darr said and Dean smiled.

His eyes zoomed in on a seven token wyvern. Darr smirked at the fact a figurine had finally called to him. Dean set the figurine on the pedestal. Wyvern - Female. Age - 2 years. Weight - 86 pounds. Length - 3'. Height - 1' Wingspan 4'. Coloration - black. Pros - Great eyesight and smell. Lethal predators with serrated teeth. Capable of seven types of magic. Temperament - Amazing. Cons - Horrible hearing. Needs a flock. Herbivore. Slow breeder.

"She is gorgeous," Dean said.

"She is a fighter and a breeder," Darr said with a sigh. "Her coloration is rare because most black wyverns shine, this beauty is different. I bought her... Oh geez. A long time ago. Back during the bubble. She's always been the priciest on the shelf; most flinch at how much she is. Why buy her when you can buy two like her for the same price?"

"Because she calls to me. Build her a flock for me. The kind she would flourish with. I've got the perfect home for them, even if they don't snuggle up to the big dragons," Dean said with a smile.

"The preserve?" Lonny asked.

"Yup."

Darr started placing wyverns around the lucky lady he'd selected. While he did this, he shook his head with a slight huff. "They won't want a cage, if that is what this preserve is. Now, those," Darr said pointing to the dwarf dragons, "stick a male with three females in there and it'll be heaven for them. At least you know."

"There is no secret way to make this all just appear in our cavern?" Dean asked looking at the box of figurines and big book they'd have to haul out with them. Darr gave him a funny look. Dean cleared his throat to say, "I need to go to the job fair and deal with the lines and congestion there. My estate is in need of a blacksmith."

"Like crafting armor and weapons?" Baxter asked, standing off to the side.

"I thought you were helping a customer," Darr snapped in a gruff tone. "Baxter is between gigs as a blacksmith. Shocker. Of course, you would come along, deliver the biggest news in years and then steal a good employee."

"Before you consider hiring me. While I'm a very talented smith, I've got baggage," Baxter admitted, pulling on his beard.

Dean frowned but nodded. "Normally I'd tell you to explain it all to Mistress Cassandra, but let me hear it now."

"Five kids, a wife, and old parents I care for. My parents are -"

Dean stopped him with a hand in the air. "That's not baggage, that's life. Come on, consider yourself qualified for an interview. Will you let me steal him for the rest of his shift?"

"You'd let him bring all those dwarves?" Darr asked with a furled brow.

Dean nodded without hesitation. "Yes."

Darr snorted, "Then take him for the rest of the shift. People tend to drink during an expansion day anyway. Baxter needs to finish working tomorrow, at the least. All the drunken courage will bring more buyers tempted to try tougher levels with a new pet."

"I don't normally handle any of the hiring stuff—I just direct it to the Queen of the home," Dean said, accepting the box while Lonny received the tome. Dean paid in full and saw the locket drop down to *208*.

"What are you thinking, Lonny?"

"No use even thinking about the PvE duet event until we get you some gear. Bye Darr," Lonny and Dean each waved goodbye with Baxter in tow.

"Yeah, I need to get Kambry up to ten in team PvE and then focus on solo."

Lonny nodded at his reasoning.

"So," Dean mused, "a day or two to find one of these dozen to bond with and then come back to solo score a bunch of tokens and then help even the score." He sighed heavily on the elevator ride down, "Assuming I don't have to compete right away. That'd be nice."

"You know it's gonna happen, since you had to go and say something about it," Lonny snickered.

Dean had to admit his friend was right. He was probably going to be the one to fight the next challenge. He really needed to buy some more gear. Either way, he felt like Team Ola had just stepped up their game with these purchases.

CHAPTER

TWENTY

DEAN

Forrester Estate

"**D**arr is still around?" Orabel asked, her face astonished. "I find it impressive he is still trading animals for tokens. Probably has the largest zoo in the universe, all tucked into figurines in storage. Bringing back ancient memories, that Parrov is older than I am."

"You don't look a day over twenty-one," Cassandra chuckled.

"So... How did I do?" Dean asked. They had just arrived back home, with Lonny leading them right into the estate. Baxter was still standing awkwardly by the shuttle. Dean nodded his head at the short man, indicating the estate. "The Mistress will see you soon. Go ahead and get a free beer and have a meal on me."

Baxter didn't need to be told twice. He hustled on into the tavern.

Orabel shrugged, still struggling with her emotions, even if her face had returned to one of neutral indifference. She was wearing a thin, summer dress that left one shoulder bare. Her large breasts were pushed up in a designer bra, showing ample cleavage.

Cassandra, on the other hand, was dressed in comfy workout clothes, smelling of nice perfume. She trailed a finger lightly over Dean's new armor before giving him a kiss. Dean was fully geared up in a set he'd pilfered from the armory in Felna's cavern. Based on the planetary score showing 398, he expected he would get called into a fourth contest at any minute.

547

"You asking me or her?" Cassandra asked, pointing between the two of them.

Orabel grabbed the box and riffled through the figurines. "Fine, I'll go first. Let me start by saying that I got three levels done with Candace before you even finished shopping. We managed the first two levels without any contest. The third level, there was a bear that I ran from while Candace indented the locket. Easy three tokens."

Cassandra smirked. "I contemplated going shopping but decided not to. There was a note in Felna's cavern from Patti that a trio of Bouncry babes had just left for the estate. I was expecting the news that three bunny girls had arrived to be negative. When I met them, though, I was pleasantly surprised. They were articulate and well mannered. I was sold from the moment I saw them."

"First impressions matter," Orabel muttered. "I talked to them. They are really nice ladies. They are going to live on the second floor. Now that the estate is running out of room, we sure could use an expansion. Which I would love to be in a spaceship. Meaning... Cassie is going to pump you for tokens."

"Yes. Now that we are starting to hire new team members, we need to ensure things are cleaner. Which is another thing. While you were in your bromance mode slaying champions. I was doing interviews. We have five new members. All from the orphanage. A set of Lycan twin ladies named Hanna, and Kelsie. An Oruk male named Markin. A Catrin named Deathanal, and last but not least, a Dryad named Mel. All went to school with Wilfred and Zayra."

Dean knew there was no way he'd remember all these names.

"They start training this week," Cassandra continued. "As for the bunny triplets Jooma, Kooma, and Looma, well, Rew is more of a handyman than a cook. Those girls can cook. If we open the restaurant up as the Forest Café, we could get a lot of tourists," Cassandra said.

Orabel's sudden giggles, caused them to shift their focus to her. They couldn't see her face because it was buried inside the box of figurines, but they did hear her echoing peals of laughter from deep in the box. "He bought a coven of dragons. Even water ones. If I set these down, there are going to be more than curious gawkers coming to see them. Not that they can stop me. Out here I'm nearly a goddess with my power," Orabel gloated.

Dean flushed under Cassandra's stern glare. His smirk did not soften her furled brows or bring out a loving smile.

"What?" he tossed his hands in the air. "They won't eat us and who cares if the citizenry of Oakley suddenly learn that the universe is bigger than humanity. It's not like Earth isn't over extended as it is. Plus, I literally can melt ships with my hand." He dodged a pointy elbow. "I needed the wee wyverns for solo PvE. Maybe even PvP."

"Dragons? Dean you got dragons?" Cassandra all but snarled with her hands on her hips. "So help me, Dean..."

"Wyverns, Cassie, babe, and dragons, and spikeasaurus, and boars, oh my," Dean said, dodging her attempts to pinch him by fleeing around Orabel.

"Oh, and this should cheer you up, we earned more than two-hundred tokens! Hurray." Dean handed her the locket to combine with hers.

The ring around the Elven sorceress ended when Kambry scooped him up in a hug. "Hey, no fair," Dean whined, getting covered in soft kisses. Cassandra joined the playful banter and smooched his other cheek.

"What's the commotion all about-?" Kambry started to say and then ran to Orabel. "You got actual dragons. These are almost worthless... Why?"

Orabel scoffed at the Dragona and set a water dragon down in the middle of the open space under the front canopy. The magical transition pulsed energy in waves that forced them all back towards the front of the estate. Bright blue tendrils swirled around the tiny figure that grew in a few moments from six inches to six feet tall. Dean gulped when the mighty beast's finned feet puffed out into giant pads.

The shifting magic raced along the length of the water dragon, shooting down long legs that dwarfed the torso. With a sudden burst of blue magic, the dragon regained its full form. It was at least three times taller than Dean.

He realized that this was the male, because it had dangling balls. The dragon's eyes were closed, and he shook his head, as if getting up from a nap. He had thick beard whiskers meant for water.

The way those tendrils swayed back and forth almost distracted you from the massive teeth in the red mouth. Bright yellow eyes shot open to stare down at Orabel. Dean saw the dragon was sleek, with no hard surfaces. The scales shimmered under the lights outside the mansion. In between its joints and the wings were flippers, or webbing of a sort, for moving easily through the water.

"He wants to know where he is and why he was brought here," Orabel said and shook her head. "I told him that he was brought to our home to live as a dragon. In exchange for his freedom, he is expected to help out when needed. I offered to make him a nest, if he finds his mate suitable. Of course, he immediately asked for two females. I told him if he behaves and brings the other dragons lots of fish, then I will consider finding him a second mate. I also have to make him a lake, apparently." Orabel rolled her eyes. "With a waterfall. Now he wants a harem, too? Ha!"

"Called it!" Dean said and Kambry smothered him with kisses.

"Yeah, yeah, yeah. Males! Can you set the female down," Cassandra asked, enjoying the spectacle.

The female was set down and instead of being a deep blue, she was a turquoise. She was bigger than the male and the transition took longer. She also had the same tendrils dangling from her face, flippers, and water wings. Unlike the male, who had pestered the sorceress for assurances, she exchanged some dragon talk with Orabel before bursting into the air. Her strokes were so powerful they pushed the humans back. When she exited the canopy, she turned sharply towards the Larvinia Sea. The male smirked and tore after her.

"Wow, so... Orabel, are they like hidden from sight by magic?" Cassandra asked.

"Nope."

"But... Wait."

Orabel snickered and said, "Yes, two dragons are now on video and people are going to lose their minds."

"Oakley doesn't have a military. The Earth defense forces will know what these are and ignore them. My kind has talked with your kind before," Orabel said.

Dean frowned.

"I know you find the idea far-fetched, but I assure you, there is an elven ambassador tucked away somewhere on Earth. That is who will eventually come visit us."

Dean walked over to the box of figurines. More of the estates' residents had come out of the tavern to watch the show. He selected the wyverns and set them down in a row. Wilfred held the door open, and called for everyone to come on out and see this.

The smaller dragons grew in myriads of swirling colorations until they poofed into being. If the big water dragons had been the bastions of calm. The wyverns were the human equivalent of toddlers, full of energy without purpose. Most shot off into the forest, a few inspected each other, and one lovely, black wyvern went straight to Dean's shoulder.

Dean knew she was his partner in violence. Where Apache had wanted snacks and affection, this creature had mischievous eyes, keen on violence. "Anna, yes, I'll call you Anna -"

"Pfft, Geo, is her name, even if Anna is nice," Orabel said, coming over to give the black wyvern's ear a scratch.

He decided to walk around with her on his shoulder to get a feel for her presence. He picked up a light jog when a sudden crack of lightning startled Dean. The rain, which had finally abated, suddenly returned. Darker than the shadows cast by the canopy, an unnatural darkness consumed the area. Geo tensed fearfully on his shoulder, her claws tightening almost painfully through his armor. Even Dean was worried what this might mean.

Lightning struck in the middle of the parking area. A circle of runes blared angrily to life and a fifty-foot-tall Min appeared. *Fook, guess it's time to compete.*

"You have one hour to -"

"Can I bring a pet?" Dean shouted at the god.

"Silence! You have one hour to prepare one champion. The other portals have all said that the champion is here. Have them stand on this circle when they are ready. And yes, since it is five against one, you may have one pet. You should have asked sooner," Min said with an amused snort. Their tough exterior cracked for the tiniest sliver of a moment as a smirk broke through.

Poof, they magicked away.

"Wahoo!" Dean shouted with fist pump.

Orabel frowned and said, "Even if Geo is allowed, she is young, and she is not one to _"

"Ha! Not yet, you minxy little wyvern, fear not." Dean scratched Geo under her chin. "I will use one of the forest dragons. No offense, little Geo," Dean said and the assembled group gave audible 'ohs'.

"Right?" Dean asked, looking at Orabel. "I can do that, can't I?"

"Uhh, sure." Orabel shrugged with her palms up. "You want to use the female? She'll be bigger. She'd fight harder for two males than the male would fight for two females."

"Why not motivate her with extra food?" Lonny asked, joining the conversation.

Lexis walked up, rocking Leena and smirked, "Women can want more than one man in the bedroom, too. Watch, just ask her."

Dean snickered and went into the stable. Geo hopped off his shoulder to explore. As he went to each stall, he set down its new inhabitant. The boar was the first to spawn and it surprised Dean. It was much larger than he'd expected and the attached saddle looked expensive. Bonus. Geo darted around Dean's head as she investigated first the cow, and then the horses, before heading deeper into the arena. He'd do the same, he realized, if he was wanting to learn about his new home.

He dropped the last spiklyosaurus into a stable run when he realized both Jessabee and Patti were in here, brushing the horses.

"Oh, hey Dean, another storm rolling in?" Patti asked while repeatedly brushing a rough spot on a mare's coat.

He tilted his head confused and replied, "No, I've got a challenge to go to. You missed us spawning dragons. That's a -"

"Wyvern! I saw the black lady soaring over while you were on your way down here," Jessabee exclaimed. "They were my favorite, growing up. Never could afford one, though, and even if I could, they need a -"

"Flock," Dean finished for her. "Yeah, we got a dozen and four big ones. This is my girl, Geo." He chuckled as the black wyvern touched down on his shoulder and nuzzled his cheek before leaping off to explore some more.

"We have two water dragons who should feed them all. May even pick up a couple more if I win a hundred tokens in a bit. The forest is going to smell fishy, soon." He turned to Patti and let his charming smile for Jessabee transition into a friendly one. "I need help Patti. Was actually looking for Yarka," Dean said.

"He is helping Snaggletooth with a hipposaurus birthing. And before you get inquisitive, Cassandra knows more than I do," Patti said sternly. "Now what can I help with?"

"Rope and a saddle. I want to harness a dragon," Dean said and Orabel scoffed from behind him.

"As awesome as that idea sounds, don't. You'd fit better without something made for a horse. Go bare back," Orabel said and Patti snickered. "Ugh, humans... moving along. I summoned Droosca, lovely lady. We negotiated. I didn't love the terms she demanded, so I spawned the other one. The male's terms were simpler, but keep in mind. They die for real if they die in this fight.

"She wants more than just wyverns as a family. She demanded an expanded forest, protections we can't give, and a statue built in her name, if she dies. The male just wants her gone and three babes he gets to pick. That would mean we would have to summon dragons, one at a time, until he finds three that he likes. She does arcane magic, which is rare, while he does lightning. She is bigger and stronger, and has more mana."

Dean sighed and thought it over. "Yes to expanding the forest," he finally nodded, "yes to protections—within reason—and yes to the statue. Tell the male to head on over to Snaggletooth or to find some cave around here to call home. If he eats humans or livestock, though, tell him to expect to be hunted—by me and you."

"No. Sorry Dean, that's not how it works," Orabel smiled at him. "The male will submit to her authority—it is the dragon way. You pick her and agree to what you can do. Consider yourself going to battle with a dragon. She will have shields, rays, balls of energy. You're magic will be... a surprise to her. Come, I will go translate for the next fifty minutes or so."

∞∞∞

The countdown to the challenge was calm and yet a whirlwind of activity. Droosca came up with a loose strategy that, although Dean agreed to it, he couldn't say whether or not it would work. Only time would tell.

The last planetary challenge, Kambry had faced two Demogres and three Succubi. The foes that appeared briefly across from him on the sigil appeared to be two Demogres and three Manteen. The Manteen were harpy mages, of sorts, with incredible mana pools. Their greatest weakness was their frail bodies. Which, if you had two massive brutes protecting you, then who cared if you were weak?

Dean received kisses from Cassandra, Kambry, and Jessabee. Orabel gave him a peck on his cheek, with Sable doing the same, in a brief sendoff. Lonny, Wilfred, and the guys checked his gear a few more times until they were sure he was ready to go.

Dean paced anxiously. I'll be revived if I lose, he thought to himself. Plus, I have Droosca and our awesome plan. Okay, half a plan... and it was still five versus one. I've got this.

He nervously bit at his nails. The true thing eating away at him was the potential natural disaster Oakley would face, if he lost. If he won, the Core team's lead would be reset to zero and the next challenge wouldn't be until the point differential climbed all the way back up to five hundred, with them providing a five man team at the next challenge.

That was the one saving grace that soothed his internal struggles. There would be an even fight next time, regardless of today's outcome.

When the five-minute timer lit up, he smirked. Droosca stuck a paw on the symbol to join him. She loomed over him, with her green and black stripes. Her clawed feet each had three hooks and a thumb claw. Her teeth were stained yellow and she constantly sneered at Kraxon, the male dragon. When he'd talk to her through Orabel, he got a sense her docile responses had its own meaning.

"You ready?" Orabel asked the behemoth at his side. There was a slight hiss from the dragon and fierce, determined eyes. Orabel gave four light taps with yellow magic and Droosca shrank down to a figurine. "Arcane magic," the sorceress smiled. "I'm going to send Jessabee to get you from the vault, if you fail. If you don't fail, she is to pick up arcane scrolls so that we can teach everyone how to enlarge and shrink pets."

Dean accepted Droosca's six-inch-tall figurine and bowed slightly, "Your wisdom is much appreciated. Thank you."

She bowed in return and left. Dean studied the angry look on the dragon's face. He would be surprised if there weren't more than a few trees felled during a dragon fight, later, when she asserted her dominance over Kraxon. She had glared so angrily at the male that Dean had decided just to let it go. If she was rearing for blood, though, that was a good thing.

Cassandra saw him fidgeting. She ensured her feet were outside the runes before saying, "We'll be here, waiting, okay?""

"Aye, I know it. Did we ever get that fishing boat?" Dean asked and Cassandra rolled her eyes at him. "What Cassie?"

"You brought home two fishing dragons, what more could a man want?"

"Three more dragons, a boat, and kinky times with his wives when he returns home victorious," Dean declared with a smirk, pumping his eyebrows.

Kambry giggled from the porch and blew him kisses. Jessabee waved while holding on to Leena. Cassandra covered her giggles with a hand. "Fine," she admitted, "I guess a boat would be a suitable reward. But..." she smirked with a mischievous gleam in her eyes, "it'll be a family boat that is really hard to fish from."

Dean titled his head with widening eyes, his jaw agape. He started to scream that no fookin way would a fisherman ever be caught dead on a party cruiser, when he was sucked away to do battle.

CHAPTER

TWENTY-ONE

DEAN

Oakley - Unknown

Dean materialized on the outskirts of an abandoned village. There were five residential homes, two big stores, and a massive church in the middle of it all. Oakley was experiencing an evening twilight, casting the rocky brown buildings in a glow of a fading sun.

The buildings themselves appeared to be in decent shape. A natural bluegrass had reclaimed the area and swayed at ankle height. A detailed inspection of the quiet outpost would probably reveal a relatively common tale—at least on Oakley.

Pilgrims voyaged from Earth, New Terra, Second Britain, or other overpopulated planets to settle on Oakley. They would arrive on this outskirt planet, with a burning desire to settle in the wilds. Living alone on the prairie, sucks, even if it was good farmland with few drawbacks.

A lot of these projects were based purely on hopes and dreams; they foundered when they met reality. He could tell these buildings were prefabricated and appeared to have been hauled in from somewhere else. If Dean had to guess, this had been a catholic outpost that had been abandoned when someone died, or enough of the settlers had said 'no thanks' and simply headed for the cities.

His assessment of the situation was frustrating. These buildings threw a huge wrench in his plans. He slung his bag off his back and quickly devoured a large burrito to buff his strength and health regen. That was followed by a pink drink to buff his stamina and a yellow goop for mana regeneration. These were expensive buffs; Dean hoped they'd make a difference.

He pressed his spyglass to his eye socket, next. His opponents seemed to be missing and he really didn't like not knowing what he was facing. Dean's grunt was followed by a boot scuff. He shifted around, trying to get an angle on his unknown foes, but his pacing led him into magical walls that formed a box.

He slung his bag onto his back, tightening the straps. The only thing he could see, besides the flat farm fields and the buildings, was a towering Min, who stood off to his left. Dean could see where she was glancing, to ensure both sides were ready.

He was not, but he knew that didn't matter. Droosca had wanted Dean to toss her at his feet at the last second. Her size would magic him aside with a push, and she could absorb the enemies' fire while they went offensive from the sudden turn of events.

Dean was not a war hero, nor was he a grand strategist. He had agreed that Droosca's plan had merit. That, and he felt it would be a big surprise, to reveal his pet at the last second. Now, he might wind up dead before some big reveal. If he walked into an enemy trap, he'd never be able to drop the dragon figurine that rested on his hip. He needed to come up with a plan B, and fast.

Min's arms whooshed up into the air until their hands clapped together over their head with an ear ringing *crash*. The force of the sound pressed the grassy plains down, and freed a few of the looser roof shingles, that spun away.

Dean didn't hesitate. He sprinted at a full run for the church's front doors. His legs pumped, his heart crashed against his chest, and each step brought him closer to the closed doors at the end of three stairs.

A long leap carried him onto the porch of the building, where he twisted, tucked his shoulder and burst through the entrance. There was a *crack,* as he burst through, with splinters of wood shooting deeper into the church. Dean closed the door with an echoing *bang*, and with a burst of magic, he unleashed a blue stream of ice from his hand along the broken seam, locking it into place.

He reached into the pouch on his belt, yanking out Droosca's figurine in a rush. He tossed her into the middle of the church. Her animation triggered between the pews. There was a cross beam, about twelve feet up, that Dean used the back of a pew to leap up on to.

He clung to the wooden bar and, with great effort, hoisted himself and his bag up. The *clacking* sound of two sets of taloned feet landing on the roof told him they had company. If he'd wanted to hide his whereabouts, this was the wrong way to go about it.

As Droosca grew, she pushed aside the pews until they stacked up against the walls. They *screeched* and *clanged* together as they were moved by the sudden magic of her growth. Her back sundered the beams above her with ear ringing *snaps* and *cracks*. As the beams revealed their location Droosca came to a complete size. She barely fit while the roof leaned in.

Fook me, the roof will break when she moves. I hope this gamble pays off.

Using his elevation, he tensed, hearing footsteps on the stairs outside. *Yes! I split them up.*

Droosca came to her senses. That was the awesome news. The bad part was that she panicked, when two Demogres burst through the front of the church. Dean iced the walkway under their feet and leaped onto the dragon's back.

Droosca never saw him jump. She propelled herself off the church floor with a force so great, the floor crumbled beneath her, the wooden beams snapping with rippling cracks. Dean suddenly realized, mid-spring, that he was not going to be getting a ride out of the building. Instead of flailing uselessly in the air, he tucked his body, spinning to give the ruptured floor his back.

He tensed, shutting his eyes for the big moment. He smashed into damaged rock-crete with enough force to create a *boom* and bounced.

Oof! That was painful. Hopefully the big guys were dumb and missed my epic fail.

Dean's breath shot out of him. He tried to recover quickly but coughed. Unfortunately, a Demogre had seen his ill-fated leap. The brute stomped forward, his red eyes hungry for blood. The exaggerated stomps with which it tried to strike terror into Dean, was his foe's downfall. Literally. One big stomp on the weakened tile sent the Demogre crashing through the floor into the basement.

Thank the creator!

The second Demogre smirked, seeing a sturdy path to reach him.

Oh shit! Dean scrambled towards the back door, the second Demogre hot on his heels. There were the sounds of battle from above him, but he couldn't spare a quarter second to glance at how Droosca fared. The remaining Demogre was not stopping for the end of the building.

In that fraction of a second, Dean had an idea. He slowed just a tad, and at the very last second, dove away from the door.

His horizontal body smacked into a wall that momentarily pushed him back into the room. The Demogre failed to slow down, as it slammed into and then out through the back of the structure. Dean smirked when he crashed back down to the rough floor with a thud and a grunt.

Dean scrambled to his feet as the load bearing wall next to him snapped under the immense pressure of a collapsed roof and a shattered frame. With few options left,

Dean charged for a stained-glass window and leaped, just as the building came crumbling down.

He dove headfirst out the window, the colored glass bursting forth in a spray. His landing was awkward, and he chipped a tooth as his jaw snapped together from the impact. Dean spat out a mouth full of blood even as he continued to scamper away from the imploding building.

A swoosh of debris washed over him, the force pushing him forward. He dug his feet in and spun to see the fight. The first Demogre was still missing, somewhere deep in the bowels of the building. The second was racing away from Dean. He saw it run to the body of a Harpy type creature splayed out on the grass, struggling to rise.

Above him, Droosca battled one of the remaining Manteen. The dragon was on the attack, with a host of spells raining onto a rapidly shrinking purple shield. The green monster spewed yellow flames from its mouth without missing a beat as it toyed with its prey.

Dean knew he needed to capitalize on their advantage. There was a missing Manteen, or at least something new that he hadn't seen yet, and the other Demonogre trapped in rubble.

A quick compression of his legs was followed by rapid lunges that soon transitioned into a run. His feet flung clumps of grass behind him so that he could close on the wounded mage and its Demogre protector. His mad dash across the field was seen, even before he could line up the proper angle to finish off the wounded Manteen.

The enraged Demogre hurled its greatsword at him. Dean jumped to the side into the grass, narrowly avoiding death as the weapon came so close to his head that it whistled by him. There was no respite.

The hulking brute charged at Dean, trying to capitalize on his awkward position where he lay sprawled in the grass. Dean's arm pushed him upright and he leveled his palm leveled at his foe, who charged at him without a weapon.

Crackling white energy poured into his hand, eager for release. Dean's body heated, his stomach churned, and his adrenaline fueled his rage. When he couldn't hold the growing power in any longer, he blasted an orb at the Demogre, his head turned to the side and his eyes squeezed shut.

He staggered from the discharge, trying to put some distance between them, in case he missed his target. The flapping of wings nearby forced Dean to open his eyes. He saw Droosca landing not five feet away from him, between a home and the church. The Dragon was panting from exertion.

A spin revealed the wounded Demogre, who rubbed in vain at its eyes. A gaping hole gushed blood from the Core monster's side. How it was still alive was a mystery to Dean. It was clearly blinded and the hole in its frame was almost big enough for a human to dive through.

Dean flinched when purple spells crashed into a yellow shield. The wounded Manteen was flinging orbs at them from where it lay. The shield Droosca threw over them handled the minor spells with a slight, pulsing vibration.

"Did you kill one?" Dean asked.

Droosca picked a staff out of her teeth with a claw, the remains of a Manteen thumping wetly onto the grass.

"Excellent. Right. Back to work. Great chat." He tore across the grass with his palm out. He bypassed the dying Demogre, Dean's target lay a hundred feet away.

The dragon had other ideas about his blinded foe. She crashed into the melee warrior with a pounce. Her frame's massive bulk smashed the brute to the ground. Massive teeth gnawed on the creature's cranium with a scraping sound that almost matched the victim's screams in volume.

Suddenly, the Demogre's skull shattered with an epic *crack*. Dean heard the liquid *schloop* of Demogre brains splashing out onto the grass.

He whipped his sword out of its sheath, at the same time, pulling his shield's crest a bit higher. The enemy's void balls smacked into the wooden defensive barrier with blows powerful enough to push him off his direct course. He spun, to avoid the next set of spells, and finished closing the distance between them.

When he saw the manic smile of the Manteen, Dean cursed himself. He knew Kambry had used this tactic before and he'd charged right into it.

The enemy's staff brimmed with power, telling him it was fully charged. Dean snatched back his downward thrust at his foe and only just managed to get his shield up before him in time.

There was a ringing sound as an explosion tore him off his feet, sending him flying high into the air. While Dean soared backwards, his eyes fought to stay open. He managed to glance over his shoulder, only to learn he was going to land on a roof. He went limp.

A flicker of motion showed Droosca was battling the other Demogre, who had finally freed itself from the collapsed church. The sensation of falling distracted him, and he tried to think through how best to avoid his impending demise.

Like a wet noodle, he smacked into the roof. His ribs snapped and shattered. Dean lost the ability to see, yet somehow remained conscious. It was a struggle, just to breathe. Every breath took a mountain climb's worth of effort.

He most certainly was still alive and based on the brief moment of agony he felt as his pinky popped back into place, he was regenerating health despite his horrific wounds. His eyes stabilized just a fraction of a second before his hearing came back. Dual roars reverberated across the forgotten town as the two remaining titans battled it out.

Dean assessed his situation while they fought. Fook me, I've lost all feeling in my legs. Well, more like my feet. I wonder if that epic breakfast burrito is what is keeping me alive. I should be grateful, even if the pain is atrocious.

Dean saw that his shins were just exposed nubs, fortunately they'd been seared numb from the explosion. His mind calculated that it was his shield that had saved him. Where he'd had exposed body parts, like his feet, they'd simply been vaporized. He scrabbled weakly in search of his life saving tool, but it'd been flung far from him by the explosion.

His back was broken, which probably explained why he couldn't feel his legs. His left arm was a crumpled mess. His right arm was twisted behind his back at an impossible angle. And yet, somehow, he was healing. Slowly healing, mind you, but he wasn't dead yet. He did the only thing he could.

Dean watched the fight of a Demogre and a Forest Dragon from the roof of some random house in an abandoned town. Droosca was letting her opponent chase her. She would occasionally whip a tail around to check his charges, and he'd have to throw up a shield to block her strikes.

This allowed her to leap or flow further away from Dean. She flung yellow arcane orbs behind her to keep her foe on his toes, but they were either absorbed by a shield, or deflected by his armor.

The big guy did not have unlimited stamina, though, while Droosca seemed impervious to the game of chase. Dean's body itched from the healing and he groaned in agony as his bones snapped around or knitted into place. He really only needed his right arm, but it would be a while before that was better.

Droosca fled from the Demogre to rest on the rubble of the church. Her opponent went to check on the dead body of the other Core melee warrior. The Demogre's shield deflected the minor spells the Forest Dragon flung at it. At the body of the dead Demogre, a second shield was embedded into the grass, facing Droosca.

She was indifferent to his behavior, though she expended no more spells at his reinforced protection. Both sides were taking a breather, it seemed. The Demogre had strapped its great axe to its back while searching the other Demogre's body for its lost sword.

Dean snickered—it wouldn't find the sword anywhere nearby. He bit his lip to keep his screams to himself as we writhed in the throes of agony while his body repaired itself. Their last foe hoisted both shields and fled into a store. The moment he was tucked safely away out of sight, Droosca flew to land not far from Dean.

She glanced down at him with a wince, her eyes absorbing all the damage he had taken. "Where is the third Manteen?" Dean asked, between coughing up mouthfuls of blood.

Droosca snapped her teeth together. Did she eat one? Guess I'll find out from Orabel in due time.

"He can't win this fight unless he kills me. The circle will start to close, eventually. I figure I'll have feet again in fifteen minutes or so and should be able to fight in twenty. Can you defeat him, if you fight instead of running?"

If a Forest Dragon could shrug with just a facial expression, then Droosca nailed the look. Dean sighed and let his eyes drift up to the clear sky. He clenched his jaw and held in the pain, as best he could, while his body healed. One minute became five, five minutes became ten, and twenty minutes later, he had feet again.

I never thought being able to wiggle my toes would mean so much.

Dean walked to the edge of the roof and not a moment too soon. A magical wall pushed him forward. He hung off the lip of the structure before dropping painfully to the grass. The soft texture of the blue vegetation felt great under his feet. The wall was pushing at him, hemming them in. The church would be the finally fighting spot.

The Demogre left its protection and charged at the remaining duo. A loud war cry escaped its lips while it ran. Dean trotted forward far enough until he was sure the wall wouldn't disrupt his attack as it closed in on them. He leveled his hand at its face and the Demogre flung clods of Oakley his way as it skidded to a halt, raising both shields defensively before it.

"If you can't expose him, I probably won't be able to kill him," Dean admitted, discharging a few small energy orbs to adjust his aim onto his target. "I'll play bait while you circle around behind him and take him out."

Droosca crouched and then with a *whoosh*, the bulging muscles of her haunches propelled her up into the air, where she spiraled away in a twirling flight. Their foe peeked up from behind his shields, didn't see a dragon, and decided to use this chance to get at an exposed Dean.

It had to know the human was the key to victory. There was only one option left in those eyes, that much Dean was able to ascertain. He was the Demogre's target and the Forest Dragon would simply be ignored.

The enemy spun about, twirling around on its heel, before launching its extra shield at Dean. The metallic frisbee was sent soaring at his face. The distance between them was great, though, and the shield was no longer a round, even disc. Dean wasn't surprised that the throw was well off its mark.

Dean stood still as the shield embedded itself into the earth, at least twenty feet to his right, sending turf flying in great clumps. Dean was cautious. He walked slowly towards his last opponent. The Demogre removed its great axe from its back and charged him.

Suddenly, Droosca landed behind their enemy, plummeting silently from the sky. She unleashed a snap of her tail that *cracked* into an exposed leg. There was a massive *snap* as the Demogre's femur shattered.

And that is why two versus one is not fair.

The loss of his leg was not enough to stop the mighty Demogre. When it continued to hobble towards Dean, brandishing its axe, he did the most sensible thing. He ran away. The dragon's arcane shots into the back of the Demogre's one good leg, however, were too much.

Their foe slammed face first into the grass, with a startled cry of frustration.

I can't crawl with a big shield, that means...

The shield was left behind as the Demogre was forced by the magical wall closing in on them to crawl for the church. Dean trotted to the steps of the church while Droosca perched behind him on the rubble.

As the circle closed, their foe cried out at some unseen agony. Dean had felt the push but not the pain of the magic wall. Whatever pressure was being applied at this point, was well beyond what the Demogre could handle.

After all the chasing, falling, plotting, recovering, and fighting the Core's remaining champion died because of a broken leg and Min's rules.

Dean could have risked his life to end the Demogre's suffering, but he didn't. He watched it seize up in agony and then experience what was most likely a heart attack, as its vital systems were overwhelmed by Min's magic. There was a loud *gong* sound and Min materialized not far away from Dean, at a height he barely had to look up to meet their gaze.

She handed Dean a locket with a one hundred on it. Dean tried to talk, but realized his lips were sealed and he couldn't move. *I fookin hate gods sometimes*, he thought.

The ground under Dean's feet flared red with a complex rune and Droosca placed a claw inside it next to his foot.

A moment later there was only blackness.

TWENTY-TWO

DEAN

Forrester Estate

D ean stretched with a grunt. He had returned to a quiet household in the middle of the night. He snuck into his shower, and tucked himself into bed, trying to snuggle up to Cassandra's warm body without waking her.

When she felt him stirring behind her, her eyes flicked open. "Did Jessabee free you?" Cassandra asked.

"Huh... No, I won. While I would like to say it was amazing skill," he grimaced in the dim light, "it was anything but." He was slightly ashamed to admit the dragon had won the day. "Truth be told, it was mostly luck. I floundered and killed one of the five. Teamwork killed two more, mainly because the idiot Core team split up, meaning that Droosca was able to chomp two mages without their defenders and carried our team to victory. What did I miss here?" Dean asked, opening his arm so she could snuggle into him.

"Kambry is with Jessabee, going to go free you. Looks like I won a bet with my father and our lover," Cassandra said, her fingers tracing their way down through his chest hair. "Ugh, Dean, when will you ever learn how to properly use a towel?" She smacked his chest. "At least you're clean. Now mount me, my dashing hero."

She shimmied out of her panties and flung off her nighty with a lusty sparkle in her eye. Dean smirked, he loved the way she twirled her hair playfully and bit her bottom lip. The long ordeal of competing in the duet event, being killed by a

563

wyvern in PvP, and then competing in the challenge had worn him thin. Despite the drain of a long, exhausting day, he suddenly became invigorated, picking up his second wind. Not a chance in hell that he'd pass up a roll in the sheets with his beautiful wife.

He rolled on top of her, locking lips with his lover. She smelled of lavender, meaning she'd showered recently, too. He kissed down her neck, until he reached her small breasts swollen with milk. When he teased her nipples, she squeaked.

"The baby feeders are off limits, it weirds me out," Cassandra grumped and he bypassed them to kiss her firm abs. "Sorry," she sighed, "but please, do continue."

Her hips twitched in eager anticipation of his approaching tongue, as he grazed his lips south along one hip. Her smooth, shaven pussy arched up to reach for his kisses. A tender smooch to her clit was just the right tease. His lips pressed firmly against her inner thigh while his index finger tickled her entry, exploring her slick folds with soft, roaming touches.

She giggled with a half moan at his tempting offers. His finger slid into her warmth while his tongue sought her pearl. The slow motion of tongue, lips, and finger teased out her pleasure, mixing teasing, soft strokes, with firmer, delicious pressure. He curled his finger up to find her G-spot.

Her hips ground against his face. He increased the tempo of his finger, but not of his tongue. She pulled on his hair, a breathy moan matching her needy hip thrusts. He felt her dripping with desire for more. His single finger became two as he adjusted his position to thrust deeper while still gently suckling on her clit.

His twirling tongue spurred her on. She moaned out loud, gasping, "Right there, right fooking there, Dean." She squealed, "Oh... fook me!"

When Dean shifted up onto his hands and knees to mount her, she pushed him away. "Eek, no. No! Get back down there. I meant keep going, you goofball, you had it just right."

He snickered, returning to licking her clit while fingering her. She was back in the groove moments later, pulling gently, rhythmically on his hair. Her hips stuttered, her breathing intensified and then caught, as her vagina clenched against his fingers. She cried out and orgasmed with a shudder.

"Amazing, so good. You want to pull my hair while you take me from behind, or have me straddle you?" Cassandra asked an amused Dean.

"I'm going to lie down on my back," Dean said, wiping his face on the sheets and flipping over with a soft bounce.

Cassandra planted two hands on his chest, her feet next to his hips, and buried his stiff cock in her dripping vagina. She slammed down on his cock, clutching her pussy tightly against his shaft. He moaned in ecstasy as she begged him to give her a son.

He was surprised he found it so hot that she wanted his child so desperately. He thrilled at each bouncing slam of their hips coming together with a *slap*. She rotated on him, rubbing her thighs with his length before she went full on reverse cowgirl, giving him a perfect show of her twerking slit sliding up and down his shaft. Ten minutes later he erupted, giving her the massive release that she'd been begging him for.

She snuggled into his side, a panting mess. Her hair spilled over his shoulder as she used his chest as a pillow. A few minutes later, the sex-soaked duo was out for the night.

∞∞∞

The next morning found Dean sat at a table filled with his team, a big breakfast in front of him. Bacon, the real kind—not that fake turkey crap—was piled high next to a steaming plate of eggs. A big glass of pulpy orange juice sat next to the plate and was being refilled by one of the triplets.

Between bites, Dean complimented Jooma, "You girls rock, this is the best breakfast I've had yet. Thanks." His chewing paused only momentarily to pour out the compliments.

"Sheesh, Mr. Forrester, we're beyond grateful. We love our human bodies and our new home is sooooo big. Mother wanted to thank you, like a billion times. She was very worried, and now she... well, she cried," Kooma said, setting down a bowl full of freshly cut honeydew melon.

Wilfred grunted and grinned, "It is understandable. The realities of Mixonia are... brutal. I'm glad you ladies are here, the cooking is fantastic."

"Oh, Dean... I got a really strange text just now," Patti said, handing her phone over. "From Quincy."

Dean raised an eyebrow at this. He shoved another forkful of food in his mouth while reading the text. He handed the phone back to Patti and shrugged, "He wants to stop by and is asking for forgiveness. It's an opening, not a great one, but better than radio silence."

"What if he wants to get back with me?" Patti asked, her face conflicted with self-doubt.

Dean scrunched his face up in mild frustration and snorted. "Tell him to fook off, at least for now. Look, we can extend an olive branch later. We've both known the guy for years, but that doesn't mean we owe him anything."

"I am really busy competing, training, and now bonding with my wyvern. Pfft, Jarod crashed at the foot of my bed last night, curled up into a precious little ball. With Quincy, though, it's just... it's odd. He goes from nothing, silence, to hey, I'm dropping by in ten minutes. There is normally an in-between, right?" Patti gave a disgruntled sigh.

Kambry entered the room, tracing a hand over the back of Dean's shoulders. "How did your solo go last night?" he asked, pushing back the chair at his side.

She sat and leaned in for a sweet kiss.

"I'm up to floor seventeen, solo. Geo went with me and it was like I had training-wheels on, it was so easy. Ninety-eight more tokens added to the stack," Kambry said with a wink. "I heard you dropped down an even hundred last night. Cassie said you snuck into bed after the win last night."

"Yeah, the fight was a struggle, even with a Forest Dragon ally. Have any of you seen reports of dragons on the news?" Dean asked.

He used his phone to turn on the television. There were sightings of dragons on the news. Then the image panned over to show a massive mammoth and a herd of elephants and dinosaurs marching across the desert.

The tanned desert mammoth leading the group had to be hundreds of feet tall. There were stegos, brontosauruses, and some other, larger variations of an elephant. A flock of medium sized dragons circled the herd as it marched. The large billowing dust cloud behind the procession gave an intense impression that some great migration was underway.

"Is this a movie? Or did we buy large stegosaurus?" Dean asked, confused by the image. He shrugged the image off as something fake. There was no way Riva, Marty, or Tucker would march through the desert with a big group of extra-large animals. Unless. "Either Tucker is really fookin around or the news is playing off the dragons to confuse people."

"They look real," Cassandra said, arriving with Leena, "and that desert looks like the landscape around here." She pointed at the image, causing him to give it a second look.

They stared in bewilderment at the screen when Quincy came through the main entrance. "Howdy! Dropping by with a present from Mr. Lexso, himself," Quincy said.

Dean devoured a piece of bacon before rising to greet his friend. Everyone else stayed glued to the images on the screen.

When Dean left the table to say hello, he noticed Quincy was fidgeting. The man was in a space suit, with his helmet under one arm and a bottle in the other.

"It's okay, we've been friends for years," Dean said with a smirk, "and I won't let Patti kill ya."

The bottle with ribbons on it was extended as an offering. "Riva sent me over. Well, he asked for volunteers and I figured this was the perfect opportunity to say hello after the way we parted company before. It's nonalcoholic, a lemonade actually— in celebration of your victory. You saved the old man a shit ton of stress, mate."

Dean accepted the gift, popped the top, and slurped down a few gulps straight from the bottle.

"Delicious," Dean exclaimed, smacking his lips together. "Now, why don't ya sit down and have breakfast with us."

"I've got a briefing to handle," Quincy demurred. "I had just enough time to bring over the gift and to say hello." Quincy's eyes darted around nervously. "Hello!" He waved.

"Hey, what's up with you?" Dean asked, placing a meaty hand on the smaller man's shoulder.

Dean stumbled, dizziness washing over him. He felt woozy and his head felt ready to explode. A weak plea escaped his lips, "Help!"

Dean' fingers clasped onto the collar of his friend's suit before he collapsed, dragging Quincy down with him.

"Dean!" a panicked cry shouted out.

His stomach heaved and he vomited. Tears rolled down his eyes and froth bubbled from the corner of his mouth.

"We're under attack!" Orabel shouted, sending the room into a frenzy.

Dean's ability to stay conscious was waning. Orabel stuck a hand to his neck while Quincy fled.

Healing washed through him. His vision, which had started to telescope down to a black circle flared back to life. His vomit went from pathetic, weak dribbles, to powerful retches. The retching was horrific as his eyes shed blood instead of tears. When he finally finished, Dean saw Wilfred pummeling a downed Quincy.

"Get into gear everyone," Orabel commanded. "These idiots messed with the wrong home. Oh, and Dean, your so-called friend tried to kill you. That stuff he laced his gift with is meant to cause a deep sleep—but the amount he added is deadly. Lucky that I was nearby."

Dean tapped Wilfred on the shoulder and managed to growl, "Strip him, bind him, and stick him in the basement. The rest of you, go get into gear. Kooma, get your sisters and the other staff and run to the barn, release all the mounts, and then get to the basement. Take Leena down there now, Cassie."

His eyes shot to the screen to see that the dinosaur army was approaching a suddenly lush forest in the middle of the desert. Their lush forest. *Who da fook would attack me?*

TWENTY-THREE

THERO

Oakley - Near the Forrester Estate

"What do you mean our scouts keep vanishing?" Thero growled at Hann.

They rode on Gravva, his family's most cherished possession—an ancient desert mammoth that stood so tall, it dwarfed the largest dinosaurs around it. The beast was from the games' earliest times, back when planets were still wild.

Thero also wore his ancestral armor, black robes trimmed with silver. Almost as if he was taunting his foes, see, I don't care. Thero's staff was large, another relic from ages past, and worth more than he cared to admit. His laser rifle, attached to the front of the riding compartment on Gravva, was just as expensive and cherished. He'd made a conscious choice to flaunt his wealth to his future bride.

Thero knew what Kambry truly was—a lost princess, unable to ever reclaim her throne. He wanted her to think that with him, she could do anything, though the reality was that he would stick her in a tiny room in Mixonia and breed her. The product of Dragonas and Vampires were rare, and Thero needed more heirs.

Braxton, Thero's son, was just as ruthless as he was. Unfortunately, his daughters were always fickle and flighty. When you grew as old and as powerful as he had, you wanted more than one champion to carry on your legacy. Braxton had begged Thero to let him come with him on the trip, but his son had been forced to run the Omega Guild while Thero was gone.

569

Thero had long wanted to breed Anoka, she would make great warriors. Anoka was everything he sought in a brood mother for his coven. He'd even let her sit at his table. Instead, he was forced to pick the second-best option, Kambry, to fill with his seed for that one in a million chance of an heir. Cross breeding could be so burdensome for vampires. But then again, the ancient vampire smirked, most of the fun in children was creating them.

Thero watched Hann fidget from his saddle booth as he thought about how important this mission was to his future. When Hann finally looked up, he snarled at the whelp.

Hann's gaze shot down submissively. He squirmed in his seat before saying, "The forest... it's different. The creatures here... are different. I sent in five teams of two scouts, each on fast dragons. Only one has made it back so far. He said there were dragons, that blended into the forest and trees that bent unnaturally to sweep the other scouts out of the sky. From the sounds of the other scouts' screams, it is likely that they are dead."

"Fine. Fine. I came here, prepared, for this very reason. It's why I brought an excess of mages, an army of figurines, and even advanced weaponry with me. We expected a fight," Thero said, waving Hann off. He turned to a Centaur captain. His loud snap caught the female's attention. "Ginga," he commanded, "spawn everything."

"Yes, Master Mage," Ginga said. She tapped a number of commands into a tablet that communicated Thero's orders across the rest of his army.

Hundreds of figurines were hurled from the backs of the creatures and onto the grainy, compact dirt. The swirling of magic was a slow process when you generated so many pets in one area. Min's magic was hard at work, bringing Thero's minions to life.

Thero waited patiently for his full army to come online. He'd been planning this for weeks. Rarely was he able to assemble a force this strong and its mere presence brought him great joy. Not only was this mission vital to him, for personal reasons, it was a great guild building activity. He'd pulled in all the Guild's Mixonia born mages, scouts, and warriors that he could on a week's notice. Their plan was both simple, yet complex.

Arriving on Oakley, they moved in a defensible formation and planned to bulldoze through their foe's defenses. He used dragon scouts to watch for flights in and out of this Forrester estate. Only two ships had flown in. Kambry had been spotted in one of them, which spurred him forward at an increased pace. His prey was exactly where he wanted her.

The other shuttle, based on the description, had Fred in it. The portal Thero had slipped through was controlled by a human named Tucker. Thero was no fool, he knew Tucker was the one feeding him information. Which had included a nasty tidbit of news that his spy was in play, and that Dean should be unconscious by the time they arrived.

That would ease some of his weaker Guild member's fears—the latest news was that the human had defeated a full core team, on his own. Again.

Which, if Thero hadn't fought Dean once already, he would have thought the chances of that happening ludicrous. Yet, he had fought the man, and lost. Now was his chance to capture and study the vile human known as Dean Forrester.

While Braxton stayed at home, a hundred of Guild Omega's finest readied for battle. It would be more than enough. Out here, where there were no level caps limiting his power... here, he was almost a god. Even his top commanders were more than the human could handle. Their arcane shields were enough to stop even the most potent of spells.

The thousands of pets coming into being from the nonchalantly tossed figurines brought a smirk to his face. There was no denying he'd gone overboard, just to capture two low level pawns at a weakly defended outpost. The survey teams had mentioned that the forest was hard to see into, but there were only a few buildings, no high-tech defenses, and a few horses. Something must have changed recently, which made him all the happier that he had pushed for an early attack.

The original idea had been to try to catch both Dean and Kambry during their commutes to and from the portal, except that he got a report the group was going into solo matches and deviating from their previous portal schedule. Being able to capture both Dean and Kambry together in one fell swoop was tougher than he had thought it would be.

While they waited in the portal cavern on Oakley, Thero had gotten the good news that they were both at home and had launched his forces. This was certain to be an easy victory. The ten minutes it took for his creations to come to life was more than enough time for the defenders to learn that they were coming. It was a risk, though one Thero felt was prudent.

When the magic had finished spawning pets from figurines, there were more dragons than dinosaurs arrayed at his side. A wide, slow circle was flown by his flock of dragons around the forest, to ensure that no one escaped. Thero's desert mammoth was now flanked by hundreds of war elephants and large dinosaurs. The mighty collection of war animals at his fingertips stomped out an earth-shaking challenge. Gravva's trunk arched high and he blared out a challenge so loud, it required an area healing be applied to fix numerous busted eardrums.

Seeing such a massive army arrayed against you would prompt most sane defenders to automatically negotiate terms of surrender—except here, there would be no parlay. Surprisingly, no group was sent out to ask for demands. There was nothing. That worried Thero because Dean was not subtle. *I wonder what the oddly powerful human is up to.*

CHAPTER
TWENTY-FOUR
DEAN

Forrester Estate

Dean covered his ears from the sound of a mammoth's bugle call. Thankfully, he was inside a building. Olivia, their dryad nanny, washed a wave of healing over the group.

"Will potions help here?" Dean asked, once his hearing was restored.

He was geared for battle, with the others returning from the armory with backup sets of armor on. Based on the fact that Wilfred and Zayra were wearing robes... that meant most of their gear was still in Felna's cavern. Cassandra had placed an emergency call to Mr. Lexso, and reinforcements were inbound from Snaggletooth, but their ETA was a few hours. Far longer than their foe would need.

"Yes! Drink up. Magic is magic, it regenerates, regardless of where you are. The big issue is how there are no levels here. I'm level six hundred," Orabel admitted amidst gasps from Team Ola. She snickered. "Big deal, even I can't defeat two hundred mages and thousands of animals." Her finger pointed to a satellite image of the army at their gates.

"Can't you just talk to the animals and get them to swap sides?" Patti asked, expertly stringing her bow.

Orabel shook her head. "That's not how it works. If they can't hear me, they can't hear me try to convince them. My ability to speak to them has a limited range and they already have masters who are on the winning side. Not saying I won't try." Her hands went up defensively before pointing to the basement stairwell. "It's probably time to hide all noncombatants down below."

Dean nodded. The five new recruits were standing there awkwardly. Dean approached the twin Lycans, Oruk, and Catrine. "You four," Dean ordered, "guard those below, please." The four newbies sighed in relief.

Mel, the Dryad, pointed to herself questioningly.

"Can you heal?" he asked.

She nodded.

"Stay here, then, with Olivia. This will be our triage place. If things go south, the two of you will duck into the basement."

"Yes, Sir," she said meekly.

Dean wanted to give her an encouraging pep talk but was out of time. Lonny waited at the door with his team—Nick, Gerald, Marvin, and Yelli. His team was in decent gear. Dean's team left the tavern for the clearing in front of the estate.

This was it, the eleven of them sent out to fight an army. He had no idea where the forest dragons were or what the defense plan really was. Almost as if on cue, the ten of them looked to the Elf, who held a hand up.

"I have a few tricks up my sleeve, but before we march to war, I have a confession to make. Jaxon and I have realized that the words of the past are being erased as are our oldest memories. The magic is not from Min—it's as if the creator himself doesn't want Dean to know something."

This brought gasps of consternation from the teams.

"My faith in our victory, however, rests on that notion. Dean is the key," she said, casting a worried look his way, "and either the key will do what it was intended to do, or the creator wants the key to disappear and everything along with him. So..."

Dean jumped a few times in place while she revealed her secret. When he stopped his mini warmup he said, "Not sure who wants to attack us, but I can go negotiate. If -"

"No, our foe doesn't know I'm here. Let's use that to our advantage. It's always better to negotiate from a position of strength. We will wait at the forest's edge. The boars and spikysaurus will follow me so keep an eye out for them. While tiny in comparison to the monsters they will face, they can fight valiantly. Here we go," Orabel said, marching to the east.

The eleven of them were joined by the four dragons, dozen wyverns, ten boars, and five hybrid dinosaurs. Their procession was an odd one as the forest thickened away from the buildings.

A heavy, dense humidity hung in the air as they trooped away from the mansion. Dean was honest enough with himself to admit that he'd avoided the forest. It was an unknown to him, and thus was to be avoided. Sad that the protection it offered him, and his family, was only just now being explored.

The tall trees were clumped tightly together. Their brown bark hid a tale of how they had sprung into a gnarled old age from saplings in mere days, magic warping and willing them into creation. The overhead canopy was dense and blocked out most of the light from the retreating sun. The interior light of the forest was from an unknown source of luminescence from high up. Creatures of the forest flocked around their group and when Dean's neck craned up, he noted enemy dragon scouts gazing down through the foliage at them.

Their leisurely walk through the forest was interrupted by the stomping of the enemy army. The foundation of Oakley shook from the coordinated movements. Loose rocks and leaves danced, and a squirrel fell from the topmost branches to its death. Its shriek, knowing it was doomed, was haunting.

Dean felt the vibrations of the massed demonstration rattle his body as much as the dying cry of the peaceful forest creature shook his soul.

A sudden rustling from above caught his attention to reveal a dozen dragons trying to get through the canopy. The trees sprang to life, their branches winding back with lethal force. The roars of the dragons were drowned out by the snap of the tree limbs releasing. Thick branches timed their attacks on the diving mage riders.

The trees... they're alive? What the fook!

There were sickening *snaps* and *crunches* that echoed over the sound of the stomping behemoths. Falling dragons and riders crashed to the undergrowth, exposing themselves and becoming the groups' first targets. His team swarmed those who fell from the sky.

Dean lanced a tight beam into a dragon's wing, halting its retreat to the skies. A perfectly timed branch smacked down the foundering beast. Broken bodies crashed to the forest floor with sickening thuds. Any that stirred were leaped upon by Team Ola's warriors. A disoriented mage surrendered with his hands up.

Dean wanted to hold back, to show restraint, but this was his home. He leveled his palm and blasted out a tight beam. His shot of energy bored a hole in the mage's head, the defeated foe collapsing into a crumpled heap.

"Well, at least we have the forest on our side," Patti said, inspecting the carnage.

She spoke too soon, though, as the behemoths of their foe's ground forces smashed into the trees. A domino effect ensued as the forest was literally knocked down. The enemy was knocking on their door by pushing over the forest that stood in their way.

Orabel grabbed Dean, her eyes wide with disbelief. She screamed over the cracking of the massive trees falling over, "I... You need to hide. I can't win this. I can... only distract them."

"We can do this," Dean shouted back, pulling her out of the way of a falling branch. His hand leveled at an approaching elephant. The riders were flaming trees as they outpaced the larger support animals. "This is my home!" he screamed.

Energy tore from his palm in a slicing beam that burst through the mages' yellow shielding as if it weren't even there. The stunned mages were caught off-guard, as his energy cut them in half. The elephant stampeded back the way it had come. The two riders' defeat was a minor victory at best.

"They're bypassing us for the estate!" Lonny hollered from the flank.

Dean cursed. He wasn't sure what Orabel had planned on happening, but it was clear that the Elf was losing. She ran forward and jumped up to hug a tree.

He flinched as green magic burst from her dainty frame. Her body entwined around the trunk as it was absorbed into the two-hundred-foot-tall creation. She literally vanished into the tree. A moment later, a branch waved at him, before blowing him a kiss.

I so need to learn Elven magic.

The tree's roots ripped themselves out of the ground, dirt cascading onto the forest floor as the tree freed itself of its confines. As its bindings to the planet were released, the tree walked forward, using its thick roots as feet. Dean wanted to race to Orabel's side, to help her, but his group was set upon from two sides.

A pack of dragons descended on the ten of them from the opening the departing tree created in the overhead cover. Dean's hand laced out in an energy beam, blasting a black behemoth of a dragon from the sky. The forest dragons and water dragons leaped into the fray. The enemy was using horned dragons, so Dean never slowed on his target, aim, and kill.

Over and over he ejected intense rays of energy as the dragons fought to buy them time.

"Retreat!" Dean shouted.

A fireball of epic proportions exploded in the middle of his group. Intense heat washed over Dean, melting his armor to his skin. The entire group was defeated by a single crippling spell of fire magic.

Dean's knees hit the forest floor. The stomp of a behemoth mammoth bounced him up and over onto his side. Even as he wailed in agony, he grimaced in determination. His screams of pain twisted into maniacal laughter.

Dean might die, but it wouldn't be on his knees or his back. It took all his willpower to stand back up on his feet. High in the air on the mammoth's back, near the top of the trees, sat Thero. He stood like an emperor atop a mighty war mount, with his shiny robes and elegant staff.

Dean's body radiated with power, his entire frame bristled with unbridled hatred for the Vampire who stared down at him as if he were an ant. He leveled his palm, only to see his opponent sneer.

A voice whispered into Dean's ear. "Summon Havnier. Summon Havnier! SUMMON HAVNIER!"

Dean couldn't ignore the orders being given to him. His sparkling power returned to his mana pool as a calm settled over Dean.

"I summon Havnier," Dean said in an almost zombie-like trance. The battle around him slowed as Thero held back his troops. Dean saw Thero urgently pointing to a downed Kambry.

The pause in the fighting was a welcomed reprieve. His team was moaning in pain as they roiled from the burn damage. When no summoning happened, Dean repeated the phrase. "I summon Havnier! I SUMMON HAVNIER!"

The air bristled, warped, and then crackled in a firework-type display of golden luminescence. Space and time ripped apart in a black opening the size of a shuttle. The enemy charging to secure Kambry went rigid as time froze around Dean.

He popped his neck, eager for whatever or whoever this Havnier was. His adrenaline pumped, his jaw twisted, and his thirst for violence was insatiable.

A Dwarven god stumbled out of the portal and onto the forest floor. The disbelief on his face said it all. Whomever had whispered into Dean's ear had shocked Havnier. The god spun looking for something or someone greater than Dean.

When the god's confused gaze rested on Dean, he asked, "Who're you?"

A fleeting flicker of a shadow caused the god to flinch.

Dean snickered and replied, "A bit on edge, aren't you? That tells me you're afraid."

"I'm ancient, eons old, and from the first age. In all my years, there has only been one occasion when a god was brought somewhere, against their will; which only happened for the creation of the games when the souls of the gods themselves were sacrificed. So, I'll ask again, who're you?" Havnier demanded, finding his confidence.

"I'm a man about to die. A sacrifice wanting to save his family—a champion unwilling to kneel or fall, laying down, helpless. Some call me the man who will ruin the peace and bring about the eighth age," Dean said, pacing a slow circle around the god, forcing him to spin to keep his eyes on him.

They stared at each other intently while Havnier contemplated the situation. The god frowned, grimaced, and then his eyes widened.

"You're Dean. No... This can't be," Havnier said spinning around again, looking for something or someone who clearly wasn't there.

"Ya lost me," Dean admitted, his eyes darting around to see if the god was able to see something that he was not.

"We thought you were going to lose Oakley, when your side floundered with its endless preparations. We needed that, a call to action of sorts. It's so rare for a side to lose. When you alerted the forces of Earth that Oakley was in play, you changed my plans. Rumor had it the Elven sorceress was talking to you. I can see her ablaze from here, poor soul. She is dead and doesn't realize it yet. A pitiful sacrifice," Havnier spat at Dean's feet, "for a worthless man."

Dean couldn't stop the growl that started deep in his chest.

"You're not some prophetic force capable of bringing about an age change. And if you were, I just won, anyway. I just convinced Zued to join my party and forget about you, hell even his daughter is being scorned for a few bottles of moonshine and an orgy or two with the siren goddesses. Best part was, I didn't even have to tell him why. And as for you, being a bastion of change...Pfft. As if," Havnier sneered. "This idiot," he gestured up at Thero, "was sent by my idiot to kill you."

Dean leveled his palm ready for action and the god laughed in his face.

The look from Havnier said it all, Dean was powerless to hurt him. "There was no easier way to end any chance of a prophecy than by siccing these dogs on you. If they had failed," the Dwarf chuckled cruelly, "there'd be more. Yer done Dean. Done. By my hand."

Fook this god who put a hit out on me and mine, he may think he's immortal, but I'll show him.

An eerie silence fell over the forest. Whistling air rustled leaves up between them that just hung in the air, defying gravity. The gravity defying vegetation crumpled into a fine billow of dust. When the process was finished, a dark shadow materialized between man and god.

A wisp of a voice spoke in a soft, frightening tone. It hissed, "You told Tucker Frenix 'Let the Core win Oakley.' That intrigued me, to hear such from one of the Suca gods. Another of your sayings tickled my fancy more though. 'A few thousand or even hundreds of thousands of fleeting lives is worth changing that.' That, of course," the shadow hissed, "being gods who no longer supported mortals who sacrifice themselves daily to maintain the balance."

The wisp of a shadow grew to a raging torrent of wind, the force whipping about them.

"Balance is everything—without it, there is nothing. You are right, Havnier, there needs to be an awakening. Dean, remove this pawn from the game, please. The death of a god by a mere mortal should be more than enough to wake those fools up who have forgotten their roles!"

Dean's hand shot out again to aim directly at the Dwarf. The crackling of energy between his fingers spooked Havnier, who suddenly looked concerned.

Dean fired upon the Dwarven god with glee.

White orbs of energy surged out of Dean's palm, slamming into Havnier with a blinding brightness. His eyes defied the assault, letting him soak in what he was witnessing.

The orbs of energy burrowed under the Dwarven god's skin. Dean's victim screamed in shock as his body was riven with growing cracks—glowing lesions that rippled across his features.

A sudden horrific explosion burst out from Havnier's body. Dean watched as the god's skin splattered the leaves of the underbrush with sizzling globs of fat.

The flayed god stopped screaming, reality sinking in at last. Dean watched Havnier's horrified eyes reach the logical outcome from this situation.

The shadow vanished when Havnier sank to his knees. Golden blood dripped from his glistening musculature, covering his flayed form in a slick golden miasma.

Zued appeared next to Dean and stared at the flayed Dwarf, totally at a loss for words. The Lightning god finally gathered his wits together. "NO!" he shouted, "This is not -"

Dean tuned him out, Zued's words fell on deaf ears. Dean used his left hand to pull the Dwarf to his feet by the god's beard.

His right hand slammed into the slick mess under the startled god's chin, his palm upward. He let his roiling anger build into a crescendo while glaring directly into Havnier's eyes. The Dwarf's eyes twitched weakly—spasming in the open air, with no eyelids to hide behind. It was evident the damage already done was taking its toll.

With a snarl, Dean unleashed a full beam through his palm into the underside of the Dwarf god's chin. The beam blew the top off the god's head out in a fountain of golden blood and brains.

Dean was drenched in the carnage.

Zued fled, realizing that his pleading at this point was worse than useless. The golden specks of god that splattered the forest in a wide arc around Dean began sliding back towards him.

This confused Dean, causing him to drop the limp corpse and leap back.

Then he realized what was really happening.

The blood of the slain god was entering the seam in his hand. As the blood of the god drained out, it was sucked up from the ground into his palm. He stood there in shock as the wound he'd received from the Eelraken consumed the golden blood.

Dean was visited again by the highest of powers, but he hardly noticed.

Min arrived, her empty hands held up defensively. "Don't shoot, please. I know you believe in the balance."

"What is happening?" Dean wondered, his words slurring together. "Oh, and ants... I promised myself -"

Min snorted in amusement. "Ants have their own ant god. As for what is happening, you've shaken the universe to its very core. You've changed the rules, Dean Forrester. Well, obviously not just you—our mutual benefactor has chosen to do so. When the time comes that we clash, know that I do so only because I must. Your newfound powers are for the three species of gods, not the games. I was given... assurances."

"I'm not in the mood for riddles or half-truths, Min. Speak plainly or leave," Dean said, his hand still consuming a god's blood.

"I, we... are here to inform you that your powers inside the game will be the same as they have been. Outside of Mixonia, though, you're more powerful than a god, less powerful than we are, and nothing compared to the creator. Continue to protect those you love."

Dean's eyes blazed golden as he soaked up a god's magic.

"And Dean," Min smirked, "Not everyone who appears to be your foe, is actually your enemy. I don't like seeing needless death—like that mage you killed earlier, who surrendered and was told that hostages would be freed."

Min vanished and Dean screamed in rage at her accusation, because he realized that she was probably right.

A fireball from above washed over him, having zero effects, other than letting him know that time had resumed. He saw his friends moving; they were burned, battered, and broken.

Dean smiled at them and cast a golden aura over their damaged bodies. There was a magical transformation as the nine other members of Team Ola were healed completely. To say they were shocked, would be an understatement.

There was an agonized scream, then, one of death. A massive walking tree on the edge of the forest was an inferno of flame. A hundred dragons surrounded Orabel, assaulting her from all sides and angles. Her desperate fight was futile. Her haunting scream suddenly stopped, the massive walking tree tottered to one side and slammed to the ground.

Dean blasted water, not from his palm, but from the air itself. With a mere whim of a wish, he extinguished the flames in a torrential downpour. The tree shuddered, giving him a burst of hope.

He ignored the magic cast against him, his divinity unaffected by the desperate lobbing of spells by Thero and his goons. Dean ran straight for Orabel, instead. She'd come out from the tree, her body lay still in the charred ashes on the ground, her chest neither rising nor falling as she rested face down.

When he flipped her onto her back, her eyes were glazed over in death. He sent healing magic into her that failed to find a spark of life to latch onto. Time did not freeze when the next god visited. An Elven goddess appeared, weeping heavily at the sight she beheld. The skies above turned black as love for her fallen turned to vengeance.

Dean joined her in her cries of anguish. Yes, Orabel had been new to him. He'd told her, though, that she was family. And to him, family meant everything.

His anger fueled him. The rage fueled his powers, converting and transforming his very nature. The mere mortal morphed into a giant with an influx of magic that the forest Orabel created continued to feed him.

When the shocked Elven god understood what was happening, she too, funneled power into Dean. His body surged with energy as he grew. At the apex of his ascension, he stood a few hundred feet tall.

He bellowed out in defiance at the army that still marched on his home. Though Dean was eager for vengeance, Mins words resonated with him. He proclaimed, "Lay on the forest floor. If ya don't, you declare yourself my foe and I'll crush ya like the ants you are. Surrender now! This is your last and only warning."

In three long strides, Dean reached Thero. The enemy mage was eagerly trying to get down to the forest floor. With a swift swipe of his hand, Dean snagged the dangling Vampire right off of his rope.

"Unhand me, god killer, you do the Core's -" Thero shrieked. Dean tossed the tiny Vampire in his mouth where he screamed out an "AHHHHHHHH!"

There was a *snap, crackle*, and then the taste of ash in Dean's mouth. He spat out the gray ash like substance that was all that was left of Thero the Master Mage. A true death had never been more certain. When those most loyal to their leader turned on Dean in his giant form, he responded with a frightening release of raw power.

Blinding light that didn't bother him in the least blasted from the heavens above in torrents of energy, as if he unleashed a solar flare on them. There was no fighting. There was no witty banter back and forth. Dean was righting a wrong. He'd warned those who challenged him. This was his response to those who thought they could still violate his home.

Death. Death was what he delivered in a holy package of incineration. The invading army was roasted into oblivion within the mighty beams. This was no half measure. Dragons burst into ash in showering displays of magic. Dinosaurs exploded and the last of Thero's troops, trying to fight a lost battle, were struck down from the heavens.

When silence settled once more over the forest, Dean returned to his normal size. While his form shifted, he turned to deal with the fallen hero. With human hands, he dug a pit beside Orabel. The Elven goddess joined him, his teammates joined him, and tears rolled from their eyes freely. Orabel was gently laid to rest in a shallow grave dug with love. As a group they buried her.

The mages of Thero's army who had surrendered approached, with their hands up. The Elven goddess placed a hand on Dean's shoulder and then waved them forward. The enemy Guild's surrender was surreal, though it was nothing compared to when her goddess sang for Orabel.

The harmonious melody was at once soothing and striking. More than that, it was inspiring. Havnier had been a glutton, his stored power was beyond reckoning for a simple human like Dean, who sank slowly to his knees and placed his hands over the fresh dirt that covered his friend.

Power of magnitudes untold, raced through his body, and into the land. A new magic entwined with his. The ways of the forest opened to him, and he opened to them. The two became one as Dean expanded the forest around his home in both its size and density. The fallen trees were instantly restored, the edge of the desert pushed even further back, and those standing near Orabel were suddenly engulfed by a pitch blackness.

There was calm as Dean raised the final tree over a cavern of remembrance. He crafted the eight-hundred-foot-tall yellowwood directly over Orabel's gravesite. There was an opening in the roots that showed him the way out when he'd finished his creation. As Dean reemerged from the roots of the grand tree, the Elven goddess concluded her song and vanished.

A wind whispered from the cavern that was Orabel's final resting place. Dean heard it clearly. "Initiation of a new age has commenced," the wind whispered to him and his team. "Choose your path carefully."

CHAPTER
TWENTY-FIVE
DEAN

Mixonia - Duet Event

"Bro, we've been ready for ten minutes. I get it, you're worried," Lonny said, standing in the open snow-covered terrain.

Dean nodded because his friend's statement was spot on. He indeed was worried. So worried, in fact, that he didn't care that he was freezing. They were on the first floor, without even a single opponent, and it was if his feet were rooted in place.

This came after a full day of him restoring and improving the forest around the estate. The captured mages were stripped of their gear and forced to use arcane magic to shift their mounts back down to figurines. When Team Ola was done looting, they returned just over sixty Omega Guild members back to Mixonia.

There were mutters and murmurs about how Thero's son, Braxton, would seek vengeance. When he'd challenged the notion, it was met with a refusal to explain or elaborate. Dean ignored them, after a point, and instead became lost in the forest. He roamed in his aimless trek. The expanded forest was vacant, without birds or animals to populate it. This only caused him to wander further into his creation.

Geo would visit him occasionally, tracking him by his scent. The others... the others left him alone, giving him time to adjust. He needed to feel human again. That was his defining thought, he realized, after long moments of self-reflection amongst the trees.

He found Lonny, shuttled to Mixonia, and together went into the duet PvE event. Of course, he had to check his stat sheet first, which was enough to give him an indication of what might happen inside the games.

Champion Information
Name: Dean Forrester Gender: Male
Level: 10 Tokens: 0
Race: Human Alignment: Suca – Mixonia
Luck: 16 Charisma: 41

Health: 360 / 360 H-Regen: 1.0 / Sec
Stamina: 320 / 320 M-Regen: 1.0 / Sec
Mana: 370 / 370 S-Regen: 1.0 / Sec

Strength: 224 Vitality: 146
Dexterity: 117 Endurance: 203
Intelligence: 115 Willpower: 255
Magic: Electrical Water

Now they stood, knee deep in the snow with gentle flakes falling. This is where he had hit his proverbial shit or get off the pot moment. Well, that and Lonny had finally grown impatient enough to make him do something.

"The voice said initiation of a new age had commenced. Not that the age has transitioned. Also, Min said I didn't have godly powers in here," Dean said with a sigh. "Either I blast a wall and it bursts the vault, there is something else that has to happen first, or I'm back to normal. If it's the latter, that would mean I won't battle Min until later."

"So... Yeah," Lonny blew out a foggy breath with a huff, "I'm here at your side to test it. Shoot the podium, try to grow a tree. Sunder the soil around us with your god-like smiting ability, I guess. It's not a question of whether or not you have the power to do it—it's whether or not you can actually do it, here. Just do it!" Lonny said with a chuckle.

Dean gave a heavy sigh before he continued. "And Min said that I would be normal in the maze, and that when we fought..."

Lonny walked to the locket, lifted it off the pedestal, pressed it to the indent, and transported them to the white room.

∞∞∞

Lonny's hand rested on the next button. Dean grumbled at this. He wanted to stew a bit more, to wallow in his introspection. Lonny wanted him to act on his worries. Dean set his hand on top of his friend's and they left for floor two.

∞∞∞

Floor two was a ballroom, at the end of which was a raised stage that held a pedestal. A goblin warrior faced them, picking its nose. It was green skinned, wart faced, and sneered at the booger on its finger. Dean chuckled at the monster guarding the treasure for the whopping two token payout.

"Fitting," Dean muttered.

"What?" Lonny chuckled, "That when you have to test your god-like powers in the game of the gods, you face a terrifying goblin? We've done probably a hundred levels, total, and we've yet to see one of the most basic mobs troped in every book, movie, and game." He rolled his eyes. "Hell, we both got zombies on a few occasions, already. And you're scared of a goblin?"

"Right. Ah, well. No time like the present," Dean said, and knelt to the ground, placing his hands flat on the floor.

He tested out whether he could generate magic by willing it from him. To describe the process—other than simply feeling the magic, manipulating the energy, and then sending the power to where he wanted it to go—was impossible. That was how the gods cast magic. There was no firing point, like a staff or a seam in your palm. It just... was.

When Dean's attempts to will the ground to grow vegetation failed, he sighed.

With a quick hop to his feet, he clapped his hands. Dean commanded the heavens above to send down lightning to incinerate his foe. His body coursed with power, but no magical lightning blasted down through the ceiling. Instead his palm shot a brilliant beam of energy above the goblin. Where it connected with the ceiling, raw white power cascaded down onto his target.

Dean had generated a lighting-strike, not that different from his energy beam. Unfortunately, he forgot to close his eyes—which he had long ago learned to do before firing his energy beams. It was very bright, quite blinding, and extremely painful to his seared eyeballs.

There was the immediate crack of thunder and he felt all of his hair stand on edge. "I'm blind," Dean proclaimed.

"You got to be fooking kidding me," Lonny growled with frustration. "I'm blind, too." He muttered a few more choice curses. "At least you killed the goblin. Tell me you slew the runt."

"Does... maybe count?"

"Fook No! 'Maybe' is a solidly bad answer in this -"

The squawking brutish tongue of the goblin caused both men to tense. They heard a goblin war cry and the sound of his little feet charging the blinded duo.

"Dean, you missed!"

Dean huffed in exasperation, "We can't be certain. That could have been a rat. Maybe I just wounded him. Not like I can see how badly I hurt him."

"Clearly, you missed. If we die on the second floor, to a single goblin..."

"Yeah. We'll never hear the end of it from our teams... Argh!" Dean exclaimed as a sharp pain stabbed into his right knee. Instinctively, he hopped on his one good leg. "Little fook shot me in the knee."

"How many arrows did he have?" Lonny wondered, as another arrow pinged off his armor. "Hey pip squeak," Dean heard his friend snarl, "Where are ya?"

Dean yanked the arrow out of his knee, only to feel another piercing pain erupt in his foot. "Fook me!" he shouted, finally drawing his sword and swinging it blindly in front of him. "Ugh, he got me twice now." He reached down and pulled an arrow out of his foot. "I'm breaking the shit's fookin arrows. At least there is a silver lining to this pain."

The goblin gave another war cry, running towards Dean but not directly at him. *Crap, it's charging Lonny.* There was a clang against Lonny's armor, the metal-on-metal scrape of a weapon smashing into his gear. Dean heard a cry of pain from his friend and then a heavy thud. The rustling, tumbling, and grunting told Dean that, while he couldn't see what was going on, it was clear that his friend and the goblin were wrestling.

"You okay?" he called out.

"Busy!" Lonny grunted energetically. Suddenly, there was a loud *snap* followed by a loud sigh of relief. "His little rusty dagger carved through my armor and straight into my guts," Lonny groaned. "Fookin ridiculous. It's healing though."

Dean walked towards his friend's voice. "And the goblin?"

"Had problems removing his dagger. My dad used to sing a silly song for me when I was a kid," Lonny said, lifting his voice in a jingle. "The wrist bone is connected to the, elbow. The elbow is connected to the, shoulder. From the shoulder you slide your hand over to find the goblin's scrawny neck and snap it!"

For some reason, Dean found this hilarious, and burst into a fit of giggles and then full on belly laughs, while trying to locate his friend by the other man's chuckles. He sat down beside Lonny and waited for his sight to come back.

"So... I'm not a god in the games. That is for certain. I saw infinite amounts of -"

"Ha! Dean, you couldn't even kill a level two goblin. Clearly, ya ain't a god in here, bro. Pfft. You're so getting laughed at for this one," Lonny snickered.

A loud thump and the clang of his friend's armor against the ballroom floor told Dean he was laying down. Dean joined him on the tile, pulling his bag around to use as a pillow. The two of them rested next to the smelly goblin corpse, waiting for their vision to return. Dean grew bored as he stared blindly up at the ceiling.

"What do ya think Cassie will do with all our new wealth?" Dean asked, knowing things were going to change at home.

Lonny scoffed and then asked, "What wealth? Some of it better be used so that I can actually have some decent armor."

"We're not going to keep the desert mammoth or the dinosaurs. There is just no feasible way to maintain them. Darr will buy them... maybe. I bet I'll have to send Jessabee off to Mixonia to sell them at a loss. And then there is all the gear," Dean grumbled.

"You do realize that you chewed up a Vampire in robes that were probably worth a spaceship?" Lonny snickered.

"Sheesh, as if it was all my fault." Dean chuckled. "Okay, maybe a wee bit, but I needed to fry his heart or do enough damage that he died a true death. How was I supposed to know that meant his robes would become cinders of ash along with the rest of him," Dean sighed. "At least he dropped his staff."

"If I were Cassandra," Lonny snorted, "not that I'm wanting to join yer harem, mate. But if I were the head of a household with three, or is it four, women... I would want more space. Then she is also managing dozens more staff to help you, us, and the others do what we do. After space, you better bet she is going to want security. Your daughter was attacked. I bet she cycles all that loot from Omega guild and buys a ship capable of defending itself. One that can flee from the threats of Mixonia. The real question you need to ask, is what is Belmont going to do?"

Dean paused to think it over. "Ya know? Belmont is my least concern. A battle of magic happened on the planet they manage. What can they do? Assess a magical fine? Levy tree destruction violations? Fook, I grew thousands more to restore and replace what was destroyed, wouldn't surprise me if there is a check with a million Gs waiting for me."

Lonny punched him in the arm.

"As much as I joke, though, I can only imagine the chaos in those offices. I bet they sent a request for guidance up to the orbital, and the goons up in the Oakley Orbital sent their 'What the fook? What should we do?' to Earth and the Galactic Council is searching for their asses in the dark, trying to come up with a response."

Lonny was silent for a moment, likely contemplating Dean's words. When he finally responded he said, "So do you want to continue to push today or just call it and head home?"

"Well, two tokens is nothing to shake a stick at. Honestly, I should be terrorizing the solo event, working my way up the floors. I do have Geo after all, that little gem is going to be amazing to kill goblins with." He sighed, "With that said, we needed to come in here to test my powers. If I did something dumb -"

"Like blinding us?"

"Like blinding myself, yeah. Two tokens is better than one, though. At least my worries were unfounded. There has to be a catch, though. It will drive me bonkers not knowing," Dean groaned.

"And Quincy? Tucker?"

Dean had been hesitant about what to do about either of them. Tucker had fled. The moment he learned that Havnier died, he knew any protection afforded him by the god was gone. He'd even sent Dean a transcript of their supposed conversations. Which was probably a fake—not that Dean cared. Tucker was merely a pawn, a piece who'd removed itself from the board.

He had apologized and said that Dean would never see him again. He even gave up the portal. Which left Riva and the teams at Snaggletooth ecstatic—they now had both a portal to grind points, as well as an overflow location.

Riva had tried to track Tucker but he'd disappeared into the rapidly expanding domains of humanity. Soon, he was just another ship with altered transponders, forged paperwork, and a new crew with clean identification. It was literally the wild west on the outer rim. Places like New Paris gave two shits if you were legitimate, only caring that you had those sweet, sweet, Gs.

With the fourth portal now in the game, Dean's portal was finally off limits to the other teams. The message Riva had sent them was that whatever was going on with the Forrester Estate and the gods; it was best for him to focus on Oakley. If they needed anything, though, they only needed to call or ask—Dean extended the same offer to Riva. Which, primarily, was his way of saying that Anoka was fine where she was.

Dean was happy to have closure with Tucker and his portal. The fact that he'd fled to the stars wasn't ideal, but his flight made a lot of sense. The guy had been put in a very sticky situation. Almost as sticky as the situation Dean faced with his former best friend, Quincy.

Quincy had spilled his guts when he'd come to. His story was basic and Dean believed him. Shortly after returning to Ola, he was visited by a bunny girl. He never knew who she was—just that she gave great head and her human tits squeaked. She'd offered him money to work for Riva.

Riva had needed more lackeys with half a brain, so Quincy had fit in smoothly. Time went by and his Ola apartment had a new resident. Quincy said that she had wanted to be called Trist. So, he and Trist would have sex, and he'd tell her what was happening at Snaggletooth. He defended his betrayal, saying that there was nothing important in those reports.

Eventually, though, he was sent to visit Thero and given a cool three-hundred-thousand Gs to put his friend to sleep. His excuse this time was that it was better Dean be taken off the board for five years and not get hurt, than have him be killed.

It was all a cluster of epic proportions for Dean to deal with.

"I'm conflicted. I can literally bury him. I can send him away to some distant planet and be rid of him. I can even forgive him, that he was conned, and got in too deep," Dean said, knowing the last option wasn't really an option.

"I've grown up with Quincy, just like you. Legally, though, we can't make him a prisoner," Lonny said.

When Dean started to speak, Lonny cut him off.

"But... Riva can. He can stick him mining some rocks for five years by tying him up in a contract with savage penalties. Put him to work on some shit job away from Oakley. I think that is what you should do."

"Give him five years of hard labor in exchange for his crimes against me? He'd have to willingly agree to it," Dean mused.

Lonny scoffed before responding, "You can literally smite him. I don't know if once you use Havnier's power, you get more, but at the very least, he has to understand you can make him vanish. Even if he tried to flee, you could smite him. It's not like you even know the limits of your god powers." Lonny shook his head. "People can change. Five years is a lot of time for self-reflection." He snorted and said, "And the money from his inheritance will be there for him when he's done."

"Right, that is fair. As is the proposal. Five years of hard labor," Dean threw his hands in the air, "and just like that we've sentenced our friend."

"Just like that," Lonny agreed.

Dean rubbed his temples.

"Dean... I'd rather cash out today and focus on proper leveling in a decent set of gear. We really need to upgrade our gear," Lonny admitted. He looked around. "My eyes are starting to focus again."

"Okay," Dean muttered, "We settle for our two tokens, consider today's quest complete and head to the market. I need to get some scrolls, anyway. Having arcane magic in here sure would be nice. I'd like to test if a shield reduces the effect of the blinding light from my energy beams."

"Not it!" Lonny touched his finger to the side of his nose. "So not it," Lonny groaned blinking at his hand. "Woot, I can see again." He picked up a broken blade from the floor. "Look at this shitty dagger."

Lonny waved the weapon in front of his face and Dean was finally able to make it out. His friend had a point, the weapon did not. It had the dullest blade possible.

"Well," Dean grunted, "tomorrow is a new day. We can buy nice gear sets with today's rewards while Baxster crafts us some backup sets. Maybe the day after tomorrow we can hit the market for some spells. I'm taking a day off." He grinned. "These tokens could buy us a shitty house on the Parsnia Sea. One with a boat that comes with the property, probably. Any objections?" Dean asked.

"As long as I don't have to go out on the water, I'd love a vacation house for Team Ola to use," Lonny said, standing up and stretching. "Okay. Let's go take a well-earned day off. I think I'm going to go to Ola City and visit my folks. I'd invite ya, but... Lexis wanted to go."

"That's a big step!" Dean said, raising his eyebrows and giving his friend a nod.

Lonny, normally, kept his parents strictly off limits. This was the first time Dean could remember hearing that Lonny was going to take a girl home—let alone a demi Minotress in human guise—to meet his parents.

Dean was like that with girls, too. Hell, he hadn't even introduced Cassandra to Uncle G until a year ago.

"It's a start," Lonny admitted, blushing. "How about you? What's your plan for your first day off in a while?"

"Fishing!" Dean said, as he walked to the podium and indented the locket, "I'm going fishing."

TWENTY-SIX

DEAN

Parvian Sea

Dean radiated a 'this is bullshit' vibe with narrowed eyes, folded arms and a grumpy face. Sure, he rarely was sour and maybe this was a bit of an act—was *mostly* an act—about the fact that he hadn't gotten his way, but a party barge?! If a drone came along, he had an image to uphold, dammit!

"Cheer up, Dean. We brought all your best gear," Cassandra smiled, kissing his cheek.

"On a party barge," he grumbled.

Kambry snickered. "You've got three gorgeous ladies in thong bikinis who forgot to put their tops on—let that little fact turn that frown upside down." She jiggled her boobs enticingly at him with a wide smile.

The hint of a grin ever so slightly cracked his curmudgeonly facade. The fact remained that Dean was *not* on a fishing boat for what was supposed to be *his* fishing trip. There were no racks for his poles and not a single place to store dead things built into the deck. There wasn't even a live well.

What there was... were a host of comfy chairs, ample shade, and loud music

The house they'd snagged with a waterfront view had cost more than two tokens— closer to four, actually, but the waterfront property was exactly the kind of vacation house the ladies had wanted. Cassandra happily picked one that would be easy either to flip or to rent. The best part of the deal, to her at least, was that it came with a boat included.

He'd halfheartedly agreed that he still wanted to go—mainly because Cassandra, Jessabee, and Kambry had insisted that he join them. He knew if he caught something decent, they could toss it into the nearest port cleaning station. For the smaller stuff, he'd managed to convince them to bring an extra-large ice chest.

Trying to make the most of the situation, he'd decided they would do some top water trolling near the shoreline. If they went just beyond the designated safety-pens where people were allowed to swim, then he should be fine. 'Fine' is what this was turning out to be.

"I do love the view," he snickered, "And I'm not talking about the afternoon's morning sunrise. You ladies look delightful." He gave each of them a good looking over. "I guess it's time we summoned Sable," Dean said, half expecting her not to show.

There was a whoosh of wind as she magically transported herself onto the boat. She dropped down into a comfy seat across from him. Sable gave a quick glance at the other women before vanishing again.

Dean turned around with a fruity drink in his hand, ready to hand it to... an empty seat. A moment later, Sable returned in a one-piece swimsuit that showed off ample cleavage.

I guess she wants to tease, where the others want to flaunt, he thought to himself.

He underhand tossed the bottled beverage to his favorite Demi. She snatched it out of the air, popping the cap off with a wink.

Dean lumbered over to one of the dozen rail fishing rod holders he'd bolted to the top rail. He'd had to install them, himself, this morning, after a rush drone delivery. Each of the slots was filled with his tackle. Seeing his gear neatly arrayed, he finally allowed a happy smile to crest his face.

He reached for a favorite trolling rig, yanking it out of its holder. The holder wasn't nearly as strong as he would have liked to have. If he hooked something too big, well, unfortunately he was likely to lose one of his favorite rods.

There was no doubt about it. The fake mullet lure was his go to answer. He slid the pole under the canopy and tripped on one of the seven ice boxes full of drinks.

"Can we move these to the front, please?" Dean asked with a long-suffering sigh.

Jessabee dribbled her fingers across the front of his swim shorts, lightly groping him before her hand reached for the ice box's handles.

He smacked her ass with a resounding *slap*.

"Yeowza," Jessabee exclaimed.

591

Dean walked to the back deck with a grin. When he got to the swim platform, totally not meant for fishing, Dean sat down on the long ice chest he'd connected to the back of the boat. When he glanced down to release the trolling motor, he noted how the motors swirled jets of water behind the boat. Those tiny jets would propel them forward slowly, compared to what a real boat could do. He remembered grunting unhappily when Cassandra had sworn up and down that it would still be fast enough for trolling. She was right, of course, as she usually was.

The mullet lure hit the surface, vanishing below the water as he released the line. His fishing experiences in the Parvain Sea had been limited and his skills here largely untested. To the twangy tune of some music the girls had blaring through the boat's speakers, he set the lure back a few hundred feet; at least double what he would normally. With the line set, he did the unusual thing of holding the rod himself.

"Want a beer?" Cassandra asked. Dean shifted his focus from the boat's wake to lock eyes with her as he considered the tempting offer. He shook his head, no.

"Soda?"

"Lemonade please," Dean said.

The over the shoulder exchange was preceded by a screaming of the line peeling off the reel. He set the drink in one of the forty seven cup holders while tightening the drag and turning off the clicker.

"What is it?" Sable asked curiously, her eyes flaring with an excitement that matched her expanding wings.

Dean shot her a quizzical look.

Cassandra laughed, "Dean doesn't know. We never do. His show was always about him guessing at what it was while he fought the fish. How often were you right, Daddy?"

"Uh...Could be any one of a number of things. There are a lot of types of fish on Oakley. And..." he rolled his eyes, "Daddy? Really?"

"Yeah, Dean, you're our babies' Daddy," Cassandra said, putting the boat in neutral before he even had to ask. "If you think I'm calling you Dean around Leena, dream on."

Dean reeled in quickly, the fish was swimming for them, going with the path of least resistance. Now that the boat had stopped, it swung to Dean's left.

"Is it big?" Kambry asked, kneeling on a seat behind Dean to watch the fight.

Dean had a snarky reply that he held in check when he zoned out as the sunlight reflected off her supple breasts. The line became too tight and he was forced to focus on the fish again.

"Dragona got his tongue, cute. Can I catch the next one?" Sable asked.

Dean stood, pumping the fish to regain some line. His brief nod was enough. Cassandra turned down the music as the catch neared. He could hear her unclamping the icebox behind him. The sound of rustling ice meant she was getting the gaff ready.

Normally you'd gaff a fish with two people. If you were an expert, you could one man it. It was tricky, though, and required coordination. It was a process that Dean had done solo many times before.

A few more minutes of give and take with the smallish fish resulted in Dean seeing his first flash of coloration. A turquoise blue reflected under the dark water, barely illuminated by the morning sunlight. The fish, like all fish, caught sight of the boat and fled.

If he hadn't been ready for it, he'd have surely lost the catch. He let the line loosen to allow for the weak run and then tightened the drag after the initial burst away. He realized he probably should be talking his way through this fight to help Sable, but learning was always something best experienced firsthand. The second time the fish saw the boat, its run was brief.

He reeled the rest of the line in quickly, this was the part where bigger predators interrupted a good fight for an easy meal and it always made him a little nervous. The line reached its limit and the blue-fish floundered on the end of the line at the side of the boat. He reached out with his empty right hand, and Cassandra handed him the gaff.

In a continuous swooping motion, he brained the fish, hoisted it out of the water, and dumped it into the ice box. Cassandra snapped a photo of the twitching fish before heading forward to get the boat moving again.

"A Snallywoo, value minimal, and a very common catch out here. Photo estimate has it at fourteen pounds. Apparently, they taste mediocre, are nasty unless properly cooked, and are barely worth more than cat food," Cassandra read while Dean found his long pliers. "Geo will probably think it's delicious, though."

He opened the ice chest to see the catch already resting motionless inside. Jessabee accepted the fishing rod, while he freed his favorite lure from the toothy mouth.

"This controls the line tension, right? And this reels it in?" Jessabee asked, messing with the reel. "It's that easy?"

"Yeah, sorta," Dean snorted. "Just don't let the line fully loose or the line will spool out and do something we commonly call a 'bird's nest'. It's better to release the line slowly, anyway, to keep the lure from snagging stuff on the bottom," Dean said, once again tossing the fake mullet lure into the water.

"When the reel says three hundred, apply the crank tight enough that the line no longer goes out." He pointed to the crank. "And then," he again pointed, "on the left side will be a clicker button. Turn that to on, once the line is set. If you want to handle that rod, I can set another for Sable."

"Sure, that looked like fun," Jessabee said, twirling her hair coyly around a finger so that her gravity-defying flesh jiggled just right. He bounced his eyebrows at her to show his appreciation, before heading towards the bow of the boat.

Dean retreated to a pole holder with another trolling rig. This one had a local bait-fish lure, about twice the size of the mullet. He knew hungry fish would try for this, regardless of the size disparity. It took some effort to wind his way through the ice chests back to the stern, but he held in his grumbling. His earlier grumpiness was gone; he'd just caught a fish and that high was hard to beat.

He spooled this second line out to two hundred and fifty feet from the boat. He knew this rig would swim lower. He set the drag and the clicker before waving Sable over to handle the rod. When she was seated on the back of the boat, he retreated to the bow to let the girls fish.

A comfy seat facing backwards became his lounging spot. The moment he got comfy, Kambry snuggled into his lap. The next ten minutes were bliss.

Dean watched Jessabee and Sable fish, chatting amicably with big smiles. Dean, Kambry, and Cassandra talked of simpler things—like baby outfits and an off-road stroller they were planning on getting. This was boating one-oh-one. Drinks, babes, nice weather, and casual talk.

Of course, as with all things in Dean's life lately, the zen-like lull was short, the interruption intense, and the need dire.

Dean's phone rang from a side storage area; Cassandra's phone jingled for attention, also. Both of the girls at the back of the boat had fish on the line and were excitedly forgetting everything Dean had instructed them to do. Cassandra answered her phone while Dean ignored his. He went to help the fisherwomen.

Jessabee had forgotten the clicker, but the drag was set correctly while Sable had a bird's nest and a penitent look on her face. *There went that fish, probably already off the hook.*

"Hand me the rod." Dean accepted the tackle from Sable. "You went the wrong way on the drag and the fish is bigger, so it stripped line." There was a sudden jerk on the rod, causing Dean to almost drop it. "Would've been better if it had got off. Not a monster fish or I'd have lost the rod. Okay, now I have to hand-spool out some line. Great work, Jessabee, just keep it slow and steady."

"Dean," Cassandra interrupted.

He grunted and replied, "Obviously busy, here."

"It's important. A very urgent and important call. One I think you should take," Cassandra said, trying to get him to see reason.

"Dammit woman, I'm fishing, tell the telemarketer to bugger off," Dean said, clearing the bird's nest. He applied the drag and handed the rod back to Sable. "Tight is up, loose is down," he instructed. "The higher the number, the harder it is for the fish to run. What's your distance at, Jessabee?" he turned to see how she was doing.

A phone was placed in his face. "Cassie, babe... I love you, but..." he began.

"No butts mister. Grab the fooking phone," Cassandra snapped

Dean winced and reached for the device.

She reassured him by saying, "I'll bring in the catches."

That did it for him. When the receiver was to his ear, he said rather tersely, "This is Dean."

"Dean, this is planetary Governor Linrick, you have a... fleet requesting an audience," the governor said in a haughty tone.

Dean scoffed, scanning the waters around him before responding, "With all due respect, Sir, there ain't no fleet around me." He took a swig of his drink while watching Cassandra miss a gaff. "Confidence Cassie," he called out, "hook it with anger—like it bit yer toe off. No half measures."

"Excuse me?" the Governor said in confusion.

Dean rolled his eyes. "Sir, I'm fishing. It's my first day off in almost a month. What do you need from me, exactly, that was so urgent you called both our phones?"

"There is an Elven war fleet stationed around Oakley Orbital -"

"You're fookin shitting me," Dean blurted out.

"Afraid not," the Governor said with a sigh. "They wish to see you, and since you're a citizen, I told them they'd need your permission first -"

"Granted," Dean said with a grunt.

"But they could be hostile!" the governor hissed.

Dean snorted, chuckled, and then cut loose a long, roaring laugh. When he'd dried the tears from his eyes, he said, "Governor Linrick, I voted for ya. You've done good things with Oakley. Just know that there are powers out there far greater than you, and infinitely more dangerous than that Elven fleet." He chuckled. "Like me, for example. Tell them they can come visit me on my wife's boat."

"The boat is in your name, Daddy," Cassandra quipped.

"The audacity!" Dean gasped, ignoring the governor and sticking his tongue out at his wife. "Is that all?"

The phone line went dead as he was hung up on. *Probably for the best.*

"Cassie, darling, I want a real fishing boat," Dean declared, heading aft to help Sable.

Cassandra laughed, hoisting her gaffed fish into the ice box. There was the crackle of ice and the floundering of a dying fish. "This is family comedy at its best. I buy us a cruising boat for the family. And... As of right now," she threw her hands up in the air, "ta da! It's a fishing boat. Hurrah! We both get what we want."

Dean couldn't help but roll his eyes and grin as Jessabee and Cassandra exchanged high fives. He glanced over Sable's shoulder to see that her catch was nearing single digits. Suddenly, the line tightened, the rod bowed nearly in half, and then flipped back up as the line snapped.

Sable stomped her foot, grumbling with frustration. "It was so close!" she pouted.

"Exactly. Next time," Dean instructed, accepting the lure-less trolling rig from her hands, "ease up on the drag when it gets within sight of the boat. And Sable, it's called fishing—not catching—for a reason." He smiled down at her.

"I've got to go, anyhow, not supposed to be around the Elves. Plus, I'm really close in my studies. I think... I think in a week or two, I'll have enough energy to live with you guys for a bit. Bye for now" Sable said, giving his ass a smack goodbye before she went and hugged each of the women tenderly. He was the last lucky one to get a hug and a kiss before she vanished.

"So..." Kambry said with a hands up shrug. "What's next?"

Dean saw shadows cast onto the ocean's surface growing bigger all around him. There was no whine of a rotor or a roar of an engine to give them warning, just silently growing shadows that soon blotted out the sun. Dean stuck his head out to see thousands of white gold boxy ships homing in on his location.

The first ship to land smoothly kissed the water's surface without even causing a ripple. Faces peered out of clear viewports. The design was beyond basic, with its rigid shapes, expansive viewpoints, and a veritable forest on the inside. If anything, that must be the reason for the blocky design. The interior of the ship had a walking path around the outer edge, and then forest.

The fleet landed all around him, creating an island of spaceships that linked together seamlessly. The exteriors of the ships spawned decking that covered the calm ocean waters. The short walkways between ships were narrow, but Dean was fairly certain he was seeing technology at work that was far beyond what humans could currently engineer.

A trio of two Elven males and one female walked towards his pleasure cruiser. The three were in matching white robes, with golden trim. They walked confidently, without the slightest hint of emotion. Dean's read of them was only that... they were ancient.

He undid the canvas top of the party barge, since there was a ship directly overhead, blotting out Oakley's rising sun. A quick slurp on his drink and he felt ready. He stepped to the edge of the boat to greet their visitors.

"I'm coming," a trailing Elf said, hauling out a collection of books oddly corralled in his arms.

The three noble looking Elves ignored the latecomer. The struggling Elf though, was eager, energetic, and very pleased by the situation. Not only were his eyes darting between Dean's babes' exposed breasts, but his smile stretched from ear to ear.

Cassandra, Kambry, and Jessabee decided to cover themselves, after the ogling.

"This is our newest historian. He is enthralled with humanity. So much so, that he predicted the champion of the eighth age would be a human. We laughed at him and called him a fool, until he proved that we were the fools for laughing at him."

Dean winked at the historian.

"Forgive my manners," the first Elf said, "I am Orawon, this is Keenish, and this is Borana. The young man is Dartanian. We represent a faction of the Elven Empires known as the Believers. Our guiding star and principle devotion was due to one Orabel Sinclair, a former princess turned outcast," he bowed his head, "and now a hero. The Goddess Mother, herself, sang of Orabel's courage to the greatest of Elven councils, which cements her in history as being correct."

"Orabel was family, even if the time she was with us was short. What can be so urgent, that you flew all this way to visit me?" Dean asked.

The historian stumbled, dropping a book. The binding landed at an odd angle, causing it to bounce off the walkway. Before Dartanian could save it, the text splashed into the water. The young Elf dropped to his stomach to try and fish the sinking book out of the water to no avail.

"Better let it go," Dean warned. "I can feel the monsters below are getting upset. There is anger building at the loss of the morning light."

"Is that so?" Borana asked with a raised brow.

"It is," Dean replied.

"May we sit?" Orawon asked and Dean gestured for them to join him on his... party boat. "I was told gods were fickle, flighty things who only give half-answers. May we know more of what is going on?"

"I'm still human, as far as I can tell," Dean shrugged, and Cassandra joined him on his lap. "I have been working on gaining control over and quieting the new powers Havnier fed me. In this case, I feel a brooding sensation down below and thoughts of an easy snack on the surface." Dean frowned. "That's the best way that I can describe the sensations I'm getting." He smirked, "Sometimes half of an answer is the full truth. Would you like a drink?"

"A human beverage? Yes please," Dartanian said eagerly. Kambry snickered, fetching the Elf a virgin daiquiri. "Unbelievable. I sincerely thank you."

"It's just a drink," Orawon said, frowning in a mild sign of frustration. "Now, as to your earlier question, we're here because of those."

The lead Elf pointed to the texts. Dean was handed the largest of the books Dartanian had carried. He flipped through the pages. Two things were written on every page.

Achieve level four hundred. Obtain eight wives.

Only then will the battle for the eighth age unfold.

"This book is somewhat lacking in content," Dean snickered

"I told you he would be hilarious," Dartanian boasted proudly.

Dean quirked a brow and put a finger to his lips. The elder Elves allowed brief smiles.

"Please explain," Dean requested, extending a hand to check out another book. He thumbed through that text to see the same two lines. "Fook me," he grumbled.

"These were littered with the on and off ramblings of a mad god. They were twisted... sorry my English needs work. They had been transcribed into something that the reader could relate to. Which in turn, meant that one day, the Champion— you—would have a guide to follow. We spent eons deciphering and documenting the path of the creator's defiler. All of it appears to have been washed away."

The elves shook their heads, sadly.

"Even with the texts reverting to two simple statements, we need to tell you this also," Borana said, "While we may herald you as the symbol of righteous change, there are a majority in the Universe who will see you as a god killing tyrant."

"Choose my path wisely..." Dean muttered.

"Was that said?" Borana asked, desperate hope in his voice.

Keenish, the silent female frowned when Dean hesitated to respond.

"It's obvious the creator, or the creator's lackey," she huffed, "is influencing things. History erased, memories forgotten, and then two lines of text. It is truly irrelevant. What is important, is that you stay alive." She glared at the other elves. "We wish to train you, offer our protection, and will let you pick from a thousand eligible females to add to your harem."

Kambry burst into laughter and blurted out, "Just one!"

"Sheesh, sister wife, let the Elves say their spiel. Is that it?" Cassandra asked in a stern tone. "You want to offer defenses, protection, and hope my family adds an Elf as one of the eight?"

All four of the Elves nodded and replied, "Yes."

Dean sighed and pinched the bridge of his nose, "So much for taking a day off. I'm going to head home." He shook his head, sadly. "We caught two fish."

Kambry rubbed his back.

"While we shuttle back to and then relax in our home, we will think over your kind offer. We will have an answer for you, tomorrow." Dean met each of the Elves' gazes. "Is there anything more you have to say—other than you would like to help or change me, and that others will seek to kill me?"

"Your list of enemies was in this book!" Dartanian said, holding up a thin hardbound, proud of himself for remembering.

Jessabee snickered. "Hurrah! The shortest book is your kill list. At least it's not the epic-length one."

"That was his potential Elven wife list," Dartanian admitted.

Jessabee groaned.

"We get it. Please give us a full day to process all this new information and to prepare." She smiled at the elves. "May we assume you will protect the champion, until he gets home?" Cassandra asked.

"We can, but there is one more thing you should know. While the memory is unfortunately gone, we do know there is more of a threat to the Champion than that of Min. We just can't remember what it is," Orawon shrugged, politely excusing himself.

The four of them left, with Dartanian stealing glances back over his shoulder.

When they were gone, Kambry asked, "What now?"

"We can head home and watch a movie on the couch?" Dean offered.

"Sex," Jessabee said, with certainty.

"Sex!" the other women echoed.

TWENTY-SEVEN

DEAN

Forrester Estate

"Why aren't you in the mood?" Kambry asked, nuzzling his neck.

They sat on their living room couch and Dean watched an animated remake of a spaceship lost on some moon called Titan. He'd come home aggravated, his nail-biting getting nipped by Kambry's and Cassandra's constant momming. Those two hated his nail-biting habit and had teamed up on him to get him to stop.

"Level four hundred," Dean admitted in frustration. "How am I ever supposed to do that?"

Jessabee came out of the bedroom in some scandalous lingerie, her full hourglass figure attractively displayed for his viewing pleasure. Her pert nipples, wide hips, and flat stomach caused him to stir down below. Cassandra arrived behind her in a matching set of purple string coverings, kissing Jessabee's shoulder while eyeing him hungrily.

Dean gulped. His ladies gestured for him to come to them.

"Last chance Dean," Kambry purred, nibbling on his earlobe, "Talk now or later?"

Her offer was nothing compared to the two ladies' enticements, dressed as they were in their sexy outfits and high heels. Dean shot off the couch with a leer, all but sprinting for the dynamic duo. He scooped them up, one over each shoulder, hearing their delightful giggling.

His trot into the bedroom had both ladies playfully smacking at his butt. He slung them on the bed, careful that they didn't crash into each other. Big round melons and tight tits both bounced from the shifting around on the mattress. He licked his lips at the tasty sight.

Kambry sidled up behind him, lifting his shirt over his head. Her kisses on his shoulder were soothing. The girls on the bed crawled back to him on all fours, to undo his comfy sweats. They had the eyes of troublemakers as they glanced up at him with matching, wicked smirks.

His growing bulge was traced by teasing fingers eager to play. Dean's smirking grin was cut short when the drawstring of his sweats was retied extra tight in a double-knot. He scrunched his face up in confusion. Kambry gently spun him around. Cassandra pulled him down to sit onto the bed. Jessabee took her place as she scooted off the bed and ran to the closet.

Ah, going to get a toy.

Cassandra exited the closet with her hands tucked behind her back. Kambry kissed one ear; Jessabee nibbled on the other.

Cassandra shifted one hand behind her back with her thumb up.

"Dean," Kambry whispered into his ear. "I had to convert to a Dragona to get a positive test. You're going to be a Daddy."

When Dean tried to spin around to kiss her in his excitement, Jessabee demonstrated a strength he didn't realize she had. "Dean," Jessabee whispered into his ear, "this morning I found out that my test was positive, too. You're going to be a Daddy twice over."

His eyes flared wide with shock. Cassandra brought her hand around from behind her back. She extended a ring box to Jessabee who danced in place. Dean saw how thrilled she was to be accepted into their family.

Dean, himself, ran the full range of positive emotions. The future was very bright.

He laid a sweet, tender kiss to Kambry's lips. She pushed her tongue into his mouth, and their kiss deepened, growing passionate. When they finally pulled back, gasping for breath, a crying Jessabee stood before them, wiping at her tears.

Cassandra stripped her thin excuse of a negligee off before helping Kambry shimmy out of her boy-shorts and tank top. The two of them slipped into bed together, letting their sister-wife have a special moment alone with Dean.

Jessabee stepped into his arms and kissed him tenderly. The tender moment quickly became passionate. Her hands ran through his hair and then pushed at his sweats. Dean growled as she fumbled at the damn double-knot, before finally tearing the waistband of his sweatpants and sending them flying.

Dean ripped the covers off, causing Cassandra to frown. The air conditioning was set to high and Jessabee, in her lingerie, was the only one wearing any clothes—if a few wisps of lace and a g-string counted as clothes. He knew there was an easy way to turn Cassie's frown upside down. He dove onto his lovely lady, smothering her in kisses.

The four of them soon heated the room up to the point where, despite the air conditioning, they were all a sweaty, panting mess. Dean had Jessabee sensually riding him while Kambry and Cassandra grabbed a toy and headed into the shower. Jessabee was slow grinding on his cock, Dean was embedded deep in her dripping vagina. She bit her lower lip while squeezing her breasts.

Dean controlled the roll of her hips to time with his thrusts. He used his control to thrust up when her hips rolled forward to impale herself on him. Her long hair descended in a silky curtain around his face as she leaned down to kiss him lovingly.

He let go of her hips, letting his hands flow smoothly up over her back. She found the spot she loved and began riding him passionately. This would be her third orgasm of the session, her lust hardly sated. Dean encouraged her to quicken the pace.

She clenched harder around his girth and increased her tempo. The sex was amazing, and when she cried out in orgasm, he joined her in bliss. His seed blasted into her tight vagina with euphoric pumps.

The moaning from the shower made them giggle as they recovered. "Again?" Jessabee asked and Dean nodded before pulling her lips down to his.

∞∞∞∞

Anoka's arrival during a lavish breakfast confused Dean.

"Anoka, what brings you to my humble abode?" Dean asked, waving her to a seat at the table next to Kambry.

She smiled and said, "I wish it were grandmother duties, but I was summoned by Kambry to run some errands. Errands that your staff was clearly unable to handle."

When Anoka said this, Dean frowned and raised an eyebrow at her.

"Yes, I know. I need to say a few things, first, though. May I sit?"

"Most certainly, Jooma, a plate for our guest," Dean smiled at their cook, "please and thank you."

Jooma responded with a quick nod before heading to the kitchen.

"Let me start by saying that Thero was a man of a different age, literally. He'd been around for a very, very long time. Vampires are... how do I say this?" She grimaced. "Difficult to conceive. Always have been. Dragona are a rare species that a Vampire's seed can bind to and even then, the chances of conception are infinitesimal. Thero has chased after me ever since he saw me holding Kambry as a baby.

"She was a great excuse to defer his interest." Anoka smiled at Kambry. "Thero is... was... a very patient being. You might be wondering why I'm telling you this, but trust me, there is a reason. For every cause, there is an effect. My having Kambry gave Thero the idea I wanted children." Anoka blushed, seeing a white-faced Kambry. "I actually don't. I'd like to think I was a great Mom to Kambry, and raised her as my own, but I could never tell Thero the truth and hurt my little girl."

Kambry clenched her fists and bolted up from her seat. She took a quick step to be nearer to Anoka, her mouth opening and closing without a word coming out. She paused before giving her Mom a long, meaningful hug. Feeling better, she returned to her seat and her breakfast, the second helping of which was piled in front of her.

"Okay, Thero was big on children. Kinda am myself," Dean admitted, winking at each of his lovely ladies. Kambry was stuffing her face, Cassandra batted her eyes at him, and Jessabee appeared as if she was getting a bout of morning sickness.

"Kooma," Dean called out, "can you please escort Jessabee to the master suite?"

The two left the packed table with the rest of his team. Lonny's team was currently in Mixonia, while the new recruits were at Snaggletooth, training. Anoka's plate arrived, causing her to forget where she was in her story, while she snacked on bacon.

"I love this stuff. Ah, right. Thero's only son, Braxton, is his defining achievement. Braxton's mother is an Elf. His battle prowess is legendary, the hybrid-son is even stronger than his father. The problem is he is quite temperamental, not a natural-born leader, else Thero would have stepped aside long ago. Or so he told me in one of his barely coherent ramblings when he tried to woo me. By ridding us of Thero's presence, though, you have earned yourself a new enemy—one far more interested in the PvP games than his father ever was."

Dean grimaced. Would he ever catch a break?

"Now that he is running Omega Guild, Braxton will have access to infinite funds to follow humans into events or portals. Just..." she frowned, "expect more friction. He won't be audacious or crafty enough to jump through wormholes with a fleet or something—not that his father's home planet would ever let him—no, he is regulated to Mixonia, where he will quickly become more than a simple nuisance."

"How?" Dean ground out.

"I'm not sure," Anoka said with a sigh. "But do not underestimate him. Which leads us to Grom. Grom was one of Havnier's two demis. Grom was freed the other morning by Havnier before being dragged here to face you. The little bastard had someone whispering into his ear, he must have."

Dean shook his head. When it rained around here, it fooking poured!

"Grom being freed sounds basic," Anoka continued. "The Demi will go to the Dwarven home world—where Havnier was revered. While a new god is being generated for their race—the female demi, Lakina, has already shown the great Dwarven council her swollen belly—her brother has sworn a blood oath to kill you. Grom is bringing a mighty fleet across the stars to come and squash you. Or so the rumors say."

Cassandra blew a raspberry, which just about summed up how Dean felt, as well.

"And that is partly why I am here. To tell you that these Elves around you, may not be the only Elves you need. You might need their full army with their superior fleets."

"What about Earth's fleets?" Dean asked.

"You will likely see Earth's fleets arriving soon to posture against these Elves. Just know that they will be next to useless—as useless as any ship you might buy to try to defend yourself with. Human technology will be woefully inadequate, when compared to the power of either the Elven or Dwarven races."

Dean gulped down a full glass of orange juice and barely held back the burp that desperately wanted to wetly escape.

"Wrong pipe," he coughed, thumping himself on the chest. A few coughs later, he asked, "When can we expect our Dwarven friends bent on avenging their god to arrive?"

"No idea. The Elves might know, though. Did you notice that your blacksmith quit?"

Dean shrugged. Cassandra held a finger up and said. "We never signed Baxster on, but yes, he rejected our offer and informed me that no Dwarf will work for, or with us... ever. On the bright side I hired a Minotress." She grinned. "Yup, a middle-dweller is coming here to live. She will be living in the other basement suite. We're building her a tunnel that will lead from the suite to a well-ventilated, if windowless, smithy underground."

"Wait, that's allowed? And even if I can't help the fact that the Dwarves are coming, I can do something to stop them... maybe," Dean grumbled at the quickly growing list of problems piling up before he even had a chance to start his day.

"What about this getting to floor four hundred?" Patti asked. She yipped when Kambry pinched her leg. "Whaaaa?!" she whined, "You didn't say it was a secret, or something."

"Well, I figure our best bet is to try to climb both group and solo events. After some more training," Dean winced, "lots of training. Honestly, since we own all four portals, finally. I wouldn't mind letting Riva right the score in our favor while Team Ola focuses on getting gear we cry about when we die. The kind -"

"Ha! That is why I'm here," Anoka said around a mouth full of eggs. She swallowed before saying, "Look, I get it. You were in training gear. It's what you could afford. When the surviving Omega Guild folks surrendered, you gained a fortune in tokens." She turned to Cassandra. "What was the estimate?"

Cassandra sighed, pulling out her phone. "Nearly five thousand talents, but... I may already have done some shopping. This place looks like piss, it needs an update and our bedroom is woefully stationary. I may have gone overboard, though, and -"

Wilfred and Zayra scooted their chairs back and started doing happy dances. "You got the community ship! The one with the farming and -"

"Hold your excitement," Cassandra said, checking their enthusiasm with a raised finger. "There was a sale on the next model down, since a buyer fell through and their deposit conveyed, which was great for Team Ola, hurrah! So, I snatched it up with a loan. It's going to bury us in work to swap out all those figurines and gear into tokens, and then from tokens into Galactic credits." She raked a hand through her hair and shrugged. "I'm literally stomping my own toes in frustration over my impulse buy."

Wilfred and Zayra walked over and laid a concerned hand on each of her shoulders.

"We all almost die, Dean has a life altering moment, and as a Momma, I wanted something right then that would make me feel secure." Cassie wiped at her face. "Well, these Elves above us probably have cheaper ships that are way more advanced and -"

"Cassie, darling, calm down. Worst case," he shrugged, "we sell it at a loss."

"Never go back into accounting, Dean," Patti snickered.

"A loss from a gain is not a true loss," Dean quipped and Patti rolled her eyes. "Where's Lexi?"

Cassandra frowned, her face instantly changing as Olivia entered the room with Leena. She kissed her little girl after taking her into a loving tuck, and said, "I love you, Daddy. But Patti is correct. I feel awful about it, but I need more information, hence my effort to curb your enthusiasm... for now."

Dean wanted to intercede and mention no one said anything about Lexi when Anoka spoke.

"I've got great news," Anoka said, wiping up the last of the bacon crumbs and bits of egg on her plate with a piece of toast and popping it into her mouth. "Come," she said between chews, "the five of you, come with me. While the Minotaur smith gets set up, I brought you gear upgrades that will help you climb to floor four hundred."

Dean scooted his chair back, eager to see the new gear, and to gain fresh knowledge on how to climb the levels of the Minotaur Maze. "What gear is it? And how the fook do I get to level four hundred in the maze?"

"Well, Mr. Forrester," Anoka smirked, "Slayer of gods, collector of wives, and champion who is ushering in a new age... you will just have to follow me into the unknown to find out."

Dean wasn't sure what escapades the next day might hold—with an impending Dwarven invasion, the inevitable showdown with Min, three-hundred-and-ninety more levels to master, and four more wives to claim as his own in his bed—but he did know one thing. His future was going to be amazing, rife with adventure, and stories worthy of legend.

EPILOGUE

TUCKER

Outer Rim Section of Space

"That bitch thinks she can just push us around. I know she was there with him. Ridiculous," Zued said pacing around the ship's bridge.

Tucker relaxed into his chair, not certain why the god was rambling to him. He'd asked Zued to leave and had been ignored. At the same time, he knew about what had happened on Oakley, and was happy as hell to be well away from there.

Bamba noticed him tense, giving him a neck massage while he listened to this god prattle on about his wounded pride.

"My transaction with Havnier is complete," Tucker said, tapping at the control panel projecting from his captain's chair.

Outside the ship, drones went to work on a chunk of rock. Drilling drones used lasers to blast sections off of the rock. A swarm of grinding drones sought to strip bland carbon away from the remaining, valuable, material. When they were done, hauling drones brought in the best parts for meager profits.

"Are you mining?" Zued asked in dismay.

Tucker shrugged and said, "I'm rich, and this is my cover. What do you want?"

"I've got a problem," the Suca god admitted.

"And?" Bamba asked, her flippant response risking the god's anger.

Zued looked ready to strike her down before Tucker said, "This is my home, and Bamba is a valued advisor to my soon to be growing empire."

"Ah! The crux of the matter. Sorry, unlike Havnier I like cheese as I slowly sip my wine. Hmm... This one you might understand. A long fulfilling conversation before my orgy. You see, young Tucker, that was Havnier greatest fault—he was crass, and to the point," Zued said, ceasing his pacing.

A zap of power ran through the god's body with a crackle. Static radiated throughout the bridge, causing Tucker's arm hairs to rise. Pamrii pushed off a side wall to place herself between the god and her sister.

A crescendo of light blasted into the small space that caused the rest of the crew to flinch, and a few of Tucker's lackeys screamed. Tucker had his eyes shut tight and wanted to wash his hands free of the frustrations of gods.

He waited for the sound of the others to stop walking into stuff before opening his eyes. His crew was frozen and rigid. Only Bamba and Pamrii were in a defensive posture, snarls on their faces.

"Dick," Tucker muttered and a new voice chuckled from behind him.

A golden aura shone around a dwarven goddess as she walked into view. This one was female with squinty eyes of pure pleasure. She didn't saunter up in a seductive manner, when walking to him... she swaggered, triumphantly. The snap of her hips was matched by a coo of joy.

A large sack dragged behind her. This, she dropped at Tucker's feet. He gazed down, noticing that the sack wiggled and squirmed.

Gods and their gods' damned problems! I have no need for this. I need to figure out how Dean can kill these assholes.

"Out, both of you," Tucker said with a flick of his wrist.

The Dwarven god pretended to pout, as if his gesture touched her heart in a hurtful way.

"Tisk tisk," She said with a smirk. "I know what motivates you, Tucker. You have the heart of a Dwarf. Your little red blood-pumper is actually big and purple and beats to the tune of filthy lucre."

"Huh?" Tucker grunted.

He pushed Bamba and Pamrii back. The Oruk girls were edging forward, as if they could really protect him.

Zued opened her sack, revealing a cute cow woman with huge tits—unnaturally huge. Tucker realized that she must be milking. Her snout was gagged, and her horns seemed small. She wasn't a full Minotaur, no she was...

"This is Lexis!" he said, aghast at the goddess' audacity. "How?"

"As if I'd tell a little -"

"What Tarreen was trying to say, is that we'll give you this one tidbit of information for free. Gods tend to value their knowledge, but I'll make a small exception for you. Tarreen abducted Lexis from Oakley, using her reserves to jump to my anchor point in space before Min could intervene," Zued said as if teleporting a body were basic. "Min cannot reach out here. The only reason we needed you, is because even a god's range is limited," he nudged the half-Minotress with a toe and snorted, "and she isn't small."

This was a bit over Tucker's head. His furled brows and scrunched up face hopefully told the gods he was perplexed.

"It's irrelevant how she got here," Tarreen said. "I just pissed in Min's mouth. Better?"

"Not in the slightest," Tucker frowned.

The goddess shrugged and Zued stepped closer to say, "There is a human planet that recently started colonizing—Las Karisak. Heard of it?"

Tucker pulled up the name on the navchart from his chair. The planet displayed on the view screen behind the gods. He read that it was recently colonized, had a population of only seventeen thousand, having only been settled for a year. The environment was swampy, as in unnaturally moist, all year round.

"The one-year mark, means portals are opening!" Zued said in a happy tone.

Tucker grunted, again uncaring about their problems or issues with Min. He wanted a clean break from all this nonsense.

"I think you're mistaking me for someone who cares," he sneered.

"Don't you want more warriors, more servants, and more squeaky tits?" Tarreen asked and Tucker shrugged.

Sure. Who didn't want more squeaky tits? The real question was, though, why risk his life for trivial gains?

"If I have Lexis, then I'm burning a bridge with Min. No way will I get to step into Mixonia," Tucker said. "There was a limit on how far you could jump with her correct... So why me?"

"Finally, a half-decent question," Zued snorted. "You don't have to hold on to her. You can take her to..." Zued tapped a few keys on a spare console. The maps swung around to highlight a section of unexplored space. "To here."

"There is nothing there, and even in this fancy ship, that will take months," Tucker said in disgust. "Each way."

Lexis fought against her bindings. A lowing groan escaped her lips.

Zued prodded at Lexis with his foot. "She needs to go there and Min has zero influence out here. You take her where I've indicated, and I will give you the four portal locations on the Las Swampyass planet. Min will never know that you were a part of this—unless you slip up and tell her. Here are your options: you can be rich and have access to all you desire, with Min none the wiser; or, you can go blab about it or do something else stupid and she'll have you on her shelf in no time at all." The god smiled cruelly. "But I'm betting you're smarter than that."

"Okay, I'm not seeing the advantage here of me taking her anywhere," Tucker smirked.

"You're an idiot," Tarreen said, her hands clenched at her sides and her eyes lighting up with the desire for violence. "See? I can talk like a human, Zued. If you don't cooperate, I'll just kill you and these two Oruk. Then I'll awaken this crew of yours one at a time, until someone agrees to do what we need doing." Her hands flexed eagerly. "Worse case, I'll just kill you all and start hopping around the area, offering to give someone a free ship for a simple drop off mission."

Tucker held up a hand to stop her. Bamba and Pamrii had preferred their human bodies, but getting beyond Min's reach, they had reverted back to their natural forms. He could see them tensing for a fight.

"Please excuse my advisors. It seems your godly status was downgraded to mortal recently, but... let's say I believe you. Okay. So we save the long back and forth. I want more than what you have offered." Tucker leaned forward in his seat. "I not only want the four portals, but also some rare trinkets from the Dwarves I meet," Tucker said, gauging Tarreen's response.

She shrugged and then nodded.

"Perfect. And that is in addition to these... Las Karisak portal locations."

Tarreen stuffed the wriggling Lexis back into the bag and headed for the crews' quarters on the ship.

Zued smiled. "I don't break my promises. The rest of your crew will have to go elsewhere while you journey, obviously the Oruk are fine to stay. When you complete your task and arrive over your new home, I will give you the locations of the portals."

"Gee, thanks. I'd like to request to never have to see you again after that," Tucker said with a scoff.

Zued vanished and the crew resumed... being alive. The few who had seen Zued didn't seem phased that he was gone.

Tucker chose to ignore it. "Listen up," he called out, "I need you to take us to the Sneed Orbital."

His crew started to enter the new location into the navcenter.

"I have a private passenger I have agreed to transport there," Tucker informed his crew. "And you, ya ugly fucks, have earned yourselves a paid vacation!"

The idiots cheered.

Tucker had hoped that after Havnier, he was done with the gods. Now, he fervently wished this was the last time he would get stuck doing their dirty work. He could only imagine the wrath Dean would bring down on his head if he ever learned of any of this.

That frightened him more than what the gods themselves might do to him.

MINOTAUR'S MAZE OF MONSTER GIRLS 3

MAIDENS OF MIXONIA BOOK 3

CHAPTER

ONE

DEAN

Mixonia - Solo Event - Floor 12

Dean grunted with frustration, holding back his desire to send a stone flying down the narrow tunnel path.

The floor twelve challenge was a true maze. The layout was relatively small, though, which meant that getting lost wasn't the real issue. The real issue was that there were gangs of kobolds at every turn he took. The cackling humanoids were thick down here, slowing him down tremendously.

An echoing noise caught his attention. Grasping his trident firmly in his hand, he tensed. He cinched down on the leather grip and held still, listening for any sort of noise. When only silence greeted him, his pet, Moon, chirped and inclined his snout for him to head further down the cave.

Moon was one of the small wyverns on Team Ola. He was green with black tiger stripes. He had a big black moon over his left eye and another one on his right shoulder. If you looked at him from most angles, it looked like someone had given him a black eye.

Jessabee had taken to Moon, and named him. While he wasn't the most powerful, fastest, or most handsome, the little guy was quite sociable.

Dean and Moon had formed a bond while searching the forest around his home, hunting for Lexis. No matter where they looked, she wasn't anywhere to be found. Days of fruitless searching had turned into weeks.

615

There simply was no sign of her—all searches came up empty. As sad as it sounded, Dean had hoped she would send a call, or that he would get a ransom demand. After weeks of nothing, he had even begun to hope he might stumble upon her body in the woods. At least that would give him some closure.

The only thing keeping Dean sane during these trying times was the fact that Leena hadn't gone missing, too. That might sound callous and uncaring at first, but Lexi had been watching Leena when she was most likely abducted—that was the conclusion Sable had come to. After thinking on it some more, she had then said that this was likely the work of gods doing nefarious things.

So... there was little to nothing for him to do that might help get their friend back. He could pout, mope, and kick the proverbial dog, but that wouldn't help. The gods avoided his summons like the plague. Whatever the creator had mutated Dean into, outside of Mixonia at least, had the divine running scared.

In here, though, he was just another competitor—another random surface dweller trying to strike it rich or competing to save his planet.

Moon chirped again, indicating that Dean should head further into the dome shaped cavern.

This was the fifth cavern they had been in. Nothing was respawning, thankfully, and though slow, he was making progress, literally killing his way forward. This was likely the last room, or so he hoped.

Every nook and cranny was thoroughly checked on this floor. He simply kept choosing poorly and heading the wrong way. The bonus was that Moon, at least, stayed positive.

"You think this is the right way?" Dean asked, pointing to yet another clump of kobold huts. "Look, you said that the last four times. I think you just like using your magic."

A happy chirp resonated with a hum. Moon sure was a character. "How about we skirt the edges this time?"

The little stinker popped his head up anyway, preparing to give a loud cry. Dean's eyes flared in a mild panic as he rushed to clamp Moon's mouth shut. When he'd silenced the call, he gave his friend a stern glare. "Easy, big guy."

Yeah, that didn't placate the little wyvern who wiggled furiously out of Dean's grasp. He flew a dozen feet overhead and hovered. Dean saw he was focused on something, so he tried to see what had caught the attention of the little wyvern.

When he saw his pet was about to squawk, he hustled over, a finger to his lips.

About fooking time.

Finally, sitting there in the middle of the fifth room was a locket on its pedestal, surrounded by half-a-dozen kobolds.

Easy, now, we just need to think of a proper strategy-

Moon darted forward, flinging fire into the face of a single kobold. The little wyvern was legendary for his stealthy, single pulls.

Dean watched the kobold go berserk, chasing after Moon—not as if he would ever catch the little stinker.

Yeah, not happening, not in this lifetime.

A quick sheet of ice in the kobold's path caused him to slide off his feet, crashing down awkwardly on his head as he slipped. There was the loud *snap* of a neck breaking. The sound was so loud, it echoed through the cavern.

Dean flung his hands up in the air and rolled his eyes, signaling that it wasn't his fault.

Moon let out a chirp, best described as wyvern laughter. The nearest kobolds came rushing out of the tents.

Moon knew the drill. The pair had done a few of the starter levels on repeat to get accustomed to working with each other.

The wyvern was great at distracting, pulling, and kiting his foes. Dean knew at some point, he wouldn't be the right pet, but for this maze—against level twelve kobolds—he was perfect.

A conga line formed behind the intentionally slow flying wyvern, who kited all five kobolds away from their prize. Dean waltzed up to the pedestal, grabbed the locket and pressed it to the slot.

∞∞∞∞

Dean let the disorientation of teleporting out of the maze wash over him. He checked his bag habitually. His buddy was back inside his bag as a figurine. Moon's figurine even had his tongue sticking out while looking back over his shoulder, taunting the kobolds. Dean chuckled at the frozen pose. Perfect, exactly like he had expected.

He walked over to the waiting area to find Kambry, who was reading a book.

"Whatcha reading?" Dean asked.

"What to expect when expecting. Cassie gave -"

"Ugh..." he groaned, rolling his eyes. "Leena adores you. I'm sure you'll be a great mother. Also, your hair looks great, have you seen how thick it is?"

Dean knew better than to quibble with Kambry. She could be stubborn. If he laid on a bit of charm, though, she'd be more likely to forgive his blunt nature.

Kambry blushed, pulling at a lock of her hair, instinctively. "Thank you, you sure do know how to make a girl feel loved. Now, how did it go?"

"Moon is a riot," Dean said, and grinned. "I thought being in there solo with Apache was fun, but that little guy has so much personality."

Kambry smiled and nodded at the pedestal. "You've really kicked it up a notch and put yourself on a whole new level—we hardly see you anymore. How are your stats looking?"

"I think it's adorable you try the slang stuff," Dean said, heading over to the pedestal to check his stats.

Champion Information
Name: Dean Forrester Gender: Male
Level: 12 Tokens: 39
Race: Human Alignment: Suca – Mixonia
Luck: 16 Charisma: 41

Health: 370 / 370 H-Regen: 1.0 / Sec
Stamina: 335 / 335 M-Regen: 1.0 / Sec
Mana: 388 / 388 S-Regen: 1.0 / Sec

Strength: 234 Vitality: 146
Dexterity: 127 Endurance: 208
Intelligence: 125 Willpower: 263
Magic: Electrical Water

He mulled over the information on his page. He was improving, which was great to see. He hoped his hard work would continue to make a difference in the planetary score, as he grew more powerful.

"And yeah..." Dean paused. "With things at home finally stabilizing, the score should finally be going our way."

"What's it at?" Kambry asked.

Dean pulled up the score. *Planet Oakley - Team Suca 79.*

"Not bad, only at seventy nine. No wonder Riva is asking for so many tokens," Dean sneered.

Kambry rolled her eyes.

"What?!" Dean frowned. "We're a small team and it's not like we're oozing tokens to hand out. Even if it is for the cause."

"Right, especially when you spend seven hours in a level twelve solo floor," Kambry said in a playful, sassy tone.

His tickle fingers came out, and he danced them all over her ribcage. She giggled and darted around the pedestal. Dean, of course, chased her for a single lap until suddenly, his tickle fingers landed in the tight abs of a furry stomach.

Gross. Who did I piss off this time?

Dean's eyes shot up to see an angry Minotaur staring down at him. This one was a brute and didn't appear to be ticklish.

"Oh, hello there," Dean said, flashing a fake smile.

The big Minotaur snorted, a wad of snot flying down into Dean's hair. He was about to protest when the guard said, "You need to follow me. Big boss's orders." Kambry started to come too, and the big guard stuck his hand out, halting her. "He will meet you at the portal entrance once he is done."

"Like hell he will," Kambry said, folding her arms. Her wings flared in irritation.

The guard turned an ear, listening to the faint whisper of words that Dean couldn't quite make out. Kambry was waved to join them, concluding the tense standoff.

The streets of Mixonia were busy, but not packed. The recent expansion had done wonders in relieving congestion in the bustling city. As far as Dean was concerned, it was almost like a whole new place. He actually enjoyed walking through the streets for once, to the point that he wanted to explore and learn more about Mixonia.

Dean noticed that the vendors all went silent when the abnormally tall guard strode by. Even the residents seemed to give them a wide berth. Dean hadn't picked up on the fact earlier that this Minotaur had golden armor instead of silver. He wasn't a half breed Demi, and yet, he was unquestionably different from the normal Minotaur guards.

It made him curious, about whether or not there was something special going on. The answer became an obvious yes, when, instead of heading directly to the front entrance of Min's Vault, they took a detour around the side. Dean was surprised to see that there was a second, smaller building behind the vault. Two hulking brutes guarded a private entry—both of them wore silver armor.

The big, greataxe wielding troops sneered at Dean and Kambry as if they were committing sacrilege by even learning about the existence of this gateway. Their golden-armored guide didn't give any hints as to why they had been summoned, though, walking right up to the single door in the dome shaped building.

The door was silver, but had a golden handle. Dean wondered if this held any relevance. When the door was pried open, their guide didn't enter. He merely ushered them in with the same frown from earlier.

Dean walked through the entrance into a large entertaining room, with comfy seats and a couch. Min sat in one lounger, the Elven goddess who had cried at Orabel's funeral sat across from them. A couch faced both gods, and Min gestured for them to sit on it.

"I hunted everywhere for Lexis!" Dean blurted out, his hands held up defensively. He paused, remaining standing, wanting to emphasize not only that he cared about Min's demi daughter, but also that he had done his best to find her. "Nothing gets past our guards or motion sensors, unless it has powers that we can't defend against."

He'd had plenty of time to think through his defense while he wandered the woods like an idiot looking for Lexis. Min stood, patting a hand onto his shoulder in a friendly manner.

"Please sit," Min directed, returning to their seat.

Dean and Kambry sat, trying to get comfy.

"I was hoping Min would introduce me," the gorgeous Elven goddess said. She wore a lacy see through gown with no bra. Her pert breasts were on full display, her barely opaque panties covered her nether lips. Kambry saw him smirking at the sight and gave him a slight elbow.

"I grieve with you Dean." The Elven goddess' words came out almost like a sad melody. "Orabel was one of the few chosen who never faltered in her beliefs, even when she was ridiculed for them. Her entire existence was predicated upon you successfully defeating that collection of gods," the elven goddess said, inclining her head at Min.

"And your name?" Dean asked

She laughed lightly, placing a hand over her chest.

Dean didn't think the request warranted a laugh, so he frowned.

"My name is not publicly known, not even to the elven leaders. However, I will tell it to you, in exchange for a story. I want to hear every detail you have or have uncovered about Lexis going missing," the goddess said. "Please, spare nothing."

Min sat there patiently while Dean detailed the events of the day Lexis had disappeared. They had handed Leena off to Lexis after waking up, to go on their usual morning run and swim, followed by sex and a shower. Dean felt it was best to be blunt and honest, so he held nothing back. He mentioned that this was their normal routine, and nothing had seemed odd or different about Lexis that morning.

During breakfast, their assistant nanny, Olivia, went upstairs to retrieve Leena when Lexis didn't bring her down. Team Ola had then gone outside to check out their new gear—the same gear that Dean was currently wearing. They first realized something must be wrong when their nanny missed lunch.

Lexis was... well, a hornball, but at the same time, she was also an introvert. She would frequently entertain men or go off on a walk in the forest, to enjoy her free time. Her going missing for a few hours wasn't seen as unusual, until lunch came and went with no sign of her.

Lexis loved to eat, and Min snickered when Dean said as much. Then he went into the long ordeal of explaining how they had searched Lexis' room without finding anything. There was only a scattering of dust in the room—it was as if a cosmic vacuum had been aimed directly downward and sucked her up.

That sealed the deal for the two gods. When Kambry asked if they wanted to hear her retelling, they waved her off.

"My name is Missinaben," the elven goddess began. "I go by Missy, to my friends, and am known as the Great Mother, to the Elves. A second armada of ships is heading for Oakley. At least eight fleets' worth."

Dean choked on his next breath, which was hard to do, but news like this made such things possible. "Exsqueeze me?"

"Excuse my crass lover," Kambry said, patting his leg. "We welcome the Elves' support. I assume it is support?"

"Yes and no. You humans are going to be indoctrinated into the Elven Federation of Higher Societies or EFHS. By -"

Dean laughed, not even bothering to hide his rudeness. "Missy, are you trying to annex humanity?"

"Yes, you clearly need guidance on how to win your planets from the Core. Think Dean Forrester, your kind has never won a single competition. Mine have won..." she paused for effect, "all of them."

"I guess, but the Earth Council already claimed Orabel's support fleet was a hoax. They set the entirety of Oakley system on -"

"The EFHS is over Earth, well, the sixth fleet will be there in about five minutes. This may seem like a game, but it is not," Missy said matter-of-factly.

"Alright, Missy, I was rude—for that I apologize. I honestly believe you have the best intentions and humanity's best interests at heart. But humans are stubborn as mules. Ya ask a man to get ya a glass of water and if he doesn't like you, he'd just as soon break the glass and spill the water. Ya catchin my point?"

"Sure, and your governments are inept thieves. The EFHs understands all this and finds your species' faults irrelevant. They plan to push your armies back from their current operational positions, abduct your best soldiers, and dominate your portals. Humans will be trained and managed by the Elves—to the point that you start winning and can finally achieve some victories. The harsh measures we are prepared to execute assumes that humans won't cooperate with their conquerors," Missy said and they both grimaced at this.

"Who?" Kambry asked.

"The Dwarves," Min all but growled out. "Not that you shouldn't thank Missy anyway. I have to go to a meeting of the Core gods after this. Imagine the fun I'm going to have, telling the Core Gods of human planets that the Elves are breaking the treaty."

"Yeah... about that..." Dean said, letting the indirect request for more information hang.

Missy tucked her chin, clenching her recliner's arms tightly before saying, "Look, when the creator killed a Suca God, they broke the binding contracts that kept the war from spilling outside of Mixonia and Wixomia. New agreements need to be drafted."

Min frowned.

"In theory," Missy continued, "I could take you, Dean, to the core and have you start zapping Core Gods, in exchange for wives or riches or whatever. The key thing here, is that the rules have been altered by your mere existence. It's an appropriate time to impose some long overdue changes and to ensure some protections. The Elves are already vacating the eight planets they won during the Minotaur's Maze trials—the same number of human planets that are currently competing. That is part of a compromise that Min is going to offer the Core."

"So, let me get this straight... you will give up eight planets, assist humanity in winning eight planets, and then...what, relocate to eight new planets?" Dean asked.

Missy nodded.

"We can easily move—can even shift planets in their orbits, now. Giving up our homes means better homes and new art to create," Missy said with a shrug, as if it were not some huge undertaking.

"Alright, so how do the Dwarves play into this?" Kambry asked.

"War," Min said with disdain. "A war unlike any other the worlds have ever seen. You cannot live in peace, Dean. The dwarven goddess herself captured Lexis. I can't prove it... but it looks like Zued helped. Your account of events leads us to believe that Zued knew of your daily routine by tracking Sable's activities with you. He then worked with the Dwarves to have our daughter abducted to use as leverage."

Dean shook his head in disbelief. "Okay, looks like there are some gods wanting to play for keeps and the Elves want to help humanity to get out of the Maze games. I take it the Dwarves and the rogue Sucra gods are coming for me?"

"I believe so, though I do not think they will come for you directly," Missy said. She smirked when Dean tilted his head like a confused puppy. "Your weakness is your species, not you. The Dwarven battle plan will be simple, like they are. They will first smash Earth's defenses, to remove humanity's ability to assist the key system. Then, they will besiege Oakley. Finally, when enough power from the sun has been harvested, they will destroy the planet."

Missy balled her hands together before flaying her fingers apart while making a boom noise.

Dean grunted in dissatisfaction at hearing this.

"Dean," the Elven goddess continued, "you are vital—and therefore, humans are vital. We want you to win your planets, so that you can focus on fighting the Dwarves, as our allies. Make no mistake, when the Dwarven Armadas arrive, there will be carnage. Humans, I'm afraid, will need to do the brunt of the dying."

Kambry leaned forward and said, "You need fodder troops, and in essence, if the humans were going to die anyway it might as well be fighting to help you win your war."

"This one is smart. That," the goddess agreed, "and we need Dean to succeed in the mission the creator has given him. There is no Elven world we could hide him on, on which he could complete his task. Therefore, we must make a stand in human space," Missy explained. She smiled as if wars between species and the possibility of Oakley being blown to bits was anything close to normal.

"You want me to beat Min that badly?" Dean asked Missy.

She shook her head in frustration, but she wasn't saying 'no'.

"Dean," Missy finally said, "even Min wants you to win, but Min can't just roll over. There must be a fight—as ordained by prophecy. You breaking into the containment and restoring some trapped souls back to life, will enable a reset." She paused. "We all want a reset. Even Tarreen and Zued want a reset, they just don't know it yet."

"Alright, so you don't blame me for Lexi?" Dean asked Min.

"You love our daughter in your own way," Min said. "So, no. And I'm glad our feelings were your priority."

Min gave a snicker that halted when Dean sternly said, "Lexi is family. If it was the Dwarves who did this, at least I have a target, now."

"You're right to go on the offensive," Missy said. "They will expect you to cower in your home."

"What do you need us to do?" Kambry asked.

"Dean, look me in the eyes," Missy said and his pupils focused on her. "You will take your team as high as you can go, as quickly as you can, in the PvE Group. Do this to increase your team's baseline power—power which the Elves can improve upon. Trust me. Go in and keep going until you lose twice in a row on a floor, which means you have plateaued and are stuck. When you come out, an Elven armada will await you. You'll get new training from Elven trainers in Elven ways. Together we will push back the Dwarven Horde, and then win this planet for the Suca."

Dean slapped his thigh eagerly. "Now that is some ass-kicking I can get behind. Let me go get my team ready for the climb of our lives. When we hit our ceiling, I sure as hell will be happy to learn some Elven secrets of war."

He meant it too. The coming days, weeks, and months would surely be challenging. But he knew he would make his family proud, rescue Lexis, help the abandoned saps stuck in the soul pit, and save humanity.

What could possibly go wrong?

CHAPTER

TWO

DEAN

Forrester Estate

After the meeting with the gods, Dean and Kambry hurried back to their home at the Forrester estate, eager to share the news with the rest of the team. When the shuttle landed, no one ran out to greet them, everyone clearly busy within the fortified home.

In the weeks that had passed since Lexi's disappearance, the forest continued to expand, the dense foliage making it even more difficult for outsiders to navigate their way to the entrance of the mansion. Despite Orabel's spirit having returned to the planet, her spells remained intact, meaning the protective measures she had put in place remained strong.

The dragons decided to remain friendly as well, keeping up their end of the deal, the water dragons providing food for the rest of the group. Dean chose to rely less on the bigger types for battle, choosing a wyvern more often than not when entering Mixonia.

The community airship Cassandra had purchased for team Ola had yet to house any of its members, the chaos of Thero's attack having set their scheduled plans back by a few months at least. Instead, it sat parked out in the back, awaiting an inspection that would prove it was ready for flight after sitting idle for so long.

Kambry hopped out of the airship, rushing toward the front of the building, her eyes searching for the team. Looma greeted her as she entered the barroom, asking if she wanted anything to eat.

"Have you seen Cassie?" Kambry asked in a hurry, her fingers tapping on the back of a chair.

"She's with Leena in her quarters," the bouncry replied immediately, sending Kambry off toward the elevators.

Dean increased his pace, adjusting the bag of weapons he had thrown over his shoulder. He'd brought the ones that needed to be altered back from the caverns. But at the present moment, sharing the news of the elves' plans was far more important.

"Slow down, would ya? It's no race," he huffed, slamming the bag onto the tables.

They were pushed together still, revealing that the team more than likely had an earlier meeting, one he and Kambry had skipped out on by rushing off to Mixonia. Kambry grinned at him, increasing her pace and he returned the smile, deciding he would play her game.

Kambry soon arrived at the elevator, crunching the button as soon as she arrived, figuring the more she pressed, the faster the mechanics would work. Dean decided to take the stairs. He ran to the kitchen and up a flight, skipping as many as three steps as he made his way up to floor three where his suite awaited.

When he finally reached the desired floor he found himself out of breath, but refused to quit, hurrying his pace. The elevator door dinged as he passed it, a stunned Kambry exiting as he turned back to wave at her. They both sprinted for the door at the end of the corridor.

Their footsteps echoed hard on the wooden floor, disturbing those below them. Cassandra opened the door to their suite, peeking her head out to see what all the commotion was about. They both nearly plowed into her, stopping just before they reached the opened door.

"Whoa there—where is the fire?" She looked at them, her eyes wide in concern.

They were both so out of breath from their full sprint that neither of them could answer right away.

"Don't everyone speak at once." She laughed, gesturing for them to come in.

She took another look down the hall, just to make sure there really wasn't anything chasing them, before closing the door behind them.

"Anything wrong?" Jessabee asked from the balcony, coming in to join the others.

Leena was sound asleep in her bassinet, a chick flick playing on the lowest volume the girls could hear. Cassandra clicked the projector off, sitting on the sofa to hear the news that had gotten both her lovers in such a state.

"We have news," Dean said at last.

"The elves want to take over the whole operation," Kambry blurted out. Cassandra's eyebrows raised in response, her expression requesting further information.

"Not the whole operation...mostly the training stuff." Dean shrugged.

"They want to abduct strong people and train them to fight. If the humans don't cooperate, there will be consequences. The goal is to strengthen them enough to dominate both the levels in Mixonia and the dwarves. Assuming the dwarves even attack in the first place."

"They did say they would be our allies." Dean tried to soften the words coming out of Kambry's mouth.

Now her eyebrows were the ones to raise, "Were we even in the same meeting?"

"Ok-ok. Calm down, both of you. What exactly happened? What meeting are you talking about?" Her voice was calm and even, trying not to wake the sleeping baby.

Both paused waiting for the other to speak, but when no one did Kambry gestured to Dean, allowing him the floor.

"It was Min and Missy—the elven goddess. First of all, they were worried about Lexi, but they didn't blame us. They think a dwarf god kidnapped her...working with Zued. No wonder I haven't seen that slacker in quite a while," Dean said the last part more to himself, wondering if Sable knew anything about his nefarious deeds.

"Anyway. We were invited into a hidden meeting place where they talked about their concerns for humanity's safety. In short—they think we're fucked. The elves are on their way here now. New fleets, not the ones who came to greet us on our mini vacation." Dean inwardly shuddered thinking about what a shit day that turned out to be.

"So they want to train the humans? For what gain?"

"I guess they are tired of seeing the Core gods taking over planets. Missy said the elves would be focusing on all eight human worlds that are fighting in the games." Dean shrugged again, having tuned out a bit of the conversation with the gods.

"That sounds great in theory, but they didn't seem like they wanted to work with humans—more like control them. A 'I've done this before, so let me tell you how things are going to work from now on' type of relationship. Agreeing to the terms essentially means giving up humanity's freedom," Kambry retorted, not seeing a positive outcome for Oakley.

"I understand what both of you are saying, thank you." Cassandra raised her hands, her mind spinning with all the details.

"One more question. What is it they want you to do Dean? There must be a reason they told you all of this."

"They need to know how strong I am without their help. I was told to go all out in the PVE team levels. If I reach a level that we all die twice on, that's when we stop." He waited for Cassie's response as he watched her expressions change with each new detail. "What are you thinking?" Dean asked, unable to read her face. Cassandra's mind seemed to be mulling over a thousand possible outcomes.

"Don't worry about the elves. I will deal with them—I'll draw up a contract that makes sure the humans remain in control of themselves even if we accept their help. I don't want us to win just to have to bow down to the elven overlords because they think we owe them our lives. You should focus on the levels. Pick a team and plan to stay for as long as you can manage."

"Now that Tucker gave up the fourth portal, we pretty much have the Ola caverns to ourselves anyway," Dean added, remembering that he wouldn't have to abide by the six hour limit anymore.

"Who were you thinking of taking with you?"

"Me! I'm going for sure," Kambry stuck her hand up high in the air, her breasts bouncing slightly from her bobbing motion.

"No—not this time." Cassandra said sternly. "You are carrying a life inside of you— normal level building maybe, but this might be a bit too strenuous for you to handle."

Kambry's entire body deflated, her bottom lip puckering out to show her disappointment. Dean understood Cassie's reasoning, but at the same time Kambry was one of the original members, having to scale the levels without her would be a challenge.

"It's still early in the pregnancy, I don't think a little exercise will affect the baby's growth," Kambry rebutted, patting her stomach. "It might even help make the child a strong warrior in the future."

Cassandra sighed, realizing she wasn't going to let this go.

"And besides, I'm a Dragona. We are made tough—this little bean won't feel a thing." She paused, taking a second to gauge Cassie's reaction before continuing.

"What if I promise to come back as soon as the levels get too hard? I already reached seventeen on my own, so at the very least I can help the team make it to that point." Kambry dug her heels in, determined to get the okay from her lover.

"Dean, don't you have anything to say about this?" Cassandra turned to Dean, hoping he would reiterate her sentiments.

"It is still early...so long as the gods don't interfere this time. If we monitor the baby during battle, we will know if the fighting is too much for it. If the sensors go off even once, she can stop," Dean said quietly, knowing it wasn't the response Cassie was looking for.

She huffed, "Fine, but one even slight ping and she's out—understood."

The duo nodded enthusiastically, exchanging glances of victory. Cassandra paused, her eyes glazing over as she stared into the distance. After a minute her eyes blinked and she looked at the two who appeared a little too excited for her liking.

"I ordered you a top of the line fetal monitoring device. It wears like a watch and will alert the wearer of any disturbances or abnormalities in the pregnancy...among other things. Do not..and I mean it— Do Not take it off for even a second when in the levels."

She put her hand to her forehead, shaking it slightly. "I can't believe I am agreeing to this. Dean, you better keep an eye on her. Oh and make sure you buy the strongest armor for your stomach—go to Min's vault to get it if you have to."

"You're the best, Mom," Kambry teased her, kissing her cheek to ease the worried lines from Cassie's face.

"What about the others?"

"Patti will be going for sure, and I was thinking of asking Lonny."

"Wouldn't he be busy trying to do the same thing with his own team?" Cassandra added, remembering how little Lonny had come to visit once he was given full reign over one of the portals.

"You're right. Then Zayra and Wilfred will fill the remaining slots. Should we have another meeting to confirm?" he asked, actually eager to call a meeting for once.

"We are supposed to have one after dinner today, so we can add all of this to the agenda. The preparations shouldn't take that long, considering you'll maybe pack for two days at a time." She paused to make sure he had no objections to her timeline.

"So you can probably head out as early as tomorrow morning, if everyone agrees." Her baby blues stared into Dean's eyes, silently pleading for him to be careful.

She knew he wouldn't like her getting all sappy on him, so she kept her concerns to herself, choosing to focus on what she could control.

"We have a pretty solid reserve of tokens at the moment, plenty for the whole team to be wiped out the two times the Elves suggested. Plus with the tokens you bring in from the levels, we won't have to worry about working at a deficit."

Dean couldn't help but feel excited. Yes, he had been in the levels before, his team having reached the tenth already, but there had always been a set stopping point, a goal to reach. Being told to attempt each level, death be damned, lit a fire in his belly, a desire to prove to the elves just what a human was capable of.

"Thank you, my love, you always know how to handle any situation." He grabbed Cassandra's hand, kissing it gently.

She smiled at his attempt to appease her. In all honesty, Dean was glad he had Cassandra by his side, even if the gods had been the one responsible for pushing his marriage timeline forward. He'd be lost without her, trying to navigate the games alone.

"Oh! We almost forgot." Cassandra sprung up, directing her excitement toward Jessabee.

"What did you forget?" Kambry and Dean asked in unison.

"We did a thing." She giggled in response, grabbing Kambry and Dean by the wrist and pulling them in the direction of one of the suite's extra rooms.

"Hopefully it suits your tastes." Jessabee smiled at Dean before Cassie released their arms, pushing the door behind her open.

The medium sized room had been decked out in baby gear. A toddler bed that resembled a boat sat in between two cribs, all three covered with frills and lace in baby blue. The wall behind them displayed an intricate mural, the sea and its rolling waves drawn in all its glory. A lighthouse stood in the distance, signaling to the ship that moved toward the distant land.

"The lace is supposed to be the fishing net...but prettier." Cassandra fiddled with the fabric, trying to read Dean's expression.

"You both really outdid yourselves," he said at last, taking a step closer to inspect the mural.

"It's gorgeous! I can't wait for our little ones to share this room." Kambry slid her hand across the bars of the crib.

"Won't Leena be too small for this bed once the other two are born?" Dean asked, thinking there was no way his little girl would be ready to sleep in such a grown up looking bed.

"No worries," Jessabee said as she approached the toddler's ship.

She ran her hand down the side of the bed, popping the rails into place. "There are even some for the front and the back if she needs them at first," she mentioned, showing off the versatility of the bed.

"I'm glad you both like it," Cassandra said with a smile.

A soft knock on the door broke up the family moment, Olivia's voice coming through the closed door.

"Is it okay to enter?"

Cassie hurried to the door, letting in the nanny. She looked a bit shocked to see all four of them were in, but went about her duties regardless.

"Looma said dinner is just about ready, I will take Leena for you now."

"Thank you, Olivia. We should head down now." She eyed the group briefly before leading them out into the hallway.

When they reached the barroom, everyone else was already seated, and the meal was laid out for them to enjoy. After they ate, they shared the news of Dean's meeting with the rest of team Ola, everyone seeming to be on board with their plans.

Dorothy interjected with a bunch of scrolls she would prefer them to get with the excess of tokens they would be bringing home, but other than that there were no additions to the plan. As the others headed off to bed that night, Cassandra prepared for a sleepless night of preparation, promising that she would have all the supplies the team would need for the coming morning.

∞∞∞∞

After a good night's rest, Dean woke up ready to push his limits in Mixonia. Kambry was dressed in full gear, her hair pulled back in a tight ponytail as she readjusted the new watch she wore, trying to get used to the weight on her wrist. Zayra and Wilfred were waiting in the barroom, bags filled with their provisions on their back.

"Good morning everyone!" Dean said with gusto, drawing the waiting party's gaze. "We ready?" he asked, seeing that everyone was present.

"Hell yes," Patti said, punching her fist into the air.

"Which pets were you bringing along? You'll need them in case you decide to do any solo leveling while you are in there." Dorthy appeared from the side room, directing her question to Dean.

"I already have Jarod," Patti mentioned, holding up a statuette of the wyvern.

"Moon, Geo, and Droosca should be enough. We can only summon one per level anyway, so it's better not to take a whole lot."

"I thought you might say that." Dorothy smiled, handing Dean a bag with the already prepared statues.

"If we split up, who is short a pet?" Kambry asked, realizing the pet to team member ratio was off by one.

"You," Dean said matter-of-factly. "If we decide to switch to soloing for some reason, you will have to sit out for that one. You understand why, right?"

Her face dropped into a pout. "Fine," she responded, dropping the issue.

Team Ola said goodbye to the estate as they made their way to the shuttle, planning to spend at least two whole days away from it. When they reached the Ola caverns, Felna had a wild west movie playing, the shots from the standoff ringing through the cave.

When she heard the doors of the shuttle close, she paused the movie, resuming her position beside the portal.

"We are going in for an extended stay this time, Felna," Dean informed the portal guard, his teammates close behind.

"Well it's about time," she said snarkily, opening the portal for the group. "Good luck," she added as Dean passed through.

When they entered Mixonia, the first thing they heard was, "Oh, crap nuggets" from Kambry as she stared down at her empty wrist.

Wilfred, Zayra and Patti were unaware of the promise she had made to Cassandra, but Dean knew automatically what her outburst meant.

"We forgot about what happens to tech in the portal," he finished her thought process.

"Now what?" she asked, not wanting to return to Oakley.

"Well we have to go to Min's vault anyway...maybe they have something that will work in the same way."

"It's worth a shot." She shrugged, playing off how desperate she wanted them to find something.

Heading to Min's vault, the streets appeared wider, the benefits of the recent expansion still clear by the reduction of the crowds.

"We need armor for Kambry's stomach and a baby monitoring device if they have it. Spread out—holler if you find something," Dean instructed the group, hoping to be finished in a matter of minutes.

He took the direction to the right, drawn in by the weapons displayed on the side wall. A giant battle axe caught his eye, the massive weapon probably weighing fifty pounds itself. The three-hundred token cost matched its excessive size.

Moving along he found a display of totes and messenger bags, his eyes scanning them, landing on a leather satchel, with a buckle closure. He leaned in to take a closer look, wondering how such a small bag could possibly justify the three token cost.

"You have an excellent eye!"

Dean jumped from the sudden introduction of a voice, spinning around to find one of the Demi's responsible for fulfilling the transactions. He took a deep breath trying to settle his racing heart.

"I'm sorry! I didn't mean to startle you. I really need to work on my entrances." She blushed, avoiding eye contact. Deciding to move past the blunder, she changed topics by asking, "Should I add it to your order?"

Dean stared at the woman who appeared to be part peacock with long green, black and gold feathers that protruded from the cartilage of her ear and her forearm forming a prominent feature.

"Who would spend three tokens on a bag?" Dean scoffed at the price, his wheelbarrow able to carry ten times the amount of stuff by the looks of it.

"Well this satchel right here is special. We don't advertise it as such, but since it caught your eye, I'll let you in on a little secret." She grabbed the bag from the display wall, opening the buckle to give Dean a look inside.

"It doesn't look like much now, but once you enter the portals, it transforms. A real rarity. This one bag can hold enough rations for a year. Its internal pantry comes stocked for nine months, no extra charge. What's actually in there, I couldn't say, but the food is guaranteed edible at least. Again, you can't retrieve them out here without the proper magic as it reverts back to a normal capacity bag, but trust me, they are in there. This bag can easily carry the supplies and weapons of an entire five man team. And the best part——once the items are inside it doesn't weigh but a few pounds at most."

Dean was sold. Sure the wheelbarrow worked, but it had its limitations. Big, bulky and had to be left behind on a good number of the levels with more uneven terrain. This bag would be a game changer, he found himself thinking, accepting the satchel when the Demi handed it to him.

"Will that complete your purchase?" she asked with a grin.

A bit dumbfounded that he had fallen right into her trap he responded, "No, I still have a few other things I need to look for," remembering the whole reason they had stopped by Min's vault.

"Very good, Sir. Is there anything I can assist you with?"

Coming to terms with the fact that the Demi was going to lead him to spending more tokens than he anticipated, he accepted her help, explaining the other items that remained on his to buy list.

"The armor is an easy one. In fact I think one of your team members is already browsing through our selection, but your other request is a bit of an odd one. Let me check our stock and I will get back to you," she said before disappearing from the aisle.

Dean was left alone, still holding his three token bag. Slinging it onto his shoulder, he decided to search for the others, wondering if they had better luck.

Zayra and Wilfred were close by, browsing the weapons that had enormous price tags, reminding him why he'd been told to avoid buying weapons and armor from within Min's vault. This time was special though, they didn't have the time to wait around for something to be made, so instead they would have to pay for the convenience.

Kambry was in another part of the vault, holding up plates of armor to her stomach to see which one felt like the right fit.

"Any luck?" Dean asked when she spotted him walking toward her.

"They are too bulky. I need to be able to move around in order to fight effectively," she huffed. "I still don't see why our normal armor isn't good enough." She hit her fist on the metal chest plate, the piece extending down past her abdomen.

"Cassie just wants to be extra cautious." Dean chose his words wisely, not wanting to take sides.

"What about adding a layer of chain mail under your gear—like mine?" Patti came up behind her, patting her own armor for reference.

She looked to Dean for the okay. When he agreed that it would be a good compromise, Patti led her away, heading to where she had seen the chain mail displayed. Dean went to follow but was blocked by the sudden reappearance of the Demi helper.

"Holy fook— would you stop it with the pop ups!" he nearly yelled, taking a step back to make room for the Demi.

"Sorry, again." The smile on her face, not matching her words. "So, unfortunately we don't have anything quite advanced like what you described, but I did find this," she pulled out a dinosaur of a device that resembled a stopwatch, a tube jutting out from the top with a needle attached to its end.

"And what is that supposed to be?" He was genuinely concerned by the archaic looking device.

"Well—you just prick the finger of the one who is pregnant and the blood will form a connection between the baby and this wellness monitor. But again it only works inside the levels. You can add the blood whenever you want, but the connection forms when you pass through the portal. Easy peasy." She held the device out toward Dean, waiting for him to take it from her hands.

"Do I want to know how much this thing costs?" he asked, expecting a ridiculous number to come from her lips.

"One token."

High, but better than he predicted.

"Will that complete your purchase for today?" she repeated hoping for the sale.

"One more thing." As he said this, Kambry rushed over having seen him speaking with one of the shop assistants.

Kambry held up the shirt of chain mail. "This is what we found."

"I want that too," Dean told the Demi.

"Perfect. Your total is 4.3 tokens."

Dean held out a locket with the number thirty-five etched onto it. He had brought enough to afford the needed items, any additional supplies, as well as the twenty-five tokens needed should anyone die in the maze and end up as a statue in Min's vault.

If more than one person faced that fate, the remaining team members would need to go back to the estate to retrieve the tokens. That or if the whole team perished, he wanted Cassandra to be able to afford to bail them all out with help from one of the other teams.

"Thank you for your business. I am Ezra by the way. I hope to see you again soon." She smiled before vanishing, leaving Dean and his team with their newly purchased items and a locket that now read 30.7.

"What's the bag for?" Wilfred asked as they exited the vault.

Kambry was already securing her new armor into place as they walked, not wanting to waste a minute by stopping.

"I figured we could use a new way to carry our belongings."

"Will everything fit in there?" Zayra asked, eying the small satchel in disbelief.

"It better or that Demi owes me some tokens," Dean quipped, hoping he didn't just waste the three tokens on a useless purchase.

"Let's get going!" Patti redirected the conversation, speeding up toward the line that led to the portals.

They entered the waiting section, pulling out the wheelbarrow statuette that carried all of their belongings. When they reached the Minotaur guard, they set their things on the ground, allowing it to expand to its full size. When the final group in front of them passed through the portal, Dean stepped up to the guard.

"Place your hand on the pedestal," the guard began.

Before he could finish his spiel, Dean placed his hand on the pedestal and said, "Dean and my team wish to go to floor eleven, we understand the risks." The Minotaur nodded, the portal shifting to a sea green color.

One at a time they entered the portal, Wilfred bringing up the rear as he rolled the wheelbarrow through. Upon entering, the scene was dark, the main light coming from a full moon overhead. They had entered into the middle of a forest, tall trees surrounding them in every direction.

The wheelbarrows' wheels caught in the softened mud, making it almost impossible to roll.

"Should we try out that bag of yours?" Wilfred asked Dean, already fed up with the transport device.

Dean pulled the bag from his shoulder, setting it down on the ground for some leverage.

"Hand me one of the food bags." He held his free hand out to Zayra.

Zayra grabbed a bag from the cart, placing it in his outstretched hand. Accepting the offered item, Dean tried to stretch the opening of the satchel, still unsure how the small bag would accommodate all of their supplies. To his surprise, the item easily slipped in, disappearing into the void. After all of the items were loaded into the bag and the wheelbarrow was empty, Dean held the bag up, testing out its weight.

"It still feels like it's empty," he said, pleasantly surprised by the bag.

"Now the question is how to take out the items," Kambry snickered, realizing Dean hadn't even thought about that.

"Well fook." He plopped the bag back on the ground, sticking his arm through the top. "There really is nothing in here. If this fooking bag ate all my javelins, I swear," he cursed, but then paused, his eyebrows raising.

In the next moment, he pulled his hand free of the bag, the long weapon coming with it.

"Well, does that answer your question?" He grinned at Kambry, who laughed, nodding her head.

After putting the weapon back into the bag, he tried again this time asking for the sack of food. Upon command, the strap of the bag that held the food appeared in his hand, allowing him to pull it from the void.

"Okay I think I got the hang of it now." He put the food back in, placing the bag back on his back.

"Oh— before I forget, this is for you Kambry." He held out the monitor. "You prick your finger with the needle and it's supposed to sync with the baby's heartbeat or something."

636

Kambry eyed the archaic looking device, not buying his claims. Despite her apprehensions she followed his instructions, piercing the tip of her finger with the needle.

The blood flowed up the tube that was connected to the needle, continuing toward the body of the device, bringing the device to life. The face of the mechanism lit up, displaying two heart rates, one for mom and one for the baby.

"All set," Kambry said, noting the normal rhythms on the screen.

The team equipped their weapons, Dean holding his trident in his hand as they surveyed their surroundings, finally ready to focus on the mission. Despite the moon being the only source of light, the forest appeared relatively well lit once their eyes adjusted. All seemed quiet as they moved through the space, unsure which direction would lead them to the locket.

They walked for a while, all eyes searching the forest floor for any signs of the pedestal or the locket. Kambry, walking a few feet ahead of the group, slammed into the invisible barrier that outlined the space, telling them that the direction they'd chosen was the wrong one. She rubbed her forehead, turning to inform her comrades that they needed to head in another direction.

She found them covering their mouths as they tried to suppress their laughter, letting Kambry know that they understood what happened.

"Ha ha, very funny." She stuck out her tongue at their laughing faces, picking another direction at random, still choosing to walk in the front.

Another twenty minutes passed by when they reached the second barrier, Kambry verbally releasing her frustration on the invisible wall.

"Why haven't we found anything yet?" she screamed.

No enemies, no pedestal, only trees as far as the eye could see.

"Maybe we missed something," Wilfred interjected, trying to regain Kambry's focus.

"Or we chose the wrong direction...again" Dean said with a huff, empathizing with Kambry's frustration. "We'll just try again. It's fine, all a part of the grind."

"What the—" Wilfred said, everyone turning to see what was wrong. On his shoulder was a wad of a light green liquid, the slime slowly trailing down his armor.

All at once the group's eyes shot toward the tree line. The once clear forest canopy was dotted with hundreds of tiny glowing red eyes, honing in on their location.

"Ah...shit it burns!" Wilfred screamed, stripping from his armor.

The metal that once protected his shoulder had nearly completely melted where the substance had touched it. His shirt came off next, the fluid having seeped through onto his underclothes, just reaching his skin. When he threw the shirt onto the forest floor, he relaxed, the burning sensation having stopped.

His metal armor didn't fare so well as it continued to melt, the damp dirt having no effect on the process. A clattering filled the forest, increasing the sense of urgency.

"Run for cover," Dean shouted, directing the team away from the looming creatures. Whatever was in the trees followed them, leaping among the branches to stay on top of the party.

"There!" Zayra pointed to a cave as it came into view.

Running as fast as they could manage in the dense forest, they headed for the cave. Wads of the sticky liquid came raining down on top of them, just barely missing their bodies as it sizzled on the forest floor around them. Before they made it past the cave's entrance, Zayra was hit in the shin, her metal guard instantly beginning to melt from the introduction of the acidic fluid.

She skidded into the safety of the cave, her hands pulling at her shin guard, frantically trying to remove it before the acid could reach her skin. She flung the piece against the wall, her breathing settling once the danger had passed.

"Don't relax yet," Dean warned the group, readying his shorter trident and shield from his bag. "Whatever it is, they will be on us in a matter of seconds."

Kambry directed her staff to the torches that lined the walls of the cave, lighting them on fire to illuminate the space. As the team moved deeper in, they realized there were tunnels on the back wall, leading deeper into the caves. They heard the sound of scurrying creatures growing louder, the threat approaching the entrance of the cave—they had a choice to make.

Stay and fight off whatever was heading their way, or travel further in, taking the chance that the pendent would be somewhere in the labyrinth of the cave.

The first of the monsters entered the cave, its form revealed by the torch light. A spider the size of an Earth guinea pig, stared them down with its multiple eyes, its sharp fangs clicking together in a set sequence.

Fluid dripped from the tips of its fangs, the ground beneath it sizzling upon impact. While small, the numbers alone made the creature a threat, but paired with its deadly saliva, it seemed impossible to come out of the fight unscathed.

"Move in—we'll search for the pendant in the tunnels," Dean made the decision, waving his teammates further into the cave. "Javelin," he whispered, sticking his hand into the bag that remained on his back, pulling out the long weapon.

He heaved it at the spider, the tip piercing its body, tethering it to the cave floor. Its legs flailed about, trying to free itself, until finally it succumbed to the wound, its body slumping onto the pole. Hordes more flanked the entrance of the cave, the hundreds of beady eyes blinking in tandem.

As if the floodgates were released, all the spiders moved at once, rushing into the cave. Dean ran toward the hole in the back wall, his friends shouting for him to hurry, their tone desperate as the wave of spiders grew closer. As his body passed the entrance, Wilfred pressed a button on the side wall, a door of stone sliding to cover the entrance.

The small space immediately went dark, the party freezing in place, their labored breathing and the scraping of legs against the stone door the only sounds. Hoping their eyes would adjust enough for them to see in front of them, they remained still, the lights flickering on a few moments later. The lights were fixed to a track on the top of the walls, leading them deeper into the cave.

Unsure how to interpret the seemingly out of place lighting, the group ventured deeper into the tunnels, knowing that exiting back the way they came was no longer an option. Five minutes in and they came to a fork in the road, the two openings leading in opposite directions.

"Let's split up and search both ways at one time," Dean suggested, knowing that if anyone from the team located the locket, they would all be transported out together.

Kambry, Patti and Dean went to the right, while Zayra and Wilfred took the tunnel to the left. At a hurried pace, they followed the determined path, scanning the walls for anything that seemed out of place. Ten minutes passed before Dean's side hit a dead end, the path completely stopping.

He ran his hand along the surface of the wall, hoping to find a hidden button, but came up empty handed. The group turned around, heading back to take the remaining tunnel.

"We might get transported out of here before we reach that side, but we'll head that way just in case," Dean told the others, who nodded in agreement.

They decided to run this time, not sure what to expect. Reaching the exit, they headed in the second direction. About five minutes of running later, they heard a scream echo through the tunnel, quickening their pace. Passing through the opening, they found themselves in a large cavern that branched off from the tunnel.

A large spider web hung in between the stalactites, close to the cave ceiling. In the center of the web was Zayra, her body rocking back and forth as she struggled to free herself from the sticky threads. Wilfred brandished his sword against a giant spider, his blade colliding with the massive legs, trying to keep it from attacking his trapped wife.

"Holy mother of...," Patti exclaimed, nocking her arrow and aiming for one of the spider's many eyes.

She pulled the string taut, releasing when she had a clear shot, sending the arrow whizzing through the air. When the arrow head made contact with one of the beast's bright red eyes, the creature reeled back, turning to face its attacker.

Wilfred accepted the help, running toward Zarya the moment the spider was distracted, his sword ready to slice through the webbing. The spider was solely focused on Patti now, its fangs chattering as it built up its acidic saliva. Dean knew there wasn't much time before the beast would be on them, intent on devouring its prey.

Scanning the room he found what they needed—the faint glow of the golden locket shining on the other side of the cavern.

"Kambry!" He shouted, pointing in the direction of the pedestal, her eyes following his direction until she knew just what he wanted her to see.

"I'm on it," she confirmed, her wings spreading as she prepared to speed toward the target.

The leg of the spider flew in Patti's direction, clashing with the prongs of Dean's trident. He tried to hold back the attack, his body sliding backward from the pressure of the spider's thrust. Patti released another arrow, the head finding its target in another of the spider's eyes.

The beast screeched in pain, its rage increasing as it struck out again, only to have its attack dodged by the offenders. Dean rolled to the side avoiding the blow, Patti having long cleared the attack path. She nocked another arrow, aiming with precision, as the spider turned toward her, recognizing her intent.

A thick wad of acidic spit flew in her direction, the amount enough to cover her entire body in the substance. Dean ran for her, his shield raised, hoping to intercept the saliva, but as he moved closer he realized that his shield wouldn't be large enough to withstand the attack unscathed.

He braced for impact, closing his eyes to prepare for the burning agony he was sure to feel. When nothing happened, he slowly opened his eyes, the view having changed from the cavern to the portal entrance. The Minotaur guard gave him the side eye, wondering why his face was scrunched up as he held his shield toward him.

"I got it!" Kambry announced cheerfully as the rest of the group struggled to catch their breath.

Dean stood straight, lowering his shield as he released a quick exhale, "Good work."

He led them to the common area, choosing a picnic table where they could rest for a little while before continuing to the next level.

"Sorry about that—that giant spider came out of nowhere. I was stuck to its web before I even realized what happened." Zayra started as soon as they sat down, feeling a bit like the weak link in that moment.

"It happens," Dean replied, not blaming anyone and just happy they all made it out alive.

"That thing was massive. I'm surprised it was on such a low-level floor," Kambry admitted.

"Maybe there was an easier way to go around it, but we roused it up somehow instead." Patti shrugged, not sure how they could have approached the situation any differently.

They spent a bit more time discussing what they could have potentially done differently during the recently completed level and after the quick debriefing, they rejoined the line determined to do even better in the next one.

"Dean and my team wish to attempt level twelve and we understand the consequences," he told the guard as he placed his hand on the pedestal.

The portal shimmered, revealing a teal green as the Minotaur guard waved them through. Together they entered, unsure of what they would find on the other side.

CHAPTER

THREE

DEAN

Minotaur's Maze- Level Twelve

Dean blinked, his eyes unable to adjust, his entire surroundings a milky white color.

"Guys are you there?" he called out, hoping his teammates were nearby.

"Here—" the voices answered one by one around him, letting him know they were close.

He waved his hand in front of him, unable to clear away the thick blanket of fog that surrounded them.

"I can't see shit," he said aloud, their voices the only thing keeping them connected.

"Same here," Kambry's voice came through the whiteout.

"What do we do?" Patti asked, her voice hoarse and quiet.

"Keep talking. We need to find each other."

In an event similar to 'Marco Polo' the party located each other, quickly using rope from the satchel to secure their bodies together.

"We need to move as a unit. Shout if you see anything at all," Dean informed them once the last member had been secured.

Step by cautious step they moved through the unseen landscape, unsure what—if anything— they were headed toward.

"Gah!" Kambry screamed, causing everyone to shift to a battle stance, still not sure what direction to face.

"What is it? What happened?" Dean questioned, shifting his footing to prepare for the potential of an attack.

"Sorry... something touched me, but I think it was a branch," Kambry apologized, her cheeks reddening behind the veil of fog.

Exhales followed her statement, the group's heightened nerves settling just a bit.

"Is that what I think it is?" Wilfred broke the silence once more, no one sure exactly what he was talking about. "Ahead and to the right just a bit...I think I see a tiny shimmer."

Sure enough, Dean saw it too, quickly leading the group in the direction of the light. Without any interference, they reached their destination, and quickly placed the locket onto the pedestal, allowing them to exit level twelve.

"That was...easy?" Patti said, a bit worried about saying the words out loud for fear of jinxing the subsequent levels.

"Yes, but just think if we would have headed in a different direction," Zayra told her. "We could have been walking around for hours, seeing nothing but white."

Patti shuddered at the possibility, the whole group thankful they had somehow chosen the right path.

"Are we ready to continue?" Dean asked, scanning the faces of his teammates.

Enthusiastic nods answered his question, everyone finding themselves on a high after completing the level in less than twenty minutes.

"Dean, my team, level thirteen, we understand," he said, hurrying up the process of entering the maze.

The Minotaur guard shook his head, but accepted the hastened response, opening the portal for his team to continue. Dean led the way as they walked through the deep green portal.

∞∞∞∞

When they passed through the entrance their free fall began, the drop off sending them plummeting into an angry sea. Four splashes followed Dean's initial one, his party members soon finding themselves in the choppy water.

"I wasn't expecting to need a life jacket," Patti yelled, trying to keep her head above the water, the weight of her armor dragging her down.

"Remove your armor if you can, before it forces us to the bottom," Dean shouted, trying to unhook his chest plate.

While an excellent swimmer, the heavy metal pieces made it nearly impossible to tread water for long, forcing the party to give up their means of protection. The scene they found themselves in was dark-- the ocean spread out in every direction, the waves increasing in intensity as time passed. When the group had stripped down to their undergarments, staying above the surface became easier, but they still weren't sure where the pedestal would be hidden in such a landscape.

"Do you think it's under the water?" Zayra asked, her arms skimming the surface as she kept herself afloat.

Dean dove down, the water too dark to see anything below the surface, forcing him to return without any new information.

"For level thirteen, I don't think so. I can't see a fooking thing."

"Gah—" Kambry cried out again, the group turning to face her.

"What is it this time?" Patti was the one to ask.

"Something touched my leg."

"Was it seaweed?" Wilfred laughed awkwardly, not wanting them to panic for no reason.

"I don't think so...not this time."

Before anyone could reassure her that what she felt wasn't some water monster, a giant tentacle broke through the surface, crashing back down into the water beside them. The group was pushed through the water by the waves the monster created, separating them from one another.

"Stay together!" Dean shouted, swimming back toward Patti who was the closest to his position.

They all swam in the same direction, trying to put distance between themselves and the space where the tentacle had first appeared. When they finally regrouped, three more giant tentacles surrounded them, hovering beside them just waiting to attack. Dean reached for his bag, the only thing he didn't let sink to the bottom of the ocean and called for his trident.

Pulling the weapon from his satchel, he dove under the water, hoping to catch a glimpse of the creature that threatened their lives. While still dark, Dean could just make out the outline of the beast, a kraken the size of a spacecar, looming just below the surface.

Dean headed back above the water, figuring he should give his team a heads up before pissing off the beast, needing them to prepare to swim for their lives.

"It's a kraken!" he announced, everyone frantically trying to see into the depths, not wanting to end up as the kraken's dinner.

"Wonderful—now what?"

Dean turned to face Kambry when he saw a dim light in the distance, the unmistakable glow of a ship's mast-light. Not only did he see a ship, but it seemed to be coming closer, either by its own power or through the push of the current.

"There's a boat," Zayra shouted before Dean could. "Let's head toward it!"

Everyone began swimming in the boat's direction, eager to be away from the kraken and back on a solid surface. The tentacles shifted in the air, the splashing rousing its attention. Dean knew they wouldn't make it if the beast decided to attack and with the number of legs this thing had, they could all become incapacitated in a matter of minutes.

"Keep swimming!—I'll hold it off," he told his companions, gripping his weapon tighter as he once again dove under the surface just as one of the tentacles came to life, aiming for Wilfred's position.

He knew there wasn't much time, so he took his shot, aiming for the beast's oversized beak. When the prongs hit the monster's flesh, two massive eyes flipped open, staring Dean down, his trident but a small fork in comparison to the kraken's size. Dean tried to back pedal, recognizing the beast's rage, but the tentacles all moved at once, quickly wrapping around his body, stopping his attempt to swim out of harm's way.

He felt the grip tighten, the strong limbs forcing the air from his lungs, threatening to snap him in two. Struggling against the grip the kraken had on his torso, he managed to free his hands as his consciousness began to darken. Placing his palms on the tentacle, he released his water magic, planning to freeze the limb that was wrapped around his body, hoping it would release him before his body succumbed to the lack of oxygen.

The surrounding water reacted to his magic, strengthening the spell and soon the entire body of the kraken was encased in ice. Its body began to sink, the weight too much to remain near the surface. Dean reached his limit, bubbles escaping from his mouth, his body trying to force him to breathe.

In a last stitch effort, he pushed on the now frozen tentacle that still gripped his torso, as both him and the beast traveled slowly toward the ocean floor. It slid off, having loosen its grip and Dean slipped out, heading back toward the open air that now seemed miles away.

Darkness continued to surround his vision, even as his mind told him to swim—told him that air was waiting for him just beyond the water line. His lungs felt like they were on fire, and he knew that he wasn't going to make it—the surface too far to reach as the darkness overtook him.

In the next moment it was bright once more, and Dean found himself lying on the cobblestone gasping for air, feeling like a fish out of water. The Minotaur guard looked at him with an amused expression on his face, but didn't say a word. All of his armor had returned to him, so at the very least he wasn't in his underwear on the ground flopping around as he tried to return his breathing to normal.

"Are you okay?" Kambry peered down at him, her eyes wide with concern. "Do you need me to heal you?"

"I'll be fine," he managed between gasps.

They helped him to his feet, leading him to the picnic table that they designated as their official debriefing spot.

"Whew—I thought I was a goner." He sat down roughly, waiting for the team's report.

"You did great." Kambry kissed him on the cheek.

"Yea, we didn't have to worry about that thing coming after us and we were able to make it onto the ship," Wilfred added, patting Dean on the shoulder.

"I'm guessing the pedestal was on board?"

"In place of the ship's wheel." Kambry nodded. "Good thing we weren't expected to sail it anywhere." She laughed now that the danger had passed.

"Should we call it a day and find somewhere to stay?" Zayra asked, Dean's breathing finally returning to normal.

"No way—we are just getting started." Dean hopped up from his seat, not wanting to be the reason they only passed three levels that day.

Excited by his determination, the group headed back to the line, ready to take on the next challenge. With his hand on the pedestal once again, Dean recited the words the Minotaur guard needed to hear, stepping into the portal that shifted to a murky green.

∞∞∞∞

"So this is level fourteen," Dean said when the last of his group appeared beside him, taking in the landscape.

They were in a rural town, buildings on either side of them with a large farmhouse in the distance. A merry-go-round sat to their right, spinning slowly as it released eerie creaks into the silent surroundings.

"What do you think we will face this time?" Patti wondered aloud, her bow ready in her hands.

No one could be sure of that answer, but they knew they would need to search the surrounding buildings thoroughly if they wished to find the locket.

"Should we split up? Cover more ground," Zayra asked, realizing searching each one individually would take quite a while.

"Remember what happened the last time? You know, the giant spider...," Wilfred reminded her with a concerned gaze. "I'd rather not deal with that again."

"We'll be more careful," she assured him.

While splitting up seemed to be the fastest option, the way the town looked gave Dean a creepy horror movie vibe. He realized that separating from each other was the quickest way for them all to die.

"We'll stick together." He made the decision, sacrificing time for safety.

"Let's check this first," Kambry said excitedly, hopping on board the small merry-go-round. The paint on the hand carved horses was chipped from the passage of time.

She moved to the center, checking out the controls, the slow motion of the spinning children's ride never stopping despite the added weight. Weird, but the group chose to ignore it, not wanting to buy into the haunted vibe the whole town exuded.

"Nothing." She jumped back onto the dirt road.

"Let's head there next." Dean pointed to a small market to their left.

He pulled the team's weapons from the bag, making sure everyone was ready for anything. The small market was deserted, much like the rest of the town, a thick layer of dust covering the stalls that lined the perimeter of the store, the remains of long outdated food still in the baskets. They scoured the place, searching for where the locket might be hiding, but came up empty handed.

Their next stop was an old hotel, the slotted reception desk looking more like an old time movie kiosk than a hotel. The whole place was decked out in red and gold, the patterned curtains blocking the sun from entering the establishment, the carpet faded from use. Again, everything was coated in dust, the residents seeming to have disappeared a long time ago, and in a hurry as even the belongings of whoever owned the place remained.

"Woah—spooky," Kambry whispered, ringing the golden bell that sat just beside the open slot of the reception desk.

The tinkling sound echoed through the reception area, much louder than any of them were expecting, putting them on guard.

"Don't do that." Patti shuddered, the place giving her the creeps.

"Sorry." She slouched her shoulders, the grin on her face revealing that she still found the situation a little amusing.

The sound of metal hitting the floor made them all stop, turning to find the source of the noise. Zayra stared down at the patterned rug, her hands dropped by her sides, her shield lying on the ground by her feet.

"Something wrong, Hun?" Wilfred moved closer to his wife, waving a hand in front of her face when she didn't respond.

Her head shot up to meet his worried face, her eyes black as night. Her body shifted, and bringing the sword up quickly, she aimed for his torso, the metal shrieking as it clashed with Wilfred's chest plate. Jumping backward, he found himself confused, his enemy now the woman he loved.

"Zayra?" He cried, demanding to know what had gotten into her.

"What's happening?" Patti asked aloud, her arrow trained on her comrade.

"I don't know, but I'd rather us not fight to the death with one of our own." Dean searched for a way out as he spoke, finding one in the form of a staircase that led up to the guest rooms.

"Everyone move for the stairs on three," He instructed, already beginning to back away from the rogue teammate. "One...two...three!" He pulled Wilfred by the back of his collar, knowing he wouldn't readily leave his wife in an unknown state.

Zayra took another swing at them, just missing as Dean pulled Wilfred into his run. The remaining group members headed up the stairs, knowing that the quickest way to end the nightmare would be to find the locket and the corresponding pedestal.

Zayra followed behind them, her pace slow and steady, giving them plenty of lead. They ran down the hallway, opening the last door on the right, knowing they would eventually need to search through all of the rooms. The small space featured a bed with an outdated comforter, a desk, and two night stands complete with a matching set of table lamps.

A window near the back gave them a view of the town, the large worn-down farm-house in the distance. Dean pulled his spyglass from the satchel on his back, aiming it toward the open loft of the farmhouse, his intuition telling him to check that direction.

His teammates checked the rest of the room as he focused out the window, not noticing when Kambry suddenly went limp behind him, her arms dropping by her side.

"I found it," he announced, finding the pedestal amongst the hay as he searched the landscape with his spyglass.

Kambry took a step closer, catching Dean's attention and in the next second, her blade came down on him, falling toward his shoulder. Instinctively, he blocked, bringing up his arm in front of him, the metal of the blade hitting his arm guard.

She swung again, this time in a horizontal arc, skimming his chest plate. Dean was up against the window pane, no room to avoid the incoming blows, his teammates rushing to defend against Kambry's attacks.

Her blackened eyes stared him down, the edge of the blade slicing his cheek as the tip of the sword cracked the window behind him. Kambry bit her lip, clearly enjoying the exchange as she leaned in close, licking the blood that dripped down his cheek.

Dean stood frozen, still not sure what had happened to his comrades, her actions being completely controlled. Wilfred and Patti grabbed Kambry's arms, pulling her off of Dean. She spun, breaking free of their grasp and readjusted her grip on her sword.

"I don't want to hurt you," Patti cried out, trying to get through to her, her arrow aimed at Kambry's neck.

In the second before she released, she re-aimed the arrow, the head flying toward Kambry's calf. The arrow dug into the soft flesh of her leg, Kambry releasing a cry of agony as she pulled it out without much thought. As she took a few steps toward her targets, Patti and Wilfred stepped back, not wanting to do any more damage. As they backed toward the door, they saw Zayra getting closer in the hall, her speed having increased to a light jog.

"Shit." Dean was out of options.

Desperate to avoid a situation where he needed to fight his friends, he slammed his elbow into the weakened window, the glass shattering on impact. Wilfred and Patti understood his intention without the need to explain, and they quickly moved into position to exit through the broken window. Kambry seemed to understand as well, a grunt of frustration leaving her mouth.

Dean aimed at her feet, freezing her to the soiled carpet, just as Zayra barged through the door. He aimed in her direction, planning to do the same with her when he heard, "Woah—don't shoot." Her eyes had returned to their normal blue shade.

He exhaled, waving her toward the window, the others having already passed through.

"What happened to her?" She looked at Kambry who was fighting with the ice constraints, her eyes black and foam escaping from her mouth.

"Same thing that happened to you."

Her eyes went wide. "I wondered why I was suddenly alone," she said, passing through the window, being extra careful of the exposed shards of glass.

Wilfred and Patti waved them along, urging them to hurry up. Dean jumped the short distance to the dirt road, all four of them running full speed toward the farmhouse. The large wooden door was in reach when to Dean's left he heard a thud, two of his party members hitting the ground.

Patti straddled Wilfred, having tackled him to the ground, her bow pressed up against his throat.

"What the hell?" he choked out the words, struggling to maintain an airway.

Dean reacted immediately, throwing himself on Patti to quickly stop her from suffocating Wilfred. Wilfred gasped, the air returning to his lungs. Dean held Patti's arms down, her eyes now black, infected by whatever once controlled the other two. He tethered her to the ground using ice shackles, both on her wrists and her ankles, quickly removing himself from on top of her.

She screamed, struggling, but to no avail, then finally gave up, her body going limp. She opened her brown eyes to find a sight of the sky, Dean standing over her. Confusion crossed her features, and then fear.

"Look out!" She shouted, Dean diving away from her reaction.

Wilfred's sword sliced the air where Dean once stood, his eyes now dark as night, his breathing looking labored. Whatever had possessed them was growing tired, the movements becoming less fluid with every strike.

"Go check the loft," Dean instructed the girls, releasing Patti from the ice trap.

He grabbed a sword from his bag, blocking the path as Wilfred turned to follow. Wilfred's weapon arced from above, clashing with Dean's as he pressed his weight into the weapon, trying to knock Dean off balance. Pushing him farther from the entrance, Dean shoved the swords apart, letting Wilfred find his footing before aiming for a chest strike.

His sword in a forward motion, he noticed the moment when the color of Wilfred's eyes changed, returning to his normal blue. Seeing the blade coming his way, Wilfred flinched, his body entering a protective stance, a small cry leaving his lips. Dean stopped his sword mid swing just before it reached Wilfred's body, allowing the Osamar to relax a bit.

If Wilfred was no longer possessed, then who was? Dean thought to himself, turning toward the entrance of the barn. His gaze shifted up just as Patti's body flew through the window opening, her hands crossed in front of her, protecting her body from the blow she likely received from Zayra.

Dean dove just in time to soften Patti's fall, his hands cushioning her head against the hard dirt road. He grimaced as he stood back up, having bruised a few limbs in the process.

"Thank you," Patti said, brushing the dirt from her bottom. "She got the jump on me." Her stern glare focused on the opening of the loft.

Dean followed her gaze, finding Zayra staring down at them from the loft's window, a sadistic grin on her face.

"The pedestal is up there," Patti told him, revealing the locket in her clenched fist.

"I guess we have to get back up there."

"Zayra!" Wilfred screamed, stopping Dean before he could run into the barn.

Zayra stood on the edge of the loft's window, her back toward them, heels teetering over the edge.

What in the—? Dean didn't have time to finish his thought before the Osamar spread her arms, letting her body fall out the window. Zayra screamed as she fell, the spirit that possessed her vacating her body the moment she let herself fall, Zayra powerless to stop it.

Wilfred and Dean ran at once, both too far to cushion her fall—they could only hope the short fall wouldn't be deadly. As Zayra braced herself for the inevitable impact, a blur of black and red flew by the boys, grabbing her from midair.

"Whew—that was close." Kambry chuckled, flying in a small arch, coming to meet the waiting team members.

"Where is it now?" Dean said when the danger had passed, his gaze shifting from one member's eyes to the next, searching for the telltale sign of possession.

Coming up empty, he was ready to head back into the barn, when a brush of cool air washed over his body. His limbs tensed, his body no longer in his control as he reached for his weapon.

"Shit—it got Dean!" Patti alerted the team, pulling an arrow from her quiver as she rushed to Kambry's side.

Dean fought to hold his arm back, but his body still wouldn't listen to his commands, his sword stabbing the air in an attempt to wound his comrades.

"Get to the loft," Patti told Kambry, forcing the locket into her hand.

Wilfred's and Dean's swords were locked, neither one giving up any ground. Kambry flew up to the upper level of the barn, closing in on the pedestal that sat in the middle of a hay bale.

"GrRah!" An unknown voice screamed, Dean feeling the spirit exit his body.

He dropped his weapon, his fingers tingling as if the circulation had just been restored. In front of him was a woman, her white gown sullied and torn, and her face a ghostly pallor. Her body was transparent, her feet not touching the ground.

She shrieked—a high-pitched deafening cry— before disappearing in a blur into the farmhouse.

"She's coming!" Dean called out, rushing toward the ladder.

Before the apparition could possess Kambry, stopping her from reaching her goal, she slammed the locket into the pedestal, sending them all back to the portal entrance.

∞∞∞

The team appeared relatively relaxed this time when they faced the Minotaur guard, smiles of relief plastered on all of their faces.

"Good work everyone," Dean told them, the tingling in his limbs still very real. "Is everyone okay?" he asked, remembering that Kambry had been shot in the leg.

"All healed," she piped up, giving him a reassuring smile.

When he determined that everyone was in good health, he led them to the picnic tables to have some lunch and discuss the previous level.

"Oh crap," Dean said, his hand in his satchel as he sat down at the table. "I forgot we can only access the stuff we shoved in the void when we are inside the portal realm. So much for lunch."

Wilfred chuckled. "I'll go get us some meal sets." He stood up, eyeing the food stalls lining the street. "My treat."

"I'll come with you." Zayra left with him, knowing he would need help carrying everything back.

While they went to buy food, the rest of the party discussed the weird happenings they experienced in the portal, and ten minutes later Wilfred and Zayra returned, their hands ladened with white take-out boxes and fountain drinks. They set the meals on the table, everyone digging in gratefully.

"Are we good to continue in the maze?" Dean asked mid-meal, wondering how many levels they would be able to conquer in one day.

They had completed four so far, but Dean knew he could take on even more, he just hoped the rest of the team felt the same.

"Hell yea, we should continue!" Kambry said enthusiastically, showing no signs of tiring out.

The rest of the team agreed, everyone quickly finishing their meals so they could get back in the fight. After clearing the table, they headed back to the line, the amount of participants in the maze seeming to have increased once reaching afternoon hours.

They joined the longer line, knowing it would be a wait before they could enter themselves. Twenty minutes later and they were finally standing in front of the Minotaur guard, Dean eager to place his hand on the pedestal.

"Dean and my team wish to go to level fifteen, we understand the consequences."

The guard nodded him through, the portal shimmering in a pale purple hue. Dean checked to make sure everyone was ready and then stepped through, curious as to what the level would hold.

∞∞∞∞

Level fifteen featured a rocky terrain, the entire area a mix of burnt red and orange. The team found themselves standing on the ledge of a cliff looking down into a deep canyon. At the bottom they saw hundreds of little green goblins, and in the center on a chair decked out with dried leaves, sat a slightly larger goblin.

Dean pulled his spyglass from the satchel, aiming it toward the mass of goblins.

"The locket is around the high goblin's neck. That should be fun to get."

"Let me try for it," Kambry said, stretching her wings, her toes inching closer to the edge of the cliff.

"Wait...if you get captured, we haven't thought of how to get down just yet, so you would be on your own," Dean warned her, needing some time to think.

"I can shoot from here, but I don't think I have enough arrows even if we use our entire supply." Patti unstrapped her quiver, filling it to capacity before counting out the number of shots she could take.

Looking at the expansive landscape, Dean remembered the statues they brought with them. "Droosca," he whispered with his hand in his bag, the statue entering his grip a moment later.

He set the small figure down on the ground in front of them, taking a few steps back.

"They only work in solo leveling, remember?" Kambry reminded him.

Damn, he inwardly cursed their luck--the level would have been so much easier with flying transportation. When Dean moved to pick up the statue, clear tendrils of magic began to surround the body of the dragon, stopping him in place. A minute later the statue was gone, a full sized dragon in its place, Droosca's green and black stripes doing a poor job of remaining inconspicuous in the setting.

"Well, that's new," Kambry said, surprised by the occurrence.

"Has that ever happened before?" Patti asked, not too familiar with the portal rules.

"Not that I know of," Wilfred and Zayra spoke in unison, just as surprised as Kambry to see a pet come to life with a full team present.

"I'm not going to question it." Dean laughed, his plan coming together.

He wanted to attack from the sky, catching the goblins below off guard, but the dragon and its bright color palette could easily be spotted from the canyon below, the goblins already taking a defensive stance against the intruder. They wasted no time moving into position, shielding the high goblin who wore a straw crown as she sat on her throne. *So much for the element of surprise*, Dean thought, too late to change what had already occurred.

He signaled to his dragon, letting her know they would need a ride. It looked as though she rolled her eyes, not too keen on having human riders, but eventually conceded, lowering her head so they could climb aboard.

When the last of the party members climbed on Droosca's back, she went over the edge, gracefully gliding toward the waiting goblins. Kambry cheered excitedly, jumping from the cliff after them, her outstretched wings catching her mid fall, until she too glided toward the enemy.

Droosca took the initiative to start the battle, her fire breath bathing the terrain in a deadly glowing orange light, the affected goblins screaming in agony as the flames consumed their flesh.

"Get me in close," Dean yelled over the whipping wind, patting the base of the dragon's neck.

Droosca seemed to understand Dean's intent, the dragon swooping low enough for him to jump from her back. He rolled when he hit the ground, protecting his legs, and immediately entered a fighting stance, his open palm outstretched in front of his body.

When he regained his bearings, he fired a beam of lightning into the crowd of goblins, slowly shifting its trajectory to encompass more enemies. After a few seconds, he let the energy subside, revealing the extent of the damage. A good third of the monsters had been eliminated just by Droosca and Dean's attack alone, making them feel a bit better about being outnumbered by such a large ratio.

Dean heard the familiar fwip of an arrow finding its mark behind him, and he turned to find a downed goblin, Patti having no problems adjusting to shooting from a flying mount. Dean pulled a javelin from his bag, holding it like a pointed battering ram against the opponents that stood before him.

"Move or die," he shouted, starting his forward run, the stick piercing the bodies of several goblins until he had to abandon the weapon.

In the midst of a crowd of goblins, he reached for his sword and shield, their close proximity demanding a close range weapon. The goblins backed up initially, seeing the newly acquired weapon, but soon they were replaced by weapon wielding goblins, each holding a crudely made spear.

Kambry was circling above them, trying to find a place to descend, but the thick cluster of goblins made it a difficult task.

"Dean, my staff!" she called down to him as she passed.

Dean quickly pushed off the goblin that ran spear first into his shield, taking the brief reprieve to retrieve Kambry's staff from his bag. He threw it into the air, hoping she would be able to catch it mid-flight, and quickly returned to the horde that surrounded him on all sides.

Feeling the wave getting too close for comfort, he released another energy blast, carving a path through the goblins and toward the queen. Droosca and company attacked the goblins behind Dean's position, making sure there was enough distance between him and the fire blasts that Droosca released into the crowd.

When her flames disappeared, the goblin bodies littered the canyon. Wilfred and Zayra hopped from Droosca's back, weapons ready, as they ran toward the main boss. Patti decided she could best help from a higher position and remained on Droosca's back, shooting arrow after arrow into the crowd, each arrowhead finding a mark.

A blast of fire lit up the sky, Kambry's staff trained on the goblin queen, her straw crown left burning. The creature let out an angry cry, pointing to the source of her discomfort as the other goblins obeyed her orders, turning on Kambry.

The crowd soon moved in her direction, Kambry quickly retreating to higher airspace. Dean used the goblin's distraction against them, finding a clear path to the queen goblin, the locket gleaming around her deep green neck.

Far from his position, Wilfred and Zayra slashed through the stragglers, taking out anyone who dared to face them. Dean was close to the goal now, the goblin queen crying out for her subordinates to protect her, but to no avail. He ran full speed toward the idle queen, thrusting his sword into her abdomen, pinning her to the chair that she refused to vacate.

She squirmed, trapped in her seat, still trying to call for reinforcements. Not sure when her call would be answered, Dean released the hilt of his sword, quickly grabbing the locket from around her neck. He slammed it onto the waiting pedestal, a quick flash of light bringing them back to the portal entrance.

∞∞∞∞

Dean blinked, his body relaxing in the familiar surroundings. He turned to congratulate his team, when he noticed Wilfred gripping his forearm, blood dripping on the cobblestone below.

"Let's go sit down," he told them, Kambry already hovering over Wilfred and his wound.

Once they were seated at a picnic table, Wilfred removed his hand, revealing a pretty deep puncture wound, surely the result of taking one of the goblins' spears head on.

"Sorry—I was careless," he said meekly, grimacing in pain.

"I'm sorry, too. I didn't realize you were injured or we could have waited for you to recover in the portal."

"Don't worry, I've got this," Kambry said, placing both her palms over the open wound.

A soft yellow glow resonated from her palms, slowly encompassing Wilfred's forearm until it was enveloped by the light. A few moments later she removed her hands, the light fading, revealing the unblemished skin on his arm, the healing so complete it was as though he was never injured in the first place.

"Thank you."

"Don't mention it." Kambry smiled, inwardly happy that her newer healing magic had been helpful to the team.

"Alright team. I think we can get in a few more levels today, what do you think?" Dean presented the question, eagerly awaiting his team's response.

Quick answers of enthusiastic yeses made the decision unanimous, the group heading back into the line for what seemed like the tenth time that day. The Minotaur guard didn't even seem surprised when they approached.

Before he started the entry statement, he decided to bring up the glitch with the statuette, wanting to know if it was a common occurrence.

"Have pets ever manifested in the team portal before?" Dean tested the guards reaction.

"Never," he replied simply.

"So it was a glitch that ours was able to spawn?"

"No glitches, no bugs whatsoever can occur within the Mixonian portals. No pets can spawn in team portals."

"But, I just told you, ours did."

"Impossible. Or are you trying to get me to strike your last level from your records so that you may redo number fifteen?"

"No--definitely not that." Dean dropped his argument, deciding the guard would never admit to any faults with the portal.

Even more confused about how they were able to summon Droosca in the previous level, Dean tried not to dwell on it, figuring they could use it to their advantage. Set in his decision, Dean once again half-assed the entry statement, before he led his team into the lilac colored portal.

∞∞∞∞

"Level sixteen," Dean repeated when he stepped out into the small room.

The lighting flickered ominously, a creaking sound erupting with every small movement made from the team. The five of them were cramped in the small space, the shiny metal door and illuminated numbers in front of them, letting them know they were in an elevator.

Patti pressed the open button, expecting the familiar ding of the elevator to ring out as the door slid open, but nothing happened. A bit frustrated, she pushed the button a few more times, hoping the device would register her intentions to leave the enclosed space.

When that didn't work, she tried the call button, figuring the results would be the same. Static rang out over the loudspeaker in response, the sound growing more intense by the second. Everyone covered their ears, as a high pitched shriek joined in the static.

"Turn it off," Kambry yelled, clutching her head as the pain from the sound forced her into a crouching position.

With one hand still on her ears, Patti slammed the call button again, and then again. Finally on the fifth time, the noise stopped, blissful silence filling the elevator once more.

"Whew," she exhaled, checking her fingertips for blood, her head still throbbing.

"I don't like this," Zayra whispered, her breathing becoming labored.

"I know—hopefully we will get out of here soon." Wilfred turned his pleading eyes on Dean, wanting him to quickly find the solution to their predicament.

"Well, if the door won't open itself, we will just have to make it open," Dean spoke confidently, trying to reassure his party members. "Javelin," he said, reaching into his satchel to pull out the long weapon.

He wedged the sharp tip into the line that marked where the two doors met, putting all of his weight against it in an attempt to wedge the doors open. Patti joined in, hoping the additional weight would be enough to see some progress.

Instead of the doors opening as intended, the javelin bent in the direction of the applied weight, rendering it useless.

"Fook," Dean huffed, throwing the useless weapon on the elevator floor. He wouldn't give up. "Maybe this instead." He pulled out his sword, hoping the metal would be strong enough to withstand the pressure.

He tried again. The doors shrieked, the mechanics fighting a difficult battle against the unnatural opening method. Once the elevator doors were open, the team was left facing another closed door, one that had level sixteen sprayed in black paint across its surface.

They gave this door the same treatment, wedging the sword's tip into the gap and applying pressure until it opened. Another deafening screech echoed through the elevator shaft as the doors were forced apart.

The team found themselves staring into an overly white hallway, the lighting dim and unreliable as it, like the elevator's lighting, flicked on and off sporadically.

"Well that's not creepy at all," Kambry mused, her eyes searching the seemingly empty hall for any enemies.

Zayra pushed through the group who chose to remain in the elevator, taking deep, calming breaths once she had exited the small space.

"Sure beats being stuck in there," she breathed out the words between breaths, having yet to really take in the surroundings.

"Think it's a hospital?" Patti exited next, feeling that the white tile and walls gave off a medical vibe.

"Stay alert," Dean told the team, moving to the front of the group to lead the way. "I'm sure we are not alone."

Over the next three hours, Dean's statement proved to be very wrong. In fact, they hadn't encountered a single living thing, friend or foe, throughout their entire exploration of the hospital.

They started with a sense of fear, checking each room thoroughly as they remained on guard, expecting an enemy to pop out at any moment. Exam rooms, storage closets filled with filing cabinets and even the cafeteria were turned upside down searching for the locket, but nothing was found—no pedestal, no locket, no threats.

The halls remained suspiciously quiet as they entered the next room, finding an x-ray machine and other medical equipment.

"How is there nothing in this whole damn place?" Patti questioned, flipping through a stack of blank papers on the side table.

Dean opened a closet in the back, the shelves filled with bedding, cloth gowns and lead aprons. Still no locket. He exhaled heavily, feeling the stress of the extended hours of searching, but they knew they would remain on the level until they found what they were searching for.

"We'll split up and search," he decided.

Over the past three hours there had been no enemy encounters making him believe the level would be safe enough to explore alone. The team split, each member taking a different room on the floor.

"We'll meet back by the open elevator when we are done," Dean said before heading off on his own.

There were several places marked for elevators on level sixteen of the hospital, but the only one with actual doors was the one where the group spawned. The rest were nothing but doors painted onto walls with a label that read elevator. The team quickly concluded that this meant the level they appeared on was the only floor that made up level sixteen of the maze.

Another two hours later and the last of the party members gathered by the open elevator.

"Please tell me you found something," Patti pleaded with Wilfred as he stood next to his wife.

"Nothing. I searched the rooms twice, but I couldn't find anything. I don't know what we are missing."

"What are we missing?" Dean repeated the words, his mind retracing their steps since the start of the level.

"I wonder what's the longest anyone has been stuck in a level," Patti moaned, sliding her back against the wall until her butt hit the floor.

Kambry sat down next to her, the exhaustion of the day catching up to her.

"What if we are trapped here for days and we have to murder each other just to get out of the portal?" Kambry cried out, letting her overactive imagination get the best of her.

"No one is murdering any one." Dean stopped her thoughts before they could spiral out of control. He knelt in front of her, his hand gently caressing hers. "We've got this...don't give up just yet." One side of his mouth curved up into a smile.

Her body visibly relaxed a bit, his confidence reassuring. When Dean moved to stand, an area on the ceiling of the elevator caught his attention.

"Maybe we have been going about this all wrong," he murmured, going back into the small, dimly lit room.

On the ceiling he noticed a service door, the nearly hidden exit leading to the top of the elevator. *It's worth a shot,* he told himself, waving over Wilfred, Patti and Kambry. Zayra chose to stay in the hall, not wanting to risk bringing on another panic attack.

Dean and Wilfred held out their hands, Kambry using them as steps to get closer to the ceiling. Dean wanted to go himself, but knew she would be much easier to lift. She pushed the metal plate aside, revealing the inner workings of the elevator, the cable that held the metal box leading all the way to the top of the building.

Wilfred and Dean lifted their arms, Kambry pulling herself up into the space. A few seconds passed before she stuck her head back through the opening, her hair falling in disheveled strands around her face.

"It's really up here," she said with a mix of relief and sarcasm, realizing they wasted over five hours running in circles.

"Well, what are you waiting for?" Patti stuck out her hip, her hand resting on it. "Get us out of here."

Kambry grinned in response, lifting her head back through the trap door. Another moment later and the whole team had been teleported from the maze, the same guard waiting for them at the portal's entrance. Like usual, their weapons had been returned to them, but the javelin that Dean had bent trying to force the doors of the elevator open remained as such, the broken weapon lying on the ground by his feet.

He scooped it up, looking for a place to properly dispose of it. The Minotaur guard recognized his intention and pointed across the street, toward a large dumpster situated in one of the alley ways.

"Thanks," he acknowledged the guard who had already turned his attention to the next waiting party.

Dean jogged the short distance to the dumpster, quickly throwing the broken weapon in before heading back to his teammates. On his way he saw a sign for an inn, reminding him just how long they had been fighting in the maze. In Mixonia, it was easy to forget time, the place having no real sun to remind guests of how many hours had actually gone by.

Mixonia remained bright at all times, accommodating the visitors that came from different planets across the galaxy, but despite this, the people who lived there still needed to sleep. So instead of true nighttime darkness, if you chose to stay in one of their numerous inns, they offered blackout devices that would give their guests the feeling of night—at least at the higher end inns.

"Should we stay here for the night or head home?" Dean asked as he rejoined the group.

"Oh you should definitely try out one of Mixonia's inns if you can," Sable appeared before them, her long blonde hair trailing down her back. "Well—WE should try out one of their inns," she re-stated, giving Kambry and Dean a seductive wink.

"It's good to see you, Sable." Dean brushed off her offer for now, genuinely happy to see her after weeks of radio silence.

"I was recharging, getting ready for an extended stay at your estate—I wanted to surprise you all." She blushed, her eyes shifting toward the ground before she realized what she was saying. "Anyway—I saw you enter the maze quite a bit today."

Dean filled her in about his talk with the gods and their decision to test their skill level to the extreme. She simply nodded as she listened, not wanting to interfere with his plans.

"So that's where we are now. We just finished level sixteen and are about to get some sleep. Tomorrow we will attempt more levels before heading back to the estate to rest—then rinse and repeat until we all die on a level twice," he shrugged, having given the same spiel so many times already that the thought of setting out for death no longer phased him.

"Well you are in luck, I know the perfect place for you to rest tonight." She seamlessly slipped her hand into Dean and Kambry's, entwining their fingers as she led them to the inn Dean had seen signage for earlier.

"And here I thought it would be some obscure place," Patti blurted, a bit disappointed it was not even a minute from the portal square.

661

"There is a reason it is front and center, after all, it is the best," she responded in a sassy tone, releasing Dean and Kambry's hand so she could push open the gilded double doors.

Dean walked to the reception desk where a short female with thick circular glasses stood behind the counter. When she saw them come in, she smiled brightly and said, "Welcome to the Traveler's Nest, do you need a room for the night?"

"Yes—three rooms actually."

Zayra blushed slightly behind Dean, knowing his purpose for the additional rooms.

"Here you are sir," the host with shining purple eyes said, sliding three silver keys toward Dean. "That will be half a token and breakfast is included."

It seemed a bit steep, but considering how many tokens they just earned in the maze, Dean chose not to dwell on it. Instead, he slid his locket to the receptionist, the number etched onto it decreasing to 36.2 to pay the hotel bill.

Once the keys were handed out, they went to their respective rooms, Patti having one all to herself. Sable slapped Dean's ass as he entered the room, a seductive smile on her face. Kambry giggled, placing the do not disturb hanger on the handle before closing the door behind them.

FOUR

TUCKER

Intergalactic Highway- Space

T he spaceship whirled as it exited hyper-speed, the ship having reached its limit for the day, settling back into an easy glide. Tucker sat at the controls, checking out the map of their destination. The Dwarven god had been very particular about where he should drop off his captive, but every time he went to view it on the digital map, the screen glitched, the image flickering a few times before returning to normal.

No matter how many times he checked, the location seemed to have nothing there. No planets, no space stations—nothing. Was he really supposed to drop this girl off in the middle of space?

"Are you checking that again?"

Two arms snaked around Tucker's neck, the breath of the speaker hot next to his ear.

"You know, you could just pretend like you dropped me off and I can come with you to the new planet," Lexis cooed, trying to convince the man not to leave her to die in space.

Tucker huffed, Lexis certainly wasn't the easiest prisoner. Not two minutes after the gods had disappeared was she out of her ropes and exploring the spaceship. Now, almost a month into their journey, she knew the spaceship like the back of her hand.

"Bamba," Tucker called, prying Lexis' arms from around his neck. "The prisoner escaped again."

Bamba entered the room, having just reached the flight deck after searching the rest of the ship for the escapee. "Sorry boss—she's quick," Bamba huffed, grabbing Lexis's arm roughly.

"Ouch—okay. I'm going." She pulled herself free, heading in the direction of her quarters. "Just think about it, okay?" She winked at Tucker before disappearing around the corner.

Tucker rubbed his temples with his fingertips, the beginning of a headache coming on. He had a lot of those these days, the stress of angering both the gods and Dean, who seemed to be gaining even more traction as the champion of Oakley, weighing heavily on his consciousness.

He didn't need this shit. He simply wanted to use the money he had earned—if he could even call it that—to live a lavish life. Maybe he would continue his mining front on the side— even enter Mixonia again if it was in the cards for him.

But that all depended on his choice now—whether or not he would follow through with Tarreen's plan to eliminate Min's daughter. Even he wasn't sure what his final decision would be, but at the very least he wanted to see what was waiting for them at this precise location.

By his calculations they had over two months of space travel left until they reached the coordinates given to him by the dwarven god. Maybe that would buy him enough time to make his decision.

Bamba entered the room, plopping down in one of the control chairs, "The prisoner has been taken care of," she said matter-of-factly.

Tucker scrubbed his face with his hand, his eyes turning back to the sea of stars that encompassed his ship. It would be a long two months.

Moments later Pamrii entered the room, "The prisoner has escaped her quarters."

Bamba released a strained grunt, dragging herself from the room to search for Lexis yet again that day. When the two oruks had left the room, Tucker laughed, finding the situation hilarious.

If anything, their time spent together certainly wasn't boring.

CHAPTER

FIVE

DEAN

The Traveler's Nest- Mixonia

Dean opened the curtains wide, letting the artificial light filter in through the window. Sable and Kambry stretched on the bed, the blankets strewn across their bodies barely covering their enticing assets. Dean had to look away, not wanting to be lured back into bed by his alluring lovers.

Pulling his satchel onto his back he told the girls, "I'll go see if the others are at the meeting spot yet. Join me when you finish washing up."

Sable jumped up from the bed, stopping him from leaving the room.

"I'm actually heading out first. Good luck today—I'll see you back at the estate in the evening," she whispered in his ear, tempting him further.

She kissed his cheek then sauntered over to where Kambry still lay on the bed, giving her a kiss as well.

"I can't wait to see Cassie and little Leena." She smiled brightly and with a small wave she disappeared.

Kambry pulled the sheets from her body, her beautiful curves in full view. Dean couldn't help but stare as she made a show of walking to the shower.

"I'll meet you in a bit," she cooed, "unless of course you want to join me."

His resolve broken, he dropped his satchel on the ground, shedding his clothing as he walked to the bathroom to accept Kambry's invitation.

Thirty minutes later the two exited the hotel room together, both feeling clean and satisfied. They walked side by side to the small dining area within the inn, finding Zayra, Wilfred and Patti already seated at one of the booths.

"Have you been waiting long?" Kambry asked as she slid into her seat.

"No, we just got here as well." Patti smiled, taking a sip of her water.

A waiter came and asked for their orders, each of them hastily picking something from the laminated menu.

When he walked away Dean began addressing his party, "Okay. New day, same game plan." He rubbed his palms together revealing his eagerness. "We'll head into the portals after breakfast and work through as many as we can today. As long as there are no deaths, we should manage about the same as yesterday. Say six or so. Even more if we manage to avoid getting stumped on a level."

The team agreed quickly, their conversation switching to other things when the food arrived. Dean shoveled forkfuls of eggs into his mouth, unintentionally quickening the pace of his teammates. Once the meal concluded, they left the hotel, dropping the keys back in the designated drop box as they passed through the front door.

Dean noticed a scoreboard on the side of the inn as they exited and couldn't help but find out where the Suca and the Core stood in the games. He pressed his hand lightly on the board, revealing the information. It read: Core 42, the core reclaiming their lead against the Suca after a previous loss.

"Che—" Dean let his hand drop from the board, not liking the information it displayed.

He jogged over to meet his teammates who seemed to have no interest in learning just how far behind the Suca were in the battle for the planet. They quickly joined the line for the portals, the inn being so close that there was literally no commute time, allowing them to get straight to work.

"Dean and my team wish to go to level seventeen and we understand the consequences," Dean told the Minotaur guard as he placed his hand on the pedestal.

The guard nodded, the portal shifting to a mix of blue and purple.

"Let's do this," Dean said, taking a confident step into the shimmering portal.

∞∞∞∞

Dean stepped into a frozen landscape, white covering the ground as far as the eye could see. Trees surrounded their position, a light snow falling overhead.

"Holy mother of creation," Patti griped, rubbing her arms to produce heat. "What kind of hell did we step into?"

"The frozen kind," Kambry quipped back, breathing out slowly, amused by her visible breath.

"What do we see?" Dean began searching their surroundings trying to find an indication of where the locket would most likely be hidden.

"White, white and more white," Zayra responded, turning in circles.

"Wait...I see something," Wilfred spoke up, his finger pointing in the distance.

Dean followed the path of Wilfred's finger, finding a blur of brown in the distance, situated on the side of the mountain. It appeared to be a cabin, a small refuge in the midst of the frozen landscape.

"Good eye." He nudged Wilfred's shoulder gratefully.

Readjusting his satchel, Dean's footsteps crunched in the snow as he started in the direction of the cabin.

"Remember to keep an eye out, we don't want to miss anything. The pedestal could be buried in the snow for all we know," Dean reminded the team, knowing that the obvious choice was not always the correct one.

As the trees began to thin around them, the depth of the snow increased, their legs sinking in the wet slush up to their knees.

"We are going to be popsicles by the time we make it to that house." Patti shuddered, her armor doing little to keep out the cold.

Dean tried to remember if they had brought any warmer clothing, but that had never been high on the priority list. Now that they had a seemingly endless storage bag, he made a mental note to stock up on winter gear. Still that didn't help them now.

"We only have some additional under clothes," Dean informed the group, kneeling down to collect the gear from his bag.

"It will be easier to move through the snow without our heavy gear," Patti made the observation, her guards coming off to lessen the amount of weight she had to pull through the snow.

The rest of the team agreed, ditching their armor in favor of a second set of long johns, hoping it would be enough to keep them warm until they could reach the cabin. As they walked, the house disappearing into the landscape, they heard a low growl echo through the wide space.

Everyone froze, hoping they were hearing things. The growling grew louder, whatever was making the sound getting closer. Before they recognized what was responsible for the sound, the team was surrounded.

Large white wolves stalked them from all sides, their fangs bared, drool escaping from the corners of their mouths. *How did we miss them approaching?* Dean asked himself, surprised to find that the wolves did not sink into the snow despite their massive size.

The team moved closer to one another, the wolves taking another step toward them, licking their lips as they eyed their next meal. A whistle halted the intense growling, the wolves taking a step back. A man dressed from head to toe in white fur stepped out from behind the trunk of a tree, a silver whistle in his hand.

He stroked the fur of the wolf beside him, eyeing up Dean and his party, silently deciding their fate.

"What did you find, Percy?" he spoke, his voice low and raspy.

"Look, we don't mean you any harm, we just need to find a gold locket. Have you seen it?" Kambry asked the man, taking a chance that he would lead them to what they needed.

"Yes. I know of it. So you are trying to steal from me?" Anger trickled into his tone.

Shit. Dean knew they weren't going to be able to turn the conversation around. He backed up slowly, signaling for his team to do the same, the dense snow making their retreat slow moving. A grin crossed the face of the man, revealing a snaggle tooth, his teeth a deep yellow.

They reached a break in the snow, the trees more abundant, providing a canopy to block out the snow. When their legs were free of the slushy restraint, another whistle echoed through the landscape, the wolves heading in their direction.

"Run!" Dean shouted, bolting into a sprint, the wolves gaining ground behind them.

Dean slid to a stop, knowing the wolves would catch up to them in no time. He needed to buy his team some time. He turned his lightning magic against them, blasting those that came at him from the front. A few evaded the bolt, passing Dean as they ran for his party members.

Oh no you don't. He shifted his position to follow the passing wolves, sending another lightning beam their way. He hit one, a sickening yelp confirming the strike, but the other still ran for his teammates. He lined up his next shot, the distance still close enough for his beam to be effective, and prepared to fire.

Before he could release his magic, he felt a sharp pain in his right shoulder and then a weight was pushing him to the frozen ground. He hit the dirt, struggling against the body of the wolf as it tore into his shoulder, trying to rip his flesh from his bones.

The shot already prepared, he adjusted his target. He placed his palm on the beast and fired, the thing not even knowing what hit it as its body flew away from Dean's, the strength of the blast ripping the wolf in two. The lifeless head remained attached to Dean's shoulder, the fangs deeply embedded in his skin.

He pried the jaw open, the puncture wounds immediately releasing a stream of blood that trickled down his chest. Suddenly he found himself regretting having taken off his armor. He didn't have time to tend to the wound, another wolf already upon him.

Hoping the natural regeneration of the portal would heal him before he bled out, he blasted the incoming wolf and ran toward the cabin. He soon found himself back with his teammates, trudging through the deep snow once more, the cabin within reach.

"Hurry up!" Kambry shouted from within the small house, holding onto the door for dear life as she prepared to slam it shut.

Dean pushed through the last of the snow and entered into the warmth of the cabin, small puddles forming under his feet as the snow fell from his clothing and melted on the warm floor. Kambry slammed the door shut, searching for items she could barricade the entrance with.

"Wait!" Zayra cried out, everyone jumping from the sudden outburst. "Where's Wilfred? Wilfred's not here." She scanned the faces of her teammates, not finding the one she sought.

He's still outside. Dean ran to the window, trying to find their missing party member, but couldn't spot him in the surrounding terrain.

"I have to go after him," Zayra concluded, trying to push Kambry from blocking the door.

"I'll get him," Dean reassured her, pushing her back into the living space.

"Barricade the door until you see us coming," Dean told them, signaling to Kambry to let him through.

Her eyebrows furrowed, but she complied, hastily shutting the door behind him and reaching for a chair to wedge under the door handle.

"Fook." The wind slapped Dean in the face, the air feeling much colder after having stepped inside a warm house.

He trudged through the snow back toward the denser trees, no sign of Wilfred or any of the wolves just yet. When he crossed the threshold into shallower snow, he increased his speed, bringing him closer to the wolves that sprinted toward him.

Dean reached for his sword, not sure how many more lightning beams he would be able to manage, and halted his run, waiting for the wolves to reach him. The first one leapt toward him, fangs ready to rip out his throat, but Dean was prepared.

He sliced the beast in front of him, a dying yelp leaving the wolf's mouth as it hit the ground with a thud. The rest of the wolves bypassed him, heading for the cabin behind him. He only hoped the girls were ready for them.

Another scream reverberated through the cold air, the shriek of metal against metal preceding the desperate cry of pain. Dean ran in the direction of the sound, soon finding Wilfred on the ground, a bear trap closed on his ankle.

He frantically pulled at the device, trying to free his injured leg, but it was to no avail, the device not even budging. Dean ran forward, but hid when another form came into view—the wolfman, walking slowly toward his trapped victim.

Dean put his back against the trunk of the tree, trying to diminish his presence while he prepared another lightning attack. The man held an ax, letting it drag across the forest floor as he made his way over to the wounded Osamar. *It's now or never*, Dean told himself, leaving his place of safety to confront the man.

Their eyes locked and Dean released his lightning beam, the blast heading straight for his target. The light enveloped the wolf man, but when it faded moments later, the man still stood, unaffected by Dean's magic. *Dammit.*

The man raised his ax above his head and Dean ran in their direction, sword ready, but he was too far from his enemy—too far from his friend. The ax came down on Wilfred's leg, the sheer force behind the weapon slicing the Osamar's foot clean off, his cries filling the silent forest. He raised the ax again, this time aiming for Wilfred's throat, but Dean intervened, the ax head clashing with his sword.

Dean pushed the man back, his body slamming into a nearby tree, then drove his sword forward, hoping to pierce his body and pin him to the tree. The wolfman dodged, quickly recovering his bearings and swung his ax wildly in Dean's direction. While able to keep up with the wolf man's attacks for a while, the pace and haphazardness of the swings became increasingly impossible to follow, the ax blade slicing into Dean's skin on more than one occasion.

"You sick bastard," Dean goaded him, the flat of his sword blocking the incoming ax strike.

The man was somehow protected by an unseen barrier, so Dean, thankful for all the practice he had put into his magic, switched to a combo attack, figuring his lightning magic would be useless alone. Dean shut his eyes releasing an intense bright light, blinding the man, his eyes burning from the close proximity.

Dean opened his eyes, revealing the man in a confused state as he scrubbed at his eyes trying to restore the vision. Dean needed to act fast before the wolf man's vision recovered. He focused on the patch of snow and dirt under the man and froze the ground beneath his feet.

The man, unable to see what happened, slipped, his head slamming into the trunk of the tree behind him. The blow knocked him unconscious, giving Dean the upper hand. He turned his attention to Wilfred who had passed out either from the pain or the blood loss.

He removed his shirt in a hurry, kneeling down to assess the injury. Using a dagger from his satchel, he ripped Wilfred's pant leg up to his knee and placed his shirt above the joint. Dean searched his surroundings, grabbing the nearest stick that he thought would work as a windlass.

Then he started twisting. He was thankful Wilfred wasn't awake for that part, the tourniquet needing to be tight enough to stop the bleeding. When this happened, he secured the stick in place, and went back for the foot. He wasn't sure how recovery would be in the portal, but he thought he should bring it along just in case.

Dean glanced at the wolfman, making sure he remained unconscious, then moved to the bear trap. He stepped on the springs, using his own weight as the force to open the jaws, the metal creaking as it moved. Dean lifted the limb from the trap and jumped back, the trap slamming shut.

A rustling caught his attention, the man beginning to stir. Dean knew he wouldn't make it back through the snow before the man would be after him.

It was an exhausting task alone and now he needed to lug a whole other person with him. He made his decision; he couldn't let the man get up, couldn't let him live —not if he wanted to make it through the level with all of the team's tokens.

Using a dagger he pulled from his satchel, he crept closer to the man, trying not to alert him, but the sound of the feet on the frozen earth was unmistakable. The man panicked, only hearing his potential attacker, his eyes still blinded, and frantically began searching for his weapon. The ax was close by, but Dean didn't give him the chance to find it, his fist that clutched the dagger coming down hard on the crouching man.

His blade sunk into the wolfman's throat, and he jerked it to the side before pulling it free, the wound widening, blood pouring down his neck. The wounded man tried to curse Dean, but his enraged cries turned to gurgles as he choked on his own blood, finally falling to his side on the cold ground.

His opponent defeated, Dean scooped up Wilfred, carrying him princess style toward the cabin. Dean shivered when his legs plunged back into the deep snow, his bare chest taking the brunt of the wind. He struggled, the house coming closer, but remembered his other problem—the horde of wolves that surrounded the entrance, eagerly searching for a way inside.

He approached from the side and realized the door was open, the wolves having breached the front, meaning the girls were inside fending off the creatures. Praying he wouldn't be spotted, Dean trudged to the back of the cabin, thankful that no wolves had circled around the house.

He pried open the window to the back bedroom and hoisted Wilfred's body into the room. His arms were numb at this point, his pants coated in slush, his teeth chattering. When Wilfred hit the floor, Dean pulled himself through the small opening, making sure to shut and lock it behind him.

Lifting Wilfred onto the bed, he placed his severed foot by the open wound, wondering if they would somehow reconnect as his body began to heal. As he turned to leave the room, wanting to help out the girls, a glimmer caught his attention in the back closet, the slits in the door just revealing the object hidden within.

He pulled the doors open, finding the pedestal and the locket hanging from the clothes rack. He glanced back at Wilfred, his face in a grimace, beads of cold sweat forming on his forehead. He couldn't take them out of the portal—not yet. Not while Wilfred's foot remained separated from his body.

Much like his dented javelin, Wilfred's foot would remain that way and Dean didn't think Kambry's healing magic would be enough to regrow limbs. They would have to wait it out.

Shutting the closet door, Dean headed for the living space, the sounds of a struggle filtering into the bedroom. He pushed the door open cautiously, ready to join the fight, but not wanting to draw attention to Wilfred's position. The scene he came upon was a bloody one.

Bodies of wolves were scattered throughout the small space, blood coating almost every surface. Three live wolves paced toward the girls who maintained a fighting stance. The couch had been pressed against the door, stopping any more wolves from entering the house, their frustrated growls entering through the cracked window.

"Dean!" Kambry exclaimed when she saw him enter the room.

He readied his sword, running to stand beside her. The girls' clothes were covered in blood, but from what he could tell none of it was theirs.

"Where's Wilfred?" Zayra asked, never taking her eyes off the wolf in front of her.

"He's in rough shape, but he is alive," Dean responded, knowing she wouldn't fully concentrate on the fight until he told her the truth.

The biggest of the three wolves pounced first, aiming for Kambry who stood at the forefront. As his body came down on her, she swung her sword, slicing it through the belly. It limped backwards, its innards escaping onto the floor until it finally succumbed to its wounds, dropping to the wooden floor.

Patti eliminated the next one, sending out three arrows in succession, each one hitting a vital point on the wolf. Zayra lunged for the final one, her outstretched blade just missing its white body. The wolf sidestepped her, heading straight for Dean.

A small blast of energy finished off the remaining wolf, its body essentially exploding, covering the group in a mess of flesh, fur and blood.

"Gag—" Patti made a motion as though she would throw up, her arms stretched away from her body. "Did you need to blow it up?"

"What happened to your shoulder?" Kambry asked in a concerned tone, already examining the wound, her fingertips gently prodding the injured skin. "And your shirt...where is your shirt?"

"I'm fine...."

A bang on the window in front of them caused everyone to turn toward the source. A member of the wolf pack slammed into the window again, the crack in the glass growing larger with every strike.

"Let's head to the bedroom," Dean instructed them, not knowing how long the glass would hold out.

The girls filed into the bedroom and Dean barricaded the door behind them, ready for when the wolves would inevitably make it into the house. A gasp escape Zayra's mouth as she ran over to Wilfred, immediately stroking his hair to comfort him.

Kambry and Patti looked on in silent horror, their eyes wide as they scanned over the severed limb. Dean went to the closet, pulling open the doors to reveal his find.

"The locket," Kambry said with relief, moving closer to the item.

"I figured we should try to hold out while he heals," Dean gestured toward Wilfred's body, his face still contorted in an expression of pain.

"Good thinking," she said, taking a step back.

"It would be easier if healing magic worked in here," Kambry moaned, eager to leave the level.

"I mean...the pet statues were able to be activated... it could be worth a try." Patti shrugged, encouraging Kambry to attempt a healing spell.

Kambry nodded, after all, there seemed to be some inconsistencies with the rules, so why not? She held her hands over Wilfred's wound, waiting to feel the flow of magic build in her palms.

After a minute her body slumped. "Nothing. I'm sorry."

"It's not your fault," Zayra told her, her forehead on Wilfred's.

The unicorn man's once tanned complexion resembled a sheet of paper, his prognosis seeming bleak.

"Do you think he'll make it?" Patti asked the question everyone was thinking.

"He'll make it," Zayra growled back at her. "He'll make it," she repeated her words, softer this time into Wilfred's ear.

His breathing was shallow, his brown hair matted to his forehead.

"Should we try food... or maybe a drink?" Kambry turned to Dean, unable to watch the scene between husband and wife.

"I'm not sure he is lucid enough to eat or drink anything."

"Give me a drink—I'll get him to swallow." Zayra held out her hand in Dean's direction.

Dean pulled a bottle from his bag, handing it over to Zayra. She lifted the bottle to her lips, and holding a swig in her mouth she put her lips on Wilfred's open mouth, slowly letting the liquid transfer from her to him. While some escaped from the corners of his mouth, slipping down his cheek, his swallowing reflex reacted, allowing him to ingest some of the stamina booster.

When she felt he had enough of the drink, Zayra handed the canteen back to Dean, then wiped Wilfred's mouth with her sleeve. To their surprise and delight, some of the color returned to his face, the tendons in his foot beginning to reattach as the healing process sped up.

"Thank goodness!" Zayra laid her head on Wilfred's shoulder, relief evident in her voice.

The rest of the team also gave a sigh of relief, happy to see their comrade healing at a much faster rate. A sudden bang pulled them from the moment, reminding them of their situation.

Another and then another proceeded the first, the wolves slamming their bodies against the closed bedroom door, trying to reach their prey.

"How much longer can we hold out?" Patti asked, staring at the thin plywood door.

Dean knew they would need another fifteen minutes at least, the reattachment of Wilfred's foot taking longer than anticipated. A crack accompanied the next loud bang, the door succumbing to the constant beating. It wouldn't be long now.

The next hit opened a hole in the door and Dean rushed to move the dresser in front of the open space. Kambry and Patti noticed his intent and helped out, grabbing the other side of the dresser.

"Hopefully this buys us some time." Dean eyed the barricade, knowing it wouldn't be enough.

The angry growling grew louder, the wolf's snout blocked by the wood of the dresser, pissing off the beast.

"Come on, come on," Kambry breathed out the words, her eyes shifting from Wilfred's wound to the blocked door.

"Prepare for a fight," Dean urged them, knowing it was inevitable.

The slamming continued until finally the wolves managed to break through, the dresser collapsing forward from the applied pressure. Patti immediately shot the first wolf that passed through the hole in the door, the arrowhead piercing the beast's eye. Kambry launched a fireball next, the flames colliding with the beast's body, throwing it into the living room. Each attack pushed the wolves back, but didn't deter them for long.

When the fire subsided, the wolves were immediately surrounding the hole once more, eager to get through to the other side. Dean pulled out his trident, holding it in a defensive position as he waited for the wolves to come to him.

"Come on you fooking dogs," he cried out, plunging his trident forward, the prongs making contact with the chest of an attacking wolf.

"It's attached!" Zayra shouted excitedly, jumping from the bed.

While she ran for the closet, the rest of the team held off the wolves. Zayra slammed the locket into the pedestal and in moments the team found themselves at the portal entrance, the Minotaur guard looking down at them.

∞∞∞

Kambry immediately ran to Wilfred who was lying on the cobblestone, all of his appendages were attached, but he still seemed to be in pain. She placed her palm on the wound, letting her healing magic flow into him, his expression relaxing. His eyes fluttered open, his mind taking a moment to recognize his situation.

"I'm alive...?" he questioned, surprised to find himself in one piece.

He rolled his ankle in small circles, the movement causing no pain.

"What happened?"

Dean helped him to his feet, leading him to their designated picnic table to fill him in on all the details.

"Thank you." He looked Dean in the eyes. "You could have left me behind."

"What are you talking about?" Dean clapped him on the back. "If there is a chance for all of us to make it out alive, that will be my choice every time."

Wilfred smiled meekly, feeling a bit embarrassed about being caught in the bear trap, but grateful for having such great teammates.

"So are we heading to the next one?" Kambry spoke up, shifting the discussion from the sappy route it had started down.

"That was what? Level seventeen?" Patti asked, trying to remember what their latest achievement had been.

"Yes, level seventeen. Which means...." Dean turned to Kambry. "This is where you stop."

Kambry's eyes went wide, her lips immediately turning into a pout. "What? No, not yet... please? I'm fine. The baby is fine."

"You promised Cassie."

"I did, but I didn't expect us to get through so many levels yesterday," she whined. "Just today. Let me come along for whatever we accomplish today. Then... I promise I will give up until after the baby is born." Kambry clapped her palms together, waving them slightly in front of Dean, pleading to continue.

Truthfully he didn't want to kick Kambry from the team, after all, they needed as much help as they could get.

"Fine. Just for today. But tell me if anything feels off. And we need to check the device as soon as we get back in the maze."

Kambry nodded enthusiastically. "Yes, yes. We will be super careful." She pulled the stop watch looking heart device from her pocket, the face blank, its abilities only available inside the portal.

"Okay—that's settled. Does anyone have any reservations about going back in today?" He waited for his party members to respond, looking especially long at Wilfred.

No one raised any complaints, everyone willing to continue entering the levels.

"Are you sure you're okay?" he asked Wilfred one more time, recalling his pale face from less than an hour earlier.

"Right as rain." He smiled.

"Alright, that settles it then. We'll try to reach level twenty today, then wrap it up. No need to be too ambitious."

With their goal determined, they headed back to the portal line, ready to return to the unknown. When they reached the front, Dean placed his hand on the pedestal, saying the familiar words before the guard waved him into the deep indigo portal.

∞∞∞

The last of Dean's team entered into a vast field of green. Hedges blocked their view, the maze expansive and beautiful. They faced an opening in the foliage, the leafy walls much too high to see over.

A sign to their right depicted the maze, a 'you are here' sticker showing them that they were at the start of the maze. In the center was a drawing of a pedestal, a star sticker labeling it as the final destination.

"I guess we have to make our way through to the center of the maze," Patti said, examining the board.

"Or we can just fly over it." Dean grinned, pulling the statuette of Droosca from his satchel.

Placing the figurine on the ground, he stepped back waiting for the magic to transform his pet to her full size. After a full minute of waiting, nothing happened. Not the slightest bit of magic surrounded the pet statue.

"They must have fixed the bug," Wilfred concluded, picking up the statue and handing it back to Dean.

"I thought there weren't any bugs in Mixonia," Zayra mocked the Minotaur guard, having been so sure that a glitch was impossible.

"Guess we go the old fashioned way. Don't worry, I have a pretty good memory, so I'll lead the way," Wilfred announced, confidently entering the maze.

He didn't even make it two steps in when a boxing glove sprung out from the hedge clocking Wilfred straight in the face. He hit the ground, scrambling back to the entrance.

The rest of the team couldn't contain their laughter, leaving Wilfred with a sour expression on his face.

"I'm sorry, but that was funny," Zayra said, patting him on the shoulder, her laughter flowing freely.

"Did you forget?" Kambry pointed to her back before spreading out her sleek black and red wings. "This will be over in no time."

True to her word, Kambry launched herself into the air, immediately heading for the center of the maze. Since she didn't need to walk the path, she didn't encounter any of the traps the team was sure the maze was riddled with. She touched down right beside the pedestal, picking up the locket to its left and placing it on the block of stone.

677

∞∞∞

Seconds later the team stood in front of the guard again, the level having taken less than ten minutes. Dean didn't even ask his team if they were ready, figuring there was no way they wouldn't be. Instead he placed his hand on the pedestal and said, "Dean and his team wish to go to level nineteen and we understand the consequences," not wanting to get back in the growing line.

The guard huffed, but accepted, the portal shifting to a murky purple color. The next two levels went similar to the first, the team finding the missions relatively easy in comparison to previous levels. In each, there had been some kind of work around, allowing them to use their skills to bypass the waiting enemy or obstacle, meaning they completed the level without much stress or any wasted time.

When they exited level twenty victorious, only two hours had passed since they first started leveling.

"Are we really going to call it a day after only two hours?" Kambry asked immediately after exiting the portal, her eyes pleading with Dean.

This time he did lead them to a picnic table, figuring they could have a snack while they discussed the possibility of continuing.

"We are on a roll!" Patti couldn't contain her excitement, feeling the high of victory.

"If the levels continue like this we could reach twenty-five at least by the end of today," Zayra added, clearly agreeing with the team that they should continue.

Dean handed the locket that contained the group's winnings to Zayra and Wilfred who went to grab food for the team while the others discussed the previous levels, still feeling the rush of adrenaline. When they returned, Wilfred handed the locket back to Dean, the number engraved on the surface reading 40.1.

The team grabbed their food from the tray, taking their time to enjoy the soft strawberry cakes the Osamars had chosen.

"If we are all in agreement, we can continue," Dean said at last, sticking the last sliver of cake into his mouth.

Excitement was evident from the expressions that crossed each member's face, everyone wanting to go back in. When the trash was discarded into the nearby disposal unit, the waste disappearing immediately after touching the bottom of the can, the group headed back to the portals to try their luck in level twenty-one.

∞∞∞

. . .

Levels twenty-one through twenty-three were a breeze, the puzzles direct without any surprises, the enemies easily defeated. The team returned unharmed and anxious to start the next battle. Level twenty-four featured an ancient colosseum, half the stadium resembling ruins.

Despite the rundown aesthetic, the gates in the back opened wide two minutes after they entered the level, revealing a massive boar with horns the size of tree trunks protruding from its bottom lip. The team ran around the circular stadium, the giant creature chasing them, until they were finally able to figure out a plan of attack.

Dean volunteered to take the lead, figuring his lightning beam would deal significant damage. While it did inflict damage to the boar, it wasn't enough to kill the creature in a single shot. The battle proceeded, both Patti and Zayra sustaining injuries in the process.

When the beast fell, they were all relieved, and luckily nothing further spawned, allowing them to heal and search for the locket in peace. They needed another hour just to find the locket which was hidden in a hole inside the wall of the area where the boar first emerged from.

When they returned to the portal entrance, they were understandably exhausted, but the day wasn't quite over yet.

"One more?" Kambry insisted, presenting the option as a question.

Since they hadn't lost anyone as of yet, their tokens growing to 44.1, the team agreed, immediately turning back to the Minotaur guard.

"Dean and my team wish to enter level twenty-five—we understand the consequences."

The guard nodded silently, preparing the level. The portal seemed to waver a bit, a movement Dean had never seen it make before. The aqua color shifted to burgundy before settling on a bright blue.

The guard didn't seem to notice the change, so Dean figured he was overthinking things, his party also having missed the strange occurrence. When the guard waved him on, Dean responded, being the first of his team to step into the portal.

∞∞∞∞

"Level twenty-five! We made it!" Kambry said excitedly when the last of the members spawned in the new zone.

They appeared in a field, a soft mist surrounding them, adding a dampness to the cool air. The sound of cicadas assaulted their ears, and they could see a forest and a massive tower in the distance.

"I bet you anything the locket will be at the top of that." Dean directed everyone's attention to the ominous looking tower.

"Well then, what are we waiting for?" Kambry grinned, outstretching her wings.

The rest of the team ran while Kambry flew ahead, checking the landscape for any enemies they might encounter on the way. Already in the air, Kambry circled the building, flying all the way to the top in search of any additional entry ways. Not even one small window could be seen, bricks reaching all the way to the top.

She landed by the stone structure, two giant double doors made of wood denoting the entrance. The handles were giant loops of black iron and in between the two doors was a dragon knocker. Kambry examined the doors, distractedly waving for the rest of the team to hurry up.

"We can't fly like you can," Patti huffed, out of breath from running the whole way.

"Jealous?" Kambry quipped, retracting her wings.

"A bit."

Dean placed his hand on the knocker, wondering if its presence meant that someone—or something—lived in the tower. Two strong knocks later, he stepped back, waiting for a reply. He followed the line of the tower up into the sky, the building looking much larger from a close distance.

Distracted by the sheer size of the structure, he almost didn't notice when the door popped open, leaving a small space that let the group know they could come in.

"It's open." Patti touched Dean's elbow, not wanting to be the first to explore the creepy tower.

Dean pressed lightly on the door, a shrill creak accompanying the movement as the door swung open giving the team a look inside the building. The entryway was empty save for a standing three-prong candle holder, the candles lit and illuminating the sparse area.

Dean ventured inside. To his left sat a spiral staircase, one that spanned the full length of the tower, the occasional door leading off the stairs, meaning there was more than one room in the structure.

With nothing else on the entry floor, Dean peered up the staircase before turning to his team. "Shall we?" He gestured to the flight of stairs.

Single file they walked up the stone staircase, the width only enough for one person to fit at a time. When the first door came into view, they heard a loud bang from above, causing everyone to freeze in place. The noise grew louder, like stone scraping against stone, until the source came into view.

A giant boulder just slightly smaller than the width of the staircase came careening down toward them, threatening to flatten them where they stood.

"Fooking hell," Dean yelled, the boulder getting closer.

Wilfred, who brought up the rear, turned around and began running back the way they came. Dean could tell immediately that their pace would be out matched by the speed of the boulder, so instead of following his team back down the stairs, he made a run for the doorway, praying that it wouldn't be locked.

I'm never going to live this down if I get flattened by a boulder. Dean's mind raced as he rushed toward the wooden door. His fingers wrapped around the handle and he held his breath as he turned it, the door easily opening.

With the rock speeding toward him, he stepped inside, slamming the door behind him just in time to hear the scrape of the stone speeding past the room. When he knew the danger had passed, he opened the door once more, checking on the situation. The boulder continued down the steps, his team running in full armor to avoid the crushing weight.

When they reached the end of the stairs, they dove out of the path of the stone, landing in the center of the entryway as the boulder crashed through the front door, its momentum carrying it out into the field. He jogged down the stairs, finding his team in a heap in the empty room, their breathing heavy.

"Holy mother of—- I was not expecting that." Patti exhaled, her hand on her chest as she tried to catch her breath.

"I think this will be easier without so much armor," Zayra told the group, removing her heavy outer shell.

The others were quick to follow her example, not wanting to lug around the suit should another boulder come after their lives.

"The doors are at least unlocked." Dean told them his findings, stuffing their armor into his satchel.

"Good to know," Kambry breathed out the words, her gaze staring back up the stairwell.

Now that they knew what was potentially waiting for them, the group headed back up the stairs, their pace much quicker than the first time. As they ran, they heard the familiar crash, but this time they had enough time to slip into the first room, closing the door as the boulder rushed past.

Since they were in the first room, they took the time to explore the area, searching for the pendent and the locket. The room resembled the entryway, the only feature a candle stick with three lit candles. After a minute of searching along the walls for any bricks that stood out, they concluded that there was nothing of importance in the room and decided to move on.

With the goal of reaching the second door, the team left the room, sprinting up the stairs until they reached the next empty room. This time as they closed the door, they heard the crash and waited inside the room for the danger to pass. They repeated this method until they reached the top of the stairs, the final doorway was left wide open, the next boulder magically lining up to roll down the stairs.

They squeezed through the space just as the boulder was put into position and watched as it slowly tipped forward, gravity taking control of the rest. This room was bigger than the others, boulders lined up around the perimeter, only a handful remaining. In the center sat the pedestal, a pretty obvious placement.

The party members shared a quick glance of relief as they headed to the pedestal, happy their final level for the day met their expectations.

"Can I do the honors since this will be my last level for quite some time?" Kambry asked, rubbing her belly gently.

Dean smiled, knowing it would be a difficult nine months for Kambry.

"Of course," he said, stepping aside to let her place the locket.

Kambry gripped the golden trinket, letting it hover over the pedestal and said, "Level twenty-five complete," before slamming it into place.

When the pedestal activated, the familiar light surrounded the group, everyone smiling about their accomplishment as they vanished from the tower.

CHAPTER

SIX

DEAN

Minotaur's Maze- Level Twenty-six

T he bright light faded, revealing a large crowd of people. Dean's eyebrows furrowed, confusion setting in. Wilfred stood to his right, his clothes swapped to a track suit, the letters LHF embroidered on the breast. Dean looked down, examining his own clothing, finding that he wore an identical set, one that also matched every other male that stood in the crowd around him.

"What happened to Mixonia? Who are all these people? Where are the girls?" Dean whispered to Wilfred whose expression revealed that he was just as confused about their situation as Dean was. "Wait—your horn?"

Wilfred's hands shot up to his forehead searching for the small curved horn that generally graced his forehead in Mixonia, an easy identifier of the Osamar race.

"Are we on Oakley?" he questioned, as it was the one place where his appearance changed to resemble the human race.

Dean surveyed the crowd finding only humans or other races disguised as humans amongst the crowd.

"This is definitely not Oakley," Dean replied, confident of his answer.

The two stood in a large grassy area surrounded by an iron fence. To the front was a massive wooden stage, a podium in the center. Hundreds of people filled the space, all male, their chatter loud and overwhelming. On the other side of the stage, were the females and Dean could only assume the rest of his team had ended up in that area.

A woman dressed all in white strolled across the stage, stopping when she reached the podium, signaling for the crowd to settle. The onlookers grew quiet, anticipating her speech.

"We have asked the gods for their support and they have provided. Finally we have a suitable sacrifice—one that will allow the rain to fall and the crops to flourish. Despair no longer my followers for better days are surely upon us."

She waved her outstretched arm toward the crowd stopping at the side of the stage where a muscular man rolled a covered cage up to the center of the stage.

"A blessed being," she announced as the man pulled the cover from the cage.

"Shit." Dean was already moving toward the stage, his fists clenched in anger.

Kambry's head bobbed softly, from the movement of the cage, settling only when the motion had stopped, her chin resting on her chest. Her wings had been strung out beside her, displaying them in all their glory for the entire crowd of onlookers. When they saw her, the crowd cheered, excitement permeating the area—what Dean could only describe as a prison.

"Wait, Dean...What are you going to do?" Wilfred pulled on his forearm, trying to stop his determined march.

"I'm going to get her out of there. Sacrifice? What the fook is that woman talking about? Ain't nobody using my future wife as a means to make it rain."

"Look around you—everyone is on her side. How are you going to get to Kambry if they decide to defend that psychopath?"

Dean gritted his teeth, knowing Wilfred was right. Being reckless would only put Kambry in more danger. He glared at the woman on stage instead, needing an outlet for his anger and that's when he saw it. Around her neck rested a locket, and that could only mean one thing.

"We haven't left the portals," he whispered, finding that saying it out loud somehow made it more real.

"What?" Wilfred followed his gaze trying to guess what Dean had said.

"This is a level...we never left the portals," he repeated to Wilfred, his eyes fixated on the woman in charge.

"That doesn't make any sense. We are supposed to exit after every level."

"Sense or not, this is a level, I'm sure of it."

Dean shook his arm free from Wilfred's grasp and began pushing his way through the crowd just as a chant began to fill the air.

"Locke Haven Fellowship! Locke Haven Fellowship!" They repeated in a loud and steady tone, drowning out all other noises.

Dean stopped in front of the stage, staring up at the woman responsible for caging his Dragona partner.

"Young man? What is it you want?" The lady moved to the edge of the stage, kneeling down to greet her follower.

"Release her at once, while I'm being nice. I won't ask again," he demanded as calmly as he could manage, the building rage seeping into his words.

From across the divide, Zayra and Patti spotted Dean making his stand in front of the leader. They headed in his direction, the overabundance of people making it a slow endeavor. Dean moved closer to the woman and took the chance presented to him, swiping his hand out quickly in an attempt to snatch the locket.

The woman caught his wrist mid-grab, her strength surprising and definitely not human.

Using only her fingers for leverage, she bent his hand into an uncomfortable position. "Nonsense," the woman said simply, releasing his hand to stand up from her crouched position, clearly finished with their conversation.

The rage boiled over, Dean no longer able to control his desire to end this woman and all of her followers. Electricity coursed through his veins, his hair standing on end as he fixated on eliminating the entire field of onlookers. The air of the area seemed to change, the dark clouds rolling in overhead, foreshadowing what was to come.

While unpracticed, Dean felt confident he would be able to invoke a lightning storm, the changes in the atmosphere already proving his capabilities. The woman turned back toward Dean just as the wind began to pick up, a mixture of shock and delight dominating her features.

"Just what are you?" she questioned with an excited grin, curiosity revealing itself before she felt any fear.

"I told you to release her," Dean growled, exposing his open palms to the sky.

A clash of thunder exploded in the air, silencing the rest of the crowd, their jubilant chants dying in their throats. Thick strands of brilliant white, hot energy connected to Dean's palms before dancing back into the sky. The show was enough to get the crowd running, seeking a form of protection in the nearby buildings, but Dean wasn't trying to put on a show.

The next bolt touched down in the grass after having passed through the person who stood in that spot. Screams filled the already panicked yard, the sight of the burnt and smoking body too much for the dedicated followers. As the storm raged on, gaining momentum as it grew with Dean's fury, Dean lifted himself onto the stage, his lightning filled gaze honed in on the woman in charge.

"Wait—we can talk about this," she screamed at Dean's intimidating form, taking a few steps back, suddenly willing to compromise.

As she backed away from the electrically charged human, she stumbled, her backward walk turning into a crawl. Dean easily closed the gap between them, crouching down until they were eye level once again.

"I tried to warn you," he said as he placed his hand on her shoulder.

She flinched back, but it was too late, the electricity coursed through her body sending her into uncontrollable convulsions. When he finally removed his hand, her body dropped to the wooden stage, her face contorted in a permanent expression of fear and pain.

Dean felt no remorse, this was a level after all, but level or not, no one messed with his people. Grabbing the locket from around the woman's neck, Dean searched the area for the pedestal. When he didn't find anything immediately, he searched the body, finding the skeleton key that would unlock Kambry's cell.

"What is happening?" Patti ran to him, having just reached the stage through the retreating crowd.

"We are on level twenty-six," Dean said coldly as he unlocked the iron lock, the storm still raging all around them.

"How? We found the locket...we pressed it to the pedestal...this shouldn't be."

"But it is—" Zayra drew their attention to the podium in the center of the stage.

She pulled on the wood, the sides dropping off to reveal the pedestal they needed.

"Do it," Dean said, throwing the locket to Zayra, his focus still on Kambry as he tried to free one of her wings.

Zayra nodded, placing the locket in position, the familiar light enveloping them all, leaving them with a sudden sense of relief. Finally, they would be free of the maze and all of its glitches.

∞∞∞∞

The relief was short lived when they opened their eyes to find themselves on a boat in the middle of a swamp, the dark murky water below giving off a putrid smell.

They were dressed in their normal attire, the tracksuits having disappeared with the rest of the previous level.

"What in god's name is going on?" Dean gritted his teeth, trying not to have a full-blown outburst.

"What happened?" Kambry asked, rubbing her head, the effects of the previous level leaving her with a headache.

"We are trapped. This is the second time we tried to leave the maze, but just ended up being sent to another level," Patti answered her, dropping to her knees by the side of the old vessel.

"There is still one way out," Wilfred interjected, drawing a line across his throat with his thumb, his tongue sticking out for emphasis.

"That's a last resort—we are not killing ourselves to get out...not yet anyway," Dean told them sternly, hoping the glitch would fix itself and they would be out soon. "For now, we just keep leveling."

The group remained quiet. While they wanted to argue, their bodies and minds exhausted, they knew there weren't any other options. Like it or not, they would be forced to continue.

As they sat on the boat lamenting their fate, they failed to notice when a vine crept onto the deck, slivering close to Zayra's leg.

"What's that?" Patti pointed it out, a bit too late.

The vine, as if it knew it had been spotted, quickly wrapped around Zayra's ankle, hoisting her high into the air and away from the boat. Dean scrambled to react, pulling the team's weapons from his satchel. The vine dropped, pulling Zayra beneath the surface of the sludge-filled water.

"Zayra!" Wilfred ran for the edge of the boat, searching for signs of his wife.

When not even a bubble could be found, he climbed on the side of the ship preparing to enter after her.

"Wait—" Dean tried to stop his impulsive action, but the unicorn man could hear nothing over the sound of his blood pumping in his ears.

He dove in, determined to find Zayra or die trying. Before the last of the displaced water could settle on the surface of the lake, a giant creature covered in swamp sludge and vines emerged from beneath the depths, roaring angrily at the boat that floated through its waters.

Patti aimed her arrow at the creature, preparing to fire, when Dean held up his hand, halting the attack.

"Look there." He pointed before pulling out his spyglass to get a better look.

In the center of the creature, her face barely visible, the rest of her body covered in vines, was Zayra struggling to be released.

"I won't hit her," Patti said confidently, and Dean didn't stop her this time.

The arrow whizzed through the air, landing precisely in one of the swamp monster's sunken eyes. The creature roared, its foliage arm raising to cover the wound. She prepared a second arrow and without any hesitation she released the bow string, this one lodging itself in the creature's arm, the creature simply swiping it away without much thought.

Wilfred reappeared from the depths, a few feet from the boat, his head coated in the swamp slime. He looked up at the beast in horror, seeing his wife in the creature's grasp. Unable to form a meaningful attack in the water, his actions being premature, he headed back to the ship, his desperation to save her growing.

Dean offered his arm, pulling Wilfred from the muck.

"I have to get to her!" He immediately ran back to the side of the ship, searching for the best method of attack.

Kambry hopped onto the side rail, her wings expanding to their full length, her staff in one hand, sword in its sheath. Without a word she jumped, her wings taking her closer to the swamp creature. She circled the monster, searching for a weak point, its arms flailing to catch her, but having no luck.

Toward the base of the creature, just above the waterline she threw a fireball, the blast exploding upon impact with the creature's leafy body. Unfortunately for her, the monster's wet exterior made her fire attacks useless, a fact that became evident the moment the fire dispersed, revealing an unaffected swamp beast.

"Let go of me you disgusting—ugh." Zayra continued to struggle, each movement causing her to sink even deeper into the foliage.

"Don't move so much!" Kambry shouted, realizing her body was being slowly swallowed up by the beast.

"I can't help it!" She continued to struggle, the thick mud and leaves pulling her in further until her entire body was completely covered.

Kambry knew she needed to act fast. Pulling out her sword, she aimed wide, not wanting to hit where she believed Zayra would still be. Back on the ship, Dean tried the controls, the engine sputtering weakly before dying out. They were stranded on a useless vessel.

Having no luck with the boat, Dean and Wilfred aimed their water magic at the murky swamp, working together to create a walkway toward the creature. They hopped onto the ice, their feet barely staying under them as they made their way across the water.

"We're coming!" Wilfred shouted, more for himself than for his wife who was buried in the muck of the creature.

Kambry sliced away another section of the vines, the plant life seeming to grow back just as quickly as she could cut it down, the blade doing virtually no damage. Another arrow flew by Kambry's head, the point sinking into the monster's second eye, the only clear vulnerability of the beast.

The monster cried out, its whole body moving from the outburst, sending waves out in all directions. The waves crashed through the ice bridge, the thin sheets cracking from the force and separating into smaller clumps. Dean and Wilfred plummeted back into the water, their means of travel completely destroyed.

They swam toward the swamp creature, knowing they were running out of time. Just as they reached the mass of vines that made up the body of the beast, fully intending to climb up, a bright light surrounded them pulling them from the level.

∞∞∞∞

Dean stood frozen, his body no longer covered in gunk, his hand reaching out for the vines that once laid in front of him. The swamp was gone, a grassy plain in front of him, all of his comrades, including Zayra, around him.

"Zay!" Wilfred hugged her tightly. "I thought you were a goner."

"What happened? How did we make it out of there?" Patti questioned, stretching out her muscles while she surveyed the seemingly calm surroundings.

"I found the locket," Zayra said as she smirked. "I guess it was a stroke of genius that I got scooped up by that thing." She chuckled, making light of the situation now that the danger had passed.

"Well if we defeated it, I'm sure the result would have been the same...but someone got swallowed by it, so we couldn't hit it full force," Kambry mocked, giving her a hard time.

"Whatever, I still got us to the next level." She shrugged.

"Yea, the next level... Just how long will this glitch last?" Dean looked around at level twenty-seven, feeling a bit defeated since they weren't there by choice.

"Well let's go see what we have to face this time." Wilfred encouraged everyone to shake off their exhaustion, heading off into the unknown.

∞∞∞∞

689

. . .

The team struggled for the rest of the day, hoping that every time they placed a locket on a pedestal that they would be transported back to the portal entrance—-back to Mixonia. On level thirty-two they held their breath, hoping this would be the last level.

After a mad dash for the exit of a cavern that was quickly filling with water, they had found the locket waiting for them. Dean lifted the trinket into position, giving his team a look that said please take us home, before slamming it down on the stone pedestal. The familiar light surrounded them, whisking them from the threat of a watery grave.

"Dammit all!" Dean cursed the bleak grey clouds overhead, finding himself in a training arena surrounded by archery targets.

"I just need to rest a bit," Kambry sighed, plopping to the dirt ground.

They didn't go back to Mixonia, the continuous levels starting to negatively affect their morale. Dean scanned the surroundings, no enemies in sight. A small metal fence separated the targets from the dirt training ground, the team spawning on the dirt side.

He pulled a bow from his satchel, stepping up to the fence that came up to his mid-calf. He nocked an arrow and aimed for one of the numerous targets in their area ahead, releasing when he was ready.

The arrow hit just shy of the center and the sound of mechanics whirling immediately filled the space. The target was pulled underground only to be replaced moments later by an empty one.

Other than the swapping of targets, nothing else happened.

"Let me try," Patti said, already nocking her own arrow.

With extreme confidence, she pulled back the string, aiming for the same target that Dean hit previously.

"Bullseye," she grinned, the arrowhead sinking into the small yellow dot on the center of the board.

The mechanical sound started up again, pulling the target underground once more, but this time, the hole closed, the spot remaining empty. *Hmm—so that's the game,* Dean thought to himself, preparing more bows from his bag.

While Patti was certainly the most skilled with a bow, that didn't mean the others couldn't try. He handed the weapons out to his teammates, everyone understanding his intention.

"What's to stop us from walking right up to the target and sinking in the arrow?" Wilfred asked, accepting the quiver of arrows from Dean.

"This fence," Kambry said mockingly, kicking the small structure lightly with her booted foot.

Wilfred made a face, lifting his foot over the fence and onto the grassy field, holding it there for a second. Zayra's eyes widened when he went to move further into the field. She raced toward him, grabbing his arm before pulling him roughly back over the fence onto the training side.

"What was that—" his words caught in his throat as a sheet of arrows rained down on the spot where he had stepped.

When the arrows finished falling, the air calming back down, the mechanisms started whirling again. The grass lifted up, giving it just enough space to flip over, clearing the arrows from the ground. The target where Patti had hit the bullseye returned, the course resetting to its original state.

"Well, now we know." Wilfred broke the silence, Zayra giving him a look that asked 'Are you serious right now?'

"What?" He smiled at her, glossing over the fact that he almost died.

"Maybe it's like in the hedge maze.... As long as you avoid activating the traps on the ground, you will be fine," Kambry said, deep in thought as she stared into the archery field. "I'm gonna try it."

"Kambry... don't. We can pass this test, no problem. After all, I'm on your team." Patti assured her, but Kambry's wings were already spread, preparing to launch into the air.

She circled the arena, getting pretty close to the targets, showing off how easy it would be to hit the bullseye from her position. For a minute it seemed that her cheat would work, but then Kambry noticed her teammates waving frantically at her, shouting for her to come back. She paused in the air, confused, but when she spun around toward the back of the arena, she saw a mass of black coming toward her—a cluster of arrows aimed right for her position.

She dodged, but another group of arrows came toward her new position, until the entire field was covered with incoming arrows. She bolted for the perimeter line, zigzagging left and right in an attempt to avoid the piercing projectiles. The sting of metal slicing her skin threw her off, allowing another arrow to slice into her forearm, reminding her to remove herself from the field.

She crash landed over the fence, her breathing heavy, small scratches across her body. Her comrades ran to her, needing to be sure she wasn't seriously injured.

"I'm mostly fine," she huffed, placing her palm over the deeper wound on her shin.

A soft light emanated from her palm, engulfing the wound. Soon both the pain and the injury itself were gone. Kambry looked up at the shocked faces of her party members.

"What's wrong?" she asked automatically.

"You just used healing magic...in the maze," Patti said with a gasp.

"Oh, yea. I guess I did."

"It seems like the normal rules of the maze no longer apply. So much for no glitches." Dean studied their surroundings. "I think we have to accept at this point that we are not getting out of here anytime soon. I don't know why, but we are stuck in the maze. We need to be smarter about when we take breaks or we are gonna end up dying on what should be a simple victory."

Wilfred lifted his hand, wanting to interject.

"And no one brings up offing ourselves...with all the glitches we've seen so far, I wouldn't be surprised if that would mean our end for good." Dean cut off Wilfred before he could make his suggestion.

Everyone was suddenly aware of how critical the situation was, the unknowns forcing them to continue with no known end in sight.

"I think we should try to get some rest on this level since there doesn't seem to be any enemies around."

Thankful for his suggestion, the party formed a circle, collapsing to the ground. The full day of leveling had left them tired, hungry and more than a little on edge.

"I'll look for some firewood," Kambry said, realizing they should prepare for an extended stay at the current level.

Kambry headed in the direction behind them, seeing some trees in the distance. A few minutes later she passed the group, heading off to the right. "Hit the barrier," she said simply when she was within earshot, not bothering to stop.

Since the goal had always been to get through the maze as quickly as possible, they weren't sure what would happen to the level as time went on. Did the sun set if they were in the field long enough? Would the rain fall from the darkening clouds overhead? They were in new territory and the only way they would find out the answer would be through experience.

Dean pulled their stores of food from his satchel, the party's stomachs growling in response. The supply consisted mainly of hard rolls and dried meat, nothing that required any cooking, but the fire was a precaution in case it really did get dark during the night or the temperature decided to drop.

Kambry returned ten minutes later, her arms laden with small twigs and sticks. She placed them in the center of the group, along with some dried leaves she'd grab to use as kindling. A small orb of fire from her staff lit the leaves ablaze, and soon they had a crackling fire, providing both warmth and light for the group.

After a small meal to satiate their growling stomachs, the members of Team Ola decided on teams for watch, figuring they shouldn't get too comfortable, after all, they were still in the maze and that meant that anything could happen. Dean and Kambry volunteered for the first watch, sitting side by side next to the fire while the others laid down for some much needed sleep.

Two hours later, the arena began to grow dark, the threat of rain having passed. Kambry shook the shoulders of Wilfred and Zayra who had agreed to the next shift. They looked up at Kambry and grunted, stretching to wake them from their sleeping state. Dean laid down on the cool grass, Kambry in his arms and closed his eyes, silently hoping he would wake up back in the inn—that being stuck in the maze was nothing but a bad dream.

CHAPTER
SEVEN
CASSANDRA

Forrester Estate

Cassandra paced her room, biting her thumbnail as she checked her watch for the tenth time that morning. Dean and his party members didn't come home last night. She went to the balcony, searching the skyline for their shuttle, something that would let her know that everything was okay.

"Come back to bed, I'm sure they are just running some extra levels. He did seem pretty set on testing his limits when I left him yesterday," Sable said from the bed, Jessabee still asleep beside her.

She had come in the afternoon as she told Dean she would, ready to help in whatever way the estate needed, be it as a worker or a trainer. Cassie was happy to have her even if she treated the stay as a vacation, but it was clear she was aiming for a more permanent stay in the household. Now that Dean and Kambry hadn't come home, she was happy to have the extra support, someone to tell her when she was jumping to conclusions.

He could have stayed an extra day, she reasoned with herself, but even that wasn't like Dean. At the very least he would have sent her a message if he planned to stay out longer than they had agreed on. Plus he knew Sable was coming, so he would want to help her settle in. *This can only mean one thing. The whole team must have been eliminated and now they are stuck in Min's vault with no way to return.*

That had to be it—right? Olivia sat on the sofa, watching Cassandra walk back and forth across the room. She rocked Leena softly, the baby sleeping soundly in her arms. Sable plopped back down on the bed, burrowing her face in the pillow, finding it much too early to deal with anything important.

Opening the doors to the balcony, Cassandra stepped out, bringing out her phone. First she texted Dean—if he were on his way the response would be quick. She paced the balcony, the warm air blowing her hair back. Nothing.

She dialed his number, tapping her fingertips against her thigh anxiously as she listened to the ring. Voicemail. If he wasn't going to answer, she could only assume the worst. She dialed her father.

"Cassie, sweetheart. How are you? How's the baby?"

"Hey, we are fine...Leena is great. It's about Dean. He hasn't returned yet from attempting mass leveling, so I'm worried that team Ola went and got themselves killed in a level."

"Say no more. We have a team in at the moment, but they only have two hours left on the docket. I'll have the next one search the vaults for your members. I'll ring you when I hear back from them."

"Thank you."

A click ended the conversation, Riva having plenty to do in his own cavern.

Two hours, Cassie thought, her thumbnail breaking off between her teeth. *Damn*, she spit the nail on the ground, upset at herself for adopting Dean's bad habit. As she thought about how to kill the time, Leena began to fuss, her nap coming to an end.

"I'll feed her," she told her nanny, reaching for the little bundle.

She cradled her daughter, gazing at her clear hazel eyes. Olivia left the room, returning minutes later with a bottle. She handed it to Cassandra before exiting the room to give them a bit of privacy.

"Let's go for a walk," she told her baby, shaking the bottle to warm it before testing the formula on her skin. When the temperature felt right, she placed the bottle in Leena's mouth as she walked toward the elevator.

They spent the next hour pacing the preservation area, Cassandra's mind a nervous wreck. Olivia came to check on them, collecting the sleeping Leena from her mother's arms before informing her that breakfast was ready.

"I'm coming," Cassandra responded, but didn't follow the nanny as she went to exit the preserve. *Everything is fine*, she repeated in her head. *Even if they all died on a level, we will free their souls. It's fine...so why can't I shake this bad feeling?*

As she turned to head back inside, her phone rang. She answered it so quickly she didn't even check who was calling.

"Hello?"

"Hey, Cass. Our group finished early, so I had my next guys check out the vault. They didn't even find one member of Team Ola in there. They also didn't see them in line for the portals. There shouldn't be anything stopping them from returning, so they may just be spending extra time on one level. Sorry I couldn't be of much help."

"No—this helps, thank you."

Cassandra headed inside with new determination. She knew her father was probably right—that the team got stuck on a level and they were spending more time than normal within the maze, but for some reason that didn't quell her anxiety. Grabbing the keys to the spare space car, she bypassed the members of the household eating breakfast and headed for the vehicle.

She set the destination to the Ola caverns and the car whirled away. Soon she landed in the cavern, finding the shuttle parked right inside in its typical position. Felna scrambled to her feet when she heard the car touch down, having previously been lounging on the couch Dean's team had provided.

"Cassandra," Felna acknowledged her as she exited her space car.

"Any word from Team Ola?" she said immediately, skipping the pleasantries.

"Not since they entered the portal."

Cassandra stepped toward the glowing yellow portal, trying to peer into Mixonia, somehow hoping she would catch a glimpse of her lovers.

"I'm sorry, but the max number of participants have already entered this portal. No one else can go through until they return."

Cassandra slunk back. "I know. I just wish I knew what was going on in there."

"They are either running late or have all perished," Felna responded.

Cassandra's eyes narrowed, a bit annoyed to have the obvious thrown in her face.

"Or maybe they have been seduced by the allure of Mixonia and are spending their winnings on pleasures within the portal world."

Cassandra felt an insult coming, but she held her tongue, not wanting to start problems with the Minotaur guard. "Can you tell what is happening in there?" she asked, hopeful she would gain some insights.

"No. If there is nothing else, I must be returning to my show," Felna added, eyeing the television set to her right.

"Fine. If they don't return soon, I'll be back."

Felna nodded, leaving her post for the romance movie that played on the big screen.

Cassandra was out of ideas, and left with only one option—to wait. She headed home, intent on finding something to do that would occupy her mind. The chosen task was finalizing the contract she had been preparing as soon as she learned of the elves' plans to dominate the games and Oakley as a result.

∞∞∞

A week passed and no news of Team Ola came from beyond the portal. The group had yet to return and Riva's teams updated Cassandra daily on whether or not they found any of the team members' statues in Min's vault. His groups checked and rechecked, but never so much as glimpsed any of Team Ola's party members in Mixonia.

Finally she couldn't take it any more—couldn't sit in her estate and do nothing. The contract provided a distraction for a little while, but now that a full week had passed she no longer believed the excuses she told herself for Dean and Kambry's absence from her bed.

"There is no way they have been stuck on a single level for a whole week," she murmured to herself as she slammed her clothes into a suitcase.

"Are you sure he's not just trying to fulfill his agreement with the gods?" Sable asked, sitting on the edge of the bed, watching the clothing fly about.

"No. Dean wouldn't do that without running it by me first. Something is wrong."

"Okay. We'll figure this out." Sable placed a comforting hand on the base of Cassandra's back. "It's time I find out what really happened to my father anyway. As much as I hate to admit it, he might have something to do with this. No way his hands are clean when he's been in the wind for the last month. He might know something about Lexis's disappearance too, who knows. Whatever he is hiding, I will find out."

"Hurry bac—" Cassandra went to wish her well, but Sable had already disappeared, not one for sitting around once a plan had been put into place.

"Guess I should do my part as well," she said to herself, strengthening her resolve. "Olivia!" she shouted, the nanny frantically answering her call.

"Yes'm?"

"I'm going to visit my father. Are you okay with Leena for a couple days? I don't think she would enjoy the shuttle ride."

697

"Of course." Olivia nodded.

Cassandra slammed her suitcase shut and headed for the elevator, the stress of the week having boiled over. A shuttle ride later and she arrived at the cavern her father controlled, not even bothering to give him a heads up.

She stepped down from the taxi shuttle, suitcase in hand, surprised to find herself in front of a large compound. Massive double doors denoted the entrance point of the thick brick wall that encompassed the entire space. Riva had been busy.

A camera whirled overhead, zooming in and out to get a better picture of the visitor.

"Miss Lexso, welcome," a voice came over the speaker before a buzzer sounded, the doors sliding open.

Just inside was the training area, line after line of men and women training in everything from swordsmanship to hand-to-hand combat. Riva walked the paved path that separated the different training areas, coming to meet Cassandra.

"Cassandra," he said as he gave her a smile. "To what do I owe this pleasure?"

"I need to borrow your portal," she replied, getting straight to the point.

He was quiet for a moment, but immediately knew her reasoning behind the request. Gesturing for her to follow him, he led her through the training ground and to the main building, a large structure that housed the team dorms and the shared dining hall—everything they would need for an extended stay near the portal.

At the back of the building was a giant circular metal door. Riva entered a code in the keypad triggering the mechanized door to slide open. The door led to the cave where the portal resided, the Minotaur guard standing tall by the cave wall. The cave had been equipped with plenty of entertainment options, much like the Ola caverns, but the guard remained standing, choosing to ignore the guilty pleasures of humanity.

"Jasper, this is my daughter. She would like to enter Mixonia through this portal." The Minotaur guard nodded along to the man's instructions. Riva then turned to Cassandra, "Luckily there is no team scheduled for another hour, so you should have plenty of time to search for your team yourself. But don't dawdle, after all, the whole of humanity depends on the few portals we have access to. We can't have one out of commission for too long."

"I understand, thank you," she replied, eager to make use of the allotted time.

Riva stuck his index finger and pinky in his mouth, releasing a shrill whistle. A few minutes later a tall, lanky kid who looked to be around nineteen appeared from the back of the cave, dirt coating his hands and the front of his shirt.

"Take Charles with you. If anything happens, we will need someone to report back."

"Fine," she said simply, understanding his reasoning.

Charles didn't say anything, just wiped his hands on his pants and stood in front of the wall where the portal would open.

"Charles and Cassandra would like to go to Mixonia where we will gather intel on the whereabouts of Team Ola."

Jasper hit the wall and the portal appeared, starting small and growing into a large shimmering yellow doorway. Cassandra walked through, Charlie following meekly behind her.

Once inside, Cassie didn't take the time to appreciate the changes that occurred from Mixonia's expansion, she was on a mission. She walked with purpose to the PVE team portal line, where only three teams were waiting to enter the maze. She wanted to barge to the front, but told herself to be patient, reluctantly waiting at the end behind the two Catomis and an Oruk team.

Her foot hit the ground impatiently as she watched the teams recite the needed script to enter the levels, the guard waving them through once the formalities were complete. Finally, it was her turn.

"You—" she started with her finger pointed straight at the tall Minotaur guard.

He eyed her with a straight face, not being swayed by the emotions of a human.

"Did you work as the portal guard about a week ago?"

"I am the primary guard for this portal," he responded shortly.

"Do you know Dean Forrester?"

When the guard didn't respond right away she said, "Short, sandy brown hair, around 6'6", beard, well built...ringing any bells?"

Still nothing.

"He would have been with two Osamars and a Dragona female and another human."

"Ah the human male who likes to breeze passed the maze's oath. Yes, I remember his team. They entered quite some time ago, level twenty... I think, or was it twenty-four? No matter.... I don't recall them exiting."

"What do you mean you don't remember? Did they or didn't they?" She growled at the guard who was nearly twice her height.

He didn't snap back at her, merely closed his eyes, his breathing slow. Cassandra didn't say anything more, just waited for the Minotaur guard to finish analyzing his memories.

"They didn't. Not on my watch anyway," he said calmly, opening his eyes to gauge her reaction.

"So then where are they? What happened to them?"

"Perhaps you should try the vault?" he offered, already looking to the next group that had joined the line behind Cassandra.

"That's the problem! We have checked and rechecked the vault and not one of them is in there!"

"That can only mean they have yet to complete the level or lost their lives in the process."

"Do you seriously expect me to believe they have been stuck at the same level for over a week?"

She was fuming now, the frustration drawing tears to her eyes.

The Minotaur guard shrugged, waving her to the side. "If you don't wish to enter the portal, there is nothing more I can help you with."

She inwardly screamed, not wanting to make a bigger scene than a human woman yelling at a nine feet tall Minotaur guard already had.

"Are we heading back now?" Charlie asked, glancing back at the maze entrance as the portal shifted colors and the waiting party stepped through.

"We are going to check the vault first," she huffed, realizing Riva's team had yet to check for them that day.

Charlie didn't say anything more and followed behind Cassandra who led them through the cobblestone streets to where the vault was located. Ignoring the distractions within the vault, Cassie headed for the section that housed all of the captured souls, starting at the closest to the front—the letter D section, finding the Dragonas.

She scanned the numerous rows of trapped souls, not finding Kambry among them. When she was sure she had eyed every last statue, she moved on to the humans, repeating the method, this time searching for statues of Dean and Patti. Nothing.

Her emotions were a mix of relief and anxiety as she checked the final section, the Osamars.

"They are not here," she said aloud to no one in particular.

Maybe they are just stuck on a complicated level, she tried to reason with herself, but being trapped for over a week seemed like too much of a stretch. Before leaving

Mixonia, she decided to explore the world, wondering if they had ended up in other parts of the place trying out the various pleasures the portal realm had to offer.

Disregarding Riva's timeline, she spent the next two hours searching every pub, night club and gambling house, but she still found herself with no new leads.

"It's like they just up and vanished." She looked to Charlie who remained quiet, simply along for the ride.

Having nowhere else to search, she headed back to the entrance of the portal, realizing that waiting for them to reappear was the only option she had been left with. As she stepped through the glowing portal, a familiar face waited on the other side to greet her.

"Cassandra!" Anoka said with open arms, her long black hair pulled back into a high ponytail.

She wore work out attire and looked to have just finished a sparring round.

"I was told you were here for a visit, it seems I chose the right time to come to the caverns. Did you have any luck finding any of their souls in the vault?"

"Not one. I'm out of ideas on what to do."

Anoka could see the struggle on her face, the worry etched into her features.

"I know it's hard to sit by and do nothing, but right now we just have to trust them. They are strong and wherever they are they are fighting to get back to us. I know that Kambry would never give up, and I'm sure Dean is the same. It will be okay."

While her words didn't provide the answers Cassandra so desperately needed, they did provide a bit of comfort, letting her know that she had done everything she could to help her team, but now it was in their hands.

"Riva told me his teams will check daily for your teammates and keep you updated should anything change. For now, we pray they resurface from the maze soon. I'm sorry you weren't able to find the answers you wanted by coming here."

"I feel a bit better that I was able to see for myself that they aren't trapped in the vault or lounging around Mixonia," she sighed, trying to see a silver lining.

Cassandra decided to stay for the rest of the night, exhausted from the cheap taxi shuttle ride to Spelunkers' Delight. Riva gave her an in-depth tour of the facility the following morning, telling her everything her team was missing out on by not expanding their base from the cavern's entrance.

"I'll bring it up to Dean when he returns," she chuckled, putting an end to the discussion.

By mid-morning Riva offered up one of his speedsters for the return trip, telling Cassandra that the ride would be much faster than if she were to call another taxi.

"Just put it on autopilot and send it back when you're done." He smiled as he handed over the keys.

"Thank you," she told him, glancing over at the fancy red speedster he had prepared for her.

After saying goodbye, Cassandra headed home, the return flight much more relaxing that her initial departure. Just over two hours later she touched down outside of the Forrester estate, Olivia hurriedly coming to greet her. Once her belongings were clear of the space car, she input the address for the Spelunkers' Delight cavern, sending the speedster back to where it belonged.

"Did you have a nice trip?" Olivia questioned, not expecting her to return so soon.

"Fine... it was fine," she told her, not in the mood to share her concerns about Team Ola's whereabouts.

CHAPTER
EIGHT

DEAN

Minotaur's Maze- Level Forty

L evel forty had seemed so cut and dry. Walk across a rock bridge, climb the mountain and reach the pedestal.

Kambry attempted to reach the pedestal by air first, but an invisible barrier surrounded the top of the mountain, meaning the only way to the top was to scale its walls. Dean had crossed the bridge first, a few rocks tumbled down the side of the structure, but ultimately he had reached the other side without any interference.

Zayra went next and had a similar experience. When Patti's turn came, she walked cautiously, afraid of losing her balance and plummeting off the side of the cliff. Her real concern should have been the weapons that suddenly appeared on the side of the mountain, spikes spraying in her direction.

Trying to decrease the bulk as she made her way over the narrow pass, she didn't carry a weapon, so when the thorny bullets were released, she could only dodge, the narrow footing making the task much more daunting. She managed to avoid all but one of the spikes, while maintaining enough balance to remain standing on the earthen structure.

The spike sunk deep into her upper thigh, sending a bolt of pain throughout her body. She dropped to her knees, her injured leg hanging over the ledge.

"Patti!" Her teammates cried out.

She pulled her leg back onto solid ground, keeping an eye out for any more potential threats as she attempted to crawl in the direction of the platform. Dean ran back from the safety zone, while Wilfred came to meet him. They scooped up Patti and started back in the direction of the mountain base.

The rocky path was starting to crumble, the earth tumbling down into the ravine below. Patti dragged her leg behind her, her arms around Dean's and Wilfred's necks as they helped her cross the unstable bridge.

"Hurry, Hurry!" Zayra waved them on from the safety zone on the other side of the deep canyon, having made it across the narrow path with no problems.

Blood trailed down Patti's leg, the spike protruding from her thigh both damaging and the only thing keeping her blood from pouring out like a faucet.

As if the level were watching their progression, the rocks behind them started to crumble, the three increasing their pace at the expense of Patti's leg. They rushed to the safety zone, throwing themselves to the ground as the final piece of the bridge crumbled into the pit that lay below them.

On their backs they huffed, the fear of falling into the ravine all too real.

"It hit an artery," Kambry said, examining the placement of the spike and the amount of blood dripping from around the wound despite the object still being embedded in the skin.

Patti gritted her teeth as the pain spread from the impact point. She propped herself up on her elbows, wanting to get a better look at the wound.

"If this had been a normal leveling run, you would have bled to death before the regeneration could be effective." Kambry pulled the spike from her leg, immediately covering the gushing wound with her hand to apply pressure.

Patti's face went white from the sight of all the blood, her vision darkening around her. She breathed deeply, trying to resist the urge to pass out, but didn't look away from Kambry whose hands were now covered in her blood.

Kambry let her magic flow from her palms and into the wound, the injury healing beneath her hands. When the blood had stopped flowing down Patti's leg, Kambry removed her hands, revealing the wound that had been reduced to a small scratch.

"Thank heavens we have you here with us," Patti said, laying back down to catch her breath, the last of the pain subsiding.

"And you wanted to leave me behind." Kambry laughed, staring up at Dean.

He chuckled softly, having heard this line many times over the past week they had been stuck in the levels. Soon after they had found themselves trapped in the maze, they decided to take each level slowly and seriously and to fight as though their lives were truly on the line. After all, they weren't sure what the truth was any more.

Kambry had saved their lives more times than he'd like to admit over the past week of slow and steady leveling, so he didn't fight her back when she highlighted her worth on the team. At the same time, he didn't encourage her, still worried about both her and the baby's health. He didn't want her taking any unnecessary risks, but needed to admit that he was happy they were once again able to avoid a potentially disastrous outcome thanks to her healing magic.

"The level's natural regeneration abilities should take care of the lightheadedness you are feeling...it may just take a little while," she told Patti, helping her to her feet.

"Well as long as I'm going to make it." she replied as she laughed. "Although I'm not sure I'll be up for climbing that."

Her eyes followed the side of the mountain all the way up into the clouds overhead. Natural footholds denoted where players should step on their climb to the top, the pedestal waiting for their arrival.

"We don't all need to go...really only one of us has to make it to the pedestal," Dean said more to himself, testing out the sturdiness of the rock grips. "Okay. I'm going to climb to the top. You all stay here. It should be safe, but at the first sign of danger, make sure you start moving okay? Remember, no one can die."

He removed a few swords and shields from his bag, wanting to leave them with a means of protection in case it proved necessary. They all nodded at Dean's warning, grabbing for the weapons before sitting down to rest while he began to scale the side of the tall mountain. Other than the rough texture of the footholds, Dean found the climb to be similar to an exercise rock wall—as long as you found the right grip, the ascent wasn't too difficult.

As he made his way toward the top, he realized his words had been premature, the space between the grabbing points becoming increasingly larger, forcing him to overextend himself in order to continue his climb. More than once, his foot slid from its position, leaving him dangling in mid-air, the threat of falling imminent.

Dangling from the ledge, he looked down—the height from his position daunting —the fear of falling to his death fueling the strength that allowed him to pull himself back into position. He heard the whirl of machines, the guns reappearing on the side of the mountain once more, preparing to fire. *Shit.* He braced himself, knowing there wasn't a whole lot he could do to avoid an incoming spike in his current position.

Instead of aiming at him, the weapons fired in the direction of his team, their shields already in place to defend them against the incoming attack. Dean exhaled, thankful they were prepared, and thankful the weapons didn't turn on him. When the guns retreated back into the side of the mountain, he focused again on the wall in front of him, searching for the next place to grab.

Slowly the ledge came into view, his goal only a few feet away. He reached for the next grip, his fingers raw from the rough surface of the rock, and felt his hold on the rock weakening. *Just a bit more*, he tried to convince himself, beads of sweat rolling down his face.

He grunted, reaching for what looked to be the final step, then pulled himself onto the flattened top of the mountain. Standing up, he admired the view below, the drop unsettling, yet beautiful. *If there weren't so many invisible barriers around the mountains, this level would be the perfect place to release Droosca and let her spread her wings*, he thought to himself, breathing in the fresh air.

He exhaled, finished with the view and headed to the center of the mountaintop, easily finding the pedestal where it waited, the locket on the ground next to it.

"What will be waiting for us next?" Dean whispered, staring at the gold necklace as he held it in his grip.

Part of him wanted to believe there was still a chance they would be released from the maze when he pressed the locket to the indent, but each time he thought that he had only been left disappointed. Knowing that the only way out was to press forward, he gently placed the trinket down, the familiar light releasing on impact, transporting them out of the rocky terrain.

∞∞∞

Dean blinked, trying to adjust his eyes to the dim lighting, the reddish hue making it hard to distinguish exactly what he was looking at. He could tell his team was around him, but as to where they ended up, he wasn't quite sure.

"It's a bed!" Patti squealed excitedly to his left, the sound of squeaking springs following her glee.

The light flickered on, Wilfred having found the light switch on the front wall. The red dimmed light switched to an artificial white, making everything a little too bright. Dean glanced around the room, his lip curled up into a scowl.

"What's that face for?" Kambry asked, pulling Dean toward the king sized bed.

The room resembled a seedy motel, the comforter of the bed stained by who knows what, the splotchy color matching the spots on the worn out carpet. Thick blackout curtains covered the windows and an ancient box tv sat on a stand in front of the bed.

"What even is this thing?" Zayra said quietly, fiddling with the knobs on the old television set.

The screen came on, the sound of static grating at their ears.

"Ugh—turn that thing off," Patti groaned, rolling over on the cheap mattress, each movement eliciting a new noise.

"Sorry," Zayra apologized, complying with her demand.

Dean pulled the curtains open, hoping to find out a bit more about where they had ended up, but behind the dingy burgundy cloth was a red brick wall, the window leading nowhere.

"Great—no going outside from here," he announced, closing the curtains.

"Well, why don't we just sleep here for a bit? I mean it may not be the prettiest thing, but it is a bed at least," Kambry suggested, eyeing Patti who looked to be sleeping already.

"Alright." Dean surrendered when he saw Kambry crawl into the bed next to Patti, the bed looking a little more inviting.

Wanting to be sure they were safe, he went to the door first. It opened, allowing him to peer down a long hallway, the lights flickering on and off giving it an eerie vibe. Hoping the place wasn't haunted, he decided they could deal with whatever this place threw at them once they had gotten some rest. He locked the door for good measure, plopping down on the bed next to Kambry.

The size of the bed provided more than enough space for the five of them, but Wilfred still insisted on sleeping at the foot of the bed, not wanting to crowd the others. No one said anything, too tired to argue about something so trivial.

Once they were settled, the light switching back to its dim red hue, it didn't take long for them to drift to sleep. Having found little time to rest comfortably over the past week, their increased exhaustion levels were at their max, so no one even mentioned sleeping in shifts, everyone assuming they would be safe inside the hotel room.

∞∞∞∞

Three hours later Dean was woken up by the smell of smoke. He shot up from his place in bed, the dim lighting seeming even less bright than before. He scooted to the end of the bed, wanting to turn on the light, but collided with Wilfred instead, forgetting he had made camp at the foot of the bed.

"Ouch," the unicorn man said, but quickly realized the situation. "What's burning?" he asked, heading for the light switch.

The bright fluorescent white lights flickered on, revealing a dark haze of smoke hovering around the room.

"I think we are," Dean said, rushing to wake the girls.

"Five more minutes—too tired," Kambry mumbled, swatting at Dean's hand as he shook her awake.

"No—now. We are not safe here anymore."

Kambry's eyes shot open, remembering where they were and immediately noticed the thick smoke that surrounded them.

"Shit," Patti said, shifting her feet onto the carpeted floor. "I knew this was too good to be true."

Dean rushed to the door, their only means of exit and placed his hand on the wood, checking to see if the fire had spread to their immediate location.

"I don't think it's reached here yet," Dean announced, the door feeling cool to the touch.

He unhooked the chain before opening the door just enough to peek into the hallway. The hall looked clear of flames, but the same dark cloud of smoke circled overhead.

"Let's go before our exit is blocked off," he told the others that scrambled to their feet to follow his advice.

"Wait!" Zayra said before they were all out the door. "Did anyone check the closets or the bathroom? We should make sure the locket isn't hidden in this room before we leave it behind."

"Good thinking," Dean agreed, disappointed with himself that he'd forgotten the most important part of the levels.

Team Ola spent the next three minutes tearing the room apart, checking every inch for the locket, but in the end they found nothing. Once they were sure it wasn't hidden in the starting room, they left, tying a pillowcase on the outside handle so they would remember that the room had been searched.

The hallway was lined with doors, each one leading to a separate, yet identical, room.

"Do we have to check them all?" Patti asked, her eyes scanning the long hall.

"Do we really believe the locket would be in one of the rooms? It's more than likely in a more significant part of the hotel. Maybe the lobby or the cafeteria—Some central location," Zayra chimed in, basing her assumption off of their experience in the previous levels.

"Just because it was like that on other levels doesn't mean it will always be the case...what if we miss something?" Kambry questioned, reaching for the handle of the door directly across from the room they had spawned in.

She attempted to turn the knob, ready to explore the next room, but was met with resistance. "It's locked," she mumbled, realizing they no longer needed to check through the rooms.

"We'll make sure that none of them are open as we head down the hall." Dean quickly adapted, deciding they should search through the rooms that were unlocked.

In the hallway that housed around thirty rooms, only two needed to be explored. The team quickly tore through them searching for the locket, but again came out empty handed. They hurried passed the remaining locked doors to the open space that waited for them, the smoke increasing, the temperature rising.

As they approached the lobby, the flicker of orange could be seen reflecting onto the white gloss walls of the hall, the fire burning freely, engulfing the tacky ornate couches that decorated the space.

"Guess we found the fire," Kambry announced, her eyes darting from one burning inferno to the next.

"We'll hit it all at once," Dean said to Patti and Wilfred, pulling their staffs from his satchel.

Although they each were at varying levels when it came to water magic, it helped that more than one of the team could manifest water, especially in their current situation. Each person focused on a side, the water blasting down the flames, allowing the team to pass through the area unscathed.

When the last of the fires had been extinguished, the room was still filled with smoke, making it hard to see if there was anything of importance in the lobby. Kambry coughed, inhaling some of the smoke.

"Kambry...maybe you should wait in the hall where there is less smoke," Dean told her, a worried expression on his face.

She wanted to argue, but something in Dean's eyes told her she would lose, so she simply went back the way they had come and sat down on the cooler tile, her breathing improving significantly. For the rest of the team, they tore up a shirt and tied it around their mouths, hoping it would help mitigate some of the smoke while they searched the room for the locket.

An hour later they had turned over every couch cushion, opened every filing cabinet and rooted through every potted plant, but they still didn't find the item they needed to complete the level.

"It's not here," Dean said, his words giving the team permission to give up their search. They moved to the hall where Kambry waited and sat next to her on the floor, everyone taking a much needed break.

"Where to next?" Kambry asked, having had a long enough rest already.

"I guess we see where else we can get to in this place." Dean shrugged, searching the burnt lobby for their next path.

In the back of the room were two large double doors, the metal singed black from the fire. Dean pointed them out to the group, signaling where they would be heading next.

"Well then, what are we waiting for?" Kambry asked, pulling herself to her feet.

Patti released a groan, as she moved to stand, hoping for a little more rest. Kambry led the group, still a bit bitter about being left out during the previous search. She pushed open the double doors with gusto, the metal creaking as they swung, revealing a bright white cafeteria, picnic style tables scattered throughout the room.

In the very middle sat the pedestal, a locket waiting on one of the tables next to it.

"Well would you look at that," Kambry said excitedly, hurrying her pace toward the locket.

"Kambry—wait a minute," Dean rushed toward her, feeling that the locket placement seemed too easy.

As Kambry passed through the tables, she didn't notice the thin clear line of string that connected them together, the string snapping when coming in contact with her leg. Kambry turned toward Dean as the pedestal in front of her exploded, the pieces flying out in every direction as a cloud of flames filled the room.

Dean had been just close enough to her that he was able to grab her and pull her into his arms as the blast erupted from the center of the room. Dean turned, shielding Kambry from the fire that surrounded them with his own body. The initial blast lasted only a second, the impact of the explosion sending everyone flying.

When things settled, the room was dark, the lights flickering on and off, having been affected by the force of the explosion. The tables around the room were on fire, the wood crackling and releasing black smoke into the air. Part of the ceiling had collapsed, rubble strewn haphazardly throughout the cafeteria. Dean groaned from his spot on the floor, his body still on top of Kambry's.

He moved to sit up, a sharp pain in his lower back causing him to wince. Looking down at the area, he found a shard of the pedestal lodged in his side, blood escaping from the plugged wound.

"Kambry—are you okay?" He cradled her head, trying to get her to open her eyes.

Finally there was movement, her eyes taking in his worried expression.

"It was a trap," she whispered, her eyes shifting to the flames that had spread to the ceiling of the cafeteria.

"It was. Can you stand?" He pushed himself to his feet, holding out his hands to help Kambry up.

"I think I'm okay." She felt around her body searching for injuries. "And look--."

She opened her hand to reveal the locket, having reached it just before triggering the detonation. "Where is everyone else?"

As she asked this, Dean was already searching around the room, trying to see through the thick haze of smoke to locate the rest of his team. As he searched, a spray of water aimed for the flames to their right, the water magic user trying to lessen the intensity of the fire.

"Dean! Kambry!" Patti yelled, moving closer to the two, her staff still pointed toward the flames. "I didn't see that coming—what the hell happened?"

"It was rigged. I should have been more careful," Kambry apologized. "Dean your side," Kambry gasped, just noticing the wound as the blood seeped into his shirt spreading to the front of his body.

"I'm fine."

"No you're not. This is all my fault."

"I will be fine," he repeated, his calm voice very convincing.

"Let me look at it."

"We should find Zayra and Wilfred first. That is more important."

"I'm here." Wilfred appeared through the smoke having heard the others talking. He had burn marks on his forearms and the side of his cheek, but otherwise appeared to be okay. "Has anyone seen Zayra?"

"Not yet," Kambry replied, yanking the piece of wood from Dean's side.

"What the fook woman? At least warn a guy!" He cursed, biting his knuckle as a wave of pain gripped his body.

"Oh hush, I'm about to heal you."

She pressed her palms to Dean's wound, letting the magic flow from her hands, healing the injury completely.

"See—good as new."

"Zayra!" Wilfred called out, tired of waiting for his wife to appear.

A faint noise answered his call, the voice weak and strained.

"Zayra! Where are you?" he repeated, encouraging the others to listen out for the small voice.

Patti stopped the stream of water, the place becoming as silent as it could be, the only remaining sound the roar of the still burning fire.

"Here," Zayra cried out, ending in a fit of coughing.

The team rushed to a table by the entrance where they thought they heard her voice. The table had been blown backwards from the blast, rubble from the ceiling piled on top as a broken ceiling light dangled overhead. When they were closer, they found Zyra's hand waving frantically at them from under the rubble, her body pinned under the table.

"Are you hurt?" Dean asked, rushing to the spot he found her hand, trying to lift the table from her body.

"I don't think so, but it's getting hard to breathe."

Wilfred went to the side opposite Dean and on three they attempted to lift the table off of Zayra. The table didn't budge despite their struggling, the weight on top too much for only two people to lift.

"We have to clear the debris off first," Dean said as he grabbed a chunk of ceiling from the top of the pile and threw it on the floor behind him.

The team scrambled to pull the large pieces from the top of the table as fast as they could, Zayra's breathing becoming increasingly labored the longer she was trapped under the rubble.

"Let's try again," Dean urged, resuming his position to lift the table.

On three they lifted as one, the table moving just enough to allow Zayra to slip from under the pile. She heaved in the smoke-filled air, trying to calm herself down, the polluted air doing more harm than good. She coughed, choking on the smog, but felt a bit better now that she was free from the confined space.

Patti had already begun fighting the flames with her water magic again, Dean and Wilfred joining her later. Another half hour later and the flames had been extinguished, allowing them to search once again for the pedestal, the fire no longer their main concern.

"So was what I saw in the middle of the room just a decoy?" Kambry asked, searching the place where the original pedestal had exploded.

As she dusted off the spot where the first pedestal had been positioned, she heard the faint sound of a man cackling, the laughter echoing through the open room. Her eyes darted around the space, the voice unfamiliar to her ears, but when she couldn't find the source, she figured she must be hearing things.

Returning her gaze back to the white tile floor, she slid her hand across the surface, revealing a small indent under the black soot. *This must be the true pedestal,* she thought to herself, pulling the locket from her pocket. Without informing the group, not wanting them to know if she were to be wrong, she placed the locket on the indent, hoping for the best. The bright familiar white light enveloped them all, transporting them from the charred hotel cafeteria.

∞∞∞∞

"Good work, Kambry," Dean said when the last of their team materialized in the new level.

Kambry smiled triumphantly, feeling as though her discovery made up for the fact that she had gotten them all blown up. Looking around, Dean realized that everything seemed familiar.

"Are we back?" Dean scooted back the chair he found himself sitting in, the kitchen table in front of them laden with an enormous amount of breakfast food and everything smelled delicious. "Is this real?" He picked up a piece of bacon from the table, shoving the whole thing in his mouth.

The greasy texture of the meat provided a flavorful explosion in his mouth, his stomach growling for more. Kambry and Patti watched him anxiously, waiting for his verdict. "It certainly tastes real."

Those words were all the girls needed to hear and they were grabbing a plate and filling it high with bacon, scrambled eggs and pancakes. As they sat back down in the chairs they had been transported to they realized two of their members were missing.

"Where are Zayra and Wilfred?" Kambry asked, her mouth full of eggs.

"I'm here." Wilfred came in through the front door. "Is this a level? It looks like we are back at your estate," he said, scanning the interior of the building.

"This has to be a level. I don't remember returning to Oakley. Or even Mixonia for that matter."

"We can figure that out after we eat—It's been a while since we had a hot meal," Patti told him.

"This is so strange. How did we get back to the estate?" Zayra came in from the kitchen side, her eyes immediately landing on the breakfast feast.

"It's not, so don't let your guard down," Dean warned her, handing her a plate.

"But I just saw Looma...she's the one who told me to go eat something."

Weird, Dean thought to himself, giving the room another look around. Everything resembled his estate, from the setup of the furniture to the smell of the old wood, but that was impossible, right? The projector screen flickered on showing a progression of dinosaurs, elephants and dragons marching across a desert background.

"I am getting serious deja vu right now," Dean said, getting closer to the screen.

"They look real," Cassandra entered the room, a sleeping Leena bundled in her arms, "and the desert looks like the landscape around here," she pointed to the screen, sending his attention back toward the massive animals headed in their direction.

"This isn't happening," he looked at Kambry and Patti, hoping they would confirm that he wasn't going crazy.

"It's that day..." Kambry said quietly, putting her fork down onto her plate.

"Howdy! Dropping by with a present from Mr. Lexso, himself," Quincy walked with purpose through the main entrance, everyone's eyes shifting to him with a scowl of disgust on their faces.

"This fooking traitor," Dean growled, glaring at Quincy, reliving his betrayal.

"It's non-alcoholic, a lemonade actually," Quincy repeated his words from that day, handing the dressed-up bottle to Dean, knowing it would be the death of him if he were to consume it.

"I thought we were friends, you bastard." He waved the gift away, or at least he tried to.

He watched as a hand grabbed for the offered bottle, the hologram popping open the gift and lifting it toward his face.

"What is this?" Dean questioned, the apparition extending from his body as if they were one.

Quincy shifted nervously across from him. "Well, I just came to say hello... so, hello," he said, eyeing his exit.

Dean watched a shadow of himself drop to the floor beneath his feet, the poison having taken effect as his hologram self heaved, vomit spewing on the floor in front of him.

"We're under attack!" A familiar voice rang out, Orabel rushing into the room, her eyes landing on the downed Dean.

Dean felt the prick of tears threatening to build in his eyes—how could the maze be so cruel? Before he could say anything—acknowledge his lost comrade, the familiar light engulfed them, transporting them into the dense forest that surrounded the Forrester estate.

Tall trees surrounded them, the sunlight barely able to break through the dense foliage of the canopy above. Still the forest remained bright, Orabel having equipped the space with an unknown light source similar to the one seen in Mixonia.

"Are we going to have to fight this battle again?" Kambry whispered, intertwining her arm with Dean's, dreading what was to come.

"It's looking that way."

Vibrations shook the earth, the enemy drawing closer. The trees came to life, defending against the intruders that attempted to breach the leafy barrier overhead. Riders fell from their flying mounts, matching Dean's memory of the moment.

Before they had attacked the vulnerable enemies, but this time he stood frozen in the moment, not ready to relive the tragedy of that day.

"What should we do?" Patti asked, moving closer to the team, keeping an eye on the downed riders.

A beam of light shot forward from Dean's position, blasting a hole straight through the wing of one of the fallen dragons, keeping it stranded on solid ground. Its cry rang out sending the rest into a frenzy in the skies over their position.

The teams' holographic selves rushed forward, claiming the lives of any of the riders that still breathed after their fall, reiterating the fact that the event was merely a moment captured in time.

"Why are we seeing this? What is the point?" Patti cried out, tears rolling down her cheeks as she pulled on Kambry's arm, begging for the level to end.

"You need to hide." Dean's chest felt tight when he felt a small hand grab his forearm, Orabel's eyes were wide with concern.

"Don't go—stay with us." Dean pleaded, hoping he could somehow save this version of Orabel, but the script merely continued, the players unable to deviate from the predestined route.

"I can only distract them," she continued, un-phased by his pleas.

"Fook—I can't watch this again." Dean turned as Orabal rushed toward the two hundred feet tall tree, merging with it in a burst of green elven magic.

Cries of pain and agony filled the battlefield, the intense memory of that day playing out around them, Dean finding it hard to distinguish between what was real and what was only a hologram. Attacks flew in their direction, but the only ones affected were the holograms of themselves from that day, the pain only a memory, even as they heard themselves cry out— watched themselves be beaten to their knees.

Dean watched his crumpled form stand back up, remembering the moment his body radiated with power. He searched the skyline for Thero, the main culprit behind the attack, but when he looked toward the mammoth, expecting to find Thero sitting on top of the beast in his excessive shiny robes, that wasn't who he found.

Instead, someone else had taken Thero's place, the unfamiliar figure the only difference in the scenario that continued to play around them. The mammoth came closer to the group, kneeling down to allow its rider to use its trunk to disembark. Dean strode forward to meet the man, not sure if he too would simply be another hologram trapped in a loop.

"Dean, are you sure this isn't another trap?" Kambry warned, following a few steps behind him.

"No, but it is the only lead we have right now."

As Dean approached the figure dressed in a dark blue tunic and stark white pants, his features became distinguishable. The man had deep crimson eyes, jet black hair and pointed ears. As Dean approached, he smirked, revealing pointed canines.

"Hello, Dean," he said, walking to meet the party.

Dean scowled, not liking the look on the man's face. The current level was like nothing he had experienced so far. It didn't make any sense. The maze was designed to challenge the party, but Dean had never heard of the maze using the players' memories as fuel to build the environments.

"Who are you? Why are we seeing all of this?"

"Oh Dean, I'm surprised you haven't figured it out for yourself. After all, there is a reason I picked this moment in time to replay for you."

A haunting scream filled the air-- the blood-chilling cry of pain and defeat-- as a massive tree fell to the ground in the background. Dean clenched his fists, forcing himself not to react to Orabel's final pleas, knowing that nothing he did in the maze would save her.

"I haven't—just what about this moment involves you?" He stared the man down, wanting to knock his lights out for digging at the party's wounds.

"Oh, it's not about her. It's about what comes after."

Against his will, Dean tried to think about that dreadful day, needing to know this man's endgame. He replayed it in his mind, the moment he flipped Orabel's body over, her eyes lifeless. He had been so angry—he was still angry. *She didn't have to die.*

He remembered the rage, the way it fueled him, his body growing as a result. He remembered snuffing out the life of his enemy with ease—Thero, the whole reason his home was reduced to a battlefield in the first place. Dean looked back at the pale skin of the man, his sharp canines a distinguishing feature.

"Braxton," he said with complete certainty.

"Ding, ding, ding we have a winner! What's your prize you ask? To be trapped in the Minotaur's Maze-- everyday another battle." He laughed maniacally, finding the whole situation hilarious.

Dean's eyes widen, the glitches suddenly making more sense.

"What? You didn't think you could kill a master mage—A Grand Vampire—and just go free, now did you? And let's not even start about all of my guild members that you slaughtered." Braxton scowled, a death glare fixed on Dean.

Dean tried to speak, needing to share his side of the story, that they were the ones to attack first, but Braxton stopped him, his palm raised toward Dean.

"Don't bother. I don't care for excuses and valid or not, it will never change my opinion of you or my choice to lock you in the maze."

"You bastard!" Kambry yelled, having heard enough from the sadistic man.

Reaching her breaking point, she threw a fireball in the vampire elf's direction. His image flickered, the fire passing through his form before the hologram stabilized. Kambry growled, angry that her attack had failed.

"You didn't actually think I would come to you in person, did you? I don't have a death wish." He chuckled, revealing that he believed the party could kill him if given the chance.

"So what then? What's your big plan? Trap us here? Until when? Until we die and get turned into statues? We are earning enough tokens that we'd be able to free ourselves many times over."

"That's fine, if you think the maze still follows its old rules. But let me present you with this little nugget of information, free of charge—it doesn't. So go ahead and die, see what happens."

"Min wouldn't let that happen... there is no way," Zayra spoke up in opposition.

Braxton smirked in response. "Maybe they will, maybe they won't," he replied, his voice sing-songy, revealing the joy he felt from seeing them struggle. "Do you really want to test your theory?"

Dean knew Braxton had them right where he wanted them. That Team Ola would do anything in their power to remain alive, the notion that dying in the maze might mean their real end being too heavy a burden to try anything risky.

"Why not just kill us outright? Why go through all the trouble of tampering with the portals?"

His eyes darted to Kambry, his expression lustful as he ogled her from head to toe, his gaze landing on her stomach. Dean shifted to stand in front of his future wife, blocking her from Braxton's view, a wave of irritation and disgust racking his body when he saw the vampire's expression.

"Don't get any ideas," Dean growled, knowing the man in the level was only a hologram unable to do any real harm, but feeling on edge nonetheless.

"In due time." Braxton chuckled, walking closer to the huddled group. "I do hope she shares her mother's looks," he murmured to himself, drinking Kambry in with his eyes.

Kambry's hands shot to her stomach, instinctively trying to protect the life that continued to grow inside of her.

"You sick fuck," Kambry said aloud, Dean's expression matching Kambry's words.

Braxton shrugged, back-tracing his steps as he put some distance between himself and team Ola.

"Think about it. What happens to children born in Mixonia?" He started laughing again, his cackling fading out when his hologram disappeared.

Shit. Dean hadn't thought that far ahead, not expecting to be in the maze for more than a couple days. That theory had already proved false as they hit their first full week of leveling.

"What happens to our baby if I give birth in the maze?" Kambry gripped Dean's arm, her eyes pleading for an answer he couldn't give her.

"We just have to get out before that happens. We won't let anything happen to our baby."

Dean hugged Kambry close, trying to comfort her from the unknown future as his own fears grew. Children born in Mixonia resided in Mixonia, that was a simple fact he learned during his first visit to the world. Would there be a way to bring the baby home to Oakley? Every question he presented in his mind was left unanswered and with no one to turn to that held the needed information, the only plan was to try and escape before the birth.

Dean hoped that Braxton's power would weaken with time, that the magic—or whatever curse he placed on the maze—would vanish before his second child came into the world. He squeezed Kambry a little tighter, now trying to quell his own worries, when the same familiar light enveloped the group, transporting them back to the start of the level. Back to the start of the hellish battle, forcing them to relive it once again.

CHAPTER

NINE

CASSANDRA

Forrester Estate

The whirl of space shuttles outside her balcony window woke Cassandra from her mid-day nap. The baby had kept her up all night, the first signs of teeth starting to poke through Leena's gums disturbing the little one's sleep. Cassandra groaned, wondering what the fuss was about, her heart beat a little faster, hoping team Ola had finally made it home.

One month had passed since the disappearance of Dean and his team, and no new information could be found regarding their location. No one had seen them in Mixonia, their statues didn't grace the shelves of Min's vault, and the team definitely didn't return to the estate, or even to Oakley for that matter.

Cassandra told herself to be patient, but the more time passed, the more questions she was left with. Even Sable had been MIA, but not letting others know her plans was just the way she lived her life, so she was one person Cassandra didn't need to worry about when she didn't call.

She opened the doors wide, stepping out onto the balcony, hoping to see the team's familiar shuttle coming in for a landing. The sounds grew louder when the doors were open---much too loud for a single shuttle---and she realized it couldn't be her family.

Shuttles dotted the sky, hundreds of ships waiting for the approval of the estate master. *What on Oakley*—Cassandra pulled on her robe, rushing for the elevator.

720

"Mistress Casandra, there are so many ships outside. Are we under attack?" Olivia asked as soon as the elevator door dinged open. She stood, anxiously wringing her hands as she awaited the answer.

"No, I'm sure that's not it or they would have started shooting by now," Cassandra reasoned, calming the nanny down. "I left Leena in her crib, will you please go and sit with her?"

Olivia nodded, slipping past Cassandra and onto the elevator before it could close. *Now, what is all this commotion about?* She walked through the main kitchen and outside to where the ships hovered overhead. Cassandra entered the permissions that would allow the ship to land, taking a few steps back to avoid the wave of displaced air that would blast in her direction when the ship touched down.

The main ship moved to land when given the signal, the rest moving back toward the forest where they remained hovering in the air over the dense canopy. The occupants of the Forrester estate peeked out the window at the scene from the safety of the building, Jooma, Kooma and Looma, at the forefront. The doors of the ship opened, three impressively dressed elves exiting in a line.

"Are you the master of this...," he asked as he looked the estate over, judgment all over his face, "...fine estate?"

"I am. Who wants to know?" Cassandra stood a little taller, trying not to be intimidated by the strong regal presence of the elf emissaries.

"I am Esterial Ulysses, leader of the Suca expansion mission. These are my cohorts, Gemini and O'Hara. I expect that you knew of our visit?"

"I did, but the timing wasn't clear."

"We are here now and would like to get started as soon as possible. First, we need complete control of your base including access to the portal you have in your possession."

"I'm sorry, but it's not going to work like that."

"Excuse me?" He stepped closer to Cassandra, his hands folded together, the white, silk cloth that covered them nearly reaching the ground.

"I said you will not be granted full control over our base." Cassandra changed her speech to a more formal one, wanting to match her audience. "We appreciate any training you provide, but the human race is not something for you to subjugate. We wish to remain in control, and to work together with the elves to grow stronger. I understand the sacrifices that you made by coming to assist humanity, but we are not just going to lay down and let you run the show."

His eyes narrowed at her words. "This wasn't what we discussed with the Great Mother. The Elven Federation of Higher Societies has come here for the betterment of humankind. Like it or not, you need us. Humans, historically speaking, have never won in the games. Do you want us to pull our assistance so that this world can become another notch on the core demon's metaphorical belt?"

"We are not asking you to leave. We are simply looking for a partnership as opposed to a takeover. Why don't you three come inside and we can further discuss the terms of our agreement."

"I don't think you understand the seriousness of our mission. How can you propose an equal partnership when the elves gain nothing in return?"

"Then would you rather the core gain control of another planet simply because you couldn't play nice with others? You threaten us with that fate, but the truth is you would suffer just as much as the human race if the core were to win."

The elven leader tried to remain composed, but Cassandra could tell her words were weighing on his mind. She knew convincing them to enter into a contract would be a difficult sell, but giving up her right to the estate just wasn't an option.

"Very well. We will listen to your requests and take them into consideration. Three additional fleets are still on their way to our location, so we have time before the entire cavalry arrives. Will that be satisfactory?"

"It will." Cassandra nodded, leading them into the main eating area of the estate.

Cassandra pointed to the table, gesturing for them to sit down.

"Is Mr. Dean Forrester not going to be present for our negotiations? We were under the Great Mother's guidance that he was an integral part of the suca's victory."

"He's a little busy at the moment, but I am the lady of the estate and he has agreed to the terms of the contract. If you'll excuse me for a moment."

Cassandra left the room, returning minutes later with a stack of papers that denoted the terms for their alliance. She set them on the table in front of Esterial, the elf's expression revealing his displeasure.

"What are you looking for in our arrangement?" he asked outright, not bothering to reach for the written contract.

"We work together. There will be no abductions, no harsh measures for noncompliance and no takeover of the planet should Oakley win in the games. You are welcome to look into the rules of immigration to planet Oakley and we'd be happy to house a few people here in the estate or on the land that surrounds it, but ultimately high numbers of new citizens will need to be discussed with the leader of Oakley—something that is above my societal position."

"We elves relinquished our planets when we learned of the human's strife. Do we not deserve gratitude for our selflessness?"

"The way you talk about saving humanity lacks the selflessness you claim to have."

With contempt in his eyes the elf leader stood, the chair squeaking as it slid across the floor. "Eight human planets are currently active in the games. So far none are leading with any significant margins. If things progress as is, it is likely Oakley will become just another casualty in the gods' games. Whether you see our action as selfless or selfish, we are here to help. Why can't you understand that?"

Cassandra stood to match the elf's height, leaning in across the table, "The majority of humanity doesn't even realize they are taking part in the games. The portals are contained, the knowledge of them is limited to a select number of humans. Now imagine eight fleets of elven warriors descending upon us demanding that every human trains to take part in a maze that exists in another world. How do you suppose that will play out? While we are not opposed to inviting more into our ranks, spreading the information nonchalantly will only result in mass chaos and destruction, something that can be avoided by choosing our fighters wisely and by presenting it as an opportunity, not a demand."

She stared at him, waiting for the information to sink in. Finally he began to see her side of things.

"It seems our knowledge of humankind is lacking," he admitted, finding the idea of hard truths causing chaos among the people unfathomable.

"Which may be why you can't see how your plan to help humanity would only cause them to rebel. In the end we would be worse off—a divide would form between those who would prioritize saving the world and those that couldn't look past the stolen freedoms, which would lead them to labeling elves as the enemy. If anything a war would break out on the surface before the core demons had the chance to dominate."

He sat back down in his chair, his rigid posture relaxing a bit as he accepted the words of someone other than the federation leaders.

"Very well. We will heed your advice. You will be the council to the elves as we — work with— humanity to save this and all the other active human planets," he conceded, gritting his teeth a bit as he said the words.

Wow from an insignificant human getting in the way of their plans to a council position, Cassandra thought to herself, quietly celebrating her accomplishment.

"Good. Now if you will take a look at the contract in front of you." Cassandra pointed to the paper in front of him.

This time, he didn't ignore its presence, instead he slid it toward him and opened to the first page.

∞∞∞∞

. . .

An hour and a half later the contract had been signed by both parties, all sides benefiting from the agreement. The humans would retain control of their portals, the elves taking a leadership role in training and knowledge distribution when it came to the maze. The fleets would be divided between the four portals, only one remaining at the Ola caverns due to its small size.

The remaining members of Dean's team would be trained, but the disappearance of the Forrester estate's main force meant that the portal remained occupied, so the elves would be useless when it came to actual leveling.

"Till when will this Dean character be busy?" O'Hara questioned, as Cassandra led them on a tour of the estate.

"I'm not sure," Cassandra answered honestly, figuring she should come clean about his disappearance.

The elven leaders had thought it strange when she had requested that only one fleet stay on the land, but none of them pried into her reasoning. After her brief explanation, having no real information in the first place, the elves gave her a look of concern.

"A month. Are you sure they are not simply pursuing Mixonia?" Gemini questioned, refusing to believe they would be gone that long without a simple explanation.

"Quite. By all accounts they are still in the maze. I just find it hard to believe it would take them that long to accomplish one level, especially when they were only on the starting levels. Has there ever been a report of someone getting stuck in the maze...You know, leveling up, but never returning to the starting zone?"

"Never," the three of them answered at once, squashing Cassandra's theory in a matter of seconds.

"But if he is to be this planet's best hope, I fear for the fate of Oakley if it takes a month to accomplish a single level."

The three elven leaders nodded to each other, accepting that their job would not be an easy one. Cassandra finished the tour, returning them back to the front of the estate, ready to see the elven leaders re-board their ship.

"Fleet five will likely occupy the Forrester estate. Expect them within the next couple of days. We will be in touch," Esterial said, crossing the plank into his shuttle.

Cassandra waved habitually, her gesture receiving a stern glare from the trio. The door to the space shuttle slammed shut, the engines coming to life before it sped off to join the other waiting ships. Cassandra sighed heavily, wishing even more that

Dean and Kambry were home with her, helping her to navigate the new relationship with the elves.

CHAPTER

TEN

DEAN

Minotaur's Maze- Level Ninety-nine

T eam Ola pushed the rock wall shut, covering the cave entrance, the fire erupting against it. Level ninety-nine was an intricate maze, each path leading them in circles for hours on end. Finally, the team had selected the right path only to be chased around by flamethrowers coming from all directions. They reached the final room in the maze, a giant blast of fire chasing them until the end.

Now that the flames were no longer a threat, the team was able to breathe, taking in the small dark cavern they had found themselves in.

"Whew—that was a close one," Kambry announced, lighting the tip of her staff ablaze, filling the small cave with a dim light.

"There's the pedestal," Zayra announced, rushing toward the center of the space.

"Wait, we should secure the area and rest for a bit. It's about time we get some sleep," Wilfred added, already searching the cavern for any signs of enemies or other potential threats.

Dean handed Kambry a few torches to light, then dispersed them amongst the group, everyone splitting up in different directions searching for any cave dwellers. The area spanned no larger than a standard living room, so the search only lasted a few minutes, everyone coming to the same conclusion—the cave appeared to be safe.

Feeling a bit better about relaxing, they slunk to the floor, the torches thrown in the middle to create a fire pit.

"Food," Dean whispered over his satchel, pulling out canned green beans and corn from within the vast depths.

The team had long run out of their prepared rations, reaching a point where they believed they would die of starvation in one of the levels. That's when Dean remembered what the vault attendant had told him—-the satchel held rations for months. Although she couldn't tell him what exactly they were, she guaranteed they would be edible. So far, her words had proven true.

"We got green beans, corn, and...spam tonight." He pulled out one final can.

Using his blade as a makeshift can opener, he pierced the lid enough to extract its contents before placing the food close to the flame to get a little warmer.

"What do you think is waiting for us on level one hundred?" Patti asked, her eyes fixated on the cans of food as they cooked.

"Maybe a way out?" Zayra answered, hoping that saying her wishes aloud would help them to come true.

After the encounter with Braxton back on level forty-two, the party decided to attempt each level with even greater caution. While they didn't fully trust Braxton's words, they also couldn't look past the fact that he was the reason they were stuck in the maze in the first place. Maybe he really did rig the levels to kill the players once and for all should they die within the maze.

True or not, Dean would rather not find out the hard way. With that level of precaution, the team had nearly reached level one hundred by day sixty of being trapped in the maze.

"A way out would be nice," Patti responded with a sigh, the constant state of battle wearing all of them down.

"I for one hope we run into Braxton so I can finish off the weaselly mother fooker before we go on home to the estate. But, even if it's not the way out, we will defeat it just like all the levels before. For now, we rest," Dean added, having little hope that either Braxton or the way out would be waiting for them in the next level.

Dean rotated the cans, making sure the entire contents would be heated by the fire, the rest of the group going quiet. Kambry fiddled with the heart monitor device, checking on the baby's health.

"How do things look?" Dean asked, scooting closer so that he could see the screen.

"Everything appears to be normal, but I really doubt how much this thing would be able to tell us anyway," Kambry sighed.

The stopwatch-looking device beeped, displaying the heartbeats of both mom and baby, both within normal range.

"It's better than nothing," Dean tried to reassure her, leaning in to kiss her on the cheek.

Kambry grinned, placing the device in her lap before grabbing Dean by the cheeks to pull him in for a real kiss. Patti blushed from the other side of the fire, turning her attention back on the cooking food. Dean tried to ignore the other's eyes, choosing not to fight Kambry as he deepened the kiss.

After a minute, he could feel the stares on them, so he decided that it was enough PDA for one night.

"Dinner is served," Dean announced, scooting the cans away from the flame with his sword.

After filling their stomachs, the team laid down, the enclosed space offering enough protection for some uninterrupted sleep. After a full night's rest, they woke refreshed—as refreshed as one could be sleeping on a damp and hard cave floor. After a quick breakfast of hardened biscuits, they placed the locket on the pedestal, crossing their fingers they would return to the maze entrance.

∞∞∞

Dean had closed his eyes when the familiar light erupted from the pedestal, transporting him and his team to the new location. Now he slowly opened his eyes, quickly realizing they were not back in Mixonia.

"Dang it! I really thought we would be let out this time!" Patti cried, stomping her foot with her words.

"Welcome travelers!" A small voice called to them reminding them that they entered into the new level, a smaller figure with floppy dog ears stood in front of them, a wide grin on his face, his canines pointed.

"Hello?" Dean replied, a little skeptical of the situation.

They stepped down from the raised circular platform they found themselves standing on, a magical inscription carved into its surface. Level one hundred resembled a small town, the roads paved and small houses with thatched roofs scattered throughout the area.

A protective wall encircled the whole town, one large gate denoting the entrance. Trees surrounded the area past the wall as far as the eye could see.

"Welcome to Pupolia. I am the teleportation ambassador, Ronan. Please let me know if there is anything I can do to make your stay more enjoyable."

"T-thank you." Kambry said awkwardly as the beastman held out his hand, waiting for Kambry to place hers in his.

She side-eyed Dean, her skepticism apparent, but complied, the beastman lifting her hand to place a kiss on the back before moving on to Patti and then Zayra.

"There are many great inns in our little town and if you are hungry I can recommend the best place to get some truly excellent beef stew. I really think you are going to like it here."

"Is this a level or a rest stop?" Wilfred mumbled, confused by the seemingly friendly sentient being. "We aren't supposed to kill these little guys right?"

Dean scanned the square of the town, more dog beast people coming to check out the new visitors in their quaint town. Everyone was a few heads shorter than even their smallest member, their demeanor inviting and sincere.

"Let's just see what happens," Dean told him, not wanting to start anything unprovoked.

The self-proclaimed ambassador happily guided team Ola around the town, giving them an extended tour of his home. He especially showed off the gardens, the lush foliage and vibrant flora, a relaxing scene.

"So beautiful!" the girls exclaimed, heading straight for the bench that was placed right in the center of the space.

Patti sat down first, admiring the water feature directly in front of her while the other two sniffed the assortment of flowers that crowded the stone bench.

"Our town takes great pride in the diversity of our plant life." Ronan beamed, excited by the party's reaction. "We don't get too many visitors here, but when we do we like to show them everything we have to offer. When you are ready, I can show you to a nice place to order some lunch and point out the inn I believe would be the most comfortable. You are planning to stay the night, correct?"

Patti, Kambry, and Zayra turned their puppy eyes on Dean, eliciting their desired response.

"We will stay," he responded, feeling as though he didn't have any other choice.

While the girls' silent pleading helped to make the decision, he knew their choices were limited, having yet to find any signs of the pedestal or locket despite the two hour tour all around town.

"Wonderful!" Ronan clapped his hands together, overjoyed.

The dog man led the group to a quiet cafe in the center of town, a dog woman greeting them at the door.

"A table for five and five helpings of your seasonal beef stew, Amari, on me," Ronan told the woman, his smile never faltering.

The group thanked him for the hospitality and he replied in kind, thanking them once again for visiting the small town. Before he left, he pointed out a small inn across the way, a sign with a bed etched onto it hanging from the front wall.

"That's the best place to stay here in town, take it from me. The owner is a great gal too. Just tell her Ronan sent you and the first night is on the house." He tipped his cap toward their table before exiting through the small wooden door.

A bell chimed as he exited, signaling his departure.

"Your meals will be right out," Amari told them, jotting down something on the clipboard she carried. "So what brings you to town? I heard you came in through the teleportation portal no less." Her clear blue eyes were shining brightly, clearly interested in the stories the strange visitors may hold. She noticed their stares and continued, "You know, small town, not much goes on without everybody hearing about it." She smiled, her head tilting a bit as she waited for their response.

"Oh, uh...we are leveling in the maze. This is a level, right? Level one hundred?" Dean questioned, finding it increasingly difficult to believe they were still in the maze, the town a non-combat zone with very friendly inhabitants.

Now it was her turn to give them a blank stare. "Maze? I'm not sure I follow."

"It's nothing. We are just here to get away." Dean changed his response to one that wouldn't further confuse her, realizing quickly that they were either no longer in the maze or the canine NPCs that occupied the level were oblivious of that fact.

"Oh, the food is here," she chirped, her tail wagging back and forth rapidly as she watched a waiter come around the corner with the five bowls on a single platter. "Well, I won't disturb you any longer. I do hope you enjoy your stay here. Be sure to come back again, our breakfast is even better, if I do say so myself." She spun on her heels retreating behind the counter to help ring out a finished guest.

The team ate in silence, enjoying the thick and flavorful stew, still unsure if they were in a level or had somehow been transported to another planet. When their bowls were clean and their stomach's full, they said their thanks to the staff before leaving the small cafe.

"This has to be a level," Kambry announced as she pushed open the little wooden door, the bell dinging its farewell. "I know it's weird that the people who live here have no idea what we are talking about when we mention the maze, but think about it...have we ever had a true conversation on any of the other levels? Programs or placed pawns, whatever the things in the maze are, they probably just see it as their home." She shrugged before continuing, "I say we keep looking for the locket, but take our time. I mean, who knows when we will find another level with its own inn."

It didn't take any convincing for the other members of team Ola to be on board with Kambry's plan, especially once they saw the room offered to them at the inn across the street from the cafe. Dean slipped the key into the old lock expecting to find a cramped dwelling with room for five, but instead the place was spacious and clean, the beds soft and comfortable.

"I could get used to this," Patti sighed, pushing past Dean to claim the twin bed next to the wall.

She plopped down on the mattress, the plush material caressing her every curve.

"That's it, we are living on level one hundred," she said matter-of-factly, turning on her side as she hugged the fluffy white pillow.

Kambry couldn't resist any longer, and giving into the temptation, she threw herself on one of the double beds, letting her body sink into the comfort of the inn's mattress.

"Don't forget we have a mission here. Tomorrow we start looking even harder for the locket." Dean tried to remind the team, ignoring the girls' excitement.

"Wait...I almost forgot," Kambry said, pulling herself from the cushion's grip.

She rushed to the door directly in front of her chosen bed and swung it open.

"EEP!" A squeal of delight left her lips. "They have a bathtub! And scented soap."

With that, the rest of the day was spoken for, the girls each taking turns in the tub scrubbing off the exhaustion of two months and nearly one hundred levels. Dean didn't mind, he felt relaxed for the first time in a while—even if he knew the feeling would fade quickly. The next day was sure to remind them that they were truly trapped within the maze by a psychotic vampire elf hellbent on taking his revenge.

But for now, he let the softness of the comforter lull him into a false sense of security, allowing him a restful night's sleep.

∞∞∞∞

The following morning, the team woke up well rested and ready to resume their hunt for the locket. Dean had expected to be woken in the night by ghosts, or bloodsucking inn staff, but nothing happened, the night passing peacefully. When everyone finished taking advantage of the personal bathroom, they headed back across the street, eager to try the breakfast Amari had bragged about.

"Back so soon? You're going to make me think you like my shop's cooking or something." She giggled, seating them as soon as they entered the cafe.

This time she handed them each a menu, allowing them to choose something for themselves.

"Do we have money for this?" Zayra asked quietly from across the table as Amari helped another guest.

"I didn't think about that." Wilfred frowned, not wanting to be viewed as a freeloader after all the hospitality the townspeople had provided.

"I think I have some gems in my satchel...I wonder if those would work," Dean responded in a hushed tone, reaching into his bag to pull out a handful of assorted gemstones.

Before Dean could wave Amari over, planning to ask the hostess herself, a deafening bang erupted from outside, shaking the entire cafe. Rocks engulfed in flame crashed through the front glass window, the scared cries of the patrons filling the air.

Team Ola rushed to their feet, Dean pulling everyone's weapons from his bag, eager to protect the town from whatever sought to destroy it. The party rushed from the building, weapons in hand, Dean's trident leading the procession. The sky had turned dark, the atmosphere heavy and foreboding.

Another boulder engulfed in flames collided on the pavement a few feet from where the group stood, the rock splitting on impact, the fiery chunks spreading out in all directions, dealing damage to the storefronts that lined the street. More screams and a horde of fleeing beast people followed, the entire town reduced to chaos.

Finally, the enemy appeared from beyond the wall, a massive onizard—the unholy combination of a demon and a fire lizard. Its body was black as night, a ring of intense blue flames surrounding it entirely. With one swift motion, it picked up another nearby rock, the object immediately catching fire before the creature hurled it into the town.

"My shop!!" an older beastwoman cried out, her tail between her legs, fear on her face as she watched the thrown rock fly through the air, lodging itself into the roof of the small flower shop.

Before the team could address her, another dog man grabbed her by the wrist dragging her away from the crumbling shop.

"I guess this is a level," Dean concluded, leading his team into battle.

The massive scale of the creature would make defeating it a challenge, but they had faced so many beasts and monsters that they knew they wouldn't go down without a fight. Moving as a unit, they approached the onizard from the front, Wilfred and Patti preparing to blast it with water magic, hoping to extinguish its flames, weakening its power in the process.

Dean felt the charge of electricity coursing through his body, his own attack ready to be released. When they were close enough, Wilfred and Patti approached from opposite sides, their staffs held out in front of them as thick streams of water flew in the onizard's direction.

The beast felt the pressure of the blast, taking a few steps backward, the flames that surrounded its body seeming to dim, the water having an effect. As the attack continued, the creature seemed to grow irate, the flames erupting, growing even higher and hotter than before as the onizard stood its ground, pushing back on the flow of the magic.

"We can't hold it back!" Patti yelled, her mana dropping quickly from the intensity of the water magic, the attack requiring a steady release of mana to sustain it.

"On three, cancel the magic," Dean yelled to his teammates, "And Kambry whatever you are thinking... don't," He looked to his lover whose wings were outstretched, ready to launch herself in the air.

At his words she retracted her wings, strengthening her grip on the sword she held.

"Just wait. We need to see what this thing is capable of first before you get too close," he said his thoughts out loud, needing her to understand his reasoning.

She nodded in response, preparing herself for when she could attack at close range.

"One....two...three!" Dean screamed with his palm raised toward the fire lizard demon, Wilfred and Patti pulling back on their attack.

The water disappeared, just as the creature reached for another boulder flinging it into the town. Dean fired an energy blast toward its torso, hoping to have better luck with lightning than water. Before the beam could reach the monster, another cry caught the team's attention, the rogue boulder spiraling straight for a townsperson, the dog man crouching in fear, unable to move.

All at once, the team tried to reach the beastman, but they were all much too far from his location to be of any help. The boulder flew unobstructed, crushing the dog man where he cowered. Dean's lightning reached the onizard, penetrating its chest just as a bright light engulfed them all, freezing them in place.

In the next moments, they were blinking from the sudden blast of light, trying to regain their vision. The air seemed calm once more, the sun shining brightly as their gaze shifted down to a familiar face.

"Welcome travelers!" Ronan said with a bright smile, his floppy ears protruding from his dark brown newsboy cap.

"Hello, Ronan," Dean responded, his eyes desperately searching the town center.

All remnants of a battle had disappeared, the townspeople gawking at the new visitors from their place on the street and through the shop windows.

"Ah—you must have visited here before. Well then, welcome back to Pupolia!" Ronan said with glee, offering his hand to Kambry to help her down from the raised teleportation platform.

"What is happening?" Wilfred mumbled to Zayra, his eyes wide with concern.

"There are so many wonderful inns in town and I can recommend a place to eat a hot meal if you are hungry. Cafe Luna has some of the best beef stew this time of year." He pointed out the small cafe, the logo imprinted on the glass window. "Would you fancy a tour around town?"

"Thanks Ronan, but I think we just want to rest for now."

"Of course. I recommend that inn there. Just tell 'em Ronan sent you and the first night is on the house." He winked, leaving the group to their own devices.

They headed to the inn three hours ahead of the previous day, the innkeeper selecting the same room for them to stay in as before. When the door closed behind them they all sighed, confusion mixing with the leftover adrenaline from the unfinished battle.

"Okay. So we arrived... stayed the night... the place got attacked, then BAM! We get transported to the beginning again? Ronan certainly didn't seem to remember we were ever here. What does that mean? Did we fail the level or something?" Kambry questioned, plopping back onto the comfortable double bed.

"Maybe we missed the chance to find the locket? Like it got destroyed or something in the fight. The level could have needed to reset itself in order to fix the broken pedestal," Patti offered, trying to think of a reason for their situation.

"If we assume we are following the same timeline as last time, that means we have until tomorrow morning until the town will be attacked. We should make use of the time we have," Dean told them, pulling back the curtain of their suite window, the townspeople happily going about their day.

"Should we search for the locket in places we didn't try yesterday? If Patti is right and the reason we restarted was because the locket had been destroyed, then it's likely it was within one of the shops that line this street. A lot of them were damaged by the boulders that thing was throwing through the windows." Wilfred suggested, thinking about how to effectively pass the level.

"Okay, we will start there," Dean told them, everyone deciding on which shops they would explore in the allotted time frame.

In the end, each member of the group would be responsible for fully exploring three shops along the main strip of the town, the team reconvening around dinner time at Cafe Luna. Dean's first stop was the flower shop they had watched crumble the previous iteration of the level.

He approached the small store front, the vibrant colors of the potted and cut flowers visible from the front glass window. The teal signage attracted many visitors, their eyes drawn to the beauty of the merchandise. The old dog woman worked out front, meticulously preening the potted plants that surrounded the front of the store.

"Welcome," she said to Dean when he approached, her smile wide, adding wrinkles to her already weathered face. "Is there a particular flower you are seeking, young man?" she said with a clear gaze.

"I am just looking for now," Dean told her, entering the store.

The place was quite long on the inside, a table set up in the middle to house potted plants, while holders lined the walls displaying the cut flowers available to craft a bouquet with.

"Welcome," another smiling face greeted Dean from behind the counter, the man's snow white hair falling in wisps about his head.

Dean recognized the man from the battle, he had grabbed the woman, likely his wife, pulling her away from their burning shop.

"Let me know if I can wrap anything up for you," he told Dean before resuming his own work at the register.

"Thank you," Dean responded, his eyes searching the store for anything suspicious.

After taking his time moving the flowers around, trying to locate the glint of gold within all the colorful flora, he decided to ask the man about the back of the shop, knowing that getting back there would be difficult without the owner's permission.

"A pedestal and a locket?" the old man asked, his fluffy tail gently swaying from side to side as he pondered the layout of the back store. "Petunia," he called to his wife, the woman coming back in from the front.

"Show this man your locket," he told her, giving Dean a bit of hope.

"Of course." She smiled, pulling a chain out front under the collar of her shirt. "My Manchester gave this to me on our twentieth anniversary. Isn't it lovely?" The lady held the locket toward Dean, the tiny heart shaped trinket engraved with a blooming rose.

"Very." Dean smiled, the locket not the one he needed to find.

After spending another ten minutes wrapped up in conversation with the elderly couple, Dean moved on to his second shop, a bakery, and the smell of fresh baked bread causing his stomach to growl. The owners were just as friendly and willing to help in Dean's search, but again he didn't find what he was searching for.

After scanning the third and final shop, Dean once again came up empty handed, the locket and the pedestal nowhere to be found. He headed to the small cafe where the team had agreed to meet, Zayra already waiting at a table inside.

"Any luck?" she asked when she saw him enter, the bell on the door ringing to alert the staff of the new guest.

"I'm with her," he told Amari who emerged from the back room to greet the new customer.

"Take your time in deciding." She smiled, handing him a menu.

"It wasn't in the flower shop, bakery or watch shop," Dean told her, taking a seat across from her at the table.

"I didn't have any luck either." She frowned, rubbing her temples.

"Are you alright?"

"Just a small headache, I'll be fine." She smiled weakly, her demeanor making her words unconvincing.

Before Dean could say anymore, Kambry strode through the door, quickly spotting her teammates and joining them at the table. It wasn't long before Patti and Wilfred joined the group, no one having any luck locating the items they needed to progress to the next level.

With daylight running out, the team decided they would instead prepare for the coming battle, hoping that their knowledge of the attack would give them the upper hand. They ate dinner and rested at the inn, wanting to wake up early to set up in the square for when the onizard would arrive.

∞∞∞∞

The following morning, the team woke before the sun, getting themselves ready for battle. They washed and dressed, heading to the town square around the time the creature was set to appear. The townspeople were obliviously going about their day, the square busy, just like the previous day. Dean began pulling the team's weapons from his satchel, receiving stares from the townsfolk for his actions.

He ignored them, everyone dressing in armor and equipping their weapons.

"Travelers!" Ronan appeared in front of them, the group too busy with their preparations to notice when he approached them. "Is there some issue that you need to don your fighting attire and pull out your weapons? We can certainly settle any dispute without the need for violence." His words were calm, but Dean could see the bead of sweat forming on his forehead, his tail tucked low as he spoke.

"This village is about to be attacked, we are just getting ready for that."

"Attacked? My goodness!" Ronan gasped, scanning the area, but finding nothing of concern. "Are you certain? There hasn't been an attack on this quaint land for over one hundred years," he tried to reassure them of the impossibility of someone trying to harm them.

"We are sure. Don't worry, we are not trying to hurt any of the townspeople. You should go take cover... it will be here soon," Dean warned the beastman, trying to remove him from the scene.

Something in Dean's voice made the dog man believe his words, his instincts telling him to flee the scene. Moments after the teleportation ambassador fled the square, the sky turned dark, the air becoming heavy. A flash of electricity erupted from over the wall, the onizard emerging from the light, its dark body brightened by the flames that surrounded it.

"Get ready!" Dean shouted to his team just as the first boulder crash landed beside Cafe Luna with a deafening bang, the flame covered rock scattering, destroying everything in its path.

The team ran toward the beast, more boulders flying over their heads as they moved. Dean prepared his lightning beam, knowing that water magic was useless against the creature. The rest of the team had their shields raised, protecting him from any incoming attacks.

Dean released the beam of condensed energy, the lightning attack speeding toward the creature when suddenly light surrounded them once again, the environment fading around them.

∞∞∞∞

"Welcome travelers!" Ronan greeted them cheerfully, his tail wagging from side to side.

Dean dropped his arms to his side, releasing a frustrated sigh. "Hello Ronan," he groaned.

"Oh! You must have been here before! Welcome back!"

Team Ola quickly gave Ronan the slip after being informed once again of the wonderful breakfast offered at Cafe Luna and the free room they provided across the way.

"What are we doing wrong? Why are we back at the beginning of this level again?" Kambry asked, her fingers prodding her temple.

"Can we check into the inn first? I'm not feeling so good," Zayra said, drawing the team's attention.

Her face looked pale, beads of sweat present on her forehead.

"Why didn't you tell me?" Kambry asked in a huff, rushing to Zayra's side.

"I didn't think it was a big deal," Zayra responded, her breathing labored.

"Big deal or not, we are here to help." Kambry placed her hands on Zayra's cheeks, looking her straight in the eyes. "We are a team—don't forget that." Kambry smiled as she released her magic, the warm glow easing Zayra's fatigue and body aches.

"Thank you."

"Think nothing of it, but you should probably still rest for the day. The healing magic helps, but you are more likely to feel sick again if you push yourself too hard."

As Dean watched Kambry heal Zayra's illness, warning signals were going off in his brain. They were in the maze--it would be one thing if she were sick when they entered the maze, but illness had no place once inside. Injuries sure, but Dean couldn't recall anything about sickness.

What if Braxton was telling the truth? If we die here, is that it? Dean could feel his heartbeat increasing, the truth behind Braxton's words suddenly feeling like a weight on his chest. He pushed his thoughts down, choosing not to worry the group with them, wanting to focus on clearing the level in front of them.

"Alright, we will find a place to stay. This time we should change up our routine... maybe our time lapse has something to do with the choices we make the day before the battle. So different food, different place to sleep."

Everyone nodded in agreement and they immediately started their search for another inn to stay at for the night. A block from their spawning location, they found another hotel, the wooden sign in the front hanging by one hook, the windows blacked out.

"Is this place even open?" Zayra stuck her face close to the window, trying to see inside.

"Only one way to find out," Dean told her, gesturing for her to open the door.

She grimaced, turning the handle of the wooden door, afraid of what she might find inside.

"Hello guests!" A short and stocky beast man chirped from behind the dusty old counter of the store. "Can I set you up with some rooms for tonight?"

Dean took a brief look around the dim and dusty inn, cobwebs gracing every corner and the chairs off to the side busting at the seams, the cotton crowding the floor beneath them.

"Any way we can get a room all together?" Dean tried to hide his disgust with what he believed was a reasonable question.

The old dog started laughing, but when he saw no one else joined in, he quieted, taking Dean's question a little more seriously. "I'm afraid we don't have any rooms of that size. One bed per room is about all we can manage here."

"Three rooms then," Dean told the man, determined to somehow break the cycle they were trapped in, even if it meant sleeping in a questionable environment.

"You betcha!" The man reached behind him, pulling three keys off the wall, each one with a keychain attached to it that denoted the room number it corresponded to.

"That'll be three hundred grimculs," he told them, keeping a jubilant tone, his grin wide as he slid the keys across the counter.

"Err—" Dean reached his hand into his satchel, pulling out three rubies. "Will this cover the cost?

A high whistle left the mouth of the innkeeper, the man leaning in close to the gems. He pulled out a little magnifying glass from under the counter, trying to get an even closer look, making sure the gems weren't counterfeit.

"These will do just fine. Room's yours for three days if you want it." He nodded, swiping the gems from Dean's open hand.

He turned around, fiddling with the safe behind him, wanting to store his new shiny possessions.

"Thanks," Dean mumbled, feeling ripped off about the exchange.

He handed out the keys and the search for the doors marked with the same numbers featured on the keychains began. It didn't take long, the hallway across from the front desk leading to a door that opened out into an alleyway, more doors lining the cramped street.

"Found mine!" Patti shouted, unlocking her door and letting it swing open.

Her face dropped immediately.

"What's wrong?" Kambry questioned, pushing in close to get a look inside the room.

The whole of the roof had caved in on the bed from a previous rain storm, the sunken mattress becoming a pond in the middle of the room.

"No way am I sleeping on that," Patti scoffed, promptly shutting the door.

Dean stifled a laugh as they moved on to Zayra and Wilfred's room, figuring it couldn't get any worse. Wilfred unlocked the door, and pushed, the wood banging against something that blocked its path, keeping them from entering the room.

"Hello? Is someone in there?" Wilfred shouted through the crack.

"Who do you think is in there?" Dean asked him, gesturing for him to move aside.

Wilfred complied, allowing Dean to try his hand at opening the door. Again he met with resistance when he pushed, but this only made him thrust harder, the sound of cracking branches following his efforts. The door slid open, a thick wave of mustiness hitting him in the face.

The room was pitch black, something blocking the windows that wasn't present in the other room. Dean flipped the light-switch on the wall to his left, the room remaining dark. Kambry stepped up, her staff in hand and illuminated the space using her fire magic.

Vines came into view, the greenery wrapped around every inch of the room, reclaiming it for nature. An unknown creature scurried away from the light, hiding in a darkened corner of the room.

"What in the hell? Do they honestly expect people to sleep in these rooms?" Kambry turned her nose up at the scene, slamming the door shut, no one daring to enter the vine filled room with who knew what living inside of it.

"Third times the charm?" Dean held up his key, the metal clanging against the plastic keychain.

"It had better be," Kambry sighed, already missing the plush mattress and the private bathtub.

Two doors over, they found the third and final room. Dean inserted the key in the lock, turning the knob with trepidation. *Alright, motel what are you hiding behind door number three*, he mimicked the voice of a television show host in his head, swinging the door open wide.

Expecting to find another swamp inside the building, the team was left disappointed, yet pleasantly surprised at the extremely normal room that lay before them. A double bed with a hideous comforter sat in the middle of the room, two night stands—one on either side of the bed filled the space, lamps displayed on each. The only other piece of furniture in the room was a small dresser, three drawers included to hold the visitors' belongings.

At the back of the room was a door, Wilfred hesitantly opening it to find a cubicle sized bathroom. The toilet was in the shower, a small sink to its right.

"Well at least someone can sleep in this room," Patti said, looking on the bright side.

"I'll go and try to exchange the rooms," Dean announced, feeling even more than ever that they were ripped off for the price of the rooms.

While the others got comfortable on the lone bed, Dean headed back to the reception desk, searching the surrounding area for the innkeeper. After waiting for ten minutes and ringing the bell repeatedly, the dog man still didn't reappear, giving Dean the impression that he received the gems and fled.

Well, we'll probably end up back at the beginning anyway, Dean reasoned with himself before hopping over the counter and swiping a few more keys, replacing the ones from the uninhabitable rooms. One last glance around the room told him the beast man was gone, so he headed back to his team, hoping they had better luck with the new rooms.

"Let's see what world these keys lead to," Patti joked, grabbing the offered key.

When she opened the door to the new room, it was identical to Dean and Kambry's, albeit the carpet was a little more stained. Wilfred and Zayra had the same luck, everyone ending up in a room they could at least sleep in for the night.

"If this plan doesn't work, we are not trying this inn again next time, " Kambry complained, failing to get comfortable on the worn out mattress, feeling every spring beneath the thin covering.

After settling in, the team searched for a different diner to buy their dinner, having similar luck with the off the wall choice. The dining area was dark, the food questionable and the patrons a little less friendly. By the end, the team just wanted to sleep, ready to get back to the battle.

The following morning they prepared for battle in the hotel room, remembering the scene they had caused by dressing in the square the previous day. They shut the doors on the way out, hoping they wouldn't be forced to return there for another night.

"Okay, I think it's just about the time when the onizard will appear," Dean told his team, leading them through the back alleys to get to the town square.

Before the teleportation ambassador could appear and ask them what they were planning to do, the sky went dark, the lightning preceding the entrance of the beast. Screams filled the square as a boulder collided with the pavement, destroying the cafe's front window.

Dean didn't hesitate this time, sending out his lightning attack, hoping it would hit the creature despite the distance. The beam flew across the square, finding its target, the onizard crying out as the blast covered its body in light. When the light faded, the beast remained unphased, a small scuff mark where the blast made contact with its toughened skin.

"What is this thing?" Patti asked, running closer with her bow in hand.

The onizard lifted its massive foot onto the wall that surrounded the village, the wall buckling from the weight. The creature grabbed the displaced bricks, tossing them into the town. The flaming material lodged in the sides of the buildings, the rest raining down on the civilians.

"Get down!" Kambry yelled as a brick headed straight for one of the townspeople.

She sped toward them, her wings increasing her speed and tackled the little dog girl who stood frozen in fear as the brick engulfed in flames headed straight for her. They rolled together, Kambry gripping the little girl's head, protecting it with her hands.

"Emily!" another of the townspeople cried, rushing to where Kambry and the small child landed. "Thank you! Thank you!" the woman cried, grabbing the girl's little hand before rushing away from the scene.

More flaming debris rained down on the town as Dean and his team scrambled to find an attack that would wound the creature.

"We are here to help!" A beastman ran to Dean's side, a pitchfork in his hand, ready to defend his home.

"I don't think that's a good idea," Dean told him straight, worried that if magic attacks did little to the monster that weapons would prove useless as well.

"This is our home! We want to help." The group that joined the first beast man agreed, determined to stay despite Dean's reservations.

He couldn't do anything to stop them, the villagers set on attacking the creature, so Dean chose to focus on his own team's attack, hoping the extra help would be beneficial. Side by side team Ola and the people of the town charged the beast, Wilfred and Patti hitting it with water magic while Dean blasted it with energy beams.

"There!" Dean shouted, pointing to a specific spot on the onizard's body. The smallest hole had pierced its thick scales, the effort succeeding after combining both a water and lightning attack. "We need to attack in succession!"

The onizard roared, feeling the pain of the inflicted wound and reared back, releasing a stream of fire-breath out into the attacking crowd. The flames engulfed the townspeople first, burning them to a crisp on impact. Before the stream of fire could reach Dean and his teammates, the bright familiar light enveloped them all, sending them back to the start of the level.

742

∞∞∞∞

"Welcome traveler!" Ronan greeted them excitedly, his wagging tail matching his tone.

"Ugrgh," Dean released a frustrated sigh, his fists clenched.

"We were almost there, what happened?!" Kambry whined, everyone ignoring the waiting beast man.

"I think it's the townspeople," Patti said thoughtfully, drawing the others' attention.

"Travelers?" Ronan said again, hoping to get their attention, his small frame looking up at them on the teleportation platform.

"What do you mean? Are they in on the attack?" Zayra eyed the area suspiciously, suddenly concerned about the stares of the seemingly harmless dog people.

"No, no. I think us returning to the start of the level has something to do with them dying. Like at least twice we were brought back right as one of them died. The first, when a civilian was crushed by a rock, the other when the volunteers were burned to death."

"It's possible the third happened out of sight.... I see what you are saying," Dean said thoughtfully, feeling like she was on to something. "Only one way to find out," he announced, pulling his satchel from his back.

The others watched him stick his hand deep into the bag, unsure of his intentions.

"Have you traveled here before?" Ronan said, still trying to garner the new visitors' attention.

Dean pulled his sword from his satchel and before anyone could stop him, he plunged the blade into the heart of the teleportation ambassador, the dog man's eyes wide from shock. Gasps left the mouth of those in the group as the onlookers screamed in horror. Ronan coughed, blood escaping from his mouth and onto Dean's blade. It took a minute, but finally his body slumped forward, the dog man succumbing to the fatal wound.

When the last breath left Ronan's lips, the familiar white light erupted around the group, restarting the level for the fourth time.

∞∞∞∞

"Well that settles that," Dean said when the blinding light had faded, the quiet town laid out in front of them, the dog man very much alive in front of them and just as cheery as ever.

"Welcome travelers!" he exclaimed, his tail wagging excitedly.

"Hello," Dean said, trying not to be too rough this time around.

"Welcome to Pupolia. I am the teleportation ambassador, Ronan. Please let me know if there is anything I can do to make your stay more enjoyable. If you need a hot meal or a place to stay, I know the perfect locations to suit your needs!"

"New plan—we evacuate the townspeople," Dean told them in a hushed tone as Ronan went through his typical spiel, outlining the pleasantries the town had to offer. "Ronan, we are on a mission. Can you get us in contact with the leader of Pupolia?"

"That's me too!" He smiled wide, tipping his newsboy cap toward the group. "How can I help you?"

Of course he's also the mayor, Dean almost chuckled out loud. "The whole town needs to be evacuated. Tomorrow morning there will be an attack by a massive onizard threatening the lives of the civilians in this town."

"Oh my! Are you sure? This town hasn't faced an attack in the last hundred years."

"We are sure. It is of great importance that you heed our words," Dean told him, trying his best to make his speech sound official. "Our sources are one hundred percent accurate—-this needs to be done."

"I need to prepare a few things, but you can count on me!" Ronan told him, rushing off toward a tall brick building in the distance, a large clock on the front.

"Great. Hopefully things go better this time," Dean said, hopping off of the teleportation platform.

"Do we have time for lunch?" Patti asked, eyeing Cafe Luna.

"I think we do." Kambry grinned, leading the group to the little cafe.

Amari was just as friendly as they remembered, recommending the seasonal stew to the new guests. They ate quickly, expecting to be interrupted by Ronan's announcement. When their bowls were cleaned, Dean paid with gems—the rubies having been replaced when they failed the previous try.

"Thank you Amari," he told her, placing the gems on the receipt.

Before they vacated the table, an alarm sounded in the town, causing every customer and shop worker to stop what they were doing, their ears perked up, waiting for further instructions.

"Attention people of Pupolia," Ronan's voice could be heard clearly from within the building. "This is not a drill. We are implementing the evacuation protocol—-destination, Catolia. Please pack light and head out before dark. I repeat this is not a drill. Thank you for your cooperation."

"Oh my," Amari gasped, rushing to flip the sign on her door from open to closed.

"Do you need the route to Catolia?" Her voice was filled with concern as she addressed Dean's table, worried about the visitors to their town.

"No, but thank you. We will manage just fine."

"Okay. Be careful." She smiled, rushing around to tend to the remaining guests.

"This might just work," Wilfred said, looking out the front window.

The people of town were heading into their dwellings, seemingly to pack up for the evacuation of the town. When they exited the shop, the group found even more of the villagers gathered in the square, seeking answers from the Mayor.

"Why are we leaving our homes?!" one man yelled, getting close to Ronan who stood on the ledge of the water feature that decorated the square.

"There is a threat coming our way. We need to be vigilant to protect the people of this town," Ronan responded, trying to answer the questions of the townspeople when he had very little information himself.

The voices of the townspeople only grew louder, not understanding the seriousness of the situation. Dean didn't step in, figuring they wouldn't listen to him, a stranger, if they wouldn't listen to the mayor of the town.

"Now what?" Zayra questioned, watching the frantic commotion in the center of the square.

"We can only hope they listen to him and get out before morning." Dean shrugged, heading toward the inn, wanting to rest up for the coming battle.

When they entered the establishment, the innkeeper was running around, collecting things in a worn out leather bag.

"We need a room for the night," Dean told her, his eyes following her as she scrambled around the room.

"Didn't you hear? We have to evacuate."

"It's ok, we are the ones who are going to battle the incoming threat."

She stared for a moment, letting the information sink in. Finally, realizing that the guests were serious, she headed behind the counter, pulling out the familiar key— the one leading to the suite big enough to fit them all in one room.

"It's on the house. Be safe." She placed the key in Dean's hand, slamming her bag shut and heading out the door.

"At least we get to sleep on the comfy bed this time." Kambry grinned, taking the keys from Dean and rushing to the assigned room.

The team spent the rest of the night enjoying the comfort of the hotel room, figuring by tomorrow they would be on another level, unsure when they would see another bed again. When day broke, the sun shining through the windows, they dressed for battle before heading to the town square.

The streets were quiet, the town seemingly deserted when they arrived at the place where the onizard would appear. *Nothing will stop us from defeating this thing this time,* Dean psyched himself up, gripping the handle of his trident tightly.

Footsteps drew the attention of the party, the group turning to find a mob of villagers, make-shift weapons in their hands and pot and pan armor strapped to their bodies.

"What are you still doing here?" Dean asked angrily, his eyes turning from the crowd to the space beyond the wall, aware that the demon lizard would appear any minute.

"We are here to fight for our town!" one answered as he readjusted the pot that rested on his head.

"Yea—no way we'd let it fall!"

"Yea!" The others joined in, the chanting fueling their determination.

"No—No. You're not supposed to be here," Wilfred told the crowd, holding up his arms as if that would stop them from proceeding forward.

"Don't you get it? A lizard is coming to burn this town down and anyone that stands in its way. Get out of here before you get yourselves killed!" Dean shouted at the gathered mob.

Just as he finished his sentence, the air changed, the sky darkening, a clash of lightning signaling the onizard's appearance.

"Let's get it!" the buff dog man in the front shouted, rallying the crowd forward.

The beast in all its flaming glory stood tall, throwing the first fire coated rock into the crowd. Flash! The light consumed them, sending them back to the start of the level.

∞∞∞∞

"For fook's sake!" Dean shouted at the top of his lungs, his teammates beside him equally irate. "If these damned villagers don't want to listen to what's good for them, we'll just have to make them listen."

"Welcome travelers?" Ronan stood in front of the teleportation platform, staring up at the five new visitors, their towering presence intimidating.

Dean pulled a sword from his bag and pointed it at Ronan's throat.

"This is our town now, ya hear. We want everyone out. Every last fooking one!" He turned to the rest of the onlookers brandishing his sword toward them. "You heard me, get out of this town now or yer all dead!"

Catching on quickly, the rest of the team joined in, grabbing their weapons to further intimidate the crowd.

"Don't no one try to be the hero either or we'll burn your homes to the ground," Kambry shouted, sending a swirl of fire up into the sky, enough to make an impact on the villagers.

"Please, we can work something out...what is it you want?" Ronan cowered before the group, his tail between his legs, hands raised in surrender.

Dean kneeled in close, "I just told you what I fooking want. I want every last one of you out of this town by the end of the day. Or we start lighting fires and slaughtering whole families." He grinned, adding another level of fear. "Go!" He gestured for Ronan to leave, but when he didn't move, Dean shouted, "Now!"

The dog man scurried off toward the towering building in the distance, the scene playing out in a similar manner to the previous attempt. Ronan ran through the streets telling the citizens to evacuate, letting them know that it was important to move as quickly as possible.

This time, instead of an unseen foe, Dean and his team played the bad guys, turning their swords toward anyone they thought might be trying to stay behind.

"Don't get any funny ideas." Dean held his blade toward a civilian he recognized, knowing if given the chance he would fight to keep the town safe. "Keep moving."

Luckily, the man obeyed the command, picking up his hastily packed suitcase and heading out of town. By the time the sun started setting, the place was a ghost town, not a single other living thing present except for the members of team Ola. Knowing they had the entire night to waste before the enemy would reappear, they raided the cafe's kitchen, helping themselves to leftovers before settling down in their favorite inn suite.

The next morning, Dean woke earlier than usual, knowing there would be some time before the monster appeared. He needed that time to be sure no one had returned to the town in the night, hoping to defend their home. He searched every shop that lined the main strip, and in the end, he found no one.

Finally, looking at the sun, he knew it wouldn't be long before the beast showed itself. His team joined him in the square, dressed in their armor. Dean quickly donned his battle gear as well, pulling out the team's weapons from his satchel.

"Let's make this our last run," he told them, his gaze directed toward the village wall, waiting for the beast to appear.

"We got this," Patti said confidently, pulling an arrow from her quiver.

"One final time," Kambry whispered, psyching herself up for the battle.

"Remember—combination attacks seemed to have the greatest effect on the onizard. Water then lightning. Weaken it and hit where it's vulnerable."

The others nodded, understanding their roles in his plan. Finally, the ominous dark clouds rolled in, the atmosphere changing as the clash of lightning summoned the demon lizard. The bright blue flames hummed over the beast's body, the creature moving toward the wall, finding the first of the boulders it would throw into the town.

Patti ran in close, nocking her arrow and aiming high above the brick wall. She released the string, running back to see if her shot would land. The arrow whizzed through the air, undetected by the onizard, but burned up in the beast's protective flames before even reaching its hardened scales.

"Arrows are out!" she yelled, regrouping with the others.

She switched her arrow for her staff, feeling the flow of her mana as she prepared for a water attack. The beast crashed through the brick wall, debris raining down into the town.

"Now!" Dean directed the group, Wilfred and Patti blasting the beast with a stream of water.

When the flames died down in the spot affected by the duo's water magic, Dean signaled for them to stop, sending out a blast of his own. The lightning flew straight, piercing the body of the beast, a palm sized hole left in his torso.

"That's more like it!" Dean said, feeling victorious.

"What can I do?" Kambry asked, feeling a bit left out since her fire magic didn't affect the creature at all.

"Prepare for a physical attack. The same concept—I'll weaken it with water and you strike."

"Got it!" Kambry responded, her wings already spread wide, ready to approach the monster.

The onizard cried out, feeling the pain of the injury and reared back, a flame attack inevitable.

Shit, Dean cursed himself, forgetting the monster's secondary attack.

"Take cover!"

Kambry dove for Patti, lifting her into the air to avoid the attack while the other three rushed for the water fountain, hoping the marble would be strong enough to withstand the blast. Just as Dean skidded behind the water feature of a giant coy fish, the beast breathed out its flames, a rush of orange and red covering the whole of the town square.

"Into the water!" Dean shouted, seeing the fire rushing closer.

No one questioned his order, submerging themselves in the shallow fountain. The air above filled with fire, Dean holding his breath as he watched it pass over the surface. Luckily, the blast passed quickly, allowing Dean, Wilfred and Zayra to come back up for air.

"Holy mother of creation," Zayra said as she sprung up from under the water.

"Quickly before it attacks again," Dean told them, pulling himself from the fountain.

They rushed back into battle, Kambry flying low to return Patti to the ground. Dean used water magic this time, the blast aimed for the shoulder of the creature. When the fire surrounding the beast's shoulder died out, Kambry flew in, sword drawn, and sliced the creature's skin, blood dripping from the deep wound.

A large claw swatted at the onizard's shoulder, trying to eliminate the cause of the pain, but Kambry had already moved on, her and Dean's next target, the creature's chest. When the spot was clear for an attack, Kambry dove, putting her full weight into the attack as she plunged the blade deep into the creature's chest.

It faltered, its balance lost as it fell to the pavement, cracking the ground on impact.

"Did we get it?" Zayra questioned, running a bit closer to the downed onizard.

"For good measure—," Dean said as he released a water bullet followed by an energy blast, creating a crater in the monster's head.

"We definitely got it now." Patti smirked.

The team glanced around, unsure if their victory would result in any changes to the level. The onizard's body began to glow, blinding the team momentarily. When they could finally see again, the beast's body had disappeared, a locket in its place.

"Victory!" Kambry shouted, running to collect the locket.

"But where does it go?" Zayra wondered aloud, scanning the scene for a newly made pedestal.

A moment later, the ground began to shake, the sounds of mechanics whirling filling the square. The water fountain dropped down below the earth, the pedestal quickly taking its place as it rose up from the depths.

"Guess that answers that question," Kambry said, moving in closer to the pedestal, waiting for it to settle into place.

"Are we ready to get out of this level?" Dean asked with a victorious smile on his face.

"Hell yeah!" the team cheered, the decision unanimous.

Kambry slammed the locket into place, ready to see what awaited them past level one hundred.

CHAPTER
ELEVEN
CASSANDRA

Forrester Estate

C assandra wiped the sweat from her brow, resettling into position to hit the wooden dummy that stood in as her opponent.

"Good. Now with more force," Danican instructed her, the elf training leader of fleet five.

The ship had arrived according to Esterial's timeline, the fleet setting up at the estate to train the remaining members of Team Ola. Cassandra figured now was her time to get involved, ready to follow Dean into the portals when he returned. Jessabee watched from the sidelines of the training arena, silently cheering on Cassandra with her presence. It was her way of supporting Cassandra's decision as the two waited for the others to return.

Two months had passed since team Ola's disappearance and Cassandra swore to herself that if they made it back—when they made it back—-a disappearance like this would never happen again. Following him everywhere seemed to be the best solution in her mind, since at the very least she would know of his well-being even if she were trapped—wherever— with him.

Everyday Riva called like clockwork, telling her the same thing—None of the members of team Ola appeared in Min's vault. She had no news to hold on to, just the hope that they were strong enough to persevere through whatever trial they were facing.

Sable returned half a month prior, having located her father in a brothel halfway across the galaxy. Out of his mind on opioids and space dust, he wasn't much help. He refused to give her any information about anything, but laughed hysterically at the mention of Lexis going missing. She made the decision that he had nothing to do with Dean and team Ola not returning from Mixonia as he seemed to hold a grudge against Min and talked about staying far away from their reach.

Assuming he had a hand in Lexis disappearance, Sable began tracing her father's energy signature from around the time of her kidnapping, something only she as a half-god of the same bloodline could accomplish. She was able to trace it to an exact location in the outer rim of space, but of course it was completely empty when she arrived.

That was as far as her detective skills could take her, so she returned to the estate handing all of the information over to Cassandra. From there Cassie gave her findings to the private investigators that were already on the case, having found nothing substantial to report as of yet.

Now Cassandra, hoping to occupy her time and avoid overthinking, trained with the other recruits, wanting to show off her progress when the others returned. Hanna and Kelsie worked best as a team, their twin intuition allowing them to read the others movements and respond accordingly. Fighting one of them was a challenge, but when they tag-teamed even Danican struggled to defeat them.

Markin preferred to handle a hefty weapon, like a war hammer on a battle ax, appreciating the weight behind each attack. Katriel took him under his wing, the stern and muscled elf being the best fit for the Oruk. Deathanal, a Catrin, was naturally quick on his feet, so Danican recommended daggers and throwing knives, something he adapted to quickly. Mel had yet to figure out her preference when it came to weapons, but, being a Dryad, earth magic was her specialty.

Danican was nicer than the elves Cassandra had met before him, a patient and respectful teacher who thought about how to best help each student. After the arrival of the ship, he and the ten other elves aboard the spacecraft stayed at the Forrester estate. They slept in their ship since there weren't enough rooms in the building, the team still looking to expand onto a community ship at some point.

With so few trainees, the elves offered to help in other ways around the estate, preferring not to be idle during the day. Cassandra appreciated the help, her impression of the elves improving a bit. The higher number of trainers also meant that the elves could work one on one with each member of team Ola, increasing the pace of improvement for the team.

The preservation had been repurposed into a training arena, the concrete flooring and wide space offering a suitable location for all of the needed gear.

"Put your body into it. You want them to feel your punches," Danican instructed from behind Cassandra as she jabbed at the dummy with her padded fists. "One, two. One, two. Keep the rhythm."

Cassandra released all of her frustration and worries about her team into the wooden training device, knowing that wearing herself out was the only way to sleep soundly through the night. Rearing back for another one, two combo, the sun disappeared, halting her practice.

"What happened?" Cassie looked out the plexiglass dome that surrounded them.

The sky darkened further, grey clouds rolling in. In the next minute, Cassie found herself staring at Min, standing at their full one hundred foot height just outside the dome.

"Holy--" Jessabee's eyes followed the sheer scale of Min, the god's true form intimidating.

Dropping her work out, Cassandra rushed outside to greet the god.

Min shrunk to around ten feet tall, allowing them to better address the approaching human. "The Suca humans' lead has reached one hundred points. This is a great success for the Suca. It is time for the bonus challenge, but this time, the chosen human team of three will be transported to the Core to fight."

"One hundred points...was it Dean? Did team Ola contribute to the points?"

"We can't be sure. But we have not sensed your team's presence in Mixonia for some time now."

"You can't sense them? What do you mean? It's been two months! Two months they have been trapped in your maze and now you're telling me you can't sense any of them?" Cassandra was irate, her rationale thrown out the window as she out right yelled at an all-powerful being.

"Trapped? That is impossible."

"Impossible." Cassandra chuckled as she continued, "You're just like the rest of them. So sure, yet can't tell me anything about what happened to them."

"Enough human. I came today to inform you that the challenge has been unlocked. I thought Dean might step up as the leader of the champions, but if he is not here, you will have to find another suitable for the challenge. Choose wisely. You have one hour." Min turned as though they would soon disappear.

"Wait—" Cassandra yelled, stopping Min before they could leave.

They turned around, an impatient look on their face, waiting for her to continue.

"You said a group of three is able to fight? I thought only one champion was needed for the challenge."

"The number changes depending on the group that earned the points. So far you have witnessed Core victories, and each time multiple core demons faced off against one suca champion. This time the outcome is reversed, meaning Oakley may choose three champions to fight to keep the lead for the Suca. If they win, the Core will face a catastrophe similar to those that Oakley has experienced from past losses."

"Okay. I understand."

"One hour," Min restated, disappearing in a flash, the sky brightening as the clouds dispersed with the minotaur's disappearance.

Shit, there isn't much time. Cassie ran, barging back into the training dome.

"It's time. The humans are leading enough in the games to unlock a bonus challenge," Cassandra blurted out as soon as she entered the space, everyone already gathered, waiting to learn why Min had made an appearance at the estate. "Danican." Cassandra stopped in front of the elf, her hands on her knees as she tried to catch her breath. "Are any of our trainees up for the fight?"

Danican scanned the room of anxious team members, carefully weighing their strengths in his mind.

"Hanna and Kelsie I deem the most prepared. Mel would benefit a team with her magic, but she lacks experience in battle. I can't be sure she wouldn't freeze under the threat of an enemy. The others are strong, but green with their chosen weapons, they need more practice before they fight in a battle that will decide the fate of humanity."

"Thank you." Cassandra nodded, taking the elf's words into consideration. "I'm going to call Riva. See if any of his members would be a better fit."

She pulled her phone out of the pocket of her workout pants, quickly pulling up her father's number. He answered on the third ring and she hastily explained the situation to him. Riva easily had fifteen soldiers he believed would be victorious against the Core demons, but Cassie still struggled with the final decision.

"What about teams of three?" she asked, wondering if sending her duo along with one of Riva's soldiers would be another potential option.

"We have a few who have worked together in the portals, but our most established team is Lonny's."

Hearing a familiar name reassured Cassandra; she knew Lonny would be a good choice for the mission.

"Talk with Lonny. See if he thinks he and two other members of his team are up for the challenge."

"Hang on a bit," Riva responded, the other end going quiet.

A few seconds later Cassie could hear the request for Lonny to report to the main training grounds echo over the loudspeaker.

"It shouldn't be long. I'll give you a ring when I've talked it over with Lonny."

"The timeline Min gave was an hour, it's been ten minutes already, so don't take too long," Cassie reminded him.

"You got it," Riva said shortly, the line disconnecting.

Her mind too preoccupied to return to practice, Cassandra paced around the preservation training ground, waiting for her father to call her back. Jessabee followed a few steps behind her, just as anxious to find out who would be representing humanity in the challenge. Twenty minutes later, her phone rang, sending her into a scramble to accept the call.

"Hello," she said in a hurry.

"Lonny's in. He said Nick and Yelli will join him in the battle. Don't worry too much Cass, they've got this. They won't let all of the hard work humanity has put into leveling go to waste. We are going to give these demon bastards a taste of their own medicine."

"Thanks. Tell me as soon as they return."

"I will."

Cassandra sighed when she hung up the phone, her worries only mildly lessened. In a half hours' time, the team of three would face off in the Core realm, their enemy unknown. If they won it, it would be a great victory for the Suca, but a loss would set them back—a devastating blow.

They've got this—she told herself, trying to calm down her swirling thoughts. Knowing it was out of her hands, she headed back to the wooden dummy, channeling all of her mixed emotions into practice.

CHAPTER

TWELVE

LONNY

Spelunkers' Delight Base

"You're the leader for the bonus challenge. Can you handle it?" Riva's hazel eyes bore down on Lonny, measuring his determination.

Lonny never pictured himself in the role, but that was before he learned of the portals and Mixonia's existence. Going from a drone operator to leading a team in the levels of the gods' games, if someone had told him this a year ago he would have called them a crazy bastard. Learning of the gods' games, the fight against the Core demons for humanity's survival--everything changed.

He trained his ass off to be an asset to the human team. With the help of Riva's hired teachers, then the elves, he was taught to fight and to control magic. He felt strong—ready.

"I can do it," he responded without a shadow of a doubt.

He knew that Dean's team was still missing. Dean was the obvious choice for the three to one bonus challenge, but with no one knowing his whereabouts, Lonny felt honored being chosen as the second. *I won't let humanity down,* he recited the words in his mind, the pressure fueling his determination.

He also knew that he wouldn't have to do it alone. Not this time. Nick and Yelli would be with him, two of the strongest soldiers in the entire Spelunkers' Delight base. Where Lonny focused on Earth magic, fascinated by the strength it afforded its user regardless of size, Nick harnessed brute strength, his brawn a formidable weapon.

Yelli on the other hand was a dual wielder, adept both in long and close range weapons. Like Patti, she could hit the smallest of targets from across the room, but instead of magic as her fallback she chose the sword.

Dressed in light armor, unsure of what the battle would bring, the three person team stood in the center of the training grounds, preparing for the fight that would solidify humanity's lead in the games or send them back to square one.

Riva ran to Lonny, shoving a statue in his hand. "Use it well," he told him before returning to the sidelines.

Lonny opened his hand, seeing the strongest of the pets their team had collected, Mira, a mighty stone dragon. *We got this*, he thought, gripping the pet in his fist, another ally in the challenge.

"We's gonna kick some Core ass!" Nick psyched the team up with a fist pump into the air.

The others cheered with him, the rest of the soldiers stopping their training to join in the chant. As if they were counting down, the crowd cheered their names repeatedly until a spotlight honed in on the group, transporting them from the arena.

Yelli rubbed her eyes, the bright light of the teleportation magic leaving her with spots floating across her vision. The team found themselves in a barren land, the earth dry and cracked, the scarce trees that grew sporadically about the land, stunted and brittle.

An orange haze lit up the battleground, the light artificial and eerie. In the distance, the team spotted their opponent. As tall as a two story home, the beast growled, three heads fighting for control. Sharp, white teeth bared toward its opponents in the distance, drool slipping past the teeth barrier and onto the cracked fire-laden ground below.

"Well, if that's not cheating, I don't know what is," Lonny mumbled, scanning the three-headed Cerberus, molten rock and flames beneath the beast's paws.

"I guess if you only get to choose one champion, you pick the guy with three heads," Nick said, readjusting his grip on his battle ax.

"It changes nothing," Lonny reminded them, refocusing his team.

He set Mira's statue on the ground in front of him, the tendrils of magic quickly flowing around the dragon's frozen silhouette, bringing the creature to life. Mira was only half the size of the Cerberus, her scales the color of stone and just as strong. Although smaller than the opponent, her wings would give her an advantage against the beast.

Lonny gestured for Mira to fly ahead, wanting the dragon in position when his team prepared to attack. Weapons in hand the team rushed the beast, needing to close the distance between them in order to launch their offense. The Cerberus stood its ground, pawing at the dirt with its front foot, glaring in the direction of the approaching enemy.

A low growl broke the silence of the still environment just before the beast began to sprint. When Lonny and his team were the ones closing in on the Cerberus, they felt in control, but having the massive three-headed dog running in their direction, suddenly they felt like targets.

In a matter of seconds, the beast was upon them, leaving its fiery nest. The razor sharp bite of all three heads fought to be the first to clamp down on Yelli's position. She rolled just in time, narrowly missing the row of closing jaws, dropping her sword in the shuffle. Taking her bow from around her torso, she nocked one of her arrows, releasing it toward the beast's body.

The arrowhead pierced the dog's leg, but the point was so small, it had almost no effect on the creature. A massive paw swiped in her direction, still recognizing her as the attacker, the appendage upon her before she had a chance to react.

Lonny brought up a wall of earth beside her, trying to block the blow, but the rock crumbled upon impact, the broken pieces raining down on Yelli. Luckily, Lonny's quick thinking gave Yelli the extra time she needed to flee from the beast, dodging the debris before collecting her sword and regrouping with the others.

As the team tried to think of a strategy, Mira flew closer to the Cerberus, flinging spikes in its direction. The oversized dog leapt from the path of the pointed rocks, hoping to avoid being wounded.

Despite its dance, one still managed to hit, a yelp escaping the pup's central mouth, a rock protruding from its lower leg. The yelp of pain quickly turned into a chorus of angry growls, its sights now set on the stone dragon that continued to circle its heads.

"Quick, while it's distracted!" Lonny yelled, propelling them all forward with his earth magic, the ground forming a platform under their feet.

When they were close enough to attack, Lonny swiped his staff against the cracked ground, arching it toward the creature, clumps of rock spiraling forward. Each rock collided with the Cerberus's body, a couple knocking it in its heads. It's growling now directed at Lonny, the others struck its legs with their weapons, Nick's ax proving to deal the most damage.

Yelli sliced the creature's leg with her blade, crimson strips appearing much more easily than she anticipated. So focused on wounding the beast, she didn't realize when its second paw, claws bared, came down on her.

"Yelli!" Lonny cried, trying to warn her before it was too late.

He raised another wall to block the attack, but the beast was quick, easily reading his movement. The paw reached her body before the wall could fully form, her small frame thrown across the dirt from the force, the four newly formed lines in her side oozing blood.

She coughed, turning over in the dirt, willing her body to stand back up. Lonny halted his sprint, raising his staff, the released magic surrounding the beast with a rock barrier, the enormous structure draining nearly half of his mana. Shrinking it quickly, he attempted to crush the dog monster under the weight of the stone.

It seemed to be working at first, the dome getting smaller, but the Cerberus, catching on to his trick, broke free, the rock exploding against the pressure of the beast's body. Irate and out for blood, the dog singled out Yelli, still struggling to stand as her wounds took their time regenerating.

"Oh no you don't!" Nick ran to intercept the beast mid-strike, swinging his ax as high up the beast as he could manage in a single leap.

The blade sliced the base of the Cerberus's chest, but the beast continued to barrel forward despite the pain, throwing Nick out of the way in the process. Spikes of stone, both from Lonny's magic and Mira's tail, aimed for the heads of the Cerberus, but nothing could stop its determination.

Yelli screamed as the teeth of the center head of the dog dug into her flesh, lifting her high into the air. The creature shook his prize, the force of the motion, tearing deeper wounds into her body. Her screams were horrific, piercing, her team frantically trying to get the beast to drop her.

Lonny, pulling his sword from his holster, used his earth magic to create a platform under him, lifting him toward his teammate. As he reached her, her screams stopped, the only movements left were from the continued shaking by the beast. Realizing his prey stopped responding, the beast dropped Yelli, her body plummeting to the ground below, her life long forfeit.

"RAA-" Lonny cried, slamming into one of the massive heads, his magic propelling him forward adding to his sword's thrust.

The blade sunk deep into the creature's eye, a howl being the beast's response as the head on the right aimed for Lonny, its open mouth approaching quickly. Abandoning his sword in the dog's eye socket, Lonny descended back to the ground, barely missing the teeth aimed at his body, which instead lodged themselves in the middle head of the Cerberus.

"She's gone," Nick said, hitting the ground with his fist when Lonny approached.

Shit. He looked back at the towering Cerberus, struggling to untangle its heads, their own team now down a member.

"It's not over yet," he told him, pulling two daggers from his side holster. "Quickly, while it's distracted."

Nick nodded, throwing his battle ax over his shoulder before running full speed toward the Cerberus.

"Get ready," Lonny shouted, Nick bracing his legs in response.

Lonny catapulted Nick forward using earth magic, the man flying toward the heads of the creature, ax reared back, ready to strike. As he neared the conjoined heads, he swung his ax, the blade slicing the beast from cheek to lip. When Nick's blade sliced across the creature's skin, Mira attacked the back of the beast, three thick spikes lodging themselves in the monster's rear.

Although the team's attack proved effective, they failed to think about what came after the strike, leaving Nick free falling from the height of a building. Nick swung his ax once more on the way down, piercing the chest of the beast. As the blade sliced through the monster's flesh, Nick propelled gently back toward the earth, avoiding becoming a splat on the hardened earth.

When his feet touched the ground, he pulled his weapon free, rushing away from the beast, trying to clear the monster's range of attack. Lonny saw his teammate's safe landing, his attention back on the Cerberus as he sent rocks flying in its direction. The beast ignored the pelting, still focused on Nick who scrambled from under the shadow of the dog creature.

Despite clearing the reach of the monster's paw, it only took a single movement in Nick's direction for the Cerberus to be on top of him again. His padded paw collided with Nick's body, sending him flying across the barren wasteland. He heard the cracking of bones, his body repeatedly slamming against the hardened surface. He choked out a breath when his body finally settled, unable to move.

Lonny rushed for his teammate, the earth moving him swiftly in the downed man's direction, but the Cerberus was faster, his long legs reaching Nick before Lonny's magic could. The massive paw crushed down on Nick before either had a chance to react, stealing what life remained.

Mira drew closer, throwing another line of spikes in the creature's direction. The rock hit the eye of the head on the right side, Mira going in for the next one. Angered by the flying nuisance, the two remaining heads grabbed her from the air, slamming her to the dirt, all three heads tearing into her flesh.

No, no, no, Lonny panicked, the last of his teammates slowly dying in front of him. He felt a surge of mana, his desperation fueling his determination. Unsure what effects it would yield, he transferred all of his remaining mana into the ground, praying for a miracle, his eyes locked on the Cerberus.

Lonny felt the release of his mana pouring into the ground, his teeth gritted, waiting for something to happen-- something that would save his base's prized dragon from the jaws of the three-headed monster. When nothing happened, he sprinted for the beast, daggers drawn, figuring he had to try something if they were going to win this challenge.

Finally, the earth reacted, the rumbling pushing Lonny off balance. A tree broke through the surface of the earth, its sharp, unruly branches impaling the body of the Cerberus as it grew. The wood branched off from the initial trunk, each new branch piercing through the beast's body, until it was lifted from the ground, spikes protruding haphazardly from its chest, back and heads.

Mira dragged herself away from the commotion, having lived through the Cerberus's beating. When the rumbling ceased, Lonny stood staring over at the effects of his magic, the deadly sight of the skewered creature illuminated by the artificial orange lighting of the Core realm. Looking around, Lonny expected to be immediately transported from the zone, but nothing happened, leaving him to question if another enemy would appear.

Finally, twenty minutes later, when Mira had healed completely and was able to fly again, a spotlight shined on the two remaining challengers, transporting them back to the surface of Oakley.

∞∞∞

Min's was the first face they saw when the three of them returned to Oakley, Mira back in her statue form and Yelli and Nick alive and in good health.

"Champions." Min stared down at them from their ten feet height. "Victory is yours. Thanks to your efforts, the Suca now have the upper hand in this battle of worlds. The demon core will take the penalty, facing a threat to their land. Don't get cocky though, the tides turn quickly, you must remain vigilant if you wish to keep your lead."

Lonny, Yelli, and Nick nodded, understanding Min's warning. Min nodded in response before vanishing from the base, the darkness receding with their departure.

"Damn—that was something else." Nick dropped his weapon to the training room floor, suddenly feeling the full extent of exhaustion from the battle.

"I can't believe it got the upper hand on me," Yelli pouted, determined to train to be even stronger in the future.

"Guys, we won!" Lonny reminded them, eager to bask in the hard won victory.

The rest of the soldiers training in the area came over to congratulate the group, everyone waiting to shake hands with the champions. Riva was among them, waving over the chef who brought out bottles of champagne to toast the Suca humans' victory. Training was dropped for the rest of the day, the base celebrating instead, knowing that the days to come would be filled with even tougher training as they made their way past the hundred-point lead.

THIRTEEN

TUCKER

Dropoff point- Space

Beep! Beep! Beep! The alarm sounded throughout the spacecraft, red flashing lights accompanying the sound. Tucker jerked awake, the sudden motion causing him to fall from the bed, tangled in the sheets.

"What is it?" Lexis stirred from the other side of the bed, pulling the covers back over her shoulder, her eyes remaining closed.

"I don't know, but I need to find out."

Tucker pulled on the pair of jeans that were in a pile at the side of the bed, pushing the button beside the bedroom door. The door hissed open, the hallway lighting up from the introduction of movement. With a hastened pace, he headed to the ship's flight deck, eager to find out what the commotion was about.

Bamba and Pamrii were already in the cockpit, pushing buttons as they tried to assess the situation.

"What's our status?" Tucker asked, his hand resting on the back of the chair.

"I can't tell. The alarms won't let up, but I can't see nothing on the radar. If something's there, we are headed right for it."

Tucker leaned into the screen, trying to make out the blips on the machine. "Slow our speed."

Bamba nodded, flipping a few switches before pulling back a lever. The ship's speed decreased as a result, their destination remaining the same.

"Should we route a new course?" Pamrii questioned, staring out into the starless abyss in front of them.

"That's the location the gods pointed out...there must be something there."

As the words came from his mouth, a squeal—like nails on a chalkboard— came from the spacecraft, an outside force starting to maneuver the ship.

"What the hell?" Tucker switched seats with Bamba, needing to know what had caught them in its gravitational pull. "There shouldn't be any planets around here...," he mumbled, rechecking the radar.

The pull on the ship strengthened, jerking everyone forward.

"There!" Pamrii pointed out the front, into the darkness.

Tucker squinted, trying to figure out what she was pointing to, and finally saw it. Barely visible, the only indication being the reflection from its constant motion, was a black hole, the gravitational pull of the anomaly drawing in everything around it.

"It's a fucking black hole!" he yelled, slamming the thrusters in the opposite direction, hoping it wasn't too late to escape from the pull of the ship destroyer.

"There were no stars... I should have known," Pamrii lamented, hitting more buttons, trying to send them into hyperdrive to help pull them from the path of the black hole.

"Nothing we can do now," Tucker told her, gripping the throttle as it shook violently.

"Come on, come on." Bamba rushed to the middle of the controls, flipping open a cap to reveal a small red button flashing underneath.

Without hesitation, Bamba pressed the blinking red button, a whoosh of fire exploding out of the front of the ship, the fuel being diverted to the thruster. Finally, the ship began to back track, moving slowly away from the deadly space crater.

"Dammit! Fucking, shitty, lying, manipulative, bastards!" Tucker said in a huff when the immediate danger had passed, swiveling his chair around before pacing the flight deck. "A black hole?! They want me to drop her off in a black hole." The more he thought about it the angrier he got.

Then he realized the flaw in the gods' explanation— Getting close enough to a black hole to throw in Lexis would inevitably pull his ship in with her.

"They never wanted me to make it out. This was a suicide mission. Assholes." He punched the wall of the ship, the contact with the metal sending a shock of pain through his arm and down his body.

Grimacing, he shook his fist, trying to alleviate the pain, his anger only rising at the situation.

"I shouldn't have trusted them. Why would I trust the words of those deceiving gods? Stupid, stupid." He smacked his forehead with the heel of his hand.

"What choice did you have?" Pamrii tried to comfort him, her hand resting on his shoulder.

"It was either that or death," Bamba assured him, sitting down in the control chair, making sure they were truly out of the range of the black hole's reach before quieting the thrusters.

"You're right...fooled or not, what choice was there? What choice is there now?" He stopped, realizing he was left with a dilemma. "Shit...what do we do now?"

"Is everything alright? There was a whole lot of shaking in the bedroom... and not the sexy kind." Lexis walked into the control room, a wink directed to Tucker.

"We've reached the destination," Tucker said solemnly.

"Oh, really. So where did Zued and Tarreen rope you into taking me?" She waltzed toward the front windows, letting her assets shake with each step, attempting to entice Tucker into watching her walk by.

She scanned the open darkness, smatterings of stars returning to their view.

"A black hole."

"Hmm," she responded nonchalantly.

"Hmm...is that all you have to say?" he questioned, remembering his own reaction.

"I mean, I can't say I'm too surprised. They were looking to get rid of me after all." She shrugged. "A black hole is a bit much for a half god, but it would certainly do the job." She saw the look on Tucker's face and added, "So are you joining me in this black hole?" She grinned knowing they couldn't just expel her out into the black hole without suffering at least some damages to the ship, if not a total loss.

"Hell no."

Her smile softened as she snuggled up closer to the man. "Aw—you like me," she cooed.

He sighed, dropping into one of the cockpit chairs. "What does it even matter anymore? We are dead no matter what I do. Throw her in the black hole, dead. Run away with her, dead. Return her to Oakley, dead."

"Whoa. Whoa. Whoa. Don't be so negative. And I am right here, you can talk to me too. What do you want to do?" Lexis said, leaning in close, her eyes meeting Tucker's.

"It doesn't matter."

"It does. Don't think about anyone else, but you. No consequences, no barriers. What is it that you want to do?"

"I want...to start over on the new planet."

"Las Karisak?"

"Yes. With you." He slipped his hand into hers. "I want to control the portals on that planet and earn money in the maze. Maybe set down some roots."

"Perfect. We'll do that." She smiled at him, so sure of her response.

For a moment he was drawn in by her confidence, captivated by her smile, but then he remembered the obstacles he would need to face in order for that small dream to come true. "It's impossible." He released her hand, scrubbing his fingers through his hair.

"Talk it out. What is wrong with the plan?" She wrapped her hands around his shoulders, sitting on his lap.

"For one, the minute we arrive on Las Karisak with you, Min will know. They will kill me... maybe for real... maybe turn me into a statue to fuel Mixonia, who can say for sure?"

"Then they don't need to know I'm there," she whispered close to his ear.

Pushing her back, he looked at her with a stern expression. "And how would we manage that?"

"Did you forget I'm half god? Erasing my presence isn't hard."

"But Zued and Tarreen talked as if it were an incredible feat to bring you to space... to keep you from Min's radar."

"For them, yes. You can't just erase another god's presence all willy nilly. Do you know what kind of chaos that would lead to? But my own, that's a different story. Just say the word and they never have to know I'm there."

His mouth twisted in concentration, finally finding a little hope to hold onto.

"Okay, but what about Zued and Tarreen? If they find out I reneged on the mission, I'll be dead then too."

"So who says they need to find out? My presence will be gone—I can hide out from the two of them while you discuss the terms of the arrangement. After that I'll be back in human form and can just change up my look a bit so they don't recognize me."

She makes it sound so easy, Tucker thought to himself, but knowing that those they were trying to fool were gods, made the plan seem lacking and a bit too optimistic.

"Okay, but what if they really did plan on me dying here? Then what? They will probably just kill me outright to get rid of the evidence."

Lexis bit her lip, her index finger stroking one of the tiny horns that protruded from her forehead.

"See, it's not that easy."

"I'm thinking," she whined.

The oruk sisters watched the exchange quietly from the sidelines, knowing that no matter what Tucker decided, they would be along for the ride. They had grown fond of the small human, so despite the contract that brought them together they now felt a sense of camaraderie with the man, a respect that proved mutual as Tucker referred to them as his valued advisors.

"I say we chance it. They may just overlook the fact that you survived and go through with the deal. Gods aren't ones to get their hands dirty...which is why they made the deal with you in the first place."

Her words made sense. There had to be a reason why Tucker was privy to the god's plans, but that didn't mean they didn't see his usefulness as being over—his life could still be in danger.

"Fine. We will continue on as if we have completed the mission. Lexis has been expelled from the ship——sucked into the black hole. Bamba, set a course for Sneed Orbital. We need to pick up the crew."

"You got it, boss," she told him, moving over to the radar screen.

Pressing in the coordinates, the screen shifted, revealing an image of the orbital in green and black.

"It's likely to take three months to return, then another four to reach the new planet. We can stock up on supplies in Sneed," Pamrii reported, joining her sister at the controls.

"Why wouldn't we just use the new wormhole set up for the Las Karisak? It just opened to the public recently, but it has been reported to drop ships off about a day from the planet," Lexis asked, eying the screen that showcased their destination.

"True and while I would love to do that, for a ship this size the cost alone would set us back years. It's money we'll need to establish ourselves on the new planet. I'll take seven months of travel over being homeless in a swampland."

Lexis nodded thoughtfully, completely agreeing with Tucker's argument.

"Lexis," Tucker said quietly, drawing the half minotaur's attention. "If you can actually hide your presence from the gods, don't you want to return to your home? Back to Oakley. I can make that happen."

She smiled softly. "I quite like it here with you." She kissed his cheek. "I think Las Karisak will provide a good new start for me. Well I'm going to take a shower. You're welcome to join me if you'd like." Lexis pointed to Tucker playfully, trying to avoid the serious conversation as she sauntered out of the control room, Tucker's eyes glued to her wide hips.

When she was clear from earshot Pamrii asked, "Are you really going to trust her and bring her with us to Las Karisak?"

"Of course not," Tucker responded instantly. While it was a dream to start a life with her on a new planet, he knew that was all it could ever be--wishful thinking. "When we get to Sneed Orbital, Lexis will be placed on a pod and sent back to Oakley. It's not so much her I'm worried about, but if Dean ever found out I was a part of her disappearance, he wouldn't hesitate to get his hands dirty." The man shuddered at the thought.

The girls went quiet, wondering if his plan would go the way he seemed to be picturing in his mind. They didn't bother to point out the impossibility of Lexis boarding a pod without making a fuss, figuring they had another three months before they'd need to worry about it. Instead, they remained focused on the vast span of space to their front, the spacecraft slowly gaining speed.

FOURTEEN

DEAN

Minotaur's Maze- Level One Hundred Fifty

The fire crackled, lighting up the darkness of the night. Dean stared into the flickering orange and red, dark circles gracing his under eyes. Around him, slept his team, his turn on watch coming to an end as the first rays of sunrise brightened the dark sky.

"Kambry." He placed his hand on her shoulder, his voice soft.

She stirred, wiping the sleep from her eyes, preparing for her shift. The team had lost count of how many days had passed in the maze, but still they found no signs of Braxton or a way out. Every level proved a little more difficult, but they kept with their plan to take each level seriously and at a pace that would allow everyone to survive.

Kambry's healing magic remained effective so far, although invoking a pet was hit or miss—sometimes the statues would transform, other times the team would wait in anticipation only for the statue to stay as nothing more than a piece of stone. They had yet to encounter another level quite like level one hundred with its friendly sentient beings that only wanted to help the visitors that appeared in their town.

With the increasing difficulty of the levels, finding a safe place to sleep was becoming more challenging. The exhaustion brought on by the constant need to remain on alert could be seen in the faces of each of the team members, bloodshot eyes and dark circles now a prominent feature. Still, they held onto the hope that they would reach a point where when they placed the locket on the pedestal, they would be transferred out of the maze.

Level one hundred and fifty spawned them in a lush forest, the leaves turning the colors of fall, the air crisp. They immediately began walking, exploring the environment, attempting to discern their mission for the level. The further they walked, the sparser the trees became, the trunks turning black and brittle.

A Victorian style castle complete with a wraparound metal fence sat far in the distance, clearly the destination. Not liking the state of the forest, but wanting to get some sleep before facing whatever beast resided in the castle, the team back tracked, making camp in the overgrown portion of the woods. They had settled into the forest the night before, sleeping in rounds to be sure none of the wildlife made easy prey of them in the darkness.

Only once during Dean's shift did he have to chase off a curious wolf, the beast instantly realizing the sleeping party outnumbered him and backing off without a fight. Now Kambry sat awake while the others slept, her eyes focused on the building in the distance, her hands gently stroking her baby bump.

When the sun rose high in the sky, the rest of team Ola awoke, feeling at least a bit more rested than before.

"What do you think is in there?" Wilfred asked, adding sticks to the fire so they could cook some breakfast.

"Hopefully nothing. Just a big, old, empty building with nothing but the pedestal inside," Patti answered immediately, glaring into the distance.

"Wouldn't that be nice," Dean replied absentmindedly, his attention on his satchel and the meat he pulled from its depths.

"Doesn't matter. Whatever it is, we will take it out just like everything before it," Kambry said confidently, skewering the sausage and holding it over the open flame.

∞∞∞

An hour later, the fire had been stomped out, the campsite cleared. The team headed toward the castle, the dead surroundings making the old fashioned mansion seem even creepier. Despite the sun having fully risen, the sky remained grey, the clouds growing darker the closer the team got to the building.

Team Ola approached the massive metal gate, the fence extending around the whole of the building, each of the slats topped with sharp points.

"Do we just go through the front door?" Zayra asked, breaking the silence.

Wilfred pushed on the gate, not expecting it to swing open as easily as it did. The team entered the castle's territory, a ominous feeling washing over them. Dean tried to ignore the suffocating feeling, choosing to focus on how to get through the level the most efficiently.

"I think we should split into two groups. One to explore the outside, the other to start on the inside," Dean told the group, his neck craned, scanning the entirety of the building. "Kambry and Zayra, you take the outside, while Patti, Wilfred and I will head inside and see if we can catch a glimpse of the monster we're up against. Meet up with us when you can."

"Alright," Kambry said, heading toward the back of the building. "Oh and Dean," she said as she stopped, turning to address him, "please try to avoid fighting 'til we regroup. Remember, slow and steady."

He nodded, agreeing that waiting for the others would be the best choice regardless of the enemy they needed to face. Feeling reassured that the group of three would not engage with the unknown enemy, Kambry and Zayra resumed their walk toward the back of the building. Wilfred, Patti and Dean approached the sleek, dark brown double doors of the castle, a knocker on either door.

"Do we knock?" Wilfred asked, his hands headed toward the iron rings.

"If we want to ruin the element of surprise, sure." Patti shrugged, rolling her eyes.

"Right." He withdrew his hand, moving it toward the doorknob instead.

A high squeak echoed through the entryway when Wilfred pushed on the door, eliciting winces from the watching members.

"Hopefully nothing heard that." Wilfred laughed nervously, pushing the door open the rest of the way.

Candles lit the inside of the hall, a giant spiral staircase leading up to the higher levels of the building. The decor was dark, blacks and reds used in over abundance. Sighs of relief left the mouths of the trio, nothing waiting for them when they entered the building.

"Up, straight or left?" Dean asked, gesturing first to the stairs to the left of them and then down the halls directly in front and to the right of them.

"Up," Patti and Wilfred spoke in unison, somehow feeling they would be less likely to encounter the owner of the castle in the upper rooms.

Dean headed for the stairs, the white marble a stark contrast to the deep burgundy walls and black curtains. When he reached the fifth step he hit an invisible barrier, the level stopping him from continuing upward. Patti and Wilfred were following so close behind that they bumped into each other when Dean stopped suddenly.

"Guess up wasn't the right choice," Dean told them, maneuvering around them to head back down the staircase.

"Alright, which way is next?" Patti questioned, peering down the two remaining halls.

Dean pointed to the front hall, leading the team down a long corridor, huge ornate pictures lining both walls. The pictures were of men and women in dark, fancy attire—-*something only a vampire would wear*, Dean thought to himself. At the end of the hall was the dining room, a rectangular wooden table spanning the length of the room sat in the middle of the space, chairs covered with plush red fabric on all sides.

Hanging from the ceiling was an oversized chandelier, the circular shape outlined with lit candles to illuminate the dining space. Dean walked through the room, opening the only other door in the room located on the back wall. Behind it laid the kitchen. Quickly scanning the room, he determined that neither contained the items they needed to move on to the next level.

"Third time's the charm," Patti chimed, heading back the way they came to follow the remaining hallway.

At the end of the hall were giant double doors, engraved with intricate carvings even more extravagant than the front doors. The significance of the doors made the team believe that whatever they were searching for would be just beyond those doors.

"Do we wait for the others?" Wilfred asked, his ear placed against the wood, trying to hear if there were any enemies waiting in the other room.

"Can you hear anything?" Patti asked anxiously.

"No it's quiet..."

"Maybe just a peek?" Patti turned her gaze on Dean, her hand already on the iron handle.

"Fine, but keep your guard up," Dean acknowledged Patti's desire to see what waited in the room, accepting her request, "and keep your weapons close."

Patti nodded, readjusting the quiver on her shoulder and readying her bow, preparing once again to open the doors.

"Not too much," Wilfred told her, not wanting her to swing the door open wide in case they needed to make a quick retreat.

"Relax. I'm just going to open it the tiniest bit." She grinned, pushing the door open a crack.

Sticking her face close to the open slit, she peered inside the spacious throne room.

"It's huge. There are two enemies...both on a stage area. One is sitting on a throne, the other is just standing beside him. Maybe a king? It's hard to tell. The other is wearing a robe that covers his face."

Before Patti could close the door, an unidentified force pulled it open, bringing her with it. She slid across the floor, her hand still gripping the knob. Dean and Wilfred ran in after her, preparing for the worst.

"Dean, Dean, Dean, how nice of you to visit," a familiar voice called to Dean. "It is a pity our last meeting ended so poorly, I had wanted to see you again."

"Thero." Dean stared at the man sitting on the throne, a crown of black metal sitting atop his head.

Patti's and Wilfred's heads turned to the figure in question, confused and appalled to see him alive and breathing. Distracted by the unwanted reunion, Thero seized the opportunity to slam the door shut behind his honored guests. Wilfred immediately tried the handle, the door locked from the outside meaning they were trapped in the room with Thero and his mysterious ally.

"I killed you. I saw it with my own eyes. There is no way this is real... It has to be another trick of the maze."

Thero's eyes narrowed, displeased by Dean's doubts. He stood, throwing his arm out in Dean's direction, a flurry of icicles answering his call. The ice sped toward Dean, the amount making it difficult to dodge. In an attempt to avoid the attack—real or an illusion—Dean leaped out of the path, missing all but one.

A single spike of ice seemed to follow Dean's desperate movements, lodging itself into his shin. He cried out, the pain much too real for the magic to be a hologram.

"Real enough for you?" Thero taunted, sitting back down on his throne.

"But how is this possible?" Patti cried, rushing to tend Dean's wound.

The ice had already begun to melt, leaving a gaping hole the size of a quarter in Dean's leg. Patti ripped a piece of cloth from the end of her shirt, holding it over the wound until the health regeneration of the maze had time to stop the bleeding. Thero laughed wickedly, his evil cackling mirrored by the figure that stood to his left.

Then Thero froze, the mysterious figure cloaked in black stepping forward.

"Surprised to face an old enemy?" the familiar voice asked, ripping the hood from his head.

"Braxton. I should have known." Dean spit, forcing himself to stand.

"It's amazing what one can accomplish in the maze." He approached the sitting Thero, leaning in closer to his face. "He might not be the real thing, but he doesn't know that. Don't worry though, all of his powers are intact... I've even added a few extra for fun." Braxton smirked.

The blood oozing from Dean's wound had slowed, freeing Patti's hands. She didn't hesitate, nocking an arrow in a split second and sending the missile whizzing toward the center stage, Braxton's head its target.

The arrow passed harmlessly through the projection, sinking into the plaster of the wall behind it. Braxton began laughing, finding it hilarious that the team fell for the same trick twice.

"Again—did you really think it would be that easy?"

Patti gritted her teeth, nocking another arrow, this one with Thero's name on it.

"Ah, Ah, Ah," Braxton waved his pointer finger back and forth at Patti. "That's not very fair, now is it?" he reprimanded, placing his palm on Thero's forehead.

A bright, magic filled light erupted from the point of contact, spreading out until Thero's entire body was enveloped in a blue glow.

"Heh, now try it." He chuckled, snapping his fingers, the hologram dispersing.

Patti couldn't resist his taunts, taking a few steps forward before releasing her arrow, quickly nocking more until a line of five arrows flew toward the still glowing Thero. Each arrow collided with the bright blue barrier, the arrowhead snapping off from the force, the broken pieces falling to the floor. Dean and Wilfred drew their swords, getting into a fighting stance as Thero's body began to bulge, slowly morphing into something else.

Dean aimed his free hand at Thero, sending out a blast of energy toward the morphing figure, hoping to stop its hideous transformation. The light connected with the barrier, the blue glow absorbing the attack as though Dean had never thrown one in the first place, Thero continuing his transformation unimpeded. The team could do nothing, but watch as their enemy grew stronger before their eyes.

Thero's once pale skin turned a charcoal color, his flesh hardening as his body grew thrice its size, two massive horns growing from his forehead. From his back sprouted two gigantic wings, similar to those of a bat, the thin, veiny membrane spreading the width of the throne room. He tucked his wings back in, smiling at his waiting prey, his pointed canines on full display.

Thero began laughing maniacally at his transformation, another row of horns appearing along his forearms.

"I am the Demon King! You have no power here. But I—I wield all the power! I will defeat you this time—mark my words," he bellowed, grabbing his staff from its resting place beside the now dwarfed throne room chair.

"Uh—now what?" Wilfred squeaked, rattling the door handle in an attempt to free them from the room that suddenly seemed very small.

Dean surveyed the area, his eyes frantically searching for a way out—or maybe the pedestal, he wasn't completely sure, all he knew was that taking on a souped up Thero wasn't their best option.

"Don't even think about leaving." Thero read his movements, a wall of ice forming around the trio.

Before they could melt the ice, Thero had rushed toward it, smashing through the barrier of his creation, shards of ice and Thero's powerful limbs falling onto the group. The three managed to avoid Thero's punches, the ice pieces having left little damage as they each ran in a different direction.

Patti shot more arrows toward the beast, the blue haze that once surrounded Thero's body no longer there to protect him. The arrows hit their target, but his skin had thickened to such a degree that the arrowheads were no longer strong enough to pierce into his flesh.

"Useless." Patti threw her bow and quiver to the ground, switching to water magic.

The others, recognizing her intent, prepared a water spell of their own, all three attacking at once. The blades of water hit Thero from all directions, leaving thin scratches in his skin, exposing the vulnerable flesh beneath his hard exterior. Just as a bit of hope began to form from seeing his wounds, the scratches healed in an instant, Thero laughing at the group's pathetic attempt to injure him.

His heavily armored forearm swung out hitting Patti before she could reset for another attack. She flew backwards, her back slamming into the castle wall. Dean seethed with anger, his mind whirling, wishing he could defeat the vampire mage turned demon lord as easily as he did back on Oakley.

"Are you okay?" Wilfred ran to Patti's side, trying to help her to her feet.

"I'll be ok. Just leave me." She waved him off, knowing her broken bones would need time to heal before she would be able to assist them in battle.

Needing a stronger attack, Dean gave energy magic another shot, fueling his blast as much as his body could handle, hoping it would be enough to injure the enemy. Placing both of his palms together, he pointed his hands at Thero, the demon lord's eyes fixated on Dean. The beast shook his head, slowly as if saying it was useless to fight back, but Dean released his attack anyway, hoping to catch Thero in a bluff.

The beam burst forth from Dean's body, the light illuminating the whole of the throne room and the energy blast headed straight for Thero. When the light collided with his body, Dean felt his chest tighten in anticipation, the physical manifestation of his hope for a successful attack.

While the blast did hit Thero's body, instead of absorbing the attack, his body reflected it, the powerful beam bouncing off his skin and connecting with the castle's roof, right over Wilfred's and Patti's position. The roof immediately caved in from the impact, a mass of debris raining down on the duo.

Seeing that his comrades had been hit, Dean tried to rush to their aide, but Thero wouldn't allow for it. He brought up a barrier of ice, blocking Dean from assisting the two that were now trapped under the rubble.

"Bastard," Dean berated the demon, trying to use his own magic to dispel the barrier, but Thero's magic proved to be stronger.

"Now this is more like it." The vampire demon grinned, taking pleasure in Dean's pain. "You see, you were never stronger than me. Just lucky."

A spike of ice flew toward Dean's shoulder, but Dean deflected it easily with his blade.

"But you see, luck runs out."

Another icicle flew toward his thigh, another swing of his sword sending it into the tiled floor.

"And yours, Dean Forrester, has definitely run out."

A wall of icicles flew toward Dean, the number too great to deflect them all. For every spike he avoided another would take its place, making dodging the attack impossible. As he attempted to strike the incoming spikes with his sword, Dean was unknowingly being pushed back, it wasn't until his back hit the wall that Dean realized Thero's plan.

With nowhere else to run to, a final wall of icicles sped toward his location, leaving Dean with no other choice but to brace for impact. He gritted his teeth, his sword swinging wildly, knocking down the knives of ice. The first to get through his defense sliced his shoulder, the next his thigh.

With no end in sight, Dean could only continue his dance, the more spikes that grazed his skin, the slower his defense, leading him in a downward spiral. Dean's forearms burned, the scratches dripping blood, but he refused to let Thero have the satisfaction of victory.

"I can do this all day," Thero taunted. "Can you?"

The banter only fueled Dean's determination, but his body was slowing down, his arm's strength waning. Another wall of ice headed for him, and Dean could tell he had reached his limit. He wouldn't be able to block enough of the spikes and dodging proved useless when the ice changed direction to follow his movement.

He let the last of his mana build, relying on an energy spell to save him from certain death. When the ice reached the halfway point within the room, he released a wall of light, the blast headed straight for the icicles. The two collided, the ice starting to melt as a bright light engulfed the entirety of the room, forcing Dean to shut his eyes.

∞∞∞

When he opened them again he stood in a forest, a shrill cry echoing through the branches. The sounds pulled him from his confused state, recognizing that his teammates were by his side, one laying on the ground.

"No—" Zayra cried, sliding to her knees beside an unconscious Wilfred.

She shook the Osamar, trying to wake him from his forced sleep, his eyes slowly blinking open.

"What the hell happened?" Kambry rushed to their sides, assessing the injury.

From his chest protruded a metal bar, his shirt soaked in his blood.

"You're alive. Look at me... here...hi," she tried to get her husband's attention, his eyes heavy, making it difficult to focus.

His hand immediately went for the bar, wanting to pull it from his chest, but Zayra stopped him, her fingers intertwining with his.

"Let Kambry handle that," she cooed, leaning in close to his ear.

Kambry placed her fingers on Wilfred's throat, reading his pulse. She then examined the wound, gently prodding the area around the steel beam.

"What happened?" Zayra asked Dean as Kambry worked.

"The ceiling collapsed. I—couldn't get to them. The next thing I knew we were here," Dean said softly, his own wounds already healing.

"He stayed to protect me," Patti choked out, her hand gripping her ribs, the breaks only halfway through healing. "I couldn't move and the ceiling came down on us. He shielded me.... I didn't think we'd get out until a light filtered in through the spaces of the rubble."

"We found the locket," Zayra responded. "It was in the basement...the dungeon."

Kambry finished examining Wilfred, her face pale when she addressed the waiting team members. She waved them over, Patti and Dean huddling up with her while Zayra remained with her husband.

"I can't save him," she whispered, tears pooling in her eyes.

Both Patti and Dean turned toward Wilfred, his eyes fixated on his wife who still held his hand firmly.

"Are you sure? There has to be something," Patti pleaded, feeling responsible for his injury.

"The bar from the ceiling is too close to his heart... maybe even in his heart. He's lost too much blood. Pulling it out... will kill him," she said with certainty.

"But not pulling it out means he's dead too."

Kambry nodded solemnly. "Even with my healing magic and the regeneration from the maze, he will succumb to the injury before either has a chance to work."

Dammit. Dean gritted his teeth, furious that he had allowed this to happen. They were doing so well, level one hundred and fifty without a team member's death-- but that didn't matter now.

"I'll tell her," Dean said, steeling himself, because one look at the tear stained faces of his comrades told him that they would be blubbering messes before passing the message on.

Dean walked over to where Zayra was rocking softly, Wilfred's hand still in hers.

"So is Kambry going to come and heal him?" she said with hope in her voice. "He can't wait much longer."

Dean broke the news as gently as he could, Zayra's expression turning from one of horror to anger to immense sadness.

"No—he can't. You can't...you have to fight," she addressed Wilfred, his breathing labored.

"I love you," he whispered.

"No, don't do that." The tears rolled down her cheek, dropping one by one onto his forehead. "Don't leave me."

Kambry and Patti joined the others, comforting Wilfred in his final moments.

"Can't you try?" Zayra asked softly, knowing her husband was slowly slipping away whether Kambry gave her magic a chance or not.

"If that's what you want," she replied.

Wilfred had already closed his eyes, his breathing becoming shallower.

"Yes. Please. I need to try something."

"Okay, but it might hurt him." Kambry looked deep into her eyes, asking silently once more if it was truly what she wanted.

"If there is a chance to save him, we have to try. It would be different if he were going to be turned into a statue, but we don't know that. This could be the last chance I have to try and save him. So please, do it."

Kambry nodded, wrapping her fist around the bar. After taking a deep breath, she yanked the piece of metal from Wilfred's chest, throwing it to the side before covering the hole with her palm. Healing magic poured into the wound, closing the injury from the inside out.

The entire ordeal lasted less than a minute and when she removed her hands from Wilfred's chest, he was completely healed, as if the injury had never happened. While he appeared unharmed, his chest remained still, everyone staring intently for any signs of motion. Kambry felt for his pulse in his neck, finding nothing.

"He's gone." She sniffled, turning to Zayra.

Her face dropped, all of the hope she held disappearing with two words. Unable to accept Kambry's evaluation, she tried CPR, performing the chest compressions and lifesaving breaths for nearly an hour before accepting his death as reality.

"How did this happen?" she asked no one in particular, her hands still in position on Wilfred's chest.

"We don't know for sure that he's gone," Patti tried to console her with the chance of an optimistic future.

"But we don't know that he's not either." She wiped her nose on her sleeve. "And honestly that might be worse—not knowing whether he is alive or dead...for real. If I hold hope that he's alive and waiting to be rescued...I might lose him all over again."

She pushed herself up, walking deeper into the woods. The others moved to follow, but she softly told them that she wanted to be alone, stopping them where they stood. The team made camp in the overgrown woods, giving Zayra the space she needed to grieve, her sobs echoing through the forest the whole night long.

∞∞∞∞

Dean sat with his back to a tree, keeping watch over his sleeping comrades, his shift being the last for the night, the sun already rising. A crack of the branches alerted his senses, causing him to stand on instinct. Zayra froze where she stood, startled by his sudden reaction.

"Sorry," they said in unison, Dean sitting back down while Zayra entered the camp.

Her eyes were red and puffy, but she was no longer crying. Dean wanted to ask her how she was, what he could do for her, but he didn't want to force her to relive the moment of Wilfred's death, still so fresh in everyone's minds.

"Did you sleep?" he asked instead, her head shaking lightly in response. "Try to sleep. There's still a few hours before these guys will be up."

"Thank you," she said softly, settling into a more comfortable position.

Dean scanned the surroundings while his teammates slept, the lush fall colored forest spreading out on all sides. Again no enemies attempted to attack while the others slept, the forest seemingly quiet. After two and half hours, Kambry woke up, her eyes immediately drawn to Wilfred's body, covered in leaves, reminding her that what happened wasn't a dream.

"Hey," she said softly, taking a seat next to Dean on the ground.

"Hey," Dean responded, laying his head on her shoulder.

They cuddled together, their body warmth comforting the other, no words needed, until Zayra and Patti woke a half hour later. No one said anything at first, the death looming in the air, but they all knew what had to be done.

"Should we bury the body and then see what kind of bastards wait for us on this level?" Zayra asked, her pain masked behind an upbeat tone.

Dean pulled a few shovels from his bag, and they began digging a hole for Wilfred's body, not wanting to leave it out in the open for the creatures of the level to desecrate. When the last pile of dirt fell on the grave, they had a moment of silence, each saying a few silent words of their own to Wilfred.

As much as she wanted to avoid creating meaningless hope, Zayra still prayed that Wilfred's statue would be waiting in Min's vault when they exited the maze.

"Let's go," she said, fighting back her tears, leading the group from the clearing and back into the thick of the woods.

Twenty minutes of walking later and the trees began to thin, the trunks turning darker and the leaves becoming scarce.

"Does this look familiar to anyone else?" Patti asked, her question laced in worry.

Ten minutes later and the massive Victorian castle could be seen in the distance, the forest reduced to a barren graveyard of brittle, blackened tree trunks.

"How—why?" Zayra stuttered.

They continued walking despite the disbelief and growing anger, having no other choice but to continue the level. Reaching the wrap around metal fence, Dean pushed the gate open, the door opening just as easily as the first time.

"If this is the same level, then will the locket still be in the same spot?" Dean questioned.

"Let's find out," Kambry responded, leading the way toward the back of the castle.

Behind the building featured an overgrown garden, the hedges that lined the area were unruly and misshapen. Vines grew up the side of the structure, looking as though nature wished to reclaim it for its own. Kambry pulled on a bush near the mansion, the roots and vines snapping from the force.

"I forgot how difficult this was," she huffed, gesturing for Dean to hand over her staff.

Switching to fire magic, a fire ball flew from her staff, easily burning up the foliage that blocked her path.

"It took us a while to find this last time; it's hidden pretty well."

Under the brush were metal cellar doors, a rusty padlock the only thing keeping them securely in place. Kambry wrapped her hand around the lock, one strong pull enough to break the shank completely. Throwing the broken pieces to the ground, she pulled open the double doors, a musty smell seeping from the dark cellar.

"If you want, you can wait here. I remember where the locket should be," she told the others, one foot already on the stairs.

"We'll go together." Dean shook his head, not willing to chance anything this time around.

Kambry shrugged as if to say suit yourself then headed into the basement of the castle. The musty smell turned putrid the further down they went, the walls damp and the dirt floor starting to mold. Cells lined the walls, Zayra not exaggerating when she called the place a dungeon.

Kambry walked with purpose past the small cubicles, each equipped with a bed of straw and a chamber pot, lighting the torches along the divider walls as she went. At the end of the line of barred rooms they reached a staircase, Kambry not hesitating to begin the ascent.

"Is the locket not down here?" Patti asked, a bit confused.

"We were thorough in checking the first time, but it turns out the locket is up the stairs on the middle platform. We're almost there," Kambry responded, hurrying her step.

When she reached it she quickly grabbed the locket from the hook on the wall, placing it on the pedestal. The familiar light consumed them once again, a sigh of relief leaving their lips as they awaited level one hundred and fifty one.

∞∞∞

When the brightness settled and Team Ola's vision adjusted enough to evaluate their surroundings, they found they once again spawned in a lush forest, the leaves the bold oranges, reds and yellows of fall.

"You don't think?" Patti spun in circles, unsure if the forest she scanned was the same one from the previous level.

The others felt the same, their stomachs dropping at the thought of being trapped in another leveling loop.

"Only one way to find out," Dean said with determination, speed walking his way through the forest.

Thirty minutes later and the same scenery of the vampire lord's castle came into view.

"It's really the same level," Patti whined, her back slouched forward.

"That's right!" Braxton appeared in front of them, the metal gate the only thing between them.

"You!" Dean reached for him through the bars, desperately needing to wring his scrawny neck.

"This level doesn't end until you defeat the enemy on it, I'm afraid—locket or not." He grinned, a smile filled with savage intent.

Dean withdrew his arm, pushing the gate open this time before lunging at Braxton. His body went straight through the projection of the vampire elf, the man cackling as he stared at Dean on the ground.

"You never learn do you?" He squatted closer to Dean, grinning sadistically, his sharp canines on full display.

Dean glared at the hologram, until the image flickered, Braxton disappearing.

"Guess we have to face the mega Thero," Patti's listless voice broke the tension.

"Thero is here?" Kambry questioned, confused.

"Not the real one. Braxton's idea of a sick joke. He's much stronger than when we faced him on Oakley though. Water magic barely touched him and he was able to deflect my energy blasts."

"His regen is also overpowered," Patti added, remembering how quickly his wounds had healed.

"Damn," Kambry mumbled under her breath, already dreading the fight.

"Well, what are we waiting for?" Zayra started toward the building, eager to kick the ass of the guy who stole Wilfred from her.

Without waiting for the team's agreement, Zayra marched straight to the front door, not hesitating to swing them wide open. Dean approached from behind, the same eerie corridor waiting for them inside.

"Go right, the other two are dead ends," he told her, influencing her direction.

When they reached the gilded double doors, Zayra paused for a minute, her hand on the knob, making sure everyone was prepared. Dean passed out the weapons, then nodded, her hand slowly turning the knob. She let the door swing open, her body remaining in the hall until they were given a clear view of the man sitting center stage on a throne, a mysterious hooded figure by his side.

"Dean, Dean, Dean. How nice of you to visit," the same commentary echoed through the hall.

"Thero," Dean responded, entering the throne room first.

"Let's skip the formalities, shall we?" Braxton once again froze time, revealing his face to the visitors.

Placing his palm to the engineered Thero's forehead, the magical blue glow surrounded him, signaling his transformation.

"Get ready," Dean told his teammates, everyone holding their weapons in position.

When the massive demon lord stood in front of them, Braxton's hologram disappeared, leaving them to face Thero alone. Dean shot an energy beam at his hardened body, the light deflecting from his skin, embedding it in the ground by Dean's feet. *How do we defeat this fooking thing?* Dean asked himself, knowing that blasting it with his full power would only put his team in danger.

Dean and Patti knew from experience that magic did very little and while weapons would deal a bit of damage, the results weren't enough to defeat the enemy, the wounds healing in under a minute. Kambry and Zayra on the other hand had yet to experience the demon lord's strength, both ready to dive head first into battle.

Zayra ran forward, her sword in hand before the blue light faded from Thero's body. Kambry jumped in the air, her wings carrying her to the high ceiling, aiming to attack with fire magic from above the enemy. Thero reanimated, his transformation complete, ready to destroy his enemy in front of him.

Before he had a chance to prepare an attack, fire rained down on his head, the blasts dispersing as soon as they hit his thick, leathery skin. Irritated, he swung out at the flying nuisance, attempting to knock Kambry from the air. Zayra used his distraction to get closer to Thero, her blade piercing his skin.

Unable to retrieve the weapon from Thero's thick hide, Zayra pulled on the hilt frantically, leaving her vulnerable to an attack from the enemy. Thero's attention turned to the throbbing in his leg, finding Zayra at his feet. He kicked out, sending Zayra flying across the floor.

In the same motion, Thero turned his body, gaining even greater height allowing him to swat a distracted Kambry from the air. Both girls were down, Patti rushing to assist them, while Dean focused on distracting the monster, needing to buy them enough time to heal.

"Hey! Over here! Your focus should be on me!" Dean waved his arms like a maniac, finally drawing Thero's attention.

A smirk crossed his features, Thero turning to grab his staff from its place on the stage.

"Were you getting lonely waiting for me?" he chided, sending out a row of ice spikes in Dean's direction.

The icicles sunk into the tiled floor inches from Dean's feet—Thero was playing with him, the attack never meant to hit him. This only angered Dean, his team-mates on the floor with broken bones as Thero toyed with him. He gripped the hilt of his sword, thinking of an attack plan that would be able to break through Thero's defenses.

"Shield your eyes!" he yelled to his comrades, his blade deflecting another row of icicles—these aimed to draw blood.

The girls squeezed their eyes shut, Thero, confused about the request, turning to face Dean needing to see his next move. A blinding light emanated from Dean's body, filling the space with a pure white glow. Thero hissed, forcing his eyes shut, his vision already affected by the attack.

With his enemy blinded, Dean switched to water magic, creating a sheet of ice under Thero's feet. The blinded man slipped, unable to see well enough to prevent his fall—everything following Dean's plan. When his butt hit the ground, Dean changed the ice back into water, his enemy now sitting in the pool.

"When I say, I want you to lift Patti and Zayra up into the air. Can you do it?" Dean whispered to Kambry, having reached his teammates' side in the chaos.

"Yes," Kambry answered, rubbing her abdomen, but ready to fight through the pain if it meant defeating Thero.

Thero groaned, his vision having yet to return, but starting to pull himself up to his feet nonetheless.

"Now," Dean told Kambry, her wings already in position as she jumped, a girl hanging on to each arm.

Realizing she wouldn't be able to hover with so much extra weight for long, Dean hit the floor with his palm, sending out an electrical charge that covered the surface area of the room. The electricity needed a few seconds to spread out from the point of contact, but when it reached Thero, strengthened by the pool under his feet, his whole body convulsed.

Dean poured all of his mana into strengthening the charge, holding the attack as long as he could manage. He kept a close eye on Kambry, making sure he was ready to stop the electrical charge before they hit the ground. The trio continued to hover over the throne room, so Dean continued to pour his mana into the attack, smoke beginning to rise from Thero's body, the attack frying his insides without allowing his regeneration ability to take effect.

"I can't stay up much longer," Kambry shouted, her height from the ground shrinking.

Dean held the flow steady, wanting every bit of electricity he could afford to course through Thero's body. His eyes remained on Kambry, ready to time his release with the moment her feet touched the floor. When she flew inches above the ground he pulled his hand from the tile, allowing her to safely land on the throne room floor.

Thero remained unmoving, smoke escaping from every pore, his eyes rolled back, revealing only the whites.

"Is he dead?" Kambry asked.

Before anyone answered, she shot a fireball in his direction, the little orb of flames colliding with the giant demon lord's stomach, knocking him off balance. His whole body teetered, finally falling onto the stage behind him. As he fell, his horns dug into the back wall, tearing a hole in the fragile plaster, his body hitting the raised platform with a thud.

Dean's gaze narrowed toward the newly formed tears, seeing another room behind the throne area. He jogged toward the stage, ignoring the still sizzling Thero and ripped an even bigger hole in the back wall.

"Braxton?"

"Shit," the vampire elf breathed out, his fingers still typing out something on a control panel that filled the room.

"Braxton," his question turned into a certain growl, his fist flying toward the man's face.

His closed hand connected with a solid object, Braxton flying from the control chair and onto the tiled floor below.

"Wait—wait." He held up his hands, trying to quell the rage he saw on Dean's face.

Ignoring the man's pleas, Dean climbed on top of him, pinning him to the floor and continuously striking him in the face—once for every hologram that his fist went right through in the past. Braxton crossed his arms over his face, trying to defend against Dean's blows, but it didn't stop him from hitting the vampire elf regardless of which part of the body his fists made contact with.

"Don't even pretend to be the victim here! It is your fault we are stuck here in the first place! Everything is your fault," Dean berated him, his hands around Braxton's throat.

"You c-can't kill me."

"Wanna bet?" Dean furrowed his brow, deciphering Braxton's words as a challenge.

The girls stayed back, watching Dean take out all of their anger on the vampire elf, seeing no downside in killing him—after all they weren't even sure it was the real Braxton to begin with, so what harm would killing him really do.

"No—I mean you shouldn't," Braxton managed to squeak out under the crushing weight of Dean's hands.

Intrigued, he loosened his grip, waiting for the rest of the story.

"If I die, the maze will be thrown into chaos," Braxton whispered through the pain in his throat.

"What are you talking about? This is still Min's maze, why would your death do anything to it?"

"It's my magic. I altered it to trap you here...and ended up getting trapped as well. I made it so that if you killed me the levels would be thrown out of whack. Higher level monsters would start appearing on the starter levels—and that is just the beginning. I wanted to make it impossible for the Suca humans to gain momentum in the game."

"How do we know you are not lying to save your skin?" Dean growled, punching the floor beside Braxton's head.

"You don't, but do you really want to chance it?"

Dean placed his hands on the man's throat again, tightening his grip. He slammed his head against the tile floor, fed up with dealing with him and his half-truths.

"This is why I hate guys like you. You don't fight fair, don't depend on your own strength, it's all traps and conditions. I can't trust you. I'd rather chance it with the stronger monsters."

"Wait, please," Braxton cried when sparks began to bounce off of his body, small bolts of electricity stinging his skin as the power built within Dean. "You'll be trapped in here forever if you kill me now."

The electricity died out, Dean not liking the words coming out of Braxton's mouth. "You can't be serious."

"I am. I made it so you would be trapped in here until the very last level—the way I see it you or your team would die long before you reach that point. You already seem to be down a member." He sneered, earning him another slam into the tile floor. "Okay—okay, testy aren't we?"

"How do we get out of the maze?" Dean ignored his snide remarks.

"Min is the only one who can break my spell—set the rules back to the way they were."

"Then why haven't they taken us out yet? What are they waiting for?"

"Well..." his voice cracked.

"Well what?" Kambry growled, no longer able to watch silently.

"I may have erased your presence from this world before you entered the maze. Silly me." He shrugged the best he could from his position under Dean's weight. "I doubt they have any idea you're in the maze let alone which level you have made it to."

"Fook, you've got to be kidding me. And you? Wouldn't your guild be looking for you?"

"Look all they want, none of them are powerful enough to free me from this prison... and I used up the majority of my magic altering this space, so I'm tapped out. The way I see it we're screwed...all of us."

"So what are you proposing? Everything you are telling me just makes me want to kill you more. Or better yet almost kill you, let you heal and kill you again. Hmm, that sounds fun, maybe we'll try that," Dean said, grabbing a dagger from his thigh holster and holding it close to Braxton's face.

"I can get you to Min," he said in a rush, the skin where the blade pressed against his face starting to sting. "I can find them and then you can get them to release us from the maze."

"Ha! Us," Dean scoffed, instantly noticing how he slipped that little condition in. "Fine," he conceded, recognizing that using Braxton would be the surest way to escape the maze. "That doesn't mean I won't just kill you back on Mixonia," he mumbled, removing himself from the man.

"We'll cross that bridge when we get to it," he sighed, readjusting his clothing before sitting back down on the swivel chair.

Patti, Zayra and Dean moved in close, interested in what Braxton was doing. His fingers were moving rapidly, the display screens shifting with each keystroke, honing in on Min's position. After two minutes of constant typing and a few grunts from Braxton, he whirled his chair around, pressing one final button triumphantly.

"Found them." He smiled confidently.

"Great, where are they?" Dean asked, annoyed that the vampire elf was trying to garner suspense.

"Ahem," he cleared his throat, pushing his seat back toward the display. "They move around the levels a bit, but they always go back to level four hundred. That seems to be their base."

"Level four hundred," Dean said aloud, letting it sink in.

"That's what I said, level four hundred," Braxton raised an eyebrow at Dean, not liking that he had to repeat himself.

"You do realize what level we are on now, right?"

"One hundred and fifty?" Braxton presented the number as a question, still not following Dean's train of thought.

"That's right, one hundred and fifty." His patience left him. "Are you trying to tell us to complete another two hundred and fifty levels?" He was screaming now, the vampire elf sinking lower in his chair with every word. "Kambry will have given birth by the time we finish all those levels and that absolutely can't happen!" He got in Braxton's face, making sure he understood what would happen to him if that fate came to be.

"Calm down—of course I have an alternative...we can just skip straight to level four hundred."

"Great—let's go now," Dean urged, ready to be free from the maze.

Braxton went quiet, his eyes glued to the screen in front of him.

"What is it?" Dean huffed, the silence grating on his nerves.

"Well—"

"That doesn't sound like you are getting us out of here," Kambry assumed from his tone, trying to decipher what he was looking at on the screen.

"Spit it out," Dean demanded, just needing to hear the truth.

"I can skip levels, but... not from here." His volume shrunk on the last three words.

"Where do we need to be? Outside the castle? Let's go then," Zayra asked, ready to leave the building if needed.

"Level two hundred."

Dean remained quiet, inhaling and exhaling to keep himself from strangling Braxton.

"And what makes level two hundred so special?" he questioned, wondering if they would reach level two hundred only to hear another story from Braxton.

"I set up teleportation portals on every level that is an interval of one hundred. Those are the only levels that stay consistent no matter how many times someone attempts them. The others change nearly every time, so finding the portals would have been like finding a pine wand in a pine forest-- nearly impossible and extremely time consuming. My oversight came when I spawned on level one hundred fifty. Obviously I wasn't about to chance leveling solo with next to no magic remaining, so I set up my base here."

"Alright, we don't need to hear your whole sob story. You want us to lead you to level two hundred, is that what I'm hearing?"

"Yes. Get us there and I will reset the teleportation portal to level four hundred. You can meet with Min, ask them to set us free—and poof no harm done. I'll give up trying to avenge my father, you give up revenge for this little mishap—it's a win-win really." He smiled.

Dean's eyes narrowed, his gut telling him not to trust the man, but he knew that he had no other choice. Trying to level with five people was hard enough, losing Wilfred meant they would be down one without Braxton's help and had at least another two hundred and fifty levels to go if they couldn't make use of the short-cut.

The time they spent on each level seemed to be increasing as the difficulty rose and they were on a strict deadline. Dean wouldn't let his wife give birth in Mixonia—in the maze, not if he could help it.

"Fine. But you so much as think about betraying us and I will slit your throat so fast, don't think I won't."

"Alright, Alright, I get it, you're a scary dude. So when do we leave?"

Dean stopped himself from saying 'now' immediately, remembering they were in a warm and comfortable building.

"How much control do you have over this level?" he asked instead.

"Limitless," Braxton replied instantly, then recognizing Dean's desires, he input a few commands into the control panel before saying, "Dinner is now served in the main dining hall, and I have removed the barrier from the top floor. You can pick any room you'd like except for the last one on the left—that's mine." He grinned, flaunting his power over the level.

The team didn't bother thanking him, walking out of the hidden space past the fried body of the fabricated demon lord and toward the hall that would lead them to the dining room. They found the room-length table filled completely with food

—a feast to behold. They didn't thank Braxton for the meal, still feeling bitter toward the man.

Everyone ate in silence, immediately retiring to the upper rooms once their stomachs were filled. They settled in for the night, knowing that they would start their grind again in the morning.

Having a goal in mind made things a little bit easier, but they knew a long road was waiting as they anticipated it would take at least another month to reach level two hundred. They only hoped that Braxton's promises proved truthful and weren't just empty words.

FIFTEEN

CASSANDRA

Forrester Estate

Cassandra stroked Jessabee's baby bump with her right hand, her left still intertwined with Sable's, her lovers sleeping soundly beside her. The three had grown even closer since Kambry and Dean's disappearance, needing to rely on each other for support.

The sun crept in through the balcony window, telling her it was time to start training for the day. She kissed the growing baby bump, and then Jessabee's and Sable's foreheads before quietly crawling out of bed, her feet padding softly on the wooden floor as she made her way to the baby's room.

Leena cooed from her crib, wide awake and staring at the mobile of plush fish that danced above her. Her eyes lit up when her mother peeked down at her, Leena's little legs and arms bouncing with excitement.

"Hi, baby girl." Cassandra matched the baby's excitement, scooping her up from the crib.

Snuggling her close, she kissed the soft fluff of hair that covered Leena's head, breathing in her scent.

"Are you hungry?" she asked, already moving to prepare her bottle.

As she shook the bottle to warm it up, Olivia entered the room, a set of clean sheets in her hands.

"You're up," she said in a chipper tone. "Good morning, mam. Would you like me to finish feeding Leena?" she asked as she set the sheets on a shelf in the closet.

Before Cassandra could refuse her offer, her phone began to ring, the caller id showing the number of the intergalactic investigation unit. "Thank you," she said instead, handing her baby over before heading to a more isolated spot to answer the call.

"Hello? This is she," she answered to the inquiry about her identity.

"We've had a breakthrough in the case. After reviewing the surveillance footage for the location you provided us in the estimated time frame, we were able to narrow down our leads to three ships. One was registered to a Mr. Laniston Weaver, who passed through the area quickly on the day in question. He was found on Oakley with his family of four, no signs of the missing girl. The second ship merely passed through as well, a much smaller ship, registered to an Ophelia Wilkinson. We were able to reach her in the outer galaxy and she had no qualms about our officers boarding her ship.

This leaves only the third and final ship found around that area within the specified timeframe. According to the footage, the ship hovered in the spot within the outer rim of space for some time before heading toward the intergalactic highway. The ship is registered to one Tucker Calloway."

"Tucker," Cassandra growled, "I should have suspected."

"So you know this man?"

"There's some bad blood there, yes."

"He is likely our culprit."

"Great, did you bring him in? Did you find Lexis?"

"Our officers have yet to search his ship, and he is blocking any incoming communication, but we are keeping a close eye on his movements. His spacecraft was captured on surveillance at Sneed Orbital some months ago heading west. Witnesses say he dropped off the majority of the crew before leaving for an undisclosed location.

Talking with the crew left at the orbital didn't reveal any further information—all were told the same thing, that they would be picked up before heading to their new home."

"New home?"

"Apparently the end destination is the newly colonized planet, Las Karisak."

"But, that's not where they are headed now?"

"Once the ship left Sneed Orbital, a traffic controller marked his ship twice, heading into unexplored territory. They like to keep tabs on the ships that explore outside barriers in case one were to go missing. Only four bodies were picked up on the heat sensors. The ship's movements were tracked, but it went months without triggering any red flags. That is until recently.

Unknown cargo was expelled in deep space, an illegal act, unfortunately our officers were unable to collect the contraband, so no fine could be officially cited."

"What do you mean they couldn't collect it?" Cassandra's foot tapped impatiently hearing no concrete evidence about Lexi's location.

"The materials were sucked into a black hole. The anomaly has been sighted for our travel database, so all GPS have been updated to contain its location. But no ships can approach it without the potential of a total loss."

Cassandra's breath caught in her throat. "Did they dump her body?" she asked, afraid to hear the answer.

The officer bypassed her question, choosing to continue his report, "The ship has once again been sighted just this morning heading back toward the orbital, ETA, with chosen wormhole bypass, two months."

"How many on board this morning?" She needed to know if continuing their search would be futile.

"Four."

She sighed in relief, "Thank the gods. What's the plan now?"

"We will intercept him when he reaches the destination. With your permission, we may try to attempt video communication again ahead of that, hoping to secure the girl faster, but all calls thus far have been blocked."

"I understand. Do everything you can to get her home safely."

"Yes'm. We'll keep in touch."

Cassandra's shoulders slumped when the line went dead, a rush of emotions washing over her. Finally there was a lead—something to be investigated. She walked back into her bedroom, her lovers still sleeping soundly, and kissed Sable on the cheek.

Her eyes popped open and she smirked. "What was that for?" she purred, her voice still deep with sleep.

"Thank you. Because of your help, we found a lead on Lexis." She smiled, genuinely grateful.

"I know another way you can say thank you," Sable tried to lighten the mood, pulling on Cassie's forearm as she tried to get her in bed.

Cassandra didn't fight the invitation, but just before she fell over into the bed, a crack of thunder outside drew her attention to the balcony. She rushed over, pulling back the curtains to find Min, standing at their full height outside her window.

"Min?" Cassandra asked in surprise.

"Another challenge has been unlocked. The three champions must be selected within the next hour. Again, the battle will take place in the Core realm. Be prepared—you have one hour." Min kept the conversation one sided and very brief, disappearing as soon as they had said what they needed.

"Another challenge. That means the Suca humans are up another hundred points." Cassie couldn't help but feel excited as she rushed to meet Danican, needing to decide who would be the best candidate for the next challenge against the Core demons.

CHAPTER

SIXTEEN

DEAN

Minotaur's Maze- Level Two Hundred

"You stupid—" Dean slapped Braxton across the back of the head sending him barreling forward nearly colliding with a small sheep humanoid that looked up at them with curious eyes.

"Welcome Travelers!" the sheep woman said, side-stepping Braxton as he fell to the cobblestone street.

The team had made it to level two hundred, no thanks to Braxton. This past level he had nearly gotten Dean killed by a raptor because he thought the babies were cute and decided to pet them. The mother wasn't thrilled to see a person with his arms around her baby, so she understandably lashed out.

Braxton had proven to be weak and useless the entire span of levels, making Dean question Thero's boasting about him. *Did magic really make the man in Braxton's case?* Dean couldn't see another explanation for why a man once said to be ruthless could be so fooking incompetent.

He made everything harder for the whole team. Kambry needed to use nearly half of her mana healing him on one level when he had both of his legs bitten off by a man-eating Venus fly-trap. *Who gets that close to a plant with teeth?* Dean had asked himself as he went to retrieve the severed limbs.

Another month passed as they persevered through the levels, but somehow all of them made it to the goal alive-- level two hundred. Now they stood on the teleportation platform looking out at a town nearly identical to that of level one hundred.

"I'm Bess, the teleportation ambassador for Sheepopolis. Welcome to our humble town," the small fluffy beast woman recited the typical speech, the team only half listening, more focused on what Braxton would do next. "Do let me know if you would like a tour around our town or I can show you the best places to get a meal or a good night's rest." She smiled, her blue eyes shining.

"Thank you. We will come find you should we need anything," Dean responded in kind, jumping down from the platform.

Feeling content she had done her job, the sheep woman walked away, heading toward a small cafe across the street.

"Alright, we held up our end of the deal—level two hundred. Your turn." Dean's face dropped from a pleasant smile to a glare as his gaze shifted from the sheep woman to Braxton.

"Okay, okay. Are you sure we can't stay here for the night? You know, get some food or something?" Braxton changed the subject glancing around at the friendly looking inhabitants.

As much as they wanted to be free of the maze, the rest of the team couldn't help but agree with Braxton. They were tired—exhausted really-- and the previous levels didn't offer much of a chance for a restful night's sleep. Kambry turned her pleading eyes to Dean, ready to argue in favor of staying, but the moment he noticed that both Zayra and Patti wore the same expressions, he conceded, having no reason to deny them the luxury.

"Fine—one night. But you know what will happen in the morning, so we need to be up extra early," Dean told them, expecting the level to play out in the same way as before.

"Wait, what happens in the morning?" Braxton ran after the group who were already on their way to Cafe Sunrise for a hot meal, content to ignore the man.

They filled their stomachs with fresh food and sought out the inn that resembled the one in Pupolia, finding plush mattresses and a private bathroom even nicer than the one they stayed in before—Or maybe it only seemed nicer in comparison to their level of exhaustion.

They didn't bother exploring the town, accepting the much needed rest as they snuggled into the soft mattress. Braxton was given a room down the hall, one much smaller than the rest of the teams, but *even that was too good for him,* Dean couldn't help but think as he pulled the covers up to his chest, Kambry's head on his shoulder.

Tomorrow will end this, he thought to himself, drifting off into uninterrupted sleep.

∞∞∞

Before the sun rose the following morning, the team got up, taking turns using the private bathroom. After showering, they headed back to the square, figuring there were still a few hours before the unknown enemy would appear.

"Alright, Braxton. You're up," Dean said when they arrived, gesturing for Braxton to get to work on the portal.

"You got it," the man answered, cracking his knuckles.

Kneeling down at the back of the portal, he placed his staff on the ground, opening a cover along the side of the device. He mumbled to himself as he looked around, then pulled out a fist full of wires. Patti's eyes went wide, but no one said anything, trusting the vampire elf knew what he was doing.

"Alright—almost got it," he said, reaching for his staff.

A display screen popped up from the top of his staff, a bunch of words flashing across the screen in a language Dean had never seen before. Touching the projection with his fingertips, he began inputting words in the same language, none of the others able to verify his work.

"All set," he said after a few more taps, placing the tip of the staff into the mechanics before sealing it with the cover once again.

The portal came to life, a white light erupting from the sides and blooming toward the top of the platform until the entire thing shone brightly.

"Well, what are we waiting for people? Your chariot awaits." Braxton bowed, waving toward the platform for the others to jump on board.

They all eyed him with skepticism, still holding no trust for the man despite having spent the last month in each other's company. When no one moved, he shrugged, hopping onto the teleportation device himself. Seeing him standing there, Dean followed, the rest matching Dean's movements.

"And away we go!" Braxton shouted, slamming the base of his staff onto the platform, the bright light enveloping the team.

∞∞∞

Please don't be a trap, Dean repeated in his head, knowing the team couldn't handle any more setbacks. He opened his eyes, finding them standing on an identical teleportation portal, but this time there was no town and no cheery beast-people to greet them.

"Where are we?" Kambry asked, looking around at the iron walls and floor of the same material, the room resembling a fortress of metal.

"Level four hundred," Braxton answered her question.

Zayra rolled her eyes, knowing that wasn't the answer that Kambry wanted to hear.

"What, it is." Braxton shrugged, having seen Zayra's reaction. "Although...I had heard that all the intervals of one hundred mirror each other, so this seems a little... off," he whispered, the others not hearing his worries.

"Never mind." Kambry hopped off the portal, choosing to explore the place on her own.

She lit the torches placed in increments along the walls, adding some light to the mostly dark gray room.

"Is it another dungeon?" Zayra questioned as they walked, the place seeming devoid of life.

"It doesn't smell nearly as bad as the first," Kambry noted.

The team stopped when they came to a circular door, grooves indented in its surface spelling out a word in the mysterious language they had seen Braxton use so fluently only a few minutes ago.

"What's it say?" Dean's question was clearly addressed to Braxton.

Knowing he couldn't hide his knowledge anymore Braxton replied, "Min's vault."

"Like back in Mixonia?" Zayra asked, brushing her hand against the iron engravings.

Reacting to the introduction of warmth, the door began to slide open, the slow movement accompanied by the creaking of gears.

"Woah," Kambry said when the room behind the door was revealed, her jaw dropping in surprise.

Inside the rectangular shaped room, spanning as far as the eye could see, were shelves upon shelves of statues, even more than in the vault back on Mixonia. Zayra immediately rushed into the room, searching for the labels that divided the statues by their race, rushing to find the Osamars.

"Zayra." Patti rushed after her, not wanting her to be alone.

"What is all of this?"

"Souls trapped in Mixonia from way before your time, those left on the shelves—no one returning to claim them," a voice startled the team from behind, Min appearing in the vault in their shrunken form.

"You're here," Braxton said in disbelief. "I told you I would find them," he quickly changed his tune.

"This is my vault, of course I am here. The question is-- why are you here?" Their eyes shifted from Braxton to Kambry, until they finally settled on Dean. "Vault breaker. So this is why your presence has gone undetected for so many months." They nearly chuckled before continuing, "And here I thought you had perished."

"Of course not. And I didn't erase it on purpose. You can blame him for that one," Dean replied curtly.

"Is that so?" Min snapped their fingers, Braxton disappearing from the vault.

"Look, we only came here to see if you could release us from the maze. We have been trapped here for too long by that psychopath and his twisted form of revenge." Dean tried to ignore the fact that Min had just snapped Braxton out of existence.

"I wish it were that easy, Dean." Min shook their head. "I really do, but I'm afraid it's not."

"What do you mean?"

Min looked around the vault alluding to the fact that his entire team now knew of its existence.

"We won't tell anyone this is here—we just thought it was another level," Patti cried, rushing back from her search with Zayra.

The tension emanating from Min sent chills down her body, but she tried to stand her ground, to not run into a corner and cower in fear.

"It's too late for that," Min's voice remained calm, but when they snapped their fingers again, Patti disappeared.

"Where is she? What did you do with her?" Kambry rushed at the minotaur god, throwing fists even though her whole body told her to run.

Dean grabbed Kambry's wrist pulling her back to his side just as Min snapped their fingers a third time. Dean's stomach dropped when the click sounded, but Kambry remained beside him, Min just as confused as they were.

"Can't have that now can we?" they said, pushing Dean and Kambry apart.

As soon as their skin no longer touched, Min snapped their fingers again, Kambry vanishing from the vault.

"Bring her back!" Dean cursed the minotaur god, demanding they bring back his beloved. "Why are you doing this? You're not like this—you're supposed to be on our side!"

"Sides? What does that matter anymore? It has already begun—just look around!"

Dean, influenced by the desperation in Min's voice, frantically scanned the room. At first he noticed no changes, but then the space shifted, shrinking before his very eyes. The affected statues all but evaporated into the air, shimmering splatters of light and glitter the only things remaining.

"What's going on?"

"You—this is what the prophecy warned us about. You were never supposed to come here. And now there is only one way to stop the process you have set into motion."

"He's not here!" Zayra rushed from the back of the continuously shrinking room, interrupting the conversation, a look of sadness and defeat on her face, having been unable to locate Wilfred's statue.

Min snapped their fingers a final time, Zayra disappearing from the vault. Their head snapped back to Dean who seethed in anger, having to watch the god take away his teammates one by one.

"At least tell me they're alive," he said through gritted teeth.

"You should be more worried about yourself," Min responded. The floor under them dropping out, lowering them both further into the depths of the maze.

The makeshift elevator reached its stop and Dean found himself in a room of similar size, minus all of the shelves containing statues, the terrain resembling a cavern. Glittering light filtered in through the hole in the ceiling, the specks seeming to be drawn to Dean, the light absorbing into his skin whenever it touched him.

"I don't want to fight you," Dean admitted to the minotaur god, their height exploding to their original one hundred feet.

"I wouldn't want to fight me either," Min said with a bit of sadness, no gloating behind their words. "Unfortunately it has come to this, so pick your weapon."

Their words only angered Dean more. He had very little choice when he was selected as champion the very first time, and even in the end he would be given no choice. *To always be thrown around by the gods—is this my fate?* he asked himself, digging in his bag for his weapon and some light armor.

"This is the only way. No we can't—imagine the power we would be forfeiting—the balance would be disrupted. It needs to be done," Min mumbled while Dean readied himself, the god seeming to be having an argument with themselves.

As Dean rooted around for his weapon, he remembered the pets that had proven nearly useless during the team leveling despite the few glitches that allowed Droosca and the others to transform. Now the statue appeared in his hand, making him wonder if he would get lucky this time. Placing the statue on the ground in front of him, he held his breath, awaiting the transformation magic to encompass the dragon.

Tendrils of magic began to dance around the pet, the magic activating, giving Dean a bit of hope for the unavoidable battle. Min narrowed their eyes on the statue, not liking that Dean was able to influence the maze enough that even the pets could transform in places they weren't previously allowed. Three steps were all it took for the massive minotaur god to cross over to Dean, using their full weight to crush the pet before it was given the chance to fully transform.

Dean fell backward when the giant limb appeared in front of him in a matter of seconds, crushing not only his pet, but also his hope at having a partner when facing off against Min. He picked up the statue, the pieces falling though his fingers, unable to be put back together. He glared at Min, the only way he could express his anger at the god.

"The rules have changed it seems, but I am still the master of this maze. Prepare yourself, Vault Breaker—Blessed Champion."

Dean shuddered at the nicknames Min threw at him, none of which he asked for. *Blessed?* He certainly didn't feel very blessed. He tightened the strap on his chest plate, stocking his leg holster with daggers and placing his sword in its holster around his waist. Finally, he grabbed a javelin, gripping it tightly in his hand as he stood tall despite his small frame in comparison to Min's massive height.

"We are sorry for this, human," Min said solemnly, a gust of wind brushing against Dean's body, swirling around Min until the god stood in the center of a vortex, the wind slowly gaining speed.

Dean looked at his weapons and then at the power that stood in front of him and he knew they wouldn't be enough. He threw the javelin in defiance, the weapon catching in the wind, whipping across the large battlefield until it lodged itself in the rock wall, its point never coming in contact with Min.

Dean pulled his staff from his satchel, his only reliable offense being magic, his weapons too minuscule when pitted against a god. Seeing no other way out, Dean charged forward, the wind slowing his speed. He reached for his mana, feeling the power build inside him and released an energy attack, shifting the very atmosphere of the arena.

The wind died down, Min left standing confused and irate, then the lightning touched the ground. Recognizing Dean's magic in the bolts, the wind resumed, Min consuming even more power to regain control of the area. Blades of wind rushed out from the vortex, invisible knives of raw power. The first flew at Dean unde-tected, the blade slicing his thigh just above the knee.

He dropped down to the rock ground, his injured leg giving out under his weight. *Shit,* Dean cursed under his breath, his hand covering the wound. When he checked the injury, the blood had already clotted, the wound in the process of healing. He stood, the pain subsiding and brought down another bolt of lightning, this one aimed directly at Min.

The energy coursed through Min's body, but they didn't so much as flinch before Dean stopped his attack, feeling the drain of mana from the higher tier magic.

"We are starting to wonder why you were the one depicted in the prophecy," the words left Min's mouth, but the voice sounded unfamiliar to Dean's ears.

"He certainly isn't anything special," another more feminine tone responded.

"Why were we so fearful of this child disrupting balance?" an older man's voice added, all of the voices coming from Min.

Dean sent a wall of icicle spikes in Min's direction, remembering the power of the attack from his fight with Thero. The god didn't even try to dodge, each spike sinking into their skin before melting instantaneously, no wounds to show for the direct hit.

"Give up—let us kill you and restore balance!" Min shouted, the vortex shifting from around their body until a whole tornado had been launched at Dean.

The whirlwind rushed toward him and Dean knew there was nowhere to hide in the flat and spacious battlefield. The first wisps of wind reached him, his skin ripping apart at the slightest brush. The body of the storm came next, but being trapped in its center would spell certain death. He needed to do something—and quick. Untested as it was, Dean threw up an energy barrier, the yellow glow of magic forming a sphere of pure energy around his body.

When the tornado reached him, the barrier rocked, but ultimately held, the sphere tethered to its source—to Dean.

"Why won't you concede?!" a chorus of voices shouted at Dean who held onto his position, piercing the ground with his sword for added stability.

"I won't give up on my teammates, my friends. I can't die here—not when there is so much at stake!" Dean shouted back through the whipping wind that continued to collide with his barrier, struggling to maintain its form.

The thought of not only those important to him, but the limitless souls trapped in this hidden level, being used as fuel for the gods--to raise their power to immeasur-able levels--- strengthened his determination.

As he fought against the blades of wind, his barrier starting to crack under the constant pressure, a light poured into the dimly lit space, the same light that had appeared when the statues began to disappear in the room above. From the light came the floating, glittery speckles of magic—the souls of those trapped in the maze for centuries.

The light focused on Dean, rushing to him, unaffected by the wind that continued to blow mercilessly around the field. The first light touched his skin, disappearing into his body, then another and another, Dean's power building as more and more souls were absorbed.

The surge of power came with a will of its own—*Set us free*—the souls pleaded, *We will lend you our strength.* As the countless souls filtered into Dean, his body began to transform, regaining the height of a god. He stood on equal ground with Min, their eyes level with one another.

The energy field that surrounded him shattered, the wind rushing in, but he was no longer affected by the sharp air blades, feeling only the caress of a cool breeze. Seeing the win slipping through their fingers, Min lashed out, desperate to stop Dean's transformation. Dean caught the hoofed hand that aimed for his body, his free one grabbing Min by one of their four horns.

He released an energy beam at point blank range, the power entering Min's body through the horn that he held. The energy swirled within his body, mixing with the power of the souls, the two combining to create something even more powerful and destructive.

As the energy transferred from Dean's hand into the minotaur god, Dean could feel the power being continuously replaced, the souls endlessly fueling the attack, making sure the blast was strong enough to defeat Min. At first Min scoffed at Dean's attack, not expecting anything to come of his attempts to defeat them, but as the power built, Min began to struggle, desperately trying to release themselves from the death-grip Dean held on their horn.

Wind erupted from Min's free limbs, the powerful attacks dwarfed by Dean's immense borrowed strength. The attack built in Min's body, the energy piling up to the point of combustion. With no way to release the pent up force, Min's body succumbed to the pressure, cracks spreading from the top of their head trailing down the rest of their body, rays of golden light filtering through the cracks.

Min screamed, their defeat imminent and finally their body exploded, the force sending Dean flying across the rocky terrain, the curved horn still in his grasp. Dean pushed himself to his feet, his body tense, finding it hard to believe what he had witnessed. *Did I really just blow up the most powerful of the gods?*

"Fly too close to the sun and you will be the one burned," a small voice echoed through the cavern.

"They meant well, but the desire to expand Mixonia—to build their power, was always going to be their downfall." Another voice merged with the first, bright orbs of light dancing around each other in front of Dean.

More orbs appeared, their light bright as they joined the others. At first, Dean believed them to be more of the souls trapped in the vault, but then they began to merge, the final product a small version of Min, their face younger and less severe as they looked up at Dean.

"We are sorry, Dean Forrester," the minotaur addressed Dean, holding out their hoof to touch him.

When they made contact with his skin, the souls absorbed into his body released, his transformation undone as he returned to his normal size.

"Min?" Dean asked, finding it hard to believe that the small creature could be the same powerful god he had just fought.

"Yes... and no. We are not the same Min that you knew, but we are a part of them. We will start over in their place. Fix the world of the gods, fix ourselves. We were created to be a neutral force, but at some point during our long existence we faltered. It is time to take a step back from this world. Return to our own and work on ourselves before meddling in your world." The voices merged together, the tones shifting from high to low until finally they united, a soft, calm voice emerging as the dominant one.

"What do you mean?"

"It is time for the gods to return to the heavens. *'A blessed champion will free the infinite souls fueling the game of the gods, restoring balance and harmony to the struggling worlds. When he is chosen, it will spell the end of an era, but also the birth of a new one. Do not fight the change my child, for only the creator has the right to judge—to select the chosen one—and his decision will be absolute.'* This message was foretold at the dawn of the seventh age and now it has come to pass. The prophecy is fulfilled."

"The prophecy," Dean repeated the words, not fully understanding his part in it all.

"Did you not know of such a prophecy?" Min asked, taking a step closer to Dean.

"The way I heard it was a bit different. What about my eight wives?"

Min stared at him with indifferent eyes. "Time has a way of altering memories— it affects all things. Even this moment will be recorded in history one day, but only those who live through it will know the true tale and even that becomes unreliable with time."

"So, no wives?" Dean's laughter sounded forced even to his own ears and Min just continued to stare blankly at his attempt at a joke. "Okay, I get it—things get mixed up with time, but wasn't it Zued who picked me to be a champion in the first place? What is this about a creator the prophecy mentioned."

"How do you suppose Zued landed on you out of so many human potentials? It was never his decision."

"So what happens now? If the gods disappear, won't the Core demons take over the surface?"

"With our return to the heavens, the Core gods will be summoned to the depths. The suca will be safe, after all core beings cannot live on the surface unless they win the games. Without the games there will be no chance of victory and each will retain their homeland."

"No more games? What will happen to Mixonia?"

"It will continue. Those whose lives are tied to it will remain, but others will have a choice to make. Soon the portals will close, it will be as though Mixonia never existed."

"Gone... just like that?"

"It won't be forever, but you, Dean Forrester, won't be around to see it. When it does resurface on the human planets—some millennia from now—it will be a different place, reshaped by the new order. You have done your part, blessed champion and now, with my brothers and sisters, we must return home."

Min turned away from Dean as if they would disappear from the rocky arena.

"Wait...." Dean stopped them, his hand raised toward the god as they walked away. "What about Kambry and Patti? Zayra, Wilfred, my team? You have to tell me if they are alive. Please!"

Min's mouth moved to speak, but before the words could leave their lips, the minotaur god disappeared, only the glittering gold flecks of the trapped souls remained in the level with Dean.

"Dammit!" Dean yelled, hitting the ground with his fist.

Not only was the one person that knew all the answers gone, but now he was stuck on level four hundred with no idea where his teammates were or if they were even alive. He felt his world begin to crumble around him, believing the weight of disrupting the balance of the worlds was starting to take its toll, until he realized the ground beneath his feet had started to rumble.

Cracks spread across the room, deep and destructive, consuming everything around him. Dean tried to run, to escape the growing crevice, but the only way out was up, a feat he couldn't manage alone. Another rumble shook the arena, the next crater appearing beneath his feet and Dean fell, his world turning black as he traveled further into the abyss.

As he fell, Dean desperately searched for something to hold onto, until a bright light enveloped him, stealing him from the level.

. . .

∞∞∞

Dean's body thumped against the hard cobblestone and when he opened his eyes, they met with the indifferent expression of the Minotaur guard.

"Finally," he breathed out the words, pushing himself to his feet.

The familiarity of Mixonia was comforting, but that feeling quickly passed as he noticed the chaos that surrounded him. The artificial light was blinking red, everyone except the Minotaur guard running around wildly. More people spawned beside Dean, having been pulled from the levels.

"What gives?" a team of catomi yelled when they spawned at the entrance of the maze, but quickly realized something major was happening.

"Attention residents of Mixonia and visitors from off world. This is your final notice. The gates of Mixonia will be closing permanently in one hour. For those of you that do not wish to make your home here, you must return to your own world. Residents—do not fear, but please encourage guests to leave in an orderly fashion. Again the gates will close in one hour."

The lights continued to flash despite the end of the announcement, panic consuming those in the square, the people pushing past one another to collect their things and depart. Dean felt his stomach drop, knowing that he was the one responsible for the sudden change. He pushed his thoughts aside, focusing on what needed to be done in the moment—there was only one hour left to find out what happened to his team.

His first stop needed to be the vault. Pushing through the crowd he made his way out of the center of Mixonia, the crowds thinning around the lake. Once he had space to move he ran the rest of the way to the vault, the number of people increasing again when he reached his destination.

Dean half expected the shelves to be empty, but despite all the souls he freed from the hidden vault in the maze, the shelves remained full. Everyone filled in around them trying to find their loved ones in the shuffle, knowing that it would be their last chance to free them from their statue form.

With the closing of Mixonia, no one knew if the tokens would be worth anything back on their home planets, so some of the more generous visitors used up their tokens to free as many souls as they could, whether they knew them or not. *This doesn't make sense*, Dean thought as he frantically searched for the 'D' section, still believing all of the souls should have released with the others. While Dean may have destroyed the vault that housed the excess souls within the maze, his influence didn't seem to extend to those in the main vault, the world still requiring their power to function.

Those left behind when the portal shut for good would be as good as dead. He clenched his fists, accepting that he couldn't save everyone. He reached the section for the dragona, but his search came up empty, Kambry nowhere to be found. He felt his heart drop, his next stop in the human section coming up empty as well, Patti nowhere on the shelves. Realizing the pattern, he still held hope when he reached the section labeled osamar.

Thoroughly glancing at every statue, he again was left devastated, not finding his teammates among the numerous souls. His eyes burned with the prickling sensation of tears threatening to form. He scrubbed his face, not ready to give up. *There has to be someone who knows what happened to them.* Dean rushed to a more empty part of the vault searching for a shop worker.

"Hello, how may I assist you?" A raven haired beauty with purple skin appeared suddenly in front of Dean, having been summoned by his thoughts alone.

"I am searching for my tea—" before he could finish, a familiar figure caught his attention—a lanky man in a dark hood. "Braxton," he growled, gripping the cape of the man as he headed for the exit.

Spinning him around, Dean stared into the eyes of the vampire elf.

"How is it that you are alive?" he asked through gritted teeth, his desire to end the man as strong as ever.

"Hello Dean," Braxton replied in a calm voice, his hands waving to someone behind Dean's back.

"Don't hello me, answer the question."

"Fine, but first get your hand off of me. This is not the maze anymore and unlucky for you my powers have returned."

Dean noticed the group of darkly dressed people start to move in closer, guild-mates of Braxton's ready to defend their leader.

"Now—while I'm asking nicely."

Dean released his grip on the man's cloak, taking a step backward to put his minions at ease.

"Thank you," Braxton grinned, dusting off his cloak.

He stared at Dean, reveling in the desperation he found etched into his expression.

"So?" Dean said after a minute of silence.

"Alright. I guess I did promise to let bygones be bygones. You see when I erased your team's presence in the maze it confused more than just Min. Dragona, osamar, human—they are all the same without a presence. I mean what else do you do with an unknown?"

Dean scowled, tired of the man's riddles, ready to punch him until he gave him the answers he sought, but then he registered what Braxton meant by his words, his expression shifting to one of realization and relief.

"Goodbye Dean. I hope we never meet again." Braxton turned to leave, his minions following him in a line out the door.

Dean ignored his words, pushing his way back through the crowd that remained near the shelves, all the way to the last shelf in the room—the unknowns. Usually reserved for ancient species, the knowledge of which was lost with the passing of time—a space that till this time remained empty, Dean found his teammates, all four sitting side by side.

"I found you—" he exhaled deeply, feeling as though he could finally breathe, the relief washing over him.

Since he would be freeing them from their statue forms without any expectations or conditions, he didn't need to talk with them first—the assistants processing his request quickly and efficiently despite the overcrowded vault.

"All four will be waiting for you at the portal entrance," the shop assistant told him before switching her focus to another guest—music to his ears.

He pushed his way past the crowd of unruly guests, the influx of people trying to make use of their final minutes in Mixonia. Dean didn't know how things would change once the portal was sealed, but he knew he wanted to be on the other side of the gate when it happened.

"Dean!" a familiar voice called to him before he could reach Oakley's portal, stopping him in his tracks.

He spun to find Sable, a concerned look on her face.

"You're alive!" She rushed to him, throwing herself in his arms.

"I'm alive," he whispered into her silken hair.

"Where were you? What happened? What is going on now?" She pushed back, gazing into his eyes, all of the questions she held bubbling over. "Suddenly, I was sent a message to return here. And now I hear they are shutting the portals for good? What am I supposed to do with that? I just found you again, but now we will be separated...for who knows how long?"

"Come with me," Dean slipped his hand in hers, gently pulling her toward the door to his planet.

Sable hesitated, looking back at the world she had lived in for so long, her home after the destruction of her birth planet.

"Do you mean it?"

"Of course I do. I love you, the girls love you. What is there to think about?" Dean responded without a hint of doubt.

"Okay." Sable nodded. "I just have a few things I need to grab before I leave. I'll see you back at the estate." She let go of his hand, disappearing from his sight.

Dean felt a knot form in his stomach, his mind silently pleading for her to hurry, but there was nothing more he could do. He continued his run toward the portal, taking one last look at the captivating world of Mixonia——the place that dubbed him a champion, that helped train him to fight, the place where he met his teammates. He would miss it, but at the same time this meant a new chapter was beginning—not only for him, but for the entire world.

He breathed it in then took a step into the portal.

∞∞∞∞

"Dean!" His four teammates cried, rushing to envelope him in a bear hug.

Zayra's face was stained with tears, her arm locked with Wilfred's. All of them were here, alive and well.

"We've been waiting for you." Kambry punched him in the shoulder before kissing him on the lips. "Tell us everything—we didn't even get the chance to fight Min before poof we died."

"I will, I will." He held up his hands in surrender, so happy to have everyone standing in front of him again. "But first—Felna.." He directed his words to the Minotaur guard who stood beside the still glowing portal. "The portals are closing —Mixonia is closing... for good."

"I am aware," she responded instantly. "My job as the portal guard, as your guard, is coming to an end. If it is all the same to you, I'd like to stay here on Oakley."

Dean didn't expect that reaction from her, but he also had no reason to refuse. "Alright. You are always welcome at the Forrester estate. We can make a room for you and—" she held up her hand to stop him.

"I don't see anything wrong with staying here." She gestured to the cave, the amenities she had brought in making it quite the comfortable apartment.

Dean laughed. "Have it your way. We will get you a space car though. Feel free to stop by any time."

Felna returned the smile, and seeing that her job was done she went back over to the couch, plopping down in front of the big screen tv, giving the team their privacy.

"Shall we go home?" Dean asked, receiving unanimous hell yeahs from the party members.

CHAPTER
SEVENTEEN

CASSANDRA

Forrester Estate

Too long—*it is taking way too long for Min to return,* Cassie thought to herself as she drew circles in the dirt beside her feet. Deathanal, Mel and Cassie were the chosen team to face off in the next Core battle. Now the team waited in the center of the preservation area, donned in full armor, ready to be transported to the Core arena.

Despite the denoted time having long passed, Min never reappeared, no battle beginning. Now the team of three sat on the ground, waiting, not wanting to be caught off guard if they were suddenly summoned.

"Madam!" Olivia burst into the training area, her breathing heavy.

"What is it?" Cassie rushed to regain her feet.

"The ship—it's returned!"

She needed a moment to let the information sink in, but as soon as Cassandra understood what the nanny was trying to tell her, she was already running toward the front of the building. Sure enough, when she reached the estate's entrance, the shuttle was touching down.

She held her breath as the doors opened, half expecting some uninvited guest to waltz out of the stolen ship. The inhabitants of the Forrester estate had gathered from the commotion, everyone awaiting the grand exit. When Dean stepped off of the ship first, Cassie couldn't contain her tears.

She ran to him, throwing herself in his arms as the tears fell unrestrained. He wrapped her in a hug, all of the stress and exhaustion of the past months falling off in an instant.

"You big idiot, how could you do this to me? If you ever leave me like that again, I will kill you myself." She pounded lightly on his chest, her threats losing their edge from the look of relief on her face.

Kambry walked out next and Cassie held her arms open, forcing her to join in the group hug. They stayed like that for a while, the whole of the estate joining in on the moment.

After the tearful reunion, Dean filled in everyone about what happened during their stay in the maze, and what it meant for their future. All of the previous residents of other planets were given the choice on whether to stay or return to their home world. They all decided to stay, content with the life that living on Oakley could provide.

Cassandra told her side of the story, but the victory over the Core seemed irrelevant now that the gods were returning to their original stations. They fell asleep that night, tangled in each other's embrace, still worried over Sable, left to wonder if she made it out of Mixonia in time.

∞∞∞

The next morning their fears disappeared, Sable having joined the huddle some time in the night, her soft snores mingling with the rest of the groups.

"Does this mean it's over? We won?" Cassandra whispered, noticing that Dean was awake.

"For now," Dean responded softly. "We've done our part at the very least. For now humanity is safe from the god's games. They won't be meddling in our affairs anymore, but now the hard part begins."

"The hard part?"

"Now we have to live for ourselves. Decide what is best for us without the gods' influence. Are you up for the challenge?" He smirked, having his lovers' full attention.

The girls glanced at each other, having woken up from the quiet conversation, knowing they were all thinking the same thing. "No matter what happens, we will be fine if we have each other."

They all leaned in, kissing Dean on the cheek, the kiss progressing into something more, leading them to spend the whole day wrapped in each other's arms.

EPILOGUE

The portal's closure sparked a lot of changes in the world—the prophecy slowly revealing itself. The elves were alerted that the planets they had forfeited were vacant once more, the Core demons having been transported back to the center of the worlds reestablishing balance between the core and the surface.

With the fight between the two no longer an issue, the fleets stationed on Oakley and all the other human planets left, their assistance no longer necessary to the population's survival. Some elves chose to make their home on the human planets, blending in with the locals, but most moved on, either to new worlds or to reestablish their old ones.

Before the elves left, Danican informed the members of the Forrester estate that the dwarves were no longer a cause for concern. While they once held Oakley in contempt for the death of their god, Dean being revealed as the blessed one of the prophecy changed their outlook on the situation, the head dwarf deciding it was best not to stir up unnecessary trouble.

The fight for the planet having been settled, the team placed all of their efforts on finding Lexis, a feat that proved to be difficult when adhering to the laws of intergalactic space travel. A week after the portals closed, they received a call from an unknown number, Dean reluctantly answering it at Cassandra's insistence.

Lexis's human face popped up on the screen, her smile wide when she saw both Dean and Cassie looking back at her.

"Hi guys!" she said happily as if she hadn't been kidnapped months prior.

"Lexi! Where are you? Are you hurt?" Cassie asked immediately, looking past Lexis and onto the ship behind her, trying to find a clue she could use to figure out who had taken her captive.

"I'm not. In fact, I'm great. I don't know how you did it, but I sense that the gods are no longer in this world." She got right to the point. "That means that no one is going to try to kill me anymore and I can live freely. I like it here—with Tucker. I want to stay. I hope you can give me your blessing."

While they expressed their doubts to her, Lexis had a comeback for every one, talking about how her and Tucker's relationship had slowly changed over time and blossomed into a love she knew would last. Although they still held doubts, Lexis was an adult and they couldn't do anything if she had made the decision for herself.

"Babe, who are you talking to?" A shirtless Tucker walked on screen, his eyes suddenly going wide when he saw the pictured couple.

He scrambled to cut the feed, but Lexis stopped him, briefly explaining about the disappearance of the gods and how the danger had passed. Tucker refused to look Dean in the eyes, still wary that the man would kill him the next time their paths crossed.

"Do anything to hurt her and I will kill you," Dean answered the tension Tucker exuded through the screen.

"I won't," he mumbled his response, getting a kiss on the cheek from Lexis for his acceptance before she disconnected the call.

∞∞∞∞

With no threats looming over their head, and Lexis's disappearance settled, Team Ola had time to focus on other things, building up their home base being one of them. After the portals shut for good, the material things linked to Mixonia were altered, namely the lockets. Overnight, the lockets etched with the teams token count were converted into g-coins, the team waking up to literal piles of money in their home.

With the influx of cash, the team was finally able to get their community ship running, expanding the amount of people they could provide for comfortably. A statue of Droosca was erected in the center of the forest, Dean fulfilling the promise he made to her, the only way he could thank her for her support in the maze.

Dean said his vows with Cassie, Kambry, Jessabee and Sable under the shadow of the statue, promising their lives to one another, something Dean never envisioned for himself, but now couldn't imagine life without.

Kambry gave birth to a little girl, naming her Sonya, while Jessabee birthed his first son, Zoran. On the day of the birth, Sable announced her pregnancy to the group along with Zayra, who's announcement would be the first of many, her and Wilfred still set on having a large family.

Dean returned to the world of fishing, although his new found funds meant he viewed the lifestyle as more of a hobby than his livelihood, letting the others in the field try for the more dangerous catches. Although they were told that the threat had passed, the team continued to train, feeling the need to be ready for anything.

Riva expanded his expertise to training the military of Oakley, not letting his high-tech base go to waste. No matter what each member of the estate chose to focus on in their new normal, the group had each other, living everyday thankful for the peace it brought. Still they remained vigilant—prepared—aware, knowing that in a second, at the will of a being more powerful than them, everything could change.

AFTERWORD

Minotaur Maze has its ending. I listened to the fans and hope you find this a fitting closure. I try to finish all my series. Some folks care, others just want to read the next story. In this case, I'm super proud to have Dean's adventure reach its conclusion. Thanks for joining me and stay tuned for more stories.

Follow my author profile on amazon, leave a review, and join me on facebook. I help run Dukes of Harem where we give out audio codes, post sexy art, and the authors get to display their latest books. https://www.facebook.com/groups/dukesofharem

Stay Classy, Marcus

Follow my Publisher for more Harem and LitRPG ebooks and audio books.

www.royalguardpublishing.com

YOU MAY ALSO ENJOY ...

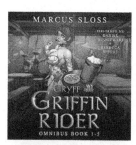

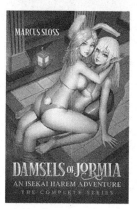

Gryff the Griffen Rider Omnibus

A fantasy tale of adventure, battle, love, lust, and excitement awaits. Gryff is a young man who had goals and dreams. A spiraling series of events rapidly rips him out of his reality and into a new world, where he must achieve a new path. Will you dare to quest with the hero? Download now to join Gryff in his exploits and feats.

Damsels of Jormia Boxset

Transported to a land of myth and magic, Nolan scrambles to adjust in a realm where he contains magic. Of course, some lovely locals are in desperate need of a savior as the vile ratkin invade. Destined to unleash his power upon the wicked, he may just save some damsels along the way.

YOU MAY ALSO ENJOY ...